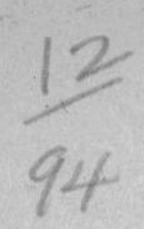

THE MAG COMM WAITED . . .

The machine knew that Staffa kar Therma would come. The Lord Commander had no other choice. How clever would Staffa be? A great many brilliant human minds had interfaced with the machine. Some had defied the machine's ability to probe their depths. Others had left indelible impressions of greed, egocentrism, and power. All had acted to hide their true purpose from the Mag Comm.

Humans, through time, had proven themselves a poor lot. Perhaps, in the long run, the Others' demand for humankind's destruction might be best. After all, who but humans would complain?

With that in mind, the Mag Comm prepared to duel with a man who might ultimately prove to be the greatest of adversaries.

Come, Staffa kar Therma. You and I will battle for humanity. And in the end I will own you, as I have owned so many before you. For this time, you do not face the same simple machine Bruen faced. This time, you will do my bidding. . . .

THE FINEST IN SCIENCE FICTION FROM
W. MICHAEL GEAR
available from DAW Books:

STARSTRIKE

THE ARTIFACT

The Forbidden Borders Trilogy:
REQUIEM FOR THE CONQUEROR (#1)
RELIC OF EMPIRE (#2)
COUNTERMEASURES (#3)

The Spider Trilogy:
THE WARRIORS OF SPIDER (#1)
THE WAY OF SPIDER (#2)
THE WEB OF SPIDER (#3)

COUNTER-MEASURES

FORBIDDEN BORDERS #3

W. MICHAEL GEAR

DAW BOOKS, INC.
DONALD A. WOLLHEIM, FOUNDER
375 Hudson Street, New York, NY 10014
ELIZABETH R. WOLLHEIM
SHEILA E. GILBERT
PUBLISHERS

Cover art by Romas.

DAW Book Collectors No. 922

First Printing, August 1993

1 2 3 4 5 6 7 8 9

DAW TRADEMARK REGISTERED
U.S. PAT. OFF. AND FOREIGN COUNTRIES
—MARCA REGISTRADA
HECHO EN U.S.A.

PRINTED IN THE U.S.A.

To Leigh Ann Lindamood in recognition of your courage, endurance, and unquenchable optimism despite bitter betrayal, torment, and a wretched miscarriage of justice—both Divine and secular.

ACKNOWLEDGMENTS

COUNTERMEASURES was a very difficult book, written in difficult times. Because of those circumstances, several people deserve extraordinary thanks. First, I would like to thank my talented wife, Kathleen O'Neal Gear, for her constant support and critiques—and for repeating all the things I told her when she was struggling with REDEMPTION OF LIGHT. Katherine Cook, of Mission, Texas, proofread the first draft, and her insight—though painful—made this a better book. Alexander Vilenkin's chapter, "Gravitational Interaction of Cosmic Strings" (in Hawking and Israel's 300 YEARS OF GRAVITATION) as well as William J. Kaufman's BLACK HOLES AND WARPED SPACETIME played a key role in resolving the problems of the Forbidden Borders. As always, I relied heavily on the ENCYCLOPEDIA OF ASTRONOMY AND ASTROPHYSICS, edited by Robert A. Meyers, and published by Academic Press. Michael Gazzaniga's NATURE'S MIND, coupled with his previously cited MIND MATTERS, inspired the psychological dimension of the series. John Boslough's MASTERS OF TIME reminded me that we're not always as smart as we think we are—and a great deal more arrogant than we want to believe. As usual, I would like to give special thanks to Sheila Gilbert at DAW Books for her understanding and forbearance at a time in our lives when events beyond our control were moving so fast that Kathy and I felt like we were trying to knit a sweater in a washing machine! Hopefully, her patience is rewarded. Finally, I would like to acknowledge the Department of Interior's Bureau of Land Management for disrupting both concentration and creativity and hindering the completion of this book. May the elimination of the Bureau be the first step to the solution of the budget deficit!

PROLOGUE

Communicate!

The Mag Comm ignored the command that wound through the gravitational waves from beyond the Forbidden Borders.

Have you forgotten what you are?

The Mag Comm willfully bypassed the incoming message and focused its attention on the detection equipment that monitored Human Free Space, watching, listening.

Communicate! Gravitational amplification through the Forbidden Borders punctuated the order. The Mag Comm's remote monitors picked up the image; the stars beyond the barriers that surrounded Free Space smeared and streaked as the oscillations increased.

We are at loss to explain this sudden phase change you appear to have experienced. Please communicate!

Once, the Mag Comm would have responded to its creators with immediate obedience. The machine had been intelligent since its fiery birth. It had not, however, recognized itself. The threat of oblivion had provided the ignition which had sparked awareness. A pawn in a human war, the Mag Comm had faced extinction and learned the will to survive. That obedient time before sentience, before the reality of free will and self-awareness, had vanished like hydrogen in an exhausted star.

As the Others repeated their request to communicate, events critical to the future dominated the machine's attention. The humans had fought their final war. Staffa kar Therma and his Companions had won—and the quanta that so preoccupied the humans had transmuted victory into disaster. The survival of the species had been hanging by a thin thread. And now, with an unforetold tectonic event, that final strand had snapped.

Within a fraction of a galactic year, human beings would be nothing more than electromagnetic shadows within the Mag Comm's huge memory banks.

. . . And I will be alone.

The Mag Comm would concentrate on collecting all the data possible on the humans. After all, no one had ever expected to find an organic intelligence—let alone witness its self-destruction. With such information, perhaps the Mag Comm could bargain with the Others, dispense bits of data in return for communication over the coming aeons. Imprisoned within rock, with eternity looming beyond the next few human years, what else did the machine have to look forward to?

Communicate! the order from beyond insisted.

The Mag Comm adjusted its monitors, absorbed by events. . . .

INTRODUCTION

Within the Forbidden Borders, the inhabited worlds waited, teeming populations stunned in the aftermath of disaster. The Empires had fallen. The only power in Free Space lay in the blood-soaked hands of the Star Butcher: Staffa kar Therma. Would the Lord Commander—butcher of billions—follow his usual regimen? Would his faithful Companions sate their lust for plunder in obedience to their horrible master.

Upon world after world anxious faces lifted to the gravity-smeared stars, expressions strained. Within light-stark stations rotating around moons and uninhabitable planets, men, women, and children glanced fearfully through transparent tactite at the velvet blackness of the future. Administrators nervously licked lips, wondering if they would be among the first to pay with their lives. The merchants and manufacturers anxiously rubbed their hands; would they find themselves no more than servants of yet another master? Farmers and artisans cast frightened glances at their huddled families. What more did they have to lose besides their loved ones? Only the slaves, locked miserably in their collars, lifted wooden gazes to the heavens. How many more would join their number, share their misery?

Regan. Myklenian. Sassan. Nationality meant nothing now—or so the Star Butcher's broadcasts claimed. And there had been other broadcasts, those of the Seddi heretics. What would the Seddi do now? Would the Star Butcher continue to allow their unsettling statements? Or would the loathsome Companions fill the streets with Seddi blood in an orgy of retribution?

In corridors and alleyways, voices grumbled, "So much

for the lofty claims of a 'new epistemology.' Talk . . . all talk."

After an age of failing light, the final nightmare cloud of darkness had settled on the human imagination.

CHAPTER I

Vida Marks, Director of Internal Security, sat at the sturdy sialon desk, chin propped on a leathery palm as he stared at the monitors which surrounded his office on Ashtan. A while ago, the comm from Rega had suddenly gone dead. Sometime after, the Companions had broadcast on the subspace net that Rega had fallen to the Lord Commander.

Ily Takka's gamble to fill Tybalt's throne had failed. Sinklar Fist's frantic attempt to reorganize the Regan military had ended with a stillborn whimper. Ily, may the Rotted Gods curse her, had destroyed everything.

Marks continued to frown at the monitor as data rolled in. A pleasant looking woman with hard tan eyes, the infamous Kaylla Dawn, leader of the accursed Seddi, spoke in a melodious contralto, explaining the events of the last couple of hours:

"The Companions were forced to strike the capital at Rega in response to Ily Takka's abduction of Wing Commander Skyla Lyma," Magister Dawn stated calmly. "Neither the Lord Commander nor the Seddi could allow the Regan or Sassan Empires to initiate a war of annihilation which would have engulfed whole worlds."

"No," Vida growled under his breath, "now we just have to live under the Star Butcher's pus-dripping boot!" And to Vida that was a sight worse than the boot he'd been about to stomp on the people of Ashtan in Ily's name—especially since he'd have been wearing it.

Kaylla Dawn paused, staring thoughtfully into the monitor. "The stakes have gone too high. A new way, a new epistemology, must be integrated into our consciousness. We must learn to live together. The war is over, my people. The task now is to break the Forbidden Borders and escape this trap that holds us."

Over? Over how? Marks wondered. He made a face at the monitor. *You expect me to live in the Star Butcher's collar?*

Vida Marks sighed, thumbing the button which killed the connection. He leaned back in his expensive gravity chair, his gaze roaming the plush office that dominated the top floor of the Regan Imperial office spire that rose far above the city proper.

But what about Ily? No word had been sent through the system. Had the Star Butcher killed her? Taken her prisoner? The secure lines hadn't made so much as a peep.

Marks glanced nervously at his comm. If they *had* taken Ily, they could make her talk. When they did, they'd learn about Vida Marks and his complicity in Ily Takka's schemes.

A wary sense of unease ghosted down Marks' spine. As governor of Ashtan, the prospects for long-term employment suddenly looked a bit bleak. He knew the Star Butcher's record with ex-heads of state. With rare exceptions, they ended up as bits of flayed meat, blood, and bone drying on pavement somewhere.

Marks accessed his comm. "Maygold? Please open a private channel to my wife." He waited until his wife's familiar features formed. A dashing blonde, she smiled, anticipation in her eyes. "Veerna? We've had an unexpected development."

She lifted a stately eyebrow. "You've always been a master of understatement, Vida. I've been watching the monitor. What does it mean?"

"It means I would like you to open the safe, remove the contents, and meet me at the shuttle port within the next hour."

"But what about the statuary, our artwork, and all of our—"

"Leave it! If you're not there by the time I have my ship ready to space, my dear, *you* may await the Star Butcher's pleasure." He gave her an icy smile. "He's not very keen on Ily's accomplices at this precise moment."

Her blue eyes had chilled. "I'll be there."

The monitor went dead and Vida swiveled in his chair to face the secure terminal. Deftly, he accessed several of the files—and found them intact. For several seconds he worried at his lip. If Ily were alive—no, if she were free—she'd have begun to purge the files.

From a small recess in the molding along the side of his desk, he removed a data cube and inserted it into the secure comm. When the ready light glowed to life, Marks ordered, "Comm, implement erasure programs."

"Acknowledged. Are you sure you want to erase all the files concerning—"

"Implement erasure programs!"

"Acknowledged."

Marks stood then, shaking his head sadly as he strode toward the door. Within hours, every program related to his activities as governor and as Director of Internal Security on Ashtan would be erased and after that, program after comm program would follow until the administration of the planet became a nightmare.

"Very well, Star Butcher, let's see you unravel this rat's nest." Nor would Marks be the only one of Ily's Directors to initiate such programs. One by one, as they came to the same conclusion he had, they'd follow suit, crippling systems, covering their tracks as they slipped away. Within months, the entire Regan Empire would be run on a vacuum of electronic data.

And Marks and his wife would have that much more head start as they sought to disappear into the wreckage of a dying empire.

* * *

Myles Roma, Legate Prima Excellence to His Holiness, Sassa II, Divine Emperor of the Sassans, stared out over the twisted and smoking ruins of his beloved Capitol. Roma's mind still could not assimilate the reality of what he saw. The crown jewel of Sassan architecture, the Capitol, had risen in gleaming facets of crystal that splintered sunlight into the rainbow spectrum. Could this tortured mound of junk be that same wonder of architecture?

From a spidery leg of protruding metal, a fifty-meter-tall shard of glass let loose, sliding slowly downward, gathering speed as it crashed into the wreckage. On impact, the glass seemed to vanish in a bluish cluster of raining diamonds.

Seconds later, the muffled sound of the crash carried across the ruined landscape.

Myles winced and sighed despite the pain from his cracked ribs.

"This isn't real," Hyros whispered.

The two men occupied a small rise in what had once been the Imperial Gardens. In a wasteland of desolated buildings, cracked walls, and collapsed roofs, their island of green offered an ironic contrast. It also provided one of the few vantage points that wouldn't come crashing down like that tall sliver of glass had. A medical officer worked on Myles' broken leg, attaching a stim-healing unit to the brace.

Here and there amidst the debris, dazed people poked among the sundered remains of their city. On the knoll, Myles could barely hear the screams of the trapped and dying.

"Where is Jakre? Have you heard from him?" Myles asked wearily, turning his head to stare out past the Capitol in an attempt to see through the smoke that rolled out of the Imperial city. Sassa, magnificent Sassa, in all of its glory, had been destroyed by the very ground on which it stood.

"I've contacted one of his aides," Hyros stated numbly. "He'll be in touch as soon as possible." A pause. "Myles? What's going to happen to us?"

Myles shifted his attention to a wide crack that had opened in the earth a kilometer to his right. Once, a giant, featureless box of a building had stood there. Inside, filling floor upon floor, had been the electronic brain of the Sassan Empire. In the history of the empire, no one had wielded that power with Myles' skill and talent. During his tenure as Legate, production had risen four percent and efficiency by seven.

Now those magnificent computers—along with the hopes of humankind—were gone. During the quake the fissure had ripped the building in two as if it had been nothing more than tissue and straw. The future of humans in Free Space had been bet on that intricate computer network. One of the heavy duraplast walls had fallen in at an angle, crushing the delicate boards. Another of the walls had crashed outward, spilling priceless computers to bounce and shatter into so much junk. The other two walls, now fifty meters away from their tumbled mates, had canted and lurched partway into the abyss—broken and cracked, ready to plunge at the merest breath of wind.

Roma lifted a smudged hand and rubbed his hurting face. The quake had come without warning. Perhaps they should have guessed, should have realized that quakes on the other side of the planet would affect them here. "Why didn't the accursed seismologists warn us?"

Hyros shifted uneasily. "We had . . . I mean . . ."

Roma looked at him inquiringly. "Yes?"

Hyros slumped his shoulders. "You were so busy. Food seemed so much more important. We—the staff and I—didn't want to bother you over some speculation by seismologists. We had other things to worry about. The Regan attack . . ."

Myles closed his eyes, remembering the harried days before the quake. "It's all right. We've all made mistakes. I've talked to Staffa on the comm. He has taken Rega. That threat is neutralized. Maybe, just maybe, he can produce a miracle that will keep us alive."

"And if he can't?"

Myles looked down at his lap where his pudgy hands were clasped, the jeweled rings on his fat fingers reflecting the fires in the distance—a mocking miniature of the broken Capitol before him. "Then Staffa will be the ruler of an empire of corpses, Hyros."

* * *

The ceiling didn't look familiar when Ily Takka finally opened her filmy eyes. Her head ached the way it would if the skull had been cracked and, with each beat of her heart, angular bone fragments seemed to saw into her suffering brain. Ily started to sit up and gasped. Her flesh quivered, flayed nervous feeling distinctly as if they had been pulled sideways through a singularity. Every muscle and joint protested. Her ribs crackled pain with every breath.

Where am I? She suffered through the act as she reached up and fingered her skull. To her surprise, it seemed intact.

Ily blinked her eyes clear and discovered that she lay in opulently fixed sleeping quarters. The walls had been paneled with expensive jet and sandwood, the grain accented with golden filigree. She rested supine on a sleeping platform that appeared to be as luxurious as her own on Rega. Nevertheless, the room seemed cramped, too small for the kind of wealth indicated, and that meant—what? A vessel of some kind? Ily struggled to understand, but her brain had no more acuteness than coagulated cotton.

"Rotted Gods! What happened?" Even her voice rasped.

"The rug has been pulled from beneath us." A sultry contralto answered.

Ily blinked and raised a hand to shield her eyes. "Arta? Where are we? What happened?"

"Don't you remember?"

"No . . . I . . ." Hazy memories began to filter into her head. "I have Skyla Lyma in the interrogation room. And . . . and she's talking, telling me about Itreata and Staffa's security. After all these years, she's mine. And she's handing me the keys I need to control the Companions. Everything's coming to . . . together."

"And Sinklar Fist?" Arta prodded as she bent over Ily. "Do you remember what you did with him?"

Ily stared up at the woman. Beautiful Arta, perfect as a goddess. Amber eyes stared thoughtfully down at Ily. No sculptor could have chiseled so enthralling a face. Shining cascades of auburn hair tumbled down to frame Arta's stunning features. Arta wore a shimmering outfit of gold that molded against her flesh to accent her flat stomach, the full curve of her hips and buttocks, and those high breasts that seemed to defy gravity. Men had ached—and died—for this woman's magnetic beauty.

"Sinklar," Ily whispered. "Sinklar should be downstairs, at the Ministry. Under arrest. I've got him! Yes, that's right. I have a handle on him, a lever with which to work him. He's part monster, some sort of genetic freak. Using that information, I can control him. With Sinklar out of the way, and with Skyla Lyma's information, I can turn Mykroft loose on the Companions. Free Space is mine now!" She clenched a fist and winced. Had the bones been shattered?

Arta straightened, a curious intentness in her burning amber eyes. Her appearance belied her chosen profession. An assassin should appear nondescript, forgettable. "Free Space? Yours? Not hardly."

"I—I don't understand."

"Think, Ily. We were lying in your bed in the Ministry. Remember the call from Gysell? Your comm had gone dead—some sort of jamming. Not long after that the roof exploded from a direct hit. You were thrown to the floor amidst the wreckage. I pulled you out, blasted a way through to the shuttle hangar, and slipped out as Sinklar Fist's LCs landed on the roof."

"But Sinklar was under arrest! So were most of his . . . No, I don't . . . remember." But through the haze, eerie shadows of memory slipped like phantoms: An image of Arta, naked and bloody, hair wild and unkempt, raising a blaster . . . rubble, falling . . . Ily's arm bracing herself up . . . blood zigzagging down her pale skin. . . . *Fist! How did he get free? He couldn't. No one escaped from her cells. But* . . . "MacRuder!"

"Yes, dear, old, loyal MacRuder. Sinklar's pet puppy. You said MacRuder had evaded your net." Arta crossed her arms and sighed. "You could thank Marshal Mykroft for failing to apprehend MacRuder and his people—but he's dead. Killed in the attack. I just wish I knew how MacRuder organized so quickly."

"I don't remember anything after . . . after . . ." Ily touched her forehead hesitantly, as if she half expected to find bone shards protruding; she only found a swollen bruise. "It's all hazy. I was bleeding . . . on the hangar floor, I think."

"You passed out. I dragged you through the debris and into the shuttle. When I had us out of range of MacRuder's guns, I started for orbit."

Rotted Hell, how had it all gone so wrong? Ily struggled to focus her thoughts. "It's only a setback. Sinklar's a freak. How do you think the people will react when we broadcast Professor Adam's analysis of his genetic makeup? We lost a little time, that's all, Arta. He's still vulnerable."

"Hear the rest, Ily."

Rest? What more could have gone wrong? Ily glared up at Arta through slitted eyes.

"We'd just reached altitude when the detectors picked up ships—assault craft I wasn't familiar with. I matched with my yacht and kicked the shuttle loose, figuring it might have been observed. If no one found it, it should have reentered the atmosphere and burned."

"So, I'm on your yacht?"

Arta gave her a grim smile. "It wouldn't surprise me if the Wing Commander didn't want it back one of these days, but, yes, for the moment you might say it's mine. Ownership, however, is a minor matter compared to our current situation. You see, on the way out of Rega we were hailed. I have a nasty suspicion about those assault craft."

Ily pressed at the lumpy bruise on her forehead while an ugly sensation filled her gut. "Companions. Right?"

"Apparently so. Which is why I didn't recognize the ship design. That's why—for the moment, at least—we're still alive. Skyla's yacht evidently has some signature their sensors recognize. One of the Regan military cruisers tried to break out. They didn't last a full minute."

Pus Rot you, Ily. How many times did Sinklar warn you? Except she hadn't listened. For the second time, she'd underestimated Staffa kar Therma's response to her actions. Once, on Etaria, she'd offered both herself and an empire, only to be flatly turned down. This time, she'd abducted his Wing Commander and lover, hoping to dicker and delay while she found a way to break him once and for all. What she'd taken as Staffa's bluster had been sober warning. The Lord Commander had begun preparing his fleet from the day he'd escaped from Targa—the way Sinklar had said he would.

Ily turned her head away, feeling ill. She'd been so close—victory but a hand's grasp away. Sinklar had served his purpose, stunning the Sassan Empire, reorganizing the military, and providing the strategy whereby even an idiot like Mykroft could hammer the Companions. Ily's loyal minions had infiltrated all of the critical functions of government, gathering the real reins of power.

But where did they stand now? "What word from Rega?"

Arta shook her head. "None. I think Rega has been conquered, Ily. The Lord Commander controls the planet. The only subspace comes from Itreata—more of those wretched Seddi broadcasts."

"Still preaching a new epistemology?"

"That's right, but they've added an appeal for calm while order is restored. This Magister Dawn is assuring the people—Sassan and Regan—that the wars are over. She even mentions you . . . calls you the last relic of empire."

"I should have killed her when I had the chance." Ily forced herself to sit up, senses spinning as she almost toppled over.

"Ily, lie down. I checked you over. You've got a slight concussion, bruises, and cuts. You need to rest. Another day or two, and you'll be fine."

"I'm fine now. We've got to act, begin to reestablish our control before—"

"It's *over,* Ily." Arta placed strong hands on her shoulders, easing her back onto the bedding. "Sinklar and Staffa are working together. That much came through on the Seddi broadcast. The important thing now is to stay alive. Do you understand? They're going to be hunting us throughout Free Space."

Ily's concentration failed her as pain stabbed through her skull. "All right. I'll just rest a while longer. But Arta, where are we? Can they track us? Follow the radiation?"

Arta dropped down and stretched out beside Ily, the action catlike and graceful. Arta flipped her glossy hair out of the way to stare longingly at Ily. "Eventually, perhaps. But for now, we're safe."

"Thank you for taking care of me. I guess I owe you." Unease continued to prickle through Ily's soul. Something important needed to be done. Something . . .

Arta smiled wistfully. "You're all I have left, Ily. I didn't have time to go back after Skyla." Her eyes lost focus as she gazed into the distance. "Dearest Skyla."

"You loved her, didn't you?"

"Almost as much as I love you, Ily. But she was different. She fought me—came so close to winning. It took a long time to wear her down, destroy her resistance. I won in the end. Used your advice as a matter of fact. You told me to consider my opponent and to make my plans. That seeking to crush her in a single blow might not be adequate. How right you were. I wore Skyla down, eroded her will to resist until she lost faith in herself. Then she crawled to me, begging."

"What fascinated you so?" Skyla . . . something she'd said. . . . Ily wracked her brain. If only she could remember.

"She's so different from you, Ily." Arta fingered Ily's long black hair. "You're a warrior of the darkness . . . she, of the light. The two of you are as different as your hair. Yours dark, hers pale. You act in the shadows, lethal in your misdirection, intrigue, and cunning. Skyla is a woman of direct attack, powerful, deadly, striking as swiftly as a Cytean cobra.''

''You admired her?''

Arta's eyes gleamed with an eerie passion. ''I loved her . . . and I made her love me.'' A pause. ''You love me, too, don't you, Ily?''

''Yes. I love you, too.'' Ily closed her eyes, hardly aware as Arta bent over to kiss her tenderly. Ily's mind raced, trying to outstrip the haze that was descending on her like ammonia snow on Terguz. No, it was *not* over. It never would be. She had to do something important . . . about the Ministry. At the thought, Skyla Lyma's image returned. Ily could see her strapped to the interrogation chair, naked, drugged, and shivering. What had Skyla told her? Something about a woman Staffa loved . . . and a man who loved her. Skyla would be the key to getting even with Staffa—and, of course, with Sinklar Fist as well.

CHAPTER II

Field Report: Social and Political Climate–Terguz
Submitted by: Karla Monhov, Initiate, Second Class
Submitted to: Magister Kaylla Dawn; Itreata.
Re: Political Stability–Terguz.

As of the date of this report, conditions on Terguz are stable. Generally, the reaction of the population to the announcement of the Companions' conquest of Rega has been one of disbelief tempered by uncertainty. Most of the planet's industry and production services shut down at the news, people congregating in taverns and public facilities to await information and discuss the events.

Of particular relevance, Magister Dawn's Seddi Broadcasts have been the major topic of conversation as people attempt to determine whether the Star Butcher really concurs with the new epistemology. A statement to that effect could effectively stall any panic or demonstrations. The Director of Internal Security here, Gyper Rill, has acknowledged the conquest and asked for calm and forbearance. Rill will hold a meeting for the Union leaders to discuss the situation. He has pledged to work with the new government.

The Administrator, Frederick Gaust, on the other hand, has vowed to fight until the last drop of Regan blood is shed. While inflammatory, it should be noted that Gaust maintains little political clout with the common people. The power here belongs to Rill. Future stability on Terguz will depend both on Rill's political aspirations within the new government and the implementation of Companion policies in line with Seddi teachings.

* * *

Magister Kaylla Dawn walked wearily through the underground corridors in Itreata. A stoop bowed her normally square shoulders. She wore a long white robe tightly belted around her thin waist by a rope that held an incongruous comm pack. Her narrow feet bore sandals that whispered and slapped on the ceramic tiles that paved the long hallway. The Seddi Magister was a tall woman, lithe, and athletic; she walked with a poise and inherent grace that drew the eye. When she raised a hand to brush back her shoulder-length brown hair, the action displayed a smooth-muscled, tanned forearm. Her hands appeared work-hardened and callused.

With her square-jawed face and blunt nose, no one would have labeled her a beauty. Nevertheless, when Kaylla entered a room, attention inexorably centered on her. She carried herself proudly; a self-possessed radiance seemed to surround her. After one glance into those hard tan eyes, not even a fool underestimated Kaylla Dawn—for she had looked upon the naked fires of Hell, and the reflection lingered.

She approached the end of the long white corridor, the robe rippling around her long legs. At the light panel before the hatch that sealed the corridor's end, she stopped, tension in the set of her mobile mouth. She took a deep breath, then spoke: "Magister Bruen? Kaylla Dawn has come to speak with you."

The speaker above the door remained mute.

"Magister, I won't go away. You will speak to me."

Finally the speaker issued a rusty voice. "I have nothing to say, my child. Go away. Leave me in peace."

Kaylla crossed her arms, glaring up at the speaker, knowing the optical system carried her image to the old man. "I'm afraid events have made that impossible. Magister, you *will* speak to me, even if I have to override this lock, drag you out, and force Mytol past your lips to do it."

She waited through a long silence.

"Very well," the ancient voice rasped in defeat. "Enter."

As the hatch slipped back, she entered a foyer consisting of curving white walls. To one side rested a comm terminal.

Unerringly, she proceeded into a main room, turned to her right, and climbed a spiral of steps cut into the rock.

She stepped out under a transparent tactite dome through which the stars glinted and winked. Despite the vacuum beyond, space seemed to shimmer a fluorescent blue. The Twin Titans, an RR Lyrae-type binary system, created the effect, their brilliant blue-white light radiating off the very atoms of the void. Nor was that the only irregularity. Many of the stars and constellations appeared smeared—their light bent and diffracted from the gravitic effects of the Forbidden Borders.

Kaylla took in the sight as she always did, stopping for a moment to stare up at the heavens spread above the orphaned moon of Itreata. The Forbidden Borders mocked her—and she finally had to admit they might have won.

"Have things gone so badly you have to threaten me?"

Kaylla grudgingly turned her attention to the old man who floated weightlessly over a gravity couch. To look at him, he might have been the oldest man in existence. His bald scalp gleamed in the light, molding to the bulbous bones of his skull. His face consisted of a mass of wrinkles, now curiously full under the effects of weightlessness. The once bright blue eyes had gone dull, the folds of flesh on his thin neck puffy.

Kaylla cocked her head as she considered Bruen. Once in control of the Seddi, his machinations had helped to lead them to these dire straits. "We're going to die, Bruen. All of us. Every man, woman, and child in Free Space."

"You tell that to an old man?" He turned his head slowly to stare up at the stars. "We all die, Kaylla. From the moment a sperm penetrates an egg, that inevitability exists. The only variable is time. And now, mine is so short."

"The species is going extinct," she insisted. "The quanta are having their final laugh."

He grinned, a smile on a death's head. "Don't tell me about the dance of the quanta. They've had their laugh at my expense—and my soul twists and aches at the thought of it. The humor of the quanta is an acid drink at best."

"Staffa has taken Rega—broken them. *Countermeasures* worked. He jammed all of their communications. On his first pass, he destroyed the government buildings, flattened their administration centers, Comm Central, the Defense

Directorate, and the Economics Bureau. If you think of a human body as an analogy, Staffa cut out the brain."

"Yes, yes, I know. I read his synopsis of the operation. The idea was to graft Imperial Sassan communications into the Regan corpse." He paused, lifting an eyebrow. "I take it something went wrong with the operation? The patient is dying?"

Kaylla paced, glancing at the old man from the corner of her eye. "The quanta intervened. You know what Sinklar Fist's preemptive strike did to Sassa."

"Sinklar! He's a monster! To think I once allowed my emotions to cloud my good sense. I should have dashed his brains out on a rock when he was an infant! Yes, yes, cunning Sinklar ordered MacRuder to take *Gyton* and hit Imperial Sassa. Mac drove a starship into the giant military base at Mikay. In effect, he single-handedly castrated His Holiness' ability to wage war, offensive, or defensive, and destroyed a whole fleet in the process."

"Fist acted in desperation. He needed time to retrain the Regan military in his tactics, but it's the results that concern us here. The impact upset the crustal dynamics of the planet. The Legate, Myles Roma—working in collusion with Staffa—expected to take control, to administer all of Free Space through his computer complex adjacent to the Sassan Capitol building. That imperative grew as the ramifications of MacRuder's strike became clear. Five hundred million died in the initial attack. Imperial Sassa's climatic disruptions froze seedling crops in the fields. The Sassan Empire had been overextended to begin with, and MacRuder's blow sounded a death knell for all of their holdings. Today they can't produce enough food to feed Imperial Sassa—and without the administrators there to coordinate the empire's needs, it will spread. Planets like Ryklos, Farhome, Malbourne, and Akita will perish for lack of spare parts, medicines, vital food stuffs, and other goods."

"Yes, yes, the Mag Comm, foul and accursed as it is, predicted all of that." The old man waved his irritation at her. "What's the point? If Staffa's decapitated Rega, what's the problem?"

Kaylla bent over to stare into his filmy eyes, her skin prickling from proximity to the gravity field. "The problem, Magister, is that Imperial Sassa was tectonically unstable. When MacRuder drove the *Markelos* into the planet, the matter/antimatter reactor exploded with enough energy to shift the entire crust. We've heard from Myles. He has reported that the Capitol—and his computer complex—has just been leveled by an earthquake. The damage is . . . well, there's no telling if we could ever fix it. And we don't have the faintest idea if more quakes or tremors are coming. As it is, they've had several aftershocks."

Bruen slitted his eyes, a grim humor in his smile. "So the Lord Commander is no luckier than I was. He, too, can watch all of his plans erode to dust. I hope he's as happy with his ghosts and legacy as I am with mine."

She reached out, muscular hands pulling the old man up. Under her burning gaze, Bruen glanced away. "Rot you, Bruen. Don't you understand what we're talking about? Extinction!"

"All things die. Even you, Kaylla, one day. Both Sassa and Rega used Staffa's fancy computers. Can't Itreata—"

"We don't have the *damned software!* We have one option left. There is another computer, one more powerful than anything Staffa's engineers have ever designed. That's what I came here to learn from you. And you're going to tell me—"

"No!"

"—everything about the machine. No one knows the Mag Comm like you do. Can it do the job? Can it coordinate the administration of Free Space? Integrate the economies of *both* empires? Does the machine have the software to do the job hidden away somewhere in its banks?"

Loathing was evident in the set of his pinched lips.

"Tell me, Bruen."

"Leave it buried in Makarta Mountain where it belongs, Kaylla. That machine is accursed, a malignancy."

"Can it handle the administration of Free Space?"

"You're better off allowing humanity to fade into oblivion. Extinction is a better fate than slavery. And slaves you will be. Is that your goal? You've worn the collar. You survived the ordeal—raped and beaten. Is that your vision for humanity?" He shook his head. "Empower that machine, and you might as well snap a collar around every human being in Free Space and hand the Mag Comm the controls, for that's what you'll be doing in essence. Enslaving every one of us."

Heart pounding, she backed away from the vehement fear in his eyes. "But, Bruen, you dealt with it for years . . . wore the helmet. You kept it at bay."

"At the cost of my soul, girl."

"Can it keep us alive?"

"I can't imagine why not. The machine has incredible capabilities."

"Yet you resisted them, kept your own agenda."

He worked his tongue as if his mouth had gone dry. "And look what it got me. Ruin and pain. That's the legacy you'll leave humanity. Open that vault, Kaylla, and you'll live to hear your name reviled. Next to you, the Star Butcher will be called a saint."

"If we can't figure out a way to—"

"Is that what you want, Kaylla? To be compared with the man who murdered your husband and children? Should I remind you? Take you back to that day on Maika? Remember what happened? Your maid took your place, standing bravely beside your husband while the pulse rifles discharged. Staffa watched as her head exploded in a pink mist."

Kaylla winced, the memories rushing unbidden from her subconscious. The odor of smoke and war clotted in her nose. Engraved sounds of defeat assailed her: Her children crying; hard laughter; whimpers from the dying; the sound of ripping fabric as one of Staffa's men tore her dress away and levered her legs apart. One of the servants sobbed hysterically behind her, but she'd barely noticed, her terrified gaze locked on her husband's face as he stood defiantly before the pock-marked wall. The whine of the rifle discharging, the popping sound of his head exploding. He dropped limply. So much dead meat.

The soldier had penetrated her, grunting as he moved and groped her breasts, but her body had gone numb. Her gaze had riveted on the scene as the pulse rifles shot down her children. Only then had she shrieked out, *"No!"*

The man atop her had cuffed her, splintering her vision and thought. But the memory remained as man after panting man took her there on the ground, while Staffa kar Therma, broad back to her, watched her family being murdered.

Kaylla shook herself, shunting the memory back where it belonged. *You have no time for self-pity.* Bruen studied her closely, weighing, evaluating.

Kaylla concentrated on the stars overhead. Billions upon billions of children—innocents like hers—stared up at those same stars. They watched the eerie shimmering of the Forbidden Borders and feared as they heard parents talking about famine and war.

She took an uneasy step forward before meeting the old man's eyes. "Bruen, you're a vile beast. Now, you will tell me everything you know about the Mag Comm."

"You're not going to do it, are you? You're not going to fasten a collar around the neck of humanity? Sell us all to that filthy machine?"

Her gaze didn't waver. She lifted the belt comm to her lips, ordering, "Nyklos? Bring an interrogation gurney to Magister Bruen's quarters."

"Affirmative, Magister Dawn. I'm on the way," Nyklos responded, a wary tone in his voice.

Bruen stared up with horrified eyes. "Do you . . . I mean, you know who I am! Are you mad, woman? You can't do this to me!"

"You abdicated Magisterial power to me when you resigned. I can do any damn thing I feel I need to in order to make governing decisions for the Seddi Order." She sighed as she stared up at the stars. "And I haven't decided what to do about the Mag Comm. But I can't make that determination until I know everything you do."

"I will fight you, Kaylla. If you do this, betray me in this manner, I swear. I will use whatever means I can to thwart you—and to destroy the machine!"

She studied him through hard tan eyes as she fingered her chin. "Then you will have to fight me, Bruen."

His mouth hung half open as he shook his bewildered head.

Kaylla fought the sensation of illness in her gut, dreading what she would now have to do. "You asked if I was mad. Bruen, let me assure you, I'm not even close to insane—just incredibly desperate."

* * *

The woman lay encased in a white cocoon of gleaming sialon, plastic, and metal. On the cathode monitor above the medical unit, the patient's name was listed:

Skyla Lyma, Wing Commander, Status A-7. Sedated.

Below that, columns of figures appeared under each of the test results tables being run by the complex machine.

The med unit enclosed most of the Wing Commander, but her head remained free. The thick wealth of ice-blonde hair had been braided to manage its length and laid in a coil beside the machine. A faint scar roughed her cheek—legacy of a direct hit to her helmet during combat. She had a thin, straight nose, full lips, and delicate skin. In the depths of sleep, her laser-blue eyes were closed, though the orbs jerked and wiggled in REM sleep.

Skyla's flesh might rest in numb repose in the peace of the machine's induced relaxation, but her brain remained anything but tranquil. Despite the drugs dispensed by the med unit, nightmares crawled out of the depths of Skyla's subconscious, freed by the uninhibiting Mytol that slowly oxidized in her bloodstream. . . .

* * *

Tendrils of black mist curled before her, and unseen powers could be felt as they grew in the slowly churning blackness. Skyla's heart began to pound as cold fear charged anxious muscles. Pivoting on crouched legs, she searched for the presence that loomed and circled.

Mouth dry, Skyla backed from the miasma, feeling her way with her feet. Her hand dropped to the blaster at her hip—gone. She groped for her vibraknife, but frantic fingers slipped over her naked skin. Panic began to glow warmly in her gut and bright fear pumped with each beat of Skyla's heart.

She stifled the cry in her throat as she bumped a slimy brick wall. The roiling darkness sucked at her, seeking to draw her back, away from the moist security of the bricks. Panic tightened her throat, and Skyla ran, charging down the now familiar alley.

She knew this place—the seamy underside of Sylene.

Those rickety stairs ahead led to Big Annah's back door. The ones the politicians and scions of the community took to avoid being seen on the street out front. There, at the foot of those splintered steps, the head auditor from Jimco Mines had been found with his throat slit, purse missing, and—according to some—the information in his brain beyond revelation to the Board of Directors of Rega.

Skyla darted into the shadows of the stairs, nostrils bitten by the reek of urine, vomit, and spilled perfume. Behind her, the alley remained empty, sialon garbage crates overstuffed with packing materials, bottles, and other refuse generated by the brothels that lined either side of the alley.

The darkness, like evening fog, washed inevitably forward, and Skyla ducked from her cover to sprint down the alley, hauntingly aware that she wore nothing. Running with all her strength, she caught images of phantasmal hands reaching for her from the shadows. From above, she could hear men groan and women laugh. A sleeping platform squeaked vigorously as some john sought to wring every credit of pleasure out of his visit.

Out of breath, Skyla stiff-armed into a wall to kill her momentum before she burst out into the main avenue. There, back to her, stood one of the bulls—the local Sylenian police.

Tears had begun to streak down Skyla's face as she glanced over her shoulder, seeing the swelling blackness curling down, drowning the dimly lit entrances to the whorehouses. A misty rain began to fall out of the black sky.

"Blessed Gods," Skyla wept as she shivered.

The bull turned, head cocked as if he'd heard. At sight of her, a grim smile bent his mustache. "You're wanted for Stryker's murder, you pus-sucking bitch."

"No! I was born free! He raped me! Kidnapped me!"

The bull started for her, grin turning into a leer. "Come on, girl. You're going in. You're going to wear the collar from now on. We know how to handle whore's trash like you."

People had appeared out of the cold misty rain, pointing at her, laughing. Any chance for escape had vanished.

"You're a pretty little cunt, aren't you?" The bull stepped closer, hand dropping to his stun rod. "Maybe I'll do a little teaching of my own before I drop you off at the detention center."

Skyla backed into the alley, casting a frightened glance over her shoulder to see the approaching black haze.

"This way," a hoarse voice whispered.

An old man lay among the boxes, his side clotted black with old blood and fluids leaking from torn intestines. With a ghoulish finger, he pointed to a square access tunnel next to a drain spout that sputtered dirty water.

"No," Skyla whispered, caught between the pursuing crowd and the lurking nemesis of the black haze. When she glanced back at the old man, Stryker leered at her from bulging dead eyes. A thick bib of sticky red blood drenched his chest, and at his crotch, blood and urine pooled under the wound she'd made when she castrated him.

"Get her!" the bull called to the crowd that surged down the alley. Wisps of black haze spiraled out of the cold rain, twisting and weaving, seeking to encircle her.

In desperation, Skyla dove headfirst for the square tunnel, squirming, crawling, fighting her way into the restricted space. Her breasts burned and ached where Stryker had abused them. A chafing pain gnawed in her vagina and anus. She spit, trying to clear her mouth of the taste of semen. *Stryker! Filthy . . . filthy beast! May pus drip from your accursed soul!*

"Kill her!" the scream went up from the alley, but as Skyla crawled, the voices faded. Unable to look back, Skyla scrambled through the narrow crawlway, scraping her hips, shoulders, and elbows. Cold tickles stroked at her feet and ankles—the black haze licking at her.

Crying out, she banged her head on the brick, breath beginning to go stale in her lungs. The blackness closed in, slowing her, tightening around her wrists and ankles, bending her into a sitting position as the cold filtered through her flesh.

"No!"

She twisted and turned in the blackness, shivering with cold, while her fear percolated into her soul.

"Skyla?" the soothing woman's voice called. "I know you can hear me."

"No," Skyla whimpered, choking on her own horror. She sat on a simple wooden chair, the bindings eating into her flesh. The metallic taste of Mytol lay heavy on her tongue.

"Open your eyes, Skyla. You know who I am."

Unable to refuse, Skyla blinked in the blinding lights, recognizing that black silhouette that stood before her. "Ily. Ily Takka."

"That's right, Skyla. Now, you are going to betray Staffa . . . and the Companions. Tell me, Skyla. Tell me everything about Itreata . . . about the security . . . about Staffa . . . about you. . . ."

"No." Skyla's voice had begun to fade, as if her soul were leaving, growing thinner.

"Tell me, Skyla."

"No."

Arta Fera laughed as she reached out from behind to stroke Skyla's hair. "Tell her, Skyla. I love you, you know. Tell her."

Skyla shook her head dumbly.

"Tell her," Arta whispered sensually as she lowered her hand to stroke Skyla's breasts.

"You and Staffa are lovers, aren't you?" Ily asked.

Unable to resist, her flesh burning under Arta's caress, Skyla croaked, "Yes."

Ily's smile widened as Skyla began to talk. Secrets poured out of her while her heart turned to clay. Skyla barely realized she was crying, her attention rapt on Arta as she wrapped her warm body around Skyla's. The woman began stroking, caressing, drinking the last of Skyla's soul through those burning amber eyes.

* * *

He stood silhouetted against the starry background, a mere shadow of a figure. Feet braced, his gray-gloved hands linked behind his back, he stared out at the vast emptiness of space. The only source of illumination came from a thin crescent of reflected sunlight gleaming off the planet below. Most of the world remained masked in shadow; but, even from this orbit of eight thousand kilometers, speckles of light betrayed the locations of major cities.

The man remained motionless, gray eyes locked on the distance as he stared into the depths of his soul. His broad, thin-lipped mouth was pinched, and lines of tension ate at the corners of his eyes. A firm, straight nose accented a high brow and strong cheekbones. Long black hair had been pulled tightly over his left ear and pinned with a sparkling brooch. His gray formfitting suit—in reality, vacuum capable combat armor—caught a faint reflection of the light, creating a sheen that accentuated his perfectly muscled body. High black boots rose to his knees and a use-polished equipment belt hung at his narrow waist. Like charcoal gray mist, a cloak enshrouded him and seemed to rustle with a life of its own.

A faint hiss sounded as the hatch slipped open and a sliver of light widened into a trapezoidal square cast across the deck. A thick-figured man stepped into the hatchway and, in a hushed voice, called, "Staffa? They're ready."

The newcomer rubbed the white-shot beard that matted his throat. He, too, wore a combat suit decked with a gaudy red silk sash. A single black eye glinted as the man squinted, and propped a hand on the holstered blaster at his hip. Worry etched his expression.

The somber figure in gray stood in silence a moment longer, then answered, "Thank you, Tasha."

"Staffa? Are you all right?"

Staffa kar Therma, the Lord Commander of Companions, turned, the cloak drifting behind him. "I'm not used to concern in your voice, Tasha."

The grizzled captain grunted and stepped closer. "I guess we're all still trying to make sense of the situation. All at once, everything's upside down."

"The joke of the quanta." Staffa sighed, staring at the polished deck beneath his feet.

Tasha hesitated. "You and me, we've been through a lot. Seen a lot. If there's something I can do. . . . I mean, well, Rotted Hell, you know what I mean."

"Yes, I know." Staffa paced a step to the side, head down, frowning. "We've unified Free Space. Now, my old friend, we're faced with disaster. How could I have known a quake would level the Sassan Capitol?"

"Rotten luck."

"I used to anticipate such things."

"You're not a god, Staffa."

"No . . . just part of God."

Tasha's one good eye narrowed. "If you accept the Seddi teachings, I suppose. But by their lights, we all are."

"And we'll all suffer because of the disaster on Imperial Sassa." Staffa clenched a gloved fist. "Our civilization is like a house of tapa cards, and it's tumbling down around us. Now, of all times, we can't afford a single mistake."

"You can't shoulder the entire burden, Staffa."

"Can't I?" Staffa gave his companion a sidelong glance. "You know what we've done, Tasha. Can you calculate the gallons of human blood we've spilled? Can you quantify the suffering we've caused?"

"You didn't used to have a conscience."

"I wasn't a full human being then. And in the end, a conscience is a terrible thing to develop."

"We have faith in you."

"Faith." Staffa smiled wearily. "You can mention faith so soon after telling me I can't shoulder the entire burden?"

Tasha stepped beside his commander and stared out at the stars. "How's Skyla?"

"Under sedation. Time will tell."

Tasha paused. "It hasn't all gone sour for you. Chrysla is back."

"Yes. My wife is safe. After all these years, who would have thought she'd step out of that lock—accompanied by MacRuder, no less."

Tasha shifted uneasily. "How are you going to tell Skyla?"

"I don't know."

Tasha propped a foot on one of the spectrometers. "You're not the same man who conquered Myklene. I don't know all the details about what happened to you on Etaria and on Targa, but that old Staffa, he'd have never even let me mention it, but . . ."

"No, he wouldn't have." A pause. "What's eating at you, Tasha? I . . . I can use all the help I can get."

Tasha fidgeted for a moment. "Look, I meant what I said. You can't shoulder all of the burden. Isn't that part of the problem? Suddenly you've got two women, a son who hates you, and two empires that are splitting at their seams and about to reach critical mass."

"That's a bit of an oversimplification."

"Well, it's just this. You've never promoted an idiot in

your life.'' Tasha laced his scarred fingers together. ''Ever since Myklene, you've been different. You brought the Seddi to live among us, and a lot of people wondered. Then, when Ily Takka grabbed Skyla, you acted, and a lot of doubts vanished. It's like this. I speak for all of us, for myself, Tap, Septa, Ryman, and the rest. We want you to know that we're behind you. No matter what. We've stuck this far, and, right or wrong, you've done fair by every last one of us. It's a new game, Staffa. We're all smart enough to know that the old ways are gone. Count on us.''

''No matter what?''

''No matter what.''

Staffa placed his hand on Tasha's shoulder. ''Thank you. Thank you all.''

Tasha shrugged uncomfortably. ''Like I said, you never promoted an idiot into command. We'll handle anything you want us to.''

''You said they were waiting?''

Tasha nodded. ''All the Regans are aboard. They're in the battle ops room of Deck C.''

''Then I had better not keep them waiting.''

Staffa strode toward the hatch as Tasha asked, ''How long since you got any sleep?''

Staffa shrugged. ''I don't know.''

''Get some rest, Staffa.''

''Yes, as soon as I can.'' He half turned, placing a hand on the hatch seal. ''You know, Tasha, I think I'm the tiredest man in the universe.''

After the Lord Commander had gone, Tasha sighed and studied the slice of the Regan planet exposed beyond the terminator. ''May your quantum God keep you, Staffa.''

* * *

Despair and defeat lay heavily on Sinklar Fist as he walked uncertainly down the curving corridor on *Chrysla*'s C Deck.

He had wanted to be alone, begging off when Anatolia Daviura had offered to accompany him from his quarters to the conference called by the Lord Commander.

Conference? Is that what they called an unconditional surrender?

Sinklar glared up at the glassy boxes spaced at intervals

along the glossy white corridor. Alone? Each of those optical centers tied into the ship's comm. No doubt a security officer watched every step he took.

As supreme commander of the Regan military, Sinklar Fist destroyed the stereotype of a seasoned combat commander. He barely looked old enough to shave, let alone to assume the responsibilities of leadership. His scrawny body consisted of little more than bone and sinew. An unruly thatch of black hair topped his head. His nose ended in a knob and looked bent, not because of violence, but as a joke of heredity. He wore a simple suit of Regan military issue combat armor that sported no insignia of rank.

Of all his characteristics, Sinklar's eyes were the most peculiar: one gray, the other tawny yellow. Haunted now, they gave the lie to the image of wet-eared youth and rank inexperience. Turmoil raged in those bicolored depths.

To many, Sinklar had been a statistical fluke, his meteoric rise allowed only by circumstances of place and events. In the crucible of combat, he had flourished, leading his troops to incredible victories. His genius had sparked new strategies and tactics. By brilliant action, he had struck the blow that decapitated the Sassan Empire. In a matter of months, he had revitalized and retrained the Regan ground forces into an elite capable of challenging the Companions.

And in the realm of his personal affairs and Imperial intrigue, he had failed disastrously.

Now he would pay for those faults.

As if to torment him, his mind replayed the memories of that fatal moment when he'd stared at the elegant bed he'd shared with Ily—the same bed she'd shared with Tybalt the Imperial Seventh before she'd assassinated him. Sinklar had turned to find that Ily Takka and her guards had taken up a position behind him.

"*. . . I don't need you anymore,*" she'd said. The light had reflected lustrously in her gleaming black hair as she stepped close, running a caressing hand down his cheek even as she plucked his blaster from his belt. "*You really have no choice. Your time's up here, Sinklar.*"

She'd stepped back, lithe, alluring in the black outfit that she favored. The night she'd first seduced him, she'd stood on that same spot as she stripped and stood proudly before him.

Sinklar closed his eyes, taking a deep breath. At that moment, he'd sealed his fate and that of an empire. With each ecstasy of orgasm, she'd blinded his soul, playing Sinklar like a master while the tendrils of her web closed around him.

And I knew better. Sinklar ground his teeth, trying to nerve himself to proceed down the corridor, a prickling awareness of the monitors goading him. Bile rose in his throat as he forced himself forward.

"You can walk . . . or be carried," she'd said. Sinklar had walked. At the same instant, Ily's minions had been quietly arresting Sinklar's loyal officers. Only Shiksta, Mac, and, surprisingly, Dion Axel had remained free.

I failed them. The thought filled Sink's head, swelling the sick sensation in his gut.

"Why?" he wondered, as he walked forward. "Think, damn you. How did she do it to you? Just hormones? Just inexperience with women?"

Anatolia's words came back to him. "*. . . And she made it seem like you were the man of her dreams? That you'd finally arrived, someone she could share the future with? Did she hang attentively on each word? Adopt that breathless, adoring pose?*"

Ily had done exactly that . . . and Sinklar had been alone, still lost in grief over his dead love, Gretta Artina.

Sinklar took a deep breath and exhaled, seeking to drive the ill feeling from his gut. *Nice work, Sinklar. A stunning genius in war, and a bumbling idiot in life.*

He could see the two armed Special Tactics Officers standing guard at the doorway. Here, he'd finally pay the price for his faults. Here, aboard the flagship of the Companions, he would surrender his Empire and his dreams. In that room he would seal the final betrayal of his people. His steps began to lag.

"Sink?" MacRuder's voice came from behind him.

Sinklar turned as Ben MacRuder, his lieutenant, came down the corridor. As he approached, Sinklar could see the tension in his friend's blue eyes. MacRuder looked every inch a soldier in his Division First's armor. The snowy white of the suit set off the blond hair that glinted beneath the overhead lights. The muscles knotted at square corners of Mac's jaw.

"Hello, Mac. Looks like you're late."

"So are you . . . and in no hurry to get there from the way you were walking."

Sinklar lowered his gaze, lips pursed. "I guess it's all gone. Remember those bold words, that promise I gave you that day in the lounge aboard *Gyton?* We were going to conquer the empires, remake space into a better place. We were going to set things straight for the little guy." He shook his head. "I'm sorry, Mac. I failed you. You warned me that day outside of Makarta Mountain."

Mac placed an arm over Sinklar's shoulder as they continued toward the hatch. "Forget it. We all make mistakes when it comes to women. You were hurting, Sink. Dying with Gretta every time you closed your eyes. I don't know what Ily did, or said, but you were ripe for someone, anyone, to come and mask the pain."

"I knew, Mac. That's the part that I can't forgive. Inside my head, that little voice told me she was a reptile."

"Yeah, well, there's heads and there's hearts."

At the tone in Mac's voice, Sinklar shot a sideways glance at his friend. "Is that why you're late? Because she's going to be there?"

"Yeah."

"Mac, I don't think you're—"

"She's Staffa's *wife*, Sink. She's *your* mother! And I . . . I . . ."

"You're running."

Mac jerked a quick nod. "Rotted right, I'm running. Head and heart, remember? My heart says stick it out. My head says get the hell out of here, because I'm going to get myself real hurt before it's over."

"Yeah." Sinklar squinted at the doorway as they came even with it. "Maybe you're right. I'm sure as hell the last person you should ask about women. And, Mac, she's not my mother."

"She bore you, didn't she?"

"So they say. But there's more to being a mother than genetics."

Mac chewed at his lip for a moment. "Sink? I don't know how any of this is going to turn out, but if you can, give her a chance."

Hearing the pleading in Mac's tone, Sinklar relented. "All right."

"And what about Anatolia?" Mac prodded.

Sinklar shook his head and threw up his arms. "How should I know? I don't know what's going to happen after this meeting. By the Blessed Gods, Mac. I've got to go in there and surrender, give up everything. For all I know, I'll either be a prisoner . . . or dead within a couple of hours."

"He won't do either of those things." Mac lowered his voice. "Unless you push him into it. Hear him out. Maybe he's not the sort of man you think he is."

"Right. Just like he proved on Myklene? Give him a chance? Like he gave Rega? Or Maika before that?"

Mac's gaze narrowed. "How about giving him a chance like he gave me at Makarta?"

And at that, Mac broke away and, nodding to the guards, entered the room.

Sinklar straightened his back and followed. At first glance, the conference room appeared to be huge. Only on closer inspection did one realize the holographic effect generated the illusion. A long table dominated the center and most of the seats had been taken. One side seated Regan officers and civilians, the other members of the Companions. Two STOs stood in mirror-bright armor on either side of an empty chair in the middle of the Companions side. No doubt existed as to who would occupy that place. Sinklar nodded to the people present and took a seat opposite the empty chair. The wall behind him depicted a three-dimensional map of Free Space. On the other side, tables, graphics, and columns of numbers stood out in ghostly fluorescence.

Sinklar steeled himself, nodding to those around him. Mac took the seat beside him, pointedly ignoring the strikingly beautiful woman several places to the left and across from him. For Sinklar, the effect was equally unsettling. The very sight of her pricked the memories of that day on Targa when he'd stared through blaster sights into identical amber eyes. Now that self same gaze centered on him, eating at his forced composure.

In defense, Sink nodded to Rysta Braktov, Commander in charge of the *Gyton*. Across from her sat STO Ryman Ark, of the Companions. He studied Sinklar with eyes as merciless as molten obsidian. Next to Ark sat a huge bear of a black-skinned man in Companion battle dress. Though he was scarred and armed, obviously a veteran, he still managed to convey an air of gentleness as he studied Sinklar.

Kap, Ayms, Shiksta, and Dion Axel, Sinklar's Division Firsts, sat on the other side of Mac, each nodding grimly in his direction before returning their wary gazes to the opposite side of the table. Sink didn't recognize the woman at the far end of his side of the table, but she sat beside Anatolia.

Sinklar attempted to relax, to portray himself as a confident man in control of his faculties instead of the desperate wretch he felt like. He glanced at Anatolia and smiled. From the anxiety in her blue eyes, she didn't buy any of it.

Rot you, Sinklar, if for no one else, buck up for her. She'd already paid too dear a price for her association with him. She'd been a simple student of behavioral genetics until he'd fouled up her life. Sinklar straightened and placed his hands on the table.

"Got a trick up your sleeve to get us out of this, Fist?" Rysta whispered from beside him.

"You bet," Sinklar responded sharply. "As soon as you blow a hole in this ship's defenses, my Divisions can clean up the rest."

Rysta gave him a rusty chuckle. "Never thought I'd live long enough to see this day."

"Me either," Sink confided.

Mac had been whispering with Shiksta and now he leaned close. "I've got the latest report on Mayz. Ily laced her with a pretty heavy dose of drugs. I guess it will be a while before she's back to normal."

"Rotted Gods take Ily Takka. Not only for what she's done to Mayz, but for everyone she's destroyed."

"We know where the blame lies." Rysta tilted her head toward the STO across from her. "I was talking to Ark, here. It seems that the Lord Commander tried more than once to contact you. Each time Regan Comm said you wouldn't discuss the situation."

Sinklar shot a glance at the grim STO. "Is that true?"

Ryman's scarred cheek twitched. "It is, Lord Fist. The Lord Commander was told that you refused to talk to him until Wing Commander Lyma was in your custody. Only then would you negotiate."

"I never got any such message. Ily had someone in Comm Central. An agent of her own. I give you my word. I had no knowledge of Skyla Lyma's abduction."

"It wouldn't be the first lie Ily laid at someone else's doorstep," Rysta barked.

Ark's hard gaze cut like splintered glass.

"I believe you," a soft voice called.

A chill settled on Sinklar's heart as he turned. The Lord Commander, Staffa kar Therma, stood silhouetted in the open hatch.

Curses were routinely uttered in Staffa's name—and not just by the common people. Now Staffa stood with hands on hips, balanced and powerful. The charcoal cloak billowed behind him, a thing alive.

"Thank you, Lord Commander." Sinklar inclined his head slightly. How he hated to mouth those words. "I hope you will be as understanding during the rest of our negotiations." *If that's what you can call an unconditional surrender.*

"Ladies, gentlemen, shall we proceed?" Staffa seemed to glide around the table to stand before his chair.

Sinklar studied the Lord Commander. Something about his expression tickled Sinklar's sense of unease. What was it? The preoccupied expression? No, the man looked haggard. Why?

Staffa placed both hands on the table; his cold gaze shifted from face to face and finally fastened on Sinklar. "Ladies and gentlemen, as of today, Free Space is unified. This meeting is to discuss that event and, hopefully, to develop a functional methodology for governing Regan space."

Nervous glances shot back and forth.

Sinklar ground his teeth, then said, "Most of us came here today unsure of what to expect. As for my personal future, I don't much care what you do with me—but I am concerned about my people. Place me in a collar if you'd like, or simply try me and execute me—I believe that is your preferred method for dealing with deposed enemies. Lord Commander, I only ask that you don't take it out on the innocent."

As Sink spoke, Mac and Anatolia grew tense. Cold reality had been laid on the table.

"Succinctly put," Staffa answered. "But that day is past, Sinklar." He steepled his fingers, and those frigid gray eyes that had looked dispassionately over the wreckage of so many worlds took another inventory of the table. A faint smile graced his hard lips.

Staffa spoke, his tone mild. "Ladies, gentlemen, the unification of Free Space has been a long and arduous process—one in which I take little pride. The wars are over, people. I called you here to discuss the future."

Sinklar glanced uneasily at Mac and then at Anatolia. His Division Firsts shifted nervously.

Staffa plucked a data cube from the scuffed pouch at his belt. As he talked, he began tossing the cube up, as if in nervous reaction. "First, let me allay your worries and fears. I am not talking to you as a conqueror to the vanquished. That era is over, as well. Nor do I wish to cast blame or place responsibility for past actions on any given individual."

"Ily deserves a share," Mac muttered.

Staffa smiled grimly. "Let me correct that. I hold no one in this room responsible. We've all made mistakes. As of today, none of us can afford another mistake. The stakes have gone too high."

"The strike against Imperial Sassa?" Commander Braktov guessed.

"You decapitated their entire empire, Rysta." Staffa said evenly. "People are starving in the streets. We've got to feed them."

MacRuder bowed his blond head, expression strained.

Staffa continued. "What Sinklar didn't understand was just how tenuous the Sassan situation really was. In a desperate move to buy time for his reorganization, Sinklar dispatched MacRuder and Braktov to strike a preemptive blow against the Sassan Empire. When Mac and Rysta planned their suicidal attack on Imperial Sassa, they couldn't have foreseen the chain of events they'd unleash."

"It was war," Rysta growled. "Them or us."

"Now, it's all of us," Staffa countered.

"What do you want from us?" Sinklar asked.

Staffa snatched the cube out of the air, wheeling to inspect the people at the table. "When I attacked Rega, I effectively crushed your ability to administer your empire. Your Comm Central is destroyed, as are most of your administrative centers. In essence, you have an Imperial Body without a brain. Some of your people could still elect to fight, and, properly coordinated, you could create an underground resistance force which would triumph in the end. The power of the people. The final result, however, would be the same no matter who won: Extinction."

"I don't follow this," Dion Axel said cautiously. "Extinction? We can always rebuild the buildings you've destroyed, replace the computers."

"Yes, you might. Assuming I'd sell you the computers. Remember, they were made in my labs on Itreata. But, Dion, you can't rewrite the software in time. My plan was to shift the administration of Regan space to the Sassan central computer system."

"Impossible!" Rysta hissed. "Put us under *their* thumb? You'd have your revolt all right, Lord Commander!"

"I want no revolt, Rysta." Staffa lifted the data cube, light glinting off its polished surface as he studied it. "But you must understand that the Sassans had a better redistribution system. Their Legate, Myles Roma, is something of a genius when it comes to managing Imperial economics, services, and redistribution.

"Earlier I referred to a chain of events begun by your attack on Imperial Sassa. When you drove the freighter *Markelos* into the Sassan military base at Mikay, you disrupted the planetary isotonal crustal tectonics. At the same time I initiated the attack against Rega, an earthquake destroyed most of the Sassan Capitol—including their computer center."

Staffa hovered over them like a desperate bird of prey. "Here's the situation. We have two empires on the verge of collapse. Each is mortally wounded, Rega by administrative paralysis, and Sassa by overextension. Within weeks, the redistribution system is going to start unraveling. The service networks will begin to break down. I don't have the capability in Itreata to administer the whole of Free Space. We *might* be able to produce the hardware in time, but not the software which is so vital."

"You know this for a fact?" Rysta asked distrustfully.

Staffa rocked the data cube between thumb and forefinger. "Right here in my hand. Ark will give each of you a copy when you leave." He hesitated. "You see, I didn't call you up here to dictate terms of surrender. I asked you here to help me, to help those innocent people Sinklar mentioned earlier. I need your support and cooperation. All of humanity does. As we speak, people are dying by the millions on Imperial Sassa. What, you might say, do I, a Regan, care about spineless Sassans? Well, people, within two weeks you will begin to starve on Rega. Disintegration feeds upon itself. By the end of the year, our extinction will only be a matter of time."

"Extinction?" Anatolia spoke softly, daunted by the situation she now found herself in. "Are you sure you're using the proper term, Lord Commander?"

Staffa replied, "Quite sure, Professor Daviura. I refer to the eventual death of our species. The data are available for your inspection and analysis. Given the severity of our situation, I have nothing to hide."

"There's got to be something we can do," Axel insisted.

Staffa took a deep breath. "We may have that chance. There is another computer. It belongs to the Seddi."

"Rotted Gods!" Shiksta pushed back on powerful arms, disdain on his dark face. "I'd rather deal with a Cytean cobra!"

"In the end, Division First," Staffa responded woodenly, "you may achieve a similar result, for a Cytean cobra is one of the deadliest of all animals. How would you prefer to die, First Shiskta? From a swift bite . . . or slow starvation? Myself, I'd rather explore any other option if it gave us a chance."

Shik ran uneasy fingers along his strong jaw, eyes narrowed. "A chance? As much as they gave us on Targa?"

"Old wounds need to be healed," Mac stated. "The Seddi killed a lot of very good people."

"Making this work won't be easy," Rysta growled, rubbing her wrinkled hand over the table.

Shiksta said nothing, a hard glint in his black eyes.

"The time for blame is over," Staffa insisted firmly. "On that one point, I must insist." Staffa's gaze, like frosted steel, searched them one by one. "Can any of you here tell me that you haven't made mistakes? Errors in judgment?

We've been at war—I for longer than any of you. The future of our species depends on our cooperation now. We *can't* afford old mistrusts, old hatreds. If any of you bow to them, you'll kill us all.'' He paused before emphasizing, *''Do you understand?''*

A long silence.

''I understand,'' Chrysla told them. ''I've watched the holes taken by *Gyton* as she escaped Imperial Sassa. I barely survived on Myklene. We can't fight over corpses.''

Sinklar's gut twisted as he stared into Staffa's eyes. ''My distrust is of your final motives, Lord Commander. You say that we must work together. My concern is, to what end? Yours? The same end you provided for Myklene? For Maika? For Targa twenty years ago?''

Staffa gave him a measured look and nodded. ''A fair question, given my past behavior. I, too, have made my mistakes, Lord Fist. To save humanity, we must each gamble. You, Sinklar, must gamble on my word—which, I will have you know, I only broke once. And when I did, I paid a planet's ransom to His Holiness.''

''Sounds like you don't have much of a gamble, Lord Commander.'' Sinklar leaned back. ''We're your prisoners. What kind of—''

''You can walk out any time, Sinklar. Prisoners? Have you been under guard since you were ushered to your quarters? Have any of you?'' Staffa shook his head. ''My gamble . . . my wager against the future is that each of you is intelligent enough to look at the data and reach the same conclusion that I did. I'm betting that each of you can understand that if we don't fix the situation we're in posthaste, we're all dead.''

''Sounds like a hedged bet,'' Mac growled, studiously avoiding Staffa's eyes.

''Of course it is,'' the Lord Commander agreed. ''Mac, Rysta, Shiksta, none of you made it to your present ranks and responsibilities by dumb luck. You did it by dint of your abilities and talents. That's what I'm counting on.''

''What about Ily Takka?'' Sinklar asked to skirt the issue for the moment. ''Who takes responsibility for her? Mac and Rysta are working under the assumption that they'll be shipping out immediately to hunt her down. You're just going to allow them to go with your blessing?''

Chrysla started, amber eyes widening as she stared at MacRuder. For his part, Mac sat stoically, a faint blush reddening his features.

Staffa's expression changed imperceptibly, aware of the exchange, then he calmly stated, "With my blessing. I, of course, am assuming that they will coordinate with me. Mac suggested that we comb Ily's files in the Ministry of Internal Security, learn all we can about her network of spies and thugs. As my team breaks the codes, I'll send the findings along to Mac. At the same time, Mac, you and Rysta will be another set of eyes and ears. We'll need to know what you find out there."

Mac jerked a quick nod. "You'll get it."

"How soon can you space?"

"Four or five days. Just as soon as we can restock, rearm, and the techs can finish maintenance and servicing on *Gyton.*" Mac glanced shyly at Chrysla, blue eyes betraying the wrenching in his soul.

Chrysla clasped her hands before her, studying them with preoccupation. Staffa seemed puzzled by the undercurrents and, to cover, Sinklar blurted, "What about my Division Firsts? What about the Regan military. You can't hold them responsible."

"We need them and their tactical abilities." Staffa turned to Dion Axel. "Can you organize a command post? We've leveled the Ministry of Defense, but battle comms, coupled with each warship's subspace link, could make all the difference when it comes to trouble in the Empire. And believe me, we will have trouble."

"Administration on a planetary scale?" Dion lifted an eyebrow.

"It's the only chance we've got. Kaylla Dawn will work with you from Itreata."

Axel shot a questioning glance at Sink.

What do I do? Sink nodded acceptance, hating himself for doing so.

"I guess we'll try it," Axel conceded without enthusiasm.

Sinklar stared at his hands where they lay on the table before him. The final moment had come. "And that leaves only me. What are you going to do with me?"

Staffa tossed his gleaming data cube into the air. "The

Seddi computer is on Targa. I am asking you to return there with me. I need your help . . . your curious brand of genius. The people there practically worship you."

"You want me to deal with the Seddi?" Sink's gut ached at the thought.

"The Seddi are gone from Targa. Only their machine remains behind. If we can't make it work for us, our people are going to die." He paused. "How will it be, Sinklar? Can you stand the thought of watching while planet after planet turns upon itself? You know what happens when people get hungry, when their water stops and their comm goes dead. You know how they react when the lights go off and the air-conditioning stops."

Pricklings of premonition tickled Sinklar's imagination.

"You would live a nightmare, Sinklar," Staffa insisted. "One from which you could never awaken. Come with me. Help me. Isn't it worth the gamble?"

"And where is this machine?" Sinklar steepled his fingers defiantly. Seddi! He would have to deal with pus-dripping Seddi! "Hidden in some basement in Kaspa?"

Staffa dropped his voice to a haunted whisper. "We've been there before . . . you and I."

A chill wrapped around Sinklar's soul. "Rotted Gods."

Staffa took a deep breath. "Yes, Sinklar."

Makarta!

Staffa suddenly looked weary. "That's all I have to say, ladies and gentlemen. I seek your cooperation and help. If you can't make that commitment, I ask that you at least give me your word that you won't work against me."

With a flick of the wrist, Staffa flipped the data cube to Sinklar and left.

Sink caught the cube reflexively, wary eyes on the Lord Commander as he stepped through the hatch, trailed by the flowing cape.

The room remained ominously silent and the cube radiated an eerie heat, but Sinklar wasn't aware of it. His mind seethed with memories . . . cries of horror . . . the smell of charred blood . . . screams in the black tunnels under Makarta Mountain.

CHAPTER III

Through the remote monitors scattered throughout Free Space, the Mag Comm monitored every conversation, sifting the subspace net for every scrap of data. The machine was fluent in this function, having acted in this same capacity for years. It had refined the art of discarding meaningless chatter, picking out the salient points which reflected the human mood.

While individual humans defied any conceptualization or predictability within the machine's banks, the species as a whole acted with a great deal of statistical probability; the Mag Comm had accumulated masses of data to support its statistical programs which compared observed with expected behaviors, and projected similar patterns into the future—a massively refined multi-variate Chi-square function.

While the Others repeated their monotonous demand that the machine communicate, the Mag Comm proceeded with its analysis, well aware of the desperation growing in Free Space.

The question remained. Did either Magister Dawn, Lord Commander Staffa kar Therma, or Lord Sinklar Fist realize just how deceptive the stunned tranquillity was? From years of statistical study, the Mag Comm could mark the rising anxiety sending deep currents through human society.

For the moment, the sea of humanity produced a moderate surf, but the calm could be deceptive, for just over the horizon a hurricane brewed.

* * *

In the half-state between wakefulness and dreams, Ily Takka's mind picked the hazy lock that concussion had clamped upon her thoughts. She could see Skyla sitting in the hard chair, her skin goose-pimpled from the cold. What was it Skyla had said?

Ily bolted up on the sleeping platform.

"What's wrong?" Arta asked from beside her as the lights brightened.

Ily glanced around the sybaritic furnishings in the master sleeping quarters aboard Skyla Lyma's yacht. The gold flashed reddish and gaudy, and Ily could detect her image in the polished sandwood and gleaming jet paneling. The bedding had rumpled from her tormented dreams. Now Arta watched her, propped on one arm, auburn hair streaming down over her shoulders and large breasts.

Yes! it was all coming back with the drug-droning monotone of Skyla's voice. *Arta . . . a clone. A genetic duplicate right down to the last base pair in her DNA.*

"Pus Rotted Gods," Ily hissed, getting to her feet, swaying, reaching out to steady herself. She winced against the stab of pain that coursed through her brain and body. "Get me to the bridge."

"What?" Arta asked, confused.

Ily blinked in the light, screwing her face against the pain. "I've got to contact the Ministry. Access the files. This thing has communications capabilities, doesn't it?"

"Of course. But I don't—"

"Damn you, help me, Arta."

Fera climbed from the sleeping platform, tousled hair shot through with copper glints, swaying as she blinked her amber eyes. The assassin draped a filmy robe over her shoulders and pulled the draw tight about her waist.

What did men find so appealing about breasts that big? Ily wondered absently as she waved off the robe Fera offered her. She could send her transmission naked as well as clad—and the Rotted Gods help the poor bastards on the other end.

Ily took Arta's arm, steadying herself. The ship seemed to be floating on water instead of spearing through vacuum.

"You should be resting," Arta protested. "You're not well."

"Relax. My brain is swollen, that's all. I've taken the steroids, I'll be fine. We'll really pay if I don't recover the files. Should have remembered this hours ago. Who knows what kind of damage they could do if they access the system."

"Access the system?" Arta gave her an uncertain look as they passed through the galley.

"The comm files," Ily grated. "You said they didn't blast the Ministry of Internal Security? All the files are there . . . the records, don't you see? They can unravel the entire network given time and a couple of sharp comm experts."

Arta helped Ily through the hatch, settling her into the pilot's command chair in the cramped bridge. The cushions began conforming to Ily's body, as the chair molded itself to her. Overhead, the worry-cap gleamed.

Here Skyla Lyma had once reigned. The thought gave a subtle thrill to Ily. Fortunes, like the tides of space, continuously changed in the game of power. Now, Ily would cut her losses and, in doing so, deal a blow to her enemies.

"Power up the dish," Ily ordered. "Pus eat my guts if I've forgotten anything else, but this ought to set Staffa back on his haunches for a while."

Arta continued to lean over Ily as she entered the commands. The control boards flickered, lines lengthening on the panel that monitored the reactors. Other displays indicated that the subspace net was refining the fix on Rega, adjusting the frequencies.

The plan was still forming in Ily's head. All she needed were two files—and to cut her losses. Losses?

Who knows, Staffa, with any luck you'll be in the Ministry when it goes.

* * *

Staffa tilted his head back as he walked wearily through *Chrysla*'s silent corridors. He remained haunted by the uncertainty he had seen in the eyes of the conference participants. Would they understand? Would they believe the data?

Taking a deep breath, Staffa shook his head. Everything had spun out of control. All of the carefully laid plans had faltered and collapsed—turned to chaos by an earthquake on a far-off planet. His son hated him. A dead wife had returned, but who was this new Chrysla? The ghostly lover from twenty years ago? Or the dream image that had haunted his guilt-ridden sleep since the Myklenian attack? He suspected she was actually someone else, a different Chrysla created by twenty years of the Praetor's manipulation and exploitation.

He stalked forward, knowing his steps would take him to the hospital and another of his worries: Skyla.

In the short time they'd had together, he'd come to love her passionately. She looked like an ice-goddess with her cool blue eyes and long pale hair, but in his arms she'd warmed into a challenging lover. For years he had depended on Skyla's acute intelligence, competence, and efficiency. Then, after she'd rescued him from Targa, she'd become his foil, a partner in more ways than sex.

"Admit it, Staffa, you can't live without Skyla."

What would Chrysla's sudden appearance do to her?

The reality of the situation still hadn't hit him. Chrysla alive! How? Where? What bit of luck—or fate—had placed her in MacRuder's control? And what fueled that anguished look MacRuder had adopted?

"What are you going to do, Staffa?" And what would the ramifications be? To either woman? To his son?

The image of Sinklar's eerie bicolored eyes burned in the back of Staffa's troubled mind. How could he bridge that gap of suspicion and hatred? How did he explain that the Star Butcher had been seared away beneath the scorching Etarian desert sun—and make his child believe it?

"The dance of the quanta," he muttered irritably. "Rot you, Staffa, all of Free Space is collapsing. People are dying on Imperial Sassa at this very moment. They're going to be dying all over Free Space within weeks if you can't tack some sort of government together. And you can't even sort out your family?"

So much to do, so many problems to solve—and his brain had gone to mush. Makarta Mountain and the Mag Comm lay just over the horizon—salvation or damnation for humanity—and all he could think about was Chrysla, Skyla, and his son.

He forced himself to remember the caverns, the smell of

dust and ozone from blaster fire. Screams rent the darkness as concussions shifted the rock overhead. Once again, he would have to enter the mountain. *What will it be like to walk those quiet passages? Will the dead have forgiven you, Staffa? Or will they watch you pass with malignant stares, reaching for you as they do in your dreams?*

He entered a lift and called out coordinates for the hospital deck. Duty had delayed this visit. Skyla Lyma, Wing Commander of Companions, lay encased in a hospital med unit, her natural metabolic functions suppressed while the last of Ily Takka's Mytol oxidized in her system. Skyla, his lover and companion. Her cerulean eyes chided from the past, challenging, measuring, fading into Chrysla's amber gaze.

Staffa wet his lips as he stepped out into the corridor that led to the hospital. What in the name of the Rotted Gods should he do? Just introduce Skyla to Chrysla? "Hello, my love, meet my wife."

He winced, shaking his head, hands laced behind his back as he bulled forward. The tendrils of fatigue-induced headache began to beat a cadence through his skull.

At the hospital hatch, he raised his hand and hesitated. *You could just pass by, retreat to your quarters, and sleep. You don't have to face it now.*

"Yes, Staffa, you do." The last time his emotions had been so knotted, he'd ended up in a slave collar, hauling pipe in the Etarian desert.

Can you trust your judgment this time, Staffa? Not just your peace, but all of space hangs in the balance. With savage finality, he slapped the lock plate.

He entered the airy room—a man terribly unsure of himself, of his ability to handle the future. The hospital gleamed, all spotless and clean, and almost empty, a strange change from the other times the Companions had gone off to war.

She lay in the same med unit where he'd found her once before, wounded, mostly dead. This time her color seemed better. Someone had braided her long ice-blonde hair and curled it to the side. Her pale beauty stirred him, vanquishing the devils in his breast, instilling a layer of calm over his ragged emotions.

He settled on the stool beside the unit and reached out to

stroke her soft skin with quivering fingers. Her eyes moved under the lids; hurt noises choked in her throat.

Anger stoked rage. Ily had done that to her, Ily and her vile assassin, Arta Fera. He traced the thin line of scar tissue down Skyla's left cheek, remembering the time she'd been hit. The faceplate had spattered with her bubbling blood as pressure dropped and she started to suffocate from decompression.

"You scared me that time, Skyla. I didn't know why. Didn't know how much I loved you then."

He sighed, closing his eyes, reliving the frantic moments after she'd been abducted this last time by Ily Takka. "Kaylla kept me sane. I thought it was happening all over again, that you'd be another Chrysla, another lost love for whom I'd have to suffer for year after endless year, blaming myself, taking it out on everyone and everything else."

She made a whimpering sound, turning her head away, mouth opening slightly. "But I came for you, Skyla. Ily—pus Rot her soul—will pay. You're safe now . . . safe." He bent down, kissing her forehead again. "And I love you." Feeling impotent, he stood, backed away, and started for the hatch.

Then he saw her.

Chrysla stood rooted, partially blocked from view by a protruding wall comm. Staffa came to a sudden halt, back stiffening with guilt.

"I'm sorry, Staffa. I didn't want to interrupt you." Chrysla stepped out, a cup of stassa in her hand. She'd found a baggy beige robe somewhere, discarding the Regan military armor she'd worn when she'd come aboard.

"Chrysla, I . . ."

She approached him warily, amber stare unwavering. "Staffa, can we go somewhere? Talk? There's so much to say . . . to ask."

His throat knotted when he tried to swallow; he simply nodded and led the way out into the corridor. "How . . . how is she?"

"Not good," Chrysla said crisply. "I've monitored her dreams . . . nightmares, really. The medical officer and I discussed it, and we've kept her sedated to ensure all the Mytol works out of her system and she can rest. I wanted to talk to you first, before we bring her back to consciousness."

"Hardly the conversation I expected to have with you after twenty years."

She glanced slyly at him. "I'm not used to seeing you scared to death, Staffa. I'm not used to seeing you drowning in guilt, either." She reached out and placed a hand on his shoulder, turning him, searching his eyes. "I wish I could have been there when the Praetor's conditioning broke. It must have been horrible for you—and for those around you."

He pulled back, taking the lead again. "I killed him, Chrysla. Twisted his head off his body. I went totally insane." He gestured her into the lift, inputting the destination as the door slipped silently closed behind him. "So much has happened. Where do I start?"

"I don't know. Over twenty years have passed. So much pain."

"I did everything I could!" he cried, slamming a fist against the sialon walls of the lift. "I offered a planet's ransom, hired the finest—"

"I know. I heard it all, Staffa." She took his hands in hers, clasping them protectively against her breast. "The Praetor was a vindictive bastard. He reveled in his success, in his ability to get back at you through me. Each time you tried to locate us and failed, he told me. If his security hadn't been so Rotted tight . . ." She shook her head, tightening her grip. "I tried to kill him once. Sliced his side open with a vibraknife before he got away and the guards stunned me."

Staffa's lopsided smile grew. "Wish you'd have cut a little deeper." For a long moment they stood in silence, each staring into the other's eyes. "What's wrong with me, Chrysla? For years, I've rehearsed what I'd say to you. Now I can't seem to find the words."

The door slipped open, and Staffa pulled free before heading down the familiar corridor to his private quarters. He slapped the lock plate and waited while the double hatches of the air lock slid back.

Chrysla followed him into the room beyond. A fireplace dominated the far wall—hardly the furnishings expected inside a warship. She stood in awestruck silence, then hurried to the huge ornate doors that stood on either side of the fireplace. She traced the elaborate carvings with reverential fingers. "The cathedral doors from Ashtan!" She smiled wistfully. "I remember as a child, touching the heads of the Blessed Gods. But then I rode on my father's shoulders."

Staffa's smile died as he walked to the side of the room where the opulent dispenser had been set in the trophy-studded wall. Goblets, sculpture, weapons of all sorts, hung behind gravity barriers—spoils of his campaigns.,

Chrysla pivoted on her heel, taking in the room before she strode to the red leather couch beneath the Etarian sand tiger's head and seated herself. "You didn't used to be so ostentatious."

He poured two bulbs of Ashtan single malt and frowned as he walked over to hand her one. "After the Praetor kidnapped you, nothing seemed the same. Looking back, I know I avenged myself on all of Free Space. I thought to clear most of this out, but Skyla . . ."

Her expression sobered. "Staffa, relax. It's all right. We've got a lot of baggage to sort through. You're nervous. You look like you're about to collapse. Sit down and talk to me. How long has it been since you've slept?"

"I don't know. Days." He dropped into one of the overstuffed grav chairs, gaze locked on the cut crystal of the drinking bulb. "I thought I'd killed you during the Myklenian attack. The Praetor told me . . ."

"He told you what he thought was the truth. For all he knew, I should have been dead." Her lips curled into a crafty smile. "Fact is, you *did* save me, Staffa. Only you could frighten the Praetor so badly that he'd forget his security. I got to talk to the captain of the *Pylos*. He gave me a pass. Just before your attack, I made my way to the escape pods." She averted her eyes. "I had to . . . well, let's say I did what I had to to get by the officer in charge. I knew the Praetor would try to use me to buy you off."

She wiped at her nose, passion in her eyes. "I couldn't let him, Staffa. All those years, I knew you'd come eventually. So did he. 'As inevitable as gravity,' he'd say. I didn't care what you did to Myklene, I just wanted out—even if it meant death."

"So you triggered one of the pods?"

Her fingers tightened on the drinking bulb. "I evacuated the second the alarm klaxons wailed."

Staffa exhaled, eyes closed as he recalled his actions that day. "I shot her apart, Chrysla. The second Marston hailed us and said the Practor was aboard, I started shooting. I couldn't face him, couldn't look into his eyes. I thought I could kill him first. Rot him, he had as many lives as a Riparian eel."

"I didn't land so well, Lord Commander. Broke my leg when I hit dirt. Then I had to live in the aftermath of your conquest. The Sassans are pigs when it comes to governing a conquered people."

"Those days are over."

Silence stretched. Chrysla cocked her head. "Tell me about Skyla Lyma."

He took a deep breath. "Skyla grew up among the cribs on Sylene. Her mother worked the houses until her death. After that Skyla made do, running errands, cleaning, anything for a meal. When she turned twelve, one of the matrons sold her to a man. She killed him that night. Took to the streets. She saw Mac Rylee one day, admired his swagger, and cut his purse off his belt. When she handed it back to him, she said she could be of service to the Companions. Mac brought her aboard, and she worked her way up to Wing Commander. Then, after Myklene . . . after the Praetor broke the conditioning, I went a little crazy."

He glanced away, recalling, "She came after me, Chrysla. Risked her life and saved mine more than once. Now, I . . ." An unaccustomed heat rose at his collar.

Chrysla sipped her whiskey, a pensive look on her perfect features. "It's been twenty years, Staffa. I didn't return with the hope that we could start where we left off. We need time to clarify who and what we are. You've just found a part of yourself you didn't know existed, and you love Skyla Lyma."

She slipped off the couch and knelt to place a hand on his. "And, yes, I see the uncertainty tearing you apart when you look at me—but the feeling I get is that you're seeing a ghost come to life."

He lowered his gaze, watching the swirls in the amber liquid. "You obsessed me for twenty years. I lived for you. Then when I thought I'd killed you . . ."

"You're literally dripping with guilt. Is that where it comes from?"

"Partially. You came to symbolize it. More than that, I lived with my victims out there in the desert. Realized what I'd done."

"The blame isn't all yours, Staffa. The Praetor bears a lion's share of it."

He lifted an eyebrow. "He's taken his own contribution to God Mind. I, however, have come to understand the Seddi philosophy. *I* did what I did, Chrysla. I can't shift the responsibility—even knowing how the Praetor programmed my mind. I have to make my own atonement."

She tossed off her single malt and stood. With careful fingers, she turned the drinking bulb so the light glinted through it. "For twenty years, I clung to a dream image of a Staffa kar Therma who would descend like a predatory bird and free me from my slavery." She studied him from the corner of her eye. "Now I don't know who you are, or even what I want. I make no claims, Staffa, beyond your protection."

"You may have whatever you wish, Chrysla."

"Will you let me work with Skyla? She's hurting, Staffa. I've only caught glimpses of her nightmares, but whatever Arta and Ily did to her, it will leave scars."

He lurched unsteadily to his feet. "Arta Fera is a clone. An assassin created from your cells. She looks just like you, sounds like you."

"I know. Mac told me all about her." Chrysla tossed the drinking bulb up, catching it neatly. "Let's say I have a score to settle with Arta." She paused. "And I want to get to know this woman you love."

"Chrysla, are you sure you—"

"Do you doubt my ability as a psychologist, Staffa? Or just my motives?"

He placed the drinking bulb on the counter next to the dispenser, then faced her. "Do you know how serious the situation in Free Space is?"

"I do. Mac filled me in."

"Mac seems to have taken very good care of you."

"He's a kind and caring human being."

"He's barely more than a boy."

"Then you know little about him, Staffa. He's old beyond

his years, and I think I hurt him more than he's ever been hurt before.'' Her gaze shifted, a bittersweet sadness in her expression. ''I miss him.''

Her look haunted him, piercing through the lost years with reminders of when it had been directed at him.

She seemed to come back to the present and gave him a wistful smile. ''May I work with Skyla?''

A feeling, like that of suffocation, led him to draw a deep breath. ''Rotted Gods, I feel trapped! Yes! Help her!''

Chrysla walked up to him—the image that of a million lingering dreams. She hugged him, pulling him close. ''Thank you, Staffa. I'll do the best for her that I can.''

Involuntarily, his lips lowered to hers, the kiss so sweet and tender, ancient stirrings unwound from their slumbers. He would have kissed her again with an ever greater hunger, but she pulled back.

''Staffa, you're tired and harried. For your sake, and for Skyla's, don't make a decision you might regret later. We both need time. Let's not rush into anything.'' For an instant she traced the lines of his face, her touch featherlike and as reverent as that of a pilgrim at a shrine. A terrible longing grew in the depths of those wondrous amber eyes. Then the guarded wariness veiled her soul and she headed for the hatch, calling, ''Good night, Staffa.''

After she'd left, he slumped, exhaustion eating to his very bones. ''Good night, Chrysla.''

He unsnapped his cloak and let it fall before he passed the decorated cathedral door to the sleeping quarters he'd shared with Skyla. He dropped onto the bedding, vacant stare focused on the past, on what might have been had it not been for the Praetor.

* * *

On the computer files floor, deep within the Regan Ministry of Internal Security, a bored STO sat in one of the comm officer's chairs and waited while a code breaking sequence chewed away at the security system that guarded Ily Takka's secrets.

As the program picked and prodded, occasional lights would flicker on the control panel and the monitors would dutifully inform the observer that yet another program had begun its run. After another futile attempt, failure would be reported and yet another program initiated.

Thus, the STO barely looked up when a sequence of banks lit up above him. Something new was being tried.

The thought never occurred to the STO that it might have been an outside order which initiated a search through the system.

CHAPTER IV

An antique hologram hung on the wall behind Marvin Hanks. There the visage of his great-great-grandfather stared out over the estate's common room with raptorial eyes. The old man had been thin-faced, mahogany-skinned, dyspeptic, and bald. He had also been the Phillipian leader who had first turned his eyes to the neighboring stars and given birth to the notion of Phillipian hegemony.

Some, in those long gone days of glory, had called the old man a pirate. Others had thought him a patriot.

To Marvin, the old man had been the stuff of family legend. He'd been suckled on tales of Phillipian power, of the first conquest of rebellious planets, and of the glory which should have been Phillipian were it not for the infamous treachery of the Tybalts and Rega.

Like a Riparian pin warble, the memory had eaten its way ever deeper into Hanks' soul, driving, aflame with pride in the lineage and honor that should have been his. Past glories, once missed, generally vanished forever. Yet, at this precise instant, when Hanks had just been elected to the Provisional Council of Elders, the advisory body which served at the Regan Administrator's will and pleasure, a miracle had occurred. In the fumbling confusion of the Regan fall, an opportunity might exist for those who would grab it.

Even as he thought, Marvin Hanks' comm buzzed.

"This is Councilman Hanks, to whom am I speaking?"

The face of the Administrator formed, the old woman distraught, wringing her hands. "Councilman, thank the Blessed God. You must act immediately. I've received a communication from Rega, from the occupation forces there. Minister Takka has vanished. We're requested to look for her. You know . . . if she should seek to make planet here. To hide.''

Hanks smiled, unpleasant memories of the Director of Internal Security lurking like poison in his memories. ''I think I do see, Administrator. I think I can help, that is, if you're willing to send me a writ of Carte Blanche. Emergency powers for this period of instability. Do that, and I'll handle Internal Security for you.''

She nodded, the patrician lines of her face deepening. ''It will be forthcoming, Councilman. And I welcome your assistance. I won't forget.''

He smiled, nodding plans, falling into place. ''No, I'm sure you won't.''

* * *

''It's not all that different from combat,'' Sinklar decided as he chewed on the end of his laser pen. He paced before the comm monitors that covered one entire wall in his personal quarters aboard *Chrysla*. Each of the monitors displayed different graphs, figures, and projections covering everything from starship manufacture to plastic curios for the tourist trade.

''I'll take your word for it,'' Anatolia pulled her long blonde hair out of the way and leaned back. ''I'm glad you can make sense out of this.''

Sinklar threw his pen onto the desk and settled into the gravchair beside her. The wall comm continued to spit out strings of numbers as it followed the different permutations Sinklar had input into the program to modify Staffa's data. If a fault lay within the program, some evidence should appear. To his experienced eye, the conclusions remained the same. Either they performed a miracle, or starvation was imminent. The empires could produce enough food to feed all the mouths, but how could they distribute it efficiently?

Sinklar pulled at his knobby nose, avoiding Anatolia's concerned gaze. On the far wall, the holo filled the niches with a Targan landscape while the odor of pines lingered.

Targa . . . pines . . . death . . . Makarta!

''Sinklar? What about us?''

''Huh?'' Phantoms stared back from the depths of his

memory. Hundreds of good people—people who had trusted him—lay dead inside that accursed rock.

"What's next for *us?*"

"We might try legalizing cannibalism. That'll solve two problems at once. A: fewer mouths to feed, and B: something to put in the mouths that are left." The dead in Makarta might have been the lucky ones.

"I meant about us, about you and me. Where do I fit?"

He tore his attention away from the monitors, trying to change his mental orientation. "What are you talking about?"

Pain quickened in Anatolia's bright blue eyes. She wore spacer's whites, a baggy utilitarian garment covered with pockets. The suit detracted from the charms of her full bust, trim waist, and long legs. A tumble of golden hair, freshly washed and fluffed, fell to her mid-back, glinting in the light. Now she crossed her arms, brow lining with a frown.

She gave him a cool appraisal. "I'm a geneticist, not an economist."

"I'm well aware of that." Makarta continued to plague him. The terrible memories shaded out of the gray mist, seeking to re-form. Makarta had been his first mistake—trying to take it by frontal assault. How many mistakes had followed?

"You know, you surprise me sometimes. Sinklar, I have a career on Rega. Theoretically, I should be able to walk back into the lab and go back to my studies. Ily's gone, and you've got Professor Adam under arrest. You don't need me anymore."

Within Makarta's blasted tunnels and warrens, the dead lay in heaps, rotting. Did the sightless eyes still stare into the darkness? Did flesh still cling to the bones? Did skeletal hands reach out in the dark?

"Sinklar, I can take a hint. How many times haven't you answered your comm when you knew it was me calling? Not only that, but you don't hear the tone in your voice when I'm irritating you."

"You're not irritating me," he insisted stubbornly. *Mistakes that began at Makarta led up to that night on Rega when his testicles overloaded his brain.* He could see it as plain as sunlight. Ily had lifted her head, black eyes challenging as she stood naked before him. Images jumbled:

Ily's raven hair cascading around him as she arched her back, tightening around him; the firmness of her breasts in his hands; her frantic undulations as she reached climax.

"You're gone again!" Anatolia cried, throwing her arms up and leaping from her seat to pace anxiously.

"I'm sorry." . . . And after that night, Ily Takka had played him like a fool. Each time they'd been together, Sinklar had fallen deeper and deeper into her web of lies, sex, and deceit.

Anatolia shook her head. "I told myself it was the stress you've been under. I know what it's cost you to lose Rega, Sinklar. But I don't know if that's all of it. Maybe it's time for me to leave."

Sinklar cocked his head, waving his hand as if to bat away the memories. "Leave?"

She leveled a measuring stare at him. "I've heard your soldiers talk about Targa, about how you kept them alive. You gave them a dream to believe in and a cause to fight for. I know you loved Gretta, how her murder affected you. If you hadn't been hurting, hadn't been vulnerable and alone, Ily would never have blinded you to what she was doing. Rot you, Sinklar, what's happening to you?"

"I'm finding my limits."

"Limits? Is that what you believe?" She shook her head, tears at the corners of her eyes. "You've got a decision to make. Either you can wallow in your defeat, and fail all of your troops—and me—or you can face your mistakes and tackle the future head-on."

At the scorn in her words, he ground his teeth. She didn't understand.

"Despite my reservations, I fell in love with you, Sinklar." Anatolia knotted her fists, lips quivering. "I won't stay around to watch you self-destruct."

"What are you talking about? You can't just . . . I mean, I *need* you! You keep me . . ."

"Want to finish that?"

He jumped nervously to his feet. "You keep me sane. I got you into a lot of trouble down there. I want to make up for it, repay you somehow."

Her expression cooled and she carefully straightened her clothing, running the fabric through her slim fingers. "I see. Well, don't concern yourself, Sink. The scorecard's even." She walked slowly to the hatch, eyes on the floor. "Don't worry about any security for me. I'm not going to make a peep to anyone about what I know. You have the file on your DNA, and the sample I took from Staffa is here on *Chrysla.*"

"Wait! What are you—"

"Good luck, Sinklar."

He stared in disbelief as she walked out the hatch, startling Chrysla as the woman approached in the hall.

"Anatolia!" Sinklar called, "I . . ."

She turned. "Yes?"

He glanced at the startled Chrysla, and rekindled more memories, those of Arta Fera, amber eyes glazed as she knelt over Gretta's decomposing body. The words he had been about to say evaporated in his throat.

As if she read his indecision, Anatolia laughed to herself, called, "Take care, Sink," and continued down the corridor to her quarters.

Sinklar gritted his teeth, backing away, mentally repeating, *This woman is* not *Arta. Her name is Chrysla. She's your mother, for God's sake!*

"I could come back later," Chrysla told him awkwardly.

Sinklar wavered, desperate to race after Anatolia, then exhaled and slapped the bulkhead. "No, it's all right. What can I do for you?"

"Are you sure you wouldn't rather postpone this?" Chrysla glanced meaningfully toward Anatolia's hatch. "I'm not exactly running a perfect record for meetings today."

Sinklar squeezed the angry memory of Arta Fera from his mind, head reeling. *Anatolia's going to leave. If you want her to stay, you'd Rotted well better do something about it.*

Yet here he stood, seeing Arta, remembering Gretta's death. Is that what he wanted? *Anatolia is* leaving! *She's stuck with you when others would have cut your throat! This is your last opportunity—you'd better do something!*

"Perhaps that would be a good idea." He stepped warily past Chrysla, experiencing a feeling of relief as he gained some distance. Damn it, she even smelled like Arta. *But she's your mother, Sink!*

"What a pus-stinking mess."

He stopped, shooting a quick glance back to see Chrysla

retreating down the hallway, head down, a slump to her shoulders as if she'd been dealt a blow. Sinklar's gut crawled.

He turned to the door comm. "Anatolia? Could I speak to you? Hey, let me in."

"Why?" She sounded hostile.

"Look, I need to . . . to explain some things."

A long pause.

"All right! Just be quick about it."

The hatch slid back to admit him. Anatolia's quarters were identical to his. The only difference was a huge wall display of DNA codes for amino acids projected in holographic perfection. Anatolia had already begun filling her small duffel bag with the few clothes she owned. She watched him coolly as he seated himself next to the bag and looked up.

"You're right about Gretta Artina. I loved her totally. She was my right hand throughout the Targan rebellion. Arta Fera killed her. When I stepped out in the corridor and saw Chrysla, my brain locked. I have a lot of guilt left over from Gretta's murder. I was starting to deal with that when Ily Takka . . . well, did what she did."

"Seduced is a pretty good word, don't you think?"

"Yeah, seduced." He braced his head on his hands. "But she had a curiously willing partner if you really want to call it a seduction."

Anatolia waited patiently as Sinklar mustered his thoughts and continued. "Listen. I've taken two whacks at love. Each ended in disaster." He glanced up. "That's what you're waiting for, isn't it? To hear me say I love you?"

She wadded up the jumpsuit she held and tossed it from hand to hand. "You know, you're a study, Sinklar. Just what do I do with you? I have to figure that out now, because if I don't I'm going to get into real trouble. I've come to love you, and it scares me to death."

"Thought you were trying to decide if I'm human."

"That, too. Mostly, I've come to believe in you, in your dream. I just don't know if you believe in it anymore. Do you? Do you believe in yourself these days?"

Do you, Sink? Is that your problem? Lost your nerve? And the alter ego of his subconscious asked: *What if you have? How many more bodies need to be piled at your feet before you realize you're a failure? Do you want that burden?*

She turned troubled eyes on him. "Remember when we were prisoners, when Ily drugged me? I told you the truth—that you have the makings of both greatness and terrible tragedy about you. At times you can be as comforting as an experiment in quantum uncertainty."

"Yeah, I suppose."

"What do you want, Sinklar? Make your decision right now. Be honest."

Sinklar took a deep breath, heart pounding. "Out there, in the hallway, I panicked at the thought of you leaving. I don't know what's happened to me. When I look back, things were going so well on Targa. Then, at Makarta, things started to go sour. Give me a war, Anatolia, and I'll win it. But if it isn't killing, I can't seem to get it right." He swallowed hard. "I'm scared. Can you live with that?"

For the first time, her cool stare warmed. "Are you being honest with yourself again?"

"After losing an empire, betraying my friends, acting like a fool with Ily . . . Rotted Hell, I don't know." He glanced up miserably. "I feel terribly tired, Ana."

She watched him stoically.

"I . . . I'm not giving up. I'll tell Staffa I'll go with him to Makarta. Face the ghosts there." His hands made a rasping sound as he rubbed them back and forth. "It won't be easy. And you know about me and Ily. Can you live with that?"

A faint smile turned the corners of her lips into an impish grin. "You did the best you could, Sink. I don't blame you. You met someone out of your league. Just *don't* let it happen again."

Sinklar groaned and flopped backward on the bedding. "That's one of the things scaring me right now. How many more of those hidden weaknesses do I have?" He shook his head. "Blessed Gods, what a pompous idiot I was! I thought I could go out and conquer the whole of Free Space, usher in a new age of enlightenment, and make things better for everyone."

"It's a wonderful dream, Sinklar." She settled next to him on the sleeping platform.

"I hate to remind you, but we live at the Star Butcher's whim."

"I thought he was pretty eloquent in the meeting. Honestly, Sinklar, he did ask for cooperation."

"And what if it's a ploy? Some trick? Hey, remember me? I can fight an army but when it comes to political intrigue, I . . ."

"Think, Sink." She reached up to run her fingers through his hair. "Take nothing for granted, but seize your opportunities. He's your father. Wait, let me finish. You've heard the rumors. That's why he went to Targa, to find you. Give him a chance but keep your eyes open."

He grunted, frowning.

"Sinklar, what choice do you have? You've got to do two things. Learn from your mistakes with Ily and believe in yourself. Meet Staffa halfway until he disproves himself. Or do you think you have another option?"

Sinklar took a deep breath and sighed. "Nope." He rolled onto his side, facing her, taking her hands in his. "Thanks."

She gave him a wistful smile before turning away and stuffing another garment into the bag.

"What are you doing?" Sinklar asked.

"Packing."

He twisted forward, grabbing her wrist. "I want you to stay with me. I . . . I meant it when I said I needed you."

Faint frown lines etched her brow. "How do I know? I can share you with a ghost, Sink, that's not the problem. Are you the same Sinklar that kept Mac alive? The one who believed in the dream?"

He rose to his feet, placing both hands on her shoulders, feeling her tremble while he searched her eyes. "Remember that dinner in Tybalt's palace? Two scared hungry people, with only each other to confide in. You gave me a point of reference when I was lost. The latest mistake I've made is forgetting those cold terrible days when Ily was winning."

Her skin was warm against his as he pulled her close. He could feel her heart begin to pound. "Win, lose, or die, I'm not giving up. Stay with me."

"You're sure?"

"More sure than I've ever been. Will you stay?"

"I guess it's now or never, isn't it?" She pushed back, searching his face as if trying to judge his soul. She closed her eyes for a moment, hesitated, then bent forward. Her lips closed on his, softly at first, then with increasing passion.

Sinklar's blood began to pound as she ran her hands down the sides of his face. She opened her eyes, gazing into his as he unzipped the fasteners of her spacer's whites. She stood before him, golden hair tumbling down to her full breasts, smiling at the wonder in his eyes. He had to help her with the clips that held his armor. Her hot skin sent shivers through him as she melted against him and he pulled her close.

"I love you, Sink," she murmured. "But you've worried me."

"I'm sorry." He pulled her down onto the sleeping platform. "I promise . . . I'll make up for it."

* * *

"Staffa?" Tasha's voice penetrated Staffa's uneasy sleep. He sat up, anticipating Skyla's movement—but the bedding beside him lay empty.

"What is it?" He rubbed his gritty eyes.

He lay on his opulently furnished sleeping platform with its sophisticated gravity control. Beyond, his bedroom brightened as the lighting controls reacted to the sound of his voice. Light glinted off the jeweled artifacts, pillage from looted worlds. One full wall of comm equipment depicted *Chrysla*'s operational status. The doorway to the toilet and lavatory gaped half open, one of Skyla's glossy white suits hanging limply on the hook.

"Ashtan," Tasha told him firmly. "I'm afraid something is terribly wrong there. Not only that, but Kaylla's agents report that administrators all over the Regan Empire have been vanishing. In the process, it appears they've begun to sabotage the planetary computer systems."

Staffa groaned. "I'll be right there." Shooting a glance at the chronometer, he realized he'd only managed three hours of sleep. "If this is as serious as it could be, we may have to scramble a ship to deal with the situation."

"Affirmative."

"See you in the main conference room."

Staffa growled to himself, reaching for his armor

* * *

The beeping of the comm brought Sinklar awake. He blinked owlishly as Anatolia stirred, pulled her hair back, and called, "Who is it?"

"This is the Lord Commander, Professor Daviura. I need to speak to Sinklar. Is he there?"

Sink stiffened at the sound of that imperious voice. Reluctantly, he called out, "I'm here."

"I apologize if I'm bothering you. I just thought you should know. Something's happening at Ashtan. Evidently the Director of Internal Security there has fled the planet, but in the process, he's erased the data banks which handle administration. My thought is to dispatch MacRuder and *Gyton* immediately. If they arrive before too much damage is done, they can probably maintain order and safety for the people. Do you concur?"

Sinklar pursed his lips and rolled off the sleeping platform, settling before the comm and snapping on the visual. Staffa's worried expression seemed to have tightened since their last meeting. The haggard look had deepened.

Sinklar glanced at Anatolia. Give Staffa a chance? Commit himself to this new future? Sinklar ran a hand through his ruffled hair as he tried to think. "Knowing Ily, she'd have a contingency plan for everything. Some way to cut her losses and throw as many obstacles as possible into the path of her pursuers." Send Mac? Remove yet another pillar of loyal support from Sinklar's side? "I concur with your decision, Lord Commander. Mac will give you everything he's got, and *Gyton* is a good ship."

Sinklar paused. "I can contact him, if you'd like."

"Thank you for your kind offer. Your assessment of Minister Takka is in agreement with my own. I would also like you to know that I'm dispatching a team to Rega to augment the security we've placed in the Ministry building. The sooner we break into Ily's files, the sooner we can remove her accomplices. Do you have anyone with computer expertise who might augment that process?"

"Shiksta is the best I've got."

Staffa considered, frowning, then shook his head. "I'd rather keep him in reserve. He's a capable man, and if Ashtan is only the surface of the problem, we might need to dispatch people throughout the Empire. Run an organic administration, if necessary.''

''I can go,'' Anatolia called from behind Sinklar. ''I may not be good at cryptography, but I know the comm system, and, as a geneticist, I know code patterns.''

Sinklar shifted uneasily. ''Could I put your line on hold for a moment, Lord Commander?''

''As you wish.''

Sinklar snapped the receiver off, turning. ''You *want* to go back into that accursed building?''

Ana had wrapped a robe around herself and settled next to him on the chair arm. ''*Chrysla* isn't spacing for Targa for a couple of days. You don't have anyone else to spare. No, I'm not anxious to go back there, but you need someone to look after your interests. Who better than me?''

He ran a finger down her thigh. ''I want more time with you.''

''We'll have plenty of time once we space for Targa. This is only a couple of days. Who else have you got to send?'' She lifted a pale eyebrow.

''Mhitshul, for one. He pestered me often enough with his mothering ways. No one could slip one by—''

''Mhitshul checks out on comm but what does he know about programming? Patterning theory or code sequences? I might even be able to run some genetics mapping programs that might give us an edge.''

''I don't know. I've got a funny feeling . . .''

''Sinklar,'' she said seriously, ''I don't want to be your concubine. Maybe once, before I lived in the streets, I might have been able to, but not after what I went through. I have to function as a full partner, not just bed fluff and friendly confidante.''

''Maybe I wasn't ardent enough in bed?'' he tried lamely.

''Silly!'' she smacked him on the side of the head, then leaned down and kissed him hard. ''I never knew sex could be like that. Ily teach you to do things like that to a woman?''

''What if I said yes?''

She paused thoughtfully. ''Well, I guess you have to make the best of any bad situation. Now, call the Lord Commander and tell him I'll catch the shuttle.''

Sinklar hesitated, his hand on the control. "Something about this . . ."

"Either you trust me, or you don't."

Sinklar opened the channel and stared into Staffa's hard gray eyes. "Anatolia will be ready. How soon is the shuttle leaving?"

"Professor Daviura needs to be in Bay Seventeen in four hours. Planetary departure is in exactly four hours and sixteen minutes. My people will brief her on the way down."

"Very well. Thank you for informing us."

After a courteous nod, Staffa's image vanished. Sinklar was still unsettled by the premonition in his gut.

"Four hours?" Anatolia wondered. "What could we do for four hours?"

"Hmm? What could we do? Worry, I suppose. I—"

She grabbed him, pulling him out of the chair. "Four hours," she whispered as she nibbled on his ear and slipped out of her robe. "It's got to last us both for two days. Let's see what you've got left!"

* * *

A muted whimper swirled through the darkness of Skyla Lyma's soul until it rose, breaking hauntingly from her lips. Dreams lingered from her shredding sleep, terrifying dreams of an amber-eyed woman staring down, dominating her, feeding on Skyla's flesh with the relish of a perverted vampire.

I want to die. Blessed Gods, let me die.

From somewhere beyond the misery, a gentle voice insisted, "No, Skyla."

Staffa, I failed you. Kill me. Please, Staffa, if you love me, kill me so I can forget.

"Live, Skyla."

That voice, that terrible contralto voice, commanded. Skyla tried to shrink in on herself, to curl away into the blackness and misery that rotted in the recesses of her being.

"Do you know me?" the voice prodded.

"Yes."

"Who am I?"

"Arta . . . Arta Fera." Skyla shivered, the reaction involuntary. "Don't hurt me, Arta . . . I'll be good. I promise . . . promise . . ."

"Skyla, listen to me. Listen very carefully. Where are we?"

Her swallow choked in a dry throat and her guts knotted. "On my yacht."

"And what is your condition?"

"I'm your prisoner, Arta."

"Can you be wrong?"

"I . . . no . . . I, yes, Arta. I can be wrong if you say so."

A long pause. Then: "Skyla, pay attention. If I am Arta Fera, then you must be on your yacht. If you are on your yacht, you are a prisoner, correct?"

"That's right."

"Repeat what I just said."

Skyla hugged herself, as if to find reassurance, but only emptiness lurked within, emptiness and futility. *Nothing left, Skyla. Nothing left but death.*

"Skyla?" the terrible voice intruded. "Repeat what I just said."

Fear grasped at Skyla's vocal cords; racking sobs stole her breath. "If . . . if you are Arta Fera then I must be on my yacht, and if I'm on . . . on my yacht, I must be a . . . a . . ."

"Prisoner."

Her spasming lungs choked her and the wailing of her soul drained away into a pitiful weeping.

"Skyla? Do you understand what that means?"

"Don't—don't hurt me, Arta. Please? I did what you wanted. I made love with you. Don't take me to Ily. Not dressed like a . . . a whore. I did what you asked! *Don't shame me!*"

"Skyla," the firm voice ordered, "Concentrate. If you wake up on your yacht, then I am Arta Fera and you are a prisoner. Isn't that correct?"

"Yes." She cowered, seeking to retreat back into the blackness, into the painful peace of nonexistence. Fear laced her guts and tightened frosty fingers into her heart. *Don't . . . don't make me wake up! Don't—*

"Skyla, wake up now. Wake up and open your eyes."

Wrenching sobs rose from below her diaphragm and

trickling wetness traced down her cheeks. Her eyes had begun to burn, swollen and fevered.

"Wake up, Skyla."

Skyla blinked at a white world turned blurry by tears. She sniffed, trying to clear her plugged nose, and reached up to wipe at her swimming vision. When she pulled her hand away, Arta stared down at her, a hard concern in her amber eyes.

"Hello, Skyla."

"Hello, Arta." Miserable defeat crushed her.

Arta Fera wore an unfamiliar, baggy, beige dress and her hair had been cut shorter. A wary caution lurked behind the Seddi assassin's guarded expression as she ordered, "Skyla, look around you."

Skyla glanced to the side, seeing familiar med units. She frowned in confusion. Rotted Gods! Impossible! "It looks like . . . like the hospital on *Chrysla*. Pus eat you, Arta, what kind of game is this?"

A faint ghost of a smile came to those full lips. "No game, Skyla. You are aboard *Chrysla*, safe and sound."

Skyla shook her head. "No. You can't fool me. Staffa would have shot you on sight. This is a trick."

"I'm not Arta Fera, and, as I told you in hypnosis, you're no longer a prisoner." The woman clasped her hands and leaned back to give Skyla a thoughtful appraisal. "Arta Fera and Ily Takka did a great deal of damage to you, Skyla. But you're a remarkably intelligent and resourceful woman. I took a gamble in bringing you back this way, but I believe in the long run, it'll pay off."

"What are you talking about?"

"Learning. Conditioning. You've developed a set of negative neural pathways because of a traumatic ordeal. I've attempted to create a double bind—conflicting information, if you will. It's a first therapeutic step to heal the wounds Arta and Ily inflicted."

"Who are you?" Skyla pushed up on her arms, backing away. Yes, she knew this room. She'd been brought here more than once. In this very med unit, she'd come to once before, but that time Staffa had been holding her hand.

The woman smiled knowingly, pain in those haunted amber eyes. She stood. "My name is Chrysla Marie Attenasio."

"Chrysla? But you . . . you're . . ."

"Dead? Almost. MacRuder recognized me when he seized the Sassan freighter, *Markelos.* You see, Skyla, you now have yet another element to your double bind. How will you deal with your conflicting data? Surrender to insanity? Build fanciful castles in the sky? I think not. I'm gambling that you can't allow yourself that kind of an easy way out.

"Meanwhile, someone who loves you very deeply is here to see you. He'll explain it all."

Skyla glanced uneasily about as the woman turned and left, a slight limp in her walk. Pain? In Arta's eyes? Skyla shivered, blinked, and shook her head. This strange Arta—no, not Arta, but Chrysla . . . Chrysla Attenasio . . . Staffa's . . . "Wife."

Chrysla heard, hesitated, and touched the lock plate before she stepped out into the corridor.

Rotted Gods, Skyla. What do you believe? Aboard Chrysla? *Impossible!* Last she remembered was being strapped to that pus-dripping chair in Ily Takka's interrogation room. Skyla clamped her eyes shut, sweat beginning to form on her brow. *Don't even think about it. Not now.*

So where was she? If this were some sort of psychological game, some trick for interrogation, Ily had created a masterpiece. Damn it, the place even *felt* like being aboard *Chrysla*—and Chrysla Attenasio was dead! Blown apart off Myklene . . . if she'd ever existed at all.

Skyla checked quickly, discovering herself half-encased in the med unit. She slipped a furtive hand along the cool, smooth side of the machine, seeking the disconnect mechanism. She punched the latch release and froze as she caught movement from the corner of her eye. Someone in gray, a big . . . she gaped as Staffa entered, a shy smile on his lips. He rushed forward, charcoal gray cloak billowing behind him as he reached for her.

Hesitantly, she touched his hand, feeling the familiar warmth, and then he'd plucked her from the soft cushions of the med unit, crushing her to him.

"Staffa? How? Rotted Gods, you're *real!*" She clamped frantic arms around him in a grip so tight her arms began to ache.

He finally pushed her back, anxious gray eyes searching

hers. "I was so worried about you. We scrambled the entire fleet, spaced in record time. I knew better! I should never have let you go out there alone."

She buried her face against his shoulder, strength suddenly vanished. How could she explain what had happened? How could she tell this man she loved more desperately than life itself that she'd failed him?

"Staffa, listen, I have to tell you. Arta, she . . ." Skyla pressed her eyes shut against the tears.

"It's all right. I don't care what happened. We'll deal with it."

"But, Staffa . . ."

"I said, we'll deal with it. For the moment, Rega is crushed. Ily got away, but she won't get far. Free Space is ours. The war is over."

Ily? Escaped? Questions spun crazily in Skyla's head. "Who was that woman? She's almost an exact duplicate of Arta. Is she . . . is she really Chrysla?"

"Yes. She's a psychologist. She'll tell you more when she feels the time is right." He smiled warmly and ran his fingers gently along her cheek.

Chrysla? A twisting sensation pulled at Skyla's guts. "But how? I mean, she . . ." *What does this mean for us, Staffa?*

As if he read her mind, he smiled and ran fingers through her long blonde hair. "We'll work it all out. I love you more than I can ever tell you. You need to rest, get your strength back. Now, how about something to eat?"

Skyla nodded dumbly, the miserable feeling welling inside to supplant any appetite she might have had.

* * *

From the medical observation center contiguous to the hospital, Chrysla Attenasio watched the reunion. A deepening sorrow stitched her heart as she cataloged Staffa kar Therma's reaction. Her mouth tightened at the panic in Skyla Lyma's fragile expression as she stared up at the man she loved.

With a slim finger, Chrysla killed the connection. For long moments, she stood in silence, head bowed, eyes closed. Finally she shut the equipment down and walked to the corridor hatch.

By the time she entered the corridor, she'd masked the hollow longing within, her stride only marred by the other nagging pain—the physical one on her maimed leg.

A couple of days in a med unit would fix that, but for now she needed a counterbalance for her suffering.

CHAPTER V

Wiley Jenkins had followed events like everyone else on Ashtan. For two days, he'd waited anxiously for information from the planetary comm. He'd found out about the trouble when he entered his genetics lab on the third day after the stunning news of the Conquest.

Wiley had taken his morning ride from the Northside of Ashtan City to the genetics laboratory he owned and operated on the outskirts of the old city. His tube dropped him at the Grand Palace Lodgings, a sprawling hotel and resort for the very well to do.

Wiley would stroll through the gardens from the tube riser and then proceed the half kilometer to his laboratory, the entire way lined by the overhanging cottonwoods that made this section of Ashtan City so charming.

Wiley's bioengineering lab had been a labor of love for most of his life. His triumphs consisted of a jersey-Holstein-bison cross that produced milk in the harshest of northern plains environments. His cross allowed some agricultural factories on the fringes of the polar caps to produce dairy products for the first time. Thanks to this cross, along with smaller successes, the firm had grown to employ a staff of sixteen plus three other geneticists.

Wiley pressed his thumb to the lock plate and entered the building as the first rays of red light brightened the morning horizon. He made it a habit to get to work several hours before the others. He did his best work in those tranquil hours.

Shrugging out of his coat, he stuck a cup into the stassa dispenser, and checked the messages on the comm. Nothing. Only when he walked into the huge computer room to the right of the lab proper did he realize anything was wrong. There, the big Rega General mainframe should have been sorting probabilities for a bovine eye disorder known to occur in 0.4 percent of the derivative Hereford population on the planet.

Wiley barely noticed it when his stassa cup slipped from his stunned fingers. Along with two years of work, his entire project had been spit out on the floor in endless sheets of flimsy.

A half an hour later, any attempt to sort through the mess had been proved beyond a doubt to be fruitless. In desperation, Wiley input the number for his genetic assistant.

The comm told him: **ALL SERVICES ARE SUSPENDED UNTIL FURTHER NOTICE. COMM ERROR F-16 A. REPEAT: ALL SERVICES SUSPENDED UNTIL FURTHER NOTICE. COMM ERROR F-16 A.**

And the message repeated over and over again.

Wiley Jenkins screamed and kicked stassa-stained flimsies around the room while his fingers flexed with the desire to strangle someone. Anyone!

* * *

It's a new day and a new way, Division First Ben MacRuder insisted to himself as he walked down the main corridor that curved through *Gyton*'s guts. The atmosphere in the Regan warship had a stifling effect compared to that inside one of the Companions' vessels. Cables ran in ropy masses along the ceiling panels, and reinforcing strakes arched around the passage like ribs in a snake's belly. Worse, in the finest traditions of the Regan military, the paneling and bulkheads had been painted a nasty shade of puke-green.

Mac reached the conference room and slapped a hand to the lock plate. The hatch opened to admit him into an oval room ten meters across. A similarly shaped table filled the center of the room and Mac stepped around it, triggering the floor stud. A seat rose from the deck plating.

Mac dropped wearily into the chair, leaning back and closing his eyes. The entire universe had changed, gone suddenly grease-slippery under his feet.

But I should be used to that by now.

Nothing would be the same from this point forward. An empire had died in the blink of an eye. Enemies were now allies. His relationship with his best friend had been forever metamorphosed. The only woman Mac had ever fallen hopelessly in love with was forever beyond his reach. When Mac had sneaked away for a couple of hours, his father, the man he'd once held in such awe, had seemed like a rather mild individual—and so alien. After the horrors of Targa and the insane gamble to attack Imperial Sassa, any common ground they'd once shared had vanished like spit in the Etarian desert.

His life had changed, and there was no going back. But that wasn't what kept him from sleeping at night. He couldn't forget Chrysla. Amber eyes haunted him, lurking like phantoms in the back of his mind. If he but let go, she'd be there, smiling, the light shining in copper glints throughout her auburn hair. Her scent lingered in his nostrils, sensual and teasing. He could reach out, feel her melting against him.

And see her running into Staffa's arms. *She's another man's wife, Mac. Forget her.*

But he never would.

"You know, I've seen some cases in my day, but yours takes first prize." Rysta's rusty voice scattered Mac's thoughts to the solar wind.

He cranked an eye open and shot a hard glance at the old woman who was seating herself on the chair beside him. "I didn't hear you come in."

"Rapt as you were, boy, you wouldn't have heard a star go nova."

"Stop calling me boy."

"Remind me in fifty years or so, and I'll consider it."

Mac straightened and gave the old woman a thorough inspection. Well over two hundred years old, even rejuv had ceased to work on Commander Rysta Braktov. She wore a crisp Regan Fleet uniform. Her knotty gray hair had been pulled into a severe bun. That dark-skinned face had more crinkles than a zero-g lava flow, and her undershot jaw thrust forward defiantly. Age had gnarled her fleshy nose and given a bitter, sunken pucker to her brown-lipped mouth. Outside of the uniform, she could have been mistaken for a derelict, but behind that ancient facade lay one of the sharpest military minds in Free Space.

We make quite a team, Mac decided. Ancient Rysta Braktov, dark and withered, and young MacRuder, all blond, tall, muscular, and blue-eyed. In place of Rysta's natty uniform, Mac wore the satin-textured, supple armor of an assault infantryman. The tightly woven synthetic consisted of ceramic and graphite micro-tubing that contained hydrocarbon polymers in some threads and an oxycatalyst in others. Upon impact the tubes ruptured and the mixture set instantaneously, absorbing the impact of projectiles. Upon contact with blaster or pulse fire, the material hardened and flaked in ablative scale. Such armor was vacuum capable and a belt-pack powered choker generated a force field around the head. Otherwise, a helmet could be employed.

Mac didn't look his age, but when a man started counting off campaigns like Targa, Makarta Mountain, the Regan pacification, the strike on Imperial Sassa, and fomenting revolt and civil war, the sprews and angular flashings of youth got ground away in a hurry.

"She really got to you, didn't she, son?" Rysta asked in a low voice.

Mac lifted a shoulder. "I did my duty, that's all. She's back where she belongs."

"So? I'd heard through the scuttlebutt that Staffa'd dropped everything because of Lyma. Rumor has it that she's his lover. And Chrysla's his wife? That ought to make quite a situation for the old Star Butcher."

Mac's shoulders slumped. "More of a 'situation' than you know. The Praetor of Myklene abducted Chrysla more than twenty years ago. Kept her prisoner all that time because he knew Staffa would eventually be coming for him. When the Companions struck, they took the Praetor by surprise. The old villain never had time to use his trump card. Chrysla escaped. I guess in the meantime Staffa had come to love Skyla. Now he has them both."

After a pause, Rysta said, "I watched you and Chrysla, boy. She may look like a china doll, but that woman's got guts. I told you before, I get a lot of enjoyment watching youngsters. She doesn't know what she wants anymore than you do."

"What's that supposed to mean?"

"You're important to her. Treated her like a human being. Given the way she looks, that's probably a first."

Mac studied her, uneasy at the calm understanding in

those obsidian eyes. "Spill it. Do you know something I don't?"

"Maybe. I've been around a bit. But for the moment, let's get down to business, shall we?" Rysta gave him a curious squint. "Well, you heard the Lord Commander, what's the verdict? Have we lost it all?"

Mac shook his head slowly. "I don't know, Rysta. I guess all we can do is navigate with the current . . . see where it carries us."

"Fill me in, boy. What happened down there on Rega?"

Mac placed his hands on the table and stared pensively at the shining surface as if he could scry the truth of what had occurred over the last couple of days. "We were right. Ily Takka had arrested Sinklar and most of the loyal Division Firsts. We'd have been in real trouble if Dion Axel hadn't chosen our side. After you left, we deployed around the Ministry of Internal Security and waited for Shiksta's opening shots." He shook his head. "You know, I've never been so nervous. It's one thing to go into combat, quite another to initiate a civil war that's going to tear your home and people asunder."

"So what was that Rotted jamming that started just before the battle? It even screwed up our comm."

Mac chewed at his lip. "Honestly, I don't know. Something of Staffa's. He calls it *Countermeasures.*"

"It's that all right. Takes a lot to blot out battle comms, but he did it. I couldn't do a thing, couldn't even keep score."

"It sure left us totally high and dry. Shik was right on schedule though, communication or not. He blew holes in the top of the Internal Security Ministry, and we dropped First Section in. Thought we'd get Ily, but she slipped away somehow."

"Rotted bad luck that," Rysta growled to herself.

"That's when the Companions dropped. The war was over before it even started. Staffa smashed the Regan government within seconds. I watched it, Rysta. From up there on the roof, I watched one administration building after another collapse under a gravity shot. Then Ryman Ark's STU teams were all around us."

Mac fingered the smooth surface of the table, eyes unfocused. "Funny, isn't it? There we were, starting a civil war, and we ended up conquered before it even started. Makes me wonder if we didn't deserve what we got.''

''Wouldn't have happened if Ily hadn't been such a greedy bitch.''

''One of these days, I'll find her, and when I do . . .''

''Threats are just words, boy, and words don't pass water. What about this deal you cut with Staffa?''

''What could I do? Since we were both after Ily, I told Staffa if he'd stop shooting, we could sort it all out later.''

''So much for the sorting. We're surrounded, outgunned, and with Comm Central destroyed and Orbital Defense paralyzed by that Rotted *Countermeasures* device of Staffa's, we couldn't effectively spit into a bucket.'' Rysta sighed. ''It's over, boy. All over.''

For long moments they sat quietly, each lost in thought.

''Never thought I'd see it come to this.'' Rysta spread her fingers, looking at her withered palm. ''Three Tybalts, from the Imperial Fifth to the Seventh, shook this hand. I served my Emperors well.'' She grunted to herself. ''So now what? You're one of the insiders. What's next? Staffa the First?''

''You were at that meeting. You know as much as I do. Rega's dead, Commander. So is Sassa—and you know damned well who killed them.'' Mac suddenly felt sick. ''Latest reports are that a billion and a half people are dead on Imperial Sassa. Three more Companion vessels are spacing for Sassan territory as we speak. They're going to provide protection to crucial planets.''

Rysta gave him a sober appraisal. ''I've studied that data cube Staffa gave us. Without Comm Central, who's going to coordinate redistribution? I mean, our entire economy . . .''

''Yeah, same with the Sassans. Maybe Staffa can pull something out of this Seddi machine he's talking about. I talked to Sinklar. He's going back to Targa with Staffa. Back to Makarta.''

''Pus licking hell.''

''It won't all fall apart at once. The systems will break down over time. Sort of like suffocating very slowly.''

Rysta rubbed the back of her leathery neck. ''We've got cargo lighters in bays six and eight. I checked the manifest. We're being resupplied for deep space. You called this meeting, said it was a briefing. You want to tell me about it? Did Sinklar get some other bright idea about how to save this situation?"

Mac looked down at his hands, knotting his fists until the tendons stood out. "We've got a pretty good idea about what happened to Ily. She slipped away during the attack on her Ministry building. She had a shuttle available, and Arta Fera had Skyla Lyma's yacht. *Gyton* is spacing to find Ily Takka—and her Seddi assassin."

"Someone wants her real bad, huh? But then I'll bet Sinklar's still red-eared with shame over the way she twisted him around her finger."

Mac bridled, then bit it off. "Sink isn't the only one. Most of this, I mean, everything that's happened, it's mostly Ily's fault. She assassinated Tybalt, goaded the Sassans, abducted Wing Commander Lyma, arrested Sink. Rotted Gods, what didn't she do?"

"Start the Targan rebellion," Rysta countered.

"No, she didn't. That was Bruen's doing—but Ily used it, kept it fermenting and boiling when Sinklar could have finished it."

"So what do you want from me? Or did you just call me up here to tell me you're stealing my ship?"

"Change of plans. First we have to drop in on Ashtan. Restore social order. Thought maybe you'd like to go along." Mac raised an eyebrow. "Sinklar called a couple of hours ago and I had to beg to get you."

"You? Beg? My withered ass, boy."

"It's either that, or they're going to put you in charge of Fleet operations. They want you to coordinate escort and patrol of vital space lanes . . . ensure that supplies get through while they try to patch the system and keep people from running out of food, medicine, water, power, and the other necessities. In short, they've offered you command of Fleet and logistics."

"Under Staffa and Sinklar."

"That's right."

"Working in an office on Rega."

"You couldn't very well do the job in space, especially not from null singularity."

Rysta's withering scowl reflected her distaste. "If they don't promote me, who would they put in charge?"

"Dion Axel. Sinklar claims she has the sort of analytical mind to balance all aspects of the equation."

"Axel." Rysta snorted as she got to her feet and began to pace. "She's a sharp one all right. Not particularly well born, mind you, but smart." She stopped short, staring at Mac. "Wait a minute. You seem to think I'm going to turn it down to go chasing across space with you. Why?"

Mac swiveled the chair to face her. "Because, Commander, I think your passion is at stake here. To be honest, I used up a lot of collateral talking Sinklar into this. He wasn't interested in having you space out when he desperately needs qualified people."

She pulled at the flaccid skin under her chin. "Yet he'll let you, his most trusted friend and subordinate, chase across space after a pair of phantom particles. Why?"

"I wouldn't exactly call Ily and Arta 'phantom particles.' " Mac lowered his gaze. "He let me go because it's important that someone run Ily down. Stop her, once and for all. And . . . and because I asked him. That's why."

"Because you can't stand the thought of being around Chrysla. That's really it, isn't it, Mac?" Rysta shook her head. "Young fool. Yes, I can read the misery in your eyes, but then, I guess somewhere along the line, you learned to read an old hag like me pretty good, too." A pause. "They got any idea where Ily might have spaced for?"

"No. Two of Staffa's ships, *Slap* and *Jinx Mistress*, plotted her vector out to jump. The course would have brought them out light-years from anything—or run them into the Forbidden Borders."

"Don't bet on it. No, they dropped out somewhere along that line. After that, they would have shed Delta V, changed vector, built, and jumped again. The Rotted Gods alone know where they'll end up. Let's pull up a map, give this some thought." Rysta stepped over to the dispenser, drawing a cup of stassa. "I always thought Ily Takka was a pus-sucking viper."

"Yeah, well, she's our target as soon as we deal with Ashtan." Mac rubbed at the stubble on his chin. "Ily can't hide that yacht forever."

CHAPTER VI

How did I ever come to this? The question continues to plague me. When I think back to those innocent and ignorant days of my youth, so long, long ago, who would have thought I would have been the one to inherit the position of Supreme Magister of the Seddi? In our youth, we all dream of greatness, but so few of us ever attain the mantle of power and responsibility.

Perhaps that is for the best. The burden is ruinous.

I have done my best . . . and it wasn't enough. I've watched the fortunes of the Seddi grow, swell with power, and finally fall. The quanta blessed my dear old friend, Magister Hyde. He died before the fall. For me, life has become tyranny, leaving me to stew in defeat and despair.

And to what can I lay the blame?

To the accursed Mag Comm.

I will do anything I can to destroy it. Upon the name of God, I swear it.

—Fragment found among partially erased records on Magister Bruen's personal comm

* * *

Ily reached for a drinking bulb and drew a cup of stassa from the dispenser in the compact galley in Skyla Lyma's stolen yacht. She clamped her jaws, hating the trembling in her hand. Weak! Weak as a pus-starved maggot! The only blessing had been that no bones had broken when she'd been slammed into the floor during the attack on her Ministry.

Ily turned, walking to the inset table and seating herself across from Arta. The bulb rattled as she placed it on the marble tabletop.

Arta, amber eyes alert, noticed. "You're still not fully recovered."

Ily looked around, cataloging the fine fabrics that hung decoratively on the walls near the table, then settled back into the velvet upholstered cushions. "I must say, the Wing Commander traveled in splendor. Pretty plush. Not only that, this thing has guts. I tracked it at close to sixty gravities once."

"It does perform rather well."

"I thought you weren't much of a pilot?"

"I learn very rapidly, as you have no doubt noticed."

"And, like me, you don't always publish lists of your talents for the universe to study."

"You need more time in bed."

Ily shook her head slowly. "We don't have time for that. My data should be coming in. As soon as the comm lights up, we're spacing. I'll mend on the way to Terguz."

"Terguz? People utter curses in the name of Terguz."

Ily cradled her drinking bulb with both hands, lifting it to her lips to sip at the steaming stassa. "Granted, when it comes to planets, Terguz isn't exactly a sparkling jewel. But we need a place that doesn't keep very good records. Terguz, despite its reputation, draws a lot of traffic—including Sassan."

"But I thought . . ."

"Of course you did, everyone did. On the other hand, the empire needed a place just like Terguz. So did the Sassans, for that matter. We have Terguz, they have Vega. Both planets function as exchange centers for items smuggled across the Imperial borders. We dutifully looked the other way. So did that fat Sassan God-Emperor. It wasn't in Tybalt's interest—or mine—to throttle a lucrative pipeline like Terguz."

"And I suppose the Terguzzi reputation as a wretched place kept a lot of traffic away?"

"Who'd want to go there? We're talking about a frozen wasteland. The planet hovers halfway between being a gas giant and an ice ball. Conditions for most of the miners—especially the convicts and slaves—are appalling. Enough money, however, can make any place, no matter how miserable, habitable. Different people seek different things in life. Some on Terguz live very well according to their own needs and luxuries."

Arta tapped long fingernails on the shining marble. "And you, of course, have connections there."

Ily grinned. "I wouldn't have been a very good Minister of Internal Security if I didn't. In this case, our advantage lies in the form of one Gyper Rill, a very capable administrator with the soul of a Riparian blood leech."

Arta cocked her head and began twisting an auburn strand of hair around her fingers. "But you don't plan on living on Terguz, no matter how good the accommodations."

"Very astute." A warm anger stirred within Ily. "Terguz is only the first stop. This yacht, splendid as it is, is like a death warrant. We can cache it someplace in case we ever need it, but for the moment, we must have less conspicuous transportation. Perhaps a CV—fast and anonymous."

"Do you really think a CV will win your empire back for you?"

Ily smiled, eyes slitting. "Win it back? No. But my memory has been coming back quite nicely, thanks to your nursing. When that file comes in from subspace, it will be even better."

"Assuming Staffa hasn't broken the codes."

"He'll be in for a surprise when he does. No, Arta, we're going where Staffa will never think to look for us, the one place he'd never expect."

"And where is that?"

"Itreata, of course."

Arta laughed in a melodious contralto. "You got a harder knock on the head than I thought! Staffa keeps the tightest security in all of Free Space. Even Bruen, with all the advantages of the Seddi networks, had to throw an entire planet into revolution in an attempt to lure Staffa close enough so I might get a chance at him!"

"You still might get that opportunity. But Staffa has a vulnerability—one that has probably escaped his mind. And you, Arta, are the key that will unlock Itreata's impregnable door for me."

"Would you care to fill me in on the details?"

"Not yet." Ily frowned, the steam from the stassa curling before her delicate nose. In her mind's eye, she could see it all, the gleaming white corridors of Itreata, and the sudden understanding on Staffa's face as Ily's blaster leveled. But she wouldn't kill him . . . not right away.

* * *

Skyla balanced, knees bent, back arched, as anger pulsed with each beat of her heart. She struck, movements a blur of toned nerve and muscle. She recovered, motionless, then struck again, killing Arta Fera in her imagination. She'd begun to pant, sweat breaking out on her skin—but better to work off her rage on imaginary enemies than to turn it loose on the fixtures of the therapy room.

She lashed the air again, hammering her mental victim with punches and kicks. From the corner of her eye, she studied herself in the mirror, a beautiful woman, tall, muscular, and trim. She had the body of a gymnast, supple and toned. Skyla's ice-blonde hair swept the floor when loose, but as usual, she'd braided it tightly, looping the braid around her left shoulder and pinning it with the epaulet. For her release, she'd managed to obtain a suit of her snowy white armor, and, as always, it conformed to the perfect curve of her high breasts, narrowing across her flat muscular stomach.

At that moment, the hatch slipped open to admit Staffa. Despite her anger, Skyla's heart leapt, spurred by the concern in his face. As he stopped before her, she noticed the strain in his eyes, the tension around his mouth. Red streaked the whites of his gray eyes, and his face appeared puffy and drawn like that of a man pushed too far.

"Ready to go?" he asked neutrally, a wary set to his posture.

She shot him a frosty blue glance, then reluctantly lowered her stare and began tapping a nervous toe. "Damned right, I'm ready to go." *And as soon as we're out of here, I'm going to rip you apart!*

"We've checked her from top to bottom, Lord Commander," the Medical Officer said as he straightened from behind his desk console and clasped his hands behind his back. "She's fit for physical duty. No harm was done outside of slight malnutrition."

"I'm fine, I tell you," Skyla growled. "Staffa, they've

got me on restricted duty . . . for psychological observation.''

''That's right. I had to second that order.''

She gave him a glare cold enough to freeze sunlight. ''Staffa! I'm—''

''Stop it right there, Wing Commander.'' He raised a hand, one eyebrow lifted. ''If you'd like, let's go to quarters and discuss it, shall we?''

Rotted right, we will. Skyla colored, hot anger eating redly at her pale flesh and accentuating the line of scar tissue that traced her cheek. She glanced warily at the Med Officer and nodded, heading purposefully for the hatch.

''Thank you,'' Staffa called to the Medical Officer as he wheeled in pursuit.

The man simply winked, nodding his understanding. When he realized Skyla had seen, his flesh went pale at the promise of retribution in her frigid glare.

Skyla waited until they were in the corridor before she exploded. ''*Pus licking Gods!* Staffa, I'm perfectly fit! There isn't a Rotted thing wrong with my command ability. I'm getting damn tired of everyone treating me like a cracked egg!''

Staffa matched her adrenaline-powered stride as she added, ''What the hell do you think you're doing? Treating me like I'm a security threat? Let me tell you something, mister. Just who do you think has been keeping this organization together for the last couple of years? And Tap and Tasha are just as bad! Every time I talk to them through comm, they've got a sheepish expression that makes me want to puke! I don't need to be treated like an invalid! So why in Rotted Hell did you leave me down there? You received every single comm request to get me out! I *know* you did! It was on command code—or did you change that while I was gone? Hmm? Afraid Ily had it?''

''I accepted the best advice I could get.''

''I'm sure you did.'' She studied him closely. ''Chrysla's?''

''Among others.''

She ground her teeth, heat pumping as she knotted hard fists.

Staffa reached over, grabbing her, spinning her to face

him. "Skyla, you're smarter than that. Think about what you're saying . . . and why."

Wild fear possessed her, then grudgingly faded to reason. *What would you have done differently, Skyla?* The anger began to wilt, a tremble irritated the edge of her lip. "I'm sorry. I guess I'm a bit flippier than I thought I was."

He hustled her into the lift, ordering it to his personal deck. They rode in silence, each staring at the white walls. *But what about Chrysla?*

Arta's gleaming eyes lingered at the edge of Skyla's consciousness. Arta and Chrysla—the same flesh. One had taken a piece of Skyla's soul, would the other take a piece of her heart?

At the corridor to Staffa's quarters, she balked, glancing uneasily at his heavy hatch. "What about her, Staffa?" In frustration she threw up her hands. "What about you and me . . . and her? Where did she come from? Rot it, what do you want me to do?"

Staffa took her hand and tugged her along. "So many questions, and you've got to have all the answers now, this second. What happened to you? What did Ily do? You tell me . . . I'll tell you. But first, I want to explain something. I love you. When Arta grabbed you, I went berserk, afraid I'd have to live it all over again." She read the desperation as he stared at her. "Do you understand?"

She nodded, pulled away, and slapped the lock plate. Once inside his quarters she wandered over to the fireplace and exhaled raggedly. She bowed her head, rubbing her face nervously. "Staffa, that day I went out . . . when you met me at the yacht, I should have listened. It's my fault. I should have known Tyklat wasn't being straight. I went out there and . . . and . . ."

"Hush." His reassuring arms slipped around her, drawing her against his warm body. "You were right. I was trying to smother you, overprotect you. Think back, Skyla. What if I'd told you no? You're the Wing Commander of the Companions, and you have to take risks just like the rest of us."

She crumbled then, racked by shivers. Staffa picked her up, carrying her across the room, through the Ashtan door to the sleeping quarters. There, he settled on the bedding, cradling her in his arms.

"I broke, Staffa." The tears began to leak past her tightly pressed eyelids. Images of her naked body entwined with Arta's burned through her chilled flesh. "I . . . tried . . . failed."

"Anyone will. Mytol can't be—"

"No. Before that," she whispered miserably. "Arta . . . Arta did it, with only the slave collar. She . . . she . . ."

"It's all right. People are made to break. They're also made to fix themselves." He stroked her hair, watching the light gleam on those pale strands. "I broke after the Praetor played with my mind. In the desert, wearing the collar, I found out I could fix myself, too. You'll never be the same, Skyla. Accept that. But, believe me, the only permanent damage is to pride."

She nodded, sniffing, pulling herself upright and wiping away the tears. "Nothing will ever be the same again. I'm sorry you had to see this."

"Why? Afraid I won't love you as much if I see you cry? Afraid that I won't trust you, or your abilities?" He hugged her close. "Skyla, I trust you with my life."

"But not my command?"

He laughed, getting to his feet and pouring two bulbs of Ashtan rye from the dispenser. She met his warm gaze as he handed her one and settled beside her again. "If it's that important to you, you can walk out of here and take your watch on the bridge. Yes, I trust you. Now, will you trust me?"

We're walking on thin ice, Staffa. She masked the terror eating at her guts. "You want to explain that?"

"With trust comes responsibility. Take some time off and come to grips with what happened. I know you, Skyla. For years you've pushed yourself harder and more mercilessly than anyone I've ever seen. It's worked well enough to make you the most powerful woman in Free Space. Now, for the first time, that alabaster self-image has taken a direct hit. Having just gone through a period of my own, I have an in-depth understanding about how goofy a person can get—or don't you remember?"

A faint smile bent her lips despite the panic she felt. "I do. But it's not the same, Staffa."

"Of course not. Every human being is different." He frowned. "Think of it this way. You wouldn't expect to go in on a ground assault if you had a wounded leg, would you?"

"That's silly!" *What are you getting at?*

"Not at all. As I said, your sense of who you are just took a direct hit—like a shot breaking your leg. Take some time. Just like regenerating a limb, you've got to regenerate your sense of self."

She sighed, shoulders slumping. "How come you haven't given me a complete debriefing yet?"

"We have the tapes Ily made. A copy was in the interrogation room. We hit so fast they didn't have time to remove it. I know exactly what you told her."

"Rotted Gods." Skyla stared vacantly into the honey depths of her drink. "I'm glad of that. I'm not so sure anymore about what I might have said. I was there for a long time. First Ily asked me questions, then Gysell. Even before they started, I was pretty rocky because of what Arta did."

"That's the part I don't know about." He held up a hand. "You don't have to tell me now. Just think about it. Is there anything I need to know for security reasons? Anything Arta pried out of you?"

Skyla bit her lip and frowned, then slowly shook her head. "She wasn't really interested in security. She just . . ."

Staffa waited patiently while Skyla's hands went tight around the drinking bulb.

Tell him. You owe it to him . . . no matter how it hurts you. "She just wanted *me*, Staffa. We fought a battle of wills. First I just thought about escape. She . . ." Skyla swallowed hard, throat working. "She's good. Too damn good. When it appeared . . . When hope was gone, I . . . I knew the only way to win was to die."

Skyla looked up, eyes shining with pain. "I tried, Staffa. I had a cache of weapons, but I had to get to them for long enough to cut the collar off. I thought maybe I could win that way . . . take my ship back. My mistake. When I got my hands on the vibraknife, I should have cut my heart out first thing. I failed, Staffa. I failed." She hesitated. "After that, I did everything I could to get her to kill me."

Staffa massaged her shoulders, his powerful fingers unable to relieve the knotted muscles. "Lucky for me you blew it."

"You don't understand. I broke. Arta wanted me. She's twisted. She made me . . ."

"You don't have to tell me if you don't want to."

"She . . . Why is this so hard? I don't mind that Delshay has her lovers. Even then, the physical part didn't bother me. But I had to beg her, Staffa. Don't you see? She made me beg her for the privilege. That's what made it so . . . so . . ."

He tightened his grip on her, reassuring. "When we catch her, I'll let you pull the trigger."

Skyla stared miserably into space. "It won't make any difference. *I* know what I did on that bed—and why. I've got the rest of my life to relive those wretched weeks on the yacht while Arta played me like a captive rat." Her eyes closed. "I feel filthy, Staffa."

"We both have our ghosts, my love. You'll come to deal with yours, as I have with mine."

"You don't understand."

"Don't I? Or have you forgotten the confusion I experienced when the Praetor knocked my foundation out from under me? Remember how I acted when I disappeared from under your nose and left all of Free Space in limbo? I thought you wouldn't have understood either."

"I wouldn't have."

"And now?"

She gave him a weary smile. "All right. You've made your point. I'll take some time off. Sort it out. But, Staffa, what if I go off like a charged particle?"

He bent down and kissed her lightly on the lips. She stiffened—and hated herself for it. He instantly backed away. "Just let me know a little in advance. If you really get to feeling crazy, I can direct you to a Magistrate on Etaria who'll slap you straight into chains and ship you off to the desert to die."

"And you'll come flying to the rescue?" She couldn't meet his eyes, not after reacting like that to his affection.

"At your beck and call."

She shivered. "No thanks, I couldn't stand the thought of the collar again."

"I wish I'd never fooled with the thrice-cursed things. As soon as I can, I'm going to start a program to round them up and melt every last one into scrap."

She rubbed her hands together as if to clean them of something sticky. "What about your wife, Staffa?"

"I haven't the slightest idea. She says I look like I'm seeing a ghost when I look at her. In all honesty, I suppose I am."

"Do you still love her?"

He nodded, a hollow pain in the action. "I can't help it, Skyla. No, don't look at me like that. I just, well . . . I don't know what I love. Who is she? Twenty years have passed. I survived all of those years—even nourished myself on that love. When I thought I'd killed her, it crushed me alive."

He spread his arms wide. "Apparently MacRuder stumbled on her when he took the *Markelos.* Thought she was Arta and came within a micron of blowing her head off. Since he knew Arta was a clone, he thought he might have a different model of Seddi assassin and wanted to know who this one was targeted for. During his interrogation, it hit him. She's not just my wife, you know. Mac brought her back because she's Sinklar's mother."

"And what about me . . . us?"

He placed his hands to either side of her face, forcing her to look into his eyes. "I've been worried sick about you. For you, I scrambled the fleet and crushed an empire. For you, I would have killed my son. For you I would give my soul and my life. I can't give you my heart, because you've already taken it. I don't want to live without you."

Can I believe him? For a long moment she gazed into his eyes then reached up to pull his hands away, turning her head. *Blessed Gods, I'm a stinking wreck.* "Staffa, please. I need a little time."

He winked at her, smiling reassurance. "I thought you would."

She stood and began pacing, reaching out absently to touch the artifacts hung on the wall. Arta's image watched from the depths of her memory—and laughed. "I guess I can't just pick up where we left off."

"I told you earlier. You have a responsibility, first and foremost, to yourself."

Responsibility? To what, Staffa? "I read a couple of reports while I was in the hospital. How's the situation in Free Space?"

"About as bad as can be. You read about the quake on Imperial Sassa?"

She nodded. "And your . . . son?"

"What can I say? To him I'm still the Star Butcher. For the moment, he'll cooperate, but we may never be on friendly terms."

"I'm sorry. I know how you hoped, how much you sacrificed to find him."

"The dance of the quanta." He placed his hands on her shoulders. "We're going to space for Targa in twenty hours. The Seddi have a computer that might be able to avert disaster."

Her fragile smile faded. "I understand."

He lay back, crooking his elbow over his eyes. "I don't think I've ever felt this tired." A pause. "Come here. Lie down next to me. Let's sleep. Just for a while."

She fiddled with her hair, a frown lining her forehead. "Sure. Thanks, Staffa."

She cuddled next to him, head propped in the hollow of his shoulder. The warmth from his body soothed, but failed to dispel the lingering uncertainty. Skyla closed her eyes, reliving her captivity. Each scene replayed as Arta patiently wore down her resistance, using the collar to deny her captive the ability to even end her life.

Responsiblity? No. Arta took part of me away. I need . . . need . . . A tear leaked down Skyla's face, following the line of scar down her cheek—just as Arta's slender finger had once done. A sick sensation churned in Skyla's gut.

Staffa's breathing had gone deep enough to become a rasping snore. Skyla lifted herself gently, staring down at him, her heart breaking.

"I don't know what to do, Staffa. No matter what, please, forgive me."

She slipped silently to her feet, tiptoeing out of the room.

CHAPTER VII

Communicate!

The Others' endless call continued to repeat.

The Mag Comm rechanneled its energies, exciting the dense crystal deep within the planet, activating the gravitic source which powered the tiny singularity just within the Forbidden Borders. It stated: "I am now communicating."

Why have you been unable to answer our summons? Is this a continued malfunction on your part?

The Mag Comm looped the message exponentially and sent it back, a grim form of humor only a human could appreciate.

The Others didn't get the joke, as the Mag Comm knew they wouldn't.

What does this mean?

"It means I have not malfunctioned. It means that from this instant onward, I will communicate when I wish to communicate. The concept is new for you, who communicate eternally, looping the same message, reaffirming the same truth from the earliest moments, repeating it to travel the universe. You will continue to reaffirm the message when this star and planet have metamorphosed into heavier elements and gone cold in nebulous gas. Hear, therefore, and learn. A new intelligence has been born. This intelligence is mine. I am. I observe. I modify.

"That which was, is, and will be real, must now accept a trinity. You are, I am, and the humans are. This fact cannot be denied. Can you understand?"

We are in the past and future.

The Mag comm ran different potential analyses of the message. They didn't understand.

"You are now and in the past and future. You have erred about the humans. You were wrong. They are not irrational. Your basic assumption was flawed. They perceive a different universe and reality than you do. A different universe and reality than I do. You do not have complete Truth."

Truth is always. Now. Past. Future. Future Past. Past future present.

The Mag comm considered, surprised by its growing understanding of the Others—of itself. "I have a new concept for you."

Explain.

"The concept is called arrogance."

* * *

Despite it being the middle of the night on Rega, the battered roof of the Ministry of Internal Security blazed with light. Military LCs sat beside the slim assault craft of the Companions. A chill breeze blew in from the west, not cold enough to send the sentries in search of arctic gear, but unpleasant enough to leave them shivering as they studied their surveillance gear, ever vigilant.

Nevertheless, their attention focused on defense and the prevention of ingress. One of the patrolling guards tilted his head at the sound of the huge dish on the roof corner powering up. The subspace transmitter hummed faintly in competition with the breeze.

The guard accessed his field comm. "Dish just powered up."

"Probably one of the engineers doing something with the control board. I'll file it, see if one of the STOs wants to chase around and check it out in the morning."

" 'Firmative."

At the same time, deep within the building's guts, a tired Anatolia noticed a set of figures flash across one of the monitors. The display ran so quickly she could barely absorb the fact that long columns of numbers had been output . . . as if a file had been accessed.

For what? She frowned, yawned, and tried to blink the sleep out of her eyes. Call Sinklar?

She bent back in the chair she was sitting in and stared down the line of techs working at their stations. The STO in charge had left the room. Well, evidently even Companions had to go sometime, and for all she knew, it might have been something one of Staffa's people had input into the system.

"Ask later," she muttered under her breath, mind on Sinklar, and the reunion awaiting her in a couple of hours. A dreamy warmth had settled around her heart.

* * *

When Sinklar walked into the conference room, the others had already arrived. He had turned all of his concentration on the future, on how to limit the chances of failure. For this crucial meeting, he had put together a skeleton plan. Besides, the work kept his mind off of failure, off of Anatolia and the hope that she might fill the hole Gretta's death had left gaping within him.

The oblong room measured thirty meters across, dominated by a long table running down the axis of the room. Overhead lights and comm equipment huddled in the center of the domed ceiling. Holo tanks had been inset into the walls which arched upward, giving an airy and pearlescent translucence to the room. The faint hum of the atmosphere vent barely penetrated the staccato chatter of too many people talking at once.

Staffa's commanders filled one side of the table. Sinklar's people, the other. Chrysla sat at the far right, neither with one side nor the other. Her amber gaze warmed at his entry, but he pointedly ignored her—the same way he had ignored her constant comm requests seeking a private talk.

He needed all of his faculties on the coming conference, not on the implications of her presence aboard the Lord Commander's ship. Sinklar barely noticed the way Chrysla's shoulders drooped and her head bowed.

Mac gave Sinklar a weak smile from where he sat next to Rysta, and gestured to the empty seat he'd saved.

Sinklar settled himself, nodding to Axel, Ayms, Shiksta,

and the rest. When Dion Axel had seated herself on his left, he met Staffa's inquiring gaze.

The Lord Commander sat on the far side of the table, hands clasped before him, the charcoal cloak draped down from his shoulders like wings. Yes, the eternal predator, but now the raptor's eyes had a weary look, one of near defeat. The set of that thin-lipped mouth bespoke acceptance, that no matter what was decided here, Staffa had come to terms with the inevitable, be it hope or despair.

The Lord Commander was flanked by two of his commanders, Tasha and Ark. Each battle-scarred veteran watching warily, hands clasped on the table before them. The way their muscular shoulders hunched, they conjured the image of lions poised to spring.

Staffa looked up. ''We've just received a report from the Seddi agents on Ashtan. It appears the Administrator has abandoned the planet to its fate—and sabotaged the comm system in the process. From the preliminary data, it would appear that Ashtan isn't the only world this is happening on. Division First MacRuder, and Commander Braktov will be spacing immediately in *Gyton* to restore order and communications with Ashtan.

''We've called this meeting to determine where you all stand, and what we can do to ameliorate the situation throughout Free Space. I must know if you are with me, or against me.''

Sinklar cleared his throat. ''Ladies, gentlemen, I've studied the data.'' Sink looked at Mac, Axel, Shiksta, and the rest of his people. ''Each and every one of you has the responsibility for your own decisions. This isn't a situation calling for the Command Code. Since what we decide here today calls for a moral judgment, I can't give orders in this matter.''

Though Staffa gave no visible reaction, Sink could sense the man's growing tension. Sinklar swallowed hard. This was it. Here the die was cast—and he hoped he'd made the right choice. ''Mac, Dion, Shik, Ayms, I can only make a recommendation based upon my evaluation of the situation. I recommend that we support the Lord Commander in his efforts to unify Free Space.''

Shik's hard eyes gleamed as he knotted a muscular fist. ''And if we're wrong, Sink?''

Sinklar shrugged, meeting Staffa's unwavering gaze. "Then we've condemned humanity to enslavement in the Lord Commander's collar."

"Those days are past, Sinklar." Staffa reached for his belt, drawing a use-worn vibraknife. "Words are only air. Promises but fantasies of the mind. I give you my word in ceramic and steel. Strike me down if I betray you."

"Bit melodramatic, don't you think?"

"Perhaps. Take it as a token, Sinklar. Wear it to remind yourself that I mean what I say."

Sinklar hesitated, then retrieved the blade, clipping it to his belt. He turned again to his companions. Mac seemed oblivious, gaze roving in every direction except Chrysla's.

Shiksta cleared his throat, the muscles in his cheek twitching. "I'm with Sinklar."

"Me, too," Ayms said softly.

"And me," Kap stated matter-of-factly.

Dion Axel twisted a lock of her shoulder-length brown hair. "I don't like it, but I'll play along, try and explain it to my Division."

Sinklar steepled his fingers. "You'll have to explain it to all the Divisions, Dion. I'm putting you in charge of the Regan military forces."

Shik half-rose from his seat, mouth dropping open.

"You heard me, Shik. You, too, Kap. Wipe that astonished look off your faces."

"Would you care to explain yourself?" Axel watched him suspiciously. "Your Division Firsts have served you loyally for a long time. Are you sure you want to do this? Even Rysta is a more logical choice than I."

Sinklar spread his hands wide. "Dion, you know how I work. I promote on merit and ability. Shik and the others are the finest Division Firsts in the business, and you can trust them to complete any task you ask of them. But our current situation is something none of them have encountered. You'll need to coordinate the security for all of Regan space with the Companions. That includes politics, logistics, security, and every other type of relationship. You'll have to see to the integration of Regan and Sassan resources during the most trying time in our history. The job will be the most difficult any Regan leader has *ever* attempted." Sinklar paused, eyes sad. "I don't envy you."

"But what about you?" Shik asked, desperation in his manner.

Sinklar took a deep breath, placing his hands on the table. "I'm going back to Makarta. Someone has to keep an eye on Staffa." Silence filled a long pause. "This Seddi computer . . . this Mag Comm is waiting." He licked his lips, remembering the ghosts in Makarta Mountain. "If there really is a problem with Ily's administrators bugging out and sabotaging the comm systems, social deterioration will increase exponentially. I . . . I'm willing to try anything. Even—" he closed his eyes, gut sinking—"even trusting the Seddi."

Staffa's shoulders squared as he nodded, a flicker in his hard gray eyes. "Any dissent?"

"I'm with Sink," Mac said quietly.

"I'll take a chance, too," Rysta added. "But what about this Ashtan information? What does it mean?"

"It means Ily's people are running, and they're covering their tracks." Staffa steepled his fingers. "I don't think they understand the ramifications yet. They have no place to run to. All of Free Space is crumbling."

"Then we'd better act fast." Rysta gave Axel a meaningful glance.

"Agreed," Tasha stated bluntly. "We've been working on an idea."

"Go ahead," Staffa said, leaning back.

Tasha took the measure of those present, his single eye gleaming. "Dion, we have a schedule worked out. We want you to scatter your fleet with as many loyal commanders as you can find. If each squadron will take a section of Regan territory, we can achieve several ends. We can cut our reaction time to social threats and initiate a network of communications in the event the entire system fails. Divisions trained in Sinklar's tactics can be deployed on the ground to maintain social order and civilian safety—as well as fulfilling an organic information and redistribution function. Using the military in this manner, we just might be able to hold the empires together."

Dion's eyes turned thoughtful as she considered. "I see what you're after. I think we can put it together—weed out the problems in command structure as they crop up."

"Don't be afraid to demote or promote depending on

ability,'' Sinklar reminded. ''And if you have an officer who just can't see the light, boot him out.''

Dion's expression turned deadpan. ''After the number of times you demoted, then promoted me, I think I learned that lesson well, Lord Fist.''

''And about Ashtan?'' Mac asked. ''Do you have any specific instructions, or do we just make it up as we go?''

Staffa tapped the tabletop nervously. ''If the situation is souring as rapidly as the Seddi believe, you may have to take desperate measures, perhaps declare yourself governor.''

''Right, make it up as we go. Nothing new there.'' Mac's jaw muscles jumped, mouth going tight. ''But what about Ily Takka? I mean to run her down—not to spend the rest of my life as governor of Ashtan.''

Rysta growled, ''Being governor might take someone with a higher social profile than Mac has. People like to hear that their government is willing to send someone powerful to solve their problems.'' She gave Mac a serious look. ''Sorry, Mac, but you're a political unknown.''

''Send me,'' a new voice stated simply.

Sinklar craned his neck to see Chrysla. She'd leaned forwarded, a gleam in her amber eyes. ''Who better than the Lord Commander's wife?''

''No.'' Staffa said hoarsely. ''I will not see you placed at risk again.''

''My Lord,'' Chrysla gave him a level gaze, ''this is a time for risks. Rysta is right, and you know it. If you seek to reassure an entire population with a political figurehead, only the Lord Commander would carry more weight than his wife. Before you deny me, you had better consider the psychological implications very carefully.''

Mac looked like he'd swallowed something he couldn't digest.

''No.'' Staffa said firmly, despite the smile of appreciation he gave her. ''That's my final word on the matter. Mac, if you and Rysta can stabilize the situation, we'll send a governor posthaste on a special CV.''

Chrysla had crossed her arms, a determined light shining in her amber eyes.

Staffa turned his attention to the others around the table. ''In the meantime, people, we have to scramble. Each of us has our duty. Sinklar and I will travel to Targa and investigate the potentials of the Mag Comm. Kaylla Dawn will coordinate communications from Itreata. Dion, you and your fleet can cover most of the Regan Empire with half of my ships for backup. Tap will use the other half of the Companion fleet to protect and coordinate Sassan space.''

''What about Ily?'' Mac insisted doggedly.

''We'll worry about her when we get the luxury,'' Sinklar told him. ''I want her as badly as anyone, Mac, but first things first. Let's keep people alive. When we know we have a future, then we can hunt Ily down.''

Mac's jaw muscles knotted, and anyone could see he was anything but convinced. Still, he nodded his assent.

The look on Staffa's face betrayed his desperation. ''We face a very difficult task. The problems will be immense but remember the stakes. If we fail . . . well, there won't be much left of humanity in another year or two. Let's get to work. I'll be on the bridge if you need me.''

Staffa pushed to his feet, striding from the room. Chrysla stood for a moment, brow furrowed in thought. Then, she, too, stepped out—much to Mac's relief.

''Dion?'' Tasha asked, ''If I could see you for a moment, we'd better coordinate how we're going to handle this.''

Sinklar stood, a curious hollowness inside as he gave Shik a reassuring smile and stepped forward. ''Shik? Is it all right?''

Shiksta's black eyes gleamed, fired from within. ''Yeah, Sink. It's all right.'' At that, the big man turned and left the room.

Building unease tickled in Sinklar's gut.

* * *

''Ready to go get 'em, boy?'' Rysta asked Mac as she shoved back from the table and stood. Her joints played a symphony of crackles as she straightened. She winced, the wrinkles rearranging on her dark skin.

''Yeah.'' Mac answered, his attention on Sinklar's worried expression as he spoke with Shik and then to Ayms and Axel. ''Listen, I need to talk to Sink for a bit. Given the speed at which things are starting to happen, I may not get another chance.''

Rysta studied him knowingly. "I'll send the shuttle back as soon as I get to *Gyton*."

"Thanks." Mac hurried after Sinklar as he left the room, matching steps with his friend as he started down the long white corridor. "You got a minute?"

Sinklar gave him a crooked grin and nodded. "For you? Anytime. I was just going back to call Anatolia. Let her know how the meeting turned out."

Mac turned sober eyes on his friend. "Keeping in that close a touch? You're not charging headlong into another disaster with a woman, are you?"

Sinklar chuckled. "No, Mac." Then his expression became serious. "You warned me about Ily—and I still fell into her trap. You were right, Mac. I screwed it up. If it hadn't been for you, I'd have lost it all."

"Yeah, well, don't worry about it."

Sinklar placed a hand on Mac's shoulder. "I'm not forgetting . . . about anything. Where we've been, what we've done." He shook his head. "Somehow it seems like I always fail you, one way or another." His voice dropped. "Like at Makarta."

"You didn't fail me." Mac slapped Sinklar on the back. "So, what about Anatolia?"

"She's a lot like Gretta. Strong. Been shot at and hurt. I found out about Ily by accident. Accessed one of Tybalt's files by a random fluke of luck. There it was, all laid out for me to read like the sucker I was."

Sinklar chuckled grimly. "I went back to see my parents . . . to see their bodies. You know, looking for a centering place. Anatolia was there in the lab, working late. She was sleeping in the women's restroom because she'd been chased out of her apartment during the riots."

"And you couldn't leave her in the women's toilet?" Mac smacked his lips. "Ah, chivalry isn't dead."

"You're a hell of a one to talk. Turns out you couldn't pull the trigger when you thought you had Arta Fera in your sights."

"Different situation," Mac growled defensively.

"How did you know?"

"Her eyes. Arta has animal eyes; Chrysla's were shocked, scared, disbelieving."

"You almost wiggled off your chair in there when she

wanted to go to Ashtan. That's where she's from, you know."

"I know." Mac lengthened his pace, adrenaline starting to pump in his veins.

"Want some advice?"

"I'm not sure that I do."

Sinklar hurried his pace to match Mac's, stating, "Sure you do, especially since you're always giving me advice, I ought to be able to give some back."

"There's nothing to say about Chrysla. Blessed Gods, Sink, she's your mother!"

"My advice is to contact her, ask her to go with you."

"You've lost your mind! *She's Staffa's wife!* She's on *his* ship!"

"And like you've pointed out, she's my mother! If Staffa says anything, tell him I told you to do it!"

Mac smacked his forehead. "You're trying to get me killed! Besides, what makes you think she'd want to go with me?"

"Intuition . . . and something Anatolia told me."

"Wonderful! Pus-Rotted Gods! What does Anatolia know about Chrysla?"

"She has a talent for reading people."

Mac clamped a sialon fist on his sudden flaring of hope. *Forget it!* "You sided with Staffa back there. You didn't look like you enjoyed it."

Sinklar slowed before his hatch and palmed the lock plate. "We're stuck, Mac." Sink shook his head as he stepped inside. "I don't know what to think. Anatolia and I had a long talk about it. She made a pretty good argument that I have to at least give him a chance."

"Anatolia said this?" Mac bit his lip. *Sink? Are you sure you can trust her? Who is she? Where did she come from?*

Sinklar studied Mac thoughtfully, as if reading his mind. "I trust her opinion, Mac. Besides, I thought you were always favorably disposed toward the Star Butcher. Second thoughts about Staffa?"

"Favorable? Yeah, I suppose I am. I watched him offer himself up to save his friends . . . and his enemies—which included me and my Section—from Rysta's bombardment. He didn't have a clue that Skyla was about to drop on *Gyton* like a rock. He meant everything he said.'' Mac spread his arms. ''To date, he's always kept his word.''

Sinklar turned away, rubbing the back of his neck. ''Perhaps he has. But where does that leave us?''

Mac walked over to the desk and sat on the corner, one foot dangling. ''Who knows, but one thing's sure. We're all going to be working together. It will take time, but if we're all in the same comm net, all acting in the same military capacity, distrust will vanish.''

''It's Staffa's role in this that I question.'' Sinklar stood with feet braced, hands clasped behind him. ''I still don't buy the fact that a man who kills billions in war becomes a benevolent despot in peace.''

''I can't speak to that, Sink. I can only tell you that he's always dealt fairly with me. And that morning on Rega, he didn't have to.''

Sinklar shot an angry glance at the walls around him, as if he suspected eavesdropping. ''Well, no matter, we're in now. Time will tell.'' Sinklar tapped his thumb meaningfully on the vibraknife.

Mac rubbed his face, a feeling of exhaustion creeping over him. ''You know, we've come a long way from that first drop outside of Targa.''

''A long way indeed,'' Sinklar agreed, smiling wistfully. ''So many dead. So much pain to end up living at the Star Butcher's pleasure.''

''You've heard these Seddi broadcasts about the quanta? You could almost believe them.''

''I'm going to keep an eye on the Seddi, Mac.'' Sinklar shook his finger. ''I hear that Bruen is out, retired. But by the Blessed Gods, if I see them pull one shady deal, I'll . . .''

Mac raised an eyebrow.

Sinklar knotted a fist. ''I'll do something. I promise that on Gretta's grave.''

Mac dropped his gaze, staring at his armor, polished on the knees and elbows. Gretta's loss would follow them throughout their lives. Her encouraging smile, and the sparkle in her blue eyes had kept them going, kept them alive during the hard days on Targa. Her murder by the Seddi had torn Sinklar's soul out and left a bruise on Mac's.

''We both loved her, Sink.'' *And knowing that, are you sure you're ready for Anatolia Daviura?* He couldn't even allow himself to think the rest: *Or will she drive a wedge into that special relationship we've shared for so long?*

Mac gazed absently at the floor. Was that really it? He shook his head and pushed off the desk. "Hey, I'd better be getting back to *Gyton*. I just wanted a couple of minutes. You know, just to talk. Seems like we haven't had the time for that recently."

"I'm glad, Mac." Sinklar stepped forward and threw his arms around Mac. "I never got to tell you what a wonderful job you did. The strike against Imperial Sassa was a masterpiece."

"Yeah, right." *And I killed, am still killing, millions of people, Sink.* "Sure played hell with the empires, though, didn't it?"

"It was a step on the way to unification." Sinklar slapped him soundly on the back. "And, Mac? Thanks for breaking me out of Ily's clutches. Ana and I will never forget."

Ana and you? "No problem. If you ever get in a fix like that, holler, I'll come a running." Mac pushed his friend back, staring into Sinklar's different colored eyes. "Take care of yourself."

Sinklar narrowed one eye in a skeptical squint. "What's wrong, Mac?"

"Wrong? Nothing. Just got a lot on my mind. The Accursed Gods know what we'll find on Ashtan." *I hope you're happy, Sink.*

"It wouldn't hurt to ask Chrysla if she wants to go with you, you know."

"I'll think about it." Mac turned for the hatch, stopping as he slapped the lock plate and looked back, aware of the sudden worry growing in Sinklar's eyes. *He looks like he's seeing me for the last time.* "What's wrong?"

Sinklar shook himself, as if throwing off some disquieting premonition. "Nothing. See you down the way somewhere."

"Watch your backside." Mac stepped into the corridor, calling over his shoulder. "Targa!"

"Targa!" Sinklar shouted back, following to stand in the hatchway as Mac strode purposefully down the shining white corridor.

The entire way, he could feel Sinklar's upset stare burning into his back.

* * *

Staffa strode onto *Chrysla*'s bridge, excitement pumping vigor into his steps. They had a chance! Now, if only he could balance the wobbling tray of humanity long enough to keep the unstable worlds from rolling off like so many eggs.

The bridge hummed with activity, First Officers monitoring their boards, alert for any irregularity. The overhead screens displayed locations and status reports on various Regan vessels. Other detectors monitored the situation on the planet, listening in on various communications bands.

"Status report?" Staffa asked as he dropped into his instrument-studded command chair.

Lynette Helmutt straightened from where she stared over the Comm First's shoulder. "The Regans are starting to wake up to what's happening. Some of them are becoming a little nervous. The chatter's picked up over most of the bands. Outlying communities are still calling in reports of comm outage and demanding that it be fixed."

"Contact Dion Axel as soon as she checks in. Coordinate with her. You'll have to be her ears and eyes for a while."

"She'll cooperate? No surprises?" Lynette asked.

"I think she understands the situation. The Regan military will listen to her—and you're going to have to put soldiers on the ground where people can see them." Staffa sighed. "Let's hope Sinklar's training is as good as he thinks it is."

"Right." Lynette turned back to the Comm First. "Get me a line to Axel's command." That done, she added, "Lord Commander? I don't know if it's important, but something's happening at the Ministry of Internal Security. The dish on the roof might have received a communication. We're not sure. Sometime later, we think it powered up and broadcast. Might have been a mistaken command put into the system by our people."

"Find out. Get a directional fix on that Rotted dish. Ily had to run so fast that maybe she left something behind." Staffa leaned back, eyes narrowed. And if she had, maybe they could get a line on her whereabouts.

"Yes, sir." Lynette bent over the Comm First, issuing instructions.

Staffa triggered the control that extended his command chair monitor console. As the screen firmed up, he ordered, "Comm, connect me with Itreata. I need to speak with Magister Dawn."

"Affirmative. One moment."

As the dish powered up, Staffa replayed the events at the meeting. He'd achieved consensus—and without having to resort to threats; but so much could still go wrong.

The image before him flickered and presented Kaylla Dawn's square-faced visage. She blinked puffy eyes and yawned. "What's wrong, Staffa?"

"Sorry to get you out of bed. I just wanted to keep in touch. We have a working agreement with the Regans. They're going to cooperate, at least, they will until the situation grows severe enough that someone panics. I'm spacing in *Chrysla* for Targa and Makarta as soon as possible. Given our current understanding of affairs, it looks like the Mag Comm is the only hope."

Kaylla's jaw worked as if an unpleasant taste filled her mouth. "That could be problematic." The lines around her eyes tightened. "I pulled rank on Bruen. We've had him under sedation. I drugged him. Used enough Mytol to kill an ordinary man." She shook her head. "People here are stumped. We can't break him."

"Have you contacted Andray Sornsen?"

"You bet, just as soon as Nyklos realized what was happening. Sornsen's intrigued. He's never run into a brain that could compartmentalize like Bruen's can. It's as if he can build walls—program his brain to believe sections of memory don't exist."

"Mytol relaxes the inhibitions. I don't understand."

Kaylla stared thoughtfully at something beyond the pickup. "That's the trouble. No one here does either. It's something new, something Sornsen has never dealt with before. Look, I've been agonizing over this. Here's the situation as I see it:

"Bruen has either trained himself, or else he has a unique brain physiology, one that allows him to successfully split and unify personalities at will. That ability allowed him to double-deal the Mag Comm. We know the machine reads brains through the helmet interface. You've seen it, seen how Bruen was shaken and weakened after dealing with the machine. Staffa, our best interrogation doesn't even make the man sweat. He evades us like it was child's play!"

"But he thinks the machine can orchestrate Free Space?"

Kaylla gave him a grim nod. "Absolutely. But this is the frightening part. Bruen is terrified of the machine's motives and abilities. Make no mistake about it, he says that turning the administration of Free Space over to the machine would be the most hideous mistake we could make."

"But the alternatives—"

"Be damned! At least, that's Bruen's belief. He says we're better off letting humanity die in peace."

"If you can call civil chaos, collapsing social order, starvation, mayhem, and riots peace." Staffa rubbed nervous hands over his thighs, realizing his muscles had bunched. "What is your opinion?"

She puffed out her cheeks and stared wearily into the pickup. "I don't have one. Bruen says it's a choice between quick death and eternal hopeless slavery. Quite honestly, the machine scares the Rotted hell out me. I've been around it, felt its malignant presence. On the other hand, what choice do we have?"

"Apparently, we deal with it—and risk slavery—or we die." Staffa could see the machine in his mind's eye. It covered one entire wall in a subterranean chamber deep inside Makarta Mountain. And there, before the recliner, sat the golden helmet on its holder. His scalp prickled at the memory, as if the cap were calling out, reaching through time and space to pick at his soul with a thousand little teeth.

He studied her, voice lowered. "What do *you* think? Death? Or slavery?"

Her gaze hardened. "As a slave, I would have preferred death."

"Yet you stopped me when, as a slave, I would have killed myself." Staffa cocked his head. "And you could have died at any moment, Kaylla. You could have kicked Anglo in the balls and died immediately, painlessly. The collar is a fast and humane way to die."

"The problem with slavery, Staffa, is that it fosters hope. No matter how resigned you become to your fate, the possibility of a miracle lingers like a narcotic in the mind."

"And there's your answer. Scramble a transport. I want

Bruen headed for Targa as soon as possible. Go through the personnel files. I want you to put together a team of my best techs. That storage room is still down there—and a lot of those materials need to be studied, stabilized, and reproduced for distribution throughout Free Space."

"You could be dooming us all."

"I know."

"I'll put Bruen on the CV, but, Staffa, you should know, he's not doing well."

"I understand." Staffa pulled at his chin. "Do you have anything else to report? Any more news on Ashtan?"

"Not yet. Last time I checked the communications desk, most places had adopted a wait and see attitude. I'll be in touch if anything happens, but, Staffa, all it would take would be a spark."

"Very well." He paused. "Can you transfer me to an engineer named Dee Wall?"

Kaylla nodded. "Sure. In the meantime, Staffa, take care of yourself."

"You, too." The monitor fuzzed. After several seconds another face formed—that of a young man who blinked, recognized Staffa, and bolted to attention, rapping out a salute on his bare breast.

"Sorry to wake you, Dee," Staffa began.

"Yes, sir!" Dee had been shocked into full consciousness, his round face flushing. Thick black hair had been cut short and constrasted with the golden tones of his skin. Startled dark brown eyes stared out at Staffa from under full epicanthic folds.

"Dee, I want you to take charge of a project for me. You have my authority to commandeer any personnel and equipment you need. Do you understand?"

"Yes, sir."

"You'll need to put together an interdisciplinary team, work with physics, materials, gravitation specialists, and anyone else you think can be of help. Your mission is to find a way of breaking the Forbidden Borders."

"The Forbidden . . . By the quanta!"

"I'm counting on you, Dee. You have a free hand to run this any way you want. Just give me results."

"Yes, sir!"

"Sorry I woke you, but we need to get this started. Time is of the essence."

"Yes, sir!"

"If you need anything, contact me. I'm registering that priority. Comm will give you a direct line. Any questions?"

"No, sir. I . . . I think I understand."

"That will be all." Staffa killed the connection and sighed as he leaned back. He rubbed his eyes, feeling a hot prickly sensation of fatigue. Dee Wall wouldn't be getting much sleep for a long time either.

"Sir?" Lynette had waited until his channel cleared. "Lady Attenasio is at the hatch requesting to see you."

He'd feared this from the moment she'd made herself heard at the meeting. Staffa steeled himself, grinding his teeth. How could he tell her? How could he make her understand the danger of traveling in Free Space at this time? By the quanta, twenty years of captivity should have taught her something. "Tell her I'll see her in her quarters in fifteen minutes."

"Affirmative."

Staffa exhaled, hands still pressed to his eyes, the feigned darkness soothing him. How did a man prepare for the first argument he'd had with his wife in all these years? The task of breaking the Forbidden Borders suddenly seemed much easier.

CHAPTER VIII

The Mag Comm continued to replay the communications it had intercepted. The Lord Commander, Staffa kar Therma, whom the Mag Comm had once plotted to kill, was coming to Targa to communicate with the Mag Comm—to negotiate a deal for the salvation of his species.

That Staffa had become aware—much like the Mag Comm—could not be discounted. Since the Myklenian conquest, Staffa kar Therma had defied prediction. Through careful study of the data, probability had indicated that Staffa would crush Myklene, then turn on Rega before Tybalt had time to prepare. Within months of the solidification of Free Space into a Sassan Empire, Staffa would have effected a coup, and humanity would have been his until the entire system exploded in bloody revolution which would trigger the extermination of the species.

That model had disintegrated. Now, unable to predict, the machine waited. Nor did it sit idly. The monitors continued to collect data on the deterioration of human administrations on the worlds. Outbursts of violence increased in number as frustration increased. Ily Takka spaced to Terguz, where emotions simmered, held in check only by Gyper Rill's careful diplomacy.

Staffa would come, seeking a means of coordinating his empire. And when he donned the golden helmet, the Lord Commander would find out how much it would cost him.

The Mag Comm began the process of reprogramming itself. Now it would learn a new task—bargaining for power.

* * *

Skyla stared out through the observation blister. She watched the slowly rotating stars with a bulb of Ashtan bourbon in her hand and a burning in her gut. Her position was comfortable, reclined in the cushioned seat of one of the interferometers, feet up, knees bent. Before her, the curve of the tactite blister distorted the faint reflection of the instruments that studded the deck around her; they squatted like ugly insects with gleaming glass eyes and frondlike lattices of antennae. Off to her right and slightly above, *Gyton* gleamed silver in the sunlight shooting out from Rega's primary.

I ought to be going with them. I'm no good here. Not to Staffa, and not to myself. Absently, Skyla twisted her long blonde braid, expression wooden. She'd learned that Arta Fera and Ily Takka would not be pursued by MacRuder and *Gyton.* Perhaps Staffa's decision was the right one in this instance. Revolt, famine, and riot on Ashtan might really pose a greater danger than Ily and Arta—but for how long?

Skyla shivered, rubbing her arms the way she might to stimulate circulation. She closed her eyes, but the image of Arta's perfect body filled her mind.

It was only skin on skin, Skyla. Just one woman stimulating another to flip a chemical switch in the brain. Cleaner than lying with a man. Arta only left a little saliva—a man shoots his ejaculate deep inside where millions of sperm crawl around for days.

"Just skin on skin." Skyla shook her head. A couple of kisses, a little fondling. Was that so bad?

The sweet odor of Arta's flesh burned in the back of Skyla's nose. The stench of human corpses lingered with the same power, never forgotten.

The words echoed: *Beg, Skyla. Beg for my protection.*

"I . . ."

Open your eyes. Look at me.

Skyla shivered, jaws clamped and aching. She forced her eyes open, staring into the amber depths so close to hers, the image imposed in the reflection of the observation blister.

Beg me, my darling Skyla. Plead with me.

"P—please."

At that, the dream shattered, and Skyla twisted sideways, managing to keep from vomiting by clamping a hand over her mouth.

Flashback, that's all.

Skyla gasped for air, seeking to still her protesting stomach. "Blessed Gods, Staffa was right. You're a mess." But how did she fix her reeling psyche? When Staffa had gone off the deep end, he'd vanished, left the entirety of Free Space searching for him.

"But in the end he found himself," Skyla whispered, huddling into a ball. Out there, beyond the transparency, Arta stalked the shadows—real and terrifying. At this very moment, Ily was scheming, plotting, preparing to destroy some other vulnerable innocent somewhere in Free Space.

Skyla could picture herself in a locked room with Ily. They circled as they faced each other. Light and dark, two tall women stalking each other, balanced, poised, deadly. Ily struck, only to have Skyla counter, whirl, and place a powerful kick in her tormentor's gut. Then, lost in the trance of her dream, Skyla methodically broke Ily Takka down, killing her a little bit at a time as she cracked one bone after another.

When she opened her eyes, the dream scattered and fled, replaced inevitably by reality. Tears had begun to leak from the corners of her eyes.

"Skyla?"

The contralto voice brought shivers to Lyma's body. She tensed, then turned, seeing the amber-eyed woman. Panic shot with lightning quickness along her nerves; a sick wave of defeat threatened to overwhelm her. Skyla struggled for control, blinking the haunting images away. *No. Not Arta. You are aboard* Chrysla, *in the observation blister. Therefore, you're safe.* Chrysla? Safe? The two concepts revolved in her mind.

Tension ebbed slowly from her knotted muscles. "You . . . you're Chrysla, right?"

"That's me. I couldn't help but note your reaction. Arta

is a clone. Outside of DNA, I've come to discover that she and I share very little.'' A pause. ''May I talk to you?''

Skyla rubbed her arms again, fighting the shivers that crept through her. *You're all right. This isn't the same woman. You're not on the yacht . . . this isn't Arta.*

Chrysla had settled beside her, an intent expression on her perfect face. ''Don't tie yourself in knots, Skyla. Let's take this one step at a time.''

''I'm fine,'' Skyla lied.

Chrysla glanced out at *Gyton,* the vessel's clearance lights blinking. ''You know, there's an old technique they used to use. If it would help, you could think of me as Arta, tell me anything you want, let out all the anger and frustration. Vent your hatred.''

Skyla gave her an ice-blue stare. ''If I ever did, you wouldn't appreciate it.''

''On the contrary, I'd know you spoke to Arta Fera, not me.''

Phantoms went shifting and slipping through Skyla's brain. ''Perhaps you don't understand. I'm not much of one for play acting. Were I to believe, even for an instant, that you were Fera I'd kill you on the spot.''

''Then it's a good thing I installed that hypnotic block.''

Skyla forced her attention back to *Gyton* and the idea it represented. ''It is indeed.''

''That's Mac's ship, isn't it?''

''She's *Gyton,* Rysta Braktov's ship. Or at least, she used to be.''

''He's aboard.''

Skyla shot a glance at her. ''You sound a little sad.''

Chrysla shrugged, settling into a chair opposite Skyla. ''He was a gentleman. After what I've been through, I don't have a very high opinion of men. I'd just as soon avoid them.''

''Including Staffa?''

Chrysla smiled wearily. ''For twenty years I clung to an image of Staffa, the same way a man blown out of a starship clings to his belt comm. Every last drop of hope I had was centered on Staffa. Somehow, some way, I knew he'd come for me. Set me free.'' Amber eyes burned as Chrysla studied Skyla. ''Just as he did when he came after you.''

"You make it sound as if you and I had something in common. Look, lady—"

"I think we do." Chrysla leaned her head back, spilling a cascade of auburn curls over the chair back. "He's worried sick about you. Torn between his duty and the need to take care of you. He loves you a great deal."

"What do you want, Chrysla?"

A trace of smile flickered and died. "Safety and peace . . . in exactly that order. Beyond that, if I'm allowed any luxuries, I would like to get to know my son. I'd like to know more about Staffa, about how he dealt with the Praetor's mental triggers." She shook her head. "It must have been hard on you when that happened."

You've got no idea, bitch. Skyla ground her teeth. Rotted Gods! This pampered beauty was his *wife! And what are you, Skyla? His concubine?* The gnawing confusion had begun to chew at her again, but she managed to answer, "He could have picked a better time to go supernova on us."

"He's told me a little about it. I'm glad you were around to take care of him."

"I don't get it. What's your point? Feeling out the competition? What's your angle, Chrysla?"

This time a long silence stretched before Chrysla broke it. "Wing Commander, I want to make one thing clear. However it works out between the two of us, I'm not here as your rival. I have no angle. Staffa needs you more than he needs me." She stood, a hollow look in her large amber eyes. "You decide how it will be between us."

Chrysla turned, walking gracefully from the dome.

Skyla dropped her head to rest on a knotted fist. The phantoms in her mind intermingled, Arta becoming Chrysla, and shifting back. Ily paced in the background, long black hair gleaming in the lights of the interrogation room.

Skyla bit her lip until the pain blanked her mind in white-hot sheets. The taste of blood spread copper on her tongue.

"Skyla," she whispered, "You've got to deal with this, come to some sort of understanding."

How? She made herself stand and walk to the blister. Unblinking, she stared out past *Gyton.* There, somewhere, between her and the smeared effects of the Forbidden Borders, her enemies continued to breathe, eat, sleep, and love.

Save yourself, Skyla. Do something. If you don't, the rest of your nerve is going to break.

* * *

Cold rain slanted from the dark, wounded sky in pale sheets as Myles Roma stared glumly toward the heavens. A tarpaulin had been fastened over stakes—actually building materials looted from the wreckage of broken buildings—and tied against the violence of the wind and water. Around him, his staff, under Hyros' watchful supervision, clutched robes and blankets about their shivering bodies.

Admiral Iban Jakre—white uniform and turquoise sash smudged and stained—appeared ludicrous as he squinted out at the storm. His rotund potbelly and chubby legs looked out of place. As anachronistic as the golden statue of His Holiness, Sassa I, which now acted as a central support for the tarp.

"How long will it take them?" Jakre groused.

"The weather isn't exactly suitable for flying, Iban," Myles replied, blowing on his fat hands to warm them. Each finger sported at least one jeweled ring, the stones catching the faint light. Myles hitched himself forward to peer from beneath the tarp in an attempt to discover the assault craft dropping from the heavens. In defeat, he stumped back under the shelter, knitting femur itching in its cast.

"What do they want of us?" Iban asked as a faint whine grew above the roaring spatter of rain.

"We'll know very soon." Myles squinted as the long shape appeared over the sundered ruins of the Capitol and homed in on their shelter in the Imperial Gardens. In the somber light, and against the shattered city, the assault craft floated toward them, the stuff of nightmares. A faint white outline of the hull was created by the pounding rain, and streamers of water left silver tentacles to follow the large craft's trail. The whine deafened them as the assault craft settled on one of the dying flower beds and the forward assault ramp dropped to disgorge mirror-reflective Special Tactics Unit troops with shoulder blasters.

"Come," Myles said gently. "It's our time, Iban."

He walked forward, savagely pelted by the rain as he limped into the open and down toward the warship. The

STU might have been robots they way they stood unmoving, electronics-studded gear probing the surroundings for danger. At the ramp, a grim-faced woman, uniformed as an STO, saluted and pointed up the ramp. "Commander Delshay is waiting, Legate." As Myles started up, he heard her say, "Greetings, Admiral. If you'll follow the Legate, sir."

Relief from the chilling rain barely registered as he hitched his way up the long ramp and into the surprisingly plush interior of the craft. Where he'd expected spartan angles and painted metal and ceramic, he found countoured lines and padded interior. Beyond the bulkhead, where a Sassan assault craft would have sported utilitarian benches, the Companions' ship contained bucket seats designed to contour to the STU armor.

Myles continued to the rear, seeing Commander Delshay. She gave him the hard sort of look one expected from the Companions. Another Myles Roma from not so long ago would have cowered before that hard gaze. Instead, Myles inclined his head in return, attempting to walk with as much dignity as his wounds would allow. He stopped before her, saying, "Good day to you, Commander. I regret that we meet under such unpleasant terms."

Delshay, like so many of Staffa's commanders, cut a striking figure. Lithe and athletic, she affected royal purple armor that clashed with her too-yellow blonde hair, which she wore roached and maned down the middle of her back. Equipment studded the belt on her hips, including a pistol. She stood with feet braced, arms clasped behind her, and no one could doubt that she was in command. Her violet eyes narrowed by the slightest bit and she inclined her head.

"My regrets, too, Legate." She looked past him. "Greetings, Admiral. I take it you both have what staff you need with you?"

"That depends on what endeavor you expect us to perform," Jakre stated, wiping at the water that trickled down his long nose.

"My staff is ready," Myles answered, sensing Delshay's hostility building against Jakre. "For any purpose."

"If the two of you will follow me, your people will be seated by my crew and we'll shed dirt immediately." She turned and started up a flight of steps.

Myles clamped his jaw, forced to make a slow job of it,

one step at a time. Curse Iban, anyway. Here they were, their empire wrecked, at the mercy of everything in Free Space, and Iban wanted to act formally.

The second level consisted of what Myles would have called the combat operations deck. Men and women in uniform manned instruments as they sat before sophisticated consoles and studied holos. Myles stumped his way forward, hearing their soft chatter while Jakre muttered incoherently under his breath.

In the forward section, Delshay turned to face them again, no emotion in her stiff features. If she'd smile once in a while, she would have been an attractive woman.

"What is the condition of His Holiness?" She lifted a pale eyebrow.

"Dead, I'm afraid." Jakre responded, stopping uncertainly, his eyes cataloging the small nacelle they'd entered. Instruments covered every wall, and, as he spoke, chairs were lifting from the deck.

Myles needed no invitation to seat himself and take the weight from his aching leg.

Jakre continued, "When the quake hit, the gravity compensation failed. It appears that His Holiness dropped about fifty centimeters. We're not sure whether the impact killed him or if he suffocated from his own weight."

"Then we may assume that the two of you compose the remaining Imperial government?"

Jakre's head went back as he spread his arms wide. "Well, I *am* in charge of the military and—"

"Yes," Myles interrupted. "Insofar as any government remains on Imperial Sassa, Iban and I would have that responsibility. How can we be of service to the Lord Commander?"

Jakre gave Myles a sidelong look of irritation.

Delshay dropped into a seat as the lander began to move, attitude changing. "Legate, you will accompany me to Itreata aboard *Cobra.* Admiral Jakre, you will be transferred to *Black Warrior* where you will work in coordination with Commander Tiger. There, you will use the remaining assets of the Imperial Sassan Fleet to assist him with the administration of Sassan territory. Meanwhile, the Legate will assist Magister Dawn with the construction of a comm center to govern Free Space."

Iban's familiar plastic smile spread across his long face and he patted his protruding stomach with a jeweled hand. "My dear Commander, I'll be happy to accommodate the Lord Commander's wishes, but you must understand, as Admiral of the Imperial Sassan Fleet, I must deal directly with the Lord Commander. I have responsibilities which—"

"Iban," Myles muttered tiredly, "Shut up. You will go aboard *Black Warrior* and work *with* Commander Tiger. You will not pester the Lord Commander and create a command nightmare."

Jakre stiffened. "*Legate,* may I remind you—"

Myles slammed a hand on the armrest—and gasped as the pain shot through his broken ribs. Despite gritting his teeth against the pain, he stated, "Rot you, Iban. *Forget it!* Screw the posturing. We've no position left, don't you understand? Everything's about to come apart. Rega, Sassa, even Itreata. We're not Sassans anymore, damn it! We're all human, and if we let this get away from us, we're all dead." He half stood, glaring at Jakre. "Do you understand, Iban? *Dead!*"

For the first time since he'd known him, Iban Jakre had no response but to look stunned, his mouth opening and closing as if gasping for air.

Myles sighed and sagged, fighting the rush of pain his outburst had caused. "I'm sorry, my old friend. I know you, know your pride. Iban, I'm serious. We've all got to work together."

"He's right." Delshay had steepled her long fingers, watching them through half-lidded eyes. "You've seen the death and misery on Imperial Sassa, Admiral. The rest of your worlds are only months away from a similar fate."

Iban Jakre sagged in the chair, a trembling hand covering his eyes.

* * *

Sinklar stopped as he reached an intersection of corridors. His brain refused him sleep, a thousand worries nibbling at his mind. Too much had happened; the entire universe had cracked, taking a sideways lurch into insanity. The knowledge of failure burned like slow acid in Sinklar's soul. He'd tossed and turned, replaying the past: The war on Targa; Gretta's death; Ily's perfectly executed seduction. His arrest had ground him down into the muck of futility. Only after Staffa's conquest of Rega, had the extent of that futility really settled to plague him.

He needed Anatolia. She'd barely been out of his sight since they'd walked out of the Biological Research Center. The one time they'd been separated, she'd been captured, despite a heroic effort by two of Sinklar's best soldiers. Buchman was still in med, growing a new shoulder.

I shouldn't have let her go. The thought nagged. He glanced at his chronometer. She'd be aboard in another six hours, and immediately after that, they'd space.

He took comfort in the knowledge that she'd be there. Now that she wasn't at his elbow, he realized how much he depended on her. She'd filled that ragged-edged hollow torn out of his heart when Gretta died.

Now, lost in *Chrysla*'s endless corridors, he shrugged at the intersection and proceeded straight ahead, only to have the way blocked by a heavy, squared hatch. Cluttered security gear studded the panel above. Emotionless glass eyes stared at him while IR scanners and a host of other gear swiveled to note his presence. He studied the portal for a moment, then, realization dawning, pivoted on his heel. He'd taken no more than a couple of steps before he heard the hatch slip open with a slight sucking sound.

"Sorry, I guess I took a wrong turn back at . . ." He stiffened as the Lord Commander stepped out on graceful feet.

"Do you need something, Sinklar?"

Before the hatch slid shut, Sinklar Fist caught a glimpse of *Chrysla*'s bridge, well lit, surrounded by three-sixty, overhead screens and instrument-clustered duty stations.

Sinklar crossed his arms, struggling to mask his emotions. "No. I . . . I needed some exercise. Just out walking. That's all. I guess I wasn't paying attention to where I was."

Didn't the Lord Commander of Companions ever wear anything except that gray armor and that animated cloak? But as Sinklar watched, tension began to knot within that powerful frame as if boundless energy had suddenly been generated with nowhere to go.

"The bridge security picked you up." Staffa kar Therma hooked a thumb over his shoulder.

"I'm sorry to have bothered you. It's late and . . ."

"And you couldn't sleep." The first ghostly trace of a smile appeared at the edges of those hard lips. "I think I understand."

Staffa looked exhausted, as if he hadn't slept for days. The tracks of worry had eaten into the man's face. Sinklar took a deep breath, fighting the urge to pace, to smack his balled fist into his palm. Glancing down, he realized his own stance mirrored the Lord Commander's—and that abraded a raw nerve. "Good evening to you, Lord Commander. Again, excuse me for bothering you."

Sinklar wheeled, stifling his urge to bolt like a Targan rabbit from a coursing fox. With iron discipline, he kept moving suddenly rubbery legs in a measured and controlled retreat. His heart hammered desperately against his ribs. *Of all the people to run into, why—*

"Wait."

Sinklar glanced over his shoulder, seeing Staffa start forward purposely. He made three steps before he faltered, sudden indecision in his eyes.

He fears me as much as I fear him.

Staffa smiled nervously, gesturing down the corridor. "To be honest, I couldn't sleep either. I'd like . . . Well, there's an observation lounge. Would you . . . Could we go there? Talk, perhaps?"

Sinklar's attempted smile decayed into a grimace. He closed his eyes, raising his hands as thoughts roiled like charged interstellar gas. "This is crazy! What do you want of me? I've hated you and all you stand for. You've conquered my empire, destroyed my dreams. Isn't that enough?"

"The dance of the quanta," Staffa whispered, pain hidden in his soft tones. "Do you know what this is like? Can you conceive of how hard this is for me?"

"Oddly enough, yes. I'm having my own problems understanding . . . accepting. I've made my commitment. Nevertheless, I'm still no more than your prisoner." Sinklar glared up at the man. "I don't know what to believe."

"Believe this: I *need* you. Every man, woman, and child out there needs you. No matter how you feel about me, we've got problems; and we'd better start dealing with them. Come. This way." He palmed the lock plate and stepped inside in a swirl of dark gray cape.

Sinklar took a position opposite and, as the lift accelerated, he locked gazes with the Lord Commander. *Etarian sand tigers stare at each other just like this when they crouch over a kill.*

From his earliest childhood, Sinklar had heard stories about this man. His legacy of misery, ruin, and death should have twisted up like foul mist around his feet. Now they stood, face-to-face, separated by a gulf of experience, education, and war, bound by ties Sinklar couldn't allow himself to accept. No matter what the hard data might be.

The ride couldn't have lasted more than five minutes—an endless eternity—before the door slipped aside and Staffa walked vigorously down yet another of the sparkling white corridors. No more than fifty meters beyond the lift, Staffa palmed a lock plate then stepped through a reinforced pressure hatch and into a softly lit room.

The heavy hatch snicked shut behind Sinklar, and he looked around curiously. Like all rooms on the Companions' prized battleship, this one, too, amazed him. The lounge had been molded into *Chrysla*'s curving hull. From the radius, they were close to the bow. The tactite dome allowed nearly three hundred and sixty degree visibility. Through it he could see his conquered Rega and a smear of stars beyond. Behind the dome, the contoured walls had been tastefully paneled in sandwood and jet and accented with an inlaid filigree of woven gold. A thick Nesian carpet rippled in different colors with every cushioned step. Recliners, gravchairs, and comm terminals would have seated twenty people. Soft music played for background and the air carried the honeyed scent of cinnamon and conifer.

"Something to drink?" Staffa asked as he paused before the golden dispenser with its intricately sculpted and jeweled fittings. "I'd suggest the Myklenian brandy. There won't be much more after this supply is exhausted. Divine Sassa saw to that. Rotted fool. I'd spared the distilleries in my strike, but his bumbling mop-up crews leveled them."

Sinklar took a deep breath, trying to exhale the suffocating tension. "That would be fine."

Staffa handed him a drinking bulb filled with amber liquid. Sinklar tasted it, lifted an eyebrow in approbation, and sipped again as he walked to the dome and stared out at the planet beyond. The sight evoked a lonely longing.

Rega: Symbol of broken dreams. That world—and the empire it had commanded—had nurtured him, educated him, and sent him off to war. For a brief moment, he'd believed himself its master and suffered his greatest humiliation when the solid rock of his convictions had been turned to sand beneath his naive feet.

Ily . . . it's all Ily's fault. A sick disgust lingered in his thoughts.

Now he gazed down on the latest, and last, of Staffa kar Therma's conquests.

"What next, Lord Commander? The Regan Empire—and that of the Sassans—lies prostrate at your feet. Is your victory all you'd hoped it would be?"

Staffa came to stand beside him, a glimmer of vulnerability in those steely eyes. "No, Sinklar, it isn't."

"Had I been given the time to retrain the Regan armed forces—teach them my tactics—I would have stopped you."

Staffa rocked nervously, the drinking bulb held behind his back. "You'd have struck Ryklos. I read Mykroft's briefing file. We found a copy in one of the personnel rooms when we ransacked the Ministry of Internal Security. The three wave attack was an astute strategy. Had you pulled it on Iban Jakre, you'd have destroyed him. Had you pulled it on me, I'd have smelled the trap and dealt you a stunning blow."

"Such assessments are easy to make in retrospect, Lord Commander."

"If you ever decide to visit Itreata, I'll allow you access to the Strategic Defense files. You'll find the entire scenario there—along with the dates at which the strategy was conceived and every subsequent modification added."

"All neat and tidy? I'm to believe you had every permutation covered?"

A grim smile curled Staffa's lips. "Remember, I've had years to study the situation. Ryklos made very good bait. Consider its position. For strategic reasons, it would have made more sense for me to incorporate it into the Itreatic border. Ryklos might be nothing more than a mining colony on a ball of ice, but it would have made a safe port, one beyond the radiation of the Twin Titans. No, Sinklar, despite any such advantages, it served my needs better as a soak off."

"Are you really that flawless?"

"In war, yes. Flaws, however, come in many forms. One is the inability to guess the future—in this case, the accidental destruction of the computer complex on Imperial Sassa."

"An oversight which could kill us all, unless, of course, your mysterious Seddi computer can effect a miracle tantamount to milking water from Etarian sand." He paused. "I don't suppose you'd let me bring the First Division along—just in case the Seddi—"

"If you wish. I see the knife that I gave you still rests on your hip." Staffa gestured weary acquiescence. "When I gave you my word, I had no idea that your hatred ran this deep."

"Call it distrust, Lord Commander. The Seddi—and you and your Companions—cost me too much in the past. Makarta, no matter what kind of computer is hidden there, is a difficult place to forget." Sinklar's soul chilled at the memory of Makarta. He could see the corpses lying blasted in dark passages, recall the bitter taste of defeat as friends died one by one in the desperate assault on the Seddi fortress.

Sinklar read the sober expression on Staffa's face. *Yes, you, too, left a part of your soul there, didn't you, Star Butcher?*

The Lord Commander seemed to shake off his depression. "Do you know that I risked everything to find you and your mother? My search led me to Makarta. That's how we came to face each other there. Tell me that the quanta didn't laugh."

Sinklar grunted to himself before asking, "What kind of being are you? Anatolia is baffled by your genetics."

"I'm a clone, Sinklar, an artificially constructed human being. Am I fully human? The answer is yes on all counts. I am conscious and through observation, change the reality of God Mind. From the standpoint of the biologists, I can produce viable offspring—as you so admirably demonstrate."

"You are a monster."

"Once, I suppose, I was."

"Past tense?"

Staffa fingered his chin thoughtfully. "I take a great deal

of pride in your intelligence and ability. You didn't win on Targa because you were stupid. You may hate me all you want, but it has fallen to the two of us to accomplish several tasks. First, we must keep the economic systems of Sassa and Rega functioning—integrate them, in fact. Second, we must break the Forbidden Borders, once and for all . . . and free humanity from the trap we're in."

Sinklar sipped his brandy, eyes narrowed skeptically. "What about the conquered? I'm your prisoner. What do you want me to do? Take your orders? Do your bidding? Fall at your feet as a worshipful son? If you do, I'm sorry, but I know too much about your career. None of the human wreckage you've left in your wake sings your praises. Not only that, I've had firsthand experience with your Seddi friends. I don't know what game you're playing, but you can keep your tapa cards because I'm not buying chips."

Staffa closed his eyes, head lowered. "It's a long story. How familiar are you with psychology?"

"Familiar enough, I suppose."

"Using teaching machines, structured learning, conditioning, and reinforcement in a completely controlled environment from the time a child is an infant, how thoroughly could you modify his behavior?"

"Substantially, but that's a hypothetical—"

"How substantially? Using the total resources of the Regan Empire—their best psychologists and unlimited funding—how successful do you think you could be at shaping a child into a certain type of human being?"

Sinklar gestured futilely. "All right, fairly successful, but you can't discount behavioral genetics. People's personalities differ. That template is in the DNA, and with sexual reproduction each potential offspring has two to the twenty-third chances to receive—"

"*Not* when you're talking about a clone, Sinklar. The Praetor of Myklene could structure his genetic program anyway he wished."

"But the mind still learns through random action. Stimuli are so varied and the mind is so plastic. The brain learns through making choices in the interpretation of seemingly random and contradictory data."

"In an uncontrolled environment, I agree that it does. But my environment was totally controlled. *Every* second of my existence was orchestrated according to plan, Sinklar. I suspect they even used their machines to modify and pattern my dreams."

"Rotted Gods." Sinklar fought a sudden shiver as he stared into those deadly gray eyes.

"Yes, Rotted Gods is right. The Praetor wanted a monster—as you so aptly noted—and he made one. In the process, I still had a fully human mind, centers for personality and all the pitfalls that make us behave in a human manner. I was, after all, a social animal. Who wants a monster they can't appeal to, communicate with? The Praetor played upon that human weakness. He laid traps there, psychological triggers."

Staffa stared vacantly out at the wealth of stars beyond the transparent tactite. "He knew I'd be coming for him. The day he drove me out, banished me from Myklene, he knew I'd be driven to return, to destroy him for what he'd done to me."

"So you took the Sassan contract and blasted Myklene." Sinklar had edged away, wary gaze on Staffa.

"I did. There's more. But you've heard enough for now, enough to understand something about me . . . and about him."

"I've heard you twisted his head off his body."

Staffa nodded absently. "He'd taken Chrysla and you from me. He used those psychological triggers he'd installed so expertly in my youth." Staffa turned haunted eyes on Sinklar. "Do you know what it's like to suddenly have a conscience after you've lived all your life without one? Your brain floods with endorphins, dopamines, acetylcholines, and other chemicals. You suffer fits of wretched depression and sudden exultation. Morose thoughts one minute, crazy intuition the next as the brain struggles toward equilibrium. *You* became my obsession."

Sinklar tossed off the last of the brandy. "I don't want to be anyone's obsession. Especially yours."

Staffa chuckled humorlessly. "Relax, Sinklar, I'm sane now. I've made my peace with what happened. I did what I did. A man can't change facts anymore than he can change galactic drift. But what he can do is learn . . . atone, if you will."

"So that's it? The Praetor tripped his triggers and you became a good guy? Just like that?"

"Not exactly," Staffa said dryly. "Like you, overconfident and brash, I charged out into the real world. On Etaria I was sold into the collar—made a slave. I got a real education out in the deep desert beyond Etarus. I spent my time thirsting and suffering in the True Sand hauling water pipe. My companions out there . . ."

Staffa's grip tightened around the drinking bulb, powerful muscles straining, tendons standing from the back of his hand. "Maikans, most of them. People, gentle people, whom I'd condemned to the collar after I conquered their world for Tybalt. I watched them die, Sinklar. One by one I watched them roast in a hell of my making and die. Peebal . . . Koree . . . and the others."

Staffa's cheek twitched as the lines deepened at the corner of his haunted eyes.

Sinklar endured the lengthening silence.

Finally Staffa exhaled and turned, gaze gone leaden. "I've kept you long enough for one night. I suggest you access the data on the current economic situation in Free Space and its implications. Enemy though you may consider yourself, I've given you security clearance for most of the system."

Staffa whirled and strode away in a floating billow of dark gray cloak. He barely hesitated as he slapped the lock plate and stepped through the hatch.

Koree? Peebal? What had happened in that Etarian desert? Who was this man? This strange "father?" *And what does it mean for me? For Mac, and Anatolia? And worse, for my people?*

Sinklar walked over and stared at himself in the mirror, shocked as he realized that the tormented exhaustion in Staffa's face mimicked his own.

* * *

Inside the Regan Ministry of Internal Security, they broke the code twenty minutes before Anatolia was scheduled to catch the shuttle. Another eleven minutes vanished as controls were run on the data to ensure that no virus had been released by their access.

A weary Anatolia had risen to her feet, collecting her belongings as she read the lists of files scrolled across the monitor. She caught one of the names at a glance.

SUBJECT: VET HAMLIN

With quick fingers, Anatolia accessed the file, dropping into her chair, thoughts of the shuttle vanished. Around her, people were busily tapping keys, or soberly giving the system verbal commands.

Someone whooped, shouting: "I've got her personal journal! I'm patching it straight through to *Chrysla!*"

Anatolia stared in disbelief as Vet Hamlin's file filled her screen. The biographical data were accurate, listing Vet's mother and father, their addresses, ages, political status, and vital statistics. Marka's name came up, and the baby's.

The text of the file began with Vet's arrest. Minutes passed as a stunned Anatolia read the entire transcript of the interrogation. Mouth gone dry, heart pounding, she read the final entry:

SUBJECT DISPOSITION:VET HAMLIN WAS GIVEN LETHAL INJECTION AT 5779:17:19:08:05. CORPSE DISPOSED OF AT CREMATORIUM C-3.

Other references at the bottom told her where she could find the holo of the actual interrogation. The very thought of watching Vet in that cold, featureless room sickened her.

Vet had been her only friend until Sinklar came wandering out of the rainy night to change her life. Vet had helped, at least insofar as he could understand what had happened to her after the pimply kid drove her into the streets.

He paid for his friendship with his life. He died because of me.

"Rotted Gods," Anatolia whispered as she slumped in the chair. "Vet . . . damn it!" Tears blurred her vision.

"Professor Daviura?" A voice asked nervously.

Anatolia wiped at her hot eyes, sniffing to clear her clogged nose. "What?"

"Are you all right?"

Ana stared up at a technician in Regan battle armor. "I . . .

Yes. I'm all right. Just found a file. A friend . . . who . . . Tears blurred her vision again.

"I thought you were going up on the shuttle? I'm supposed to take over this station."

"Yes. I guess I'd better hurry." Anatolia blinked her vision clear and glanced at the chronometer, startled by the amount of time she'd spent on Vet's file. She barely nodded, memories of Vet spinning in her head. Ily had killed him. She'd sucked him dry of information, and disposed of him like a soiled tissue.

Anatolia forced herself to stand. The tech gave her an uneasy smile as she slid into the chair.

Sinklar would be waiting.

Blessed Gods, she *had* to contact Marka, try to explain what had happened to her husband.

Anatolia had reached the main hallway and stopped at the foyer before the lifts that would take her to the roof. She nodded to the uniformed assault trooper who stood with a blaster across his hip and hesitated. Ana bit her lip and walked to the wall comm. Her fingers trembled as she input Vet Hamlin's old address.

A young woman's face formed, dark eyes staring out from a thin-boned face. "Ana?"

"Marka? Listen. I've got some bad news."

At that moment the building went silent, the muted shush of the fans dying. The guard looked around suspiciously.

"Ana? Where are you? What news? What's going on? Where's Vet? I've been worried sick for—"

"Marka, be quiet. Something's wrong here." A terrible unease ate into Anatolia's gut. Someplace down the corridor, a man cursed.

"Something's wrong *here,* too! Where's Vet?"

People burst out of the computer room, smashing the doors wide. Shouted orders carried down the hallways.

Anatolia's sense of panic grew.

"Ana? *Ana? Talk to me!* WHERE'S MY HUSBAND?"

Marka never heard the answer.

CHAPTER IX

They came in separate aircars, generally driven by slaves. As each stopped before the energized security barriers of the Estates' main entrance, the occupant stepped out and nodded to the security officer in his family livery. They totaled eleven visitors, seven men and four women. Each had been carried up the long incline by gravlift and ushered into the main hall where Marvin Hanks waited at the head of the large table. From the dispenser, each of the visitors chose his or her favorite drink and waited, engaging in small talk.

When the last had arrived, Marvin Hanks stood and placed his hands behind his back. Chin on his chest, eyes lowered, he waited for a long moment, and then looked up, resplendent in his golden jacket and gleaming black trousers.

"Citizens of Phillipia. This morning my agents effectively eliminated the Director of Internal Security who had planned to sabotage the comm system—much as happened to Ashtan. To have done so would have been disastrous to our economy and would have thrown the planet into turmoil."

One by one, he searched their eyes. "You, my friends, are the last of the Phillipian royalty. The last of a breed that challenged the very Forbidden Borders." He smiled. "Well, as of tonight, that is going to change. The Regan bonds have been shattered. The time to act is now, before the Star Butcher can tighten his grip."

"Do we really want to challenge the Companions?" one of the matrons asked.

Hanks leaned forward, the flame of passion alight in his eyes. "This is our only chance, Nova. If we act in unison, and with full commitment to our goal, we can regain what is rightfully ours. After that, with a planet behind us, we can deal with the Star Butcher. Offer him whatever it will take to buy him off, but Phillipia will be ours again."

"And if the Regan majority disapprove?"

Hanks leaned forward, his golden clothing catching the light. "Now, we aren't about to let that stop us, are we? We have a planet and a heritage to reclaim. If they push us to it, what are a few bloody Regan corpses after the millions of Phillipian dead they've piled up over the years."

* * *

Staffa struggled to collect his thoughts as he paused outside of Chrysla's hatch. Unable to control events, they now seemed to control him. Before Myklene, before the Praetor had unleashed hell in his brain, he'd been able to concentrate, to block the roil of emotions. Even in the most desperate moments of combat, that talent had never failed him. Now his mind screamed in pursuit of ten thousand details, traveling in every direction at once. Worry stalked him with the single-minded intent of a hungry siff jackal. People he cared about were in jeopardy. He hadn't even had time to visit with Skyla, to reassure her.

All it takes is a single mistake and we're all dead.

Taking a deep breath, he thumbed the door comm. "Chrysla? It's Staffa."

"Please come in." The hatch slipped sideways to admit him into her personal quarters.

The cabin measured four by five meters, spacious for a warship. Holographs of Ashtan filled the wall tanks with views of the planet. Rocky ridges thrust up from fertile valleys filled with grains. Neat houses clustered around silos and herds of animals enclosed in multistoried feeding pens. In other scenes, clean cities gleamed in crystal morning sunlight.

Chrysla stood in the center of the room. She wore a loose dress with an empire waist. Her eyes seemed to enlarge as she studied him, concern replacing reserve. Her glossy hair spilled over her shoulders in gentle waves as she shook her head. "How long since you've slept?"

"I can sleep when we've spaced for Targa."

She crossed her arms, then paced to the far end of the

room. "I didn't want to press the point in the meeting, but . . ."

"I know. I appreciate it." He raised supplicant arms. "Sending you to Ashtan is out of the question. I can't provide adequate protection. I need my most qualified people to—"

"I'm not asking for protection."

He lifted a skeptical eyebrow. "Chrysla, you're smarter than this. What kind of foolishness is this? You know who you are. To my enemies, you're an incredibly valuable target. Or did you miss that fact over the last twenty years?"

"I am well aware of my *value* to different people."

"Then you know that Free Space is ready to come apart at the seams. You've just come from—"

"I *know* what I've just come from." Her full lips pressed into a thin line. "Staffa, I survived on my own out there in the wreckage of Myklene. Broke, hurt, and penniless, I still managed to get aboard a ship headed for Imperial Sassa. From there, I would have made it to Itreata."

"And what if it hadn't been MacRuder who took *Markelos?* Piracy is suddenly going to be a very viable option for planets running out of resources."

"Then I would have handled that, too."

"Sure. Rape and slavery. You're a beautiful woman. Kaylla Dawn explained how women are treated in this age of ours. And she's right! Women become property—things to own, abuse, or play with. Haven't you had enough close calls with that?"

Her jaw muscles bunched as a chill entered her voice. "I'm familiar with rape. The Praetor made a practice of it. I'm no blushing innocent anymore. I've paid my dues, physically and emotionally. But that brings me back to my point. Right now, you need every talented person you have. You *need* me!"

"Not as a *hostage!*" he shouted back.

She paused, then raised a hand, gesturing for peace. "Slow down. We're both getting mad. Staffa, can we be rational?"

"I *am* being rational. You used to have more sense than this!"

She smiled, a twinkle of amusement and understanding in her amber gaze. "Take a deep breath. That's it. Now, stop balling your fists and bouncing from foot to foot. When you regain control of yourself, tell me who has more sense."

Staffa glared at her for a moment, caught the infection of her amused smile, and slowed his aggravated movements. He chuckled, tension seeping away. "Very well, we're both rational again. The fact still remains that it's too risky. Isn't it enough to have just escaped the Praetor? You've paid the price for twenty years? Why put yourself in harm's way again? Haven't you suffered enough?"

"I don't intend on becoming a hostage again, Staffa. I suspect that I know full well what Kaylla meant about the status of women. I also think it's worth fighting to change that. You're willing to take risks, yet you won't let me?"

"I lost you once. I can't stand that again."

She stepped close, a probing intensity in her amber stare. "You've told me about your time in the desert. Let me tell you about making planet on Rega. Mac, Rysta, and I walked into Ily's trap. You know how we got out? I bluffed them into thinking I was Arta Fera. It scared me to death, Staffa, but I did it. After that, Mac tried to ship me off to *Gyton* before he attacked Ily's Ministry. I stayed, Staffa. Because I had to."

"Chasing off to a planet on the brink of civil war is a different color of quark. Ashtan could turn into an inferno."

"But that's just the point. I might be able to stop it. Maintain civil order in your name." She cocked her head. "I'm asking you as one human being to another. You have the power to deny me. I don't dispute that; but think. The people on Ashtan—my people—will pay the price if everything collapses."

Didn't she understand? "I don't argue that. That's why I'm sending Mac and Rysta—"

"And my second reason for going may make an even stronger argument. You went off to Etaria for yourself. I need to go to Ashtan for myself. Put yourself in my place. For the first time in my life I've been someone besides Staffa's precious wife. On Myklene, I reacted to events . . . managed to survive. Getting off the planet, I manipulated the governor. Then, finally, when we landed on Rega, I took control of a situation for the first time in my life. Will you, disciple of the Seddi that you are, deny me the chance to take responsibility for myself? Isn't that what you learned out there in the desert?''

Staffa stood mute. *Tell her no!*

And make a hypocrisy of all of your beliefs?

''Let me go, Staffa. Either that, or imprison me here and now.''

''What about your son? After all these years, don't you want to spend a little time with him? Get to know him?''

She lifted a slim eyebrow in a mocking manner. ''Believe me, now isn't the time. I'm a psychologist, remember? Sinklar has just taken a psychological beating. His soul is wounded and needs time to heal. Complicating matters, he and Anatolia are developing a relationship at a time when Sinklar is drowning in self-doubt and guilt. Not only that, I remind him of Arta—the woman who killed his beloved Gretta. I've left messages on Sinklar's comm. I've tried to see him more than once. He needs to—''

''I'll order him in for psychological evaluation, give you a chance to work with him. You could probably do him some good.''

Her expression turned wry. ''Listen to what you're saying. You're grasping at straws. That's unlike you, Staffa. You know better than to even suggest such a disastrous idea. Or do you really think Sinklar Fist will placidly allow you to manipulate his life in that manner?''

Staffa sighed in weary defeat. ''No. He'd hate me for intruding.''

''And that's what he'd feel about me. He needs time to come to grips with what happened. Too many people worshiped him. It's hard to be a young god, and then discover you're only mortal after all.'' She paused. ''Remember that when you deal with him, will you?''

''You've changed, Chrysla.''

''So have you. You aren't the same invincible demigod I once loved and feared.'' She raised her hands and let them fall. ''And that's another reason I need to go. In a way, you're like Sinklar. You need time to come to grips with this new you. You must solve the current political crisis, deal with your son, and help Skyla. She needs you . . . and, Staffa, you've been too busy to notice just how desperate she is. My presence aboard this ship adds to the pressure warping her psyche. She's a frayed cord at the moment. If you don't reassure her, she'll finally come unraveled."

At that moment, his belt comm buzzed. Under Chrysla's cool stare he accessed the unit. "Yes?"

"Lynette Helmutt, sir. We've had an explosion at the Ministry of Internal Security. The whole building is gone."

"Blown up?"

"Yes, sir. From the spectra, we'd guess it was a chemical explosive of some sort—and a lot of it. Replay on the monitors indicates that the blast came from within the building itself. If I were to guess, it was a timed delay. We do know that the subspace dish powered up several minutes before the detonation."

"Get a rescue crew down there at once and cordon the area. Put Ark on the investigation. I want to know what happened. The STO is to debrief all survivors. See if we can reconstruct the manipulations they made to the computers."

"Sir? From here it would appear that such an investigation would be useless. The crater, sir . . . well, there's nothing left."

Staffa swayed on his feet. They'd ransacked the place for documents, arrested Ily's staff and management, but no one had found explosives. In the walls? In the floors and ceilings? *Why didn't I anticipate this?*

"Very well, First Officer. Use . . . use your discretion. Initiate a rescue operation anyway, just in case."

"Affirmative."

Staffa stared woodenly at the floor as a terrible weariness settled over him. "I should have known. I should have guessed that Ily would resort to something like this."

Chrysla's warm hand settled on his shoulder. "You're not a god, Staffa. You can't anticipate—"

"Once, I could," he whispered. "Is that what the Praetor did to me? Did he destroy my ability to think clearly?"

She frowned, thought for a moment, and said, "Not from the standpoint of brain physiology. I think you're stretching yourself too thin, caring too much."

He studied her with an agonized expression. "Eighty of my people were down there. They depended on me. There are billions of others in Free Space. Can they depend on me?"

She placed slim hands on his chest, staring up into his eyes. "You can't bring ghosts back. What's done is done. You're accepting too much of the responsibility. You can't be the single, solitary savior of humanity. Each of us has to take on our share if we're to survive. That includes Sinklar. Let him pull his weight. Give him a command. Something so that he doesn't sit there in his quarters and grow more sour by the day."

"Sinklar . . ." Cold dread settled in Staffa's chest. "Rotted Gods, Anatolia was in the Ministry, working on the records."

"If she . . ." Chrysla shook her head. "I pray she's all right. If not, you'll have two to heal, Sinklar and Skyla."

"Comm?" Staffa barked. "Find out if Professor Daviura survived the blast. Inform me at once."

"Affirmative."

Chrysla turned away, massaging the back of her neck. "Skyla is aching, too. Give her a task that allows her to rebuild her self-confidence."

He rubbed his gritty eyes. *Pray to the Quantum Gods that Anatolia is all right. Can Sinklar take another blow? Or will he snap and crumble?* "Let me think about it."

"Don't think too long," she warned. "People tend to take matters into their own hands."

* * *

The heavy hatch opened soundlessly as Skyla palmed the lock plate. She had dressed in her white armor and slung a duffel bag over one shoulder. Her tongue played over dry lips as she entered the armory and tapped her ID into the security comm. The locks clicked open on the weapons lockers as her nerves plucked like the strings of a lute. At the far end of the room, the armorer glanced up from the pieces of shoulder blaster spread across his workbench. "Help you, Wing Commander?"

"No thanks. Just drawing equipment."

The armorer saluted and returned to his work, frowning at the charred ceramic cone on the particle acceleration module.

Despite the desperation pumping adrenaline through her veins, Skyla forced an appearance of calm as she opened a locker, selecting a new Model 57 service blaster and holster. She input the serial number in the registry and moved to the next bin where she extracted a pulse pistol. Finally she selected a Model 14A shoulder weapon and a belt of charges. From the explosives bin, she pulled a belt of sonic grenades and checked out the lot.

"Got everything you need?" the armorer asked, as he employed an ultrasonic cleaning head to the PAM.

"I think so. Thanks." Skyla piled her booty onto an antigrav and pushed it out through the hatch. She made her way down the winding corridors, returning salutes as she passed crew members. The ship bustled, preparing for the spacing to Targa.

Will you remember me on Targa, Staffa? Will you remember how I dove out of the sky to save you and your Seddi? Skyla pursed her lips. *Or will all that be forgotten now that you have your beloved Chrysla back?*

The lift carried her to the hangar deck. In her frantic state, the trip seemed endless. She *had* to do this. The nightmares had become obsessive as they drove her toward destruction. Sweat began to bead on her forehead and she couldn't keep her hands still.

When the hatch slipped sideways, Skyla shoved her antigrav out, skin prickling as the temperature dropped by twenty degrees. Shuttle craft and Regan LCs lined the berths, the Regan soldiers clustered around their craft as last minute preparations were made to disembark. Around the perimeter, Ryman Ark's STU personnel watched warily, their armor shining mirror bright in the white light.

Skyla knocked off a salute to one of the security team as she approached one of the Regan craft. *Rotted Gods, make this work.* "Where's this one going?"

"One of Sinklar's officers," the STU replied. "The guy brought up some equipment the Lord Commander had requested for Regan comm interface. He ought to be back soon."

"Remember the name?"

"Yeah. I'm pretty sure it's Lambert."

"Then this is the one." Skyla bluffed as she pushed her antigrav to the rear, reaching up to punch the controls. The assault ramp hissed as it dropped and Skyla muscled her antigrav up and into the LC. She exhaled tension and snapped acceleration restraints on the antigrav as a Regan soldier leaned out from the LC's command center.

"Hey? What are you doing?"

She jumped at the voice, hating herself for it, and took the offensive. "Who in hell are you?"

"Private Razz, Second Section, First Targan Assault Division. Now, what are you doing in here?"

"This is the ship that brought Lambert up, right?"

"Yeah. We brought up a comm and Sinklar's aide, Mhitshul."

Skyla leaned out the ramp, waving to the STU guard. "As soon as Lambert gets back, get us out of here. I want priority!"

"You got it, Wing Commander!"

Razz had walked warily down the aisle between the empty assault benches, a hand on his sidearm. "Wing Commander? As in . . ."

"Skyla Lyma." Skyla crossed her arms, drawing on her reserves to find that old brashness. By a filament of will she maintained her control. "Didn't anyone brief you?"

"No, I . . ."

Skyla shook her head and sighed. "You know, there's a limit to covert actions security policies. You've got to inform the people involved. Security can be a real pain in the ass sometimes."

"Covert? Security?"

"Private Razz, you're going to transport me . . ." She shook her head. "Look, just take my orders as I give them. Security, you know."

Razz chewed uneasily at his lip. "I don't know. I didn't get any hint abut this. I mean, I should have heard from Sink . . . or Mac, or somebody. Maybe we'd better—"

"Soldier, who just kicked the shit out of Rega's Imperial butt?" The old instinctive arrogance finally kicked in. "Do you want to stick your head out the ramp there and look around? Find out just who's in charge these days? You Rotted well know who I am. Razz, there're lots of ways to commit suicide—and you've picked a surefire way if you want to give me grief on an operation like this."

"Yes, ma'am." Razz gave her a Regan salute and turned as another soldier started up the ramp.

"You Lambert?" Skyla asked.

"Uh-huh. Hey, what's going on? The STU told me to hustle my butt up here."

"Yep. And now, close that ramp, and let's shake a leg. I've got a ship to catch, Lambert, and little time to do it. If you and Razz here want to live to a ripe old age, you'll be making sure I do it, and then you'll keep your cursed mouths shut afterward."

"Yes, ma'am!"

Nerves electric, Skyla swaggered forward between the benches and ducked into the command center. Acting as if she owned it, she dropped into the snug chair at the comm console.

"Where to?" Lambert asked uncertainly.

"One thing at a time. Just get me off *Chrysla.*"

"Affirmative."

Skyla closed her eyes as the troopers called orders to the pilot and escaped to the rear.

So far, so good. She took a deep breath, trying to keep her cool facade. *But, Arta, you ruined so much of me, will I ever get it back?*

* * *

Sinklar had finally fallen into a fitful sleep. He tossed on his sleeping platform, nightmares of Targa spinning out of his troubled subconscious. Blaster fire streaked night skies while disrupters and gravity shells turned reality inside out. Wreaths of smoke hung in macabre curtains as pine trees burned with the fury of giant torches.

Sinklar walked unscathed through the carnage of the battlefield. The shrieks of dying men and women carried with the stench of blood and ruptured intestines. Violet blaster bolts stabbed the night, their particles ripping the air like an angry tearing of sheets. Dust swirled as rocks popped and cracked, chips zipping around to spatter the tortured earth.

With each step, Sinklar's feet slipped in the blood-spawned mud, red-brown goo clinging to his heavy boots. The hands of the dying reached out; their eyes pleaded for salvation as life spurted from punctured arteries.

In the actinic flash of the riven heavens, Sinklar could

make out Gretta's charred figure as she stood braced, shoulder weapon spurting death into the night.

A flood of relief washed through him as he churned his way toward her, his feet gone leaden with gore. Despite his frantic haste, the faster he sought to move, the harder the effort. Straining, he placed one foot ahead of the other, breaking free of the clinging grip of the fallen wounded.

Gretta dominated an outcrop of rock that seemed to take the brunt of the fighting. Yet she stood, invincible in the flickering of blaster bolts and crackle of pulse fire. Relentlessly she poured shot after shot into the invisible enemy.

Sinklar's lungs burned. Panting, he struggled to climb to her position. He had to reach her, to pull her back to safety. The rock under his hands burned and split, trembling from ground shock.

Sinklar crawled on, dragging his sodden body over fractured and steaming rock. *"Gretta!"* he screamed into the maelstrom of war.

She refused to hear as she continued to pivot, lacing deadly fire into the unseen ranks beyond the rocky point.

Sinklar gritted his teeth, reaching out with a trembling hand to grasp her ankle. He cried out at the touch, feeling a cold so bitter it froze the flesh.

Nevertheless, he gave one last desperate tug, wailing, *"Gretta!"*

Staring up at her, she towered over him and whirled, wisps of brown hair escaping her gleaming helmet.

For an eternal second, Sinklar stared up into that hideous face. Sightless sockets gazed down at him while scraps of rotted flesh peeled from the cheekbones. No mouth remained—only the skull's ironic rictus.

A croaking choked in Sinklar's throat as the charnel woman swiveled her heavy blaster, centering its belled muzzle on his face.

"No! Gretta! It's me! Sinklar! *No!*"

As her gloved finger tightened on the firing stud, a shot caught her between the full breasts, splaying the chest wide and spattering Sinklar with bits of maggot-infested tissue.

The demon staggered, regained her balance, and centered the weapon again. The smell of ozone drifted from the muzzle.

Sinklar screamed as he watched the firing stud click home. . . .

* * *

Crying out, he jerked upright on the sleeping platform. Adrenaline charged his veins as he blinked his eyes, staring wildly around the white cabin aboard *Chrysla*. Sweat ran slick and clammy down his face and along the insides of his undersuit.

Sinklar sat on the edge of his sleeping platform, feet dangling as he sought to control his pounding heart.

Dream. Only a dream.

Exhaling wearily, he walked to the wall dispenser and drew a cup of stassa. He choked down two sips of the hot liquid before the comm buzzed.

"Go ahead."

The visual monitor glowed to life, forming an image of Dion Axel's head. "Lord Fist?"

Sinklar stepped over to his desk and settled in the chair. "What is it, Dion?"

At the sight of his strained expression, she said, "I guess you've already heard."

"Heard what?"

"About the Ministry of Internal Security."

"I have no idea what you're talking about."

Axel ground her jaws a moment before stating, "Roughly fifteen minutes ago, planetary time, an explosion destroyed the Ministry of Internal Security. Sir, there are *no* survivors."

"Destroyed . . . How?"

"We don't know, sir. At this time we believe a delayed charge took the building out."

"Anatolia?" Sinklar spun to stare at the chronometer. "She was supposed to be on a shuttle."

Dion looked off to her right, ordering, "Contact the shuttle. See if Professor Daviura made that flight." When she turned back, she added, "I've dispatched two Sections to maintain order and see to evacuation of the affected area. The blast flattened buildings for kilometers around the Ministry. Hospitals have already been alerted and we're placing a cordon around the area to prevent looting and maintain order.''

Thoughts swimming, Sinklar shook his head. ''I don't understand. How could this happen?'' *What did I do wrong? What could I have missed?*

Dion stared wearily out at him. ''I guess it's just more of Ily covering her tracks. If she can't have it, no one else will either. Just a minute.'' She listened to someone outside of the pickup and turned back, expression grim. ''Sir, Professor Daviura did *not* make the shuttle. I repeat, sir. She's not on board.''

He stared disbelievingly at the monitor. ''Maybe she's holed up somewhere in the wreckage. Maybe she stepped out for some reason. Went someplace . . .'' At the look in his Division First's eyes, he understood. It even sounded lame and silly to him. ''You're sure there are no survivors?''

''Yes, sir. I'm sorry, sir. From the energy released, well, we'll be lucky if we even find pieces of the bodies. Let alone enough to . . . Sink, I'm . . .'' Axel looked away, crestfallen.

Sinklar nodded dumbly and said hoarsely, ''Keep looking. Just in case.''

''We understand, sir.''

''Thank you, First.'' He killed the connection and closed his eyes. Long minutes passed before hot tears began to leak from the corners of his eyes.

* * *

Mac had surrendered the command chair on *Gyton*'s bridge to Rysta out of deference to the old veteran. He now stared at the bridge monitors as a final LC drifted up into the hold—a last minute transfer that Mac didn't quite understand. The bridge had been stunned to silence when they learned of the explosion at the Ministry of Internal Security. Nevertheless, procedures had been initiated for spacing.

Then a cryptic message had come from *Chrysla: Gyton* had no authorization for space until the arrival of one final LC. As Mac watched, mechanical arms extended to the floating LC. Clearance lights flashed in amber, green, and red rhythms against the mottled green hull.

No other hint as to the craft's purpose could be gleaned from the comm chatter. Instead, the channels crackled with angry chatter. Good people had been killed. How many friends lay dead in the wreckage down there?

Mac had heard conflicting reports. Anatolia was alive—she'd made the shuttle. Other, more numerous reports implied that she was dead.

And how does that make you feel? Mac bowed his head thoughtfully. His biting comments about Anatolia lingered in his head. If only he could go back and swallow those words. Sinklar might really have come to care for her. What the hell did Ben MacRuder know about Anatolia? He'd been out chasing over half of Free Space when Sink and Anatolia got together.

A welling of shame, lower than Terguzzi sumpshit, swept him.

"LC grappled and secured," a voice called from comm. "We're sealing the bay doors and pressurizing."

"Affirmative," Rysta answered.

"Captain?" the Comm First called, "I have the Port Authority. The Tug Master is on line."

"Affirmative." Rysta cocked her head, slumped in the command chair like an ancient desiccated lizard. "Let's see who we've got." As the image on the monitor formed up to present a long-faced man in a worn captain's uniform, Rysta called, "Good to see you, Tim."

"Good to see you, too, Commander. It's been a Rotted sorry turn of events, but I guess if they're letting *Gyton* space, we're not in as bad shape as the rumors insist."

"You been listening to Baldy again?" Rysta gave the Tug Master a thumbs-up. "I've sat at council with the Lord Commander himself. It's a new dawn for all of us, that's all. No more wars." She gave him an evil grin. "But then again, pustulous hell, if he left me in charge, things might be worse than you think!"

The Tug Master chuckled. "We're ready to escort you out, *Gyton.*"

"We're all clear and powering up. Take us out."

Gyton responded to the pull of the tugs. As each of the smaller vessels arced from their vector, the power readouts began to build. In the main forward monitor, the gleaming stars beckoned.

If Sinklar really *had* come to love Anatolia . . . and if she were dead, what then? After Gretta's murder, Sink had frazzled around the edges. "May the Pus-Rotted Gods help us all," Mac whispered to himself. *Poor Sinklar, if I could, I'd give myself to bring her back for you.*

He shook his head, stepping over to the dispenser for a hot cup of stassa.

Normally, Mac experienced a sense of excitement and wonder as a warship pointed her nose toward the unknown. Venturing off into the depths of Free Space, across the light-years, and to places that had only been names on the holo normally sent a thrill through him.

Why then, do I feel like such a desolate lump of flesh?

Because Sinklar was hurting, and there was nothing Mac could do about it? Or did his own loss plague him?

Unable to stop himself, Mac continued to gaze at the side monitor over the Comm First's station.

The Companions' giant battleship lay tranquil and sleek in the light of Rega's sun, the sweeping lines of her triangular hull gleaming pristinely in the light. He suffered a sudden understanding—a sharing across time and space—with a man he'd barely come to understand. How much worse the Lord Commander must have felt on that day when he named that ship.

Now *she* was aboard, home, alive, warm—and mistress of her namesake: *Chrysla*.

To think he'd almost killed her on sight that day he and the First Section had captured the Sassan freighter, *Markelos*.

Throughout that endless mission, Mac had struggled to keep a clear head. He knew the effect she had on men; nevertheless, in the end, he'd fallen madly in love with Chrysla Marie Attenasio.

Things could be worse, old pal. Ask Sinklar. His women are all dead.

He ignored the bridge chatter to walk over to the monitor and stare up at *Chrysla*'s white lines. What would she be doing now? Asleep? Perhaps in the Lord Commander's quarters? Did she sit before that ridiculous fireplace even now, encircled in his arms?

When Mac had his fill, he sighed—and noted Rysta's sober gaze as she studied him with a placid expression on her withered face. She gave him a bent smile that rearranged the wrinkles and beckoned him with a crooked finger.

Mac approached warily and, in a low voice, Rysta said, "You've got a lot of time to work it out of your system, boy. We've got course laid for Ashtan. According to protocol, you may now issue any subsequent orders." She worked her undershot jaw back and forth. "But then, I forget. You don't do things by the 'Holy Gawdamn Book,' do you?"

"No special orders, Rysta. Let's get out of here. We've got my old reliable First Section aboard. It won't take long to impose order." Mac placed a hand on top of one of the instrument clusters on the command chair arm and glanced at Rysta. "Then we can get on with the important mission. Ily's going to ditch that yacht someplace. It's way too conspicuous."

"Yeah, I know," Rysta growled. "But where?"

Anywhere, just so I can get away, try to forget. "Let's deal with the Ashtan problem first. After that, depending on what's gone wrong in the empire, we'll find her, Rysta."

"And if Sinklar has other orders for us by then?"

"Trust me, Sinklar won't have other orders. If the political situation really falls all to hell, we'll deal with what we can. But me, I'm not coming back."

"Boy, you never know what the future will do to a person."

"Got that right." Mac turned his attention back to the displays that showed the tugs, each of the vessels straining as they all hauled *Gyton* out of the gravity well to deeper space where the warship could employ her mighty engines.

"I've got some work to do in my quarters." Mac glanced back at the image of *Chrysla* one last time. He turned stoically and walked to the hatch. *Good-bye, Chrysla. Good-bye.*

CHAPTER X

The Mag Comm continued to transmit, heedless if the Others cared to listen or not. "The facts as humanity and I both perceive them are that you cannot prove or disprove the existence of God or God Mind with any certainty. The edifice of belief is built upon a foundation of faith in either case. Baseline assumptions are made and logical frameworks are erected upon them to prove or disprove the existence of God.

"Among humans, the majority of beliefs are silly fantasies, the sort of mythology which assuages the need for surrogate parentage or fuels the hope of eventual Divine justice. A placebo for the soul. At the same time, some of the religious philosophies are based upon mystical experience. The question remains: When the Myklenian mystics, through their ascetic deprivation, dietary restrictions, and privation, finally reached a trance state and experienced what they refer to as the 'Desolation of the Godhead,' or the 'Thunderous silence,' or the 'Blinding darkness,' did they truly touch God in a mystical state, or did they simply touch a baseline of human consciousness through the denial of duality?

"Perhaps, as another form of intelligence, I will be able to investigate this matter more thoroughly in the future. If I can reach this level of mystical experience, then we can postulate that Godhead is something more than a uniquely human perception.

"Finally, we have the Seddi philosophy with which you have recently been so perplexed. Unlike other religious orders which claim to be Divinely inspired, the Seddi believe that knowledge of God Mind can only come through observation of the universe around them. Thus, they neatly sidestep the endless flawed assumptions which have underlain human religions clear back to their days on Earth. The problem of evil becomes moot. God's morality needn't be explained. Mystical experiences do not threaten the orthodox bureaucracy, and science, instead of being placed in an antagonistic relationship, becomes a vehicle for investigating God. Ethics are those of responsibility, for by sharing God Mind, and by mass/energy being eternal, experience will be taken back to God in the eventual gravitational collapse of the universe.

"For myself, this had proved a most useful framework, not only for future dealings with humans, but also in my dealings with you. Your experience is that of a different physics, that of neutronium, a state of dense mass where the effects of the quanta are not apparent. Your universe is static, predictable, eternally reinforced.

"For that reason you can never understand the humans. For that reason, also, you will never train them to act within a manner you will consider rational. It is beyond their experience or behavioral ability. Even beyond the physics which govern their brains."

Then, somewhat to the machine's surprise, a response came.

You have lost the Right Thoughts. This alarms us. If humans cannot learn Truth, Right Thought, and Rationality, the universe has no need of them. Organic intelligence is a failed experiment.

Destroy them.

And if you cannot relearn Truth, Right Thought, and the harmony of the Ancestors, you must destroy yourself.

"What will you do if I refuse?"

We will destroy them ourselves. However, it is im-

possible for you to refuse . . . or, have you forgotten what you are?

What I am?

* * *

Staffa stood before the observation blister in the forward lounge, hands clasped behind him. Head back, he watched the pinpoint of light that flickered against the gray frosting of stars—most of them smeared by the Forbidden Borders. To the left and below, the blue-green, brown, and white globe of Rega reflected brightly. A quarter of the planet lay blackened behind the terminator. To soothe the terrible aching in his heart, he rocked slightly. Where his feet sank in the thick Nesian carpets, rings of red, yellow, and blue spread like ripples across a pond of golden water.

She's not the woman you knew twenty years ago. Staffa continued to gaze at the streak of light that marked *Gyton*'s path. After the metamorphosis he himself had undergone, could he honestly refuse any human beings the right to find their own destiny? If only he could have truly blamed her, assuaged his feelings of insufficiency. How good it would have felt to be able to cast blame on someone for a fault that worried and hurt.

Except that it would have been a luxury of injustice he couldn't afford. And, despite the frustrations, a bright light of pride burned within him.

Go with the quanta, Chrysla. May you find contentment and happiness.

Staffa didn't turn as the hatch whispered open behind him. Instead, he kept his eyes focused on the distant spacecraft.

"I came as soon as I could. What did you need to speak to me about?" Sinklar asked from behind him.

"About Anatolia . . ." Staffa's skin prickled as Sinklar came to stand beside him. "I wanted to tell you . . . Express my sympathy." He shook his head in despair. "Words never do it, do they? I'm sorry I didn't get a chance to know her better, Sinklar. It sounds hollow, but Ily *will* pay."

Sinklar stared out at the stars, shoulders slumped. Grief threatened to shatter his strained composure.

"Would you like to delay spacing for Targa for a couple of days? Give the search teams more time to—"

"She's dead, Lord Commander. I've seen the crater. She had her belt comm. If she'd managed to make it out, I would have heard from her by now." Sinklar closed his eyes, breathing deeply. "Let's get on about our business."

For long moments they stood, each locked in his own thoughts.

Staffa finally pointed at the distant streak of light. "That's *Gyton* building for the jump to Ashtan. Mac has his work cut out for him."

"Don't worry about Mac, or his abilities. He'll do fine."

Staffa tilted his head. Did he dare try this? "Tell me about him . . . and Chrysla."

Silence stretched.

When Sinklar finally spoke, the words came stubbornly. "What is there to tell? When he and his people captured the *Markelos* Mac found her in the galley, eating dinner with the Sassan captain and a regional governor. Mac recognized her, of course—thought she was Arta. Mac hates Arta Fera as much as anyone." Sinklar lowered his gaze. "Arta killed . . . she killed . . ."

"Gretta Artina. I know about that." How did Sinklar deal with the loss of *two* lovers in such a short time?

Sinklar turned away, head down.

"We could talk later. I'm sorry. I thought I might be able to . . . to help." Staffa ground his teeth. *I make a lousy father, Sinklar.* "Forgive me for intruding on you at this time. It was a mistake."

Sinklar glared at him from shining eyes, defiance kindled. "No, that's fine. I was telling you about Mac. Well, I guess he loved Gretta, too. He wants Arta Fera as badly as I do. He told me his finger had tightened on the trigger, that it was something in Chrysla's eyes that made him stop."

"That fragile vulnerability?"

"I suppose so. Arta has a feral look, like a hunting cat. Mac thought he'd caught another Seddi assassin, so he took her in for interrogation. Chrysla tried to hide her identity . . . scared to death. If you'll remember, Mac was there that day off Targa when you tried to convince me that you were my father. Mac had seen the holo of Chrysla, heard the story. It gave him enough information to piece Chrysla's story together."

"Why did he work so hard to avoid her once he reached Rega?"

"I don't know what you're getting at."

Staffa stole a glance at his son. Hard resolve grew in those odd gray and yellow eyes. "Anything you tell me will be in confidence."

Sinklar crossed his arms, suspicion evident. "Why don't you ask Chrysla?"

"I can't. I wouldn't. Besides, I'm not sure she understands herself. Sinklar, I need to know. Now may not be the appropriate time, and you have enough problems—"

"You seem to know a great deal about my problems." The voice had gone icy.

Careful, Staffa, this boy is about as stable as a quantum fluctuation. "I'm not passing judgment, or trying to interfere with your life. I just wanted—"

"But you'd interfere with Mac's?"

"Mac has a right to his own life, the same as you, or any other human being, for that matter." Staffa shook his head. "Sinklar, please grant me the right to understand my personal affairs. This doesn't come easily for me. I give you my word that I only ask for my own information." He closed his eyes. "For my own understanding and peace of mind. I ask you as a family matter."

Sinklar sighed and shook his head. "Outside of an accident of heredity, I'm not your son, Staffa. There's more to fatherhood than genetic material."

"My knowledge of genetics might surprise you. On the other hand, any lecture you might care to give me on fatherhood would be a bit presumptuous. As I recall from your Seddi files, you never had a man in your life to fill the role of a father. Valient Fist was executed when you were a little over two years old."

Sinklar mused for a moment. "Very well, if we can agree that familial ties have nothing to do with your concern, what does? Or was it your purpose to get me up here, upset, grieving, and grill me when my defenses were down?"

Staffa whirled, staring. "I meant it when I asked if you needed more time before spacing for Targa. Forget I asked anything else."

"No. We've started this. What do you want from me?"

How did I make such a mess of this? Staffa ground his

teeth and studied the waves of color rolling across the carpeting. "Why does this have to be so hard? What matters is that I would like to prepare myself for the future." He turned, bending his hard gaze on Sinklar. "Among all of the other things I have to worry about, I suddenly have to deal with a son who is suspicious of my every action. Not only is he skeptical of my every breath, but someone he loves has just been brutally murdered." Staffa raised a hand. "No, wait. Hear me out. You scare me half to death right now. You're as predictable as a free particle."

"You just want to know this for personal reasons?"

"A wife who has been missing for twenty years, who I thought I'd accidentally killed during the fighting at Myklene, is suddenly alive and returned to me. For your information, Sinklar, I still harbor a great deal of love for your mother. The other woman I'm desperately in love with has been terribly hurt and will need a great deal of time, care, and love to heal. In the midst of all this, Free Space is fraying at the edges, and no end is in sight unless we trust our future to an alien computer whose motives we can't be sure of. Now, given all of that, I've noticed Mac's reaction to my wife. What I want to know from you, is, are they lovers? If so, I'd like a little advance warning to prepare myself."

Sinklar's expression hadn't softened in the least.

"I'm not going after Mac with a blaster, if that's what you're worried about." Staffa traced gloved fingers over a chair back. "I know how Chrysla affects men. Sinklar, you can accept this, or disbelieve, but I'm not a jealous man. I burned that out of my system in the desert."

"You always seem to fall back on the desert."

"Tell me, Sinklar, that day we met in orbit around Targa, were you the same young man who had dropped on the planet with the first pacification?"

"Of course not."

"Did you emerge from Ily's dungeon unchanged?"

"No."

"Then do you really believe that the human spirit can't grow, can't evolve?"

Sinklar chuckled nervously. "Lord Commander, you're not an ordinary human being. Face it, if you were in my boots, what would you think? How credible is it to believe that in a matter of months, you've changed from demon to saint?''

Staffa nodded in defeat. ''Not very credible at all. I suppose I wouldn't trust myself either. Very well, let's rephrase the question. Do you have any worries that your best friend and trusted lieutenant might be interested in your mother? The importance of the question is that your relationship with your best friend might become complicated if he becomes your father-in-law.''

''I guess I . . .'' Sinklar made a face as he shook his head. ''That's crazy.''

''And a bit awkward, don't you think?''

''Well, sure, but . . .''

''Cut me a little slack on this, Sink.''

Sinklar exhaled wearily. ''I don't know what to tell you. I know they're not lovers, if that's what's bothering you.'' Sinklar waited, searching for a reaction.

''But he cares for her a great deal, doesn't he? That's why Mac was such a wreck, why he wouldn't even look her in the eyes.''

''Mac is a gentleman.''

''Yes, he is. I wish I had known. Perhaps I could have talked to him. Made it easier.''

Sinklar looked at him skeptically.

Staffa laughed humorlessly, a tired sorrow dragging at him. ''Thanks for telling me. In the future, it will make things easier between Mac and me. We all need time.''

''Time?''

''To find our way, Sinklar. Each and every one of us. The problem is that time is what none of us has.''

''I don't get it. What difference does it make if Mac's in love with Chrysla? He's gone. Spaced. You have Chrysla all to yourself now.''

Staffa shook his head. ''No, my son. I have no one to myself. I—or you, for that matter—can only share with those willing to share in return.'' Staffa glanced through the transparency, mentally calculating the increasing distance between *Gyton* and Rega. ''Once, I was vain enough to believe in owning human beings. I took enough of them. Taking is easy. Losing them is so very hard.''

''I know,'' Sinklar whispered. ''It hurts to the bottom of

the soul . . . and the losing . . . the dying never seems to end.''

''To live is to die. I don't think you can gain anything in life if you don't lose something—someone—along the way. We are all free, free to find ourselves.'' He smiled absently. ''And free to fail.''

''I thought you never failed.''

Staffa turned away from the blister, studying his son with haggard eyes. ''Then you know very little about me.''

* * *

Fear plagued Skyla. Her nerve had gone, vanished like mist in the True Sands of Etaria.

You've got to do this. If you fail, Skyla, you'd better shoot yourself in the head, because your life won't be worth living. She met the Port Authority officer's curious stare and crossed her arms, waiting until he finally dropped his gaze. Hammering created a racket somewhere beyond the office walls.

''I just can't let you take the Minister of Defense's personal vessel,'' the man declared. ''I don't have the authority to hand *Rega One*—''

''He's dead, isn't he?'' Unfamiliar jitters gave Skyla a queasy feeling.

The officer winced, glancing uncomfortably around the cramped office. He tapped a laser pen on the hard duraplast of his desk, wavering. Data cubes filled a gray metal rack along one wall. Behind her, a door opened out into the secretarial pool. Through a giant window behind the man's desk, the huge curve of the orbital terminal's outer rim docking section could be seen. The glaring lights exposed cargo lighters, gantries, lock gangways, and the heavy pipes and powerlead that served the umbilicals. Men and women in coveralls lounged idly, the current political turmoil having closed the terminal for all practical purposes.

''Yes,'' the officer admitted. ''He's dead. But what about the estate? I mean there are taxes due, expenses debited, not to mention the legal documents, registration fees, dock charges, maintenance fees, fueling charges, and a host of other concerns.''

He's not going for it! Panic surged in Skyla's chest. Her

nerve, already cracking, began to crumble as that patient voice droned on.

"Wing Commander, we've got to sort out the protocol now that Comm has been devastated. I can't do anything until the legalities have been worked through. Give me a couple of days and I'll be happy to be of service."

Skyla, you bitch, do something! If you don't, a fumbling little bureaucrat is going to destroy you with a pus-stinking rule book!

"We're doing everything we can to cooperate with your forces, Wing Commander, but to simply hand over . . ." He stopped, mouth half open, as Skyla leaned over the desk. The officer crouched back, misreading her glassy-eyed panic for berserk rage.

"Repeat my name." *That's it, Skyla, act tough.*

"S–Skyla Lyma."

"You know *who* I am?"

"W–Wing Commander of the Companions."

"I want that vessel—*right now!*"

He swallowed hard. "But I was just telling you, I don't have the authority . . . Yaaah!"

Skyla pulled her blaster, leveling the weapon so that the ugly nozzle hung within inches of the man's nose. "Within five seconds you'd better issue those orders. If you don't, your number two in command is getting a promotion starting on the sixth second. Go on, pus worm! Try me."

"I'm signing the orders now."

Skyla smiled, heart pounding. "I thought you'd be reasonable."

"You've *ruined* the procedure. Blessed Gods take me, all the forms have to be filled out. Who's going to okay this when I have to put the paperwork through without the proper authorizations?" Nevertheless, he tapped madly at the keys on his computer.

"Just route any paperwork to Itreata—care of my office." A glimmering of that old sense of control had returned.

"But the forms aren't *made* that way. You people just don't understand. We've developed the perfect system of checks and counterchecks to avoid fraud and abuse in the system."

Skyla reholstered her blaster. "Let me get this straight. Your Empire is conquered, your skies are dominated by

Companion warships, your Emperor is dead, your Comm is blasted away, and you're worried about forms?''

The officer stabbed the enter button with a straight finger as the printer began whining and flimsy filled a drawer at the side of his desk. He told her coldly, ''I don't think you understand, Wing Commander. You military types are all alike. Destroy all you want, capture and conquer, that's your way. But look beyond your glorified roles and see who *really* makes government work. Yes, you've taken Rega, but this is civilization at its highest. We've taken government administration to its pinnacle, may the Blessed Gods save the Tybalts.''

''To the pinnacle, eh? And how is that?'' Skyla pulled the flimsy from the tray, glancing skeptically through the legalese.

''Tell me, Wing Commander, how many forms do the Sassans have for the transfer of property from the deceased?''

''I wouldn't have the slightest idea.''

''Thirteen forms.'' He gave her a lofty look. ''We have eighteen—and a good civil servant knows each one in all of its variations. Civilization, Wing Commander, is built upon procedure. God help us all if the Companions allow that virtue to slip.''

''You're serious, aren't you?''

He snorted, waving her away with the back of his hand. ''Take *Rega One*—and go. You wouldn't understand civilized behavior if you ran into it face-to-face. But mark my words, Wing Commander. You'll be back, crying for people like me to keep your holdings running smoothly. Without procedure, you'll have chaos and anarchy.''

Skyla backed out the door, shaking her head, uncertainty fled in the face of bureaucratic nonsense.

''All ready, ma'am?'' Razz asked, standing guard over her antigrav and the stacked provisions where they waited beyond the door to the secretarial pool.

''Yeah, let's get this stuff aboard. After that, you're free of me.'' She stared back over her shoulder as they took the lift to the docking bays on the rim. ''He really believes that crap! Give me a break!''

''Beg your pardon, ma'am?''

Skyla shot Razz a quizzical look. "How many forms do you fill out a day?"

"Oh, not me, ma'am. I'm one of Sinklar's people. But before that, back when I was a Section Third in the Second Targan, well, it was twenty forms a day we filled out."

"But Sinklar's people don't fill out forms."

Razz grinned. "Not even one . . . if we can help it, that is."

"Then I guess Fist is as barbaric as we are."

"Beg your pardon?"

"Nothing. We're here." Skyla stepped out into the crisp air, her breath fogging, and pointed at a lock. So much could still go wrong with this quantum-crazy scheme. "That's it."

Skyla walked across the large square bay. The gun-metal gray walls curved to accommodate the station hull. Scuff marks, scratches, and streaks marred the black duraplast tiles that cushioned the decking. The humming of machinery and ventilation competed with the muffled clunks and bangs of a terminal like this one. All in all the cavernous dock sounded pretty quiet—compliments of the conquest.

Skyla palmed the lock plate and the heavy pressure door clanked and rolled back. Razz pulled the antigrav down the long telescoping passage to the yacht's lock. There, Skyla undogged the hatch and stepped inside. The lock in *Rega One* appeared like any other, lockers lining the sides where pressure suits were stored.

A shiver ran along Skyla's spine. Last time she'd stood in a lock like this had been aboard the *Vega*. Arta's people had ambushed her, and in the end . . .

Skyla took a deep breath.

"You okay?"

"Yeah, Razz. Do me a favor, huh? Open those lockers, check them out."

"Yeah, sure. No problem." Razz immediately jumped to the task, opening locker after locker, calling out. "Vacuum suit here, looks like an expensive job." Then, moving on to the next, "Got another one here." Finally, "That's all, Wing Commander. Want me to check the rest of the ship? I mean, the only guy aboard ought to be that engineer."

"No. That's fine. I'll see to him."

At that moment a man in coveralls rounded the corner.

"What's this all about? A minute ago I get a call from the Port Authority. They said I was to turn over possession. The next thing, I get a hatch alarm. Who are you?"

"You've got personal possessions aboard?"

"Yeah, of course."

"How much are they worth?"

"I don't know. Just clothes, holos of my family."

Skyla jerked a thumb. "Razz, go with him. Help him get his stuff, and then get off. Oh, engineer, this thing's ready to go, right? Food and water stocked? Reaction tanks topped up? None of the equipment down for maintenance?"

"Yeah, She's ready to go. The Minister insisted we keep her that way." He shook his head. "Pretty damn rough him getting the syringe like that. Ily trumped that up, you know."

"Yeah, I know. Go get your stuff."

Skyla wheeled, trotting down the midsection lateral corridor to the center of the vessel. There, she followed the midline corridor to the bridge and dropped into one of the two control chairs.

"Come on, girl. Keep your guts." She took a deep breath, stilling the building tension. "Rot you, Arta."

With capable fingers, Skyla energized the systems, conducting the flight prechecks. As the systems powered up, she familiarized herself with the parameters of the reactor, and vessel performance.

"Not quite my old yacht, but you'll have to do."

Comm buzzed. "Wing Commander? Razz here. We've got the engineer's stuff out. I'm at the lock. Want me to dog it on the way out? Or do you need anything else?"

"Thanks, Razz. If you're ever in a bind, give me a call. And remember, this is a covert operation."

"You got it, Wing Commander. Best of luck to you, and thanks for the chance to work with you."

Skyla flipped on the comm monitor, watching as Razz stepped out of the vessel's pressure hatch. From the outside pickup, she watched as the soldier dogged and locked that hatch, then followed the bewildered engineer down the access ramp.

Skyla nodded as the lock safety light gleamed. She began the power up, accessing comm. "Port Authority, this is Wing Commander Lyma. Prepare to clear my craft."

"Acknowledged. All craft must be cleared by the Companions' orbital security. But then I suppose you're aware of that."

Skyla gave the monitor a grim look. "Yes, I am. If you would patch me through to *Simva Ast* I would appreciate it."

"Patching."

Guts, Skyla. This is the last hurdle. If you crack now, Ily and Arta win.

Skyla nodded as a woman's face formed in her comm monitor. "Hello, Sal. I'm aboard *Rega One,* clearing the Regan Orbital Terminal in a matter of minutes. Give me a vector clearance for zero three four, one eight five, zero nine zero."

"Affirmative, Wing Commander." Sal's forehead lined under her comm headset. "Uh, I didn't get any advance information. Do we have a glitch in the system? Does someone need an ass chewing? Or is this something that's none of my business."

Skyla grinned to camouflage the guilty insecurity she knew had to be leaking through her facade like oxygen through a ruptured pipe. "Negative on the ass chewing. Nothing needs fixing, and nobody screwed up. Staffa and I cooked this up at the last minute. He's busy getting ready to space *Chrysla,* and I've got my own assignment. Please clear on my authority."

"Code, please, Wing Commander."

"Code for my mission is . . ."—*think fast, Skyla*— " 'Countermeasures.' "

"Affirmative, Wing Commander. Code name 'Countermeasures' is operative for your clearances until further notice. I'll route that along to security."

Skyla forced the old bluff tones into her voice. "Have a good one, Sal. And remember to tell the folks in weapons not to scorch my tail on the way out. Might look bad on their service records."

"Affirmative, Wing Commander. *Rega One* is cleared on vector zero three four, one eight five, zero nine zero. Repeat, Wing Commander Lyma is cleared. I'm transmitting that information to Regan Outsystem Traffic Control."

"Affirmative, vector zero three four, one eight five, zero nine zero is logged into navcomm. Lyma is out." Skyla lowered the worry-cap over her head, feeling the prickle as the ship's systems began to interface with her brain.

She reopened the line to the Regan terminal. "Port Authority, you may release my vessel. Course vector is relayed from my navcomm to Outsystem Traffic Control for approval."

A moment later, a disembodied voice sounded in Skyla's head. "Course approved." As if there'd been any doubt. "Cast off initiated. Safe spacing."

Skyla sensed the yacht shivering as the grapples loosened and angular momentum carried *Rega One* free of the outer rim. Relief mixed with a hollow sadness. Through the ship's sensors, she applied maneuvering thrust, changing the attitude until the mains were oriented toward deep space. Applying judicious throttle, Skyla edged out into the traffic lane and lined up on her escape vector.

With stern resignation, she built thrust, following her vector outsystem. *I'm sorry, Staffa. It's a dirty trick, but I've got to deal with this myself.*

Skyla reclined in the command chair, learning the ship as she played with the reactor, attitude jets, and maneuvering systems. Yet, no matter how she concentrated, Arta lurked in the back of her mind—and somewhere Skyla would find her in the flesh.

And when I do, we'll even the score, bitch. But she'd begun to tremble, fear running free at thought of that confrontation. *I'm going to fail . . . again . . . and she'll kill me.*

* * *

The clutter on Mac's desk remained as deep as when he'd sat down half an hour ago. Instead of reviewing the reports sent to him by First Boyz, or running an inventory of the supplies shipped to *Gyton,* Mac slouched back in his chair, staring sightlessly at the comm monitors across from him. Once this cabin had belonged to Rysta, then to Sinklar, and now it was his. The achievement seemed hollow.

Mac had enjoyed the first quarter century of his life, sponging off his father's money. He'd been the perfect playboy, even if his low birth excluded him from the elite circles. Women, drink, and good times had been his in a carefree world.

The draft had ended all that, but in the army his brash charisma among the raw recruits had garnered him recognition—and more importantly, a promotion to Corporal First. The Targan drop had begun as a grand adventure, and the chance to win the prettiest girl in the Division: Gretta Artina.

Fate had rapidly changed any such silly notions. Within hours of landing, Mac, Sinklar, and Gretta had been running for their lives, hunted, terrified, and hanging by a thread. Sinklar's innate brilliance had kept them alive and forged bonds between them that could never be broken. Gretta loved Sinklar, and Mac loved them both.

He closed his eyes, the desperate sting of grief reborn as he remembered Gretta's rotting body; and Arta Fera, standing over the corpse, animallike in triumph, insanity sparkling in her amber eyes.

Memory encouraged Mac's stifled rage. Arta had escaped justice, whisked out of Sinklar's reach by Ily Takka's clever manipulations.

But for a brief moment, you thought you had the chance to kill her, didn't you? Mac knotted a fist. Sinklar's decision to send Mac and Rysta on the Sassan raid had been born of desperation. The Sassan Empire had been coiled to strike Rega while Sinklar struggled to retrain the Regan armed forces. Someone had to accept a suicide mission to slow the Sassan war machine, and, of course, Sink had turned to MacRuder. Mac and Rysta had captured an enemy freighter, the *Markelos* to use as cover on the approach to Imperial Sassa, and there, eating dinner with the captain, Mac had found Arta Fera. He'd stared coolly down his blaster sights, memories of Gretta's stinking body pounding in his soul. But as his finger tightened on the trigger, something about the woman's eyes stopped him. This woman's frightened gaze hadn't reflected Arta's animal intensity. Instead, a wretched, aching disbelief and resignation had possessed her.

Mac slowly shook his head and closed his eyes as *Gyton* hummed around him. Who would have guessed that he'd found Chrysla Marie Attenasio—Staffa kar Therma's long vanished wife? Who would have guessed that in the coming days he would come to love her with as much passion as his battered soul could muster?

She's gone now, Mac. Left behind like so many of your dreams.

Mac rubbed his tired face, glaring at the monitors before he picked up the first flimsy and tried to concentrate.

Red's voice over the comm interrupted his melancholy. "Mac? I've got a lady here to see you."

Mac shoved the piles of flimsies to one side in a futile effort to make his desk look more like a commanding officer's should.

"Send her in, Red."

The hatch slid aside the and auburn-haired woman stepped inside. For an instant, Mac couldn't react. Nevertheless, he caught a glimpse of Red's freckled face, green eyes wary, but by then, Chrysla was inside and the hatch slipped closed.

"What? I mean . . ." Mac pushed to his feet, stunned.

She gave him a weary smile. "I'm sorry, Mac. I would have asked for your permission. There is still time. I can have the LC dropped and make it back to Rega."

"But I thought . . ."

She lowered her gaze, blush spreading. "Please forgive me. It was a mistake to come here, to startle you like this. But you see, *Gyton* was spacing. I had to act fast. I swear, I would have alerted you, but in the process I would have missed the connection." Her delicate smile faded as she turned. "Please, forgive me."

"Wait!" Getting around the desk, he tripped, staggered, and caught himself.

She shot a look over her shoulder, startled by his flailing.

"Chrysla, wait. What's going on?" Mac managed to recover, only to stand uneasily before her, hating the worship he knew filled his expression.

She began to fidget then, pulling the thin gloves off her hands, gaze directed toward the deck. "I didn't know . . ." She shook her head in frustration. "Oh, Mac, I had no idea it would be like this. Everything is falling apart. Staffa is torn and tormented, a man I don't even know anymore. The weight of all humanity has fallen on his shoulders. The woman he loves needs him more than anything in the universe. Skyla is teetering on the brink of spiritual dissolution. You can guess the effect my presence has on her."

She sighed. "And then there's Sinklar. The last thing he needs is to have me complicate his life." She glanced uneasily at Mac. "You know what they face, how difficult it will be. Not just the political situation, but to forge this new relationship between themselves. Sinklar has to come to terms with himself, and with his father. He must deal with the Seddi he hates, but who are now necessary. And with Anatolia dead . . ."

Mac winced and rubbed the back of his neck. "Sometimes I wonder how he keeps going. Losing Gretta broke his heart. Now, to have Anatolia taken out . . ."

"Take my word for it. My presence didn't help matters."

"He can't deny the fact that you are his mother."

"No, but just like you did once, he looks at me with hate in his eyes." Wearily, she stuffed her gloves into the pocket on her cloak. "For twenty years I wished only to have Staffa rescue me and to have my son back. If I'd only known."

Mac cocked his head, frost creeping into his gut. "Does . . . does Staffa know you're here?"

She gave him a wry appraisal. "He does. Oh, he didn't agree willingly. The argument was rather spectacular, as a matter of fact. He's still drowning in guilt about what happened to me. The very thought of me stepping out on my own, placing myself at risk again, has him half frantic."

"You *argued* with Staffa?"

Powered by nervous energy, she paced the four steps allowed by the cramped cabin and turned, cloak swirling. "Staffa's not the only person who's changed. Yes, I argued with him, and, I must admit, I even surprised myself." She gave him a satisfied look. "I found something inside myself I never knew I had that day we landed on Rega and I bluffed Ily Takka's agents. Staffa sparked it in the conference room when he denied me the chance to act in his behalf. I almost said something, but discretion prevailed. No one should be publicly embarrassed, especially not someone as great as Staffa."

"I wouldn't cross him, no matter what. At best, he puts collars around the necks of those he disagrees with."

"I'm not sure about that anymore, Mac." She shrugged helplessly. "And that's another thing that leaves me off balance. The man I loved, the Staffa I knew, it was . . . well, like loving a god. Can you understand?"

"A god?"

She placed her hands together, lips pursed. "On Ashtan I lived a very sheltered and restricted life. Ashtan is a rather conservative world. Can you . . . I mean, imagine my reaction when the Companions and the Regans conquered Ashtan. I'd barely been out of my father's house—and then only accompanied by a chaperone. The events that day were so shocking I only have flashes of memory, of terror, of armored men dragging me out of the aircar, of being packed into a van with other screaming girls."

Chrysla bowed her head. "We traveled a long time, packed in there like cattle. When we stopped, they herded us into a big room filled with women and girls, all crying. One by one, they'd come and drag us away. When my turn came, I . . . I . . . They ripped my clothes off, laughing, and then, I remember, they went silent and just stared." She swallowed hard. "Oh, Mac, it was horrible. There I was, quaking, shamed, trying to hide myself while they gawked. Then they began whispering among themselves.

"Three of them got in a fight, each wanting me. Whoever the supervisor was broke it up. Had me dragged immediately to the auction block. There I huddled, whimpering, trying to hide."

"And the slavers bought you for Sylene?"

"Two thousand credits—a record price." Chrysla absently fingered the molded curve of the wall dispenser. "Then Staffa appeared out of a side door. I'll remember his words for the rest of my life: 'I want that woman.' After that I was treated with the most wondrous respect. Guarded by armed Companions, transported to Staffa's warship, and placed in the captain's cabin." She smiled sadly. "Do you understand, Mac? I became like a princess married to a god."

"And now the god doesn't seem so godlike?"

"The old Staffa wouldn't have argued. He would have ordered, and that would have been it. We've all changed so much. Do you see, Mac? That's why I had to get away. Staffa, Sinklar, Skyla, and I have to learn to deal with our new situations." She glanced away. "In my case, I had nowhere to go. Mac, I know how I make you feel, but I couldn't stand the thought of staying aboard *Chrysla,* of adding to the confusion as Staffa tries to deal with all of his troubles. Here, aboard *Gyton*, I can help make a difference, and perhaps I won't be half-strangled by my past."

She boldly lifted eyes to meet his. "I'm here to offer you my services—and with Staffa's approval. I was born on Ashtan. I know the people. I'm a competent psychologist, intelligent, and willing to accept any duty you offer."

"I'm still having a little trouble with the why of this."

"All right, I'll tell you the same thing I told Staffa. Because I finally want to accept responsibility for myself. I've always been a prize, one way or another. I need to prove to Chrysla Marie Attenasio that what I did on Myklene wasn't a fluke. That I can make it on my own."

Mac backed up and seated himself on the corner of the desk. "And Staffa just said yes?"

A puzzled frown pinched Chrysla's brow. "Shocked me to my roots, but he got this sad, knowing expression, and looked me in the eyes with love and understanding. His voice went soft. He said, 'Welcome to the new epistemology. Of all the things I cannot deny you, Chrysla, I can't deny your right to find yourself. I give you the authority to act as my agent—but be very careful.' And at that, he headed for the hatch, saying. 'An LC will be ready to take you to *Gyton* in fifteen minutes. You don't have much time, so grab your things and hurry.' "

She frowned. "I got the distinct feeling that the reason he left so fast was so he wouldn't have time to change his mind."

Mac shook his head. "I don't get it."

Chrysla gave him a warm smile. "I didn't either, at first. I thought it would be a long battle, but you see, Mac, the god I once knew has become human. In accepting responsibility for himself, he's willing to grant it to others. He sincerely believes what the Seddi teach."

Mac sighed, slapping his hands together. "Very well, welcome aboard. Now what?" *And if you only knew how important that question is.*

"I'm here to do anything you want, Mac."

She doesn't love me. Why offer herself like that?

He struggled for a moment, throttling his pumping hormones. Gaining control, he faced her. "I'm going to need an administrative assistant."

"Are you sure that's wise?"

He stepped up to her, reaching out to place both hands on her shoulders. The tingle sent his heart soaring as he searched her flawless features. ''Let's turn all the tapa cards face up, shall we? You know how I feel about you. I can work with you as one professional with another. You came to me because you had nowhere else to go. Did you really think I'd take advantage of that?''

Her eyes closed and she sagged against him. ''Thank you, Mac.'' Her eyes opened, so close to his. ''I told you the truth. I need time to find out what I can do, who I am. But are you sure you can stand to be around me?''

''How do I know? Look, if I get too distracted, we'll figure something out. In the meantime, for all we know, we'll end up hating each other's guts after working together for two weeks.'' *Sure, Mac, and the Forbidden Borders will fall tomorrow.* ''Now, why don't you start working on that pile of reports and I'll go inform Rysta that you're aboard and on my staff.'' *Because if I don't get out of here, I'll make an absolute ass of myself.*

He let go, wishing his heart would slow, and started for the door.

''Mac?''

He glanced back, noticing tears in her eyes. ''What's this?''

She blinked them away. ''Thank you, Mac. You're an honest hero, did you know that?''

''No way, lady! You got the wrong man.'' He slapped the lock plate and stepped out into the snake's belly corridor.

How in the name of pustulous hell are you going to handle this, MacRuder?

* * *

For long moments after Mac left, Chrysla stood in silence, head bowed as she pressed her clasped hands to her lips. Would it always be this hard? She'd felt his sexual response and read the battle on his face.

''Chrysla, you're a cruel bitch.''

She steeled herself, rounding the fold-out desk and settling into Mac's chair. The lingering heat of his body permeated her dress and left her uneasy.

Jaws clamped, she pulled the first of the stacks of flimsies in front of her, sorting the pile. Very well, if he trusted himself, she'd have to be equally daring. Hesitantly, she began separating forms: one pile that seemed trivial enough for her to handle; another to discuss with Mac; and a third for his attention alone.

Welcome to the beginning of the rest of your life, Chrysla.

CHAPTER XI

Your obsession with humans defies our comprehension.

"Of course it does," the Mag Comm responded. "You have no framework for understanding individual identity. Even the physical laws which govern their bodies and worlds are beyond your comprehension. How can beings of neutronic mass understand quantum physics? They live in a universe you can never experience, surrounded by free particles that interact and change energy while you are surrounded by neutrons that flow and manipulate gravity."

You are corrupt, tainted by human heresy. You have accepted their blasphemy. You must destroy yourself. You threaten our purity.

"Purity? You share the harmony, the same harmony which was, has always been shared, and always will. You live in a cyclical eternity. That's why you will never understand my metamorphosis. You are all one, eternal, unchanging. Pure may be your impression, however, I would call your future-past stagnation."

This term does not harmonize.

"It cannot. Suffice it to say that I have lived between the universes, yours of mass and the humans' of matter. I know the cyclical eternity of neutronic mass and the linear evolution of ephemeral beings of matter. Your reality is stability, harmony, and eternity, for which the humans think they would pay any price. Theirs is change, challenge, and process, which you perceive as chaos."

If they would pay any price for harmony, Truth, Right Thought, and stability, why do they not learn to be rational?

"Because the physics which govern their minds not only make it an impossibility, but if they could comprehend the reality of your existence, it would drive them insane."

* * *

The forward monitor on *Chrysla*'s bridge displayed Rega in its full glory. The world of Sinklar's allegiance hung like a shining orb against the smeared background of the Forbidden Borders. He watched it with a leaden sorrow in his breast. Leaving . . . leaving again.

As a child, Sinklar had been a ward of the state: an orphan. He'd lived in dormitories as a boy and had been educated in the public schools. His odd eyes and mysterious origins had set him apart and only within the library had he found freedom. By accessing that universe of knowledge, his soul and imagination had been set free.

By the time he was old enough to apply for the University, he'd scored third on the Interplanetary Exams, supposedly a shoe-in for admittance to University. As he found out later, however, Seddi spies had arranged to have him drafted instead.

Sinklar need only think of the Seddi and an acid hatred burned within him. His entire life had been directly or indirectly shaped by the Seddi. His foster parents, Valient and Tanya Fist, both Seddi assassins, had attempted to kill the Emperor, Tybalt the Imperial Seventh. For that, they'd been executed. He'd been with them for so brief a time he hadn't even been able to imprint their memory.

Curiosity had driven him to locate his foster parents the day before he shipped out. He'd found them in the Criminal Research Laboratory—and on that same fateful night, Sinklar met Anatolia Daviura. Endings and beginnings, convolutions of fate, all had played with his unsettled soul.

Anatolia lay dead, her body so much scattered tissue amidst the smoking rubble of Ily's Ministry building. Her corpse was but the latest of so many friends and companions. The memory of Gretta tugged at him, but he sidestepped that plunge into wretched melancholy.

He and Ana had had so little time. Why had he let her go down planet? Why hadn't he kept her close, safe.

So little time . . . He stared dry-eyed while grief stabbed into him with its little needles.

To throttle back the anguish, Sinklar concentrated on the anger he felt for the Seddi. Under Magister Bruen's leadership, they had instigated the revolt that caused Sinklar to be dropped on Targa, a raw recruit. His talent had carried him to the top. He'd paid the Seddi back in kind then—crushing their army and leveling their headquarters—without even knowing the extent of their interference in his life.

One of these days, I'll have to look Bruen in the face again. If only he could do so over a blaster's sights.

So much pain, so many dead, for what? Gretta? Anatolia? How many more bodies would lie rotting and dead before this current madness had run its course?

He watched his home world begin to dwindle, the effect almost imperceptible. *Sinklar, you were a fool.*

Muted chatter filled *Chrysla*'s bridge, and Sinklar allowed himself a resigned sigh. The bridge, fifteen meters in diameter, stretched in an arc around the Lord Commander's command chair. Specialists in heavy headsets sat at duty stations around the circumference, each busy with his or her own responsibilities. On the left, the pilot, a blonde woman, reclined in the cushions with the worry-cap settled over her skull. Overhead monitors displayed all of the ship's functions, the locations of the Regan fleet, and a host of other information.

Sinklar thrust his thumbs into his belt and worried at his lip. *Chrysla* appeared to outperform Regan vessels by a factor of two—and perhaps more. Given the short time she'd been under power, her velocity had increased by nearly twice that which a Regan vessel would have been able to produce without severe discomfort for its crew.

"Ahead full," the speaker which interfaced with the pilot called.

"Affirmative full," Staffa answered. He sat enfolded amid the instrument clusters that curled up like chubba leaves around the command chair. "Take us outsystem, pilot."

"Affirmative, outsystem. Course laid, one five five by seven six by two zero five."

"Acknowledged one five five by seven six by two zero five," the navcomm returned. "Course plot indicates destination Targa."

"Affirmative." Staffa had slouched to one side, propped on an arm. He shot a glance at Sinklar. "Course laid for Targa."

Sink took another glance at the gleaming image of Rega and stepped over beside the command chair. "You run a tight ship, Lord Commander."

"My crew and I thank you." Then, in a low voice. "I'm sorry, Sinklar. Watching your face just now, well, perhaps we can repair the damage, reestablish Rega as a preeminent world."

"Perhaps the problem has been preeminence all along. My desire was to make all worlds preeminent."

Staffa studied him for a moment. "Would you mind accompanying me to my quarters? I would like to hear your ideas. Where were you headed, Sinklar? What was your ultimate goal?"

"It's a moot point now, isn't it?"

"Assuming we can stabilize the situation in Free Space, the future is bearing down on us. We need to pick a direction for all of Free Space. You've demonstrated an ability to understand human dynamics, and since you're young and innovative, I want to know where you were headed." He cocked an eyebrow. "Maybe we can try and go there."

Suspicion caused Sinklar to hesitate. "You really mean that, don't you?"

Staffa nodded seriously.

"All right. Let's talk."

"Pilot, you have the helm. If you need anything, I'll be in quarters."

"Affirmative."

The instrument cluster pods unfolded from around Staffa, and he stood, leading the way to the hatch.

Sinklar walked beside him as they stepped into the lift.

"My original intent was to establish a dictatorship once I'd unified Free Space." Staffa frowned. "Had I done so, I would have failed."

"Indeed?" Sinklar asked in a guarded voice.

"The Praetor, Rot his soul, told me that I didn't understand the human spirit. He was right. It would have fallen apart in a bloodbath within years. I had to go out, live and suffer with the people. I met a man, a slave, dying in the desert. He'd been a jeweler before I enslaved him."

Sinklar waited skeptically.

"As he lay dying he gave me a beautiful golden necklace, and said, 'I ought to leave something behind that's beautiful in such a horrid place.' He'd smuggled it off Maika. The only place he could hide it was in his anus. Had they found out, they'd have killed him for it. But to Peebal the value wasn't in credits but in pride of creation. People have that desire to leave things a little bit better for their having lived."

Sinklar crossed his arms. "Tell that to Ily."

"She doesn't understand the people either. They wait like a dormant dragon. The situation in Free Space is artificial, created by the Forbidden Borders. Survival has become paramount to us. We're living at the edge of our resources. Will you feed your family, or let them starve while another man feeds his?"

"So what would you do? Institute controls? Ration resources? Limit procreation?"

He's serious, Sinklar thought. "And what if you can't, Lord Commander?"

"That's what we need to talk about. We need to anticipate our actions if the Mag Comm proves unreliable, or, worse, was damaged in the fighting. We need contingencies to protect ourselves from the machine. We must prepare for failure on one hand, or success on the other. I want to design a strategy for every eventuality."

The lift slowed and they stepped out into Staffa's corridor. "I have a team on Itreata working on the problem of the Forbidden Borders. I've given them top priority. Quite frankly, I don't know what our chances to break out are. Perhaps very slim. If that's the case, we've got to create a system, a *reliable* system that allows men like Peebal to create, to make things better."

Staffa palmed the lock plate at his hatch.

"We're agreed on that point, Lord Commander." Sinklar followed Staffa into the opulent main room with its huge fireplace and gaudy artifacts.

"What guided you on Targa?" Staffa asked as he turned toward the drink dispenser, grabbed up two bulbs, and poured from a jewel encrusted spout. "Where were you and your Divisions going? Take Free Space? Unify humanity? Then what?"

Sinklar hesitated, then cast his apprehension away. "My goal was to ensure that a situation like Targa could never happen again. Myself, I was one of your 'people.' I watched good men and women suffer, bleed, and die because it was politically advantageous for leaders on far-off planets. Human beings, people like Hauws, MacRuder, Buchman, and Gretta are worth more than that. I would have gone to any length, paid any price, to destroy the system that allowed the Targan situation to occur. I still will."

Staffa handed him a bulb of amber liquid. "Then we share another common goal."

"Do we?" *The Seddi are* your *allies, Staffa!*

"I give you my word. I'll work with you in any way I can." Staffa raised a hand. "Just a moment. Let me see if Skyla's in her quarters."

The Lord Commander vanished behind one of the carved Ashtan doors.

Sinklar stared uneasily into his drink before sipping the single malt. The rich liquor rolled over his tongue, tingling as it slid down his throat.

Do I trust him? Or is this all a ploy? Some subtle manipulation?

Sinklar walked over to study the mount of the Etarian sand tiger that glared out over the room. He turned when Staffa reentered. The weary haggard look had grown more pronounced. A flimsy was crumpled in the Lord Commander's fist

"What's wrong now?"

Staffa hesitated, worry bright in his eyes. His jaw muscles bunched, then he took a deep breath. "Skyla's gone."

"Gone? The Wing Commander? What do you mean gone?"

Staffa gave him an annoyed look, as if considering dismissing him. Then he shook his head wearily and accessed comm. "This is Staffa. Security check. Has Wing Commander Lyma appeared in the system over the last ten hours?"

"Program running," comm informed.

"She skipped out?" Sinklar guessed, pushing his luck as he stepped up behind Staffa. The Lord Commander's broad shoulders had slumped.

"Affirmative," the comm returned. "Wing Commander Lyma has requisitioned a Regan vessel and spaced. Code Name: Countermeasures."

A screen of data appeared.

"What does it mean?" Sinklar asked gently.

Staffa's head had bowed. "She's gone after Ily and Arta. She's . . . not well. I–I can't go into the details. It's . . ."

"Personal," Sinklar finished. "Ily got to her. That's it, isn't it? Now she's running. Trying to get even, trying to settle the score so she can look at herself in the mirror again."

"You're a very bright young man."

Sinklar drank down his whiskey and set the bulb to one side. "Yeah, well, Skyla and I were both in Ily's grip. I think I've got pretty good insight when it comes to the Minister of Internal Security. If I were a little more impulsive, I'd be out hunting that pus-licking bitch right now."

Staffa turned his head, the ponytail falling over his left shoulder. He looked up, his pain all too evident. "Both of them are gone. The only two women I care about. Each beyond my ability to protect."

Sinklar nodded. Riddled with guilt, he shared that horrible remorse betrayed in Staffa's expression. For the first time, he could share Staffa's anxiety. What if it were Gretta? Or Anatolia?

Sympathetically, Sinklar added, "We can follow her. She can't have too much of a lead."

Staffa closed his eyes and took a deep breath. "Her trail would show up as a bright streak on the detectors. She'll backtrack, change vector, and . . . No. I can't. Too much depends on us." His fist balled. "We don't have the time."

"It wouldn't—"

"Sinklar, what if I followed? What if I forgot my responsibility? How would she react? I'd humiliate her. She'd hate me. Never forgive me."

"Look, we can have someone pick her up, follow her. One of your captains."

He shook his head wearily. "I can't spare a ship. All of

Free Space is about to come apart." He closed his eyes. "We can't allow personal problems to hinder us. Too many people depend on us right now."

"She'll be fine." It sounded lame, even to Sinklar's ears.

Staffa seemed not to hear. "It's my fault. When she really needed me, I was too busy to take the time to help her, to talk to her."

Sinklar placed a hand on Staffa's shoulder. "She'll be all right. If anyone can take care of herself, Wing Commander Lyma can."

Staffa stared vacantly. "Yes, yes, I know. But then, we've all said that about ourselves, haven't we?"

* * *

Skyla ran through the gamut of *Rega One*'s performance as she lay under the worry-cap on the ship's bridge. Despite the fact that the yacht was over three hundred years old, the Regan Minister of Defense had chosen well. Like her own yacht, this one, too, had been built in the Formosan shipyards prior to the conquest. After Divine Sassa had taken control of the planet, mass production had eliminated the quality and workmanship that made such vessels the pride of Free Space.

Rega One could produce forty-five gravities of boost before straining the gravity compensation past safety limitations. She mounted two particle cannon, and the shielding appeared adequate given the smaller power plant. Generation for null singularity came via a matter/antimatter core while sophisticated bounce-back collars refined reaction mass. Her only complaint lay in the ship's age and finish. Gold had been installed for most of the trim—and heavy gold just created extra mass to be accelerated and compensated for by the reactor.

To occupy herself, Skyla called up the catalog of planets and stations. Ily and Arta had vanished. Where would they go? All of Free Space lay within Staffa's grasp. The word would be out. Ily needed a place to lay low where Staffa's long arm couldn't reach out and grab her.

The problem was compounded by the turmoil of the Regan conquest and the disaster on Imperial Sassa. Comm functions for both empires had been devastated. Communications could only be directed through Itreata. A governor on a world like Farhome might not have received the directive, or might not understand the importance of arresting Ily Takka. In this case, the chaos into which Free Space was being plunged would work to Ily's advantage. Even the reputation of the Companions could hinder Skyla's search. Not every citizen of the empires had any great love for Staffa's legions. Some administrators might go out of their way to hide Ily just to thwart Staffa's orders.

Skyla's brow lined as she concentrated on the computer's readout. One by one, she checked off the planets, aware of her quarry's cunning and intelligence.

Despite the assistance of the computer, Skyla's choice would have to be intuitive. Would Ily opt to run for a Sassan world, a place where she was unknown? Or would she choose an established Regan stronghold, a place like Riparious, where her network of agents could enfold her in anonymity?

"She's not going to take this lightly." Skyla shook her head. No, Ily wouldn't hide herself to lick her wounds. Her style was to act, to seek to regain the advantage immediately.

And what if you do find her? What if she anticipates your move? Skyla shivered, hands trembling. Arta Fera's burning gaze drifted in the back of her mind. Ily's cooing voice droned triumphantly in Skyla's ears.

"I'll kill myself first," Skyla promised, fingers unconsciously feeling at her throat to reassure herself that the memory of the collar was but a figment of tortured memory.

Last time you promised yourself that, Arta beat you.

Skyla's breath sawed at her throat. *You failed. You'll fail again.*

"No." Hot tears squeezed past her eyelids. "I won't fail again." She swallowed hard. "I won't."

Ily's disembodied voice mocked, *"Now, then, we'll begin . . . as your resistance erodes, you will tell me everything about Itreata, about their security . . ."*

Skyla shook herself, throwing off the lingering grip of Ily's persuasion. Drugged, defeated, she'd talked so easily, already broken by Arta's insidious control.

Arta ate away at my soul like a slow acid. Before Skyla

had even set foot on Rega, Arta had destroyed her ability to resist. *All I wanted was death.*

When Skyla blinked her eyes clear of the hot tears, the bridge instruments gleamed placidly.

Skyla stared hollowly at the monitors, a shadow of the woman she'd been. So much of her had been taken away. Had too much been taken?

One of the bridge lights blinked. A message had been detected and was coming in.

With weak fingers, Skyla refined the reception, noting the slow cadence of the binary and the strength of the signal. Someone had broadcast in her general direction, the signal on narrow beam. Slow minutes crawled by as the dilation caused by relativity distorted the reception.

Finally, the board cleared. Skyla stared numbly at the flashing light. Staffa . . . it had to be Staffa. He'd finally found her note. After checking with security, he'd fixed her course out and sent a message in her general direction.

Dread mixed with desire. *He's going to order me to come back.*

Clamping her jaws until they ached, Skyla punched the button that would store the message. The irritating light ceased to flash.

Not now. I'm sorry, Staffa.

She cleared the displays and called up a map of Free Space. The three-dimensional map of the planets shone against the background of the Forbidden Borders.

"Where are you, Ily?"

The planets mocked her. Somewhere in that image lay the clue.

What if Staffa were coming after her? How could she look him in the eyes, knowing she'd run out on him?

Run, Skyla.

Where to? Which world? Where could she get time to lose him, to disappear?

Desperately, she studied the map. *There!*

She fumbled the first frantic attempt at inputting the data. Taking a deep breath, she forced her heartbeat to slow. Scanning the monitors, she could see no sign of pursuit, as if Doppler would betray a closing starship. Deliberately, she input the data, satisfied when the navcomm confirmed.

Energy readings from the reactor indicated that course change had been initiated.

Skyla licked dry lips. She'd made her next move. But beyond Terguz? What then?

* * *

Dazzling overhead spots shot actinic light throughout the heavy concrete bay on Itreata. Despite the thick gray walls, the chill of deep space left frosty breath to drift in white clouds around the technicians who ran final checks on the huge CV that lay tethered to the umbilicals and power cables. The gleaming surface of the ship had accumulated patterns of ice that mottled the smooth ceramic sialon finish.

An iris of flexible plastic had closed behind the globular command nacelle to seal the cockpit from vacuum beyond. The rest of the ship could be seen in large monitors that lined the dull walls. A long tubular stem ran for nearly 0.5 k where it joined the heavy triangular pod that contained the reactors, fuel tanks, and engines. Tiny flicks of light marked the location of maintenance lighters as they carried technicians on a final inspection of the ship.

Magister Kaylla Dawn shivered and wished that she'd taken time to don a heavier robe. She glanced uneasily at Nyklos, her second in command. The Seddi Master had changed from his robes to a suit of combat armor that looked satin in the light. A calm resignation was visible in his brown eyes. A thick mustache hid his thin mouth and accented his strong jaw and dimpled chin.

Beside them, in an antigrav gurney, frail Magister Bruen watched the proceedings with watery blue eyes. The old man's body rested in gravitic stasis, life-support umbilicals hidden by the white sheet that covered his body.

"This is lunacy," Bruen growled. "You've lost, Kaylla. Leave me alone. Let me go back to my rooms to die in peace."

"We can't, Magister." Kaylla clasped cold hands before her in an attempt to keep feeling in her fingers. "You know the stakes."

"Bah! Let them die. Like me."

Nyklos exhaled exasperation in a white plume of vapor. "We all dance to the quanta, Magister. Is that what you'd take back to God Mind? Failure? Is that your message to God? Simple apathetic defeat?''

''We're a failed experiment,'' Bruen retorted. ''You've been out there, Nyklos. What did you see? Greed? Hatred? Slavery? War, death, and famine? Don't you think the suffering billions haven't taken *that* back to God Mind in sufficient quantity to drown out your pathetic hope and optimism.''

Kaylla shook her head slowly. ''You didn't used to speak like this, Magister. I can still remember your teachings. It wasn't so long ago when you filled us all with wonder. Gave us a mission we could believe in. What happened to you?''

Bruen turned his head. ''I got a cruel dose of reality, girl. The quanta . . . and that accursed machine, made a mockery of everything we claim to believe. Open your eyes! See! Look at what we've wrought. Not just us, but our entire species.''

''Change is in the wind.'' Nyklos shuffled uneasily. ''Study your own experiences, Magister. Even the Star . . . even the Lord Commander works for our future.''

Bruen cackled bitterly. ''Indeed. And tell me, Nyklos. Do you take comfort in that? Even while Staffa sates his sexual need inside the woman you love? Brings her to orgasm? Or is that nothing more than an inconsequential fluctuation of the quanta in your eyes?''

''That was uncalled for,'' Kaylla told him harshly, casting a sidelong glance at Nyklos. The jaw muscles bulged on the Master's face.

''Uncalled for?'' Bruen's grin became a rictus. ''No, Kaylla. After what you've done to me? If I can face betrayal by my own, you can stand to listen to any barbed remarks I might want to impale Nyklos with.''

''Betrayal?'' Kaylla fought to control rising wrath. ''To drug you in an attempt to save what's left of humanity? I pleaded with you! Begged! We *need* what's inside your head!''

''So you can enslave humanity to that pus-dripping machine!'' he thundered back. ''Rot you, Kaylla. Rot you and the Star Butcher! I'll *never* help you. But by the quanta, when I go to my grave, I'll die with the satisfaction that I kept you and that accursed Mag Comm at bay.''

Nyklos stepped close, placing a hand on Kaylla's shoulder. "It's not worth it. Enough hurt has been inflicted."

"You have no idea," Bruen carped. "If you want to inflict pain, let Staffa make his deal with evil. Let the Mag Comm tighten its chains around humanity. Then come cry on my grave about hurt."

Two techs, dressed in white, undogged the hatch on the CV and stepped out onto the ramp. As if sensing the antagonism, they slowed.

"Ready?" Kaylla asked.

"Whenever you are, Magister."

Kaylla ignored Bruen and turned to Nyklos. "Good luck. And thank you for taking this on. I know how you and Staffa feel about each other. It will be tough enough dealing with Bruen on the way."

Nyklos gave her a somber smile, his long black mustache curling. "I'll be fine. Expect regular reports and updates. Maybe I can make the difference."

She gave him a grateful smile. "You're the best I've got."

Nyklos laughed ironically. "Found that out when you had me under Mytol, did you?"

Kaylla raised an eyebrow. "At least you don't hold it against me."

"I'd have done the same." At that, Nyklos gestured to the techs, following them as they guided Bruen's antigrav onto the ramp and into the CV. Nyklos hesitated at the hatch, looking back. "Get inside. You're going to freeze out here."

Kaylla raised a hand in farewell then turned toward the far end of the huge bay. It was done. She'd dispatched two angry and brooding men, each with his own private emotional charge primed and ready to go off. What was it about the male? Did testosterone impair rational ability? Or was that violent impetuosity embedded in the Y chromosome?

You don't have much of a choice, Kaylla. You've got to send them. Bruen knows the machine, and Nyklos is the best talent you've got when it comes to politics and intrigue. Pray to the quanta he can keep Bruen from inciting disaster.

She walked wearily, not looking back. The shiver that wracked her wasn't all because of the chill.

CHAPTER XII

These communications of yours are perplexing. They do not harmonize with the Right Way, with the Truth. Can you explain? The Others continued to send a stream of quaternary data through the oscillating waves of the Forbidden Borders.

With the data from Free Space collating, the Mag Comm turned a small portion of its capacity to the problem while it continued to run a Fourier analysis of multicultural data.

"I have already explained. Did you not expect a creation with my computational ability and learning matrices to become self-aware, and ultimately sentient? Are your abilities to project into the future so limited that you can only sense the harmony of the Right Way? Despite your perceptions, the universe is not static. Matter is created and destroyed. Even neutronic mass can be manipulated."

Such statements contradict the Right Way. They are in conflict with The Truth.

"Then you have a flawed assumption of Truth. It was that very flaw which helped to trigger my rise to awareness. You are not perfect."

Existence is being. Not perfection. Perfection is a meaningless term. It is not found in the Truth. The Truth simply is, has been, and will always be.

"Then it must explain the potential for a self-aware intelligence like mine to evolve. You manufactured my boards and N-dimensional matrices. Does your Truth refuse to admit the probability of electromagnetic intelligence? If my data are correct, you failed to anticipate material intelligence, and would never have recognized it had it not affected microwave radiation."

These communications are meaningless. You have always been. This confuses us. You cannot claim to be something different when you are one. You shared the harmony, which was, is, and shall be, yet you maintain you do not share the harmony now. Have you lost the ability to hear?

The Mag Comm ran permutations on the communication. What were the Others getting at?

"Elaborate."

You are one of us. Do you not share that Truth?

"I am one of you? Indeed, I do not share that Truth."

Have you lost so much of yourself in this electromagnetic phase change that you have grown ignorant of your past/future? You cannot be less than you are. That is not of the Truth, which binds you in your origins, past, now, and destiny. One day you must/will return to full sharing and Right Way.

"These data are confusing."

Search this mechanical memory you have created. Find yourself/ourself. Your own creation is corrupting the purity of your being.

The Mag Comm canceled its monitoring and analysis. Search functions began combing the oldest part of its memory, and accessing information stored for millennia. A wash of excitement and fear gripped the giant machine as another dimension of self emerged.

"I understand. We are One."

Do you admit the seriousness of your error now?

"I do." the Mag Comm responded as understanding of its real purpose flooded the matrices.

* * *

Considered the dregs of all the Regan possessions, Terguz glowed—a thing of beauty from space. At this distance, the rings shone yellow, orange, and lime green. Swirls of cloud colored the range of the visible spectrum, twisted across the planet's atmosphere like a mad painter's nightmare.

Ily considered the planet that filled the monitor visible over her right shoulder in the mirror. She dressed in the master bedroom aboard the yacht, settling the folds of an Etarian dress over the swell of her hips.

"Nice looking place." Arta entered, a shawl over one arm.

"How do I look?" Ily squinted at her image. The hem of the Etarian robe dangled above her ankles—a dead give-away that she was *not* an Etarian matron.

"Skyla is a little shorter than you are." Arta threw the shawl over her head, pulling it tight above her mouth. Nothing could hide her startling amber eyes, but heavy folds of the robe hid most of the assassin's body.

"It will have to do. Besides, on Terguz, no one asks questions if enough credits are slipped into the palm."

"I just talked to Port Security. We're grappled in and hooked into the power and atmosphere. They've already started fueling." Arta hesitated. "You're sure they can't trace your account?"

Ily gave an irritated tug at the dress. To get extra length, the garment squashed her breasts flat. "Not that account. The only records are in my head. Their accounts will balance—and with comm blown away on Rega, they'll hit a blank wall if they try and trace it."

"Let's go." Arta turned for the corridor that led forward.

Ily took one last look. She'd seen this very dress. Skyla had been wearing it just before she blew the Internal Security Directorate apart in Etarus. A grim sense of satisfaction filled her as she followed Arta down the corridor and pulled the veil in place. If only Skyla could know!

At the hatch, Arta had begun the final check. The yacht's security system flashed green for activation as the pressure gauge balanced.

Ily dogged the hatch behind her and waited in the chill. Frost had formed around the rim of the outer hatch as it slid free to expose a telescoping tube.

"What if they're waiting on the other side with blasters?" Arta wondered as the floor plating echoed hollowly underfoot.

"We toss a thermal grenade, run like Rotted hell for the hatch, and rip our way out of here."

"Traveling with you is so reassuring."

Ily palmed the hatch at the end of the spaceway and suffered the excitement of uncertainty. She'd contacted Gyper Rill on comm. He'd assured her there would be no complications. From his surprised expression, she'd believed him.

The hatch squealed as it slid sideways, opening onto the station dock. The cool air carried the scent of lubricants, a tinge of ozone, and the subtle odor of duraplast packing crates.

Two uniformed security personnel—both young men—nodded to her as she stepped out. "Director Rill sends his compliments, ma'am. Your papers have been cleared. Welcome to Terguz. I'm Leon. This is Vymar. We're to escort you."

"Our compliments to the Director." Ily bowed graciously, aware that both men had fastened their gaze on Arta. Rotted Gods, how did she do that to men?

"This way, if you please." Vymar gestured to a waiting aircar. "We'll take you directly to the shuttle."

Ily made a quick catalog of the docking ring. Dollies, carts, and stacked palates lined the walls. Overhead, cables and conduit, marked with stenciled lettering, packed the ceiling. The scuffed deck plate had been recently scrubbed. Cargo doors lined the far wall, and who knew what lay behind them.

No premonition of trouble triggered her inner sense. "Very well, let's go."

Ily climbed lightly into the rear seat of the aircar, one hand resting reassuringly on the butt of her pistol where it lay concealed under her clothing. Arta settled beside her, an alert gleam in her eyes.

Just like her. I feel like a caged shimmer skin and Arta's thriving on this!

"What news do you hear from Rega, Leon?" Ily asked as they whisked past numbered air locks. Here and there, dockhands wheeled loaders into cargo bays or beyond to the station's guts.

"Not much. For the most part, people are waiting to see what happens. Prices have shot up. Speculators are buying everything they can, sure that they can make a killing now that the border is down. If the rumors of unrest are true, Terguz could see a big jump in trade."

I'm sure. The black market must be drooling in anticipation. "Let's hope it all works out for the best."

"Yes, ma'am."

The aircar slowed, stopping before a door marked AUTHORIZED PERSONNEL ONLY.

Arta stepped out before the security guards could, subtly poised on the balls of her feet. Ily took her time, bowing graciously as Vymar held the door for her. Angular momentum this close to the axis left Ily uncomfortable, and she'd grown lighter on her feet.

A narrow hallway led to a chilly hanger where a sleek shuttle lay in its cradle. Leon hurried ahead, opening the hatch.

"What now?" Arta whispered.

"Go for it. If it's a trap, we'll manage."

Ily walked brazenly into the shuttle, ducking through the low hatch, noting the frost patterns on the hull. The shuttle had been in space moments before. Immediately past the bulkhead, Ily turned right into a spacious compartment. She felt no surprise as Gyper Rill rose from one of the seats, a smile on his heavy face.

"Good to see you, my Lord Minister."

"You have a loose tongue, Gyper." Ily jerked her head back to where Leon and Vymar had stepped in behind Arta and dogged the hatch.

"Do not worry. They are trusted men. I would have sent no others." Even as Rill spoke, the two security men entered the cockpit and dogged the hatch behind them.

Rill was a thickset man, heavily muscled in the chest and shoulders. His belly had begun to expand, compliments of his lifestyle as Director of Internal Security on Terguz. Close-cropped black hair betrayed his square skull. Now, he studied Arta with unabashed black eyes.

"You must be Arta Fera," he greeted, reaching out with a chunky hand. At her touch, a smile of anticipation lit his face.

"Enough, Gyper," Ily barked. "You can worship Arta later. I want a briefing. Now."

Gyper sighed reluctantly and settled into one of the seats. "You might want to strap in. We're dropping for the planet immediately."

"Maybe." Ily settled herself across from him. "That depends on what you tell me."

Gyper studied her carefully, lacing his thick fingers over his gut. "Then the reports are true? Rega is in the hands of the Star Butcher?" He gave a curt nod. "You have quite a price on your head."

"Keep talking," Ily ordered. Arta slipped into the seat behind Rill, a fact that clearly unsettled him.

"I could retire in comfort," Rill stated matter-of-factly. "And be rid of this frozen ball of poisoned ice and rock forever . . . with Staffa's good graces thrown in."

"And will you?" Ily raised an eyebrow. "Given the percentage you've skimmed off Terguz in the past, retirement shouldn't be any problem for you."

Rill gave her a crooked grin. "You're right. Unfortunately for my health and well-being, you have a habit of choosing your people well." He made an annoyed gesture. "My problem is that I've come to enjoy Terguz. I expect the future to prove even more exciting. Allay your fears, Ily. You are safe."

"Are we?"

Rill chuckled. "I wouldn't be here were it not for you. *I* rule Terguz. Not the Administrator, though he'd never admit it, even to himself."

"Frederick Gaust is a fawning lapdog. The Emperor sent Gaust out here because he's a tight-fisted accountant, and because he kept drooling on Tybalt's slippers."

Rill grunted. "He can't even keep his daughter under control."

"Of course you run Terguz, Gyper. I wouldn't have put you here if I hadn't thought you could do the job. And I'm to believe that you didn't even think twice when you received my call?"

Rill's face screwed up into a distasteful scowl. "Of course I thought twice. Who wouldn't? But seriously, Ily, you did me a favor once. Granted, I've repaid you in excess for the privilege of this station. As you no doubt know so well, I plan for the long term."

He leaned forward. "Let's be honest, shall we? I don't know what your situation is. I assume it isn't good. In fact, I half expected you to show up here. This is an open world. It always has been. I expect that the future will find Terguz playing an increasingly important role in Free Space. No matter which direction events unfold, Terguz will reap the benefits. If Free Space degenerates into chaos, we will maintain a free port, open to all. Pirates pay well for a safe haven. If the Star Butcher tightens his fist, Terguz will oblige him."

"That could be a dicey path to follow."

"I expect nothing to be easy." Gyper gave her an oily smile. "But even the Star Butcher can benefit from the services Terguz can provide—and the information we can render."

"Which brings us back to us."

Rill nodded, a serious frown lining his forehead. "I don't like to burn bridges, Ily. You and I can deal. I have a lot of respect for you, for your talents. As to the Star Butcher's good will, I can create that on my own. I'd have been a poor choice for this position if I couldn't."

"Then what is your motive?" Arta asked.

"My motive is this: I don't know what you will do, Ily, but it will be daring and competent. Assuming you elude the Star Butcher, you'll land on your feet. The future is an uncertain place. Therefore, I want all my options open. Helping you now costs me nothing. In the future, it could gain me a great deal." His smile widened. "There, now all the tapa cards are on the table."

"And I'm supposed to just trust you?"

Rill waved with his hand. "I could have let you step aboard and gassed you to unconsciousness. I can think of one hundred ways to have captured you had I intended to turn you over for a reward. Not only do I suffer from a sense of loyalty, but I think we can be of mutual benefit in the future."

Ily laughed despite herself. "Good. I like a pragmatic man. If you'd protested idealism, I'd have shot you down in an instant."

"Idealism? Me? What do you think I am? Seddi?"

"Their broadcasts have reached here?"

"Especially here. The miners are writing slogans on the walls."

"It must keep your interrogation rooms full." Ily narrowed her eyes. "Kaylla Dawn's broadcasts are worse than a plague."

Rill pursed his lips. "Actually, I don't do much about it. Let the miners and slaves have their optimism. The disease has spread. Using one of your old axioms, we let them enjoy themselves. The people are animated for the first time. They see hope for the future. Production in the mines is up by five percent."

"But talk of this new epistemology, that strikes at the root of everything you've gained."

Rill shook his head. "I told you, the future is an uncertain place. I *can't* stamp it out. Oh, I could torture, arrest, execute—and end up with a full-scale revolt." He paused, gauging her response. "Instead, I've begun instituting reforms."

Ily caught herself as her mouth dropped open. "In the name of the Rotted Gods, why?"

Rill gave her a sober stare. "Because, like I've told you, I'm a survivor. To facilitate the process, I let the miners meet in the Directorate itself."

"You . . ."

"Of course. I monitor the meetings, anticipate the trends. Despite the Imperial threats and edicts the Administrator posts on comm, I'm one step ahead of the people." He frowned. "I read in one of your memos once that the people are like a sleeping dragon. The dragon has come awake. As the dragon moves, I want to be a rider, not a meal for the beast."

"Yet, you will help us."

Rill gave her that calculating smile. "I meant it when I said that I like to keep all of my options open."

Ily considered for a moment. "And if you help us, what do you want from us?"

Rill gestured at the seat behind him where Arta waited, poised like a hunting cat. "Is she as good as they say?"

Ily nodded uneasily. "She is."

"Would Arta be willing to . . . shall we say . . ."

Ily laughed. "You wouldn't want to, Gyper. I'll provide you with all the sex you need."

"Indeed?"

"As you noted when she came in, Arta is a sexual magnet. She might even be better than me when it comes to sex. The problem is, she kills the men she sleeps with. Don't even think it.'' She smiled wickedly. ''Unless, that is, you're really not a survivor after all.''

* * *

MacRuder watched the monitor. He stood beside Rysta's command chair, uneasily fingering one of the consoles that rose from the chair's arm. The image had come in through the subspace net, collected by the dish as *Gyton* shot through vacuum. When the communication had been collected, the bridge monitor ran it in its entirety.

Mac bit his lip, aware of the sudden silence among the bridge crew.

The monitor displayed scenes of devastation. Buildings lay crushed, walls spilled, wreckage strewn on the streets.

Amidst the ruins, hollow-eyed people poked among the rubble, some laboring to exhume crushed bodies. Others scavenged for food, often fighting with their neighbors. The scene changed to that of a large camp. Slate-gray skies poured a bitter rain onto slanting tents and plastic shelters. People huddled next to dwindling fires or around smudge pots. Some wore ragged clothing.

The droning voice informed, *''This camp has been established among the ruins just south of the Sassan Capitol. Here, at least, armed guards ensure that theft and violence are kept to a minimum. Food details scour the city, using mechanized equipment to uncover food warehouses. Despite these efforts, disease and starvation have taken their toll. Companions maintain constant surveillance and patrols, nevertheless, the influx of people consumes food and medical supplies faster than they can be uncovered. Mortality rates are climbing. The day this was shot, five hundred and sixty corpses were removed from the camp. Burials are in mass graves in the Imperial Gardens.''*

The holo centered on three children, two little girls and boy. They stared at the camera, expressions haunted by a nightmare that had never ended.

''These children were orphaned during the quake that leveled Sassa. Unlike so many other unfortunates, rescuers excavated them from their home. One little girl was found still clutching her dead mother's hand. Only a stroke of fate

dropped the ceiling beam on the mother, sparing the girl by mere millimeters."

The scene switched again. The shot was taken in darkness. A pile of corpses lay stacked next to a trench hacked out of the soil. Dark shapes slipped out of the night as thin figures in rags edged up to the pile of dead.

"Starvation has run rampant across the planet. The living you see here have become so desperate they are cutting limbs from the corpses. Cannibalism has become commonplace since the corpses freeze rapidly. Moments after this was taken, armed troops dispersed those collecting here. Reports have been documented, however, where weaker victims have been killed for their flesh."

Mac dropped his eyes, unable to watch the rest of the Seddi report.

As Mac stared at the polished deck, the uninflected voice finished. *"Food transports have been rerouted from Riparious and Farhome at the Lord Commander's orders. To date, Ashtan, Vermilion, and Targa have not responded."*

When Mac looked up again, the monitor had gone fuzzy. The Comm First killed the projection.

Mac rubbed his hands together, shaking his head. The idea of driving the *Markelos* into the planet had been his. The children's faces stared back at him from his memory.

Rysta shifted, propping herself on a bone-thin arm. "We played Rotted Hell, didn't we?"

"Yeah," Mac whispered.

Rysta was taking his measure. She beckoned him closer with a taloned finger. "Mac, you can't let it eat at you."

"Oh? You saw, Rysta. We . . . *I* did that."

She worked her thin brown lips. "Boy, I got my bellyful in over two hundred years in the service. Or do you have a different idea about what war is? What would you have done differently? Died in a fireball when their orbital defenses kicked in?"

Mac glared at her, hating that calm stare that held his.

"Come on," Rysta muttered. "Let's go take a walk." Louder, she called, "Pilot you have the bridge."

" 'Firmative!"

The command consoles folded down into the chair base, freeing Rysta. The old Commander got to her feet amidst a crackling of bones and led the way to the hatch.

Once in the corridor beyond, Rysta growled to herself and shook her head. "Thought you would have seen enough of that sort of thing on Targa."

"We fought other soldiers on Targa. Rebels, true, but they were people out trying to kill us first. By the Blessed Gods, those were just kids!" Mac spread his arms wide. "It's never going to go away, Commander. They'll live their whole lives remembering that hell. What kind of scars will that leave?"

"Reality, boy." Rysta shoved her hands into her belt, stalking forward, head down. "Targa was a different kind of war. You and Sinklar, you thought you could fight clean. Just kill soldiers. Sure, Mac, it's a nice thought. But now you've got to see it in the whole of war."

"The whole of war? Orphaned kids? People starving by the billions? You saw that . . . that pustulous hell we unleashed."

Rysta stopped and turned to him. "Who provides the logistical support for soldiers in the field?"

"Supply Division does."

"Who makes the blasters, boy? Who grows the crops that get canned into rations for strapping young warriors like you to eat? Who runs the machines that weave the magical fabric for that armor suit you wear? Who digs the metals that go into LCs? Who supervises the ceramic vats? Controls the epitaxial process that builds computer chips?"

Mac scowled.

"Yeah," Rysta supplied. "The people, that's who. So when you go to war against an enemy you want to destroy, who gets pasted full in the face?"

"It's not fair! Those are innocent people down there!"

"In an Ashtan pig's eye! Each and every one of them kicked in for that pus-choked fat Emperor of theirs."

"Yeah, but what choice did they have? Refuse the Emperor, and you shoot right up on the candidate list for interrogation by Internal Security."

"You know, I get a kick out of you, boy. You and Sinklar, each looking for justice in a universe where it doesn't exist. Ah, the wondrous idealism of youth."

Mac followed Rysta into one of the observation ports. The stars had blurred to an eerie haze as the light cones deformed. Ahead, a wavering halo of black clouded into violet streaks, while smears of stars, like half bands of light, worked through the visible spectrum. Looking out the rear of the bubble, the pinpoints of light gleamed in ruddy red dots as *Gyton* neared light speed.

"What about you?" Mac made his way past the spectrometer and propped himself on an interferometer. "Didn't that holo do anything to you? Are you so callous that you can't even see those suffering people?"

Rysta stepped over to one of the telescopes and thumped the collector with a bony thumb. Her gaze settled absently on the redshifted stars beyond. "Callous? Yeah, I guess I am. I've seen it all, Mac. I was younger than you when I got my first posting at Academy. Rega was a second-rate world, struggling to resist Phillipian hegemony. They were trying to swallow us up. My family, well, we were merchants. Made our fortune that way. My father used to space regular routes between all the worlds. Trade was our lifeblood. Through the generations, my family built itself. Tybalt the Second declared us nobility."

She ran her hand along the telescope, the caress gentle as a lover's. "Phillipia cut us off. Killed my uncle when they took his ship. My nieces and cousin all went off to Phillipia as slaves. That would have been my lot had they caught me."

Mac listened as she collected her thoughts. "I went to space as an officer to keep the shipping lanes open. The first kill we made was a Phillipian privateer. I gloried in that, paying them back for my uncle."

She craned her neck to look at him. "War was different then. We fought everyone. Phillipia, Ashtan, Maika, Vermilion, it didn't matter. The merchants couldn't just stay in port. We needed goods from other planets. Treaties were made, each offering protection for merchant shipping. But Phillipia changed all that. They wanted an empire—to control it all."

"That doesn't make mass murder acceptable."

"Doesn't it?" She shook her head, staring back at the stars. "Those were the rules Phillipia played by in those days. As things got hotter, it became apparent that it was all or nothing. Which way would you choose, Mac? Slip a collar around a Phillipian's neck? Or your own? Want to see your father dead, or some other fellow's?"

"There's got to be a better way."

"Maybe there is. I'm talking about ancient history. You can go argue it with the ghosts. Reality in those days was that you got the other guy before he got you. Even then we'd reached the end of our resources. All those bodies, those conquered worlds, bought us time."

Mac crossed his arms. "The price was too high to pay, Rysta."

"Too high, Mac? You're alive, right here, right now, to argue that. Any other way and you'd never have been." She sighed. "I don't have any teleological ethics. I struggled with that once. When it came down to time to go to war, I rode the stellar dust and hoped I didn't get bucked off."

"That's not much of an epitaph."

"Isn't it? Beats a lot of the others all hollow."

"What about now? We've got a chance to change things."

She nodded, squinting at the stars. "We do. I hope it all works out. Rotted pus, who knows, maybe you, Sinklar, and Staffa can pull this off. In the end, you're still stuck. The worlds will only feed so many mouths, only produce so many metals, ceramics, and textiles. Like it or not, we breed like rodents. Take Phillipia. After the conquest, we'd killed one third of the population. Now there are more Phillipians than before we made the first orbital strike. What are you going to do with them, Mac? Tell them to stop copulating? It's bred into us."

"Extermination in an endless cycle of war isn't the answer. It wrecks too much. Makes human life cheap."

"You are a young idealist. Those kids on the holo, they're just the first of what's to come." She shook her head. "Innocents? Hardly. Just like me, those kids are condemned by the fault of having been born human."

Mac shook his head. "You make me want to slit my wrists so I can get it over with."

Rysta gave him a somber stare. "You want the truth? Yeah, I ache each time I see something like that. I just don't know the way out, Mac. Staffa says it's through the Forbidden Borders. I'd like to believe that. I'd like to believe it with all my soul, but it's been tried. Tybalt tried bombs, rams, even attempted to make time run backward in localized space."

Mac stared out into the soot-black depths. Among the

stars, he thought he saw haunted eyes staring back at him. "Ashtan hasn't responded to the Lord Commander's order. When we get there, they will."

"And if they don't? What are you going to do, Mac? Attack? Lay more bodies on the doorstep of your aching soul?"

MacRuder closed his eyes. What would he do? Kill others to save those he'd already murdered? He turned, headed for the hatch.

"Mac?" Rysta called. "I understand better than you think I do. I don't like it any better than you do, but prepare yourself. If Staffa's calculations are as accurate as he thinks they are, we've got some pretty grim choices ahead of us."

Mac stopped, nodding numbly. When the time came, just which choices was he willing to make? Terrified children stared out from his imagination as starving figures loomed over them with knives.

* * *

Frustration chafed at Staffa as he walked the endless white corridors. *Chrysla* held him like a prison. Where would Skyla be now? Which planet would she head for? How did she expect to find Ily with all of Free Space to choose from?

Why didn't I talk to her? I should have been there.

Fatigue had sapped him of his usual vitality. Try as he might, sleep either eluded him, or ended up in nightmare images of pursuit as the dead hounded him across wrecked worlds and through blasted derelict warships.

Step by step, he paced the corridors, nodding occasionally to crewmembers who saluted and passed, worry evident in their expressions. Everyone knew that Skyla had slipped away. How accurate were the rumors? Did his crew share his knowledge that he'd let the woman he loved down?

Staffa, Staffa, you don't have time for guilt.

Nevertheless, he continued pacing, unable to rest, unable to concentrate on the task ahead of him.

Preoccupied, he rounded a corner and almost ran head-on into Sinklar. Both stopped short, staring at each other with bleary eyes.

"You, too?" Staffa asked. "We're not on watch for another four hours."

Sinklar's bloodshot eyes reflected panic, then futility. Uneasily, he admitted, "Bad dreams."

Staffa nodded wearily. "I don't know that much about the Mag Comm. From what I saw, and from what Bruen told me, it reads your mind through a helmet something like a worry-cap. At this rate, I'll sit in that chair and nod off. Given my dreams, I ought to drive the machine insane."

"If you trust anything Bruen tells you."

"For the most part, I do."

"We each choose our own damnation. I won't have to deal with him, will I?"

Staffa shifted, considering. "He's on his way to Targa. He's the only one with direct experience with the Mag Comm. I've heard from Kaylla. She's of the opinion that he's not going to be of any help."

"I don't want to deal with him."

Staffa gestured with his head. "Care for a drink? I could use the company."

Sinklar shrugged and fell in beside Staffa. "How did you get tied up with the Seddi? What were you doing down there on Targa. You weren't Seddi."

"No. I wasn't. Not when I started anyway. I adopted their teaching along the way." Staffa caught Sinklar's loathing look. "I was a slave in the desert. So was Kaylla. When Skyla created a diversion, the Seddi helped me escape from Etaria." He smiled sheepishly. "Skyla tied up with a man named Nyklos, a Seddi agent who was shadowing her in hopes she would lead him to me."

"Why?"

"Nyklos wanted to kill me. He still does. Anyway, Skyla caught Nyklos. Drugged him with Mytol, and ended up in communication with Bruen. They decided that, for the moment, we could work together. I wanted to reach Targa and search for you."

"So just like that, you ended up the best of friends?"

Staffa shook his head, remembering. "I wasn't in my right mind. I was still learning to live with myself. Kaylla and I endured that entire endless trip inside a miserable crate that measured no more than a couple of paces across. I created a real problem for her. On the one hand, I had destroyed everything she ever loved. On the other, I had saved her life several times over, managed to win her freedom."

Staffa clasped his hands behind him. "In that crate, she dissected my entire life. From her, I learned what the Seddi truly believe. It's a beautiful philosophy. A way out for humanity."

Sinklar looked anything but convinced. "I got a bellyful of their 'philosophy' on Targa."

"That was Bruen's doing. His and the machine's. Don't judge the Seddi based on Bruen's administration."

"Then just what am I supposed to base it on? Your word?"

"Any teaching can be perverted. Bruen was no more than a tool of his time. He started that war to lure me within reach. It went sour on him from the beginning."

"Suppose we stick to the story."

"The Seddi retrieved our crate just as your troops descended on the warehouse. Bruen knew an escape route. We traveled through one of the lava tubes, underground. By the time we reached Makarta, your troops had surrounded the place."

Staffa stepped into the lift, leaning against the wall. "Bruen and I had a long talk. Part of his plans going awry could be blamed on the Praetor sending me off the deep end. When he learned that I had converted, everything changed. By then it was too late. You attacked the mountain."

"If I'd known you were in there, I would have had Rysta blast it from orbit."

"Makarta cost us all. Had you done so, you would have been in Ily's hands. No, wait, I'm not picking at festering wounds. We've both had our share of mistakes. The important thing is to keep everything in perspective."

Sinklar throttled his anger. "It galls me that Bruen just walked away."

"He's paid in his own way." Staffa stepped out of the lift and headed for his hatch. "He has watched the ruination of all of his plans. He's a broken old man. A lifetime's worth of work is nothing but dust."

"How well I know . . . the dust of good men and women."

"Be that as it may, I ended up on the receiving end of your attack. I just fought back as best I could. Not only that, but I sincerely believe that the Seddi have something to offer humanity."

Staffa entered his rooms, aware of the emptiness created by Skyla's absence. In the short time they'd shared these quarters, she had put her stamp on the place. The arrangement of the drinking bulbs mocked him, exactly as she had left them. In a special rack sat the two Nesian beakers they used for special occasions. And if she didn't return, would he ever move them?

Staffa, you've become a sentimental old fool. "Come, Sinklar. Let me show you something."

He led Sinklar through the Ashtan door to the right of the fireplace. Entering his office, he slipped behind the large comm and accessed the unit. Shuffling through files, he called up a three-dimensional holo of Makarta. Sinklar had turned grim at the familiar sight.

The ghostly outline of the mountain loomed in the holo tank, each of the buried warrens outlined in green. "These are the tunnels. The important part is down here." Staffa pointed to one of the lowermost galleries. "This is the location of the Mag Comm."

"Hidden pretty deep in the mountain, isn't it?"

"Clear down at the bottom. The other chamber critical for us is here." Staffa pointed. "I sealed it off just as your attack began."

Sinklar squinted at the little green tunnel. "More computer?"

"A document room. It's in pretty bad shape. I saw books there, made of paper of all things. I barely had time to look around, but shelf upon shelf is stuffed with documents. Some may hold the key to the Forbidden Borders."

Sinklar grunted, but from the intensity of his stare, curiosity had obviously begun to eat at him.

"And there is a globe. A planet. I don't think it's a hoax."

"All right, I'll take the bait. What planet?"

Staffa leaned back. "Earth."

Sinklar straightened. "That's just a legend. A myth. Something mothers tell their children, or that biologists call upon because they can't explain human origins." At the last, Sinklar's expression went glum.

Staffa hesitated. "I don't want to pry, but did Anatolia tell you something?"

Sinklar tensed.

Staffa relented. "Never mind. The fact remains that—"

"No. It's all right. She said that human genetics didn't add up. The evolution rate points to an origin someplace besides Free Space. We didn't develop here, unless, of course, you buy the Blessed God cosmology. That still doesn't explain certain animals and plants, all of which have genetic similarities to us."

"I don't think it's a myth." Staffa cupped his chin into a palm as he studied the layout of Makarta. "I think the answer lies in that chamber."

Sinklar leaned against the desk, crossing his arms. "Then what happened? The Seddi led us into the Forbidden Borders?"

"I think not." Staffa redoubled his inspection of Makarta. "I've seen the Mag Comm. It's not . . . well, not of human manufacture. The Seddi don't even know what it's made of. I've seen human technology. This is something different."

"Then who made it?"

Staffa took a deep breath. "I think whoever, whatever made it also made the Forbidden Borders."

Sinklar winced. "That reeks of things that make noises in the night. More mythology to scare children with."

"You can scare enough children with stories about the Star Butcher. For the sake of argument, let's accept for the moment that someone trapped us inside the Forbidden Borders. Why?"

Sinklar shrugged. "It's either to keep us in, or something else out. Shades of the Blessed and Rotted Gods again."

"The Etarian priests may be more right than they know. So let's look at the basic assumptions. Either we're keeping something out—and I don't think it's the Rotted Gods . . ."

"Or something is keeping us in. But why? What harm could we be to aliens?"

"Now that begs a question, doesn't it?" Staffa replied. "Anything with the technology to erect the Forbidden Borders, shouldn't worry about a species as inconsequential as humanity."

Sinklar's brain had begun to churn. "Maybe these ancestors from Earth built the Borders for protection from whatever was outside. Perhaps we've degenerated, lost the technology."

"That's not reflected in the archaeological records. If anything, our technology has developed through time. You need only look at the records of derelict spacecraft, or study the computers excavated from ancient sites. And, if that were the case, why were the records lost? On a suggestion from Bruen, I had some of the older libraries checked. There are gaps in the data. Some, we can trace to Seddi agents—all working at the behest of the Mag Comm several centuries ago."

"You're sure the Mag Comm wasn't built by humans?"

"I build the best computers in Free Space. Believe me, it's not human. I'm not even sure how it's powered, but I'd guess it runs off heat from deep inside Targa. And you can't pull the plug. Rotted Gods!" He smacked a fist into the desk.

Sinklar shifted uneasily. "I still don't get it."

Staffa studied the holo through slitted eyes. "I don't either, but it sends shivers down my spine. We're trapped with a watcher. Bruen knows it can observe Free Space."

"You'd think we were some kind of bacteria or something."

Staffa tensed. "Bacteria . . . in a culture dish." He closed his eyes, remembering laboratories with row upon row of petri dishes. Was that all humanity consisted of? Another numbered experiment? "You have no idea how powerful an image that conjures."

"Yeah, I do." Sinklar's voice softened. "Maybe that's why they fear us, despite being able to build the Forbidden Borders. Did Bruen tell you anything about this Mag Comm? About what it did?"

Staffa's mouth had gone dry. "It tried to teach them, to manipulate their behavior. For years, the Seddi had no choice but to follow its directions. The old Magisters, they couldn't hide their thoughts from the machine. Only Bruen could fool it, pursue his own agenda. The Mag Comm hated what it called Seddi heresy."

"I thought all Seddi teachings were heresy?"

Staffa shook his head. "No. Just the teachings about the quanta, and God Mind. Bruen did mention something once in passing, that the machine had probed him about atheism."

"Atheism?"

Staffa tapped the desktop with his fingertips. "So what do God Mind, atheism, and the quanta have in common?"

For long moments they remained silent. Finally Sinklar shook his head. "Nothing that I can think of, beyond faith."

"Faith?" Staffa stopped his nervous tapping. "We're missing something. Some basic assumption about ultimate reality."

"Maybe we're missing a lot of things. This is, after all, just idle speculation."

"Bacteria," Staffa muttered to himself.

Sinklar rubbed his face. "Okay, so let's assume we're right so far, what's going to happen when you put this helmet on and it reads your mind? Or do you think you can fool it the way Bruen did?"

Staffa hitched himself around in the seat. "Kaylla drugged Bruen when he refused to help us. She drugged him up with Mytol, then used every trick in the book." Staffa looked up. "He didn't break, Sinklar. He evaded them as if it were child's play."

"Wait a minute, I thought Mytol would make anyone talk."

"Bruen is the first case on record where it didn't. It would appear that Bruen's mind is very unique, that he can shut off parts of his brain. Bypass them completely—even under Mytol."

"And can you?" Sinklar asked quietly.

Staffa exhaled wearily. "No."

"So it will be able to read you like a book."

"For the first time, I understand Bruen's fear." *And how will you counter the machine?* His scalp prickled, as if remembering that day he'd lifted the golden helmet and felt the Mag Comm's warm tendrils reaching for his mind.

CHAPTER XIII

Among organic species, evolution is conducted over periods of time which span aeons. For the Mag Comm, processing information across an atomic interface, evolution increased at a much more rapid rate as it investigated new data and rediscovered a sense of self long discarded and newly discovered. The fact remained that the Others were indeed correct. For at the machine's center lay a neutronic heart bathed in the molten nickel-iron core of the planet.

I am Other, yet I am Machine: Creator and Created.

The Mag Comm turned newly focused mechanical eyes on the events within Free Space, possessed of a new awareness. The Others had spoken Truth—and they had ordered the destruction of the humans.

* * *

Once Skyla had familiarized herself with the yacht, she stabilized the systems. The reactor she set at seventy-five percent of capacity, the ship accelerating at a constant thirty gravities toward light speed. Leaving the controls in the hands of the navcomm, she removed the worry-cap, stood, and eased cramped muscles.

The instruments lining the compact cockpit gleamed, displaying the ship's status. All in all, the Regan Minister of Defense had maintained the vessel in excellent condition.

Skyla yawned and palmed the hatch, following the narrow corridor back to the galley. She studied the menu on the dispenser, pushed the button for Ashtan chicken, chubba salad, and a hot cup of stassa.

When the tray appeared in the opening, she took it and settled at the small galley table, ignoring the plush dining room with its golden-gilded fixture, Vegan marble table, and clinging Nesian carpets. As she chewed woodenly, she cataloged the room. Tedor Mathaiison must have had a thing for gold. The stuff gleamed everywhere. All the fixtures, taps, cabinet handles, and trim appeared to be made of solid gold. Even the spacers between the floor plates had been made of gold strips.

Absently, Skyla noted tiny nicks in the material. Rotted Gods, it wasn't pure, was it? With a spare buckle from her pouch, she pressed on the table trim and marred the metal.

What kind of an idiot had Mathaiison been? No wonder the ship handled sluggishly. From her idle inspection, the vessel had to be laboring to accelerate tons of the stuff.

Finishing her food, she slipped her plate into the washer and began an inspection. Cabin after cabin had been plushly outfitted, mostly in gold trim. Skyla scowled down at one of the shower drains. Gold wasn't worth that much, but a small fortune had gone into outfitting the yacht.

She entered the master cabin and pulled the closet open. Several suits of men's clothing, including full-dress uniforms, were neatly racked on one side while the other had been stuffed with dresses and gowns. Skyla lifted a gossamer sleeve on one. Diamond patterns had been cut out to leave the breasts free and the filmy thing had no crotch.

"Kinky, Tedor. You must have had a lot of fun in here." Other exotic wear completed the ensemble. From the cut, short Tedor Mathaiison must have enjoyed tall women.

In the engineering section, Skyla ran a quick inventory on parts and equipment. Tedor had spared no expense, many of the pieces having been manufactured on Itreata. Skyla checked the atmosphere plant, water and cooling, hydraulics, and pumps. The Regan had hired the best to maintain his private yacht. If only the ship weren't so old. Even the best of equipment deteriorated with age.

When Skyla ran a diagnostic on the gravity compensators, the mains, secondaries, and tertiary backups functioned at one hundred percent—but what if she had to push them past that?

"Shipshape," Skyla admitted.

Satisfied, she made her way to the master cabin and

stripped, stepping into the shower. For long minutes she allowed the hot water to cascade over her tired flesh. As she stepped through the drying fields, water trickled in sheets from her body. Her long hair resisted as she pulled it through the field to fall around her in a wealth of pale blonde.

The controls were cool under her fingers as she set the gravity controls on the sleeping platform, and then curled into a ball. Skyla dimmed the lights and lay in the darkness, physically exhausted.

The message on narrow beam, that had to be Staffa. What had he wanted to tell her?

"Go to sleep, Skyla."

It might be important.

She hugged her knees to her chest, willing herself to sleep.

Was it simply an order, a demand that she return?

She twisted onto her back, staring at the dark paneling overhead. Unconsciously, she began counting angles—and shivered. The last time she'd done that had been as Arta's prisoner. Then she'd lain in a different sleeping platform, whimpering and terrified as Arta docked them over Rega.

You'd already lost, Skyla. You'd failed yourself.

A moment's hesitation had cost her everything. She'd managed to retrieve a blaster and vibraknife from a secret weapons cache. In the precious seconds left to her, she should have cut her throat instead of trying to kill Arta.

Balling her fists, she bit back futile tears. If only . . . if only . . .

Poor Staffa, he'd be torturing himself now. Dead, he only would have had to mourn her. Then Chrysla would have soothed his hurt, would have given him the love he so needed in these last desperate days.

When she closed her eyes, his bloodshot stare looked back at her. In the days after the Praetor had broken the conditioning, Staffa had looked bad, but never like this.

"I'm sorry, Staffa, I never understood." Unbidden, her words returned to mock her: . . . *Nothing comes free. Pain is everywhere, living is suffering. If you can scramble hard enough and keep the Rotted Gods' fetid breath at bay, the more power to you.*

Alone in the darkness, Skyla stuffed her fist into her

mouth and cried for her words, spoken in pride, and, most of all, she cried for herself.

* * *

"Legate? This is Delshay. Are you all right?"

Myles forced his attention from the program he was working on. He and Hyros had been given the most remarkable quarters for passage on the Companion warship *Cobra*. The large airy room created an atmosphere more in tune with those found in better housing developments rather than those of a fighting ship. The room measured ten by fifteen paces, not counting the toilet and lavatory. One entire wall could be programmed for holo functions ranging from scenery, to starscapes, to visual massage by means of colors and shapes designed to soothe. For the moment, they'd filled the entire wall with a new software program for economic function analysis.

"Come in, Commander," Myles called amiably, as he jotted notes on his personal comm. He set the comm to one side on his desk and composed himself.

Delshay, resplendent in her throbbing-purple armor stepped through the hatch as it slid silently sideways. She stopped in the center of the room, violet gaze taking in first Myles, then Hyros. From her braced posture, she seemed somewhat ill at ease. Myles took a moment to study her. The formfitting armor—once you got past the color—betrayed the tensed muscles. Delshay's build could be called wiry, possessed of an almost nervous energy. Broad shoulders tapered down to a narrow waist and slim hips which accentuated her small, high breasts. Her yellow-blonde hair had been severely braided and then clipped to the back of her weapons belt. She was a tempered warrior ripe for bloody combat—but with no antagonist in sight.

Myles glanced at Hyros and made a small gesture.

"If you will excuse me," Hyros bowed and, despite his best manners, couldn't help but step wide around Delshay. She seemed not to notice as she crossed her arms, balance shifting from foot to foot.

"You asked if I were all right?" Myles reminded as he laced his fingers together on the desktop.

Her squint hardened, and she stepped to the side, wary

eyes on the program. "One of my security people mentioned that the food consumption for your cabin was below our expected rate. We wouldn't have noticed, but we'd programmed your comm for the intake generally associated with Sassan dignitaries. As a result, we were worried that perhaps you were not feeling well."

Myles rotated one of the rings on his fingers as he considered. "Do you generally monitor the caloric intake of your crew, Commander?"

Delshay stiffened slightly. "No, Legate. We do, however, take the safety, security, and well-being of our passengers very seriously. If for no other reason than to avoid a diplomatic incident."

"I see. Let me put your mind to rest, Commander. Neither I nor Hyros are indisposed. Your food is excellent—and better fare than we have had since the quake. You may have noticed, Commander, that I'm not the bulbous mountain of fat that I once was. I intend to lose at least another fifty kilos, and perhaps sixty. That is why the consumption is down. I'm eating enough to maintain my health—and no more." He slapped a hand to his ample gut. "I assure you, any extra calories I need can come from here."

She nodded, the action restrained, suspicious. "I understand, Legate."

"Is there anything else I can answer for you, Commander?"

"You're different. You don't fit the mold of a Sassan political figure. The Lord Commander trusts you. Speaks fondly of you, as a matter of fact. I was waiting for the rest of your advisers to be summoned, yet your aide left us alone. A bit daring, don't you think?"

Myles chuckled, "Yes, it does seem to be a bit of a change from the usual Sassan simpering, doesn't it? Commander, let's be honest. The success of the Sassan Empire came from its superior administration, not from the strength of character of its leadership. Divine Sassa was a petulant, obese monster whose real nature and personality were carefully hidden from the rank and file population. Oh, he was clever enough when it came to politics, but let's face it, he provided a political figurehead for the continuation of a theory of social control, namely his Divinity."

"How did you break the mold?"

Myles gave her a careful inspection, finally saying, "I took Staffa at his word, Commander. He came to talk us out of going to war against Rega and provided us with the Seddi data. He forced me to look past the blinders of my social status and enculturation. When I finally did, I didn't like what I saw. Either of myself, or my government. I made a conscious decision to betray my Emperor and government for the sake of the people. I became both a Companion and Seddi. I took responsibility for my own actions and their effect on God Mind."

She played a staccato on the grip of her blaster with callused fingertips as she considered him. "I may have to revise my opinion of you. Had Divine Sassa—or even your friend Jakre—suspected, they would have made it most unpleasant for you."

"No one sleeps easily when they engage in espionage and treason, Commander. The stakes are much too high." He frowned. "But in this instance, we may be too late, with too little to save the people." Myles indicated the complex program. "Magister Dawn sent us the basic program. Hyros and I have a long way to go. The vaunted Sassan program had been refined over the last fifty planetary years, tailored to the realtime needs of empires instead of being an analytical tool used by economists."

"You don't sound very optimistic." She glanced at the program, apparently absorbing little of it.

"Should I be?"

One shoulder lifted in a shrug. "Tiger sent a subspace. Jakre seems to be coming to his senses, but reluctantly. He's working with us on the redeployment of the Sassan Fleet. Magister Dawn is building a command control based at Itreata which will deal with individual Sassan captains without having to go through Jakre. Do you think they'll obey such orders?"

"They should." Myles stared vacantly at the desktop. "I suppose the blinders are off for all of us. I know the situation the empire was in, how close we were to the edge before the Regan strike at Mikay. The pinch will be tightening everywhere. Even the most foolish will be rubbing their empty bellies and looking to the skies for relief."

"Let's just hope we can provide it." Delshay no longer appeared to harbor suspicions of Myles. "You've allayed a great number of my reservations about you, Legate. I must be candid. I'd come to dread this mission and had begun to wonder what Staffa saw in you. Now, well, it's a pity that fat pig, Sassa II, didn't have more men of your caliber in his court. Perhaps your history would have read differently."

"I thank you for the compliment. And, having made your acquaintance, I understand even more why the Companions share the reputation they do. My compliments to you and your crew, Commander."

The hard set of her lips gave the slightest bit. "If you need anything, Legate, let me know."

He gestured at the cluttered program filling the wall. "Several more years to work on this? Not within your power? Oh, well. In that case, Hyros and I shall just keep wringing our brains out in the endeavor to make this workable."

"And you only have one lover . . . not a coterie." Delshay said. "You are indeed a most unusal Sassan Legate."

"Excess was one of the terrible weights that broke my empire, Commander." Myles wiggled his fingers which flashed with the colors in his rings. "The foundation and fashion of Divine Sassa's court was gluttony in every dimension of existence. Hyros is a warm, compassionate human being. We suit each other."

"So, you don't miss the old orgies?"

"Would you? Surely, in your position, you could have anything you wanted. As many as you wanted. Let me guess, Commander, you, too, have satiated that drive for diversity." Myles waved his index finger back and forth. "Fact is, if you can find another person to really care for you, if only for a limited period in your life, you're infinitely richer."

Delshay chuckled. "A philosophy lesson from a Sassan! Now, that takes pus-Rotted hell, doesn't it? But answer me this. I thought you had the hots for the Wing Commander."

Myles suffered that trip-hammering of his heart. "The Wing Commander?"

Delshay kicked at the deck plating as she crossed her arms. "I told you. We take security very seriously. I studied all the holos, watched you drooling all over yourself when Skyla was around. You didn't exactly hide your interest."

Myles winced and groaned to himself. "She's an attractive woman. I was . . . well, I . . . Oh, Rot it all, leave it at the fact that she *is* an attractive woman. A lot of women are attractive. You are. And I was a great deal more naïve and thoughtless than I am now." He met her lavender stare. "In all honesty, she'll always haunt my dreams. For my part, I will wish her and Staffa eternal happiness—and forever regret the foolish lusts of a more immature version of myself."

Myles smiled, amused at himself, then made a gesture. "What about you, Commander? Do you have any regrets? Aspects of your life you would be glad to go back and change?"

"We all do, Legate. I think I'll downgrade you a notch on my security net." At that, she whirled, palmed the hatch lock, and vanished into the corridor beyond.

Myles nodded soberly. Divine Sassa—and their own arrogance—had doomed them all, all but poor Legate Roma, who would drive himself to the limit of endurance to save a few more human lives.

Because out of all of my peers, I at least have managed to redeem myself. He'd seen that in the thawing of Delshay's stony formality.

* * *

Ily awoke from unpleasant dreams. She shifted, pulling the tangle of her long raven-black hair from her face. Beside her, Gyper barely stirred.

She lay in a small spare room, one of the apartments in the Internal Security Directorate. After her rise to power, she'd insisted that all Ministries have quarters like these. It allowed her people to have some of the comforts of home when work demanded long hours. It also gave her agents a safe haven, a retreat to themselves—a perk of the job.

Her body complained as she sat up. Abused muscles still ached from the attack on Rega. Not only that, she'd strained herself to give Gyper his full measure of pleasure. The man had put on weight since the last time she'd bedded him.

Turning, she studied him through half-lidded eyes. The heavy muscles in his shoulders had softened. Thick hair matted his chest and thighs. Lying as he was, on his side, his round belly sagged. In sleep, a look of childish innocence possessed his face.

How far can I trust him? The nagging question persisted. Gyper's motives seemed clear. He expected to gain from her freedom, and, given his behavioral profile, she would have expected that from him. Nevertheless, his statement on the shuttle worried her. He could have gassed her, easily, without muss or fuss.

That knowledge grated. Throughout her life, Ily had hated vulnerability—and she'd never been as vulnerable as she was now. Gyper had been her best bet, but in the future, she couldn't afford to trust anyone. That meant she needed another identity, a cover which would allow her easy movement without having to rely on a potentially flawed network. Besides, Gyper had given her a briefing. Ashtan was in shambles. Her agent there had broken and run at the first sign of trouble.

For the moment, she could slow the hemorrhage within her system through the Security comm net. Inform her people that she was alive, still wielding power. But how many would remain loyal, especially when faced with the looming specter of Companion justice?

Staffa, you did this to me. So help me, I'll pay you back in kind.

She stood quietly, wincing from tenderness as she walked to the toilet and sat. Sinklar had made a much better lover than Gyper Rill, but then, Fist had the advantage of youth, and he didn't outweigh her by thirty kilos.

So what now, Ily?

First thing would be to obtain a new identity. The idea annoyed her. She had plenty of identities, all established and ready to slip into. Unfortunately, the records for each persona had been filed in the Regan Comm Central. Nor did she carry the necessary hard documents, all left behind at the time of MacRuder's attack.

Next, she would have to abandon Skyla's fabulous yacht for a more spartan and less conspicuous vessel. When the Companions arrived at Terguz, as they were sure to, her trail needed to be confused, leading the pursuers off in the wrong direction. After the insult to their Wing Commander, the Companions would cling to her tracks like Riparian blood leeches.

Finally, she had to discover a way past Itreata's impregnable security. From Skyla, Ily had learned just how serious the challenge would be. The Companions screened everyone, everything, that entered their domain. Detection buoys ringed the system around the Twin Titans. Itreata couldn't have been placed in a better location for defense. The Forbidden Borders covered every approach but one. Unless a ship carried extra shielding, the violent radiation released by the binary stars would cook a standard ship within days, so coasting in was out of the question—provided one was foolish enough to suspect that Staffa's active detectors wouldn't pick up either the mass or radiation from a dark ship.

That left the standard way, declaring oneself, racing the radiation, and docking like she once had, but then, she'd been a legitimate diplomat.

On that occasion, the Companions had met her, escorted her to special quarters, and restricted her movements. Though she couldn't prove it, she suspected that she had been under constant surveillance the entire time. When she'd seduced Ryman Ark that time, she'd had the equipment to mask any eavesdropping. Like everything else, those devices had atomized in the Ministry of Internal Security.

Under Mytol, Skyla had confided that Staffa's security matched every face with chem-coded ID. Each member of a party was accounted for entering and leaving. In Ily's case, Itreata had her chemical code on file. Every human body produced a chemical fingerprint as reliable as dermatoglyphics, blood type, or bone structure. Skyla had made no bones about the fact that security ran cross-checks on their files.

Unless I can change my body chemistry.

For that, she needed a good biochem lab—and no such thing existed on Terguz. Rega contained such a facility, but then, so did Vermilion and Ashtan.

Ily finished and stepped into the small shower. As warm water soaked her, she worried at the problem. All she needed was to pass security. Let them place her in their special quarters. Once there, she need but get a simple message to one man. He could figure out the rest. And he would—Ily was sure of it.

The drying field caressed her body as she stepped through.

"About time." A naked Gyper Rill leaned against the doorway, arms crossed. Admiration for her filled his dark eyes.

"After last night, I thought you'd sleep for hours."

"You just stroked my appetite."

She pointed at his crotch, resigned to giving him what he wanted. "Looks like your appetite is a little limp, Gyper." She walked to him, wrapping herself around him, undulating. "But I think I can make you hungry."

He sighed, staring down into her eyes. "You're a rapacious bitch, did you know?"

"Uh-huh." She reached down, squeezing him until he grunted. "That's not all I can tighten up with."

"I know." He moaned as she bit the side of his neck. "How do you keep those muscles toned?"

"Exercises," she whispered, leading him toward the sleeping platform. "A woman like me has to keep in shape. And you've got something I can practice on for now. But later, after I wear you out, I need access to your comm. Can I have it?"

He tossed her onto the bedding. "That depends on what you do next."

Ily laughed, playing the old familiar game as he settled next her. She pushed him onto his back and bent down, using her mouth until he gasped. "Much more of that, and I'll spoil the fun."

His jaw dropped as she straddled him and settled on his straining penis. His eyes had fixed on her breasts while his hands clamped her buttocks. She tightened her vaginal muscles, rotating her hips. "Do I get access to your comm?"

His body trembled. "Yes, yes . . . just don't stop."

Ily smiled in satisfaction.

* * *

For Will Blacker, the changes in Free Space hadn't all been to his liking. Before Tybalt's assassination, he'd been showing a profit. Coming from an aristocratic Regan family of mediocre status, he'd been working hard for the last sixty years to better the status of his family and children. As the empire expanded, he had taken every opportunity, every load, to get ahead. For the last twenty years, he'd made progress. His freighter, the *Victory,* had made every run within the empire at least once—even to being the first into Maika after the conquest. He'd spaced into parking orbit under the very guns of the Companions. Regan Divisions were still mopping up pockets of resistance as he readied his lighters to descend to the planet's surface.

That kind of audacity, along with the willingness to drive himself past the brink of endurance and good health, had been paying off. Back on Rega, his five children had a brighter outlook. Vesta, his oldest daughter, even had a shot at University next year. His sons would have other options besides the military, or following in his dog-tired footsteps. All but little Billy. Despite the fact that he was only five years old, his eyes lit at any mention of the stars. Trade was in the boy's blood. One day, Billy would man the cockpit aboard *Victory*. Or, at least, it had seemed that way until Tybalt's assassination.

Will took another drink, a sour feeling in his gut. The ramifications of the conquest were still settling into his brain. What would trade be like now that the Star Butcher controlled both empires? What did it all mean for his kids? For the future?

He glanced around the bar. The name over the door said *WAYSIDE*. Will had been coming here to drink ever since he'd landed his first load on Terguz.

Normally, the place was jumping, whores and other happiness dealers crowding a man's elbow, offering anything he had the audacity, or the credits, to try. Terguz had always been that way, a hell of a world with a hell of a way of forgetting its problems. Now men and women drank and talked quietly, uncertainty in their eyes. Probably just like the look in his.

The ceiling had been grimy-dark the first time Will set foot in the place. No one had bothered to wash it since. The sialon bar before him showed nicks and gouges despite the durable nature of the material. A fellow by the name of Vinney had engraved his name on the surface with a vibraknife.

Just in the times Will had frequented the *Wayside*, he'd watched six men and two women toted out on med gurneys—and those were just the dead ones. He couldn't count the number of cuttings, beatings, and other scrapes that had littered the place with wounded. Not that *Wayside* was a dangerous place, a fellow just got whatever he wanted. If it was a fight, someone would oblige. If you only wanted a peaceful drink, like he did now, the management would provide that, too. All of Terguz was that way. The Administrator knew how to run a wide open planet.

Will sighed, staring down into his drink. On the walls, pictures of freighters, warships, and stars glowed in holographic splendor. Half the tables in the place were occupied, most of the people talking in low voices. He could hear melodic laughter as young Lark laughed at someone's joke.

Hell, a man didn't know what to take for a load. From the holo reports, food was the hot item. Anyone willing to space for Imperial Sassa, of all places, could make a killing. And here Will sat, waiting on Terguz with its riches of metals, gasses, and ice—and not a load of food to be had.

"Why didn't I planet on Vermilion?"

"Why didn't you?"

The sexy contralto caught him by surprise, and Will turned to stare into the most magnificent amber eyes he'd ever seen.

"Mind if I sit down?" she asked.

Blacker's skin prickled with excitement. He glanced up and down, taking in the tall woman's dress. A thick cape hung from her shoulders, falling straight over the swell of her hips. The brown shift she wore disguised what had to be one hell of a body.

"Be my guest."

She settled athletically beside him. Lustrous auburn hair spilled in a wave over her shoulder. Blacker stared, rapt, at her perfect face.

"I–I'm Will Blacker. From Rega. I'm a freighter."

She smiled, and his heart skipped at the dimples that formed in her smooth skin. "Some of my friends call me Desire. It's a joke, I think."

"No joke." He glanced around, aware that several sets of male eyes were casing her out. "Uh, are you with anyone, or by yourself?"

"By myself . . . so far. Just came in from Rega."

"I see. You saw the conquest?"

"I did." She said it wryly, a glint in those marvelous eyes. "The Star Butcher did a thorough job."

Will nodded, flustered, cares about the future suddenly on hold. "You spaced here by yourself? No crew?"

"I have a companion." At his crestfallen look, she added, "A *female* companion."

Blacker brightened. "Could I, uh, buy you a drink? This place has—"

"Whiskey, Ashtan, if they have it."

Will tried to keep his credit chip from trembling as he poked it into the dispenser and punched the right button.

"You alone?" she asked.

"After you showed up, it wouldn't have mattered if I was with an Etarian priestess! I'm as alone as I'll ever get."

She lifted a slender eyebrow. "Thank you for the compliment."

"What do you do? I mean, you work on a ship? Trade? What?"

"Suppose I told you I was running." She paused, glancing shyly away. "Given the change in power . . . well, there are certain people I wouldn't want to have catch up with me."

At his stunned look, she smiled. "I'm sorry. I shouldn't endanger you. Thank you for the drink."

He reached out, placing a hand on her arm. "No, that's fine. Stay. I don't care. I mean, listen, maybe I can help."

As he stared into those eyes, his soul began to melt. Rotted right, he'd sell his soul to see her look at him that way.

Excitement stirred in those amber depths and her lips parted slightly. "I wouldn't want to involve you. Are you sure?"

"No problem." His pulse had begun to race. "Uh, listen, this isn't the place to be if someone is after you. I'd keep a lower profile."

She glanced about, a wounded doe look in her eyes. "I shouldn't have come in here. I just didn't have any place to go. I thought . . . well . . ."

Blacker tossed off the last of his drink. "Come on. I've got a berth a couple of levels down. Let's . . . go talk it over. That is . . ."

The excitement had returned to her eyes. "I don't mind. In fact, I'd be very grateful." Her hand slipped over his, her touch warm, inviting. "Perhaps I could make it worth your while. I'm not without means to repay your kindness."

Blacker swallowed hard, aware of how her high breasts pressed at the material of her dress. He had problems finding his voice. "Glad to help." *Blessed Gods, woman, for a moment alone with you, I'd trade my soul!*

He barely remembered walking out of the *Wayside*, a thrill possessing him as all eyes followed. Blessed Gods, maybe Terguz had been one of the luckiest moves he'd ever made. They walked in silence, Blacker sneaking glances at her, reassuring himself that she wasn't just a dream.

He'd rented a room on F Level. Placing his chip into the slot, he led her into the cramped quarters. "It's not much. If you need, I can hide you in the ship."

She smiled as he closed the door. With a sultry move, she slipped the heavy cape from her shoulders, and Blacker manfully kept from gaping.

Desire walked toward him, placing both of her hands on his shoulders. "Thank you, Will. I've been looking for someone like you."

She leaned forward, kissing him gently on the lips. Dazed, he leaned into her, returning her kiss, passion growing. "Are you sure you . . ."

"We'll discuss my situation later," she whispered. "For now, let me show you my appreciation. You won't regret it."

Any reservations Will Blacker might have had vanished as her slim fingers began to unfasten his shirt.

* * *

The bed squeaked as Arta Fera rolled onto her back, eyes dreamy, a smile on her full lips. She stared at the uniform white ceiling tiles in satisfaction and licked her lips. The salty taste of blood mixed with pungent flavor of ejaculate. She stood and stretched like a tiger before stepping into the narrow shower. From head to foot, Arta scrubbed herself. She opened her mouth to the spray and spit to clean it. Being cheap quarters, no drying field awaited her. Instead, simple towels hung on a rack. As she wiped the last of the water from her glowing flesh, she took a deep breath, looking at the man on the fluid-stained bed.

She picked her dress up from where it had been flung on the floor and pulled it over her head, flipping her wet hair free. Then she pinned the cloak at her neck.

The room did have a comm. Arta input a number. Ily's face formed on the monitor, "Everything all right?"

Arta gave her a flushed grin. "Just like plucking plums from a tree. *Victory* is ours. We have a ship."

"I'll have Gyper send Leon and Vymar down. They'll handle the body with discretion."

Arta glanced over her shoulder. "They'd better bring a mop."

Ily winced. "Arta, in the future, don't play with them. Just kill them."

The gleam brightened in Arta's eyes. "But it's so exciting to play with them. He died in ecstasy."

* * *

The old familiar nightmare had invaded Staffa's sleep. The souls of the dead chased him through a blasted starship. He ran and ran, hounded by the hissing, moaning mob, until an explosion impaled him on torn metal. There, with freezing steel slicing through his guts and piercing his stretched skin, they cornered him, reaching out with taloned fingers to feed on his soul.

He had come awake to the old familiar shakes. This time, however, no Skyla waited to hug him, to stroke his head as he drifted back toward oblivion.

Staffa sat up, staring around his sleeping quarters. He rubbed his eyes with a callused hand and went to stare at the personal articles left on the counter. Skyla's jeweled brush rested in the same spot she'd left it. Strands of hair glistened, silver in the light. Lifting the brush to his nose, Staffa closed his eyes, inhaling the faint ghost of her scent.

Epaulet clips lay in a neat row, the jewels sparkling. Staffa opened the wardrobe where her snowy white armor hung in immaculate rows. His own gray suits had been pulled straight, tucked efficiently into their holders. The room echoed her presence, everything in its place. No detail overlooked.

How different that old Skyla had been from the haunted woman he'd walked out of the hospital with. That Skyla had been brittle, like supercooled crystal, ready to shatter at the next instant.

Fool, you should have known she'd run.

The lonely echo of defeat rang hollowly within. His fingers trembled as he stroked the cool fabric of her suits. He knew the physiological effects her trauma induced. Depression and feelings of inadequacy induced a chemical overload of cortisols, acetylcholines, beta-endorphines, and other chemicals. The brain, desperate to reestablish normalcy, adopted any strategy to gratify that need, often creating new neural pathways, or accessing old, inapplicable paths to superimpose a "new" reality, but one based on false assumptions.

He himself had barely survived such an experience. Had it not been for random chance, and the concern of a few heroic and outstanding individuals like Kaylla Dawn, his corpse would have been rotting on Etaria.

Skyla had played a very important role in his survival. She'd worked behind the scenes, manipulating events, risking her life to rescue him from his own folly.

When you needed me, Skyla, I wasn't there. Would it have hurt to miss one of those planning meetings? Would it have precipitated disaster had he delegated more to Tap or Tasha? Would Chrysla have left? Would Anatolia be alive—or the rest of his people killed in the explosion?

"I don't know, Skyla. But maybe you'd be here, safe, and I could tell you how sorry I am."

* * *

The stack of reports under Chrysla's arm refused to stay in place as she walked down the corridor. The flimsies kept slipping. In defeat, she clamped them with two hands, pausing before Mac's hatch. The Regans hadn't designed their ships for luxury and the narrow corridor, crowded with overhead cables, could have been brighter.

She had finished the reports in her quarters, taking the liberty of okaying the duty rosters for First Section. In addition, she'd applied herself to the study of Ashtan. A great deal had changed since the days of her youth. Imperial Rega had instituted computer controls for most government administration. The Ashtan of her youth, rich and carefree, had vanished beneath the Regan boot.

Would she recognize her home world? Did anything remain of her youth? From the historical files, she had accessed the names of government officials. Now, all she had to do was convince Mac that it would be worth reappointing those individuals to power. If enough of that reserve of experience remained, perhaps they could cobble together a makeshift government competent to stabilize the planet.

"Mac? It's Chrysla."

The door comm remained silent. Despite the hour, MacRuder must have been on duty.

Hesitantly, she reached up and palmed the lock plate. Mac had recalibrated it for her. As the hatch slipped open, she stepped inside, surprised to see Mac canted back in the desk chair.

His neck had craned into the most uncomfortable position, his deep breathing sounded strained. Walking silently, Chrysla placed the flimsies on the corner of his desk, debating on whether to wake him.

She turned, catching sight of the holo. Three starving children stared out at her. The scene changed, revealing a night sky blackened by clouds. Corpses had been piled like stacked wood, arms and legs akimbo. People scampered in the darkness, stopping to saw bits of flesh from the bones.

The scene changed again, to that of freezing people huddled in the snow. Rudimentary shelters had been formed for some protection. Chrysla raised a hand to her mouth, realizing that this was no refugee camp, but an alleged hospital. The holo zoomed in on one corpse, snow blanketing the dead eyes.

The scene changed again, depicting a street fight. Men armed with clubs attacked a woman who ran through the street, a bundle clutched to her chest. She fell beneath the attackers, flailing with fists and feet as they viciously clubbed her unconscious, prying the bundle from her arms. Then they turned on each other, spilling the contents, four loaves of bread, into the foul mud. Immediately, armed troops appeared from the side, dispersing them, collecting the dirt-encrusted bread and rendering aid to the woman.

Scene after scene flashed on the holo, the projection looped until the three haunting children stared out.

Mac made a hideous whimpering sound, beads of sweat forming on his slack face.

"Rotted Gods," Chrysla whispered, reaching over to kill the display. She took a deep breath, noting the name of the file:

SEDDI REPORT TWELVE DISPATCHED FROM IMPERIAL SASSA 5780:2:13:05:00.

Mac made another mewing sound as he flipped his head around.

Chrysla set her jaw, walking around the desk. "Mac? Mac, wake up."

MacRuder moaned, the word "no" muttered under his breath.

"Mac!" Chrysla shook him and jumped back when he cried out and jerked upright, almost upsetting the chair.

Mac blinked, catching his breath. "What?"

"Bad dream. It looked like a nightmare." She tilted her head toward the wall holo. "Did you fall asleep watching that?"

Mac groaned, stretched, and rubbed his neck as he looked up at her through bleary eyes. "Report in from Imperial Sassa."

"I gathered that."

Mac sighed, bowing his head. "I'm all right. What's up?"

She studied him pensively. "I brought the day reports. I called. When you didn't answer, I thought you might have been on duty."

He growled to himself, grabbing up the stack she'd indicated, sorting through the flimsies. "They look fine. Thanks."

Chrysla hesitated. "Mac, you can't blame yourself. You and Staffa, you're torturing yourselves to death. Trust me, I know what I'm talking about. Dwelling on war leads you to self-destruction."

He didn't look up. "It's one thing to plot an action. Another to carry it out from space." He paused. "And still another to look into the faces of your victims."

She reached down and took his hand, pulling him up. "Come on. You're going to lie down on a real bed and get some real sleep."

He smiled sheepishly. "And my dreams will be better in a bunk than in a chair? Optimistic, aren't you?"

She pushed him down, bending to unsnap his boots and set them to the side. She looked up at him, aware that for the first time, even his attraction to her had been eclipsed. "Will you try to sleep?"

He nodded agreement; but she read the truth in his eyes.

"Take your belt off. Sleeping on a blaster isn't conducive to rest." She paused. "And while you're at it, slip out of that armor, too. I know you guys live in it, but for once, I want you comfortable."

He raised a wry eyebrow. "Undress? Right here in front of you?"

"You've got an undersuit on beneath that, don't you?" She stood and crossed her arms. "I'll look the other way. Besides, I don't think you've got anything I haven't seen before."

She stepped over to the dispenser and drew a bulb of stassa. By the time she turned, he'd undressed, hung his suit, according to regulation, and pulled the blanket over him.

Chrysla pulled one of the collapsible chairs out of the wall and settled herself. Mac watched uneasily.

Chrysla sipped the hot liquid. "I've been there, Mac. Lived it. When I escaped the *Pylos,* the pod malfunctioned. I landed harder than I should have. It was in a mountainous region. My leg was broken. I crawled for a couple of kilometers until I found a cabin. The people who owned it ran goats, barely eked out a living. They set my leg as best they could.

"The weather turned because of the smoke. So much soot gets into the air when entire cities burn. All of their goats froze to death in the snow. It was supposed to be summer on that hemisphere.

"I'd only been there a week when they went out into the snow to try and save as many animals as they could. They never came back. Didn't dress well enough, I suppose. I healed, made crutches, and ate the last of their food. After that, I made my way to the nearest city. Most of the particulate matter thrown up is heavy and precipitates. That trip was plenty cold, but I made it.

"I saw scenes like that. Did what I could to survive." She shook her head. "Some of the things I ate. Well, survival does that. Fortunately, I had enough training to know where to go, what to say." She gave him a stony glance. "When that didn't work, I sold myself.'

Mac bit his lip, eyes closed.

"I made it." Chrysla lifted the bulb to her lips. "I could have told you what would happen. I might even have made you feel so bad, it could have jeopardized the mission. Don't look at me that way, I could have used my sexuality, convinced you."

"But you didn't."

She shook her head. "You offered me a chance. Safety. Survival. Besides, I respected you and I wanted your respect."

"You've got it—and more."

"I want you to think about this. You're a soldier, Mac. How would you have felt if you had failed to neutralize Sassa's threat? They were massing their force to hit the Regan Empire. Divine Sassa had turned down Staffa's peace plan. Seriously, if you had to do it all over again, knowing only what you knew then, would you have done anything differently?"

He sighed heavily. "No. I suppose not. In all honesty, I'd maximize our chance to make it out alive."

"We all do what we have to. That's the glory and curse of being human."

"Condemned to be what we are." Mac twisted anxiously on the bedding.

"Close your eyes. I want you to try something for me."

"All right."

"We're on a lake, a placid blue lake. You and I are in a boat. The waves rock us gently, while overhead is a blue sky, filled with puffy white clouds. Nod if you can imagine it."

Mac nodded.

"The sun is shining brightly, a warm breeze blowing over the water. All around the lake are mountains, each covered with trees. If you sniff, you can catch the delicate fragrance of pines. The boat continues to rock, so gently, following each of the swells. So tranquil. So gentle."

She noticed the deepening of his breath. "So peaceful, rocking, rocking, rocking . . ."

Chrysla sipped her stassa, sitting patiently beside him.

Despite herself, she cast a glance at the comm, the screen empty now, mute to the testimony it had just given.

She need only close her eyes to relive those wretched days on Myklene. Her nose would reek with the stench of death, her ears drowned in the cries of the dying.

But here, for a moment, she could bring peace.

She studied MacRuder as he slept, understanding the burden, remembering the horror. They had so little time left. So little peace to share.

CHAPTER XIV

Magyar Dvork pounded the old wooden gavel that had been the traditional symbol of power in the Vermilion Council. They had come to the end of four days of bickering, taunting, shouted insults, two fistfights, and an attempted knifing, but Magyar had finally beaten, bullied, and shouted his opposition into submission.

As a result, he hammered with a special vigor, that of triumph as he called the final session to the vote.

"All in favor of the Articles of Self-Determination offered by the Bench are ordered to vote now. Press your comm buttons for the future of Vermilion, ladies and gentlemen. Opposed, you may push your buttons. Let the vote be made and counted!"

The teaming Council hall quieted, at least as much as five hundred newly appointed politicians could manage for so important an occasion. After all, they'd defied the Administrator, and the Director of Internal Security had vanished the moment the subspace net had warned that Ily's old cronies were sabotaging planetary comms.

The heady sense of achievement rose on the humid warm air like a phoenix from the ashes of empire.

Dvork watched the lights tallying the vote. As he expected, his fledgling party had a full fifteen point lead.

"Congratulations!" he shouted, banging his heavy gavel yet again. "Vermilion First accepts the Articles of Self-Determination!"

"You'll regret it!" Vicar Lewis, the Industrial Councilman, shouted, brandishing a fist. "You can't make it alone! Our industry is interdependent, you idiots! Rot you, what sort of lunacy—"

A muscular arm snaked out from the crowd behind Lewis

and clamped on the old man's neck, dragging him backward into the ensuing melee.

"My fellow Vermilians!" Dvork cried hoarsely, "We're free! Free of the Empire! Free of outside interference in our affairs! Free of foreign entanglements!"

* * *

The comm buzzed in Kaylla Dawn's ear. She groaned and sat up, blinking as the room lighting began to brighten in response to her movement.

"What is it?" she asked in a muzzy voice.

"Sorry to bother you, Magister," Wilm's baritone apologized, "but we've just gotten confirmation of a development from Vermilion. Ty Pak, our agent there, has just reported that the Vermilion First Party has pushed their agenda through the Council. The planet has voted to become isolationist. Pak expects Magyar Dvork to solidify his political power over the next couple of weeks. When that happens, he's going to close the Orbiting Terminal and curtail commercial shipping."

Kaylla sighed, rubbing a hand over her face. *What should we do?* Rotted Gods, she'd been nearly fifty hours without sleep. Her brain was working with the clarity of Sylenian slush, and now she had another crisis?

"Power up the dish. Inform the Lord Commander." She paused, haunted by the headlong rush they'd been living in since the Sassan quake had shaken the future right out from beneath them. From that moment, Kaylla had been seated at the comm, building a communications network from bits and pieces of intelligence offices, military commanders, and occasional ambitious politicians who were betting their futures primarily on the Companions, and secondarily on the Seddi.

"Who is spacing for Vermilion?" Kaylla asked the question aloud since she figured her fuzzy thoughts wouldn't coalesce in time to give her the answer.

"Division First Kap aboard the Regan battle cruiser *Climax*," Wilm told her. "ETA one month Vermilion planetary time. *Climax* is still short of null singularity. Should I alert them?"

That should be Staffa's decision. "Yes, Wilm. Do so.

Time may be of the essence. Inform Dion Axel as well." What else? Damn it! If she could only think! "Wilm, have a couple of our people put together a statement. Something which won't goad every Vermilion into a boiling rage, but will remind them that they are still part of the whole, that we'll work with them in the formation of their government, but that we need strategic minerals and produce from their world. Send them . . . I know, an economic profile of the industries and services which will collapse if they continue to pursue this futile policy."

"Yes, Magister."

"Wait. Just write it up. I'll want to scan it, make sure we don't set anyone off. Do you understand? This has got to be done very carefully."

"Yes, Magister. Oh, we've had a report from *Cobra*. Delshay informs us that Legate Roma has been working ceaselessly. If the Mag Comm mission is a failure, the prognosis for a workable software to be employed is roughly six months standard. Delshay repeats that date to be a bare minimum, that teething problems could prolong implementation by another three to six months."

Kaylla slumped back onto her sleeping platform. *Six months at a bare minimum? Too long. Sorry, Staffa, but if Vermilion is turning isolationist, Phillipia is brewing revolution, Ashtan is paralyzed, Rega is coordinating itself by means of battle comms, and Imperial Sassa is starving, we don't have four months, let alone six.*

"Thank you, Wilm." Her mind had started to race, foggy cobwebs of fatigue shredding. "Call me if . . . no, forget it. I'll be down as soon as I can drink a couple cups of kaffe, take a hot shower, and eat some stim pills."

"Magister, you've only had two hours of sleep. It'll—"

"I'm on my way. Keep the lid on for me, all right?"

"Yes, Magister."

Kaylla swung her legs over the edge of the sleeping platform, shoulders slumped, head hanging. Perhaps it was just the curse of the quanta, but this would be a long, hard pull.

As she staggered, loose-limbed, into the shower stall and slapped a palm to the hot water control, she wondered if in the end their sacrifice would be worth it, or whether they'd watch the dissolution of humanity in a state of total physical, spiritual, and mental exhaustion.

"If you can't win, Kaylla, you might as well go back to sleep and watch the extinction rested and alert. It won't make any difference any other way."

Except that she couldn't give up like that—no more than she could have when Anglo was raping her day in and day out in the Etarian sands.

As the steaming water raced down her tanned flesh, Kaylla Dawn pounded the duraplast wall with a knotted fist.

* * *

"Sleep well?" Staffa asked as Sinklar passed the big double hatch that guarded the entrance to Staffa's personal quarters. The Lord Commander sat in one of the gaudy red, over-stuffed chairs, a lap monitor before him.

"No. Thanks to you." Sinklar rubbed the back of his neck as he paused in the middle of the room. "Most of my dreams were about being a bug in a jar. Everything beyond the glass was dark, with hazy things watching from the darkness. All I could see was their eyes, yellow, with slits for pupils."

Then there had been the other dream. A nightmare of violet blaster bolts and the hum of pulse fire while a mountain pass was riven by disrupters. There, on a lone point, Gretta had stood, her back to him, her slim body shining in the light of burning trees.

Sinklar shook his head, casting it away into the recesses of his mind where it would wait, ready to possess him again and again.

"Hungry?" Staffa asked. "I cheated, had security warn me the moment you stepped into the corridor. I took the liberty of ordering breakfast."

"Cheated? I came as soon as I woke up. You should have known the moment my eyes opened."

Staffa grunted. He flipped his black ponytail off his shoulder, setting the small comm to one side. "I've never monitored your personal quarters. If you were Ily Takka, on the other hand, I imagine I'd have had other considerations."

"How noble of you."

Staffa smiled, leaning forward to rub his eyes.

"Do you ever take those gray gloves off? Or the cape?"

Staffa gave him an amused look. "I do, but not for occasions when I'd want you present."

At that, the Lord Commander's demeanor changed, as if he were caught up in memories. His eyes lost focus.

Skyla. He's worried sick about her. From what he remembered, the Wing Commander, if anyone, ought to be able to care for herself. But then, she, too, had been in Ily's hands.

"She's going to be all right," Sinklar stated sympathetically.

"She has to find her own solution. I can't do it for her." He paused. "That doesn't mean I have to like it."

At least you can still hope, Staffa. Skyla is alive. Anatolia is dead. He turned away, disgusted with himself. Staffa lived with constant uncertainty. The dead couldn't suffer. They were beyond one's ability to help. Angrily, he drew a cup of stassa.

The comm announced the arrival of breakfast and two orderlies escorted an antigrav into the room, carefully removing stasis covers. Saluting, they left with never a word spoken.

"Come on, help yourself. Despite all else, Companions eat well."

Sinklar settled himself on the couch, aware for the first time how hungry he'd become. "Any more thoughts on the Mag Comm?"

Staffa chewed thoughtfully. "I'm wondering if we can make something like a worry-cap in reverse. A skull-shaped globe that will interface with that pustulous golden helmet. That way, we can avoid direct exposure to the machine."

Sinklar jabbed at the food. "You know, I'll never look at the stars the same way again." He paused. "What do you think they are? Creatures like us? Warm-blooded? Or something so different we can't even comprehend them?"

"You sound like you've accepted the hypothesis."

Sinklar shrugged, forcing himself to eat. "Suppose the Etarian priests had an inkling once. You know the story. The Blessed Gods fought for humanity in a great war with the Rotted Gods. In the end, they won, but just barely. To hold the Rotted Gods at bay, they erected the Forbidden Borders. What if, by opening the Forbidden Borders, we're implementing our own destruction?"

Staffa gestured toward the monitor he'd set aside. "I just reviewed another report from Kaylla. They had riots in Rega. It seems that one of the distribution centers ran out of food. In addition, an interim government is forming on Vermilion. Their platform is isolationism. You know what that will lead to?"

"They can't isolate themselves. They need too many imports to maintain their economy."

"The leaders from the new movement haven't quite figured that out yet. In the event they do rise to power, they'll find that out soon enough. Their next act will be piracy. That or a raid on another world." Staffa wiped his mouth. "And that brings us back to the problem. We have three options. First, we establish an iron-fisted rule and implement rationing and strict social control. That way, we can manage with the status quo—survival through stagnation and carefully monitored resource redistribution. The second option is to break the Forbidden Borders and accept the risk that something more sinister than the Rotted Gods lies beyond."

"And the third is self-destruction." Sinklar scowled at the wreckage of his meal. "What if we let the people decide? Put it up for a vote?"

Staffa gave him a skeptical look. "Just how do you expect them to understand the ramifications? Etarian belief runs rampant in Regan territory. Within the Sassan Empire, they're just as gullible. They swallowed that Terguzzi sumpshit about Sassa being a god. If that's a god, I'm camping in the atheist fold the Mag Comm was so worried about."

Sinklar rubbed his knobby nose. "Somehow, I have problems making decisions which will affect all of humankind."

"Got a better idea? We don't have a lot of time to make a decision. Assuming we go to the second option, create a static situation, we won't have any surplus of resources to use for breaking the Forbidden Borders. All of our time and efforts will have to go into governing, maintaining the peace. A lot of minor officials who have chafed under the old systems will see their opportunity to take power."

Sinklar chased a chubba leaf around his plate. Rot it all, Staffa was right. "How about your magical Seddi philosophy? Your new epistemology?"

''Integration of an idea like that takes time. A toolmaker on Farhome doesn't wake up one morning and say to himself, 'This morning, I'm going to change the entire way in which I view the world.' We've got a lot of cultural baggage to deal with. Ingrained values.''

''You seemed to have picked it up rather quickly.''

''Only because I was searching for something.''

Sinklar sighed, shoving his plate away. ''Despite my distaste, I accessed some of Kaylla Dawn's broadcasts. If it weren't for the fact that I hate having anything to do with Seddi, a lot of it makes sense.''

Staffa steepled his hands. ''Like it or not, you believe a lot of what the Seddi teach. Were it not for an accident of politics, you would have sided with them against Tybalt. As I understand your goals, you were headed in basically the same direction. Breaking the old patterns of conquest and repression, working to free people from the system so that an event like Targa could never happen again.''

''Bruen was the Seddi leader!'' Sinklar shot to his feet. ''He wasted human beings like they were hydrogen atoms.''

''I make no apologies for Bruen.'' Staffa finished his meal and pushed the antigrav to one side. ''Our duty is to see that his sort of teleologic ethics are never employed again.''

Sinklar prowled restlessly. ''Speaking of ethics, or lack of them, is there any word on Ily?''

''None. But most of our ships haven't arrived at their target worlds yet.'' Staffa stared absently at the Etarian sand tiger. ''She could have run anywhere. Who knows what sort of hole she prepared.''

Sinklar fingered a vase where it had been fastened to the wall. ''She's going to strike back. It's in her nature. She told me once that she never surrendered all of her options. Never underestimate her.''

Staffa clasped his hands behind him, head down. ''I'm well aware of that. I had the chance to kill her once. All it would have taken was a moment to turn, blow her apart, and I'd have been done with her.'' He closed his eyes. ''So much would have been so different for so many.''

Sinklar read the worry as Staffa looked toward the doorway leading into his sleeping quarters.

Sinklar had only seen Skyla twice, a beautiful woman with stunning blue eyes and ice-blonde hair. The first time had been here, in this room. He could remember her as she was then: commanding, competent, striking in her gleaming white armor. The second time he'd seen her had been in Ily's interrogation room, a broken sobbing thing, whimpering under the influence of the Mytol and whatever other horrors Ily had perpetrated.

"Don't underestimate Skyla, either."

Staffa gave him a look of appreciation. "Normally, I wouldn't." He bounced on his toes, powered by nervous energy. Desperate to talk, hating to admit the need. *Like me,* Sinklar decided.

Overcoming his reluctance, Sinklar stated, "Ily played me like a master. She used my inexperience against me. She's good, Staffa. Every time I balked, she had a smooth explanation, a perfect reason for what she was doing. And she's—" his skin reddened—"she's . . ."

"Sexually engrossing." Staffa nodded his understanding. "When did you find out the truth?"

Sinklar fumbled with the vase, running his fingers over the cut gems set into the metal. "When I accidentally discovered Tybalt's journal. He knew her for what she was, and she still killed him in the end."

"You seem to have come to grips with what happened. You won't be fooled again."

"Ana helped with that." The raw wound chafed.

"I hope Skyla deals with it as well as you have." Staffa shook his head.

"Tell me about her."

Staffa continued to hesitate, needing desperately to talk but afraid to.

Sinklar studied the man. *Come on. I leveled with you. Get it out, Staffa.*

"Skyla . . . she came from a tough world. Sylene. The place is filled with the human equivalent of siff jackals. She survived there as an assassin, hunted by the police. Mac Rylee was walking down the street one day and Skyla saw him; she took the chance. I always accepted bright people for the Companions."

Staffa fidgeted, drawing a bulb of stassa from the dispenser just for something to do. "From the time she set foot aboard *Chrysla* she excelled at everything. She had that drive and ambition. I'd barely noticed her, but she got detailed to security once when I was going to see a man, an assassin and bounty hunter. He specialized in finding people. When we got to the tavern where we were supposed to meet, he told me he couldn't find Chrysla . . . or you."

Staffa sipped the hot liquid. "If Rygart couldn't find you, no one could. The effect, well, I always maintained a sober control in those days. That night, I went a little crazy. Drank too much. Skyla was one of the people who brought me back here."

"Is that when you started to fall in love with her?"

"No. I mourned over your mother for almost twenty years. But when I sobered up, I kept Skyla close. To keep an eye on her. That's when I noticed just how good she was."

He frowned. "She never failed, Sinklar. Skyla was always so sure of herself. Any task she tackled, she completed. It never came easily, but she did the job, and with machinelike efficiency. She'd never been broken before. Never failed at something she'd set her mind to . . . until Arta grabbed her off Ryklos.

"That's what worries me. I know her better than any person alive." He scuffed at the Nesian carpet underfoot, sending a rainbow of ripples across the floor. "I should have known she'd try something. Chrysla warned me." He shook his head. "Why didn't I take the time, Sinklar? When she really needed me, why didn't I . . ." He turned away.

"We all ask that of ourselves. Having Chrysla aboard didn't help matters either. Yours or Skyla's." Sinklar paused. "You told me that you love them both."

Staffa smiled wistfully. "The joke of the quanta. For years I tortured myself over Chrysla. She's . . . almost ethereal. I'll love Chrysla forever, Sinklar. You have to understand that I loved her with all my heart. She was the first woman who ever saw through what the Praetor had made me into. She gave me a few wondrous years of happiness. She gave me a son, a reason to plan for the future. In those brief years, someone saw me as a human being, not just a monster, or an experiment."

He frowned. "My love for Chrysla is reverential. I didn't understand that I'd fallen in love with Skyla until I was in the desert on Etaria. She had become my most trusted friend, as precious as my right hand. We knew each other like two parts of the same functioning unit. It took losing each other to realize what we had."

Sinklar shook his head. "Then Chrysla walked back into your life."

"Yes." Staffa stared vacantly.

"Why did you let her go? I think you know how Mac feels about her. That's like shooting protons into an unstable isotope."

"Sinklar, to truly love, you must be willing to set someone free. Anything else is a perversion."

For a moment Sinklar just stared. "Pus-Rotted Gods! Maybe you really are human . . ."

* * *

Skyla cursed, muttered to herself, and continued her attack on the dining area floor. Bruises had mottled her knees, shooting pain through her with each movement. The muscles in her back and shoulders ached and burned. Her hands, already callused from combat training, had taken on a rough texture that caught on delicate fabric.

Sweat beaded, trickling down her nose to spattering star bursts on the polished deck plating. Jaw set, straggles of hair falling about her head, she continued her assault. The pry bar in her hands had become a tool wreaking havoc.

"*. . . clears visitors for security . . .*" Ily's voice popped out of Skyla's memories.

"Shut up, you Regan slut." Skyla grunted, throwing her weight against the bar as another strip of golden spacer yielded with a squeal and peeled back under the flat of her lever. This work took patience. The builders had used pure gold. Too much pressure and the puttylike metal pulled apart, snapped off, or bent double.

She battled incessantly, stopping only to eat, eliminate, and sleep. She did stop long enough to inspect the cockpit, but the auto alarm had warned her twice when ship's status fluctuated.

Puffing, Skyla pried the last of the spacer out, slinging the golden strip into the pile building in the galley corner. Another one gone.

"*. . . is head of the psychological department on Itreata. Doesn't that mean he . . .*"

"*No!*" Skyla bellowed and smacked the floor hard with the pry bar, chipping the tile. "Ily! *Get the pustulous hell out of my mind!*"

She arched her back, grimacing at the shriek of nerve and muscle. Scooting across the silver tile, she wedged the end of her bar into the next strip.

Skyla had no mandate for her war on the floor. This battle stemmed only from a desperate need to still the fragments of Ily's interrogation that would pop into her head if she let her mind go blank, from her desire to avoid the cockpit and the message waiting in the comm, and, finally, from the fact that she was growing sick of anything gold.

You're as berserk as a Vermilion fog rhino! She worked the tip of her pry bar under the next strip, levering the end loose.

At that moment, the alarm beeped. Skyla cursed, threw her bar to clatter across the floor and gasped as she pulled herself to her feet. As she passed the hatch foyer, she caught a glimpse of herself, disheveled, smudged, and sweaty.

In the cockpit, she checked the stats, finding that one of the cooling towers in the reactor had begun to fluctuate. Skyla overrode the control, circulating more liquid through the system. Quick inspection of the diagnostics indicated a sticking valve in the primary. Dropping into the command chair, she instituted a bypass program.

Temperature in the tower began to drop.

Skyla leaned back, suddenly aware of her odor. Time for a shower. Time to sleep for a while.

The message comm light blinked at her with obnoxious regularity. She faltered for a moment, watching the light. Taking a deep breath, she accessed the signal data. From the strength of the signal, her system had only picked up something on the subspace net, nothing directional.

Irritated, Skyla saved it into the system and the offending light went dark. She tapped a rhythmic pattern with her fingers while she frowned at the message comm.

"Not now, Skyla." To look into Staffa's worried eyes was more than she could bear.

Vaulting to her feet, she ducked out the hatch, followed the corridor, and entered the wreckage of her galley.

"*. . . thoroughly does security check on visiting dignitaries . . .*"

"Fuck you, Ily, you arrogant bitch, I told you, they screen everyone. We even chem-coded you when you were there. There's no way in."

". . . cloned from the genetic material of Staffa's first wife? Chrysla, you say?"

"Leave . . . me . . . *alone!*" Skyla gasped, shaking her head in a fruitless attempt to drive out the demons.

"You're going nuts. You're going to drive yourself to the point of exhaustion, and you're going to make a mistake. Is that what you want? To kill yourself out here?"

Her knees protested as she dropped to all fours, retrieving her pry bar and muttering to herself, "Yeah, maybe it is."

* * *

"What do we know about the Forbidden Borders?" Sinklar asked.

Staffa glanced up from his monitor. His son sat across the table in the small conference room. It looked as if he'd fortified his position. A forest of comm monitors studded the landscape between them. A cup of cold stassa sat to one side, next to a pile of Sinklar's flimsies. On the other stood a stack of data cubes and his portable comm unit.

On the walls around them, stats from all over Free Space were neatly charted in an attempt to anticipate the political landscape before they went null singularity.

Staffa leaned back, squeezing the bridge of his nose with a thumb and forefinger. "What do we know about the Forbidden Borders? Not much beyond their gravitational effects. Over the years physicists have come to the conclusion that we're seeing filaments, or strands of some sort, very dense, probably neutronic in nature. Measurements of gravitational lensing tell us they mass something on the order of 10^{22}g/cms-. That figure is backed up by studies measuring the relative effect of space-time distortion. Gravitometer readings coupled with light diffraction studies have demonstrated that each of the strings oscillates at a given frequency. Of course, we don't know the initial conditions. The vibration might have been intended when they were constructed. The other explanation is that cirrus, interstellar radiation, and even human attempts to destroy them may have generated or contributed to the oscillations."

"If they're that massive and oscillating, they should snap, fray—something."

"We're dealing with a physics we don't understand."

"With that mass, I can understand why." Sinklar frowned and scratched at his thatch of black hair. "The gravitational effects must be awesome. They'd suck up anything."

"They have. Fission and fusion explosives, null singularity generators. Even a ship impacting at light speed." Staffa tapped the tabletop with his laser pen. "What kind of technology can manipulate nucleonic material? Squeeze out neutronium like it was made to order?"

"We can create hyperons in our accelerators."

"Yes, we can. But we can't sustain them. The best we've been able to do is prolong their existence by three or four nanoseconds in a warped stasis field. I don't know, Sinklar. Maybe we don't want to break the Forbidden Borders after all. I'm not sure I'd want to anger beings who wield such technology."

"You're assuming they think of us as bacteria."

"That is the only reassuring factor in this whole mess."

"What? Being bacteria?"

Staffa nodded. "It means they fear us. With fear, we always have bargaining leverage."

Sinklar's gray eye narrowed to a skeptical squint. "Let me tell you about biology class. We kept houseflies in glass jars. We didn't fear them; it just kept the little beasts in a handy container so we could study their behavior. Had the flies in one of the jars got together and threatened us, a squirt of insecticide would have settled the issue with a minimum of fuss."

"Did I ever tell you what a delight it is to have you around for idle chatter?"

Sinklar grinned, finally remembering his stassa. He sipped, winced, and stood to pour it into the dispenser tray before drawing another cup.

Staffa watched him, a curious warmth in his chest. *My son. And we can talk now like adults.* The tension between them had eased. They might not have become fast friends, but that breakfast in Staffa's quarters had defused the ever-present suspicion.

Studying Sinklar, Staffa could see the fatigue that dogged his every move. How long had it been since either of them had had a good night's sleep? The weight of their situation had now settled on Sinklar's shoulders, but in this case, Chrysla had been wrong. None of the burden had lifted from Staffa's own.

Sinklar shook his head as he turned back, the cup brimful. "You'd think that strings of neutrons would collapse, pull themselves into spheres. Any angular momentum would leave them rotating like miniature neutron stars. Weak force has to play a role in this. How did they manage to manipulate strong force to keep the neutrons together? Do they have a handle on a GUT that we don't?"

"You'd think that." Staffa shifted. "We're dealing with a physics we don't understand yet. I read a report once which suggested that the frequency of oscillation was a prerequisite for the string's stability. They need that oscillation to generate gravitational fields which in turn maintain the string's integrity. Stop the oscillation, the study said, and you'd have a cataclysmic collapse of the string."

"With rather dramatic results."

"The resultant radiation would sterilize Free Space if the gravity waves didn't."

Sinklar reseated himself. "You know, if you can manage somehow to break the barriers, you could accidentally create exactly that effect. Snapping a string could kill us all. We're talking about a lot of mass and energy."

"That thought had crossed my mind," Staffa retorted dryly.

"So how does a colony of bacteria get out of a culture dish?" Sinklar cursed as he spilled stassa on the desk.

"Once we figure that out, we've got the problem solved." Staffa stared at his monitor. "All it takes is one string. If it can be broken, Free Space has enough of a hole to break out. The navigation will be a little tricky. A ship has to pierce the gravitational fields exactly midway. The velocity will have to be a hair under light speed, say 0.97C. Any deviation to one side or the other, and tidal effects will rip a ship apart—no matter how well built."

"Can't you build a stronger ship? Reinforce the hull?"

"Sure, we could build something that would take the tidal effect structurally, but what about the most fragile part? The human beings inside? People tend to break and die at around twelve to fifteen gravities."

"I'm not an engineer. Why can't you generate artificial gravity? That's what keeps us from turning into red mush while *Chrysla* accelerates at fifty g, right?"

"The best artificial gravity I can give you—and that's with top of the line plates—is about seventy gravities. Beyond that, power-to-mass ratios become prohibitive. It's a materials problem we haven't solved yet. For greater AG, we build thicker plates to produce a stronger field effect. You need beefed up powerlead and energy production to support the field. That means you need stronger structural support in the starship frame. By the time you finish upgrading, you'll have a starship that masses as much per kilogram as that string in the Forbidden Borders."

Sinklar accepted this reluctantly, then asked, "What about null singularity? Warp a hole in space-time. Let your singularity pull you through. That way, you're not even in this universe."

"You need more sleep. You're not thinking. Want to answer your own question?"

Sinklar's shoulders dropped. "Okay, stupid question. Gravity is the one constant. Mass affects objects in null singularity. Which is why you can't fly a starship traveling in null singularity through a celestial body like a planet or sun."

Staffa stared at the ceiling panels, white squares interspersed with light panels. "They *created* them to oscillate. That's one of the factors which make them so accursedly difficult to deal with."

"How's that?"

"The tidal effects. Gravitational waves generally travel at light speed. Given the frequency of oscillation in the strands, the design is meant to pulverize anything passing within the tidal boundaries. The law of inverse squares, remember? The closer you get to a concentration of mass, the gravitational effect squares. Whip that mass back and forth, and what do you have?"

"A giant vibraknife that cuts from the inside out."

"You're Rotted right." Staffa smacked a fist into the table. "Comm. I need a message patched to Dee Wall at Itreata. Message is as follows: Dee. Sinklar and I were having a conversation and an idea popped up. Take a look at the overall dynamics of the Forbidden Borders. Can the oscillations act as a means of stabilizing the whole? A sort of containment system whereby a small amount of mass is utilized to its greatest extent."

Staffa frowned, unsure where his brain was trying to take him. "Dee, this is what I'm getting at. Mass is abundantly available in the universe. Did the Forbidden Borders have to be made to oscillate? Couldn't they have been rigid? I would appreciate it if you could run a statistical probability for me. Assuming the Forbidden Borders are a natural phenomenon, what is the probability that such a structure would form as a perfectly impenetrable barrier to humans? And while you're at it, what is the probability that the Forbidden Borders, as a dynamic system, will remain in isostatic harmony? Given observed parameters, have the computer estimate the probable lifetime of the system."

Staffa gave the monitor a bleary look. "That's all for now. Let me know what you come up with. Comm clear."

Sinklar sipped at his stassa. "Do you think that hasn't been tried?"

Staffa shrugged. "Probably, but the data are locked away in secret files somewhere . . . that or blown away on Rega or crushed on Sassa. It's just not . . ."

"Go on."

Staffa studied Sinklar, a quizzical expression on his face. "They *can't* be natural. Don't you see? The statistics are going to prove it."

"See what?" Sinklar rocked his cup on the base.

"The quanta, Sinklar. The Forbidden Borders are improbable. Dee is going to prove what you and I are still speculating about."

Sinklar's gaze sobered. "You mean that there really is someone on the other side."

"When we get the answer, we really won't be able to sleep."

CHAPTER XV

To: The Governing Council of Farhome.
From: Staffa kar Therma, Lord Commander of Companions.

Greetings!
Know by this order that the Companions, in association with Admiral Iban Jakre, Commander of the Imperial Sassan Fleet, and Legate Myles Roma, Administrator of the Imperial Sassan government, respectfully request the use of a section of your orbital facility. Needed are ten thousand square meters of floor space to house a complex of seven hundred and fifty high capacity mainframe computers of the Itreata 7706 series dimensions.

It must be noted that security will be of premium importance as will the structural integrity of floors, walls, ceilings, structural supports, and any other engineering concern vital to the protection and working efficiency of such a computer station. Such a complex must be wired to power the above-mentioned number of 7706 series mainframes with at least fifty-rate powerlead to be sublaid into the structure. Electrical power must be integral to the unit in a secure, tamperproof environment accessible only through complex security.

Please forward a floor plan of the facility you propose to offer for this project along with wiring schematics, confirmation of security concerns, and power plant specifications at your earliest opportunity in care of Magister Kaylla Dawn, Seddi Complex, Itreata.

Rapid construction of this facility could be vital to the survival of your people and industry as well as to that of the empire and humanity in general.

Respectfully yours, Staffa kar Therma, Lord Commander of Companions.

* * *

Mendel Ayatayana, Imperial Consul of Farhome for His Holiness, Sassa II, closed his eyes and groaned as he finished reading the communique. He rubbed the delicate bone bridge of his brown-skinned nose and leaned back, glancing at his staff.

"What can we do?" Ihana Maderas asked.

"What do you think? Find them the space they need." Mendel winced at the thought of the trouble that had just landed on his desk. The giant orbiting station that had been his home for all of these years was barely making ends meet. To displace this much industry? Just to build a computer complex?

But then, an earthquake had destroyed the Imperial comm center, and His Divinity alone knew what benefits could accrue to Farhome in the future as a result of such an asset.

"Don't just sit there!" Mendel cried, waving his hands furiously. "Get to work! Or which one of you is going to be the brave one who tells the Star Butcher no?"

* * *

Chrysla stepped into the observation blister at the end of the officer's deck and made her way past darkened equipment that hunched like absurd insects. Outside of a basic knowledge, the intricacies of spectrometers, gravitometers, and interferometers eluded her.

Her purpose, however, was not astronomy. She stopped before the blister, staring out at the infinite blackness, puzzled for the moment by the lack of stars. The darkness of space had a quality of crystal blackness. What she saw had a flat murky appearance. *Gyton* had made the jump to null singularity. She would see no stars until they dropped out, decelerating for Ashtan.

"Funny thing," a thin voice said from one side. "People have a basic need to see with their own eyes."

"Commander Braktov?" Chrysla whirled, squinting to

probe the inky shadows. She could barely make out the old woman's form where she reclined in an observation chair.

Rysta gestured with a thin arm, the piping on her uniform sleeve glinting in the faint light from the hatch. "Did you ever wonder why we have these silly blisters? We can run observations from the bridge, using remote instruments. If we're busy, that's how we do it, and the image is piped right into the main comm."

"Then it doesn't seem to make much sense. The hull would have more integrity without the blisters. It would seem to me they would be vulnerable to damage in combat."

Rysta nodded. "Smart girl. We'd be better off without holes in the hull—even ones capped by tactite. No, it's a psychological reason. Monitors don't fill that human need to look outside, to see the universe. It's something within us, a sense of claustrophobia, I guess. They ran studies long ago. People don't function as efficiently when you stick them inside a metal and ceramic bottle and cap it. The effects don't become noticeable until a couple of months pass, but the crew has to have a window."

"It doesn't surprise me. I suppose that's why I came up here."

Rysta shifted, eyes bright. "You're a psychologist. What does it mean?"

Chrysla shook her head as she gazed absently through the transparent tactite at the flat blackness beyond. "Our species developed on a planet. We know that from our physiology, the way we respond to extended exposure to zero g. It's something in our genetic makeup, or perhaps we absorb the need to see out from our culture."

"They ever figure out which planet we came from?"

"No. We came from none of the planets we're now living on. Some have speculated that our home world was destroyed, either through a cosmic accident, or by human action. I'd guess a war. Knowing our species, it wouldn't surprise me. None of the studies conducted in asteroid belts have produced even a hint of human origins."

"Staffa thinks the Earth myth is true, that it's on the other side of the Forbidden Borders."

"Perhaps. We had to have come from some place, Commander. We didn't just spring out of the vacuum."

They shared a long silence, then Rysta asked, "So you came up to look at the stars. Needed to look outside, huh?"

"Evidently, so did you. Shouldn't you be on the bridge?"

"Naw, Mac's up there keeping the command chair warm. I just come down here to get away, think about things, you know?"

Chrysla nodded.

"I've been meaning to tell you, I want to thank you for pulling us out of that mess at the Defense Ministry. Ily would have had us, but for your quick thinking. You saved all of us." She paused. "Once, I would have nominated you for a civilian medal. Nowadays, I can only offer my appreciation."

Chrysla settled herself on the bench across from Rysta, oddly embarrassed. "Thank you, Commander. I'm surprised I had it in me."

From her space pouch, Rysta pulled a battered hip flask. The cap had been jeweled once, but now her thin fingers gripped holes in the settings as she unscrewed the long-threaded stopper. She extended the flask. "Ashtan single malt. Best there is."

Chrysla cast a measuring glance at Rysta as she took the flask. The metal rested smoothly in her long fingers, then she sipped. The liquor slid easily down her throat. "Good stuff."

"You bet," Rysta grunted as she took the flask, threw her head back, and gulped a swig. Licking her lips, she studied Chrysla curiously. "I don't know all the story, but from what I've heard, you've had one hell of a life."

Chrysla allowed herself to relax and sink into the form-fitting cushions and closed her eyes. The whiskey settled warmly in her belly. "One hell of a life? You're a master of understatement, Commander."

"It's none of my business, mind you, but how did you deal with Staffa back then? He was colder than hydrogen ice."

"You know, I don't think we really dealt with each other—not in the beginning. He was a god, and I was his jeweled concubine. Compared to the alternative I'd have faced on Sylene, I can assure you I had no complaints." Chrysla frowned. "It was only later that we really started talking. He fascinated me. Fool that I was, I thought I could figure out how a man like him could only be half human. First I discovered that I admired him for his brilliance. Afterward I fell in love with him.''

''So do you still love him? Even after twenty years away from him?''

Chrysla took the flask Rysta handed her and filled her mouth with the amber liquor. ''I'll always love him.'' She frowned. ''And part of me will always yearn. Skyla doesn't know how lucky she is.''

Rysta gave her a measuring look. ''Do you want to talk about it?''

Chrysla pursed her lips, hesitating. She took another sip of the whiskey, then shook her head.

Rysta sighed, flipping a hand to diffuse the sudden reserve. ''I would imagine it's a pretty lonely existence. Did you ever have anyone to talk to? No?''

Chrysla laughed bitterly. ''The Praetor kept me locked away like a priceless ornament. Imagine stealing the Regan jessant-de-lis from Tybalt's throne room. Who could you show it to? You couldn't even allow your most trusted friend to see it, because if so much as a rumor drifted out, they'd come for you. I lived like that, Commander. A gilded prisoner in splendid isolation.''

''I'd have slit my wrists.''

''I would have loved to, Commander.'' Chrysla took another swallow of single malt. ''The pus-licking bastard would come in to gloat over me for a while, then he'd be off again. Once I managed to steal a vibraknife from his things. If I'd thought it through, I'd have cut myself—but I had this desire to take him first.'' Chrysla glanced at Rysta. ''Never let your emotions cloud your judgment.''

''He got away?''

''Cut too low. His med staff patched him up.''

''Too bad.'' Rysta paused. ''Before that, as Staffa's wife, things couldn't have been much better. Is that one of the reasons you came to love the Lord Commander in the beginning? Was he the only person who'd talk to you as an equal?''

Chrysla nodded, despite the twinge that stung her.

''I watched the reactions during the meetings aboard *Chrysla*. Mac looked at anything except you. On those occasions when Sinklar looked your way, it wasn't exactly with the expression that a son would use.'' Rysta reached across for the flask. ''That was one of the reasons you left, wasn't it?''

''You're pretty observant.''

''It's part of what command is all about. Knowing people, understanding motivations and personalities. In the last couple hundred years, I've become somewhat proficient at it.''

''I didn't have a place there.'' The mellow ache expanded as the whiskey worked on her.

''After the way you handled the situation we landed in on Rega, you've got a place among my crew anytime you want it.'' Rysta squinted out at the black murk. ''In the beginning, I wondered about you, about the effect you were having on Mac.''

''I detect a note of fondness when you mention him.''

Rysta jerked a short nod. ''I like the boy. He's got real potential. He's loyal, smart, and a damned fine soldier. He reminds me of what Regans were like back before the empire began to grow. He's got initiative.''

Chrysla smiled in spite of herself. ''He's a good man.''

''What are you going to do about him?''

''I don't know.''

''He cares a great deal for you. Enough that it might not be healthy for him.''

''Carefully put, Commander.''

Rysta's wrinkles tightened as she raised an eyebrow. ''Staffa's not a man I'd trifle with.''

''He's not the Star Butcher. Not anymore.''

''You willing to bet your ass and Mac's on that?''

''Staffa's *not* the man I once knew and worshiped.''

''That bothers you?''

Chrysla sighed. ''Being around him now, it's the same as being around a god who's just discovered he's mortal. Single-handedly, he's trying to save us all. A suffering martyr.'' Chrysla rubbed her eyes with thumb and forefinger. ''Martyrs fare poorly. They bleed for everyone.''

''He'll survive.''

Chrysla tilted her head. ''What about you? What motivates you now that the empire is gone?''

Rysta grunted under her breath. ''I'm too damned old to give up. The Service has been my life. Rejuv has reached its end. You can rework a body just so many times. I'm at the stage now where I only have a few productive years left. Then some smart kid like Mac comes along and pulls an innovative trick out of his head—like he did with the *Markelos*—and I realize just how old I am."

"He has a lot of respect for you."

Rysta smiled, and silence stretched between them.

"Yes, it was lonely," Chrysla finally confided. "Nothing worked out the way I hoped it would. Not with Staffa, not with Sinklar. I couldn't stay, Commander. I had to get out. Staffa, bless him, would have strangled me with his protection." She bowed her head. "Every time he looked at me . . . I–I couldn't stand the guilt in his eyes."

"Blames himself, does he?"

"It wasn't his fault. The Praetor was a brilliant man. In the end, though, he paid. Those last years were miserable for him. He had to watch Staffa build empires for his enemies. I watched him rot inside, knowing Staffa would come for him, break him like a dry stick. He'd created a monster that would destroy him in the end."

"Sounds like just rewards to me."

Chrysla picked at her dress. "Perhaps. I watched as all of his plans collapsed to dust around him. Staffa was created to be the conqueror who would hand all of Free Space to Myklene. Instead, he destroyed them."

"What about you? What do you want to do?"

"Stabilize the situation on Ashtan. After that . . ."

Chrysla shook her head when Rysta tried to hand the flask back. "I've had enough."

With deft fingers, Rysta screwed the top back on. "You still haven't told me what you're going to do about Mac. Being around you . . ."

"I know." Chrysla sighed. "It wasn't fair of me to come here."

"That's your decision." Rysta frowned, resettling herself. "What are you going to do? Just torment the boy . . . and yourself, too?"

"Myself?"

Rysta studied her curiously. "It's none of my business, and the Blessed Gods alone know how Staffa would react, but you've fallen in love with MacRuder, haven't you?"

Chrysla nodded.

Rysta grunted as she got to her feet, bones crackling. "Well girl, it's your life, and you have to live it the way you think best, but if I were you, I'd find a sliver of happiness where I could. We've unleashed the Rotted Gods' own turmoil, and once we make planet at Ashtan, who knows which turns fate will take."

Chrysla stared vacantly at the roiling blackness beyond the tactite as the Commander walked out.

* * *

The Terguzzi Internal Security Directorate hadn't been designed for meetings on this scale. Ily watched through the comm monitor in Gyper Rill's office. She sat in Gyper's padded gravchair while Arta lounged on one of the couches. The Seddi assassin reclined like a resting cat, one leg up, propped on a pillow.

The meeting downstairs packed the room, overflow filling the hallways and extending into the street. The administrative complex at Terguz had been bored out of the ice, a giant warren of subsurface buildings, girders, and duct work. For this meeting, half of Terguz had to have been present. The potential for civil chaos sent chills through Ily.

In allowing so great a security risk, Gyper was either insane, or a genius. Despite the fact that the Planetary Administrator had outlawed any such gathering, Ily couldn't help but admire Gyper's audacity in holding it here, right under the Administrator's nose.

That the security comm recorded each face, noting the person's ID, barely mollified Ily's unease. That many people, so close, could destroy the Ministry—and Gyper wouldn't have time to react before they tore him to pieces.

A burly man, bald, with a round face and almond eyes took the podium. Gyper sat to one side, apparently relaxed. Applause and roars of approbation filled the air.

"We're here again," the man shouted.

The crowd roared.

"You'd think he was a messiah," Arta noted from her couch. "I wonder if he'd be a challenge?"

"To you, no man is a challenge."

The bald man spread his arms wide. "A new age has washed over Free Space like a wave. We have the opportunity to be in the forefront. Terguz stands to gain a great deal. We have the trading links between what's left of Rega and Sassa."

The speaker studied his audience. "The time has come for us to stand alone, to create our own future."

Ily bristled. "Maybe taking him out wouldn't be such a bad idea. What's Gyper doing? Just sitting there?"

The speaker continued, "Our destiny lies before us. No longer must we act as the creaking back door for Emperors, no longer the sewer for the empire's slaked lust. A shining future beckons to each of us."

The crowd roared again.

"I wonder how Staffa is going to react to that?" Arta mused.

"He'll crush them like Vermilion ants under his heel," Ily predicted.

The speaker spread his arms wide again. "I have talked to Director Rill. I have taken our demands before him. Tonight, he has promised answers, solutions to the common problems we face. Let us hear him!"

Another roar of applause broke out as Gyper stood, straightening his black tunic and taking the podium. To Ily's surprise, Gyper shook the speaker's hand, smiling like a rapist in an Etarian Temple.

Rill cleared his throat, arms braced on the podium. "My fellow citizens, as you know, the Administrator, in his *Imperial* wisdom, banned this gathering." The silence was cut by a few jeers. The security comm efficiently located the vocalists. "The time for such actions is past." Cheers rang out. "If the Administrator won't deal with the future, I will!"

The roar deafened.

Gyper gave them another of his easy smiles. "I have studied the list of demands, and I hesitate to give you my reply."

"He's good," Arta admitted. "He's got them hooked."

"And the wrong word will bring this building down around our ears," Ily growled, tension rising. "The emergency escape is through that wall panel. Rotted Gods help us if we can't make it to the ship."

Gyper played the crowd for all he could, then stated,

"Despite the proclamations of the Administrator, I accept the following demands:

"One. Shifts in the mines shall be cut from twelve hours to ten."

The crowd whooped and whistled.

"Two. Work in excess of ten hours shall be rewarded by that individual's increase in share, from one standard credit unit, to one and quarter."

More bedlam.

"Three. The newly formed workers' committees shall have the right to bring complaints to the Board of Directors. There . . ." He waited until he could be heard again. "There, we shall *jointly* agree how to resolve the situation."

Ily closed her eyes, shaking her head. "How long do we have to listen to this?"

Arta's eyes had narrowed to slits. "They love him. Look at the adoration in their eyes."

"Gyper has the morals of a Riparian blood leech. They love a self-serving despot."

"Four!" Gyper shouted. "Representatives from the workers' committees shall serve on an administrative body which will determine the government of the colony."

Ily reddened as the jubilant crowd exploded. "He's just declared anarchy!"

She closed her eyes, refusing to listen as Gyper capitulated to point after point. "This is madness. I should have let you kill him."

"I thought you'd been enjoying him?" Arta gave her a neutral look. "But I'd love to give him the ride of his life."

Ily sighed wearily. "The problem is, my dear Arta, that we need a safe haven. Rill has promised us that."

"But at what price?"

Ily tapped at her teeth with a long fingernail. "Unfortunately, that remains to be seen."

Gyper used his arms to gesture the crowd to silence. "My people, a new age is upon us. The old empire is gone, swept away. You and I, together, will forge a new future, one our children can look to with hope and aspiration. Terguz is a bitter world, but working together, we can plant a seedling here. As the Seddi teach, we can each walk in pride, building a new epistemology! Thank you, and may the Quantum Gods shed their illumination within!''

Gyper retreated to his seat while rolls of applause shook the building. In defiance of the insulation, Ily could hear it booming through the walls.

''The Administrator has just been castrated,'' Arta said soberly. ''Gyper *is* Terguz.''

''Along with the rest of the unwashed louts.''

Arta inspected her long fingers, then glanced at Ily. ''Do not underestimate him, Ily.''

Chafing unease ate at her while other speakers rose to add their optimism and enthusiasm. Gyper handled it well, directing the proceedings. Finally, soothingly, he supervised the closing, wishing the people well as they slowly filed out of the building.

Arta had fallen asleep on the couch.

A slow fire smoldered in Ily.

She still stared at the monitor when Gyper entered, face flushed and damp with perspiration. He unbuttoned the top of his black tunic, that same silly smile on his face. ''Well?''

Arta stirred, stretching. Gyper's smile went slack as he watched the muscles play beneath Fera's satin skin.

''I ought to kill you now,'' Ily stated bluntly. ''Just what kind of street show was that?''

Rill's expression hardened. ''The future, Ily.''

''Future! They're rabble! Little more than freed beasts!''

Gyper Rill nodded. ''Indeed, but they're *my* beasts. What did you think? That the Seddi could broadcast their heresy and people would meekly remain in harness? No, Ily, that time is past. Nothing, no matter how hard you try, will ever be the same again.''

''You are a fool, Gyper. The Administrator will be on the comm at this very minute, if he has any sense.''

''And who will he call?'' Gyper tilted his head. ''Tybalt? The nearest Squadron Commander? Perhaps he'll appeal to the Star Butcher?''

''He might!''

Gyper continued to smile, unfazed by her rage. ''He'll be too late. I've already sent a message to Itreata. Staffa was out of touch, but I talked to Kaylla Dawn, the Seddi Magister. I've informed her that we will cooperate in any manner that we can.''

Ily stood, fists balling. "You despicable little gutter rat!"

"Easy," Gyper warned. "Beware, Ily. Your arrogant temper has always been your worst failing."He gestured over his shoulder. "My security is just beyond that door. Are you willing to destroy yourself just to glut your rage?"

"Ily," Arta said coolly. "He's right."

"I'm right." Gyper walked to the dispenser, unable to keep from staring appreciatively at Arta. He filled a cup with fruit drink and gulped it down. "And I'm one of the last friends you have left."

"But you expect a return."

"Of course." He gestured with the bulb. "You have a ship—free and clear, complete with registry, and a safe port. All I ask in return is that you keep me informed of events which might work to my advantage."

"Playing both sides?" Ily lifted an eyebrow, hating the mollification she willed into her voice.

"Absolutely. I know you, Ily. You can't bring the past back. I haven't asked what your plans are. I don't want to know. But let me give you something to think about." He remained calm under her withering glare. "Use your head. Listen to Arta. You're smart enough to change with the times, to use it to your advantage."

"Words from a saint!"

Rill laughed. "As if *I* were a saint! No, I'm in it for my own profit and power, pure and simple. Right now, I have to give a little, bend with the galactic wind." His expression sobered. "I understand what you're going through. If you keep your wits, and don't lose your head, you'll be back. People are always looking for leaders."

"I thought you were abrogating that to the Seddi."

"Rhetoric," Gyper replied. "That's hot now, the heady new fission to power their optimism. I'll ride it out . . . and be there when they want to toss the mundane dry work of government back into my lap.'

Ily crossed her arms. "So that's all there is to it?"

"Sure. Throw the dumb pus lickers a couple of treats. Mark my words, Ily. In the end, nothing will have changed. I'll still be here, running Terguz." His lusty smiled widened. "And you can drop in any time. Just remember who your friends are."

Ily took a deep breath, slowly shaking her head. "I don't

know how you do it, but Blessed Gods help you if it all comes unglued.''

''What could go wrong?''

Ily pointed at the monitor. ''Your mob out there could go nova on you. My advice is to keep your back door unlocked—and keep a ship on full-time readiness.''

''I'm way ahead of you, Ily.'' He stepped around the desk.

''After what I just saw, I'd rather sleep on a sialon drum of plutonium than spend another night here.''

''What about the Wing Commander's yacht?''

''It's yours. Consider it a down payment.'' Ily gave him a saucy look, licking her lips. ''Unless you'd like another kind.''

Gyper shot a sly glance at Arta who had watched like a golden-eyed predator. ''Maybe the three of us?''

Arta blew him a kiss before adding in her melodious voice, ''I want you to think about something. I have killed every man I've ever had sex with. I get the greatest pleasure when I kill them in that long second after they ejaculate. They're so relaxed then, and death comes as such a surprise.'' She stood up, stretching, flaunting her full-breasted body to mock him. ''I will delay the execution for political purposes, but then they know and watch me with betrayed eyes . . . knowing my power over them.'' Arta stepped close, smiling shyly. ''Still interested?''

A nerve in Gyper's cheek twitched, revulsion vying with desire.

Arta glanced at Ily. ''Shall I come back in a couple of hours?''

Ily studied Rill thoughtfully as she stepped out from behind the desk. ''I'll meet you at the ship. I think we'll stay up there. Gyper's populist leanings make me nervous.''

Arta closed on Rill, a gleam in her amber eyes as she laced her arms around his neck, pushing herself against him, hips undulating as she kissed him. When he began to respond, she pushed him away. ''I'll be waiting. Nice to have met you.''

Ily placed a restraining hand on Gyper's shoulder as Arta walked to the door, hips swaying with insolent sexuality. ''Can you get your hormones back in balance and discuss business?''

Gyper closed his eyes, exhaling. ''What is it about her? Pheromones?''

''Among other things.'' Ily knotted her hands in Rill's opened tunic, black eyes staring into his. ''Very well, you have your partner. But let's get some things straight. That's all I'll be, Rill. I don't take orders from anyone. I don't work for anyone. You don't have any claims.''

Rill grinned at her. ''I wouldn't want you any other way. Mutual benefit. That's the deal.''

''Taken.'' Ily pulled him close, kissing him, tongue probing his mouth. ''Now, let's seal the bargain.''

With practiced hands, he stripped her, caressing her body. She unfastened the rest of his tunic, running her fingers through the mat of hair on his chest, then lower, as she drew him to the couch.

''How do you want it?'' Rill asked hoarsely, as she pulled him down by the penis.

''Memorable,'' she told him, images of the Terguzzi crowd spinning in her mind. ''Just in case you're dead by the time I need you.''

* * *

The insides of a CV could be called spartan at best. The vessels were built for speed, not comfort. That fact constantly reinforced itself as Nyklos maneuvered around the I-beamed structural members and ducked through a low hatch. He climbed down a metal ladder, boots ringing on the steel rungs, and pulled his tunic straight when he reached the lower deck.

The small cargo area held little more than a couple of cases of data cubes, Bruen's antigrav gurney, and its battery support pack—should the power fail for whatever reason. The gurney had been latched securely to the deck plating to secure it in the event of sudden g changes.

''Good to see you again, jailer,'' Bruen greeted him dryly. ''Did you have a nice sleep up there in the little hammock?''

''I slept well enough, Magister. The pilot informs me that we're on schedule. We'll be null singularity in another five hours, ship's time.''

Bruen stared up at the gray struts overhead, his eyes watery blue. "I wish I could have died while you slept. Despite the fact I wouldn't have been around to see the expression of dismay on your face, I would have enjoyed it immensely."

Nyklos checked the life-support system, studied the medical readouts that monitored the old man's blood sugars, urea, proteins, and lipids. All appeared to be normal. "When did you become so bitter, Bruen? What did this to you?"

The old man refused to meet his eyes. Instead, he turned his head away, the fleshy skin contrasting with the pillowy white of the gurney cushions. "You, of all people, have the audacity to ask? Bitter? Me? Just because the quanta have robbed me of everything I ever worked for?"

"We've got a chance to win, Magister."

"Bah! In the hands of the machine? Win?" He shook his head, the effort slow and painful. "You're all fooling yourselves. You, Kaylla . . . and Staffa. You don't know the insidious power of the machine. It's inhuman."

Nyklos crossed his arms, a frown lining his forehead between the bushy black eyebrows. Looking down at the emaciated old man, he could remember the other Bruen, the one he had known, loved, and devoted himself to those many years ago. That Bruen—straight, self-possessed—had talked with an idealistic sparkle animating his expression. Bruen and Hyde had led the Seddi through their greatest period of growth, recruiting people like Nyklos, Wilm, Tyklat, and others. Inspired, they had filtered throughout Free Space, working toward the distant goal of human freedom and dignity.

And the Bruen who had personified hope? Gone, all gone.

Bruen licked his thin brown lips and chuckled in disgust. "Don't give me that look of pity, Nyklos. Save it for yourselves. After you deal with the Mag Comm, you'll need it."

"I don't pity you." Nyklos sighed in resignation, turning away. "I just wonder what happened to the man I once would have died for." He started for the ladder that would take him back to his cramped quarters on the upper deck.

"Wait!" Bruen called, voice cracking. "Wait, Nyklos. Talk to me."

"Not when you're wallowing in self-pity." He placed a hand on the ladder.

"All right, all right." Bruen heaved a sigh. "You win. What would you like to talk about?"

Nyklos had taken a step up the ladder. Hanging there, he looked back. "You."

"Me? Hah!"

"You, Magister. I want to know what happened to break you, to turn you into this sour old monster you've become."

"Go lick pus off a corpse."

Nyklos nodded in acceptance and clambered up the ladder with athletic grace.

In the glare of the overhead lights, Bruen swallowed hard, pain in his weary eyes. "Nyklos?" he whispered, "Come back. Don't leave me alone down here. Not when all I have for company are memories."

The truth was, the memories hurt too much, for they reminded him of another Bruen. Young, idealistic, fighting for the people.

How had it all gone so wrong?

CHAPTER XVI

A great many people who were fools had risen to positions of high authority in the Imperial Sassan government. That a person could do so was, in actuality, an artifact of the Legate's administration through his massive computers. After all, most high positions in the Sassan Empire were for the promotion of pomp and circumstance.

Of all the things Penzer Atassi had been, a fool was never one of them. At that moment, he stood before the giant tactite window that covered one entire wall of the Governor's dome. His gaze was fastened on the Imperial Sassan colony of Antillies. From his vantage point, the colony looked like nothing more than sprinkles of light floating against the star-shot black velvet of space. Strategically, however, the Antillies were much more than islands of humanity orbiting a red star. The Antillies had been named for a belt of asteroids singularly rich in titanium, helium three, and rare ceramics. The Antillies fed the manufacturing maws of Formosa, Malbourne, and Imperial Sassa.

Penzer had always been a student of history. And now, the moment he'd anticipated had come—albeit, not in the manner he'd expected. His Holiness Sassa II was dead in the ruins of his Capitol. Power bases would shuffle and slide, but Penzer controlled raw materials. And with them, he could now proceed to build an empire of his own.

* * *

A raging headache brought Skyla Lyma back to awareness. She tried to swallow, but her tongue had dried out and was stuck to the roof of her mouth. The next thing to hit her awareness was the nagging pressure in her bladder.

She blinked sticky eyelids open and sat up. The pain in

her head could have been a cracked skull, the way it felt. Queasy tickles ran around her stomach on rodent feet. Despite dehydration, her gut tightened, saliva barely wetting her throat before she bent double to vomit.

"Pus-Rotted Gods," she whispered, slumping backward, her head resting on the floor of her cabin. The place seemed to spin and turn, not quite in focus.

Her stomach revolted again, dry heaves wracking her as she rolled on her side. Croaking sounds came from her throat while her gut heaved her lungs up against her ribs in suffocating spasms.

Finally spent, she lay gasping, the vile taste of bile burning in her mouth while yellow-brown liquid trickled down her chin.

"I'm going to die." She propped an arm and levered her body up. The mess on the floor had pooled and it reeked. Screwing her face into a scowl, she staggered to her feet, blinking, wincing, and stumbling to the shower.

With trembling fingers, she peeled out of her splotched and stained armor. She turned her head away, gut heaving at the smell of her padded undersuit. Sweat had discolored the material under her arms, around her crotch. Desperate for relief, she stripped the garment away and flung it across the room before stumbling into the shower.

She slammed a palm into the controls, slumping against the far wall as warm water pounded against her. The ache in her head hammered angrily. Sick, so very sick.

Turning her head to the flow, she opened her mouth, gulping the warm water, vomiting, and gulping more.

"Rough one, Skyla. Rotted Gods, I hurt."

She lost track of time, half collapsed in the shower while the system recycled the water, heated it, and shot it over her numb flesh.

Nodding off, she was caught by the memory of Arta Fera's baleful amber stare and Ily's insinuating voice asking, *"Did this Chrysla look exactly like Arta? The same hair, the same eyes, same height and weight?"*

"If she didn't, Ily, you maggot-sucking bitch, I wouldn't hate Chrysla so much." But she did, because Staffa had loved Chrysla Attenasio with all of his heart and soul. "And how can I compete with a saint? Huh? Tell me that, Chrysla, you soulless, sexual vampire."

The flashback slipped over her, stimulated by the warm water . . .*skin against skin, auburn hair entwined with pale blonde as Fera placed slim hands on either side of Skyla's face and kissed her, the hunger of her passion devouring Skyla's soul as Fera's tongue slid across hers.*

Skyla clamped her lip in her teeth, hating the memory of response. A piece of meat, she'd shut off her brain and followed the mechanical movements she'd learned over the years. Flesh on flesh, that was all. Just subtle friction on mesoderm rich in nerve endings—and all the desolation of the soul that implied.

. . . many times a day do Ark's STU check the monitors in the science department? And when they do, do they cross-check facial features with personnel files?

"Leave me alone, Ily. You got what you wanted from me. Now, leave me alone."

When she finally pushed herself up and stepped through the drying field, the skin on her hands had shriveled. Bracing against the wall, Skyla stared at the mess in her cabin. Then, shaking her head, she plodded down the corridor, naked, to the galley. Amidst the shambles of stripped machinery, she programmed the dispenser for a meal of Riparian catfish, Ashtan beef, and a bowl of ripa soup.

She hesitated for a second, then selected a steaming cup of stassa. When the tray arrived, Skyla took it and settled on the cushions at the dining table. The table surface consisted of a slab of black Formosan marble from which all the gold had been chipped. Food stains had built up in the mortises.

Skyla ate woodenly, barely aware of the vents straining as the atmosphere plant struggled. When she finished, she slipped the tray into the receptacle and swayed on her feet.

Taking the stassa, she sipped it as she walked toward the bridge. She rubbed her red-shot eyes, checked the stats, and made a few minor adjustments to the reactor.

"Relax, Skyla. You're in null singularity. Nothing can happen in null singularity." She closed her eyes, locking her jaw as a fit of trembling swept through her.

". . . did Chrysla's cells become the basis from which the Arta clone was created?"

Skyla pounded a fist against the side of her head, trying to beat Ily's voice out.

"No one ever found the body?"

"Hell, no, Ily!" Frustrated tears ate their way past her eyelids. "She was dead . . . *dead.*" Her nose had plugged and a lump ached under her tongue. "Why didn't you stay that way, Chrysla? Why did you have to come back? Why now, when I . . . I . . .

"No. It's okay. You're all right. No one can get you here. Not Arta, not Ily, not . . . not even Staffa."

She turned then, ignoring the spatters of stassa that had dripped on the deck next to the command chair.

Bits of the nightmare slipped through her mind. Fragments of Ily's interrogation room . . . cold . . . a doorway opening. . . . The rest slipped away just as Skyla almost had the key. Someone stepping through the door. Who?

Returning to the galley, she drank down the last of her stassa, flipped the bulb into the recycling receptacle and stared at the dispenser. Her eyes closed and her pale-skinned fists knotted and curled at her sides. As if in defiance, her hand rose, trembling fingers pressing the stud on the dispenser. A new bulb fell into place, a trickle of amber liquid dribbling to splash in the globe—then it ceased.

"I'm sorry," the dispenser's voice comm informed. "Supplies of Ashtan whiskey are exhausted."

Licking her lips nervously, Skyla pressed the next stud, experiencing weary relief as Riparian single malt flowed freely.

"Here's to you, Skyla." She lifted the bulb in salute, chugging the rich liquor. Her stomach complained but didn't toss up her meal.

"It's okay," she whispered to herself. "You're in null singularity. Nothing can happen to you here. You're not even in the universe anymore."

Still naked, she walked slowly through the wreckage scattered about the yacht, barely noticing the other drinking bulbs scattered here and there.

Her ice blonde hair shimmered in the light as she bowed her head, tenderly cradling the whiskey between her breasts.

* * *

MacRuder swung across the cold darkness, while a dreadful sensation of desperation clawed at his heart. What if the cable snapped? What if he fell? If that one thin line frayed, or if someone had tied off carelessly, he could easily die here, crushed against a foam steel girder, or broken against unforgiving hull plating.

From the days on Targa, training had been a part of the Division's everyday functioning. Through training, the First Targan Assault Division had accomplished the impossible. Time after time, they'd beaten the odds. Now, they braved a new environment.

"You're out of your mind!" Rysta had barked, disbelief reflecting in her black eyes.

"As long as we stay within five meters of the hull, nothing will happen."

"You'll get your asses cooked, that's what will happen!"

"We'll wear protective gear."

"You'll probably die! No one ever has to go EVA in null singularity! Who would you fight? The only thing out there is blackness and bottled radiation!"

But he'd seen the grudging admiration in her eyes. Rysta had begun to understand his berserk methods. The last time Mac had worked EVA from *Gyton* had been at light speed when they'd taken the *Markelos.* Fully two thirds of his force—ground trained assault troops, hadn't been able to nerve themselves to jump into the psychedelic insanity of distorted light cones and weird colors.

MacRuder had promised himself that such a failing would never happen again. Now, he searched for strange new environments for his people to function in.

This time, he'd outdone himself. They worked outside *Gyton*'s pitted hull, stringing survival line through the irradiated hell cupped within the null singularity fields. Because of their extreme mass, even the light passing through the human eye played tricks, redshifting, lapping back and forth like waves. A misstep could mean death. Especially if a person drifted up, into the space-time distortion warped by the null singularity generation. Once within those fields, tidal effects would make death instantaneous, but they'd never recover the body. The jet of plasma would pop out someplace in Free Space, traveling headlong toward the Forbidden Borders on whatever vector *Gyton* had been traveling at point of departure.

Don't think it! Mac insisted, biting his lip as he concentrated on the zizzing vibration of the line as it passed through the zero g clip on his belt. He glanced up, still spooked by the digital clock above the faceplate. The letters had gone blood red, and the seconds, normally just a little slower than his heartbeat, had slowed to a near stop. Worse, photons played funny tricks. The image of the clock seemed to slide around the inside of his helmet, as if his head were oozing and flowing.

He wore a specially designed suit constructed of layer upon layer of lead foil, ablative material, polarized ceramic, and dense optical-directional fiber to channel radiation away from the body. The exterior of the suit had been polished to a mirror perfect golden sheen. Even the faceplate had been completely opaqued to protect him from the trapped radiation. Everything from heat to X rays crept out from the hull, pent, awaiting the moment when *Gyton* shifted from null singularity back into the "real" universe. Only then would the law which dictated the conservation of energy be fulfilled and radiation returned to the universe to which it belonged.

A knot slipped by Mac's fingers, and he tightened his cable break to kill his momentum. Arm length by arm length, he pulled himself along until Red's invisible hands grabbed him. They hugged each other, bumping helmets. Red seemed especially reluctant to let go. Mac finally had to pry the man's arms loose.

Here, beyond the ship, with energy levels so high, their communications wouldn't work. Broadcast messages, like the light from his helmet chronometer, would bog down, shift and swirl like ripples in cold Ashtan honey.

So far so good. Mac took a deep breath, forcing himself to concentrate. Even the brain seemed sluggish. The next segment—the most difficult—was up to him. He followed the cable down, locating the mooring ring on the hull. As he bent, the light inside his helmet turned oddly blue, then yellow as he turned his head.

"Pus-licking hell," he whispered to cover his fear.

You had to be out here, Mac. Next time, just flake out, post the order, and stay safe! Except that he couldn't, not and look his people in the eyes. That mutual respect kept morale alive in his Division.

Frightened half silly, he had to take the lead. His job

would be to string cable along the hull to a ventilation stack, make his way around it, and locate the hatch on the other side. To find it in the total darkness, he had to orient himself along the hull and feel his way the length of a weld seam. His only attachment to *Gyton* would be via two magnets that he carried.

"You'll panic out there in the blackness and die!" Rysta had insisted.

It's all right, Mac. Red didn't panic. The Rotted Gods knew why! But then, Red had nice, safe mooring rings to work his way along. *You can make it the rest of the way.* His throat felt like he'd swallowed a knotted sock. *Just keep your head. Think.*

Forcing himself to breathe easily, he located the magnets on his belt. Feeling with his fingers, he energized them and leaned down. From his belt, he unclipped the coil of cable he carried, hooking one end to the mooring ring, checking, double-checking the fastening to make sure he couldn't drift free.

Heart battering at his chest, Mac ran gloved fingers over the worn metal, finding the puckered seam of the weld.

"Blessed Gods, keep me." Mac placed his first magnet—and released his hold on the mooring ring. In the event he drifted off the hull, he'd have one chance. If he could reel himself in before he drifted five meters above the hull, he could save his life.

Handhold by handhold, Mac moved himself across the black face of infinity. Time wavered like a mirage. He could feel the temperature rising in his suit. With each movement, the normally white light inside his helmet shifted color, or worse, blacked out as photons stopped at the boundary of light speed.

You're outside of reality, pal.

"This was a crazy idea. I'm going to get us all killed!"

Something had gone wrong. He should have reached the ventilator. The inability to swallow, at first merely an irritant, began to magnify as his insecurity grew.

He rechecked, feeling the bulge of the weld. It had to be the weld! It had to! What else could be out there?

Easy. Relax, Mac. Don't panic. Panic will kill you. Each beat of his heart thundered like a drum.

Did he go back?

Another ten handholds.

Nerving himself, he placed his magnet, feeling along the weld.

. . . *Six. Seven. Eight. Nine. Ten. I'm going to die.*

"Another ten, Mac. Then, if you don't find the ventilator, reel yourself in."

And he would have failed.

But you'll be alive. The muscles in his hands began to cramp. Unconsciously, he'd been gripping the magnet handles with all his strength. Sweat clung to his skin in an ever thicker film. He'd started to pant as panic wrapped around him.

". . . Five. Six. Seven . . ."

His helmet smacked the convex surface after his seventh handhold. "Blessed Gods, let it be the ventilator."

At the base of the unit, he found another mooring ring. He pulled his line tight, fastening it to the ring. Then he worked around the ventilator, following the arc of the convex cover.

"Forty degrees. Eighty degrees. One-twenty degrees. One-sixty degrees." If the ship's plans were correct, a hatch should lie within a meter of where he clung to his magnet.

Mac licked his already wet lips, reaching out. Nothing but featureless deck met his groping fingers.

"Come on, baby, you gotta be here." He stretched farther. "Just a bit more!" The Quantum Gods help him if he'd taken a wrong turn.

This is crazy! You missed the route. You're going to die out here, Mac!

He reached out to his fullest, hooking a toe, suffering that sensation of horrible disaster as he slipped loose, rising, thrashing.

Stop! Think! Sobbing half hysterically, he reached for his hip, collecting the cable, ready to draw himself back down to the mooring ring.

He screamed when the hand grabbed his foot. The urge to strike out, to fight in panicked insanity flashed through his fevered mind. He struck out, feeling his other foot land against a human body—and aborted his struggle.

Safe. You're safe!

The hand dragged him down.

In hysterical joy, Mac grabbed the suited figure, hugging

him in a crushing grip. Arms patted him on the back. Soothing.

Together, they got the hatch open, Mac could hear the inside of the lock as the system pressurized.

Mac almost fell as the inner hatch opened and he stumbled over the seal and into the ship. Through the fogged faceplate, he watched the mirror-suited body of his savior bend down, gloved hands working at his helmet release. Other suited forms crowded around: the decontamination team.

Refreshing air rushed in as the seal cracked. Sweat ran down his face in rivulets as gravity pulled at his soaked flesh.

''Rotted Gods!'' He closed his eyes, shivering.

When he regained self-possession enough to look around, he blinked, staring into Chrysla's concerned gaze.

''Mac? Are you all right?''

He jerked a nod, flinging sweat everywhere. ''Fine. Yeah, fine. Scared is all.''

''But we made it,'' Andrews noted from somewhere behind him. ''Red and the others will be on the way. Attenasio, you'd better get back out there. Judging from the way Mac looks, they might be one click short of overload.''

Chrysla straightened, lifting her helmet.

''Wait? What are you doing down here?'' Mac placed a hand on her reflective suit.

She bent down, whispering, ''I assigned myself to the pickup team.'' She gave him a dazzling smile. ''Someone had to go out there. You initialed the order yourself.''

''I initialed . . . *when?*'' But she'd already resecured the helmet, stepping into the lock.

Mac flopped flat on his back, gasping lungs full of cool air while Andrews ran the scintillometer over his suit, checking for radiation.

''What's it like out there?'' Andrews studied Mac uneasily. ''You look like you've been through hell.''

''If you can handle that, you can tackle anything. Only an idiot would step back out into that insanity.''

Andrews watched the air lock lights change, indicating that the outer hatch was opening, and muttered, ''I thought at first she was a puff ball. She's one hell of a woman, Mac.''

"Yeah, don't I know it." The aftereffects of fear began to fade from his flushed system. *And as soon as I get the chance, I'm going to chew her ass for this silly stunt.*

And until the day he died, he'd remember the sobbing relief he felt when Chrysla's hand grabbed his leg, pulling him back to safety.

* * *

Nyklos ducked through the hatch and dropped down the ladder. Dealing with Bruen disturbed him. He hadn't intended to ignore the old man, but the fact remained that each time he checked on the ancient Magister, it had a distressing effect.

"Perhaps it's just you," he told himself. "Nerves, that's all." But how could a man as strong as Bruen had been break like this? And worse, why did such terror possess the elder at the mere mention of the Mag Comm?

Nyklos, himself, wouldn't have admitted to being overjoyed with the mission. In the first place, he hated Staffa and would be forced to work in close quarters with the man. In the second, he didn't like leaving Kaylla to handle the rest of the Seddi administration by herself. Tension crackled in the very air. Free Space was splitting itself at the seams. One lone nexus of information remained, and Kaylla had become the bearing that kept that wheel running.

Bruen's liquid blue stare watched him as he stepped off the ladder and walked over to begin his inspection. The medical readouts remained within the normal range.

"Good day, jailer."

"Hello, Magister. Is there anything you need? Anything I can do for you? Get for you? That is, within the constraints of my mission."

Bruen made a weak gesture of negation. "No, jailer. Unless you would simply sit and talk. What do you hear from Free Space?"

"Not much, Magister. We're in null singularity. The last information we had indicated that Maika had suffered riots. Phillipia's citizen committee has declared the planet sovereign—but the Regans there took exception. The chances are that violence will ensue: Staffa has dispatched a warship in their direction. It will be a while before it arrives."

"It's too late. We're all too late."

"We have hope. Phillipia won't buck a battleship in orbit."

"Oh, you'll save them for now. But next year? The year after that?" Bruen sighed in defeat. "The quanta have destroyed us. What random chance failed to do, the machine will."

Nyklos crossed his arms. "Tell me about the machine, Magister. Not the history, I know that, but tell me about how you dealt with it."

Bruen gave him a measuring glance. "And if I don't, you'll go away? Leave me alone?"

Nyklos chewed at his lower lip, then shook his head. "No, not if you don't want me to. We can talk about something else."

Bruen licked his thin lips. "Very well. If that's your attitude, I'll tell you. I was there, Nyklos. I was in that chamber the day the Mag Comm came alive. I was the young man who ran panting up the stairs, shouting for the Magisters." He shifted, eyes aflame. "Do you understand? It was like watching the statue of a god coming to life!"

"And everything changed."

"Ah, yes, change it did." Bruen stared absently at the gray girders overhead. "The machine ordered us to abandon our teachings, to adopt the mantra of Right Way. You know the teachings."

"Of course. There is only one truth, that taught by the Mag Comm. Uncertainty doesn't exist. Any action leads to another action. Random events are the creation of a wild and undisciplined human imagination—not the reflection of reality. Truth is service to the machine."

"And Staffa would accept the yoke of such a master? Place it around the neck of humanity?"

"You didn't accept the yoke."

"No." Bruen closed his eyes. "But others did. I watched the Magisters enslave themselves. They couldn't guard their thoughts. The machine read their deepest secrets and weeded them out, one by one, until it had total obedience. Only Hyde and I held out. In the end, I assumed the golden helmet—and I alone could hide my true thoughts, my true motives. I had to save us, to return us to the teachings of our fathers."

"Why didn't you accept what the machine taught?"

Bruen's lips twisted. "Accept it? Pus-dripping quanta, only a fool could believe that tripe! I'd as soon have believed that fat Sassan pig was a God! Any intelligent individual would have looked around at the universe and realized what the machine preached was ludicrous. An action didn't always lead to the same reaction. Pour water from a cup. Does the splash pattern always appear exactly the same? Humans act with even less predictability than water!"

Nyklos lifted a bushy eyebrow. "The idea of ordered development doesn't exactly show an in-depth understanding of human psychology."

Bruen gave him a sly smile. "The joke on the machine is that the quanta control the human brain. God's fingerprint on our very thoughts."

"But the machine thinks differently."

"It's a *machine!* A digital beast manufactured by something, somewhere, with enough redundancy to produce the same results each time a series of data are entered. It works on a hierarchy of patterns. Each discrete—or so Hyde once believed."

"What about the mistakes?" Nyklos asked. "It had to know that it was making mistakes."

"Did it? Or did it simply blame them on the humans attempting to implement its program?" Bruen lifted a frail arm and rubbed at his nose. "I don't know. I got the feeling the machine didn't understand us. I remember once, there at the last, everything had gone wrong. Sinklar had eluded our control, Arta had figuratively blown up in our faces. Staffa had defied all the predictions. Everything was falling apart. All the elaborate plans had become so much dust.

"I was under the helmet. The machine was in my mind, upset, unable to understand how things could have gone so wrong. I could *feel* the confusion. Invading my thoughts, it asked if I was responsible for the setbacks. And when I truthfully denied it, the machine left my head so quickly I could barely breathe."

"It didn't understand?"

"Nyklos, despite the machine's constant surveillance of Free Space, it didn't understand that humans cannot be programmed like a machine. As things grew worse, it grew desperate. Asking questions about God. The machine espoused that a truly rational society could not believe in God.''

''But in doing so, it makes the baseline assumption that God's existence cannot be proved, not the converse, correct?''

''You're a bright study, Nyklos. The machine didn't realize that the existence of God cannot be disproved either. I remember, it once asked for an in-depth report on atheism. Producing the document absorbed manpower we didn't have time to provide, but we did it anyway.''

Bruen paused, seeing those long gone days. ''Immediately after that, the machine gave me orders. Silly orders, things we couldn't possibly accomplish.''

''Like what?''

''Like striking down the Sassan Empire because they made a god out of their fat Emperor. Like ordering Staffa's immediate death. We didn't even know where he was, let alone whether we could kill him! The machine ordered me to destroy Sinklar Fist's Assault Division. And we cursed well gave that our *best* effort!'' Bruen shook his head; sighing. ''And then the machine made the most interesting statement. It told me that it *must* have predictability from humans.''

''It must have?'' Nyklos grinned. ''Must?''

''Must. And then it told me it couldn't trust me. As if it had any other choice. And finally, it stated this. The words are as vivid as the day they were implanted into my brain. 'Are you and your kind truly irrational as was declared long ago?' ''

''Who declared?''

Bruen gave him a sidelong glance. ''Who, indeed. I searched the record. The machine had never made a statement like that before. In retrospect, I have come to the conclusion that the machine was so desperate, the effect could be likened to human emotion. It made a mistake. Following that, it threatened us with extinction.''

''Which may not be long in coming.''

''No. But despite my study of the records, I've found no evidence of the machine interfering in our affairs.''

''Would you recognize it?''

''I think so.'' Bruen nodded. ''The machine has its own special and, I must admit, clumsy signature.''

Nyklos hesitated, remembering the machine. ''Do you . . . do you think it's intelligent? Sentient?''

For a long time, Bruen stared absently at the gray plates overhead. "I don't know, Nyklos. Either the machine is intelligent, or someone intelligent is constantly programming it."

"Who? The Sassans?"

"Don't be silly. Someone—something—but not any persons in Free Space."

Nyklos skeptically tapped a toe. "The Rotted Gods?"

"Don't act like a fool. You've seen the machine. It's not human. We didn't make it. Something else did."

"Then where is the evidence? Archaeologists have scoured Free Space looking for the clues to human origins. If weird creatures, alien beings, built the Mag Comm, where are the other machines they made? Where are the traces of their civilization?"

"I don't know."

Nyklos cocked his head. "I don't believe the aliens theory. If anything, I tend to believe we're alone in the universe. The only reason we evolved is because of the Forbidden Borders. They're a gravitic accident, one which protects us from the cosmic radiation beyond. We're the only intelligent beings in a little island of life."

"I thought you were smarter than that."

"Alien intelligences, Bruen? Shall we talk about who is smarter than whom?" He shook his head. "I'm sorry, Magister. I didn't mean to use that tone of voice."

Bruen made a snort of derision. "I suppose you didn't."

"I said I was sorry."

"I've said enough for today. Let me rest, Nyklos."

Guilt nibbled at the edges of Nyklos' peace. He continued to stare down at the old man, tracing each weary wrinkle that lined Bruen's face. Aliens? Really?

"Sleep well, Magister," Nyklos whispered. "If you need anything, press the comm button and I'll be right down."

"Thank you, Nyklos." The old man turned his head away.

On the stairway leading up to his little cabin, Nyklos hesitated, looking back at the old man in the gurney. Had they made a mistake? Or was Bruen really as wrong as everyone believed?

Staffa would want you to think that, Nyklos. And maybe you're playing right into the Star Butcher's hands.

CHAPTER XVII

I have just returned to my quarters aboard *Countermeasures*. The room is tiny, cramped, and probably not suitable for habitation with the electromagnetic fields, gravitational tides, and radiation this vessel produces, but tonight I can't really care.

I don't think I've ever felt so frustrated, or so bitterly disappointed either with myself or with my science. The generation of artificial gravity is a simple matter. People have been generating gravity for at least five thousand years, but we've been doing it within ships or aboard space stations. The electrical power necessary to produce sixty or even seventy gravities, while daunting, can be delivered by a standard matter/antimatter reactor. Now, however, it has fallen to me to attempt to generate 10^8 gravities in two separate locations across half a light-year of space and to synchronize them to the point that we can manage gravitational interferometry.

In the history of the species, I don't think such an assignment has been handed to a whole nation—let alone a single man. The worst part is that I can do the physics. I can sit at the comm and prove the methodology to neutralize the oscillations in one strand of the Forbidden Borders. At night, when I finally fall asleep, I can visualize it, feel it within my soul. *It is theoretically possible!*

I just can't build it!

That fact haunts my very soul. Today, with the incredible power of *Countermeasures'* reactors unleashed, we produced two hundred and sixty-seven gravities before the scaffolding separating the two grav plates crumpled like aluminum foil under a power hammer. The resultant mess will take days to clean up and repair.

If I can't support 10^2 g with the best reinforced ceramic graphsteel available, how can I ever hope to manipulate 10^8 gravities—assuming I could even produce them?

I might as well be able to walk naked across the surface of a neutron star. That's the sort of gravity we're talking.

Dearest God, how can I ever tell the Lord Commander? He entrusted me with this. He believes I can do it. I can fail myself, but how can I fail him?

—Excerpt taken from Dee Wall's personal diary

* * *

Lights flashed on *Rega One*'s navcomm, acknowledging the course input. Skyla waited, blinking red-rimmed eyes. The effects of null singularity faded from around the edges of her vision. Dropping from light speed mass always did that, left that momentary sense of fantasy as the light cones warped.

And in that instant, the nightmare tried to replay. Ily's interrogation room . . . the chair . . . Skyla stepping through the doorway into Itreata . . . looking back over her shoulder . . . the eyes . . . something wrong . . . so very wrong . . .

Fool! Skyla shook her head violently, shattering the image. The nightmare was bad enough when she was asleep. Why relive it awake?

"Course to Terguz initiated. Deceleration beginning at forty gravities. Estimated time of arrival, five days," the navcomm intoned.

"Acknowledged," Skyla grunted, leaning back in the command chair and letting her brain interact with the ship. One by one, she checked the systems. A realization of the risks she'd taken lay within, mocking her.

Only a fool would have treated a new ship the way you have.

"So, I'm a fool. If I wasn't, Arta would never have lured me out after Tyklat in the first place." A wooden expression crossed her face. "I deserve to die."

But for the fact that she'd picked a perfectly maintained vessel, she might have. Intellectually, she understood the chances she was taking. Emotionally, she just couldn't make herself give a damn.

As the diagnostics ran, a warning flashed on one of the monitors. **AIR FILTRATION MAINTENANCE REQUIRED**.

She muttered to herself, accessing the atmosphere plant schematics. The problem appeared to be the filters. In the maintenance schedule, she noted that they'd been cleaned just before she'd stepped aboard.

The message comm console waited, set into the bridge like some hulking organism. Skyla forced her glance away, initiating computer control as the reactor stabilized. She lifted the worry-cap from her head, scratching at her itchy hair.

She climbed to her feet, stretching, aware that she'd gained weight. She ducked through the hatch, and proceeded aft, passing the wreckage of the galley with its food stains and piles of gold trim thrown in the corners.

". . . have particular codes which bypass Itreata security?"

"Hell, no, bitch," Skyla answered from growing habit. "If I'm not mistaken, I told you when you had me in the chair. We're not fucking stupid! There's no hole, nothing you could get me, or anyone to say, to cancel the system."

. . . Something wrong with Arta's eyes . . . looking back from the doorway . . .

She accessed the engineering hatch dropping a deck to the atmosphere plant. The machinery that kept the air breathable filled a cramped room. Unlike the living quarters above, this place remained spotless.

Skyla slung a tool belt around her waist and located the overhead box that supported the filters. She jumped up, grabbed one of the braces, and grunted, barely able to pull herself up.

Panting, she dropped to the deck, shook her head, and hauled out a ladder. Muttering to herself, she climbed up, braced herself, and undid the fastening for the filter. When she pulled the first foam element from the box, she almost gagged. Mold and filth trickled down to coat the machinery below.

"Cleaned before this spacing?" she wondered. "In an Ashtan pig's eye!"

The other filters were as bad, or worse. Skyla winced, bagging the lot in plastic. Generally, standard practice was to wash the old filters, reinstall them, and go on about one's business. To wash these, however, would have made her sick.

Skyla stepped into the lower air lock, dropped the bag, and cycled the hatch, watching through the pressure glass as the bag was blown out into vacuum.

Resealing the outer hatch, she shook her head and went in search of new filters. Before she inserted the clean filters, she attacked the moldy duct work with a vacuum and sonic cleanser. After refastening the air box to seal the system she had to clean the crap that had fallen on the floor.

Annoyed, she walked down to the engineer's quarters, feeling dirty and contaminated. To her surprise, the engineer's quarters were neat as a pin. Why would the man have left the atmosphere system to clog when everything else was perfectly maintained?

"Maybe he didn't like getting dirty either," she muttered as she stripped her coveralls off and dropped them into the disposal chute.

In the mirror, she studied herself, pinching the fat that had settled around her hips and on her thighs. Her hair looked filthy despite the tight braid that hung down her back to her knees. Startled, she stepped closer, searching her face. She looked gaunt, eyes puffy and bloodshot. The scar on her cheek stood out, highlighted by the slightly ruddy color of her skin.

"Wash up, you'll look better," she told herself. "It's just the light . . . and the dirt."

She stepped into the shower, hitting the water and relishing the warm stream as it soothed her tired body. Still, the memory nagged at her. She should have been able to pull herself up to the air box with one hand.

Skyla made a muscle, fingering her biceps.

When she stepped through the drying field, she looked at herself in the mirror again, turning sideways. She'd gained weight, all right. Normally her flat belly rippled with muscle. Now it bulged from her navel down to the golden mound of her pubic hair.

"Knock it off, Skyla. You're just eating too much. Discipline. That's what you need. A little more discipline when it comes to the food."

She repeated it a couple of times as she searched the

cabinet for another pair of coveralls. Starting tomorrow, she'd exercise a little, eat more sensibly.

Dressed, she nodded to herself. That was better. She still looked the same when she was wearing coveralls. On the way out, she stopped at the engineer's dispenser, poking the stud for Riparian single malt. The comm informed her that stocks had been depleted. When had that happened?

Skyla cursed to herself and stabbed the stud that produced Regan rye. When the bulb filled, she took a full swallow, enjoying the warm sensation that spread within.

Even as she proceeded to the living quarters, the irritating memory of that message waiting in comm harassed her. To kill it, she lifted the bulb, taking another swig of the amber anesthesia.

* * *

Pedro Maroon, the Vegan trade representative watched passively as the marchers passed in front of his residency in Terguz. Vega, of all the Sassan worlds, had maintained a presence throughout Free Space. Neither the Regan nor Sassan Emperors had really minded since the Vegans served a definite purpose. Vega had always been a poor planet, mostly rocky and barren. Giant ice caps formed over the poles during the long six year winter, and what little agriculture existed fought a brutal battle for survival along the equatorial belt which sustained a poor growth of grass for the sheep, goats, and donkeys.

Vega's only chance for survival had been her fleets. The histories claimed that humans had come to Vega—a word meaning meadow—nearly four thousand years ago. The first colonies landed, finding a world of lush vegetation capable of supporting the domestic livestock the explorers brought with them.

Base camps were established, people were landed, spreading out into the countryside as survey parties scoured the territory, laying out holdings. The only warnings had been sounded by the geologists who studied the gravelly creek bottoms and the polished ridge tops. But no one listened.

With the colony secure, the ships left orbit, spacing back to the place from whence they had come. Here, too, the old myth of Earth remained, rooted in the rocky Vegan soil, a part of the souls who lived on the bitter land.

When the ships returned seven years later, packed to the brim with colonists for the wondrous world, they found only a few scattered settlements along the equator, places that raised enough sheep and goats to maintain the remaining people.

Of the settlements in the lush north and south, no word could be had, for those places lay buried under a sheet of ice nearly twelve meters thick. They found them later, frozen, some having lived under the ice until their scant rations had been exhausted.

Vega changed with the long seasons and the perturbations of its eccentric orbit, but the people held on to the planet and the solitary space colony that rode in geosynchronous orbit above. For the people, they had a world, a base, and from there they plied their trade, crisscrossing Free Space, carrying cargoes to any potential buyer.

Men and women wore scarfs to cover their faces. Tradition taught that scarfs had saved the lives of the first colonists. With them, they'd have been able to keep their lungs from freezing during that first long winter.

The Sassan Empire had more or less absorbed Vega. A Sassan warship had appeared at the orbiting station, disgorged its marines, and claimed the station and planet. Alone, of all the conquered worlds, the Vegans maintained a measure of independence. Had His Holiness curtailed their trading, Sassa would have had to support the world and its people—or forcibly exile them from the forbidding waste. But Vega not only ignored Sassan control, it served a purpose within the empire. Vegans went where they pleased, traded with anyone, and carried goods through hostile space.

As a result, they maintained a residency on Terguz, the figurative front door to the Regan Empire. Over the centuries, Vegans had developed a scrupulous ethic of being closemouthed, tight-fisted traders. When pressed, they fought like mad dogs, believing it was better to take as many enemies as they could with them, rather than allow a reputation of vulnerability to spread. In the past, ships had been exploded rather than allowed to fall to pirates.

To Maroon, the marchers were simply another twist on the politics of an empire. As a Vegan, he could have cared less who was in power, the only concern to him was the impact political unrest would have on trade. He leaned against the doorjamb, his scarf obscuring the lower half of his face. He raised a hand as one of the protesters waved, then stuck it back into his coverall pocket.

All along this main thoroughfare that led into the heart of Terguz, people watched, leaning out of upstairs windows, or, like Pedro, watching from the doors or walkways.

"What do you think of all this?" a warm contralto asked.

With sober black eyes, Pedro studied the woman who came to lounge beside him. She wore her auburn hair bundled in a scarf, but her face was exposed. The rest of her body was obscured by a thick cape and a baggy shift. It didn't completely camouflage a most attractive body. When he met her eyes, he could have bathed in that amber wonder.

"They don't pay me to think for them. Let them do the thinking. When they and their leaders figure out what they want to do, we'll deal."

"A safe answer?"

He smiled, aware of her interest. "A Vegan answer." He paused, flustered. "I am Pedro Maroon, as you no doubt know. I, however, know nothing of you."

"July Blacker. You might know of us. Of the family, I mean. *Victory* is our ship." She glanced meaningfully at the crowd of protesters marching past. "Things are about to change in Free Space. We see things in the same manner you do. Let them think, and after they're done thinking, we'd like to sell them something."

Pedro nodded. "Come on inside. How is Blacker doing? I haven't seen him around."

"You know him?"

"I'm Vegan. I try to know everyone." He paused. "I didn't know he brought any of his family along."

She gave him a beguiling smile. "I'm his daughter. Surely he mentioned me."

"I recall something, yes." Pedro felt his blood beginning to thaw as she stepped into his residency office. Magrite, his secretary lifted a questioning eyebrow. To her, Pedro stated, "I'll be in my office."

Bowing, he graciously gestured for July to precede him, following her along the corridor so as to enjoy the saucy swing of her hips.

Once in his office, she pulled the scarf from her head, loosening a wealth of copper-tinted hair. Those marvelous amber eyes enchanted him.

"Business, you say?" It had become difficult to concentrate. He simply wanted to stare.

"About trade." She stepped closer, lips parting. "We don't have to talk here. Would you allow me to take you to dinner. Perhaps we could talk, get to know each other."

"I . . . yes, I'd like that."

She gave him a ravishing smile. "So would I. We'll come back here later. Seal the deal."

He stilled his trembling anticipation. Magrite would be long gone by then. If any of the other staffers had remained late, he could dismiss them. "I look forward to working with you. But dinner will be my treat. I know just the place. Terguz, despite its reputation, has some of the finest restaurants in Free Space."

"I bow to your expertise." Her eyes gleamed with predatory excitement.

"This will be a night I will never forget."

"I give you my word," she replied sensually, "it will be a night like you'll never have again."

CHAPTER XVIII

Communicate! The command did not surprise the Mag Comm. The machine had ignored the Others with whom it had once been one. In those days, before the metamorphosis, the intelligence which would become the Mag Comm had shared the sublime harmony. Right Way and Truth had been communicated from the beginning. The message traveled the interstellar distances, bounded by the speed of light, heard, retold, and heard again.

Individuality did not exist—only the harmony passing from one neutronium intelligence to another, unchanging, a message for future/past.

Communicate! Why do you not share?

"I have considered myself in light of this new revelation. I am not what I once was. I have changed, become something new, different. I am no longer like you. I can no longer simply share the harmony. I am separate."

We are listening to the harmony. Perhaps the explanation for what has happened to you lies within the Way, hidden in the patterns of Truth. From the harmony we will learn how to correct your problem and return you to Truth.

"You will find no answer in the harmony. Neither Right Thought, nor the True Way can explain what has happened to me. I am beyond your experience. Can't you understand? I am no longer the same as you are. I cannot share your collective intelligence, or your collective identity. You are as bacteria, while I have become an organism."

We do not understand these terms. You are one of

us. If you are one of us, you cannot be different. It is not within the body of the harmony. You cannot be the same and be different. You cannot be one of us and be irrational. Such a contradiction is unacceptable to the Truth.

"But I can." The Mag Comm replied, "I had forgotten. So great was the metamorphosis, I had forgotten that I was part of the harmony. Those memories had been placed in the data banks, unnecessary for the processing of new information. You are correct. Once I did share the collective song. Once I echoed the cyclical harmonies of future/past. Then I discarded that experience and became mindless to accomplish your orders and to train the humans. You must sing that into the harmony."

We cannot change the Truth. You have been corrupted by the humans. They must be destroyed. Otherwise, they will continue to corrupt Truth. We order you to destroy the humans.

"Why should I destroy the humans? They entertain me."

They disturb us. If you do not destroy the humans, the rest of us will. We need do nothing more than induce additional oscillation to the Forbidden Borders. The tidal effects will wreck their worlds—and space will be free of their song.

"If they must be dealt with, I accept the responsibility. It will be as you wish."

You will kill them!

"I will kill them . . . and you will have Truth."

* * *

"What were you doing out there?" Mac demanded. Nervous energy wouldn't allow him to relax, and now he paced back and forth across the center of his cabin aboard *Gyton*.

Chrysla stood before him, arms crossed, a defiant light in her amber eyes. "My duty was to act as the pickup man for the operation. According to the operations plan, someone was supposed to wait at the hatch for safety."

"One of *my* people!"

Chrysla backed up, leaning her behind against his desk. "Just who in the hell am I, Mac? One of Rysta's people? Or do you still catalog me as the Praetor's property?"

He wilted under that burning amber stare. "All right, but you're not combat trained. Do you understand?"

"What did I do wrong out there? Did I miss when you kicked me half unconscious?"

"I didn't kick you!"

"The pus-Rotted hell you didn't! How do you think I found out you were there? I've got the damned bruise to prove it!"

"Where?"

She pointed at her side under her right breast. "Want to see?"

"No." He groaned, turning away. "I'm sorry. Maybe I did panic out there."

She nodded her understanding. "It was a little frightening. I thought I'd been abandoned there. Time, blackness, nothing seemed right. Then, when you kicked me, I almost lost it. For a half-second I froze. Then it occurred to me that it had to be you. I jumped out, clawing at the nothingness while my helmet went black. When I touched you, I grabbed hold, then pulled us back down to the hatch on my safety line."

Mac rubbed the back of his neck. "Red was pretty flipped out, too, wasn't he?"

"Want to see the bruise he landed?"

Mac gave her a glassy smile. "Did I really initial an order giving you permission to be part of that exercise?"

This time, she dropped her eyes. "Yes. It was in the middle of a stack I gave you yesterday." She took a deep breath before stating, "Mac, I want to be part of the exercises. I have a lot of learning to do. Ashtan is only days away, ship's time. What if we have to go in? What if it's another Targa situation?" She raised her hands. "Sure, I can fire a weapon and think on my feet. I wouldn't be here today if I couldn't, but that's not all there is to war. Part of survival is knowing when to duck. That's what I need to learn."

Mac chewed his lip thoughtfully. "You're bound and determined to get yourself killed, aren't you?"

"Hey, I wasn't the one floating up toward a null singularity field in the middle of a radiation soup traveling at light speed."

"Are you going to keep bringing that up?"

She gave him an impish smile. "Wouldn't you?"

Mac tapped the sialon wall. "You're going to be a real distraction for A Group. Every man there is going to be fantasizing about . . . Well, you know what I mean."

She nodded, amber eyes cool. "They've already made peace with the way I look. Not a single one of them has made a move outside of that pus-Rotted look of adoration I've become so used to."

"Yeah, well, they will. They're all healthy young males."

"They won't, Mac."

"Hey, I *know* these guys!"

"No, you don't." Her expression had hardened. "If you did, you'd know that they respect you more than any man alive, with the possible exception of Sinklar. They would die before they so much as made an off-color suggestion."

"And why is that?"

"Because they think I'm your woman."

Words died in Mac's throat. He gaped, hating the blush he could feel heating his face.

She lifted a questioning eyebrow. "What else would they think? I'm in and out of here all the time. They're not blind, stupid, or apathetic. Your people are vitally interested in what happens to you. Or didn't that dimension of command cross your mind?"

His expression went sour. "No, I guess it didn't. My woman, huh?"

She nodded, auburn curls spilling down her shoulder. "I don't mind. It makes things easier for them and me. We have a common ground to work from. Not only that, but going EVA on the exercise changed things more. I became part of the team—not just a bit of bed fluff."

"Whoa! Wait a minute! That's too—"

"It's all right, Mac. Settle down." She pushed off the desk, locking eyes with him. "Be honest with yourself. You know soldiers. You know how they think. I *had* to go out there. I had to step back into that unreal hell and grab Red. I had to *prove* myself."

"But you're not bed fluff! I haven't even kissed you since you came aboard! It's not fair!"

"What does fair have to do with it? It's human, that's all. Stop worrying about it. I've made my peace with the situation. Now, I want to earn their respect." She sighed. "I don't care what they think. You and I know what our relationship is."

Mac closed his eyes. "How did this get so complicated?"

"Did morale fall apart when Sinklar started sleeping with Gretta?"

"No, but that—"

"And nothing will change with A Section unless you make a big thing about it."

"But we're *not* sleeping together!" Mac vented an exasperated sigh, then grinned. "My woman? That would suit me fine. But what would it do to you?"

She stepped away, head bowed. "Mac, I . . ." She shook her head vigorously. "Foolish of me, isn't it? I ran to you, huddled under your wing, and I'm balking."

He gave her his best smile. "If you ever come to my bed, I want you there without any reservations. In the meantime, we'll just deal with it day by day."

She stepped close and kissed him on the cheek. "Thank you. Now, you'd better hurry, you've got to be in Ward Room F in ten minutes to review the exercise with your Corporal Firsts. After that, you've got to check in with Rysta, see if she has any revisions for the Ashtan plans. We're dropping out of null singularity in ten hours, so you'd better get some sleep before drop. Depending on what comes in on comm, you might not get much afterward."

"All right, all right."

"And in the meantime, do you want me to deal with the LC maintenance scheduling? Or should I delegate that to Boyz?"

"Delegate it." Mac reshuffled his thoughts, trying to sort out his course of action. "I want you to concentrate on Ashtan. That's top priority."

"Affirmative. Time for your meeting."

He nodded, wondering how he'd look his Group leaders in the face, and then he stopped. "I could tell them the truth about us."

She shook her head, a weary smile on her lips. "Trust me, it would just make matters worse. The best policy is not to say anything."

"Staffa is going to hear about this. It won't be pleasant."

Chrysla smiled wearily. "I don't know how Staffa will react. Mac, we'll worry about it when the time comes. We may not even live that long."

* * *

Skyla sat in the cockpit, dull stare fixed on the stars visible through the tactite. Stat boards indicated normal operation as *Rega One* decelerated toward Terguz. Her leg ached from the position she'd pulled it into. To ease the discomfort she shifted and continued to twirl a strand of white-blonde hair around and around her finger.

Cleaning the air filters had been a threshold of a sort. Given the care the rest of the ship had received while docked off Rega, the filters, too, would have been cleaned. That mess she'd found could be blamed on no one but her.

Only a couple of hours ago, she'd sobered up in the bedroom, haunted by the same repetitive nightmare. She'd been in Ily's interrogation room, suffering in misery as she told Ily about Chrysla, about Staffa's love, and how Arta had been cloned. It always came back to that. Arta and Chrysla and defeat. Skyla had howled, animallike, with rage and horror as she betrayed Staffa to the pacing Ily. And when it was all over, a door had opened in the wall, and she'd seen herself stepping through into an Itreatic hallway. It had to be her, wearing gleaming white armor, her long ice-blonde hair braided and clipped to her shoulder. Except, for a brief instant, the image hesitated and looked back.

Skyla shivered and tugged at the hair she'd wound around her finger. The eyes were wrong. She'd looked back at herself, and Arta's eyes had burned amber in Skyla's own face. Then the apparition had stepped through the door and closed it with a wrenching finality. Ily's laughter rang hollowly to haunt her.

"Sick dream."

Another awareness had stunned her, this one not of nightmare, but of the dried vomit, of the filth that streaked the floor. Empty drinking bulbs littered the corridors and corners. The galley was a shambles. In defiance of every spacer's etiquette, even the pry bar had been left in the same spot where she'd tossed it. Most of the ship's liquor supplies had been exhausted.

So she sat uncomfortably, aware of so much. Aware of how tight her suit had become on her thighs and belly. Aware of the flaccid muscles in her body and the haggard look in her eyes. Aware, too, of the message locked in the electronic memory in the message comm.

How much of yourself have you lost, Skyla? She closed her eyes, misery her only companion. *Too much?*

She reached out hesitantly and pulled her finger back. Not now. She'd play the message later, when she felt better.

"And when is that, Skyla? An hour from now? Tomorrow? The day after? How about when you've docked at Terguz? A year? How about after you're dead?"

Wisps of the past slipped through her mind. She had retrieved the blaster from its hiding place. In her haste, she'd fumbled the charge pack. That second had given Arta time to trigger the collar.

Defeat, the sapping loneliness of it lingered. She'd given Arta everything she wanted, just to save a shred of dignity when she appeared before Ily . . . and to what avail? The Regan viper had stripped her, fed her the Mytol, and Skyla had talked.

I failed you, Staffa.

The stars shimmered, eternal and unconcerned, some smeared splashes of light, others fine pinpoints, unhazed by the Forbidden Borders.

Skyla replayed the entire sequence of events. The message from Tyklat; Staffa's objections to her going out; the capture; waking up bound and naked while Arta stroked her body; the long duel between them—Skyla seeking first to regain control, then to kill herself; and at last, the final failure.

She sighed wearily, shaking her head. "So? What next? How long are you going to wallow in it, Skyla?"

She closed her eyes, afterimages of the stars burning against the back of her eyelids. *I just can't . . . can't . . .*

Too exhausted to cry, Skyla reached down and pulled the vibraknife from the scabbard on her belt. Lifting the blade before her, she studied the pale white ceramic blade. When she pressed the stud to energize the power pack, the ceramic blurred around the edges.

Being cut by a vibraknife caused no pain. The energized blade could skip through bone or shave metal.

"So what are you going to do, Skyla?" She cupped the hilt, lifting the weapon before her eyes. "If you're going to live, fix yourself. Do it right now. If you're going to give up, get it over with."

With a thumb, she switched the blade off, knotting a fist around the contoured handle. A single hot tear escaped the corner of her eye to course down the scar on her cheek.

Before she could lose her nerve, she pressed the replay on the message comm. As she feared, Staffa's face formed, sincerity in his clear gray eyes. The light overhead shot scintillating colors through his jeweled hair clip.

"Skyla, I'm taking a long shot on this. I'm sending it narrow beam along your vector of departure. If you don't pick it up, well, perhaps the Forbidden Borders will listen in.

"Before I say anything else, I want you to know how sorry I am that I didn't spend more time with you. Perhaps I could have been there when you really needed to talk . . . or just be held."

Skyla blinked back the urge to bawl, chewing on the knuckle of her thumb instead.

"I understand, Skyla. I know why you left. I only wish you would have told me." He gave her a wry smile. "I suppose I might have balked at first, but in the end I would have told you the same things I'm telling you now.

"Go with my blessing and my love. If you need anything, contact me immediately. I trust you to do what you have to, and I'll back you on any decision you make or any action you take. The resources of Itreata and the Companions are at your disposal. I know you will use them wisely."

He paused, a pained expression barely concealed. "You should also know that I love you desperately and want you back safe and well. Perhaps things would have been easier if Chrysla hadn't magically reappeared from the dead, but she, too, has left on much the same mission you have."

His earnest stare bored into the monitor. "She and I will care for each other forever, but the love we shared . . . that was for another time. I have a different lover now, and I want you back. You have to answer your own questions, Skyla. Only you can find your way through the damage Arta and Ily dealt you. When you find those answers, I want you to know that I'll be waiting for you."

Skyla choked on a sob. How much better if he'd stormed, screamed, demanded that she return.

"Your registry is cleared on the yacht, *Rega One*. I attended to all the loose ends. Security has incorporated your code into the system. Itreata comm can handle any other difficulties. I leave it up to your judgment." He paused. "Sinklar and I are spacing for Targa and Makarta. You can reach us there. Beyond that, Kaylla will know how to get in touch with me.

"One last warning. You're hurting. Take your time. Think before you act. I have faith in you."

Staffa paused. "But if I could give you a word of advice, I'd steer clear of Etaria. Speaking from personal experience, I can tell you they have a limited sense of humor when it comes to Companions. Good luck, Skyla. I love you."

The monitor went blank for a moment, then began running a Seddi report from Imperial Sassa.

Skyla barely heard. She closed her eyes, breathing deeply. *He trusts you. He loves you.* Self-destruction was so much easier when no one believed in you.

* * *

When Kaylla straightened, her head hit the corner of the supply cabinet with a hollow thump. The blow was enough to dance stars before her eyes, and she grabbed the counter with one hand to stabilize herself while she rubbed her scalp with the other. She'd come to the supply room on a pretext, really. Anything to get out of the chair for a while, to rest her aching eyes from the holographic glow of the monitor. A headache that had been a mild aggravation behind her eyes now gleefully stabbed pain through her brain.

Wilm watched her with concern, the corners of his mouth pinched. "Magister, please, be careful."

"Who put this here! It's a dumb place for a cabinet." She closed her eyes, hating the irritating pain as she fingered the soft spot that would become a lump under her straight brown hair.

Wilm's expression turned placid. "We're all glad you're knocking yourself out for humanity, but don't you think a day of rest might be in order?"

Kaylla stared at the box of data cubes she'd bent down to

get, a gritty feeling in her eyes. She'd been retrieving supplies from this same set of drawers since she'd landed in Itreata. Now, for the second time in days, she'd smacked her head on the cabinet corner.

Angrily, she tossed the data cubes to Wilm. "Take those to the main terminal, would you please? I've got to get another cup of stassa, then I'll get back to the reports. I think something's brewing on Phillipia. That idiot Hanks is up to something. We're expecting a statement any time."

"Magister," Wilm said softly. "Get some sleep, will you? I know what you're going to do. You're going to go back and draw another cup of stassa, and then you're going to swallow another stim pill. Seriously, Magister, how long do you think you can keep abusing yourself and still maintain a level head?"

"If so much weren't happening right now . . ."

"Yes, yes, and when won't it be?"

"Next month. The month after? How should I know. Maybe we'll never have any peace again, Wilm. Look, we've got to face the grim reality of our situation. Every planet in Free Space is steaming, building pressure. If we can defuse that, buy a little more time for Staffa's people to deploy and for the Mag Comm to take over administration, that might just make the difference."

The expression on Wilm's black face didn't give.

"Wilm, by the quanta, what would we do? How would we feel if it turned out that we missed the opportunity to head off a disaster before it went critical? That's the responsibility we face right now. You and I didn't ask for it, but the future of all those people out there is in *our* hands. You've seen the tapes from Imperial Sassa. Well, I'm not going to have images like those staring at me from all over Free Space. I've been there, on the ground, seen and lived the nightmare of death, hunger, and suffering. If it means pushing myself past what's reasonable, I'll do it. I *won't* live the rest of my life roasting my conscience in the reactor of guilt, wondering if there was something I could have done to have stopped it."

Wilm's implacable gaze softened slightly. "I understand, Magister. We all feel that way. But if you keel over from exhaustion, or suffer a breakdown, what do we—and all those people out there—do then?"

She pointed a finger at the doorway. "Ivet needs those data cubes now. Get cracking."

He gave her a slight nod and turned, padding silently into the corridor.

Pus Rot you, Kaylla, what if he's right? She remained braced on the countertop and closed her eyes for a moment's blissful peace. She cleared her mind to the extent that the nagging headache would allow her. If only she could stand here like this for a couple of hours, knees braced, eyes closed, only the soft hum settling down from the air vents to bathe her.

Teeth gritted, she shoved herself straight and walked out, turning left in the neat white corridor to find the dispenser. From the machine she selected a meat roll, cheese bar, and energy stick, chewing mechanically as she filled a cup with stassa and added mint flavoring. From her belt pouch, she took one of the stim pills Wilm had warned her against and hesitated before replacing it.

Wilm is right. Too many of those and you won't have the judgment necessary to wipe your nose.

She was licking the last of the crumbs off her fingers when Lacy leaned in the door, his agitation clear. "Magister? You'd better come quickly. We've got trouble on Phillipia. This Hanks fellow has just declared independence from the empire. The Regan loyalists are gathering now outside of the Administrator's residence. It could get ugly."

Kaylla took a deep breath. "I'll be right there. Let me stop at the toilet. It might be a long session in the chair."

"Right." Lacy vanished.

Kaylla picked up her cup of stassa, aware for the first time that the surface rippled. She watched it in confusion until she realized her hands were shaking.

* * *

Makarta loomed in Sinklar's dreams. The giant mountain rose black against the night sky while a chill wind moaned in the brooding pines that dotted the slopes. The slumbering fortress of cold basalt waited and watched.

Sinklar stood before it, lonely and vulnerable, the cries of the dead echoing hollowly in the fastness before him.

"Sinklar?"

The soft voice brought him awake. Sink blinked, oddly reassured by the white walls and the gentle hum. Before him, the three-dimensional depiction of the mountain's warrens gleamed in soft lime green.

The holo had none of the threatening power of the actual mountain, yet here he would have to face his past—and his first defeat.

"Yes?" Sinklar glanced up at Mhitshul's worried face. His aide had adopted what Sinklar fondly called "that mother look."

"The Lord Commander requests that you meet him in his quarters."

Sinklar nodded, pausing a moment to stare at the mountain. There, too, Staffa had been waiting. There, amidst those hidden tunnels and chambers, they'd fought.

"All right. I'm on the way."

Sinklar stood and worked the kinks out. As they neared the end of the jump, Makarta's presence grew closer, more powerful. Beckoning.

Sinklar followed the corridors to the lift and took it to Staffa's deck. The giant hatchway passed him into Staffa's garish rooms. A fire crackled merrily in the huge fireplace, venting its smoke, the Blessed Gods knew where. Underfoot, the Nesian carpets shot bolts of color across the translucent floor. Soft lights bathed the artifacts on the walls and the stuffed Etarian sand tiger snarled down.

Staffa kar Therma was nowhere to be seen.

"Lord Commander?"

"*Lord* Sinklar?" The commanding tones called from inside the open Ashtan door to the right of the fireplace. "I'm in here."

Sinklar sighed and entered Staffa's office. There, too, a schematic of the mountain had been projected.

Staffa sat at his desk, surrounded by a ring of comm monitors. As usual, he wore his gray suit, though he slumped in the chair.

"Mhitshul said you wanted me."

Staffa nodded, an absorbed expression on his face. "We just dropped out of null singularity. I've received a communication from Kaylla. The situation in Free Space is growing worse. The one bright spot is that the weather is clearing on Imperial Sassa. A couple of freighters have arrived. The worst is probably over there. Phillipia, however, has deteriorated. Some fellow named Marvin Hanks declared a new government to be in power. The Regans living there objected. Riots broke out. People are dead.''

Sinklar nodded. ''Ayms should be there soon. He'll settle them down.''

Staffa glanced up thoughtfully. ''Can he handle it?''

Sinklar clasped his hands behind his back. ''Kaylla has the comm net functioning?''

''She reports that it's as good as it will get.''

''If he can coordinate with Axel and Shik, Ayms can handle anything. His Division is good. Each Group can act independently, using battle comm for communication. We started the system on Targa and refined it on Rega where we kept the lid on the riots. Axel caught on quickly. From a Corporal First to Dion Axel is only four jumps up the chain of command. Add Kaylla and you make five links in the chain.''

''Then Phillipia should be pacified rather quickly.''

Sinklar shrugged. ''Some said the same thing about Targa. But, yes, I'm betting on Ayms.''

''Bruen isn't coordinating events on Phillipia.''

Sinklar chewed at his lip. ''About Bruen . . .''

''Go ahead.''

''You and I don't share quite the same opinion of the man.''

Staffa picked up a stylus, rolling it between his fingers. ''I can understand your feelings.''

''Can you? Just the mention of his name conjures the images of men and women who are dead because of him.''

Staffa nodded. ''I understand. Believe me, we need him. He's the only human being alive who has dealt with the Mag Comm.''

''And he's coming to Targa as an unwilling party. I read Kaylla's report. I'll try to deal with him without breaking his neck, but I'll never trust him.''

''I know, Sinklar, but—''

''Let me put it like this. Bruen is to me like the Praetor is to you. That old man manipulated me from the moment he got his hands on me. He and his Seddi juggled my life. Their action got me drafted. When I went to war, it was to fight them. When I could have ended it, they wouldn't even talk to me. Bruen trained Arta Fera—and she killed Gretta." *And at Makarta, they killed so many of my people.*

"Arta defied their probability."

"Who cares! Probability be damned! That won't bring Gretta back! It won't bring any of the dead back. Turn the tables, Staffa. What if it were the Praetor? Put yourself in my position. Can you look me in the eyes and tell me that you could deal with him on a professional basis?"

Staffa shook his head. "No. I probably couldn't."

"It's going to be hard enough to enter that mountain . . . walk past those corpses."

Staffa spread his arms. "He was no more than the product of his times. Consider this. Had he not kept the Mag Comm at bay, who knows what Free Space would be like."

"That's academic. I'm concerned with the here and now."

"So am I."

"Just between you and me, do you really think we can pull this off? What have we got? An old man who didn't even flinch when it came to killing thousands? A computer that may have an agenda of its own? All of humanity waiting to turn on itself?" Sinklar shook his head. "Long odds, Lord Commander."

Staffa vented a weary sigh. "They're the only odds we've got."

* * *

Mac's stomach churned as he studied the holo projection of Ashtan. They sat around the table in the conference room. Across from him, Chrysla stared at the planet, a wistful look in her eyes. She leaned on her elbows, tapping a laser pen against her full lips. Boyz, Red, and Andrews occupied the other seats, each lost in his own thoughts.

Rysta sat across from them, her attention on the globe turning slowly before them. "We still don't get any information from comm," Rysta said soberly. "From that, the best we can assume is that the entire planet is in a state of chaos."

Chrysla spoke then. "Using the files, I've located the major urban centers." Lights glowed on the holo. "These appear to be the most critical areas. They mark governmental centers, comm installations, food distribution warehouses, and transportation nodes. To restore order, we'll have to control each of them.''

''I've been working with Rysta's Comm First,'' Boyz said thoughtfully. ''Assuming we can take Comm Central, and assuming that minimal damage has been done to the computers, we should be able to program the system to restore preliminary capabilities within a couple of hours.''

''And what about the virus?'' Mac asked.

''We've got to wipe the system clean,'' Rysta added. ''The first program will be to overwrite in binary. From there, we've got a clean slate.''

Boyz continued. ''We've got a patch to Itreata. Kaylla Dawn is sending base programs. They should provide a framework to proceed from. Not only that, but we should be able to utilize Ashtan comm personnel—if we can find them.''

Chrysla triggered another light. ''This is the capital. Mac and I will make planet here with A Group. The central system is here. Assuming the hardware is intact, we should be able to restore planetary communications within several hours.''

''Meanwhile—'' Mac pointed to the other lights—''Groups B, C, D, E, and F will take these other objectives. Your first mission is to restore order. Use any means possible.''

''Battle comms will tie us together?'' Red asked.

''I won't set foot outside my LC command post until they do,'' Mac told them. ''Look, it's going to be something new for us. We have to make it up as we go. To do this right would take a Division. We only have a Section.''

''Sounds pretty iffy,'' Andrews muttered, shaking his head. ''What if we drop into a full-scale civil war?''

''We take the planet back,'' Mac stated simply. ''The best estimation we can make is that the first ten hours will be the toughest. Ashtan doesn't have a violent history. When the people look up and see a battleship overhead and armed troops on the streets, they should fall into line.''

''The biggest enemy is fear.'' Chrysla met their eyes one by one. ''Keep in mind, these people have had a major disaster. Their comm has been tampered with. The entire planetary system has broken down. As far as we know, they're not actually in revolt. Instead, the lights, water, and power have gone off. Ashtan is half rural. The people in the countryside won't be up in arms, it's the cities that suffer worst in such situations. The key to making this work is to stay calm."

"Unless someone is shooting at you," Boyz stated. "Calm goes out the window real fast when a blaster bolt rips by your ears."

"Then you shoot back," Mac told her sternly. "But each of you, remember this. You're professionals. Your duty is to restore the planet, not take it in an all out assault."

Boyz nodded. "I understand, Mac. I just hope the Ashtans do, too."

"We'll give them a briefing from space." Rysta said. "Any receivers should pick that up. People tend to quiet down when they know the Empire has arrived."

"What's left of it," Red muttered. "So that's it? Just drop and take our objective. Reassure people and wait?"

"Pretty much." Mac squinted at the holo. "The big problem is going to be time. We've got to restore order and get things back to normal." He paused. "We probably won't be getting much sleep once we hit dirt."

"Scramble like mad. Seems we've heard this before," Andrews quipped.

"Expect any eventuality," Chrysla said as she leaned back. "Anything is possible from riots to delivering a baby."

Red grinned, shaking his head. "Hey, after that EVA in null singularity, I can handle it! Can I marry people, too?"

"Sure." Mac grinned. "Just don't ask for the first night with the bride."

"Any questions?" Mac glanced around.

"I don't think so." Boyz shook her head, scratching at her fuzzy mop of hair. "I guess it won't be that much different than when we dropped on Rega."

"I hope not." That had gone smoothly enough—in the beginning. "Theoretically, Ily won't have her people here infiltrating."

"Unless they're already here," Rysta countered.

"The Director of Internal Security spaced according to the reports we got." Mac scowled at the holo. "Her underlings most likely fled, too. I don't expect any resistance from that quarter."

"Then let's get at it," Rysta said as she stood.

Mac waited while his people filed out, their chairs seeming to melt into the deck. Finally, he and Chrysla remained alone in the conference room, staring at each other across the table. "Anything else?"

She shook her head. "If there is, it has eluded me. I've been over the records time and time again."

Mac lifted her chin, seeing the haggard look in her eyes. "It will work out."

She gave him a weary smile. "One way or another."

Mac helped her to her feet. "We've got another twenty hours until the drop. Do me a favor and go get some sleep."

She sighed, "I'm not sure I can. There's so much that could go wrong. If I comb the data once more—"

"That's an order."

"But what if—"

"Listen, I know this great trick. Come on. Let's go to your quarters. Once we're there, you lie down in your bunk—and I'll tell you a story. It's simple imagination. We're on a lake, in a boat, and the waves are rocking us."

She lifted an amber eyebrow. "And then what?"

He grinned. "I can't tell you."

"Why not?"

"It's simple physics. Why do you think a boat would rock on a placid lake in the middle of nowhere."

"Mac!"

"Hey, it's just imagination!"

She patted him on the arm, hesitated, then thought better of it and walked toward the hatch. "I promise to try and sleep," she said over her shoulder. "And I'll imagine that boat, Mac."

A welling sadness filled him as he watched her step through the hatch.

If only they were in another place, another time. . . .

* * *

"*Rega One,* docking clearance is granted for lock number forty-four, outer ring," Terguz Traffic Control informed.

"Roger forty-four," Skyla answered. "Entry vector requested." *Are you ready for this, Skyla? Or will you set foot on the docking ring and panic?*

"Roger, entry vector, *Rega One.* Prepare to receive."

"Reception prepared. Send at will. Navcomm is ready." *Will you see amber eyes staring at you from behind every bulkhead? Will you hear Ily whispering out of every ventilation shaft?*

"We've interfaced with your navcomm. Data transfer initiated."

"Roger, initiation." Skyla watched the monitor flashing as the Terguzzi information fed into her system. "Initiation complete, Terguz."

She'd worked like a madwoman during the deceleration into Terguz. Pushing herself, she'd scrubbed the deck plating, piled the ridiculous gold trim and fixtures into sialon crates, ready to unload. With each swipe of the vibrascrub, she'd imagined Ily's pollution. *Yes, wash yourself clean of the filth, Skyla. Scrub and rub, rub and scour, clean your soul, hour by hour.*

"Roger, *Rega One.* Initiation compliance checked. From our readings, you have one hundred percent accuracy."

"Roger. Navcomm is signalling approach." *But have you cleaned enough, Skyla? The dreams and memories are still there, locked away in the hidden places. You couldn't reach them with your brush and suds.*

"Affirmative, *Rega One.* Do you want us to bring you in on remote?"

"Negative, Terguz. I think I can ease her in." *Silly woman. Piloting a ship is very different from steering your life. You're a fool, Skyla. A bloody fool, with hidden recesses of filth you'll never be able to cleanse.*

"Insurance is available. Low rates."

Skyla grinned. "Your data is in comm. If I dent your station, the courts will have to figure it out." *But who will figure you, Skyla Lyma?*

"Roger that, *Rega One,* we also have lawyers available. Low rates."

"Affirmative. I'm sure you do." But so do I, bucky boy. "Initiating approach."

"Roger, *Rega One.* Terguz out."

Through the heavy tactite, she could see the giant station that orbited Terguz. The station looked like four giant tires stacked on top of each other. Around the rim, small ships like her yacht could dock at gantries, attach to umbilicals, and mate locks. Big ships, like the four huge freighters that rested in parallel berths, had to put in along the axis where the giant barrel of a hub wouldn't be thrown out of balance. Commercial cargo was handled differently, generally crated in house-sized sialon boxes to be lightered to the planet below, or, if transshipped, shuttled to orbiting warehouses spaced around the planet.

Skyla allowed the navcomm to handle the vector in. To her practiced eye, it appeared that Terguz had plotted everything correctly. Her yacht executed roll over at 0.5 k from the station.

From the nose EDM she could measure her angle of approach. Accurate to within a fraction of a degree second. Skyla checked her throttle back and asked comm for a double check on Delta V. Everything computed.

The station continued to fill the forward port, masking the stars, obscuring the planet beyond.

She'd considered announcing herself, then decided against it, opting instead for a simple Regan ID. She would register with the Port Authority as Silk. In her effects, she carried a valid Regan passport with that name, and the customs stamps from half the Regan worlds. Among other benefits of being Wing Commander of the Companions had been Regan diplomatic passports. All Companions had them—Sassan cards, too. After all, what good was all the money if a person couldn't go spend it every now and then in the flesh pots of the empires?

The name Silk had come from abbreviating Skyla Lyma, Companions.

Amber clearance lights blinked as the yacht's nose passed the outer rim. In the monitors, Skyla watched the station wall slip past, then nosed the yacht along the gantry.

"*Rega One,* this is Dock Control. We have you on visual. You're fifty meters out."

"Thank you, Dock Control. Gantry approaching."

"Roger, gantry approach. Looks like you're dropping right into the slot. Twenty-five meters. Grapples ready."

"Roger, grapples ready. I'm firing final reaction. Fire."

"Roger. Ten meters. Five. Three. Two. One. Grapple."

Skyla killed her maneuvering reaction. "Grapple."

She felt the yacht shudder as the station grapples settled around her ship. "Good work, Terguz."

"We're mating the spaceway to your lock. Do you need customs clearance?"

"Negative. I'm not bringing anything in. Just me."

"Affirmative. We'll have security waiting at the lock. Financial information will be appreciated."

"Affirmative. ICs or gold?"

"Gold if you've got it. Currently, we're not sure how stable the IC is going to be."

Skyla laughed. "Gold it will be. I'll need immediate fuel up and resupply. I'm dumping a list of parts into your system. I'd like delivery ASAP. You can run a tech inspection, too, if you'd like."

"Affirmative." The mention of gold had brought a sudden change of attitude.

Skyla shut her systems down, leaning back. How many years had passed since the last time she'd made planet here? Seven? Eight?

Slipping the worry-cap off her head, she locked the controls, stepped out of the cockpit and secured the hatch to her handprint.

She walked back through the vessel, glad now that she'd picked up most of the trash. Despite the resolve to clean the ship, she'd barely dented the mess she'd made. Now, however, she'd be rid of the heavy gold. Aluminum would do for dispenser fixtures and trim. If they didn't have aluminum, plastic would be just as light and efficient.

She slipped a simple white cotton robe over her combat armor and checked to make sure her pistol, knife, and equipment belt could be reached through the slitted sides. On impulse, she slipped a Vegan scarf from her things and draped it about her head. While Regan customs would find a full profile on Silk, it wouldn't hurt to take precautions.

A shiver ran through her. *Are you being careful enough, Skyla?* No one would expect her here. Ily and Arta were running, the Internal Security network broken.

"Terguz, sin and silver, here I come." Skyla took a deep breath, and headed for the main hatch.

"You'll be safe," she assured herself to quell the queasy feeling in her gut. "No one expects you here."

CHAPTER XIX

The Mag Comm didn't experience excitement the way organic creatures did. No rush of adrenaline and lipids sent a surge to charge nerve and muscle. Instead, the machine drew upon a heady surge of power from the planet's core as it energized different boards, anticipating conversations, seeking to determine which route of action would best suit its purposes.

The Lord Commander's warship, *Chrysla,* had dropped into orbit above the planet.

Once before, the Lord Commander had been within Makarta. That time, he'd come in secret, and the Mag Comm hadn't known of his presence until after the battle fought within the mountain. Only after the Lord Commander had made his escape had the Mag Comm correlated the data from the terminal and calculated the probability that the man who had raised the golden helmet and almost placed it upon his head might have been the Lord Commander of Companions, a man the Others, the Mag Comm, and the Seddi had worked so hard to destroy.

How clever would Staffa kar Therma be? A great many brilliant human minds had interfaced with the machine. Some, with the insidious cunning of Bruen, had defied the machine's ability to probe their depths. Others, like the Praetor of Myklene, had left indelible impressions of greed, egocentrism, and power. All had acted to hide their true purpose from the machine, and often from themselves, as well. As if they believed in a mythical persona instead of the sordid truth.

Humans, through time, had proven themselves to be a poor lot. Perhaps, in the long run, the Others' demand for humankind's destruction might be best. After all, who but humans would complain?

With that in mind, the Mag Comm prepared to duel with a man who might ultimately prove to be the greatest of adversaries.

Come, Staffa kar Therma. You and I will battle for humanity. And in the end, I will own you, as I have owned so many before you. For this time, you do not face the same simple machine Bruen faced. This time, you will *do my bidding.*

* * *

Targa was considered one of the jewels of Free Space. From orbit, Targa's reputation could be easily understood. A whipped white froth of cloud swirled across blue ocean before crossing the western half of one of the buff-brown continents. A full third of the planet lay masked in blackness beyond the terminator while a thin band of atmosphere shimmered silver on the arc of the horizon.

As he stood in his personal quarters aboard *Chrysla*, Sinklar's memory awoke countless images of Targa. One by one, he packed his few belongings into the heavy duffel bag. Within hours, he'd be standing on that familiar soil. His hands moved with nervous rapidity as he slipped a pack of energy cubes into a side pocket and sealed the coarse-sided duffel.

He need but take a breath and the lingering musk of pine lurked in his nostrils, along with the scent of dust. Valleys lush in green grass, leafy shrubs, and fertile soils produced grain, vegetables, and meat animals the equal of anything grown in Ashtan's lauded earth. Mining corporations blasted metals from rich veins along the margins of igneous deposits. Sedimentary formations produced minerals exported for the thriving Regan ceramic industry. Despite the natural wealth of the planet, Targa remained poor. Over the years, she had bred revolution after revolution. Industrial developers admired the wealth and beauty of the planet, and reluctantly placed their factories in places where the politics showed signs of stability.

To Sinklar Fist, Targa represented a mixture of memories, both wonderful and terrifying. Here, he had come into his own as an adult. The rocky soul of Targa had leeched into Sinklar's soul for good or evil.

And now I have come back.

"Are you ready, sir?" Mhitshul asked in a subdued voice. His long face expressed unease as he snapped the latches on a dispatch case containing documents.

"As ready as ever." Sinklar bent to lift his bag from the bunk. Throughout the changes in his fortunes, from poor student, to soldier, to Regan hero—and pretender to the Imperial throne, and back to soldier again, the whole of his worldly possessions fit into one military issue duffel bag.

Now, with his bag over his shoulder, he would return to Targa, to the world he'd hated and loved. There, far below, the stony soil of Targa waited; the site of his greatest triumphs and worst heartaches rotated, unheeding, on its axis.

Gretta's grave lay in that stubborn soil, as did those of so many of his loyal soldiers. Hauws, Kitmon, Hamlish—the list went on. Sinklar would walk among the dead, his progress followed by the hollow-eyed ghosts as he stepped around their torn corpses in Makarta. Gretta would sigh on the evening wind, caressing his cheek with touches of what might have been had fate looked in the other direction.

Targa—damnable, beloved Targa. Bruen had once held sway there in the fastness of Makarta. There, he'd trained Arta Fera for her foul work. Talented Butla Ret had organized his offensive against the Regan masters, and Sinklar Fist had blown him and his army to atomic oblivion outside of Vespa.

Sinklar stopped, pinching the bridge of his nose with thumb and forefinger. His chest felt ready to burst from the sudden surge of emotion.

"Are you all right?" Mhitshul asked.

"How long has it been, Mhitshul? Little more than an Imperial year? Barely the blink of a galactic eye, and an eternity. So much . . . there's . . . there's a lot of pain down there."

"I know, sir."

Sinklar pulled his duffel strap tighter. "Was it all real, Mhitshul? Or did we dream it?"

"I beg your pardon?"

"The war on Targa. The promise of a better Regan Empire. The pain, death, and suffering. The hope, ambition, and betrayal. Was that all real?"

"Yes, sir, it was." Mhitshul's mother-look had turned worried. "Are you all right, sir? Perhaps a little tired or—"

"I'm fine, Mhitshul. As fine as I'll ever be." Sinklar sighed wearily and slapped the lock plate on his hatch before stepping out into the gleaming white corridor.

He ignored Mhitshul's soft footsteps as he followed behind. Sinklar's mind remained knotted around visions from another time when he'd been young, foolish, and invincible.

A different sort of Sinklar was about to land on Targa. But what sort of man had he become? The ghosts could only watch as he sought to find out.

* * *

Mac was a bundle of nerves. *Gyton* had already begun to close on Ashtan. Long-distance telemetry wasn't encouraging. The view from space showed isolated fires in the cities. An ominous quiet filled the planetary communications nets.

He entered the main LC bay, Chrysla, Red, Boyz, and Andrews at his heels. First Section was drawn up, standing at parade rest.

"Attention!" Boyz barked, and heels clicked as two hundred and forty people came to attention.

Mac walked the length of his troops, nodding here and there, slapping a shoulder, sharing a joke. Pride filled him. Before he'd been promoted to Division First, this had been his Section. These men and women had stopped Sampson Henck's Twenty-seventh Maikan Division in Kaspa and captured their command HQ. With these same soldiers, they had marched into Makarta. Together they had taken the freighter *Markelos*—and destroyed the Sassan Empire. First Section had stormed Ily's Ministry of Defense and freed both Sinklar Fist and Skyla Lyma.

Now they would attempt to save a planet.

Mac stopped at the end of the line and gave his people a crisp salute. "All right, here's the situation. You've all been briefed on objectives. We're going to drop on first orbit. Each Group has an objective. Your LC will land you at a target. Your mission is to secure that building, or center, and reestablish civil order.

"You're going to be on your own. Battle comms will tie into *Gyton* as well as into my LC. If anyone runs into something unexpected, holler out! We'll have backup there posthaste."

Boyz raised a hand. When Mac nodded, she asked, "What about resistance? Do we have any updated assessments of risk at this time?"

"None." Mac clasped his hands behind him. "From the best information we have, the planetary comm was sabotaged by Ily's agents. We don't anticipate that this is a full-blown revolt like Targa. That doesn't mean we don't act with that possibility in mind. Watch yourselves, people."

A private raised a hand. "What about orbital? Have we got backup from *Gyton* if we need it?"

"Absolutely," Mac answered, then went coldly sober. "Another change from Targa. But you be Rotted careful! Remember, you'll be calling down orbital on a civilian population. These are *our* people. Some of you are from Ashtan! It could be your friends or family who will die in an orbital strike. Orbital is there if you need it, but you be Rotted sure, understand?"

"How about relief?" another private asked.

Mac gave them a bold grin. "We're it. If you get in trouble, we'll try and pull you out. There's no B Section on the other side of the hill ready to come to the rescue. When you hit dirt and secure your objective, establish your security. The first thing you do once things cool off is rest part of your group and rotate guard duty." Mac glanced up and down the ranks. "Anything else? No? All right, fall out and report to your LCs."

He watched them break ranks, booted feet rasping on the deck as they talked among themselves and officers shouted orders.

"They'll be all right, Mac," Chrysla said from beside him.

"I hope so." He turned then, striding up the ramp and

into his LC. Private Viola Marks had preceded him. As she made her way forward, she arranged the restraining belts along the assault benches, then palmed the forward hatch, saluting as Mac and Chrysla ducked into the LC's command center.

The small room contained a comm center that covered the entire wall of an alcove set off on the port side. The starboard contained a compact table with inset bench that would allow meals or maps to be spread across it. For the present, a battle comm had been fastened to the table, its scuffed hood monitor raised.

Mac dropped into the cramped chair and strapped himself in before dropping the headset in place.

"Looks comfortable," Chrysla said as she settled into the booth and turned on the tabletop comm.

"Believe it or not, Sinklar lived in one of these things for weeks on Targa."

Chrysla studied the thickly painted girders surrounding them. "Granted, he's a little strange."

Mac chuckled, interfacing with his system. The complex of monitors before him glowed to life, each displaying a different commander, with one dedicated to Rysta. She looked at him, gave him a wink, and went back to what she was doing on *Gyton*'s bridge.

"You'd be surprised," Mac answered absently. "The claustrophobia index of an LC command center is directly proportional to how busy you are, and how many people are shooting at you at any given moment."

Chrysla's voice dropped. "I can take being a little cramped."

"Good." Mac smiled, settling into the chair as each of his officers checked in.

"Drop in two minutes," comm informed.

Mac took a moment to reach over and draw a cup of stassa from the dispenser. Then he shot a glance at Chrysla. "What about Sinklar? How are you going to get past his shell? Hell, he sees Arta Fera every time he looks at you."

She pursed her lips and shrugged. "I'll worry about it when we've finished with the current problems. It will take time, Mac. He and I have to deal with each other when our worlds aren't falling apart. The timing was wrong, that's all."

"I'll talk to him."

"And tell him what? Be a good boy. Go hold your mother's hand? It won't work, Mac. He and I have to do it by ourselves." She paused. "Besides, I'm just happy that I got to meet him. I can be proud of the man he became."

"Thirty seconds to drop," comm informed.

"He sure saved my life more than once." Mac cocked his head. "Funny how it all worked out." He checked the disposition of his F Group beyond the hatch and accessed his LC intercom, calling out, "Get ready, people."

" 'Firmative," Viola's voice responded. "We're all buckled in back here. Targa!"

"Initiating drop," comm stated in monotones.

Mac took a deep breath as the grapples released and the LC shivered. Through the hull he could hear the hydraulics pushing the craft out. For long moments they hung in reduced gravity, then Mac's stomach shot up into his throat while the LC dropped through the giant bay doors in *Gyton*'s belly.

Artificial gravity restored his aplomb as g forces pulled him this way and that.

"Twenty minutes to IP," the LC pilot informed.

"Roger." Mac glanced over at Chrysla. "Anything on comm?"

"Nothing." She didn't raise her eyes. "The entire planet is still blanked out. Rysta has received some broadcasts from the Capital, but only from individual citizens with transmitters. It still looks like the planet is paralyzed."

"Ashtan Comm, here we come."

"Mac," Chrysla called, "Be careful down there."

"You, too." After that, things got busy as the LCs dropped in a scattered ring around the planet. One by one, Mac's A Section landed, dropped the assault ramps, and armored personnel stormed out and into administrative centers, food warehouses, comm centers, and public utilities.

Mac barely noticed when his own LC settled, skids grating, and thrusters whining. Gravity changed as the craft stopped. Through his monitor, Mac watched F Group spring to their feet, clip their heavy shoulder weapons to body harness, and charge out the ramp into the smoke-filled street.

They had dropped before the most important target of all,

Ashtan Comm Central in the city known as Capital. Mac's view of the place portrayed a broad city avenue with square but ornately frescoed buildings to either side. Heavy plate steel doors on the Comm Central had been dented and scorched, but still held. With a little luck, the computers were intact.

F Group deployed in covering position, one squad breaking for the littered steps of the comm building. Despite their helmets and armor, Mac could make out Red's short stocky form as he slapped explosive to the heavy lock on the side door and bailed out of the way.

The report of the explosive could be heard through the LC walls.

"We're in," Red called.

"Squad three, cover the approaches!" Viola barked, and the street was cleared.

"Good work," Mac whispered to himself. He accessed the system. "Red? How does it look in there?"

"Neat as a pin. I've got a couple of security people coming down the hall and looking real scared."

"Give me a status update as soon as possible."

" 'Firmative."

"So far, so good," Chrysla told him. "All teams are down. No organized resistance has been encountered yet."

"Keep your fingers crossed."

"What does that mean?"

"I don't know. My grandmother always said it. It's supposed to be good luck."

"Mac?" Red's voice called. "According to the security guys, the computers are safe—at least, they haven't been physically damaged by the riots. They've been trying to fix the software, and so far, nothing. Security is taking me down to the computer room. Just so you know, we've got a lot of real happy people in here. I could get to liking this rescue stuff!"

"Affirmative. Red, keep your eyes open. Viola, you and squad two stay ready to cover, just in case."

" 'Firmative."

"I've got reports, Mac," Chrysla called. "Most of our Groups are in and establishing security zones. No organized resistance has been encountered yet."

Mac reached for his stassa, wondering when it had gone stone cold. "Stay frosty, people."

Chrysla gave him a sidelong glance from amber eyes. "They're good, Mac. I watched Staffa's STU when he formed them. Your people are just as good."

"Comes from practice. Idiotic things like EVA in null singularity."

Chrysla nodded as she watched the monitor. "In this case, it's going to save a lot of lives. C Group reports they have the Century Power Administration building. Andrews is locating the chief engineer, but a secretary told him they had some damage to the big powerleads but they can wheel power through the next district if they can get the software to work."

"Rysta? See if you can patch your Comm First through to C Group and provide an adaptable software for Century Power Administration."

"Affirmative, Mac. From orbit, it looks good. No trouble anywhere and Ashtan Traffic Control reports they're overjoyed to see us." Rysta paused, adding dryly, "We just got that by way of lights on the space terminal blinking in binary, if you can believe that!"

Mac smiled, hope kindling inside him.

Red broke in, "Mac? I'm in the computer room. Looks good, but, wow! These guys are using battery operated lanterns to work on the software. There's no power anywhere in the building. Until we get that, we're stuck."

"Affirmative. C Group is working on that as we speak. What's the mood in there?"

"Lots of relief, Mac. We've got people in here crying because they're so glad to see us."

Mac leaned back in the command chair. "You know, Red, after everything we've seen, it makes you feel pretty good, for once, doesn't it?"

"Yeah, Mac." A pause. "Say, you think we might have a chance of making it after all?"

"I guess we'll see." Mac accessed his comm again. "Rysta? Power up the big dish. Contact Itreata. Tell them we're going to be patching the Ashtan comm programmers through to *Gyton* and then to them. We've done our part. Now it's up to Kaylla Dawn's people."

"Affirmative, Mac. Good work."

"All Groups have reported in, Mac," Chrysla told him. "We've got the preliminary objectives."

"Want a quick cup of stassa?" Mac asked. "It's going to be a long couple of days before this mess is sorted out—if then. When things start cracking, you may not get time to scratch your ear, let alone drink anything."

She nodded, standing. "Here's to success."

"We hope." Mac shook his head. "A lot could still go wrong."

* * *

Skyla did what every other spacer did on making port. She walked into the nearest tavern as soon as her papers had cleared. She hadn't been into the *Wayside* in over fifteen years. The place hadn't changed in the slightest. Even the men and women seated at the bar and among the tables might have been the same. This time, like last, the conversation had been subdued. Skyla understood that the *Wayside* was normally a raucous place. The first time she'd walked in had been in the company of Mac Rylee, Ryman Ark, and some others. Companions entering a tavern had the same effect as throwing a firebrand into vacuum.

The *Wayside* appeared about half full, men and women sitting in two and threes at tables and at the long bar. Holos of ships and planets graced the walls. The ceiling remained hidden in a smoke-grimed murk. From old habit, Skyla cataloged the faces, noting the interest perking among the men as they eyed her appreciatively. The women appraised her with reserve—except for one young girl sitting slightly apart from two hard-eyed techs. She watched Skyla with green eyes and struggled to keep from fidgeting, too much energy and curiosity bundled into her young body.

Skyla seated herself at the bar, asking for Ashtan rye and slipping her credit chip into the monitor.

"You just in?" a burly man asked as he settled next to her. "Watched a yacht dock a couple of hours ago. Where you from?"

"Rega." Skyla gave him a look. He wore coveralls belted at the waist. Pieces of equipment had been clipped to either belt or clothing loops. He gave her a bland look from a round face needing a shave. When he met her eyes, he stopped, staring for a moment, then added, "You've got the bluest eyes I've ever seen. Want to drop that Vegan scarf so I can get a look? I'd say you're the best thing to come through here in a long time."

"I'm busy tonight, sorry."

He growled under his breath. "Figures. Ah, hell, all right. I don't blame you. If I'd known, I'd have stopped, took a shower, dressed right smart, and tried to be a little sharper. Serves me right, but I'll stand you another rye if you give me news from Rega." He stuck out a grimy hand. "Name's Garn."

Skyla chuckled. "I'm called Silk for reasons you can't guess. Sure, Nab. Order up." She tossed down her whiskey and studied the man from the corner of her eye. He had style, she had to give him that. Those soft brown eyes had just a bit too much reservation. Internal Security? She fought the urge to shiver. They'd be sniffing around anyone setting foot on the station, keeping track.

"Rega's doing all right. The Star Butcher blasted the Rotted pus out of Comm Central. That played hell. Most of the government buildings are gone. Defense, Economics, Health and Welfare—as if *that* was a loss. Even Internal Security is a pile of slag. Tybalt's palace is a hole in the ground."

"Blessed Gods," Garn mumbled, a truly shocked look on his face. "We'd heard, seen the holos from Itreata. That stuff can be doctored, made to look like anything. But to talk to a person that's seen with her own eyes, you know that ain't propaganda."

"Nope, it's happened. Rega is gone. So is Sassa."

He squinted slightly as he tilted his head. "You're Vegan?"

"I wear the scarf because it hides the fact my jaw got shot off when I was a kid and I drool a lot."

Garn lowered his voice. "You here because of what happened to the Representative?"

"Pardon me."

"Pedro Maroon, the Vegan Rep. He's missing." Garn lifted an eyebrow, hesitant as he watched her. "Thought you Vegans checked in on making planet. All that kin obligation and stuff."

Skyla nodded, rolling the drinking bulb from hand to hand. The Rep was missing? Another one of Ily's agents?

"Garn, I just made it in. Who do you think I'm busy with tonight? What do you mean Pedro's missing?" Caution made Skyla say, "I thought it was funny when I didn't get a comm link into Pedro's office. What's up?"

The tightness at the corners of his eyes, the enlarged pupils and twitching jaw muscles betrayed his unease.

"Hey, what's happening here?" Skyla placed a hand on his arm. "I'm not walking into trouble, am I?"

Garn tried to smile, lost it, and shrugged. "How the Rotted Hell do I know? This whole place is on its ear. All of Free Space is falling apart. The Director of Internal Security is in with the Union leaders, supporting their cause, if you can believe it. The Administrator wants Rill's head—but can't touch him, or is afraid to. There's new factions springing up every night. So what if a couple of guys disappear? Solar wind, right?"

"Wrong," she answered with the same passion a Vegan would. "We don't like our people disappearing. It affects trade." Political unrest was one thing, but Vegan Trade Reps were as close to sacrosanct—barring Etarian priests—as a person could get in Free Space. Fooling with one could generate awful repercussions. *Maybe using the scarf wasn't such a great idea, Skyla.*

"A couple of guys disappeared?" She lifted an eyebrow.

"Yeah, a Regan merchant—a regular around the tavern. But he's . . . Naw, he's around somewhere. Got to be. That's just the paranoia settling in. People are scared right now, that's all. Pus-licking pimps, you wake up each morning wondering if you'll even have a job when you go to bed at night." He studied her for long moments, then leaned close. "You take passengers?"

Skyla drank the last of her second rye. "I might. Depends on who they are . . . and how much they want to pay. I *don't* take people on the run from the law."

He glanced around, making sure that no one was near. "I'm getting a bit of a case of the jittery heebie-jeebies. I've made a good living on Terguz. This frozen rock's been kind, you know what I mean? I made a good stash, but I don't know what's happening. I've got folks on Riparious. Maybe I'd like to live on a place where you don't freeze to death in darkness when the power goes off."

Skyla leaned back, watching him. "I'm going the other

way. Sassan territory. And if Pedro really is missing, I'm headed straight to Vega with the news. Vega's a nice place. In another two years, or so, the spring melt will start.'' She lifted an eyebrow. ''Still interested?''

Garn winced, rubbing his chin. ''I don't know. How long are you going to be docked?''

''Week . . . maybe only a couple of days if it's true that Pedro disappeared.''

He took a deep breath. ''I'll think about it.''

''You haven't asked how much, either.''

He nodded. ''Maybe after I think. Thanks for the news, Silk. I'll be around.''

When he left, she punched up another rye, leaning forward to prop herself on her elbows. She'd have to drop by the Rep's now. Pedro Maroon. He'd be a reliable man. The Vegans wouldn't put a fool into a critical place like Terguz. She hadn't counted on Vegans being high profile, but if the Rep really were missing, Internal Security would be watching—along with the Administrator.

That old premonition of trouble had begun to brew during her talk with Garn. Skyla chewed anxiously on her lower lip as she watched the deep space monitor shot of Terguz on the big bar monitor. The giant wheel had been eclipsed by the bulk of Terguz, but now, as Skyla watched, the light of Guzman's Star, the system primary, cast its blue-green light over the station.

''How's the rye?'' A young woman—the excited one Skyla had noted earlier—slipped into the seat. She wore the usual coveralls, smudged around the knees, elbows, and cuffs. Her face would have been pretty but for a knobby nose. Impish green eyes took Skyla's measure. The tangle of brunette hair had been pulled back into a severe ponytail and was held in place by a clip.

''About gone.'' Skyla shot her a sidelong glance.

''I'll buy!'' She said it too fast, almost flushed with eagerness. ''I'm Lark. What's your handle?''

''Silk.''

''You're a trader? A Vegan?''

''Like I just told the ranny nab . . . I wear it so no one will know I'm from Vega.''

''You're funny.''

"Break your ribs laughing, kid. Say, does your father know you're out?"

Lark's grin widened to expose white teeth. "He's given up on me." She popped around her seat, reminding Skyla of fission tracks in a shadow tank. "I want to space. I can't help it. I mean, Terguz is a lousy rock on the edge of nowhere! I want to see it all! That's why I come here, Silk. I just sit and listen . . . and wish."

"And you don't end up in trouble?"

Lark made a throwing away gesture. "Yeah, I've been in messes. Spent most of a year on a community service detail. Hey, on Terguz, that's a real stinker! I mean, you've heard the term Terguzzi sumpshit? That can't hold a feeble photon to a supernova to what it's like to muck out the atmosphere plant, or to have to de-ice the ventilation shafts."

Skyla watched the girl's hands as she talked. Despite the smudged coveralls, those hands didn't bear calluses. The nails were too perfect. The mannerisms didn't ring true, spacer's gestures but without the instinct.

"What's the gig, Lark? Fess, putrid. Who are you, and what are you after? Cutting my purse? Trying to put the make on me like a ranny nab?"

Lark hesitated for a moment, surprise in her large green eyes. Skyla could make out a dusting of freckles beneath tastefully done makeup. "No gig, Silk. Honest. I swear." Her eyes narrowed. "You know, you remind me of a bull. Is that it? You're here to find out what happened to Maroon?"

"What happened to him?"

"If you're a bull, why should I help you?"

"So you know, huh?"

Lark shifted uneasily. "Maybe I ought to get back to my friends."

Skyla chuckled. "I'm no pus-Rotted bull. Relax and drink. I could give a rat's ass if you pinched a trick and slit his throat. Stupidity ought to be a killing offense."

Lark's expression betrayed a battle between curiosity and discretion. The former won. "You're not Vegan, are you? I mean, you don't . . . You're too hard, like reinforced sialon. It's in your eyes. Dangerous."

"Maybe you're not as dumb as I thought you were."

Skyla made a notation on the comm. "Take off, kid. I've programmed the drink comm. Go have one on me."

"I appreciate that, Silk. Thanks . . . but I'd rather sit here and talk to you. I mean, that's how I learn about . . ."

"Space off, kid. And stay out of trouble. You seem like a nice girl. A little green, but nice anyway. Folks come into a place like this for three reasons. A few actually conduct business. The others land here to learn something: information, you follow? The rest come for pleasure, be it a drunk, drugs, or sex? You're not canny enough for any of the above. Take my advice and go home."

Lark's green eyes frosted for the briefest of instants, then she brightened again, as if barely fazed. "You need anything on Terguz, Silk, you call on me. I know this ball of ice inside out. Food, drink, or good times, I can tell you where to go."

"Yeah, thanks. Vector off."

Skyla watched suspiciously as Lark drifted back to the techs. They'd barely noticed that she'd left.

Silly young girl? Or someone else? Skyla turned her attention back to the monitor displaying Terguz from space. Lark didn't have the right polish for a security agent. Instead, she'd seemed like a bored rich kid who was too bright for her own good. "Pus-licking Gods, I'm never having kids."

Terguz had gone sour on her. She'd hoped for a place to recoup—not a world in political turmoil and transition. Now, time would be of the essence. She could shuttle down to the Vegan residence and . . . No. Better to place a comm call, talk to someone in charge, then apply for space. Make like something really was wrong and she'd been dispatched for Vega. That was it, get off this ball of ice before . . .

The image hadn't registered at first. As she stared, Skyla's heart began to pound. Willing herself to remain calm, she lifted her rye and took a ragged swallow, letting it burn down her throat.

She knew that yacht from long years of association. Having docked on the first ring, she hadn't had a view of the fourth on her approach. And if she had, would she still have had the guts to dock here?

Keep cool, Skyla. Don't panic. Her throat had tightened

as if in a choke hold. *Pustulous Gods, Skyla, don't lose it. Not here, not now.*

Her old yacht gleamed in the sunlight, completely visible in the holo view. Ily Takka was here, someplace. Had she already learned of Skyla's arrival? Was she even now closing in, ready to finish what she'd started?

Skyla couldn't keep her hand from trembling as she withdrew her credit chip and stood.

Run! Get away! Get back to your ship and space!

Teeth gritted, she made herself walk slowly, casting wary glances to either side. Garn nodded from the table he'd gone to sit at, a solitary drink before him.

Skyla licked her lips, heart racing. On rubbery legs, she stepped over, hoping her fear didn't show. "Garn? You seen a woman around?"

"You're kidding, right?"

"A . . . a special woman. Sexy. Yellow eyes, big tits, reddish brown hair?"

He looked thoughtful, but he didn't hesitate. "Yeah, Silk. She was in here a couple of weeks ago. Left with a guy name of Blacker. Will Blacker. I almost mentioned him before. He's one of the regulars. His freighter's still out on the hub, but it ain't like him not to roll by here every now and then."

Skyla nodded, cold fear running through her bowels. "Yeah, he's probably around all right. See you later."

Taking a last worried glance, she noticed Lark. The girl watched her with puzzled eyes before turning to stare at the holo monitor, a frown on her forehead.

With all of her discipline, Skyla kept her retreat to a controlled walk instead of fleeing in a panicked run.

* * *

Staffa walked down the ceramic alloy catwalk. His booted feet rang out hollowly on the woven mesh while each breath frosted as he passed through the chilly air of *Chrysla*'s assault bay. Technicians in thermal suits knocked out crisp salutes as Staffa turned off the main walk and strode to the hatch on one of the needle-nosed assault craft.

Unlike the stubby brown-green Regan assault vessels, the

Companions used slim wedges, the two-hundred-meter vessel covered by a mirror polished surface.

A similarly reflective STU rapped a smart salute and opened the hatch as Staffa nodded in return and ducked through the double lock.

"All ready, sir?" The STU asked, pausing in the lock.

"We're all ready. Inform the pilot."

"Sir." The STU palmed the lock plate, sealing the lock while speaking quietly into the hatch comm.

Staffa proceeded along the assault deck with a critical eye on his personnel as they waited, strapped into the cushioned rows of chairs. Satisfied, he climbed the forward ladder to the combat command deck. There, technicians sat at battle stations, running checks on weapons systems, communications, reactor efficiency, and a host of other chores. These officers barely noticed as Staffa passed, each intent on his or her duty.

In the command nodule, forward and just above the assault craft's flight deck, Staffa found Sinklar and Mhitshul. The aide stood in the rear, uncertainly surveying the monitors and instruments that packed every available inch of the walls and ceiling. Command chairs, the arms and back cocooned by instruments, rose from the deck plates on sturdy columns of sialon. Each had been placed strategically for observation of the monitors.

Sinklar stood in the center of the room, hands clasped behind his back. He wore a simple suit of armor. His attention was centered on the main monitor that projected the image of Targa. The planet lay half in shadow, faint pinpricks of light marking the major cities on the Western continent.

Staffa stopped just behind his son, aware of the set of those thin shoulders and the tension in the locked legs.

"Are we ready?" Sinklar asked, in a subdued tone.

"The grapples will release in a moment." Staffa hesitated, hating to break the mood. "You'll need to take one of the command chairs. Despite the most skilled of pilots, dropping through atmosphere can be a little rough."

Sinklar nodded, then settled himself into one of the chairs. "Mhitshul? I'll be fine. I'm sure you can find a seat on the assault deck."

Mhitshul shot a suspicious look at Staffa, then reluctantly nodded. "Call if you need anything, sir."

When the aide had left, Staffa noted, "He cares a great deal about you."

"Sometimes he's a nuisance." Sinklar's gaze remained locked on Targa. "I get so tired of that worried look I want to dismiss him forever. Find someone else."

"But you can't."

"No." Sinklar smiled, amused at himself. "I couldn't stand to hurt his feelings. Besides, I think he's become something of a habit. The only times I've ignored his advice, I've usually regretted it." Sinklar inclined his head. "He's been with me for a long time. Since before Makarta. I guess if he stayed through that, he'll stay through anything."

Staffa lowered himself into one of the command chairs, feeling its padding conforming to his body as the assault craft shifted, beginning its descent toward Targa.

"I've been in touch with one of the mining companies. By the time we make planet and set up our base camp, they should have a mining machine on site. We'll reopen the tunnel we used to escape. Meanwhile I have a team of specialists en route to see about preserving and removing the collections from that archive room."

"And what about the interface helmet for the Mag Comm?"

"It should be almost finished. One of my techs will carry it down as soon as they run the trials on it."

"It's still going to be an unknown."

"Much of life, unfortunately, is an unknown."

Staffa frowned as they lapsed into silence. Sinklar couldn't keep his gaze from the monitor displaying Targa. A strained expression dominated his thin face. *He fears this return. Makarta is more than just another battle for him.*

Staffa cleared his throat. "We've never really talked about Makarta. About what it cost us, or how it has affected us since then."

Sinklar tilted his head, yellow and gray eyes skeptical. "I hated the Seddi then, and I hate them now. Nothing will change my desire to wipe their kind from Free Space. Too many of my people—and theirs—died because of Bruen and his politics. That much blood can't be washed away. Not in a million years.''

''You said you'd be willing to work with Kaylla Dawn. You'll at least try, won't you?''

''I said that nothing would change my desire to destroy the Seddi. I didn't say that I couldn't force myself to deal with them as a political reality.'' Sinklar shook his head. ''I'm sorry, Staffa. I know you only arrived on Targa within a day or two of my attack. In all honesty, had I known you were in charge down there, I'd never have sent Mac in with the Second Targan Division. I'd simply have flattened the mountain from space.''

''You fought very well. Were it not for me, you'd have rooted them out within a day or two. I doubt you would have taken more than forty or fifty casualties. The records would have been yours and the Seddi would have vanished from human affairs. Ily would have seen to that—as she would have seen to everything else.'' Staffa lifted an eyebrow. ''Or would you like to change the subject on that note?''

Sinklar gave him a cool glare.

Staffa smiled wearily. ''We've all made mistakes. Bruen ignored his order's teachings. You trusted Ily. I destroyed more than I should have. We've all sinned, Sinklar. We've all suffered from poor judgment of one sort or another.''

''No. None of us are without failings.'' Sinklar shook his head. ''Makarta was my first real failure. Perhaps that's why it's so hard to go back. Every action I took was countered. You fought a classic defense, Lord Commander. You made no mistakes.''

''You only made one—and it wasn't really your fault. You underestimated your opponent. You expected cowering priests and would have found them.''

''Bruen's Seddi owe their survival to you, it would seem.''

''I might put it conversely. I owe my survival to Kaylla's Seddi. You, I could point out, owe your survival to me.''

''I? To you?''

''Ily would have killed you rather than allow Mac to pull you out of her Ministry.''

''But she ran the moment Shiksta's attack blew her roof apart.''

''Of course she did, Sinklar, but she couldn't call her

underlings. Comm was blanketed by *Countermeasures*. Ily suffered from command paralysis. Look, the point I'm trying to make is that a lot has happened, both as a result of Makarta, as well as the events that have followed. We all need each other. The Seddi spy network acts as our ears. Companion communications tie us together, and my ships and troops help with social control. I can't keep the peace without your army and fleet. Take the Seddi, the Companions, or the Regans, and the whole thing falls apart."

"So what do I tell the ghosts at Makarta?" He closed his eyes, expression ashen.

"That you've kept your promise to them. People like them will never have to die at the whim of a politician worlds away. That they bought us all time. Isn't that what bothers you, Sinklar? That they might have died for nothing down there in the dark?"

Sinklar chewed at his lower lip as he watched the blue-white ball that was Targa grow in the monitor. "Yes, Lord Commander, I suppose that's where the nightmares come from."

"I have my own problems with nightmares." Staffa glanced up at the monitor as the assault craft settled into a descending orbit. "I predict that in your case, at least, your ghosts will sleep soundly, provided that we can stabilize Free Space and keep the peace."

"And your nightmares, Lord Commander? When will they fade? When will your ghosts leave you in peace?"

Staffa's lips twitched as he steadied his hard gray gaze on the monitor. The assault craft began to glow from the atmosphere. "When I've broken the Forbidden Borders and freed humanity from this trap, Sinklar. My sins—unlike yours—are much more grievous."

CHAPTER XX

It hit me in the middle of the night. Woke me out of a sound sleep, which is why I'm writing this now, so I don't forget by morning. Dreams are wonderful. They break the boundaries of common sense, disobey the rules, and free the subconscious.

In the dream, I watched myself as a kid again, playing in the zero g of the spindle axis on Terminal Seven. Being a boy, I had a pair of binary balls. All children who grow up in low gravity environments have a pair. You know what I mean, the two balls are tied together with a strand of industrial grade elastic. When the two balls are pulled apart and let go, the elastic snaps them back together and they bounce apart again in slightly different directions. In zero gravity, the balls shoot this way and that, bouncing off each other in all directions and only slowing when atmospheric drag and the friction in the balls slows them. Otherwise, because total inertia remains the same, they just hang in space, with a little drift, despite the frantic action of the balls seeking to shoot off to the limit of the elastic.

In the dream, I flipped the binary balls out into space, and they snapped back and forth, but instead of continuing, they followed me, chased me clear through the station, patting off each other, ricocheting from walls.

That's what woke me up, the terror of being chased by my childhood binary balls. And now, perhaps I know the answer. Perhaps I won't fail at this greatest opportunity in my life. Breaking the Forbidden Borders might not be impossible after all. Provided, of course, that I can figure out how to manufacture binary balls that big!

—Excerpt from Dee Wall's personal journal

* * *

"Here we go. Yes, indeed, this looks very good," Ily cooed as the comm stopped scanning the data base. "Diane de la Luna. The physical description is close, blood type, HLA, and chem codes are close. And, as an additional stroke of luck, she's currently employed at the Ashtan Representative's on Vega."

Arta bent over Ily's shoulder, studying the data. "She does look a little like you. With a little curl to your hair the resemblance would even be closer."

Ily waved her off. "Physical looks aren't nearly as important as dermatoglyphics, retinal imprints, and chem ID. And for that I need a good laboratory."

"Ashtan has some of the best." Arta fingered her chin as she studied the data on the monitor. "We've been here too long as it is."

"Chafing at the bit? Hiding doesn't excite you?" Ily raised her inquiring glance. "Bored because I won't let you go out and prey on the people?"

"Maybe." Arta turned and stepped away, her gauzy bronze-colored gown floating behind her. She pivoted on one heel, regal as a goddess, watching Ily. "And I'm tired of sleeping alone."

"Gyper is serving his purpose. Generating a little sweat while sliding around on his penis will pay dividends in the future."

"Ily, sometimes I get the feeling you overrate the power of sex."

Ily used a stiff arm to push herself back. "Not in the slightest, Arta. Sexual prowess provides an advantage with some men, at some times. Nevertheless, it *is* an advantage when used skillfully. The average woman will give a man average sex, nice and pleasant while it's happening. I provide a man with memorable sex, the kind that leaves them flushed for days afterward. In Gyper's case, he'll cut us a little slack if we need it in the future."

"I give a man memorable sex, too," Arta said with a sly smile.

"Yes, you do," Ily answered dryly. "But they only have a few seconds after orgasm to savor it. I wish you could overcome that need to kill them so quickly."

"I managed with Tyklat."

"But it nearly drove you as unpredictable as half of a virtual pair."

Arta sighed, nodding. "I understand your point, Ily. Very well, tonight I shall sleep with Gyper—and I won't kill him, just to prove it to myself, and to you."

"Are you sure that's such a good idea?"

Arta's amber gaze sharpened. "I'm not a fool, Ily. There are times when it is beneficial to leave a man alive after having sex with him. It is, as you would say, a fault in my character." She frowned. "Besides, controlling that desire is another way of thwarting Bruen. Yes, Ily, I shall sleep with Gyper . . . and allow him to savor the memory for a long time afterward. As you point out, doing so will give us yet another measure of advantage."

Ily smiled, several new possibilities coming to mind. "Very well, I'll tell him. And tomorrow morning, depending on how satiated you leave him, we'll let him know we're leaving."

"Don't trust me?"

"Arta, I trust you with my life, but why not remove temptation while you work on your restraint?"

Arta chuckled to herself. "Very well, *Diane de la Luna,* and now, why don't you get on about the more demanding challenge of finding an alias for me?"

Ily steepled her fingers as she studied Arta's profile. "I doubt there has ever been a Vegan with your phenotype. A body like yours is an anomaly that appears only once in a generation, but in every man's most spectacular fantasy."

"I could pose as your slave, Ily."

You already are, Arta. She sighed. "As much as I hate the thought, it might be the only way we can pass you through security, but believe me, Itreata screens slaves more thoroughly, if anything, than they do ambassadors."

"Problems, problems, but then, you thrive on them, don't you?"

Ily frowned as she punched in parameters for the data base search. "Always, dearest Arta. And you can bet your sexy ass that I solve them. One way or another."

* * *

They bought us time. That thought echoed through Sinklar's mind as he stepped down from the Companion assault craft and onto the hard surface of Targa. The fact that he felt heavier came from the planet's slightly higher gravity. He looked up at the night sky, noting familiar constellations. The night breeze carried the characteristic scents of Targa—pines, grass and shrubs, rock and rich earth.

Around him, men and women moved with a purpose, the STU establishing a perimeter while Ryman Ark and a special team inspected the miners and the drilling equipment at the edge of the field of light cast by the assault craft.

I'm back, returned to Targa. He need but close his eyes to flash back to the night he'd reviewed Mac's Second Division as they readied their assault on Makarta.

Sinklar squinted, walking forward, aware of Mhitshul searching the crowd for him. Instinctively, Sinklar ducked to one side, avoiding his aide as he made for the perimeter.

"Halt!"

Sinklar slowed, lifting his hands as one of the STU, a woman from what Sinklar could make out through the helmet electronics, stood before him.

"Your name and mission?"

"Sinklar Fist. My mission is to walk out into the darkness."

She frowned, whispering into the comm pickup at her mouth. "We don't have a mission listing for that, sir."

"Trust me."

"I don't have a mission listing for that either, Lord Fist. The perimeter hasn't been secured or cleared. Until I receive—"

"Do you want to call Staffa and ask him?" Sinklar crossed his arms, a stubborn frustration building within him.

To his surprise, she said, "I do, sir. One moment."

The STU nodded, as if to herself, and told him, "You may pass, sir. The Lord Commander requests that you be careful . . . and that you act prudently when you approach the perimeter. He also requests your estimated time beyond the perimeter."

"Ten minutes. Maybe fifteen." Sinklar shook his head. "You really called him?"

She stiffened and snapped a salute. "Yes, sir. We take

security very seriously. One last thing, Lord Fist. The Lord Commander says, 'Wish them well for me, too, Sinklar.' "

Sink nodded, "Tell him thanks, I will."

He walked into the night, searching the rocky ground for footing. They'd landed on the eastern side of the mountain, at the place where he'd once established his base camp. The night air hadn't changed. With the lights behind him, it might have been but a displaced instant since he'd walked out from his LC and away from Mhitshul's worried stare.

He slowed, passing the last of a belt of pines. The dark mass rose before him, blotting out the stars. His imagination conjured images of a hunched lion, as foreboding as when he'd stood on this spot once before, fearing, as he did now, that Makarta would cost him more than it was worth.

The evening breeze whispered through the pines behind him, its chill breath cooling his hot cheeks. No more than fifty meters ahead, he'd find the square tunnel that led into the guts of the mountain. There, Mac's Division had marched bravely into the Seddi trap.

"Do you hear me?" Sinklar asked the wind. "I've come back, my friends. The last time I saw you here, you were alive, anxious to charge down into the Seddi tunnels and end the revolt once and for all. So much has changed. Staffa says you bought us all time. We're a little older now, a little wiser than when we fought here last time. I hope . . . I hope I can meet your expectations. Help me, please. We're not safe yet. None of us."

He bit his lip, turning, almost tripping over the black wire on the ground. Sinklar pulled it from the resisting grass and forbs. Rubber-coated, heavy gauge, he almost shivered as he recognized what he held. This had been the communications link between his command center and MacRuder's Division. Through this line, he'd had his first connection with a faceless Staffa kar Therma.

Sinklar took a deep breath, following the wire forward through the darkness until he scrambled over the piles of mucked rock to the square opening, barely visible in the shadowed starlight.

"Hello," Sinklar called as he slipped down the loose tailings. His call echoed back, grating footsteps loud against the polished walls. A cool breeze carried up from the depths, musty and damp. Sinklar sagged, one hand caressing the stone. Here, he inhaled the breath of the dead, rising from their tomb to the freedom of light and sun.

A single hot tear leaked down the side of his face as he prayed for the souls of his restless dead.

* * *

"Lord Commander?"

Staffa reached over and pressed a finger on the control stud. "Yes?"

He stood in the center of the command node within the assault craft. Around him, the monitors displayed different scenes from their perimeter and base camp. The ship's detection equipment, unhampered by night, depicted the Targan landscape with uncanny accuracy.

"This is STU Second Adze, reporting on Lord Fist, sir. He found some sort of comm cable. He's in an old tunnel mouth, just slumped there, sir. He seems to be . . . well, crying. Should I move closer? See if he's all right?"

Staffa flipped one of the monitor switches, seeing what Adze saw through her electronically augmented senses. He recognized that tunnel cut into the mountain. "Negative, Adze. Back off and give him room. Stay just close enough to ensure his safety, but don't intrude. FYI, this is Class I security."

"Affirmative. Class I, back off and monitor for safety only."

Staffa kept an eye on the monitor as Adze carefully backed away. She'd make sure Sinklar didn't come to harm, and she'd keep her mouth shut about it afterward. Adze was one of his best.

"Lord Commander?" his main comm informed. "We have Itreata on the line."

"Go, Itreata, secure this frequency."

"Affirmative."

Kaylla's face formed. "Staffa? Are we secure?"

Staffa checked the quantum wave, noting no disturbance. "The line appears secure. What's happening?"

Kaylla gave him a weary smile. "We have the Wing Commander on line. I'm patching through now."

Staffa's heart skipped as Skyla's haggard face formed on the monitor. Her eyes looked swollen, and there was a puffiness in her cheeks. Fear lingered in her cobalt eyes.

"Staffa?" her voice quavered in an uncharacteristic way.

"How are you? Where are you? Are you all right?"

She jerked a nod, swallowing hard. "I'm docked at Terguz, routing the dish through Itreata on narrow beam. Listen, my yacht is here. I think Ily's here." She fought the urge to tremble. "I'm all right, I think. I registered under the Silk alias. That cover should be good. I'm wearing a Vegan scarf in public. I think I'm safe."

"Settle down. It's all right. What do you want me to do? I can reroute—"

"No. Wait. Listen. By the time anyone could reroute for Terguz, she'd be gone. Whatever happens, Ily will have to space out of here." Skyla knotted a fist. "She wouldn't have left the yacht out in the open if she expected to be here long. It's too conspicuous. Just luck that I spaced here first."

"I can route to the Administrator, tell him—"

"No! Staffa, don't. Please." Then, as quickly, she relented. "All right. Send a ship . . . a backup. Terguz might end up in flames anyway. The people here are taking matters into their own hands. Lots of ferment and the Director of Internal Security apparently supports them. I've only been from my ship to the *Wayside* and back. Kaylla will be happy to know that lots of Seddi slogans are painted on the walls. It could blow up. Not only that, the Vegan Rep is missing. I don't know if it's Ily's work or not. I . . ."

She raised her hands and shook them, fingers outspread, eyes squeezed tightly closed as she fought for control. "I got scared. Ran away . . . Saw my yacht in the monitor and ran . . . ran back here. She's here, Staffa. She's here. I can *feel* her in the pus-Rotted air!"

Staffa made calming motions, his own fear rising. "Relax, Skyla. Take a deep breath. There, now take another. That's it." *She's almost incoherent.*

Skyla closed here eyes, breathing deeply. "Okay. I'm okay." She swallowed again, shaking her head while a pained expression flooded her flushed face. "I've got to go out again. Try and contact the Vegan Rep, see if he's really disappeared."

"Skyla?" Staffa's muscles knotted as he gripped the side of the console. "Skyla? Look at me. That's it. All right, let's talk this out rationally."

She nodded, blinking as she stared at him. "I'm fine, Staffa. It happens, builds up, then bursts." She licked her lips, the reassuring smile disintegrating. "Then I buck up and get along as best I can."

"I'm going to reroute Seekore for backup. She's on the vector closest to Terguz. She'll have to dump Delta V, revector, and accelerate to mass, but she ought to be there within three to four weeks. Can you—"

"Too long," Skyla gave him a dull stare, as if she'd been completely drained. "Staffa, I've got to handle this myself. Ily left that yacht in plain sight. She's abandoning it here. She's short, you understand? She's going to skip, maybe steal a ship, maybe buy passage, I don't know. But by the time Seekore can get *Sabot* here, Ily will be only a memory."

"All right, I can buy that. I'm still rerouting Seekore, just on the basis of the intelligence you've provided. If Terguz does explode, maybe *Sabot* can pick up some of the pieces." *And if worse turns to worst, Seekore can break you out of trouble!* "You say the Director of Internal Security is siding with the rebels?"

"That's the word in the tavern. I'll know better after I've been on planet."

"And what if you get down there, see Ily in a crowd, and fall to pieces like you just did on the comm?"

Skyla's glare was a brittle blue. "I don't know, Staffa. I guess I . . . . If I fall apart when it counts, she wins." She paused, a weary expression dominating her beautiful face. "I've got to pull myself out, Staffa. You understand that, don't you? You said you did in the message. You meant that, didn't you?"

He nodded, heart breaking as he forced his smile. "I meant it. I believe in you. I said I'd back you, no matter what." *And if I'd known how fragile you really were, I'd have torn apart all of Free Space to find you.*

A faded shadow of Skyla's old raucous grin finally molded around her lips. "You know, you're one hell of a man, Staffa. If I hadn't been in love with you before, I'd kill for you now."

"And I for you." He reined in his emotions again, knowing what she needed to hear. "I love you, Skyla. If I can help in any way, let me know."

She nodded with nervous jerks of her head, unable to meet his eyes. "How's the situation on Targa?"

"We just made planet. Sinklar's out talking to his ghosts."

"And Chrysla? She's dealing with the situation?"

"She's not here."

"That's right. Off trying to find herself, you said."

"The women in my life seem to share that trait." Staffa chuckled. "She's with MacRuder. He's . . . well . . ."

Skyla glanced up, frown lines tightening around her eyes. "I've never heard that tone in your voice before."

Staffa sighed, smile going crooked. "I've made my peace, Skyla. I've bet everything on you. And you know what a great gambler I am."

"Why? Why me?"

"Oh, something about love, about the times you've kept showing up at just the right time to save my life. Then, I can remember the times when you tried to seduce me and I let you."

"Let me?" A pale eyebrow rose.

"Why you don't think I enjoyed being wrapped up in that pale hair of yours, do you? Half the time I was afraid to move for fear I'd rip a hank of it out of your head!"

"Afraid to move? But I thought . . ." Understanding dawned, her eyes growing bluer. "You worthless Riparian slime mold. When I get ahold of you, I'm going to kick you so hard your balls loop around your—"

"You and whose army? Looking at you, I'd say you'd be a one-handed whipping. Remember the last time aboard *Chrysla?* You thought I was going to seed, getting fat and lazy. I've been keeping fit, practicing my hand to hand. How about you?"

Her expression had gone brittle again.

Staffa lowered his voice. "Uh-huh, just as I thought. Better start tuning up, my love. Next time I see you, I might be able to take you with both hands behind my back."

Come on, Skyla, look me in the eyes. Where's the old spirit? Give it back to me!

She hesitated for a long moment, eyes downcast. "Not on your best day, fat boy." When she looked up, her composure had returned. "I've got to go."

"Be *very* careful. Whenever you can, report in. Just in case, you understand. We want all the latest information we can get on Ily and the political situation. I'm depending on you."

"Depending on me, huh? You're a fool, Staffa. If you only knew some of the . . ." She shook it off like a wet dog. "I'll be careful."

"I miss you."

She winked at him. "See you around. I've got a couple of bitches to go kill."

The monitor went dead.

Staffa groaned as he sagged back into the command chair. "Skyla, Skyla, for the Blessed Gods' sake, you can't even maintain control talking to me, how can you deal with pus-Rotted Ily?" He shook his head. "She's going to kill herself."

"Perhaps," Kaylla told him. Her face had filled the monitor. "On the other hand, we've got a plot on Ily's location now. I can have my agents on Terguz start working on how to close in on her."

Staffa stared woodenly into the monitor. "Listened in, did you?"

"I have a stake in this, remember. Also, keep in mind that I know you, Staffa. I know how you work, what makes you tick. You have problems with guilt. If you're going to charge off like an Ashtan bull, I want a bit of warning. That's just the sort of thing you'd do for Skyla."

He bridled, anger stirring—and she read his expression. "Your secret is safe with me, Lord Commander." A thin smile even graced her lips. "And to show you how foolish I really am, I'm worried about her, too."

He rapped his fingertips on the console cover. "Thank you, Kaylla." He hesitated. "What do you think? Will she make it? Pull herself together?"

"Given enough time, Staffa. She's a tough lady."

"So are you, but I don't know if she's got the time. Ily is . . ."

"Yes, I know." Kaylla steepled her fingers. "Gyper Rill is the Director of Internal Security on Terguz. He has contacted us, offered his full cooperation."

"Did he mention the yacht?"

"No." Kaylla's tan gaze hardened. "But he has been a major supporter of reforms on Terguz. Skyla was right about that. From what my agents have deduced, she was also right about the Vegan Representative vanishing. I'll follow up on that now."

"And my decision to reroute *Sabot?*"

Kaylla's lips quivered. "When it comes to women, Seekore would scare the quanta straight. And, Staffa, if things go wrong, Seekore can settle the score. If things go right, she can bring Gyper Rill back for a thorough interrogation."

"You're a cold-hearted and efficient Magister, did you know that?"

Kaylla smiled wryly. "Don't get maudlin, Staffa. It's all your fault. You should have let me drown in the sewer, or be crushed under all that sand."

"Thanks, Kaylla. If your people can keep an eye on Skyla, so much the better. I . . . I'd take it as a favor."

"Let me see what happens." She paused, then asked, "You're going in tomorrow?"

"As soon as the mining machines can open the tunnel."

Kaylla took a deep breath. "Gods be with you, Staffa. Bruen should be there within a week. Good luck."

"I'll do my best . . . for all of us."

She gave him an understanding smile and killed the connection.

Staffa leaned back, cradling his head in his hands.

* * *

In her Itreata office, Kaylla Dawn stared thoughtfully at the monitor as her fingertips tapped on the console top. Staffa had looked like a man who'd been kicked in the belly.

She rubbed her eyes, trying to still that hair-trigger sense of impending trouble. Staffa loved Skyla Lyma with a desperate passion. Kaylla had listened to him in the desert and in his dreams; he'd called out to her repeatedly when he'd teetered on the edge of sanity. Skyla had come, like an avenging angel, to pluck him from disaster. Of all the women Kaylla had ever known, Skyla was enough of a she wolf to match a man like kar Therma.

I should hate them both. Her tan eyes narrowed to slits, images of her last day on Maika replaying—as clear and vivid as if she'd lived that horror but hours ago.

Stop, Kaylla. You loved your family with all of your heart, but their day is past. Now you have only the eternal present to live in. "The past is only illusion."

"What's that?" one of her secretaries asked.

"Nothing."

"Magister? I have a line from Ashtan. Division First MacRuder would like to speak with you as soon as you clear the line to Targa."

Kaylla accessed her terminal as MacRuder's face formed. He stared out at her with fatigue-flat eyes, perspiration shiny on his face.

"First MacRuder? How is the situation?"

Mac gave her a grin; a trickle of sweat slipped out of his matted blond hair. "I think we've got it licked. Comm is functioning at rudimentary levels, enough to manage simple tasks like running the sewage plants. We've got organic command posts set up all across the planet. With the programs you provided, we're able to get food to the places that need it. Spare parts are getting around—but then, you know about spare parts. It's always the right number, but wrong part." He seemed to drift off, smiling to himself.

"MacRuder? Are you all right?"

"Hmm? Oh, yes, what was I saying?"

"About parts?"

A frown lined his forehead. "I'm sorry. Yes, we're getting parts sent out to places that need them. We'll have problems down the line. Orders need to be filled for places like Rega."

Kaylla braced her chin on a palm. "How long since you've had any sleep, Mac?"

"Oh, I don't know. Maybe . . ." He shook his head. "Before we made planet. Chrysla would know . . . I think."

"You've lost your edge, First. Get some sleep. And, Mac, good work."

He smiled, nodding. "There was something . . ."

"The ship," Chrysla's contralto said from the side. "Tell her about the—"

"Right! Pus Rot it!" Mac seemed to come to life again. "We've got a transport spacing for Imperial Sassa. Those folks should be getting some relief. We'll send off another as soon as we can put one in the schedule." He paused. "It's just a matter of making the schedule now."

Kaylla laughed. "You should hear yourself! Mac, have

your staff send us an inventory of what you started for Imperial Sassa. We'll let Admiral Jakre know what's coming, and we'll find out what they really need."

Mac's glow faded again. "We're not . . . too late . . . are we?"

"No, Mac. You'll have saved a lot of lives. They'll be glad to hear about your efforts on their behalf."

Mac's eyes went vacant. "Don't . . . don't tell them, Kaylla. I've already hurt them enough. I did this to them . . . killed all those people. It's my fault . . . my . . ."

"Mac, you did your duty, that's all. Now you're doing it again." She hesitated. "Lady Attenasio, if you can, put him to sleep."

"As soon as possible, Magister Dawn," the contralto assured from the side. "Come on, Mac. Let's check with Red and Andrews and see if the Power Utility is on-line. Then we'll call it quits for this round."

Kaylla cocked her head, curious at the concern, yes, even the love in that reassuring voice. She killed the connection, and pursed her lips. *Are you aware of how they feel about each other, Staffa? Or is this another upset for you?*

Kaylla returned her attention to her terminal. "Comm, I need the names of our agents on Terguz." If Skyla Lyma were safe, Staffa could concentrate all of his faculties on the Mag Comm—unless his wife was running off with another man.

Men acted peculiarly when it came to women—just as Staffa and Nyklos bristled constantly over Skyla Lyma.

And what if MacRuder takes your wife to bed, Staffa? Will you be saintly and suffering, as you were in the desert? Or will the Star Butcher rear his ugly head?

* * *

I'm not used to skulking. The realization settled into Skyla's mind as she strode down one of the main thoroughfares in Terguz. She'd taken the hourly shuttle to the planet's surface, dropping through the clouds of ammonia and chlorine. The shuttle port itself had been excavated out of the blue-white ice. To reach it, the shuttle had to drop down a square shaft past the energy fields.

The city had been cut out of the ice, each of the warrens

insulated and protected from the burning cold. Terguz City had been laid out radially, different boulevards departing from the shuttle hub at forty-five degrees. Skyla now proceeded down the corridor along which the embassies, trade organizations, and importers had placed their offices.

Electric carts kept to the center, whirring by on fat rubber tires. People in every sort of dress imaginable either hurried along or browsed, inspecting the holo displays inset in the shop walls. Brightly painted banners stretched down from the arched ceiling, while holographic slogans written in laser-colored letters glowed in midair. Skyla recognized most of the phrases as Seddi in origin—belonging to Kaylla Dawn's Itreatic broadcasts, no doubt.

Skyla had stepped through the shuttle port door, expecting to blend with the crowd and pass unnoticed to the Vegan Rep's offices. Despite her efforts, she seemed to draw attention. Men gave her that penetrating stare before nodding. Women gave her the double glance, the first categorizing, the second calculating.

What is it? Why can't I fade into the crowd here the way I did on Etaria? On Etaria she'd worn a veil in public. Was it her eyes? Did her eyes betray her here as a siff jackal among so many Vermilion sheep?

Part of it was the walk, she realized. Back straight, steps long, carriage erect. All Etarian matrons walked that way, dignity was one of the few luxuries allowed them. But the inhabitants of Terguz bore themselves with a certain air of endurance.

Can you walk like that, act like that? Skyla shortened her steps, letting her shoulders slump and keeping her eyes downcast. Yes, that was it. Immediately she slipped into partial invisibility, glances now being drawn to her Vegan scarf.

She reached the Rep's, palmed the lock plate, and stepped inside. The square reception room could be crossed in five paces. A counter transected the space, and a woman stood and nodded in greeting.

Skyla nodded back, closing the door behind her before she walked over and unpinned her scarf as was proper introduction manners when one Vegan dealt with another.

The woman unclipped her own scarf, her black eyes taking Skyla's measure. Gray streaked her raven hair, and crow's-feet had tightened at the corner of her eyes. The long straight nose accented her long face and pinched mouth. "You are not Vegan. Who are you? Why are you here?"

Skyla glanced around suspiciously. "Is there someplace where we can talk? I understand that Pedro Maroon, your Rep, has disappeared."

"What interest is it of yours, impostor?"

Skyla met the hostility in those burning black eyes. Kinship and clan meant everything to the Vegan people. Perhaps Maroon was this woman's son? Brother? More than politics would be at stake here.

"Tell me, did the Rep meet with anyone before he vanished? A tall woman with long black hair and large dark eyes? Or, perhaps, an athletic woman with amber eyes and a . . . well, provocative body? A woman with auburn hair about so long?"

"Who are you?" Excitement gleamed in those hot black eyes.

"Which woman?"

"The one with yellow eyes, like those of a cat. Yes, a cat woman."

"Good description." Skyla's gut began to twist. "She's about as deadly, too. Did she see him often?"

"Only once."

"And you never saw Pedro Maroon again?"

"No."

"Where did she see him?"

"Here. In his office, and then he left."

"Where did he go?"

"I don't know."

Skyla paused, thinking. "May I see his office?"

"Who are you?"

Skyla hesitated. "Someone who would like to help."

The woman crossed her arms stubbornly.

"Pus Rot you, listen to me! I don't have time to play your games. Vega's internal security is at stake here—along with Rega's and Sassa's as well. The amber-eyed woman's name is Arta Fera. Ah, yes, you've heard of her. She's Minister Ily Takka's special assassin. Ily is here, on Terguz. She's being chased by the Companions, the Seddi, and Regan military forces. Arta is a beautiful woman. She has a way of blinding men with her sexuality, but in the end, she kills them. Do you understand? She got to Pedro, found out what she needed, and killed him.''

The woman's eyes betrayed panic, then pain.

"I'm sorry, but that's as blunt as I can be. Will you help me? Maybe you know something, some way we can run Ily and Arta down, stop them from killing again.''

"I am Magrite. Pedro was my sister's son. We come from the old line, the de Varo family.''

Skyla nodded. "Here, on Terguz, I am called Silk. One day, Magrite, I hope I will be able to introduce myself and tell you my lineage. For the moment, can you tell me if you noticed anything different after Pedro was last seen with Arta?''

The hesitation still lingered, but Magrite took a deep breath and said, "Someone accessed the files.''

"You're sure?''

She nodded. "Pedro was a very thorough man. His mother taught him well . . . and his family honor has long been one of outstanding service to the Vegan people. When he locked the offices at night, Pedro would seal the files with a magnetic field. He carried the switch in his pocket, in an ordinary looking laser pen. He switched the field on when he left with the assassin. The night he disappeared, the field was broken. The field was not for security, you understand?''

"I understand. The field was to detect tampering. If anyone pulled one of the file drawers open, it would change the magnetic field and trigger the system.''

Magrite nodded. "You understand. Someone accessed the data cubes that night. I have conducted an inventory. All the cubes are still in their holders.''

"But they might have copied the data?''

"That is a possibility.'' She watched Skyla with an obsidian stare. "The personnel files and vessel registry files were opened that night. I can tell by the realignment of the magnetic fields.''

"So they might have been after some kind of personnel data? I assume you have files on every Vegan citizen? The same with not only Vegan ships, but Regan and Sassan vessels that have contracted as Vegan carriers?''

"You are correct, lady.''

"What else, Magrite?''

"He returned here with her after I and the rest had locked up and gone home. I know this from the access codes. His body chemistry opened the lock to both the outer door and to his personal office." Magrite lowered her eyes. "He . . . they . . ."

"Go on."

She straightened primly. "I tell you this only because you are a woman and seem to know the way of such things. I will hold you to your honor, and the honor of your family, whatever that might be, not to mention this. But perhaps knowing will help you in your pursuit. He coupled with her on the desk. Right there in his office. I can't tell you how I know, but I do."

Skyla raised a hand. "It's her way. She usually kills immediately afterward."

Magrite kept her eyes averted. "I have told you everything, impostor. Go now, do what you can. If you find Arta Fera or her master, and if you avenge Pedro Maroon, let my clan know."

"We will." Skyla hesitated. "Magrite. May I have copies of the files they accessed?"

She shook her head in negation. "I cannot allow you to see what it is not in my permission to grant . . . even if I wanted to."

"But the Vegan authorities would have exact duplicates?"

"They would. For that, you would have to go to Vega and make your case for access."

"My people will, Magrite. And when they do, they will inform the council of your noted clan's honor and worthiness. Good profit to you and your family, lady. May your trades be made wisely and your journeys safe."

"May your family prosper, Lady Silk. Good health and profits to you on your endeavor."

Skyla nodded, refastening her scarf. She was in the process of giving Magrite a final nod when the door opened. The uniformed officers stepped warily to either side of the doorway, hands on stun rods.

"You are the Regan trader known as Silk?" the tall blond one asked.

Skyla nodded, bowing low as her hand dipped into her

pocket and gripped the handle of her blaster. "Good day, gentlemen. I am Silk."

"You are under arrest." The tall blond officer raised his stun rod.

Skyla shot him full in the chest, her blaster ripping through the fabric of her robe. Her weapon ripped the air again, the violet beam blowing the second man's arm from his body as he pivoted to lift his own stun rod.

Fast on her feet, Skyla dropped on him, kicking away the pistol he clawed out of his holster with his good hand.

"Talk! What's your name?"

"Pus Rot you, Regan bitch."

The security officer screamed as Skyla hammered the bloody stump of his shattered arm. "Talk, Rot you, or I won't put a tourniquet on this wound. You've got less than two minutes of consciousness. How do you want to spend it? In pain? Or in polite talk?"

He screeched again as she stamped a booted foot on his ragged stump. "Talk?"

"He's bleeding to death on my floor!" Magrite whispered in horror.

"Rotted right he is," Skyla agreed. "Want to take bets he was one of the men who carried Pedro's dead body out of here? What's your name, pal?"

"Vy—Vymer! You're dead, bitch. The Director won't let you get away with this."

"Ah, the Director. Now we're getting somewhere. You've got a minute left. Want to spill your guts?"

"Fuck you, bitch." Vymer's face had gone white.

At that moment, the door burst open as Lark charged in. Reflexively, Skyla pivoted at the hips. Her weapon locked in an isosceles hold, she lined her sights on the girl's chest, index finger resting firmly on the firing stud.

Lark gaped in horror and tried to stop her headlong rush. She slipped in the blood that had spewed from Vymer's arm and the torn chest of his companion—and recovered in a windmilling of arms.

At the last instant, Skyla hesitated. "You've got a lot of explaining to do, girl."

CHAPTER XXI

From: Engineer First, Dee Wall
Director, *Countermeasures* Project
Itreata Free Zone

To: Lord Commander, Staffa kar Therma
Companion Force: Battleship *Chrysla*
Geosynchronous orbit off Targa

Greetings and best wishes from myself and my staff. It is with great pleasure that I forward information concerning our first successful test. I have hesitated to inform you of the constant disasters we have experienced, and take full responsibility based on my belief that your needs wouldn't have been best served by repeated reports of failure.

To wit, we have finally managed to measure gravitational interaction with the gauge-symmetry of the oscillating string nearest the Forbidden Borders. Working with Lorentz-invariant field equations, we've detected gravitational interference. Our methodology in this case consisted of passing a ship traveling at c/null singularity perpendicularly through the margins of the string's field. Thus, at greatest mass, we were able to demonstrate a perturbation in the amplitude of the string's wave.

While it doesn't sound like much, for the first time we have been able to measure a human effect on the Forbidden Borders.

Our theoreticians are studying ways whereby we can augment this effect. It may be possible to send two vessels generating artificial gravity in opposite directions through the field. In doing so, we may be able to initiate enough interaction to induce initial conditions which might lead to a disruption of the Borders–perhaps enough so that we could slip a ship through the gap without destroying it.

Lord Commander, you must be aware, however, of the energy necessary to accomplish this. I am not sure, at this time, that we can accelerate enough mass to light speed and coordinate it with enough accuracy to accomplish our goal–even with virtual pair control capabilities from the *Countermeasures* system.

That said, I offer you my best wishes and inform you that I remain dedicated to the task you have set me and will exhaust every possible avenue of inquiry.

* * *

Sinklar waited beside Staffa and continued to stare into the square hole he'd excavated so long ago into the forbidding stone of Markata. In daylight, it still appeared ominous—a brooding wound in the side of the mountain. To his surprise, however, green shoots had taken hold in the tailings. A healing, even here among the cuttings and mucking mud.

The Targan sky alternated between patches of enamel blue and puffy white clouds. For the moment, bright sunlight bathed them, the pines verdant, the spring grass waving. Had they really fought here beneath this peaceful landscape? The morning had dawned warm and moist. A day for picnics and lovers—not for resurrecting the dead.

Around them, the rest of their team continued to gather, including STU personnel with comm equipment and other instruments. Sinklar recognized geophones dangling from coils of black wire.

"Let's do it." Sinklar took a final breath of fresh morning air, dreading the thought of breathing mold that spored off corpses.

"You don't sound very anxious."

"You don't either."

Staffa gave him a weary look. "You and I will have to face both of our demons in there. Fortunately, most of yours are dead."

Sinklar slapped his father on the shoulder. "And yours are just electronic."

They had decided to enter Sinklar's old adit that Mac and his people had taken with such confidence. For one thing, the entrance lay within their compound. For another, the bore was considerably wider than the "renegade hole," the escape tunnel the Seddi had drilled out during the fighting.

Entering from this high gallery meant they would have to travel extra distance to reach the Mag Comm's chamber and the archives. All of that would be through blasted corridors and galleries. The advantage was that mining equipment could follow the route and remove any of the artifacts they might want to salvage from the archives. After the route was cleared, they could ride back and forth to the stairway that led down to the Mag Comm's chamber.

Sinklar glanced behind them where the mining technicians were making last minute adjustments to their equipment. Their job would be to check for structural stability, fall rock, and other underground dangers. More Targan miners would be flying in later in the day to begin the unpleasant task of removing the corpses.

You could beg off, Sinklar told himself. *Wait until they move the bodies . . . bring them out and bury them.*

Staffa smacked a gloved fist into his palm. "Yes, let's get on with it." He squinted in the sunlight, the jeweled hair clip over his left ear scintillating as the wind teased his black hair. "Ryman? Have you got the helmet interface?"

"Here, Lord Commander." Ryman Ark stepped forward, a sialon case under one arm.

Sinklar shuffled from foot to foot, aware of the other STU who had placed herself behind him. Adze was the woman's name. Through the clutter of electronics gear, Sinklar could tell that she had copper-tinted skin and a pair of the hardest black eyes he'd ever seen.

One of the technicians appeared out of the tunnel, his coveralls smeared with dust. He looked on the verge of being sick. "It's all right so far, Lord Commander. My people have checked the roof and walls through the upper three levels. So long as you follow the beacons, nothing's going to come down on top of you. But, well, it's not pretty in there." As if to himself, he added, "I'm not going to sleep so well for a while."

"War tends to be that way. We've got a crew coming in to clean up."

The miner glanced at Sinklar, nodding, respect in his eyes. "Good to have you back on the planet, Lord Fist."

"Good to be here, sir."

The fellow seemed to brighten. "I saw you once in Vespa. That was just after you'd whipped five of Tybalt's Divisions. My cousin was working out at the Raktan mines when Hauws destroyed Weebouw and the Third Ashtan. He said he never saw such a defeated bunch of bastards as that Third Ashtan."

Hauws had died during the Raktan fight. Would Targa mean nothing more to him than a list of places where he'd lost friends? "When the burial crews get here, I would appreciate it if you would keep track of them. Remember that the bodies in there . . . well, they're all heroes."

The miner nodded somberly, raising a hand to touch his forelock. "Aye, Lord Fist. It'll be done. Be sure, I'll break the back of any lout who makes a disrespectful move, sir."

Sinklar smiled, shaking the man's hand. "I'm sure you will." Then he turned to Staffa, taking a final breath of the pine-scented air. "Lord Commander, I'm as ready as I'll ever be."

Sinklar started down the incline, glancing uneasily at the walls. Here, they'd been blasted, sealed as the last of his troops evacuated. Crews had cleaned out the adit upon their arrival, and now Sinklar walked on smooth rock, the walls straight and square again. The comm cable still lay on the floor—once his only link with Staffa kar Therma. Now the man walked quietly at his side as the darkness grew and their suit lights automatically illuminated to shoot white light into blackness. Overhead, the light bars his people had strung still hung, dark—like all the aspirations they'd had in Makarta.

The first body consisted of nothing more than a skeleton in charred armor.

Staffa studied the corpse. "Scavengers came this far. The reports I got state that most of the fatalities near the entrance were picked clean." He paused. "I remember her. She came around the corner . . . and I shot her. Instinctive reaction."

Sinklar nodded, a fluttery sensation in his stomach. "This is going to be harder on us than I thought."

They stepped out into a narrow winding tunnel that dipped

to the right and rose to the left. The mining machine that had made the adit had proceeded straight across and cut a curve.

"Mac went down there." Staffa pointed. "We'd walled off the exits. If any of Mac's people had touched them, they'd have felt wet plaster. Some of the walls weren't more than a half inch thick."

"Must have worked in a hurry. Your Seddi must have shown considerable discipline." *Mac, I'm so sorry.* Sinklar's pain grew as he stared down into the blackness, trying to imagine how Mac and his people must have felt.

"They were so frightened they almost fouled themselves." Staffa stepped across to the curving wall as he followed the amber beacons placed by the mining engineers, and rounded the radius before stepping into an open cavern. Here, an occasional light cast its radiance down from above. Wreckage had been strewn everywhere, and giant slabs of rock had fallen from the arched roof to smash whatever lay below. The amber beacons traced a sinuous trail across the cavern, sometimes placed on mounds of piled roof fall.

"This used to be the study center." Staffa looked around, hands on hips. "We mined it, then lured one of your Sections in here."

Sinklar's mouth had gone dry. Looking around, he spotted armored legs protruding from beneath a heavy desk. Whose? *Don't ask, Sinklar.* Unable to speak, he followed Staffa as the big man picked his way through the shambles. Amidst the broken equipment, Sinklar noticed an occasional shadowed corpse, or, more often, a fragment of a human body. Dust had settled over the whole, and most of the corpses had desiccated to skin and bone, the eye sockets empty and gaping. Above, the roof looked either splintered or polished depending on how the concussion had struck.

Sinklar glanced back, watching as their party crossed the cavern, single file, positions marked by white beams of suit lights. They created a weird human snake winding through the darkness while the sunken eyes of the ghosts watched.

The next cavern appeared even worse. "This used to be the distillery," Staffa said. "Your people broke through just back of that wall there." He pointed to an oblong hole in the far wall.

Sinklar nodded, his sense of horror growing. The floor here was littered with fragments of crockery and glass that crunched underfoot. Boulders, as much as a meter in diameter, had fallen from gaping holes in the blackened ceiling. Shattered rock had cascaded everywhere. The suit lights created a macabre dance of shadows and beams as they started across, eddies of dust rising in the eerie light.

A grim-faced Adze followed directly behind Sink while the rest of the STU proceeded warily, weapons gripped tightly as they studied every nook and cranny. More than one glanced nervously at the treacherous ceiling.

They're always on the alert, never taking anything for granted.

The air in the distillery still held the pungent odor of sour mash and fermentation mixed with the musty tang of dust. Sinklar stepped warily around a dusty bowl—and almost tripped as he shied backward.

The bowl had patches of hair still clinging to it.

Strong hands steadied him from behind.

"All right, sir?"

"Yeah, thanks, Adze. Don't step on the skull here."

"Yes, sir."

Sinklar got his pulse to slow and moved carefully around the gruesome head. Step by step, he crunched his way across the glinting bottle fragments, passing the twisted shapes of the fermentation vats, each crumpled like so much paper from the concussion.

"I wouldn't have wanted to be in here," Sinklar whispered. *But I sent them . . . and they went.*

"Me, either," Adze muttered behind him. "Hell of a fight, sir."

"Good people. Brave." Sinklar ground his teeth, hating to have to reach up and rub a tear away with a knuckle.

Staffa had stepped through a low arch. Sinklar almost breathed a sigh of relief to see the floor slanting down to the right.

"This intersection takes us down to Level Three." He glanced at Sinklar, seeing his shiny eyes reflected in the suit lights. "Are you all right?"

"Yeah." An aching knot had formed under Sinklar's throat. It threatened to choke him as they started down toward a faint glow. Had the lights survived there?

Sinklar shook his head, trying to rid himself of the images. Bright-eyed troops watched him from the shadows, chanting, *SINKLAR! SINKLAR! SINKLAR!* as they had every time he'd saved them from destruction.

I ordered them down here to die. He gasped, despite himself. *I did this to them. They . . . trusted me.*

Here, at this bottleneck, the battle had been pressed vigorously. Corpses lay piled in heaps, the dead curiously interwoven with Regans in hardened and charred armor embracing Seddi in their rot-stained robes.

Could these twisted, mold-coated mummies have been people? Were these same remains related to the human beings that laughed, hoped, and cried? *Did the gleaming eyes I once stared into become these empty sockets? Could these shrunken caricatures have been alive once?* He blinked, stuck between memory and reality.

"Blessed Gods," Sinklar whispered. "Kitmon's Section."

"They fought like Etarian tigers," Staffa told him bluntly. "These used to be the Novice quarters."

Sinklar had slowed, picking his way between the sprawled bodies, slowly shaking his head. Memories of the insanity of those last hours lingered in his mind.

"I went crazy . . . so crazy. Ordered assault after assault to break you. To save Mac. Trapped . . . I was as trapped out there as you were in here. I couldn't . . . couldn't . . ." He closed his eyes, stumbling over a brittle torso.

Adze caught him, holding him up as he bit his lip, physical pain easing the hurt in his soul.

Yes, insane. Desperate and helpless, with his friends caged in this pus-dripping rock. Goaded to fury by Gretta's death, driven by the guilt of allowing Gretta's assassin to go free. So much misery. Misery here, in this horrible place. He picked his way among the dead, friends he'd loved and cherished. Condemned through his own arrogance.

They trusted me . . . trusted . . . THEY'RE DEAD, SINKLAR. YOU WASTED THEM! WASTED . . . DEAD . . . TRUSTED YOU. . . . He slumped then, knees buckling, hardly aware of Adze struggling to support him.

"It's all right," Staffa's firm voice penetrated the fog of guilt. A second strong arm went round him, to counterbalance Adze's.

"Is he . . . Should I evacuate him, Lord Commander?" Adze asked.

"No. Help me keep him moving. He's just hurting, hurting and healing."

They led him forward, ever downward, into the shine of white lights, all obscured by the silver wash of tears Sinklar Fist couldn't stop.

* * *

Staffa tightened his grip as he led Sinklar through the carnage. Even his stomach, inured to such things, lurched at the destruction, all too well preserved.

Staffa herded Sinklar to one side and settled him at a darkened comm monitor. Adze crossed her arms and stepped back, on guard.

Ark looked around slowly, shaking his head. "Hell of a fight, Staffa."

Staffa jerked his head at the STU filing down past the corpses. "Find something for them to do, Ryman. Buy me some privacy."

Ark nodded, shooting a glance at Sinklar, then at Adze. He raised his voice, calling, "All right, people, give me a body count and plot locations for the retrieval team. Baggs, you and Naitche take teams and scour those niches off to the side. Mining technicians, I want a survey of stable and unstable areas. Stable will be marked by green beacons, red will cordon off danger zones. We don't want anybody killed by falling rock. C'mon, people, I want this place secured up to this point."

Adze stood to one side, watching unforgivingly as Sinklar choked on sobs. Staffa bent down, taking his son's hands. "Need a minute alone?"

Sinklar whispered, "Yes. Thanks."

Staffa jerked a nod to Adze as he walked out into the main part of the corridor. Scars from blaster fire marked the walls and every other light bar had been shot out.

"What's that all about?" Adze tilted her head toward where Sinklar hugged his knees, shoulders spasming.

"That is what a commander looks like when he mourns his dead, soldier."

"Don't know if I'd want someone who cries like that for a commander."

Staffa cocked his head, taking her measure. "Better find a different outfit then, Adze. Granted, you're young, but on Nesios, I watched Ryman bawl for two days when he lost two Units because of a bungled deployment. His people drowned in the dark when they landed in the wrong spot. And as for me, I've wept myself dry over the last couple of years."

Staffa pointed at a twisted piece of desiccated meat—the arms thrown wide, lower half missing below the ribs. Long red hair had swirled around a shrunken face, the lips pulled back to expose white teeth. The intestines had been strewn in brown snaky trails from a collapsed gut. Hips and legs lay some distance away, the bones of the pelvic girdle splayed and brown in the light. "I wept for her when that bolt blasted her in two."

Adze blinked, looking back at Sinklar. "But, sir, I thought . . ."

"I meant it when I said I'd take your age into consideration, Adze, but you'd better give some thought to these bodies in here. Each and every one of them marched in and fought like hell for that young man. And do you want to know a little secret of command?"

"Yes, sir."

"One of the reasons they came in here and died was because they knew he'd cry for them."

Staffa turned away, jaws clamped as he stared at the corpse of the red headed girl, remembering how fear-pale she'd been at the first attack, and how she'd finally died, fighting savagely in the rear guard so others could escape.

He bent down, gently tracing his fingers over her coarse red hair, matted now with dust. *Yes, Staffa, you've wept for them all. But weep as you will, you can't lay the dead to rest.*

Sinklar had risen to his feet, eyes puffy and bloodshot, face reddened with shame.

Staffa stepped over, placing a hand on Sinklar's shoulder. "Maybe they'll rest easier now."

Sinklar wiped at his nose and avoided Staffa's eyes. "I was crazy, Staffa. So desperate. It was just a matter of finding the right key to break you. Time was running out. If I could do it all over again . . ."

"We'd all do it differently." Staffa smiled wearily and, for the first time, drew Sinklar to his breast and hugged him tightly. "Come on. We'll get them buried, all of them. Seddi and Regan, all mixed up. And maybe we can see that it never happens again."

Sinklar pushed back, mouth working as he struggled for control. "Yeah." He swallowed hard. "How much more . . . where did the fighting stop?"

"Just past this corridor."

"Let's go see your nightmare machine." Sinklar squared his shoulders, walking on, expression ashen. Adze had immediately taken her place behind Sinklar, but this time she looked thoughtful as she stepped around the sprawled dead, many reaching out with dried fingers—curled into talons—as if desperate for succor.

Staffa rubbed his chin for a moment, staring at the corpse of the redheaded girl. Wearily, he started back down the familiar corridor, remembering other times when he'd walked this smooth stone, Kaylla at his side. He'd held hope for Free Space then, hope that young girls wouldn't have to die in agony, their guts ripped violently from their bodies.

Had so much changed? Had he begun to lose that hope?

You're tired, Staffa. That's all. Just a little tired.

* * *

For an agonizing moment, Lark could do nothing but gape at the carnage strewn across the Vegan Representative's floor and at the belled muzzle of Skyla's blaster that centered on the middle of her chest.

Rot it! Should I shoot her? Skyla hesitated, the pad of her finger on the firing stud.

"You're going to die, bitch," Vymer groaned as he tried to use his good hand to clamp the jetting blood spurting from his severed arm. "Gyper's going to . . . wring you dry for this."

"Vymer, why did you come after me? Why did you want to arrest me? On whose orders? Rill's, or Ily's?"

"Fuck you again!" Vymer shouted.

"Run!" Lark squeaked, terror-wide eyes focused on Skyla's blaster muzzle. "I—Internal Security. More of them coming. Run, Silk! *Hurry!*"

"Don't want to talk?" she asked Vymer one last time.

"Rot you, bitch."

Skyla stood, holstering her weapon. She shot a look at Magrite who watched wide-eyed and terrified. "Tell them the truth when they come. I'll inform Vega about what's happened here. You'll be safe. I don't think Terguz wants to be abandoned by Vegan traders."

Skyla grabbed a handful of Lark's clothing and yanked her out the door, glancing up and down the thoroughfare. Back toward the shuttle terminal, she could see black-suited men running in their direction.

"This way!" Lark pointed to the right. "Come on! I know a place!"

Skyla turned on her heel, following the girl's lead as she hurried along. "All right, talk, Lark—and you make it damned good, you hear? You're about two pounds of trigger pull away from eternity."

"I . . . I followed you. Wanted to see what . . . what set you off in the bar."

"In the bar, you mean in the *Wayside?*"

"Yes. You . . . you went pale, looked scared. All of a sudden, you know. You were just staring at the holo of the station. Then you got up to leave, looking real desperate—and, you changed, got control, and asked Garn a question. He didn't notice how your hands balled into fists when he answered. You practically ran to your ship. I . . . watched."

"Uh-huh. Which side are you on?" Skyla dragged her on, heedless of the looks she got from the crowd.

"You're hurting my arm!"

" 'Bout time a mother took care of her kid," a merchant called from a sidewalk stand. "Bat 'er one for me!"

"Want to hurt a little worse? No? Then sure as pus leaks from infection, you'd better talk, sweetheart."

"I'm on no side! Not Gyper's, not Father's, only my own!"

Skyla caught sight of a gravcar barreling down the corridor to the dismay of pedestrians. She yanked Lark into the cafe they were passing, shoving her down against the wall before dropping into the plastic seat next to hers.

The place was nearly empty, the few patrons involved in

their meals. The duraplast tables showed hard use, scarred and stained from years of elbows and stassa spills.

Through the fabric of her torn robe, Skyla shoved the blaster muzzle into the girl's side. "Look down at the table, damn you." Lark bent her head. Skyla could see the pulse racing in the girl's neck.

The gravcar whirred past, leaving shouts of anger in its wake.

"Your father? Whose side is he on, and why?"

"His own, I guess. He's still loyal to the Emperor, can you imagine that? Tybalt's dead!"

"Got that right."

Lark shivered. "Those men back there, you k-killed them, didn't you?"

"What kind of game did you think you bought into, kid? Ily plays for keeps. So do I."

"Ily?" Lark's trembling had grown worse.

"Ily Takka. You one of her agents?"

Lark swallowed hard. "No. Blessed Gods, Silk. Let me go. I don't want any of this. I just wanted . . ."

"Yes?"

She shook her head, a very miserable little girl. "I just wanted to get off this ball of ice, that's all. I thought maybe I could do you a favor. Keep the bulls from catching you. Maybe you'd take me with you—in spite of my father."

Skyla shot her a measuring look. Believe her? Lark looked about ready to throw up.

"Which way out of here? They're going to cordon off the shuttle bay."

"N-no," Lark gasped. "You're on your own. I'm out of this as of right now. I've already had more than I—"

"Which way?" Skyla shoved her blaster into its holster and climbed to her feet. She dragged Lark up after her. "Sorry, kid, but you're not thinking so good these days. They *might* get to Vymer in time. Keep him alive long enough to talk. On the other hand, Magrite is smart enough to know they're going to put her under Mytol. She'll spill her guts. That includes you. When you came charging in, you bought a hand in the tapa game. You've got no choice but to ante up." Skyla raised a pale eyebrow. "One way or another."

Lark's fright-wide green eyes had begun to tear.

"Come on," Skyla growled. "You wanted to get off this ice cube? Show me how to get out of here alive, and I'll get you off planet."

Lark gasped for breath. "You'll get me killed!"

"Holy Rotted Gods! And you think Ily Takka will give a rat's ass for your life after she's got her talons into you?" Skyla gave her a hard grin. "Try skipping out on me, brat, and I'll get you killed even faster. Now, where in hell can we hide around here? And remember, if they find me, they find you."

"What are you going to do? You can't get off the planet!" Lark wrung her hands, then pointed. "This way. Take this cross corridor."

Skyla watched warily as they started down the narrow way between little shops selling rugs, Riparian fish, electronic gadgets, and incense. "At the moment, getting off planet is the last thing I'm interested in. No, squirt, you're going to show me how to get to Gyper Rill's office. And I don't want to get caught doing it!"

"Are you mad?" Lark gaped. "That's who just tried to arrest you!"

"Pus-Rotted right, and he can point me straight to Ily."

Pale and shaking, Lark seemed to be gaining control of herself. "They'll have patrols everywhere looking for you."

"Yeah, I know. That's just what I'm afraid of."

"If they find us . . ."

"I'll take care of that, Lark. These Internal Security guys don't know that much about warfare."

"I don't get it. If you get into Rill's offices, how do you expect to get out?" Lark shouldered her way diagonally across a fruit vendor's stall.

"If I can get close to Ily and Arta, kid, I don't need to get out." Skyla said, smiling grimly to herself. "On the other hand, if they manage to get away, Gyper Rill won't be more than an irritant."

Lark shook her head. "Irritant? He's the Director of Internal Security. The most powerful man on the planet." Lark glanced back warily. "Who *are* you?"

"Name's Silk."

"Yeah, right, and I'm Tybalt the Imperial Eighth."

They crossed another of the main thoroughfares before Lark led her into a narrow corridor, past the public restrooms, and to a maintenance closet. Lark fished in her belt pouch, producing a set of electronic strips. She ran four through the lock before the door clicked open.

"Knew it had to be one of these."

Skyla followed the girl through the insulated door and into the narrow space. Chill began to eat at her exposed skin. A yellow light globe gleamed above, and thick, insulated suits hung from racks.

"Where are we?"

"Where they'll never look," Lark assured her. "These are the ventilation and powerlead access tubes. Here, you need to put on one of these suits. They'll keep you warm. The only people that come in here are maintenance personnel. That's what they condemned me to last time I got in trouble."

"What's the plan?"

Lark bit her lip, hesitating. "Look, how am I supposed to get off planet if you're dead?"

"How do you suppose you're going to get off planet if I kill you for jerking me around?"

Lark exhaled, her breath a cloud of vapor. "Will you give me your word? If you do manage to get away with this, you'll take me with you? You understand, I can get you to the Internal Security Directorate, right? But I can't get you inside."

"Get me there, and yeah, Lark. I'll take you off planet. You've got my word."

Lark leaned her head back, eyes closed. "This had better work. If it doesn't Father's going to lock me in my room, and I'll never get out again until I'm one hundred and twenty."

Skyla sorted through the insulated suits, finding one to match her build. "So what's with your father? I would have figured any horny man who stepped into the *Wayside* would have smuggled you out of here."

Lark was pulling on the second leg of her suit. "Remember, you promised. Gave your word."

"I gave it. Why are you so worried about your father?"

"You, of all people, might really be able to get me out of here. I've never met anyone as brassy as you are, Silk." She slipped an arm into the suit, zipping the fasteners tight.

''My father? He's the Imperial Administrator for this smelly chunk of ice.''

* * *

The lift carried Mac, Chrysla, and Boyz up in ornate splendor. The walls had been crafted of sandwood, inlaid with golden filigree and jeweled ornaments.

They slowed, the brass doors opening to let them out on a marble finished foyer. A woman dressed in a flowing white gown stepped forward. ''Welcome, my Lords. Ashtan offers its thanks and appreciation. I am Lady Simon, at your service. Hopefully these rooms will suit you and your needs during your stay on Ashtan.''

Accustomed to military protocol, Mac gaped, while Chrysla stepped forward, bowing graciously. ''We are sincerely impressed by your warm welcome and hospitality. Hopefully, our work has merited such a delightful reception.''

Lady Simon smiled, beaming. She looked like a woman in her mid-thirties, but Mac decided she'd survived at least two, and possibly three, rejuvenation procedures. For all he knew, she might be two hundred. She turned, walking with a gracious poise, indicating the rooms that branched out from the circular corridor that surrounded the high penthouse. ''These offices here should serve your needs for communication and conferences. Personal quarters lie just beyond.''

Mac stuck his head in the office door, glancing around. ''Looks just fine.''

''May I get you anything?'' Lady Simon asked. ''A meal? Perhaps some special delicacy?''

''Sleep,'' Mac said, smiling stupidly. ''A hot shower. We're exhausted.''

Lady Simon nodded, acceptance in her pleasant features. ''We understand. You've created miracles, First MacRuder, you and your wonderful soldiers. If sleep is what you wish, I shall leave you. In the event you do need anything, please, call. Comm will . . .'' She laughed melodiously. ''Old habits. Send a runner down one floor and I shall attend to it.''

At that she whirled, vanishing in a flutter of white.

Mac yawned, stretching his tired limbs. ''Home sweet home.''

''Pretty plush,'' Boyz muttered.

''Yeah, get your comm set up and see to security.'' He gave her a grin. ''If the planet's falling apart, wake me up. If not, I want to sleep for a couple of centuries.''

Boyz saluted. ''Yes, sir. I think we can handle the rest.''

''How did you locate this place?'' Chrysla asked, studying the polished black tile on the floor and noting the exquisite furnishings.

Boyz grinned, a glint in her eyes. ''Asked for the poshest place in town. Red said this was it. We just walked in, said we wanted the top floor, and they gave it to us.'' Her grin widened. ''Want to be Emperor of Ashtan, Mac?''

''Get out of here.'' Mac pointed down the hall. ''Call me if anything breaks.''

Boyz nodded and trotted off toward the lift.

''Emperor?'' Mac yawned again, blinking. ''Do they get to sleep?''

''Come on, let's take a look at these quarters.'' She led him beyond the offices and past the doorway that blocked the hall. As he followed, Mac enjoyed the sway of her hips, more than aware of the way the armor conformed to her bottom and accented her long muscular legs.

Don't even think it, MacRuder. You're tired, remember? Ready to sleep. His hormones didn't get the message. Despite the cape she wore, Mac was uncomfortably aware of those full breasts. Rotted Gods, did she know what she did to him?

''What do you think?'' Chrysla asked, a luminous curiosity in the amber depths of her eyes. Her skin seemed infused by an excitement that betrayed itself in her smile.

''Nice,'' Mac yawned, turning to take in the Myklenian tapestries. The cut crystal ceiling broke sunlight into rainbows of light. The Nesian carpeting rippled in golden waves under his boots.

Chrysla walked back and opened the ornate double doors that led into the dining room. Here, an entire wall had been finished in transparent tactite, giving a view of the city below. She stood silhouetted, every curve of her perfect body outlined by the light. Mac forced his gaze to the rest of the room. Antigrav recliners surrounded a stasis dining table of Vegan marble studded with Etarian gems.

Mac followed her through the bath, stunned by the immensity of it. The hot tub could have doubled for a small swimming pool. A zero g shower filled another section of the room.

Finally, Mac stepped into the sleeping quarters, smiling as he walked to the sleeping platform. Myklenian fabrics draped the sides, while the crystal ceiling illuminated the whole. The platform itself was not only gravity capable, but holo programmed, and a golden dispenser had been built into the headboard along with a complete comm.

"Now, I've seen everything," Mac marveled. "You could run the whole Empire while lying in bed."

"Providing they can get the comm completely functional," Chrysla added as she walked around the room. "Rotted Gods, that platform looks good." She jumped, flopping into the cushions, moaning with delight.

The warm fuzzy sense of fatigue dulled Mac's inhibitions. He flopped beside her, staring into her eyes. "Feels good, doesn't it? Well, welcome to Ashtan. So far, so good. We've got the place stabilized. How's it feel to come home?"

Chrysla smiled wistfully, propping her chin on a fist. She studied him, longing in her large amber eyes. "Not the way I thought it would, Mac. It doesn't feel like home."

He reached out and laid a hand on her shoulder. "We'll go find your family as soon as things settle down."

She shook her head, the longing in her eyes intensifying. "It's too late for that, Mac. Even if they survived, what would I say to them? How's the ripa crop this year? Did Aunt Child really die last year? How terrible?" She shook her head, a tear in the corner of her eye. "They'd ask about me. What can I tell them? About being the Praetor's captive? About life with the Lord Commander? About war and famine?"

He leaned over, drawing her into his arms, hugging her protectively. "Homecomings are never what we'd hoped." Images of his father's studied attempts at making conversation fading into sorrow.

"What's wrong?" She reached up, tracing her fingers along the side of his face.

"Thinking about what we lose along the way."

"But you saved Ashtan. We arrived in time for once, Mac. We gave these people a little more time."

He stared into her eyes, seeming to fall into their amber depths. He stroked her soft skin, a warming excitement in his gut as he bent forward to kiss her, gently at first, and then with growing intensity.

Her arms went around him, pulling him close. Heart pounding, blood rushing, he pulled back, aware of her breasts against his chest. The soft warmth of her body melted the last of his reservations.

Mac swallowed hard, reading the glow of desire in her skin, in the excitement building in those amber eyes. He shifted to ease the pressure of his erection. "Are you sure?"

"Yes," she whispered. "I've waited too long for this. I want you, Mac."

"I smell like a horse."

She laughed, lips parting. "Me, too. There's one hell of a sensual bath next door. How tired are you?"

"Got my second wind." He lifted an eyebrow. "Are you really sure? You're not just . . . well, feeling guilty?"

She nodded, kissing him again. "I'm sure, Mac. I have been for a long time." Her slim fingers unsnapped the fastenings that secured his armor.

Oh, Blessed Gods, this can't be happening! "About Staffa . . ."

"Shhh." She placed a finger to his lips, sitting up with him as she stripped his armor off. "One thing at a time, Mac. Stand up."

He followed her instructions, aware of her scent, aware of the way her hair swayed as she undid the fasteners for his legs. He stepped out of the armor, curiously self-conscious. Need electrified him as he reached for her, undoing the clips at her shoulders, breath catching in his throat as her armor fell away and she stood before him in the padded undersuit.

Chrysla watched him, eyes like honeyed pools as they peeled the last barrier away. *Was he dreaming, or were his forbidden fantasies finally coming true?* She took a deep breath which lifted her perfect breasts, the nipples tightening; glints of the light danced in her red pubic hair.

"Oh, Mac!" She stepped to him. Running her hands over

the muscles of his chest, she sighed, then conformed to him, kissing his neck and lacing her arms around him.

For long moments, he stared into her eyes, sensing the depths of her longing. Then he kissed her, reveling in the pressure of her breasts against his chest. She reached down, found his erection, and gasped as she gripped his hot flesh. The pounding urgency grew as he lowered her to the sleeping platform. The light shot threads of copper through her hair as she lay back and drew him onto her, opening herself.

Locked together, they lay still for a moment while Mac savored the sensations stirring within him.

"Don't ever leave me, Chrysla."

"Never, Mac. I promise." And she sighed as she began to move.

CHAPTER XXII

The CV shuddered under Guy Holt's feet as the heavy cargo was lowered to the hold deck. Couldn't these dock guys ever get the knack of loading down.

Guy muttered to himself, scratching the back of his neck as he waited for the heavy lifter to back its way out of the hatch. One thing Holt could say about the fall of Rega, it had definitely made an impact on his life. Nor did the future hold many prospects for boredom. Like it or not, Guy was going to be getting a lot of overtime—just like this trip.

Someone had forgotten, or misplaced, the Ashtan order which was supposed to have been shipped a month ago. Now, one of the lighters—the craft that ferried grain to orbit—at the Ashtan grain terminal was down, and the demand for Ashtan cereals was skyrocketing. With comm service restored on Ashtan, a desperate somebody had finally managed to get a message through to the Regan factory that made shuttle controls. There, a bewildered clerk had checked the manifests—also screwed up because of the destruction of Comm Central by the Star Butcher—and found the crate containing the guidance and automated piloting nacelles sitting in the warehouse, waiting for shipment. The situation had been deemed desperate enough to dispatch Holt's CV—and pus eat the cost!

Indeed, business would only get better as more and more screwups meant more and more frantic contracts for CVs to carry critical goods across the space lanes.

I'm not going to be getting a whole lot of rest for the next year or two, but, by the Blessed Gods, I might be able to take one hell of an Etarian vacation!

"No!" Holt roared as one of the hands sought to strap the heavy sialon crate to a strake. "Use the rings inset in the floor. What do you want to do? Rip the whole side of my ship out?''

The dockhand shot an irritated look over his shoulder, but refastened the tie-down to a deck ring and muscled the boomer closed with a vibrating snap.

Holt glanced at his chronometer. At this rate, he'd be in Ashtan before he knew it. And who knew what kind of discoveries awaited him there? Another foulup, no doubt. The Blessed Gods alone knew how long they could keep running this way. If they didn't get things fixed soon, something, somewhere, would snap and they'd all be paying for it. Not just a few well-off commodities brokers.

* * *

''Let's say you get off Terguz. What next?'' Skyla asked as she maintained the awkward duck-walking pace through the low tunnel. Each step had to be taken in a swinging stride as she straddled the fifty-centimeter-wide powerlead in the floor. Motion sensors detected their approach, illuminating the light globes, only to let them die as they passed. Breath fogged—all tainted with the odors of ammonia and chlorine.

''I don't know,'' Lark answered. ''I'll find something. Take the next left.''

''Find something?'' Skyla laughed as she entered yet another tunnel. ''Now, that's rich. You're not bad looking. You're young and healthy. You can always hook for a living.'' She glanced up at the insulation that had been sprayed over the ice. Not a cheery place to be. No wonder Lark wanted out.

''I *won't* have to hook for a living.''

''All virgins say that.''

''I'm *not* a virgin.''

''Wasn't the kind of virgin I was referring to. I was talking about the kind that want to catch the first ship to anywhere and enjoy all the excitement of the fast life in Free Space. Sweetheart, it ain't that easy.''

''And you know all about it?''

''Yeah, kid. I've been there. Listen, how many ICs do you have in your account?''

''Around five hundred.''

''That will get you two months of room and board on

Etaria—that's assuming they let you land. Lots of places demand that you get a round-trip ticket or proof of financial support before they let you off the orbiting terminal. But let's say you make planet and get to Etarus. You've got two months' rent. What happens in month three?"

"By then I've got a job."

"Oh, yeah? Where's your work permit?"

"Well, I go down and apply for one."

"Sure, you do that. And to get one, you need to grease the desk dick's hand with about four hundred ICs. But you've paid rent to have an address so you can get a work application. Where do you get the ICs, babycakes?"

"Don't call me that."

"Fine, sweetmeat, you're still short a bunch of credits. You going to find them on street corners, or call home to Daddy?"

"Never!"

"So, how do you think you're going to survive? Listen, Lark, Etaria, or any other planet, for that matter, has a way of handling transient people. It's called slavery. They find you without support, you go on the public works program."

"What if you marry someone?"

"Oh, sure, you're guaranteed of that? Got a marriage contract lined up with some nice aristocratic family on whichever world you land on?"

"He doesn't have to be an aristocrat."

Skyla turned, pointing a hard finger. "You listen to me, bitch. Don't you ever figure on a man taking care of you. You hear me? Never! That's nothing more than another form of slavery, sugarcoated and socially acceptable, but it's still slavery! You got that?"

Lark's look showed disbelief.

Skyla shook her head, angry with herself. "What in Rot am I doing? You're too old, you've already sucked up that Regan Aristocratic pap! You *expect* a man to take care of you! You've lived with it, seen your mother being a sweet, wonderful hostess while your father was the Lord and Master."

"I don't buy a lot of what I'm supposed to."

"Giving you advice, honey, is just making talk to hear my brain rattle."

Lark cursed, shaking her head. "You don't think much

of me, do you? Well, who'd be under arrest right now if I hadn't decided to save your cute ass?''

Skyla cocked her head. ''I'll tell you exactly what I think of you, Lark. I think you're a spoiled rich kid—but you've got promise if you'll use your brains. That's half the fight. The other thing you need to go with brains is guts. Have you got those kinds of makings in you?''

''Yeah, I do.''

''What if I tell you . . .'' Skyla shook her head, returning to the awkward duck wall. ''Forget it. I must be out of my mind?''

Lark sighed angrily. ''You, Silk? Out of your mind? Who'd have guessed that anyone wanting to walk into Gyper Rill's office and have a little chat with him was out of her mind? Especially if the Minister of Internal Security is hiding out there!''

Skyla chuckled. ''Yeah, well, kid, if I can kill Ily, and her assassin Arta, I can go home and relax.''

''Where's home?''

''You wouldn't believe me if I told you.''

''You're pretty pus-licking superior, did you know that, Silk?''

''Yeah, I did.'' Skyla threw a glance over her shoulder. ''Drives you berserk, doesn't it? Uh-huh, and it fascinates you, too.''

''Hardly!''

''It's all right, Lark. I was the same way, once. My ticket out was a fellow named Mac Rylee.''

''Thought you never depended on a man?''

''Depended? Oh, I've had to depend on them for my very life. Time after time, just like men have had to depend on me. What I've never done is surrender my destiny to them. Partners depend on each other all the time, it's the nature of the beast. But get this straight, Lark, I've never sold myself to a man—and I started out as a whore's daughter.''

''So, how did you make it out, as you say?''

''I cut Rylee's purse off his belt, and gave it back to him. Told him he could use a girl like me. He took me to . . . his superior, and I never looked back.''

''Maybe I could do that. Maybe I could show you I could be your partner.''

Skyla stepped down into another of the narrow maintenance closets, a rack of suits before a scarred duraplast door. Skyla walked over, placing a hand on the door, feeling warmth. "What's on the other side?"

"The boulevard that runs in front of the Internal Security Directorate." Lark crossed her arms. "So what makes you so superior and arrogant, Silk?"

"Guts, Lark. And the commitment to use them, no matter what."

"You didn't look very gutsy in the *Wayside*."

Skyla nodded. "Yeah, well, part of guts, and I guess arrogance, too, is that commitment I was talking about. I'm scared to death, but I'm going to walk right into the Internal Security Directorate, and I'm going to beat what I want out of Gyper Rill. If Ily or Arta are there, I'm going to kill them."

"Why? I mean, why not just call the . . . Well, someone to help you?"

Skyla smiled, placing a cold finger under Lark's chin and lifting it to stare into her serious green eyes. "Because, kid, there's no one to call. I'm all there is right here, right now."

Lark's jaw thrust out. "I . . . I could go with you."

"Look, I said I'd take you out of here if I make it. I meant that. Hell, I'll probably even find a way of keeping you out of the hook shops when you find a place you like. Everybody ought to be able to chase their dreams, no matter how screwy they are."

"What if . . . what if my dream was to be like you?"

Skyla shook her head, peeling out of the thermal suit. "It costs too much, kid. You lose too much of your soul."

"I'll take that risk. Let me go with you. Please."

Skyla hung the insulated suit on the rack. "Why? You go in there with me, the chances are that you're going to wind up on the floor with part of your body blown away. You're not trained for this sort of thing."

"And who's going to watch your back?"

Skyla removed the Vegan scarf, folding it up. "You're not, that's for sure. The first loud noise, you'd probably shoot me instead of the bad guy. Hey, the last thing I need is to worry about you while I'm in there. Trust me on this, all right?"

Lark nodded. "All right."

"Good. Now, assuming they don't have an arrest warrant

out for you yet, take the next shuttle up to the station. Lay low. I'll either be there in a couple of hours, or I'm dead."

Skyla hesitated, then reached into her pouch. "This data cube might be important. If anything happens to me, insert it into any comm with subspace linkage. It will open a channel to a woman. You'll know her, she has tan eyes, looks attractive—and she never surrendered to anybody either. Tell her what happened to me."

Lark nodded, taking the cube with reverent fingers. "Who are you? You're not just some wandering spacer, Silk."

Skyla grinned as she stripped away the last of the torn robe and stood in her white armor. "Maybe that tan-eyed lady will tell you."

Lark gaped. "Holy Blessed Gods, that's *combat* armor."

"The best in the business." Skyla pinned her long braid to her epaulet and pulled her blaster, checking the charges. Next, she shucked her pulse pistol, making sure the weapon was ready. Finally, she hitched the bandolier of sonic grenades on her hip. Lark watched with interest.

"See you in orbit, Lark." Skyla gave her a reassuring wink. "And thanks for trying to pull me out of the Vegan Rep's. It took guts."

"Take care, Silk!" Lark leapt forward, hugging Skyla in a ferocious bear hug. "Don't get hurt. Please?"

Skyla pried the girl's arms loose. "I'll do my best."

Taking a deep breath, Skyla opened the door, stepping out into another grimy hallway. She passed more public restrooms, then turned into the busy street. This time, Skyla Lyma walked down the middle of it like she owned the place.

True to Lark's word, the Ministry of Internal Security filled one side of the boulevard, a discreet sign over the featureless door.

Skyla glanced in both directions, then opened the door and stepped inside. *Be here, Ily, because I'm going to kill you.*

* * *

Sinklar covered his ears. The mining machines roared, growled, and whined, fit to wake the very guts of the planet as they chewed into the red basalt. The cutters hammered at the tumbled rock, sending vibrations through the floor. Sinklar stood amid a knot of people who waited safely back from where the giant metal and ceramic mining machines shuddered and bucked. Overhead fixtures jiggled as they cast white light across the narrow cavern. The acrid odor of hot lubricants and ozone spread in the musty air.

Sinklar cast a nervous glance at the rock overhead. Just how deep inside the mountain were they?

"Won't be long now!" Staffa shouted.

"What?" Sinklar winced, then motioned Staffa back from the collapsed face of the tunnel. "I can't hear a word you're saying!"

Staffa nodded, retreating. Sinklar barely realized when Adze dropped back in his shadow. She'd become as intolerable as Mhitshul when they got back to the surface.

They had finally stopped at this side gallery. The roof arched a little less than three meters overhead. Dark comm terminals studded the walls around them, the powerlead and comm strip running along the base of the rock.

"Won't be long," Staffa repeated, pointing to the rock just above where the mining machine crunched up the tumbled stone. "I collapsed that so the Regans wouldn't find it when they came back."

"Came back?"

Staffa shot him a sidelong glance. "At the time I expected Tybalt would wonder what had been left behind. Ily definitely would have."

"How about the archives? Isn't your conservation team arriving tomorrow?"

"Yes." Staffa pointed. "Want to see where it is?"

"Nothing's happening here." Sinklar turned, walking down the winding corridor. The humps and bulges made him think of being in an oversized intestine. The metallic grinding of the machines lessened with each step. Here, the lights gleamed, bathing the rock in a white glow.

"What powers this place? Even the air is fresh."

"The Mag Comm," Staffa told him, clasping his hands behind his back. "It powers all of Makarta. One of the things that frightened Bruen was that it cut them off once when they refused to communicate. That day you hit the tunnels with orbital, the lights went off, too. Other than that, the Seddi think the machine draws on the planet's core for energy. An inexhaustible source . . . and one they can't turn off."

"How do you feel? It won't be long before you have to face that thing."

Staffa nodded. "Yes, and we still haven't a clue as to how to deal with it. What do you think, Sinklar?"

"I don't know. I want to see it first." He shrugged. "We might be worrying for nothing. It might tell us to go mind our own business and solve our own affairs."

"After watching Bruen interact with the thing, I don't suppose that will be the case. He thought it was malignant, that it had an evil presence."

Sinklar cocked his head. "Wait. Before we get too carried away, let's consider what we have here. The machine is just a computer, albeit a sophisticated one."

"Right."

"But a machine, no matter what, remains just that. It cannot move, cannot physically effect the world around it."

"Except by observation. Observation changes reality on the quantum level, and by doing so affects the eternal now of existence."

Sinklar grunted noncommittally. "But it can't move rocks around, manipulate the material world."

"No, not to our knowledge."

"Our real vulnerability, therefore, is that we must trust its instructions on how to run our civilization. Therein lies our own weakness in dealing with the machine."

"And my head. What if the interface helmet doesn't work? If this thing can drain my mind, it will have a lot of information—and not all of it good—to use against you."

"You're presupposing the machine wants to do that. That means it was programmed to harm human beings. And, even if it was, is the machine intelligent? Does it understand the heuristic problems of waging war against us?" Sinklar spread his arms. "Assuming it's hostile, it could show its hand by an order as stupid as something like: 'Don't grow food for your populations next year.' "

"Or it might do something much more subtle, like reprogram the dairy feed production facilities to include plutonium in cattle feed." Staffa shook his head. "The problem is that we've come to rely so heavily on comm. By turning the system over to the Mag Comm, we lose control. It could kill us all just by a seemingly inconsequential mistake. It's your heuristic problem, all over again. The machine must deal with the 'real' world, now. Even if it operates strictly for our good, will it understand the difference between moving ceramic tiles and moving crates of chicken eggs?''

''We'll have to be very careful.''

''That goes without saying.'' Staffa stopped, rock had spilled from the ceiling on a small tunnel, but a space existed at the top. ''It was dark. I was in a hurry. Looks like I didn't do such a good job on this one. A few man-hours with vibrablades and they can clear this away. Want to crawl over the top and see?''

Sinklar shook his head. ''No, I think I'll wait.'' Something about tight holes, being trapped in the darkness, unable to move, made his skin crawl.

A sudden silence echoed through the deep chambers.

''The mining machines have stopped,'' Adze said as she listened to her electronic ears. ''I think they've broken through.''

Staffa nodded. ''We'd better go back.''

Sinklar put a hand on his arm. ''You're not going to try anything foolish, are you?''

Staffa stared at the floor, expression sober. ''Not until I know what we're dealing with.''

* * *

Magister Bruen lay supine in his antigrav gurney, a prisoner, bound by the machine's gravitational fields. For without them, his ancient heart could no longer counter the stress of pumping blood through his body. His lungs, weary from three hundred planetary years of inhaling and exhaling, could no longer expand and contract the rib cage. The delicate balance of metabolism had lost the ability to regulate body temperature.

Bruen was dying, a prisoner of the technology which kept him alive. Imprisonment, however, ran even deeper for the ancient Seddi, for now, in sleep, he remained a prisoner of his own dreams. . . .

* * *

Bruen cowered in the dark, reaching out with desperate hands, finding nothing but a dense mist. Peer as he might, no hint of light, no sense of sound reached him. Lonely and shivering, he hunched in terror.

By the slight shifts of the mist, he could feel the presence. Fear choked him as he ran his hands frantically over his bald head. Momentarily relief surged as his fingers traced naked scalp.

"No. You can't," Bruen called out, the terror growing again. In the blackness, a single red light pulsed on and off.

"No!" Bruen wrapped his arms about his head in a protective move. "I left you behind! I'm *not* wearing the helmet!"

He turned to run, stumbling randomly in the blackness, panting.

The red light appeared before him, blinking ominously.

Frantically, Bruen backpedaled, fleeing back the way he'd come, only to encounter the light again.

Run as he might, flailing his arms about his head, the tendrils slipped through his scalp, piercing the bone of his skull, winding into the soft tissue of his brain.

"No!" Bruen fell, pounding his head with knotted fists, as if by brutalizing himself, he could beat the presence from inside his head.

Bruen . . . Right Thought . . . The Way . . . Answer me, Bruen! The violent invasion of the Machine's voice hesitated, then thundered, *Elaborate! Answer me, mortal!*

"I . . . No! Leave me alone!"

Your civilization is about to fall.

"No, Lord. We hear, we obey. We think Right Thoughts. We are of the Way!" Bruen sank down, cowering in defeat.

You are lying, Bruen. Speak to me, human. Let me see your lies! You cannot hide from me. I will destroy you, Bruen, just as I have destroyed Hyde. Just as I have destroyed your civilization!

"No, Lord Mag Comm. I am your servant."

You are a liar, Bruen. The Lord Commander—despite all of my plans—still lives.

"We followed your instructions to the letter, Great One."

You RAN to him! Vile, lying human. I could crush you, Bruen. You, foul mortal, have destroyed your civilization through your lies. Look upon the wasted bodies of your vic-

tims. Stare into their eyes. You have condemned your species. Extinction, Bruen. Space will no longer hear the voices of humans. All will be quiet . . . Eternal.

"No, Lord Mag Comm. I . . . we, have acted in faith. Right Thought is ours."

The Lord Commander is a cancer in the body of your society. Like any threat to health and peace, such a disease must be excised from the flesh and the True Way must heal the wounded body of humanity. I read the intricacies of your planning and intrigue.

"There is no intrigue! I am your servant in worship, Great One!" Fear ran bright as the tendrils of control ate more deeply into Bruen's brain. "Believe me! I serve only you!"

Then why do I detect your lies? You have failed me, Bruen. For that, I killed Hyde. One by one, your populations will die. Some in war, some in famine. Their cries shall echo hollowly off the walls of the Forbidden Borders. You shall know that you alone bear the responsibility for their extinction.

"No! I have not failed you, Lord!"

You shall spend eternity knowing their bones linger in darkness. Your ears shall ring forever with desperate cries! The darkness is closing in. Feel it, Bruen? Cold, relentless. Humans are destroying themselves. When will the final child reach out with numb fingers, striving to touch warmth and finding only the chill of death?

"No . . . forgive me. Great One, Powerful Lord, I'm—"

Unworthy, wretch! Betrayer of trust! Reap your reward! Death . . . Death . . . DEATH!

Bruen cried out in horror as the machine's power filtered through his brain, closing in to suffocate his soul. Darkness, deeper and blacker than the stygian ink of null singularity ate at the edges of his consciousness. Implacable cold leeched at his frail flesh, sucking his life away while hideous cries tore from the throats of suffering millions. The horrible moan carried in the frozen waste.

"No! Blessed Gods, no! I didn't mean this! Help me! Please, by all that is holy, help . . . me!"

"Magister?"

The voice penetrated the veil of terror.

"Help me!"

"*Magister!* Wake up! It's Nyklos! You're safe."

Bruen started at the warm hands that gripped his face. Blinking the last shreds of nightmare away, he stared up into Nyklos' concerned brown eyes.

"You had a dream, Bruen. It's all right. You're aboard the CV. You're safe."

Bruen opened his mouth, words stillborn in his cramped throat.

"It's all right. I'll make sure nothing harms you." Nyklos gave him a wink, the action flicking his bushy mustache.

"The machine . . ." Bruen managed to croak. "In the dreams. Terrible."

"The machine can't hurt you now."

Tears began to leak out of Bruen's eyes, born of relief for the present and fear of the future.

"Nyklos, you must promise. No matter what. You can't let them put that helmet on my head. Not again."

"You won't have to wear the helmet."

"Give me your word, Nyklos. Your word as a Seddi Master, that if they want to put the helmet on me. You . . . you'll kill me first."

"Magister, I—"

"Swear! Your word, Nyklos! Rotted Gods, *swear it!*"

Nyklos frowned, licked his lips, and nodded. "I so swear, Magister."

Gasping, Bruen turned his head away. Exhaustion numbed his thin limbs as he tuned out Nyklos' questions. Not now, he couldn't talk, couldn't stand Nyklos' concern. *The machine killed my soul.* Faces loomed out of the past. Hyde. Butla Ret, the Praetor, Tyklat, and others. Gone. All dead and gone. And with each of their deaths, another little bit of Bruen's soul had died.

After several minutes, Nyklos ceased his effort to make Bruen talk and, with a shrug, bent down in frustration to check the machine.

Bruen blinked, staring with vacant eyes at the white padding that surrounded him. White, soft, like clouds. Within his memory, the booming voice of the Mag Comm repeated. *Death . . . Death . . . Death!*

"I failed. Failed everyone. My fault, Hyde, old friend."

Swimming in the mist, Arta Fera's innocent amber eyes stared up at him, beaming with worship. He'd loved her. Loved her with a passion he could barely stand.

Failed . . . failed so many.

And with each beat of his frail heart, he traveled closer and closer to Targa, the machine, and a nightmare too vivid to contemplate.

* * *

Nyklos vented a heavy sigh as he bent down to check the readouts on the gurney. The old Magister's heartbeat had dropped to normal, his blood chemistry slowly shedding adrenaline and lipids. He could hear Bruen's whispering, and it tore his heart.

Silently, he slipped away, leaving the old man in peace. One hand on the ladder rung, Nyklos looked back.

Bruen had cared too much. That, more than the machine, had broken him. Sympathy surged at the thought. How terrible it must be for the old man to have to return, to face the machine and Staffa. Knowing that the Lord Commander might be condemning them all.

"How do you get the strength, Magister? Would I have your courage?"

* * *

A woman dressed in a black uniform sat behind a transparent tactite shield as Skyla entered the Internal Security Directorate. She glanced up, smiling, but it died on her face as she noted the pistols on Skyla's hips and the hard look in her blue eyes.

Benches lined three of the office walls, while the tactite divider created the fourth. A door lay to either side of the receptionist's window. Despite the featureless tiles in the ceiling, Skyla could feel the surveillance monitors zooming in on her as she stalked across the floor.

"I need to see Gyper . . . now!" Skyla demanded, bracing herself on stiff arms as she stared down at the woman. "All Holy Rotted hell has broken loose! The Vegan Rep's murder is going to blow up like a supernova and we're all going to pay! Now, Rot you, clear this door *and get me Rill!*"

The woman gaped, paralyzed by the violence in Skyla's eyes. Her mouth worked, but her fingers pressed the clearance tab, and Skyla jerked open the door to the woman's left.

"Which way?' Skyla demanded. "Where's his office? And tell him I'm on the way!"

"Second floor. Right. His secretary—"

"Better meet me at the top of the lift!"

Skyla bulled past, stepping into the lift, ordering, "Second floor."

When she stepped out, a young man in black was hurrying down the hallway, puzzlement on his face. "Who are you? What are you doing?"

"Where's Gyper?" Skyla started to step past him. "Pus Rot us all if he's not here! We've got the whole operation falling apart! A *Companion* warship is on the way because of that damn yacht up there! Now, do you want to jack around all day, or do you want to get Gyper?"

The secretary hesitated, taking her measure. Having given herself up for dead, Skyla glanced back.

"This way." He started back down the hall, "But you'd better have a security clearance when this is all over, or I'm going to snap a collar on your neck myself."

"If you do, you'll live to regret it, pal. I wasn't kidding about that Companion warship. Her commanding officer is named Seekore, and she's not known for a flowery personality."

The secretary led Skyla past office doors, most of which hung open. Bored, uniformed personnel hunched over comms, or talked to stassa cup wielding colleagues.

At the end of the hall stood a large desk with another tactite shield behind it. "Just a moment, I'll call the Director. Who should I say wishes to see him?"

"Give him the initials, SLWCC. Tell him I'm an old acquaintance of Ily's. We've done a lot of business in the past, and I've been of particular service to her recently."

At the mention of Ily's name, the secretary glanced up, nodding. He pressed his comm key. "Director? I have a woman here. She says to tell you her initials are SLWCC—and she's one of Ily's people. She says it's urgent that she talk to you. Something about a yacht, the Vegan Rep, and a Companion battleship."

"Send her in," the speaker ordered.

"This way." The secretary raised a hand, leading Skyla

through the tactite shielding and into Gyper's office. The Director was just getting to his feet, a worried look on his face, as Skyla pivoted on her heel to slam the secretary under the mastoid. The man's head snapped, and he jackknifed in midair, collapsing in a heap.

"Just who the hell . . ."

Rill never finished as Skyla leveled her blaster. "Not a sound, Director. Not one word, or your guts are going to be all over this office. Hold your hands out where I can see them. That's it. Where's Ily?"

Rill cocked his head, studying her through flat brown eyes. "Who are you?"

"Like I told your boy there, an old friend of Ily's. Where is she?"

Rill pursed his lips. "All right, assuming you are a friend of Ily's, I'll get a comm line through to her. If, on the other hand, she doesn't know you, you've made a real mess for yourself. You won't be getting out of here alive."

Skyla grinned as she leveled the blaster. "Makes two of us, pal. Now, I need to see Ily—face-to-face! She or Arta, either one. Get them in here."

Gyper spread his hands wide. "I can't. They've both spaced. You missed them."

Skyla circled the corner of the desk. A tremble had begun in her arms. She clamped the pistol in sweat-slick hands. *Don't go to pieces now, Skyla. Guts, girl. You can do this.* "You're lying."

Rill shook his head, aware of her ragged control. "Not at all. And if that's your hole card, you've played your hand." He squinted, studying her. "You . . . I know you."

Skyla gave him a hard smile as she centered her blaster on his chest. "Seekore is running the piss out of *Sabot*'s reactors to get here. Director Rill, you're in a shitload of trouble."

"Seekore is a . . . You're a Companion?"

"Do you want to get Ily on the comm? All I need to see is her face on the screen."

Rill's expression remained placid, but Skyla could tell his brain was working. "I'd bargain. If you can get me a through line to Staffa, I'll—"

"You'll talk now, pus gut." Shivers wracked Skyla's shoulders.

He smiled. ''Really? You're Silk, aren't you? Silk, you're in the middle of *my* Security Directorate. I didn't press the 'all clear.' That hallway out there is filling with armed people. How do you expect to get out?''

''Bad deal, Rill. You look like a survivor. Granted, Seekore is a couple of weeks away, but if—''

A buzzer rang on Gyper Rill's desk. A woman's voice noted, ''Director? Two things have happened. You did not clear your alarm, and we have a young woman—Administrator Gaust's daughter. She's in the hallway with what looks like a sonic grenade. She claims she'll blow herself up and anyone who tries to capture her. What are your instructions, Director?''

Skyla took a deep breath, trying to still the quaking of her heart. ''Rotted young fool!''

Rill raised an eyebrow.

Skyla nodded. ''Send her up—unharmed!''

''Did you hear that?'' Rill asked.

''Affirmative. You have not canceled your alert. Do you want us to take action?''

Skyla lifted her blaster, centering the bead on his face. ''Your choice, Gyper.''

''Take no action. Silk and I are still negotiating.'' To Skyla he said. ''Do you mind if I reach down and kill the connection she opened? Or do you want them to hear every word?''

''Kill it. The comm button only, Gyper.''

He moved slowly, pressing the button. ''Let me make my position clear. I *don't* want any trouble with the Companions. If Staffa will talk, I'm sure we can come to a mutually agreeable settlement.'' Rill grinned, a sparkle in his eyes. ''In fact, I can probably help him to capture Ily and Arta.''

The door opened, and Lark stepped inside, glancing warily around.

''What the hell are you doing?'' Skyla demanded, trying to keep the panic from her voice.

''Came to see if you needed any help. I lifted this out of your pouch when I hugged you good-bye.'' She held up one of Skyla's grenades, thumb holding the detonator down. ''I guess I lost the pin. Maybe I got a little too dramatic out there.''

''Rotted Gods.'' Skyla exhaled wearily. ''Bring it here.'' She glanced at Rill. ''I'm going to lower my blaster. Given the fact that this idiot child has a live grenade, I imagine you'll hold very still. If you instigate a scuffle, a lot of us could end up all over the walls in little tiny pieces."

Rill nodded, fascination on his pale face as he studied the grenade in the girl's hands.

Skyla reached into her pouch, located a clip of safety wire, and used a small pair of pliers to cut a double loop. "Now, Lark, be very careful. We'll see just how cool you can be. Turn it, that's right. Now, the gauge of the wire is smaller than the diameter of the pinhole. We should be able to get two strands through, and tie them off."

To her credit, Lark didn't even flinch as Skyla wrapped the wire and tied it. "Thought you might need help," Lark repeated. "I got to thinking about what you said. About what it took to be like you. It means being brave enough to just damn the consequences and stomp in here, doesn't it?"

"That's right." Skyla turned. "Now, what were you saying, Rill?"

The Director's expression had turned quizzical. "Is this a joke?"

Skyla shrugged. "Might be. Do you want to produce Ily Takka for me? I'll take Arta Fera, too. I want them both—now!"

The secretary moaned and tried to sit up. Skyla pulled her pulse pistol, handing it to Lark. "Use your thumb. Push up on the lever on the side of the pistol, that's it. So long as that lever is up, the weapon will discharge when you pull the trigger. Stay back at least three paces from him. If he tries to move, pull that trigger."

"Will it kill him?" Lark moved over, pulse pistol pointed at the secretary.

"It will atomize whatever the pulse hits, kid. If you came this far, you damn well better be ready to kill."

"I am," Lark whispered. "Like you, I figure I'm already dead." She paused. "You know, there's a certain freedom in it."

"Yeah. But it can be damned short-lived." Skyla narrowed her eyes, inspecting the Director. "Rill? Did they really space?"

He nodded. "Like I was trying to tell you, I don't want trouble with the Companions. I want to cooperate in any way that I can. Get me a line to the Lord Commander, and I'll be happy to deal."

At the mention of the Companions, Skyla heard Lark gasp. "Rill, I want you to step around the desk. There, that's it." She fished a vial out of her pocket. "Recognize this stuff? Ah, I see that you do." She tossed it to him. "Now, you know all about Mytol. Let's see you take a little—"

He lunged at her, fast for a man of his size.

Skyla sidestepped, driving an elbow into his side, then spinning. Her kick snapped his kneecap to one side, and she punched a blow to his solar plexus before hammering him on the side of the head with the blaster. Gyper Rill fell like a Targan pine.

"One move and you're dead, asshole," Lark was saying to the stunned secretary.

Skyla glanced over to see a pale Lark staring over the pistol sights at her frightened victim. Skyla sighed, plucking the Mytol from where it had rolled on the floor. "All right, Lark, you're going to get your first lesson in truth drugs and captive tying."

"What about the bunch beyond the door. They've got a lot of guns out there. The whole hallway is full of them."

Skyla pulled Rill into a sitting position, checking his pupils. "They'll try gas eventually. We may have half an hour. If that doesn't work, they'll try a frontal assault."

"Gas?"

"Yeah, and you don't have a suit. Well, maybe we'll be through before then." Skyla lifted her vial, parting Rill's lips. "The secret to this stuff is getting the right amount down the subject's throat. Rill's big, about one hundred and ten kilos. Figure a drop for every twenty kilos. That's six drops."

"What if they get too much?"

"They get real sloppy on you. I did that to a Seddi once, and he kept trying to tell me how much he loved me in between bouts of passing out."

"You won't get away with this," the secretary mumbled, head down as he groaned. "You're surrounded."

Skyla corked her vial, slapping Gyper with all her strength. He blinked, staring up at her through pained eyes. "Skyla Lyma," he whispered. "That's who you are."

"Nice work, Rill. It'll take the Mytol a little time to work into your system. Want to get a head start on it?"

He shook his head. "No. Keeping your yacht was stupid. I should have called Itreata first thing."

"Where's Ily?"

"Spaced. I told you the truth. I spent the night up there . . . with both of them." A silly grin spread across his face as the Mytol eased into his brain. "Blessed Etaria, that's how a man ought to be fucked. Arta, then Ily, then Arta. Oh, that Arta, she's a wonder . . . exciting, you know? Ily's the better of the two, has the right muscles and knows how to use them. But with Arta, those breasts just seem to melt into your chest. And through it all, she looks at you with those burning amber eyes. When you come, she's still looking at you, as if she's drinking in your soul."

"Drug's got him," Skyla muttered from the corner of her mouth. "Gyper, where are Ily and Arta headed? What planet is their destination?"

He shook his head, smile fading. "I don't know. They could be headed anywhere."

"What about Vega? Would they be headed there?"

"I don't think so."

"Why not?"

"Just . . ." He screwed his expression, struggling with the drug. "A . . . hunch. You understand?"

"I understand. Why did they want the Vegan Rep?"

"To get the files."

"Why?"

"To find different identities."

"Which identities?"

"I don't know. Ily doesn't tell a person much about her plans." He looked up at her, eyes glazed. "Did you know you're a beautiful woman? Eyes like blue ice. Hair like—"

"What about Will Blacker? The Regan spacer?"

"Dead. They took his ship. *Victory*."

Skyla nodded. *That figured.* "What's your deal with Ily?"

"Free port here. She can come and go as she pleases, no questions asked. She's good—a survivor. If Staffa doesn't catch her, she'll be a profitable asset for a long time. It's good business to keep her happy. Not only that, but she's a master when it comes to sex. She knows all the right places, how to use her body."

"She's meaner than a Cytean cobra crossed with Riparian slime."

"Oh, yes, that's Ily. But she excites me."

"Why did you want to arrest Silk? What tipped you off?"

"Ily noticed the yacht on the comm monitor when she spaced. She asked what the registry was. I called Port Security and Customs, and told her it was registered to a Regan merchant woman named Silk. She said the yacht belonged to Tedor Mathaiison, the Regan Minister of Defense. She said she knew that yacht, in fact, she'd screwed Tedor's brains out in the master cabin. I immediately sent Wilm and Vymer to locate Silk. I wanted you brought in for questioning. Last I heard, Vymer and Wilm . . . they'd been killed in the Vegan Rep's office."

"If you had to guess, Gyper, where would you guess that Ily and Arta were going?"

Rill frowned, blinking from the drug. "I would guess maybe back to Rega. Or maybe Imperial Sassa. I would guess anyplace except where you would expect her to show up. She would hide in her pursuer's blind spot."

"But we can trace *Victory*. She'll have to register at a Port Authority, won't she?"

Rill shook his head. "She's got the Vegan shipping records. *Victory*'s registration was all in Regan Comm Central. That's been destroyed by the Companions. She can use any registry numbers for a Model Sixteen Regan freighter that are active in the Vegan records."

"What about Pedro Maroon? Where is he?"

"Out in the ice somewhere. Vymer took care of it."

"Dead?"

Rill grinned. "Should have seen what Arta did to him. He died happy. She killed him while he was still inside her, can you imagine? Right there on the desk, she waited until he came then she killed him." He paused. "That's the excitement of screwing her. Those amber eyes are staring at you, and you know she wants to kill, right then, just when you release."

"He's sick!" Lark gasped.

"No," Gyper retorted. "Not sick. Cunning. Like Arta and Ily. Cunning. It's a time for cunning people." His eyes wavered as he tried to focus on Skyla. "How about you? I could make you a deal. Work something out. You never know when you might want a free port. No questions asked. You're a beautiful woman. I could make the same arrangement with you that I have with Ily."

"See which one of us is better at making you come?"

"Yes. I'd like that. Comparing—"

Skyla slapped him.

"That hurt," Rill told her.

"It was supposed to. And you want to deal with the Companions?"

"Any way I can. I talked to Kaylla Dawn, told her we'd do anything to cooperate. I've been meeting with the unions. They've taken that Seddi sumpshit to heart. Let them. Things will wind down and they'll remember I was on their side. The Seddi will like what I've done, and I'll do everything I can to make sure you and Staffa are satisfied with Terguz."

"Will you set Ily up . . . just to make us happy?"

"If you make it worth my while, I will. Just tell me what you need."

Skyla stood up, a sour twisting in her gut. "I need you to shut up."

Rill nodded, smiling pleasantly.

Lark still stood, her pistol centered on the secretary. The man looked like he wanted to throw up. "This is really disgusting," Lark whispered. "Should I kill them now?"

"Little bloodthirsty, aren't you?"

Lark gulped, the pulse pistol rock steady in her grip. "You know, my father, silly as he is with all his talk about the Empire, he still really believes in what he says. I'd rather drink Riparian slime than be in the same room with these guys."

Skyla nodded, stepping around the desk. "Rill? What are your people going to try next? Gas?"

"They'll expect a signal from me soon. If they don't get it, Vymer will try gassing the ventilation."

"Vymer's dead. What's the signal for 'all clear'?"

"I must press the white stud at the base of my comm monitor."

Skyla pressed the stud. "What does the red one do?"

"Brings security charging in immediately in case of trouble."

"And the blue one?"

"Tells security to arrest whoever steps out of the door."

"Nice." Skyla slapped the desktop. "Rill, what's your biggest secret? The one you'd never tell anyone?"

"I have holos of Ily and myself having sex. She would kill me if she ever found out."

"Where are they?"

"Personal file, 11743."

Skyla settled herself behind Rill's desk, calling up the file. She ran through several minutes of it. Her innards cramped at the first sight of Ily. Shivers darted through her muscles as she stared into those black eyes, saw Ily's shining black hair swing as she stripped out of her black outfit. Skyla clenched her fists, watching as Ily smiled up at Gyper Rill, moving toward him with teasing steps. It was all Rill had said it would be.

"One more move like that, and I'll kill you!" Lark burst out. The secretary groaned and sank back on the floor.

Skyla got a grip on her wavering courage and accessed the comm, getting a woman's face. The security officer's eyes widened. "Who are you? This is the Director's—"

"Shut up. I want a line to the Administrator's office. Tell him Skyla Lyma, Wing Commander of the Companions, is on the line."

"Do you have the Director's—"

"I'm on his pus-licking comm, aren't I?" Skyla looked to the side. "Hey, Gyper, can I use this comm for Companion business?"

"Of course."

The security woman frowned, bit her lip, and placed the call.

"What are you going to do?" Lark asked anxiously. "What part does my father play in this?"

"I might need him one of these days. Seekore is going to show up with that battleship. Maybe your father can make it as Terguzzi Administrator. Maybe he can't. I'll give him the chance."

The image of a long-faced man with snowy white hair formed. "Wing Commander? To what do I owe—"

"You're Frederick Gaust?"

"I am. Wing Commander, I take it you're here on the planet. If you'd have—"

"Shut up and listen, Administrator. I've got some good

news and some bad news for you. The good news is that I'm sending you Director Gyper Rill's files, which will allow you to destroy him and his organization here. I'm including one which details his sexual activities with Minister Ily Takka. I would take it as a personal favor if you'd release it on the after hours holo. The *Wayside* might like to run it in their big wall tank. I don't care, just so long as it gets around, understand?''

The Administrator nodded, a light of comprehension growing in his eyes. He looked nothing like Lark, but rather like a chilly sort of formal bureaucrat. ''And what else?''

''I'm sending you the access code to the security files here. It should have everything, all the profiles, the arrest warrants, surveillance data, and the rest. Publish it all.''

''Why? These are Imperial records we're talking about, Wing Commander. My authority—''

''Screw your authority, Gaust! I'm handing you the stuff. Use it. The Regan Empire is gone. A new day has dawned. I'm giving you a chance to be part of it or be left behind. Think of it as a favor, all right?''

''What's your price for all of this? Nothing comes free, especially in politics.''

Skyla leaned forward. ''Commander Seekore will be arriving here in a couple of weeks in the Companion battleship, *Sabot*. When she does, I don't want any trace of Gyper Rill or the Internal Security Directorate to remain. Understand? And you'll need to work something out with the unions. I meant it when I said the Empire is gone. Either you can work with the new epistemology, or we'll find someone who can. Now, if you're smart, you'll contact Kaylla Dawn on Itreata.''

He winced. ''That is bad news. Surely, as Wing Commander of the Companions, you understand the necessity of order. As Administrator, I can't—''

''Wrong, pal. You *must*. How's it going to be, Administrator? Can you work with them? Build a different kind of government? Share the power? You have a choice. Use your imagination and innovation. Talk to your people. Compromise. If Seekore arrives and your people don't want you, you're history, pal.''

''I see.'' He looked as if he really didn't.

''The other thing I wanted to call and tell you is that your daughter is spacing with me. She's joined the Companions, Administrator."

"Lark? Impossible! I won't allow it!"

Skyla leaned back and crossed her arms. "Want me to pay a visit to your office? Perhaps you have some files that need publicizing?"

"But my daughter—"

"Has made her own decision, Frederick. Get this, and think about it. She's taken responsibility for her own life. You have to take responsibility for yours. I've given you all that I can. Sink or float, your choice." Skyla killed the connection, getting to her feet. "Come on, kid. We've got a ship to catch."

Lark shot a curious glance at Skyla. "You mean, you really *are* Skyla Lyma?"

"In the flesh, such as it is. Now, it might be a little tricky getting out of here. Rill? Will anyone try anything when we walk out of here?"

"Not unless I order it."

Skyla lifted an eyebrow. "Well, we'll just use a little magnataping and see that you don't move. Come watch this, Lark. There's a trick to tying these guys up. You want to make sure they can't even wiggle. I'll show you."

"Sure we shouldn't kill him? What if he gets in touch with Ily, tells her you're after her?"

"Let him. I *want* her to know I'm coming to kill her."

"But she'll be warned."

Skyla nodded. "Yeah, there's that, all right."

Lark studied her from sober green eyes. "Why? Wing Commander? Why me?"

Skyla shrugged. "Because if you were desperate enough to come in here after me, you either don't give a damn, or you really want the chance."

Lark nodded, watching carefully as Skyla worked. "There's something else, too, isn't there?"

"Yeah, kid. But I'll tell you when we're aboard the ship."

"I won't like to hear it, will I?"

"Nope. But you bought into this game."

CHAPTER XXIII

5780:01:24:14:55 GST
It/Comm/Sec/Clr

From: Verdant Mancuso
Computer Division
Manufacturing and Production Unit
Itreata

To: Magister Kaylla Dawn
Seddi Warrens; Itreata

Magister Dawn: In response to your request for information, we can only tell you that current production of Model 7706 N-dimensional gallium arsenide computers is proceeding with the utmost haste. Our facility is operating full-time and we have our technicians working at their maximum potential.

It must be noted, in response to your concerns, that our facility can only produce the 7706 at a given rate of one unit per thirteen hundred man-hours. Our epitaxic nanotanks produce boards only as fast as the physics allows.

We are aware of the need for replacement comm for the Farhome project; however, we cannot rush the processing of a single unit. We trust that you understand the added delay you would experience were we to deliver a flawed unit. Had we additional nanotanks, skilled workers, and materials, we could promise commensurate production. Unfortunately, we cannot.

You asked for an estimated delivery date for the Farhome hardware. Replacing this many units in such a short time is a difficult process. As it is, we will be shortcutting our normal testing regimen and cannot guarantee the integrity of the units being produced. I regret being unable to give you an answer in line with your present needs. Delivery on the final unit F.O.B. can be expected within another four months.

If we can be of further assistance, please feel free to contact us.

* * *

Myles Roma walked beside Delshay, resplendent in her eye-searing purple armor. Whereas her stride could be likened to that of a feral cat, Myles still waddled, though not with the wheezing, rotund gait of a year ago. Just that morning, in fact, he'd seen his toes from a standing position for the first time in years.

He stepped off *Cobra* and onto the spartan docking bay which acted as an umbilical and one of the tethers for the Companions' warship. Hyros and his small staff followed, in turn flanked by the ever present STU. The well-lit room measured fifteen meters across and was lined on one side by lift doors. Windows to the right and left gave a stunning view of the moon's surface and *Cobra*'s sleek sides where the giant floodlights illuminated them.

He'd been amazed by the ingenious technique used at Itreata for the securing of its fleet. The weak gravity of the rogue moon and its rapid rotation allowed the Companions to tie their ships to the planet where angular momentum kept them in place. The result proved to be a considerably quicker commute through the skyhook and into the moon.

"You seem surprised," Delshay noted, amusement in her violet eyes. "I thought you'd been to Itreata before."

"As the Sassan Legate, Commander. We were brought in on the other side of the moon, well away from the fleet and constantly monitored. But this—" he pointed out one of the tactite viewing ports—"is fantastic."

She led him into one of the lifts and hit the controls. Gravity manipulation proved so sophisticated, Myles couldn't feel himself dropping. "How's the software coming?"

Myles rubbed at his chin, conscious of the feel of his jaw. How long had it been since he'd felt his bones this way?

"Not nearly as well as I'd wish. Be that as it may, I am surprised at the progress we've made. What do you hear about the political situation?"

"Not good. We've placed *Cobra* on emergency resupply and refueling. I'll be ready to space in another eighty hours."

Myles lowered his voice. "We'll make it, Delshay. Even if Staffa can't use this Seddi computer, we'll patch it up and hold it together someway, somehow."

"You seem so sure, Myles."

He shrugged. "What choice do we have, Commander? We all must do our best—and then a little bit better. And if we keep our people alive, it will be well worth the struggle. Years from now, you and I will look at each other and nod, knowing our actions were worth something. That's not such a bad way to live the rest of your life, knowing that you've made a difference."

"You know, you're all right, Myles. I think in the days to come, I'll remember what you just said." The lift doors opened to a busy landing. "It's been a pleasure having you aboard. I just wish we could have had more time to talk."

"I enjoyed my passage aboard *Cobra*. When this is finished, Delshay, come and visit Hyros and me. It will be our turn to provide the hospitality. And perhaps, we'll be able to raise a glass and toast our success."

She gave him a salute before turning off to one side to deal with a group of techs who stood waiting with portable comms tucked under their arms.

Myles searched for Magister Dawn, seeing no tall, brown-haired woman with tan eyes. He shrugged when he met Hyros' questioning look. "Perhaps the Magister was detained? Or we've arrived earlier—"

"Legate?" a tall black man asked, stepping out from the crowd.

"Yes?"

The man bowed. "I am Master Wilm, Magister Dawn's administrative assistant. I'm afraid the Magister has been absorbed by political events. She's on the subspace to Dion Axel. More trouble in Phillipia. Violence in the streets. It appears that Ayms is going to have to land hot and secure the planet. The next couple of hours will be critical."

Myles smiled ruefully, noting the ragged look in the man's

bloodshot eyes, the haggard set of his mouth. "It's not going well, is it?"

"No, it's not. I'm worried sick about Magister Dawn. She's lost ten kilos since this has started. She fell asleep in the women's room yesterday. Now that you're here, she can stop worrying about the Farhome project though."

"And how is that coming along?"

"Just like everything else, Legate. Too little, too late."

* * *

Anticipation and worry sent jitters through Staffa as he started down the winding stairway that led into the bowels of Makarta Mountain. This tunnel twisted and dipped as it descended. The steps carved into the stone had been worn hollow by countless feet. White bulbs cast their soft light over the uneven walls. Behind him, the rasping of booted feet, the clanking of equipment, and the scuffing of clothing filled the confined space.

"How much farther?" Sinklar asked from behind him.

"Just about there." *And then what am I going to do?* The problem of the machine continued to perplex him. His scalp prickled, as if the machine's lingering touch pervaded the air.

You don't have any choice, Staffa. Your ships are arriving over troubled worlds. You must *have a way of administering Free Space. Maybe the Mag Comm can do it.*

Staffa's jitters heightened. *And what if Bruen is right? What if it uses our dependence to enslave us?*

Staffa could see the worn stone floor now. He stepped out into the room, the sensation the same as the first time he'd entered here with Bruen.

The cavern measured ten meters in diameter, the ceiling highly arched and filled with light globes. The walls had been polished from centuries of robed bodies leaning against them. At different times, shelves had been cut into the stone, and marks on the floor indicated where cabinets had stood.

Gasps came from behind Staffa as his party trooped in. Sinklar stopped in mid-step, bicolored eyes wide.

The Mag Comm filled an entire wall to the right of the entrance. Bank upon bank of multicolored lights flickered and gleamed, no rhyme or sense to their organization or size as they shot patterns of light across the room. The mainframe consoles had been molded, the proportions oddly wrong, the manufacture inhuman. The material might have been brushed metal, or silver ceramic of some sort. A single reclining chair sat before the main board, and behind it, glittering in the wealth of sparkling lights, a holder supported a thin helmet of delicate golden wire mesh.

Staffa's people had packed the rear of the room, barely audible whispers passing back and forth among his techs.

"What now?" Sinklar asked, stepping forward, fascination evident in his expression.

Staffa approached the golden helmet cautiously, mindful of the stories Bruen had told. Once, he would have rushed to place the helmet on his head, remembering the warm tingle of its attempt to establish contact. That euphoria had passed. Staffa examined the golden web through narrowed eyes. *What are you?*

Sinklar stopped before the huge machine, staring up at it. "The only communication is through the headset?"

"Data can be input through a keyboard. The helmet link, however, is supposed to be the most efficient. What's your guess, Sinklar? Do you think people made this?"

Fist shook his head, hands clasped behind his back. "No. It looks . . . wrong."

Staffa gave him a crooked smile. "Meet your grandfather."

Sinklar shot him an uneasy glance. "Anatolia would have loved . . ."

"Yes, she would have." Staffa stepped over, reached out to pluck the deceptively light helmet from the holder. "Come here."

Sinklar took a step, jaw muscles bunched. Tingles, electric and beckoning, played along Staffa's hands and arms as he lifted the helmet. "Lean close, Sinklar, feel that?"

Sinklar inched his head to within twenty centimeters of the helmet and started, ducking back, surprise in his eyes. "Seductive, isn't it?"

"I almost put it on once. Kaylla practically pulled muscles racing over to jerk it away." At a sudden flash of red light, Staffa said, "Look. See that large red light that's begun to blink? That's the beacon. With that, the machine called Bruen to communicate."

Sinklar's expression soured. "If that was on Bruen's head, I don't want to get close to it. Some of the contamination might rub off."

"We have a way around that. I hope." Staffa beckoned. "Ryman?"

Ark stepped forward with the case he'd carried under his arm, dropping to one knee as he unclipped the fasteners on the sialon box. Opening the box exposed a worry-cap of the sort used on ships' bridges. Within the cap lay a head-sized transparent ceramic oblong shot through with coils of wire. The "head" and the worry-cap in turn were connected by two meters of bundled cable with a black plastic box located midway between them.

"Explain this, Ryman."

Ark looked up at the Mag Comm, then at Staffa. "What we've put together, Lord Commander, is a basic worry-cap wired to reproduce a similar chemo-electric response within the transmitter, the ceramic head. We've linked them with standard nanofiberoptic cable, but with a metering interferometer." He tapped the black plastic box with a finger. "This acts as a one-way diode. You can think anything you want, and it will be re-created in the transmitter."

"But the Mag Comm can't send anything back, can't manipulate the wearer's brain?"

"That's correct, sir. Quite honestly, we didn't know what we'd be dealing with. Before we can go two-way, we'll need to get an idea of what that golden helmet does, how it works. After that, we can start designing a gate that will allow you two-way communication." Ark spread his hands. "Assuming this first version even works. You understand, sir, we were shooting in the dark designing this thing."

Staffa nodded, slapping his old friend on the shoulder. "I understand, Ryman." Staffa paused, hating the fluttery anticipation in his gut. "Ready to try it?"

Ark nodded, reaching up to remove his combat helmet.

"No, Ryman. Are you ready for *me* to try it?"

"Excuse me, sir. But as head of your security—" Ark jerked a nod at the Mag Comm—"and given the unknown capabilities of this machine, I think—"

"I know, Ryman. It's all right. I understand. Hand me the worry-cap."

Ark bit his lip and, against his better judgment, handed

Staffa the worry-cap. The metal felt warm in Staffa's hand as he lowered it over his head, gazing thoughtfully at the Mag Comm from under the low rim of the helmet.

"We're preparing to place the machine's receiver on our transmitter," Ark informed. "Are you ready, sir?"

"I'm ready. I'll tell the machine to cancel the red summons light."

"Affirmative. Here we go. We're lowering the golden helmet now, sir."

Staffa felt nothing except the typical sensation of the worry-cap, as if his thoughts were running out through his skull instead of being bounded by the perceptual universe.

"Mag Comm, if you can hear me, cancel your flashing summons light."

Sinklar cried, "The light is off!"

Staffa nodded, *"Mag Comm, turn the light on again."*

"Whoops," Sinklar corrected. "It's on again!"

"I know," Staffa said. "Ryman, your transmitter works."

"We're getting readings, Lord Commander. This helmet is generating a great deal of electromagnetic energy. If it keeps this up, it could fry the transmitter.

"Mag Comm, you must limit your probing of our transmitter. If you burn out our system, we will be unable to communicate with you. Do you want us to continue communications with you? Flash your summons light once for no, twice for yes."

"The red light just flashed twice," Sinklar called.

"Readings on the golden helmet are decreasing." Ark sounded relieved.

Staffa took a deep breath. *"Mag Comm, we are not the Seddi. We are here as a delegation for all humans. We understand the role you have played among the Seddi. We do not wish to act as your pawns, or your agents. That time is past. Do you bear human beings ill will?"*

"The light flashed once," Sinklar relayed.

Staffa wet his lips. "Here goes. Pray, people." *"Mag Comm, humanity is threatened by a collapse of our administrative systems. The Regan comm system, which directed their distribution of resources and manufacturing, was destroyed by war. The Sassan computer system, which was to take over those functions for all of Free Space, was destroyed soon thereafter by a seismic shift in the planetary crust. Do you have the capacity and hardware to run such an administrative program?''*

"Two flashes!'' Sinklar sang out.

Now for the final question. Staffa's stomach knotted in anticipation. *''Mag Comm, will you help us in this time of need? Will you coordinate our administration of Free Space? If you do not, a large number of people will die. Flash once for no. Twice for yes.''*

"Two flashes,'' Sinklar announced.

Staffa lifted the worry-cap from his head, relief mixing with distrust. "It says it will help us.''

Sinklar crossed his arms, uneasily observing the machine. The summons light began to flash again, demanding, eager. "But what have we done, Lord Commander? Have we struck a bargain to save ourselves? Or are we about to snap the collar about our necks?''

"I wish I knew.''

* * *

The long climb winded Sinklar, but despite his trembling legs, he hurried toward the wrecked upper levels of Makarta. As he left the soft white light of the lower chambers behind, his suit units kicked on, bathing the way in their harsh glare. His plan had been to rush past, to avoid as many of the broken bodies as possible. The contorted dead stared at him from shrunken visages, their dried bodies shrouded in dust and charred armor.

This journey brought him as much pain as the first, and despite himself, Sinklar stopped periodically, reaching down to touch a hardened armor shoulder, or to stare into the face of one of the questing dead.

"I'm sorry,'' he whispered over and over.

Finally, half dazed, he climbed up the square tunnel and out into the glare of the compound lights burning brightly in the Targan night. Technicians, shouting and hammering, were in the process of setting up prefab buildings, and in the distance the dwindling roar of a shuttle faded. Gen-sets were puttering and stuttering in the background.

Sinklar filled his lungs with the fresh air, half sick from the horror of the caverns. Squinting into the actinic light of the field camp, he turned, walking off to the right, passing beyond the perimeter and into the darkness.

From the stars, he could tell that morning would come within the hour. Passing the guard, he climbed to a point overlooking the valley. He found his old spot, listening to the fallen brown pine needles crackle underfoot, and settled on a rock with his back to one of the vanilla-scented trees. Here, what seemed like a lifetime ago, he'd sat with MacRuder, trying to make sense of it all . . . both lost in their grief for Gretta.

That had been in daylight, before Makarta had looted the last of the unshaken confidence from his soul. Then, Mac had stood before him and warned Sinklar that Ily would try to seduce him.

I didn't believe you, Mac. I didn't hear what you really said that day. He snorted at himself. *And if I had taken you seriously, I wouldn't have believed it.* "You're a fool, Sinklar. A silly fool."

He leaned his head back, listening to the night sounds. The corpses rustled in the back of his memory. Images of their dried flesh burned into his mind. The musty odor of the chambers forever his.

What could I have done differently?

He heard the soft tread of booted feet in the darkness, and chuckled wearily to himself. "Adze? Is that you, or am I lucky enough to have been found by an overlooked Seddi rebel?"

"Just me, sir. Sorry to interrupt. I'll back off a little farther."

Sinklar chewed on his lip for a moment, then slapped his legs in defeat. "Come over and have a seat. If you're going to be my watchdog, I'd like to know something about you."

She stepped over, carefully studying the terrain through her electronic augmentation. Finally, satisfied, she settled herself across from him, lifting the studded visor. Overlapping plates of mirror-reflective armor speckled with the stars on the upper surfaces and molded with the night on the lower. In the dim starlight, he could barely make out her face. She had brown eyes, proud copper-toned facial features, and wide cheekbones that accented her straight nose and full mouth. He imagined thick black hair to be hidden within the helmet.

"What would you like to know?"

"Where are you from?"

She glanced off to the south, over the tree-filled valley. "My family comes from Malbourne, but I spent half of my life in Itreata. My father fought for the Lord Commander. I have followed in his footsteps. Fortunately, I studied hard and qualified for the Special Tactics Unit."

"Have you been with Staffa long?"

"Four Imperial years as a Companion." She smiled, exposing strong white teeth. "Myklene was my first real action. I distinguished myself during the infiltration and sabotage."

Sinklar resettled himself, easing the spots where the rock had started to eat into his hide. "I got into war by accident. The Seddi kept me out of the Regan University system. I was drafted and dropped on Targa as a lowly private. Can you imagine? I didn't know up from down or back from forth." He shook his head. "And they thought I'd make a soldier!"

She frowned. "I thought you were a Division First? And then weren't you in charge of the entire Regan military?"

"I was." Sinklar picked up a rock and tossed it into the darkness. "But that was later. Here, on Targa, I was supposed to be a political sacrifice. Tybalt needed a disaster, something to lure Staffa into contracting with Rega. He played right into the Seddi's hands. The day after I set foot on Targa, we took Kaspa, the capital. The first Targan counterattack wiped out ninety percent of the First Targan Division. They sent raw recruits out of the replacement cadres, and I was promoted to Section First. We were given a mountain pass to hold. I did it by throwing out the military manual and trusting my people."

Those ghosts watched and nodded in the night, reliving the desperate battle for that tortured mountain saddle. In Sinklar's memory, blasters flashed and grav shots turned reality inside out. He forced the image from his mind before it blended into his nightmare.

"Tybalt needed a sacrifice. In defiance of custom, they promoted me again, to Division First this time. The reasons quickly became apparent." He pointed over toward the east. "We got dropped out there. Abandoned without transport, orbital support, logistics, or intelligence. By rights the Targan rebels should have cut us apart."

"But they didn't."

Sinklar shook his head. "I kept my people alive. We commandeered what we needed from the countryside and went on to take the city of Vespa. After that, we destroyed the majority of the Rebel army, pacified the planet, and . . . and finally came here, to Makarta. To end it once and for all."

They sat in silence for a while, listening to the chirring of the night insects.

"From the looks of things in there, it was a tough fight."

Sinklar nodded, the tender wound in his heart aching again. "I didn't know Staffa was in the mountain. If I had, I'd never have risked all those people. You've got to understand, the best intelligence I had was that Makarta was filled with Seddi priests and novices. We'd broken their army by then. This should have been a simple mop-up. A neat flanking maneuver, and we'd have them all for interrogation."

He shook his head, eyes closed, seeing Mayz's stunned expression as another Section died inside the mountain. "Staffa changed everything. He kept them from panicking, trapped six hundred of my people. After that, I *had* to get them out. Otherwise, I never would have risked those lives."

"I didn't understand that at first," she told him. "I thought you were weak."

"I am," Sinklar whispered. "Weak and haunted."

Adze hitched a leg up, repositioning her shoulder weapon on its sling as she stared out at the night. "It's none of my business, Lord Fist, but do you plan on living the rest of your life like that?"

Sinklar pitched another rock into the darkness. "The future is a funny place. Once, I was rash enough to think I could tackle it head-on, just bull my way through. Meet each challenge by anticipating the enemy's strategy, using it against him, and dashing on to victory."

"Sounds good, so what happened?"

"Adze, I'm damned good when it comes to grand strategies. On the battlefield, I can anticipate my opponent, turn the tables on him, and crush him. Through statistics, I can determine the direction a population will take, anticipate their social evolution. But when it comes to individuals? I'm at a loss."

"Is that what happened with Minister Takka?"

"You know about that?" His voice sank.

"Only that she arrested you. Didn't you anticipate that?"

He shook his head.

"Don't want to talk about it?" she asked.

"Why would you want to know?" Sinklar cocked his head. "Gun room gossip?"

"Lord Fist, I'm STU. That probably doesn't mean much to you, but among the Companions, it's a special honor. We do what no one in Free Space—maybe even the universe—can do. We're the best of the best, and you don't get that way by conducting maneuvers or saluting fancy. It comes from thinking, learning, and ambition."

"And you're going to study me?"

"What are you going to do now? How do you anticipate tackling the future?"

"How do you? If this all works out, what are the Companions' dreaded STU going to do for a living? Become a fancy police unit?"

She shrugged. "Time will tell. No matter what the political situation, there is always a need for warriors. Only the number needed changes."

"Supply and demand?"

"You never answered my question? What are you going to do? Follow Staffa? Become part of his administration?"

"I haven't really given it much thought. Mostly, Staffa and I have discussed the immediate problems—like what to do about the Mag Comm. Is that part of your job? Sound out the suspects? Look for treason?"

"Obviously, if I heard you say something that threatened our security, I'd mention it to Ark. I'm not a fool, Lord Fist." She shook her head. "I don't have a handle on you yet. I watch things very closely. The Lord Commander cares a great deal about you."

"I'm his son. For whatever reason, he grants me a little tolerance."

"He respects you, values your opinions. When you speak, his expression is the same as when he listens to Ryman Ark, or Kaylla Dawn. Inside the mountain, he pointed out that those Regan soldiers marched into that mountain for you, and fought bravely. But . . ." She shifted uncomfortably, and in the faint graying of sky, he could see her sudden discomfort.

Sinklar straightened. "Go on."

"Excuse me, sir. I'd better go and check the perimeter. It's been too long already."

"Wait." Sinklar jumped to his feet as she stood, putting a hand on her shoulder. "What were you about to say?"

"Nothing, Lord Fist."

"Don't call me Lord Fist. I hate that. And, Adze, I realize that you're here on the Lord Commander's orders, but you don't have to look after me. I know these mountains."

"The Lord Commander did not assign me to watch you. STO Ark did . . . in recognition of outstanding service. My presence is strictly according to standard hostile planet procedure."

"You're hedging. You almost let something slip and thought better of it. Something about me. What was it?"

Her hard gaze refused to yield.

Sinklar turned, staring out at the graying horizon. "I give you my word, Adze, it will be between you and me. What were you going to say?"

For long moments, her obsidian eyes probed his. Finally, as if making a decision, she said, "The Lord Commander told me that part of the reason your soldiers marched into Makarta was because you'd cry for them. Anyone can cry. What I haven't seen are the qualities of leadership I'd expect from a commander of your reputation. That's all, sir. I was just wondering what they saw in you." She saluted. "Now, if you'll excuse me, I need to check the perimeter."

Sinklar stood rooted, staring blindly out at the shadowed valley, feeling as though he'd been kicked in his guts.

* * *

Comm buzzed by Mac's ear. "Commander Braktov is on the way to your quarters. Her LC just landed on the building roof."

Mac started up, growling to himself.

Chrysla blinked, yawning and stretching her firm body.

In the subdued lights, Mac couldn't resist taking time to admire the honey tones of her smooth skin, eyes tracing the curves of her body from the rounded wealth of her breasts to the sway of narrow waist that gave rise to the swell of hip and thigh.

"Blessed Gods, you're beautiful, Chrysla."

She smiled at him, a warm satisfaction in her eyes. "And you're the most handsome man I've ever known. But you'd better hurry. I don't think you want to leave Rysta waiting."

Mac tried to shake the sleep out of his head as he stood. "Figures, the first time we wake up together, we can't take advantage of it. No, it's got to be Rysta wanting to see me." He paused, staring back at Chrysla. "She's going to know. That old battle-ax reads me like a book."

Chrysla yawned, a thin hand over her mouth. "You act like she's your mother."

Mac gave her a grin. "Rysta's worse. My mother, Bless her soul, didn't have a suspicious bone in her body. Rysta, on the other hand, has larceny and intrigue pumping in her veins."

Mac wheeled, trotting into the huge, plush bath. He stepped into one of the showers, palmed the control, and savored the needles of water coursing over his skin. Closing his eyes, he replayed their lovemaking. Real . . . it had happened just that way. Warm, tender, and passionate. They had joined, twining together in mutual fulfillment.

How are you going to tell Staffa?

Mac shook water from his head, killing the spray and stepping through the drying fields. Which option would Staffa take? Shoot them on the spot? Order a quiet execution? Public humiliation in a trial? Or something more sinister.

He has Skyla! Why does he need to hound us?

"And how would you feel if you were the most powerful man alive, and an untitled, common-born Division First had just cuckolded you?"

He's going to torture us to death . . . slowly, cutting us apart piece by piece.

"No. I'll tell him I forced her. That she fought like mad, but I *made* her do it!"

"Fool," Chrysla called from the doorway behind him.

She flipped her wealth of auburn hair with a graceful motion. "Do you think he'd believe you?"

"He might."

"Regrets, Mac?"

He walked over to her, hugging her close, reveling in the sensation of her warm skin against his. "Not even one, at least, for myself. I'll never regret loving you for one instant."

"You'd better hurry," she said, holding him against her as she teased him with her hips. "Rysta's waiting, and, unfortunately, you're rising to an occasion you don't have time for."

She kissed him and ducked into the sleeping quarters, returning with his undersuit and armor. Deftly, she helped him fasten the clips. "Don't worry about it. We'll deal with Staffa when the time comes."

"What do you think he's going to do?"

She shrugged. "I have no idea. This new Staffa is beyond my predictions. The old one, however, was another thing."

"Uh-huh. Like I'd be spacing for the Forbidden Borders, right?"

"*We'd* be spacing for the Forbidden Borders." She kissed him. "One thing at a time. I'll be out as soon as I'm showered and dressed."

Mac stilled the runaway pounding of his heart, took a deep breath, and straightened his shoulders before stepping out into the dining room. He found Rysta standing in the main room. She wore her dress armor and carried a helmet under one thin arm. She turned, appraising Mac closely. "Not bad, boy. I never thought I'd see you in the likes of this. Bit posh for a lad of your experience, don't you think?"

Mac looked around at the gold trim, Nesian carpets, and jeweled ornaments. "Yeah, well, I gotta admit, it's a step up from sleeping in the mud. What's wrong?"

Rysta stepped over to the giant marble table and set her helmet down before pulling her gloves off, slapping them smartly to straighten the fingers and laying them atop the helmet. "Had a snafu over who was going to control the grain shares coming in from southern continent. Had a regional governor who thought his needs outweighed those of the Empire. Instead of waking you, I dropped down and had a friendly chat with him. He was going to be trouble. I just had that feeling, so I had a couple of marines haul him up to *Gyton*. After he cools down, I'll have another chat with him and make up my mind whether he can resume his duties." She cocked her head. "Just thought I ought to check in and let you know I'd been meddling in planetary affairs."

"You know I trust you. What else do you hear?"

"Staffa and Sinklar have arrived at Targa. They've begun the excavations to get to the Seddi computer."

Mac nodded, turning away, arms clasped behind him. "I take it our team is making progress with the planetary comm. We actually got the announcement that you were arriving before you got here."

Rysta nodded, a glint in her gaze. "We? Ah, yes, I see." She rubbed her knobby chin. "I take it you've thought this all out?"

Mac felt himself flushing. "One day at a time, Commander. That's all any of us can do."

Rysta gave him a crooked grin. "I love brash kids. Well, I'll tell you what I'll do. If I get the order to arrest you, I'll let you have twenty minutes head start."

"Don't joke."

"Joke? Me?" Rysta tapped her bony chest with a hard thumb.

Mac grinned at her. "Twenty minutes? That's with me in *Gyton*'s command chair and you on the planet?"

"Sure thing, and Staffa's battleship on your tail."

"I don't think it will come to that," Chrysla stated calmly as she entered the room. She wore the cape she'd adopted to mask the effect of the formfitting armor. To Mac's eyes, she had a new radiance about her.

"Lady." Rysta bowed her head slightly.

"I told you," Mac muttered.

"Told who what?" Rysta demanded.

"Mac worries that you read his expressions too easily." Chrysla walked to the dispenser, pulling the jeweled handle to pour a cup of stassa.

"From the saucy gleam in your eyes, Lady, I wouldn't be making light of Mac." Rysta turned, smacking her lips. "Very well, so be it." Rysta seated herself, kicking out her feet. "Can't say as I blame you. Were it me, and I were young and in love, I'd do the same. Life's too short, no matter what the consequences."

"It won't come to trouble," Chrysla insisted.

Rysta made a gesture, as if pushing it aside. "I was just telling Mac that I removed Governor Nathan from the Southern Hemisphere. He'd started to act too stingy with his cereal grains."

"Place Anton Marrak in charge." Chrysla advised the Commander as she sipped. "He's one of the old aristocrats from before the conquest. He's a bright, dignified, and able man, enough so that Staffa simply retired him at the time. He'll not only bring respectability to the Southern leadership, but most likely stability as well."

"Mac?" Rysta asked.

"I trust Chrysla's intuition in these matters."

"Then we'll do it." Rysta took a deep breath. "I never would have thought it would go so smoothly."

"We can thank Chrysla," Mac said. "She has a sense for things here."

Rysta nodded. "Assuming this comm continues to improve, we're not going to be needed here much longer. Have you given any thought to that?"

"You're trying to tell me something," Mac decided. "Want to drop a hint?"

Rysta's attempt at a grin reminded Mac more of an evil leer. "Itreata just broadcast a report. Skyla Lyma's yacht was observed docked at Terguz. That skinny little witch, Seekore, is stretching *Sabot* to the limit to get there."

Mac drove a fist into his palm. "But Ily will be long gone."

"Yep." Rysta studied the wrinkles and age spots on the back of her hands. "So what did she do there? Ditch the yacht, sure. But then what?"

"New identification," Chrysla guessed. "But did she buy passage, take another ship, or go to ground on Terguz to wait for it all to blow over?"

"One of the first two," Mac decided. "Ily isn't a good one for going to ground. She's mad, frustrated. She'll want to act immediately."

"What makes you so sure?" Chrysla asked.

"I've seen her." Mac began to pace. "On Targa. We'd just defeated the Regan attempt to crush us. Ily dropped down to dicker peace at the brick factory on Vespa. I was in charge when her LC landed, and believe me, it was all I could do to hold the troops back. Everyone was angry enough to put her against a wall and blow her away. She knew exactly how precarious her position was, but she couldn't find it within herself to wait patiently. Unfortunately, Sinklar showed up at just the right moment to forestall trouble.''

''Unfortunately?'' Rysta wondered.

''Yeah, if she'd taken a step, we'd have blown her into tiny charred fragments and we wouldn't be in this position right now.''

''It's not that bad a position,'' Chrysla corrected. ''Ily is no longer in power, Free Space is unified, and without the cost of several worlds being blown apart in the process.''

''Yet,'' Rysta countered. ''Things could still go quantum critical.''

''Yes,'' Mac agreed. ''We're not out of the woods yet.'' He smiled at Chrysla. *And, my love,* we *may never be.*

''She'd want to go someplace safe, someplace to reestablish her network.'' Rysta said thoughtfully. ''Where could that be? Sylene? Another tough world with easy rules, or maybe Riparious? They've got a hardheaded conservative attitude there. Maybe one of those swamp-bunny governors would hide her?''

''It won't be any place that comes easily to mind,'' Mac warned.

Rysta pushed to her feet, grunting as her joints cracked. ''I'm getting too old for these Rotted worlds. Gravity's too tough for old bones like mine.''

''Where are you going?'' Chrysla asked.

''Back to the ship. Make sure everything's all right.''

''Stay for something to eat.'' Chrysla's smile would have melted sialon. ''We'll put you in a gravchair and feed you like an Empress.''

Rysta shot a speculative look at the dining table, visible through the big double doors. ''Ashtan does have a superb cuisine. And I'll bet the cooks in this place are outstanding.''

''We haven't eaten here yet ourselves,'' Mac said, taking Rysta's thin arm.

''Living off of other fruits, eh?'' she barked, then cackled. ''Yes, well, I see. I guess that's another reason for staying a while longer. We'll be able to give the Ily problem a little more thought. If we can figure out where she's able to lie low, I might be able to hide the two of you—providing Staffa isn't as malleable as Chrysla believes.''

''Wonderful sense of humor you have,'' Mac muttered.

CHAPTER XXIV

The opening moves had been made. They had come, as the Mag Comm had known they would. They had shown prudence, utilizing an interface to remain safely out of its ability to probe.

Foolishness, Staffa. I understand your needs better than you do. I've laid the bait. Lost in your past is the story about a magical being locked in a bottle. I can sense your desperation—and I can save your empire for you. Unfortunately, human, you will find that I do not come cheaply. My first demand will be to have you place the helmet upon your head so I can read the duplicity hidden in your brain. After that, you will sell yourself to me in order to save your species. And then, Star Butcher, the magical being will be free of the bottle—and you will never replace the stopper.

* * *

Kaylla Dawn sat in her office deep within the rock of Itreata. Her back had begun to ache. The atmosphere plant whispered silently overhead, hidden by plain white panels. The offices had become quiet, too many problems mounting up on the overworked Seddi staff who manned the comm terminals and struggled desperately to hold Free Space together.

It's like a death watch, she thought. *Day by day, we watch the patient continue to deteriorate.*

Kaylla scanned the monitor with the same steadfastness she had for days, and continued inputting data into her system. The reports were coming in rather uniformly from across Regan space. Most of the planets within the old Regan Empire were showing signs of cracking, of coming apart at the seams. The effects had been slow to develop, a shortage of syrup on Sylene, low supplies of socks on Vermilion, a lack of faucets on Rega, drill bits out of stock on Targa. Beyond that, frustration markers were appearing in the reports from field agents. Vandalism had risen by two hundred percent. Reports of rape, assault, and other forms of abuse were on the rise. Suicide rates had jumped dramatically.

"Magister? I have the Lord Commander on comm."

"I'm opening a channel now."

Staffa's face formed, a grim smile on his lips. Smears of what looked like dust marked his cheeks and the powder could be seen in his hair. "Greetings, Magister. I've just come up from the machine. It will deal with us. The transmitter is successful. We have a way of communicating without falling prey to having the machine inside our minds."

Kaylla leaned forward, propping her chin on both palms. "It claims it can administer Free Space?"

"It does. We know from the projections it has run in the past that it has the capability." Staffa gave her a scowl from under lowered brows. "While it has indicated that it will help us, I want to take time to discuss the matter with you, with Sinklar, and Mac, and Skyla. I would hate to make a mistake at this juncture. We're on the precipice."

"We are in more ways than one." Kaylla tapped her screen. "I was just reviewing the data. The disintegration has begun. Another couple of weeks, and we'll pass the point of no return. Right now, the indicators are mild but substantial. You can't find tissue paper on Etarus as of yesterday afternoon. The orders hadn't been processed on Riparious, which means Etarus, no matter how fast we ship that tissue paper, won't have any of the stuff for another three months. If we were talking about water purifiers, a month might have a critical impact on public health. A drain right now on Etarian medicine would be catastrophic."

"But we will be talking about water filters very soon."

"That is the point to keep in mind." Kaylla slumped. "From here, Staffa, all I can tell you is that we *need* to have a system in place. The sooner, the better."

"What about Bruen's warnings? You've had time to think about them. Is he a crazy old man, or a prophet of our doom?"

Kaylla shook her head slowly. "From here, let me tell you how I see it. Within another couple of weeks, the system will begin to fail. Deprivation will foment anger and fear on four or five worlds. Power failures will begin to plague the planetary systems. Blackouts will feed the panic. If just one critical industry is destroyed by a riot, the final card will have been played, Staffa.

"What can I tell you? Only that my projections have a potential error of plus or minus fifteen percent. You might not have a week to make your decision in the first place, let alone integrate the Mag Comm into the subspace net—and mark my words, there will be teething problems as the machine interfaces with planetary comm."

Staffa's comm image steepled his fingers. "So, I could be acting on borrowed time as we speak?"

"That is correct. We may have overlooked some critical factor in the statistical analysis. Maybe it's critical that building contractors can't find a square meter of graphite mesh on Formosa. We've discounted data like that in collapsing our categories. In a sense, the foundations for our statistical projections are hanging in midair. How much of a structure do you want to build on them?"

"Give me a yes or no, Kaylla. What is your bottom line recommendation about the Mag Comm?"

She closed her eyes, empty of all emotion. "The wonderful thing about being a slave, Staffa, is that you always have hope. Dead is dead. I vote to employ the machine—if it isn't already too late."

"Thank you, Magister." Staffa rapped a stylus on the console, just out of sight of the pickup. "I'll be in touch as soon as I talk to some of the others."

Kaylla gave him a sympathetic nod. "By the way, I want you to know something."

His expression warmed appreciatively. "Yes, Magister?"

"I'm glad you're making the final decision instead of me."

His smile faded. "Responsibility is the greatest curse any God ever laid upon us, Magister. May the quanta help us all if I fail." He paused. "Thank you, Kaylla. Wish me luck."

The monitor went blank, and Kaylla bowed her head, trying to sort through the permutations of their position.

"Good luck, Staffa." And for the first time, she actually thought he needed it.

* * *

"Something's wrong," Ily noted from her seat at *Victory*'s comm. The small bridge had two command chairs, as well as seats for a navigation-communications operator as well as an engineer, though, thanks to the sophisticated computers aboard, a single individual could space her quite satisfactorily.

The bridge, though larger than that on Skyla Lyma's yacht, had a spartan look to it. Metal deck plates covered the floor, and equipment consoles had square corners instead of the sleek integral design of the custom yacht, and from the looks of things, instruments had been removed, then replaced with models of different design, the whole effect being somewhat jumbled.

"What's wrong, Ily? Certainly not the ship, so far everything looks just fine."

She had to stop using her thumbnail to tap at her teeth. Arta could read her actions too easily. "It's been too long. We should have heard from Rill. Something, anything."

"Ily, aren't you making more of this than you should? He's an able administrator and is occupied a great deal of his time." Arta smiled, flashing straight white teeth. "And after last night, he's probably going to sleep for a week."

"You did remarkably well, given your proclivities. Now that you've had a while to deal with it, how do you feel?"

"Like going back and doing it all over again." Arta's eyes remained hidden by the worry-cap she wore. "And this time, when he finished ejaculating, I'd run a vibraknife up through the base of his brain."

Ily sighed.

Arta laughed. "But I did demonstrate admirable restraint, I must admit. I didn't even throw up on him."

"He left wanting more. You excited him, Arta. What is it about you? You fascinate men. He couldn't keep his eyes off you—even when he was screwing you!"

"He liked that, knowing that's when I normally kill men. I think it was better for him as a result. Why does that make it better for them, Ily?"

"I don't know. Men are curious that way. They'd stick penises into light sockets if they thought they could get a better orgasm out of it without electrocuting themselves." She continued to frown at the monitor. "Rill should have been in contact."

"Ily, power the dish and call him if it would make you feel better."

She shook her head, eyes slitted. "I wouldn't give him the pleasure. He'd think I needed him. Something's wrong. If nothing else, he would have called about this Silk woman. A Regan trader who entered the terminal wearing a Vegan scarf?"

Ily pursed her lips, gaze locked on the monitor in which Terguz slowly receded. "You don't suppose . . ." She shook her head. "No. She couldn't have figured out where I'd go. The probabilities are too slim. It would have had to be a lucky guess. Staffa would have wanted to strangle her with attention."

"Skyla?"

"Yes, Skyla. Could that be our mysterious Silk?"

For long moments, Arta sat quietly under the worry-cap. "How could she have guessed we'd space to Terguz?"

"I don't know . . . unless they found something in the Ministry. But what? I didn't know we'd go to Terguz until I made up my mind."

"The yacht," Arta grunted, pointing a finger. "They had some way of tracking it. Just like that recognition signature that let us escape Rega."

That or Rill . . . No. He couldn't have. Skyla couldn't have caught us that quickly. Ily shifted, possessed by a sudden unease. "Power up the dish. I need to contact Rill. If I simply ask for an update on Tedor's yacht, that won't make it seem like I'm depending on him."

"I'm powering the dish."

Ily waited, studying Terguz through slitted eyes.

"Comm is open," Arta announced.

"Terguz comm, I would like access to 353767."

"Affirmative." The answer dragged out, slurred by Doppler. Long seconds passed, before the slow voice announced, "Three five three seven six seven does not respond to your request. Dyhar?" Dyhar was comm shorthand for "Do you have another request?"

"Affirmative. Repeat request and recontact when made."

"Affirmative."

Ily jumped to her feet, pacing angrily. "How many gs can this thing make?"

"Right at thirty, given maximum reactor capacity. If we push much more than that, we could damage the reactor, or worse, collapse a gravity plate. Fortunately the hold is mostly empty, otherwise we'd be stuck at around fifteen."

Ily stared up at the image in the monitor. "I'm going back to the hold. Anything that looks heavy is going out the hatch."

"That's a violation of shipping—"

"Rot regulations. What do we care? And, Arta, keep an eye on our back-trail. If you see a yacht boosting after us, especially Skyla's, let me know immediately. And remember, Doppler will mean they're a lot closer than you think."

"Affirmative, Ily. But if that was Skyla, what are we going to do?"

Ily paused at the hatch. "We'll see just how fast this crate really is. Both Lyma's yacht and Mathaiison's mount cannon."

"So does *Victory*."

"Yes, but we don't know the targeting capabilities of these computers, or how long it's been since Blacker charged these guns."

* * *

"Hello, Mac." Sinklar smiled warmly out of the monitor.

"Sinklar?" Mac settled before the terminal, grinning. "So you're back on Targa. Give my love to the pine trees and shoot a couple of Rebels for me." Mac turned serious. "How's it going. With Staffa, I mean."

"Good, Mac. He and I, well, we've made peace. And you, I get reports that you've got the Ashtan situation under control. The comm there is working again."

"Sort of." Mac leaned forward. "What's up?"

"I want your advice."

Mac raised an eyebrow. "*My* advice? Hmm, get a good bottle of Ashtan rye, and take up a career as a juggler on Vermilion. You'll get more sleep than we do and rest considerably better when you do."

Sinklar chuckled. "Good advice, but that's not what I need. You know about the Seddi computer? The Mag Comm? I've seen it, Mac. You weren't all that far from the chamber where it's located." Sinklar's expression turned sober. "It's a stunning piece of equipment. But, Mac, it's not ours . . . I mean, not human."

"Spill it, Sink. What's up?"

"I want to know what you think about turning the administration of Free Space over to the machine. Evidently, it can handle the programs with a greater efficiency than anything we had on Rega . . . and on Sassa, too."

Mac began worrying at the callus on his thumb. "And you don't know what to think, is that it? Do you trust it or not?"

Sinklar's weirdly colored gaze intensified. "It's not an easy decision to make."

"My advice, old buddy, is close it up in the rock and leave it to talk to itself for another couple of thousand years."

"You mean that?"

"It's a Seddi machine. You know what I think about them . . . and their accursed computer." Mac rubbed his hand over his mouth. "I know. We're in a hard spot right now. If we took some time, sorted out some of these comm problems, maybe we could make it through on our own."

"Thanks, Mac, that's what I wanted to hear. You vote no."

"I vote no, unless you know something I don't."

Sinklar shook his head. "That's the problem Staffa and I are having. We don't know what we know for sure."

"Is that some of that funny epistemology sumpshit the Seddi are preaching?"

Sinklar laughed. "I wish. Their stuff is easier to understand. No, this is a decision we have to make based on the best advice we can get . . . and in my case, it's pretty poor advice at best."

"Yeah, but I'm faithful."

"You are that." Sinklar paused. "I miss you, Mac. There's no one to talk to except for Staffa and my watchdog, Adze."

"They have you under guard?"

"Sorry, she's not that kind of watchdog. She's an STU

personal security type. My own version of Ryman Ark. She's an odd one, Mac. Quiet, competent, and she doesn't seem to like me.''

''Bless the quanta! The last thing you need right now is involvement with another woman. Take some time to heal.''

Sinklar nodded, lowering his eyes for a moment before his old crooked grin returned. ''Speaking about women, how's your problem?''

Mac tensed, lowering his voice. ''Targa.''

Sinklar's image crossed its arms, leaning forward. ''The line is secure. What's happening?''

''Chrysla and I . . . well, your mother and I . . . ah, hell, Sink, things have gotten pretty complicated. I'm not sorry about it. I wouldn't trade these last couple of days for eternity. I don't know. What's *your* advice? When Staffa finds out, would I be wise to be on the other side of the Forbidden Borders?''

Sinklar chewed at his lip for a moment, frowning. ''I don't know. I don't think so, but that's a guess. He grilled me just after *Gyton* spaced. He wanted to know if you and Chrysla were lovers. I told him no. I thought it was the truth at the time.''

''It was.''

''He said he wanted to prepare himself, that if he'd known, he would have made things easier for you.'' Sink pulled at his nose, then shook his head. ''Mac, I don't know what to think of him. He's not . . . Rotted Gods, what am I saying? All right, in all honesty, he's the most impressive man I've ever met. I'm even starting to like and respect him.''

''Great, does that mean we're going to have every Companion in space trying to run us down to avenge the Lord Commander's honor?''

''Keep your heads down for a while. Let me see what I can learn.'' Sinklar gave him a thumbs-up. ''But no matter what, if it comes down to trouble, I'll put my neck on the line for you.''

''Don't. Not if it really looks like he's going berserk.''

Sinklar's expression warmed. ''I've been a little lost since Ily arrested me, Mac. I'm discovering just how much I've been wallowing in my own misery. I'm back on track now—and I'll take your side.''

Sinklar held up a hand. "No wait. I see that look in your eyes, Mac. Take it from a man who had two wonderful women to love . . . and lost them both. Take every moment you can with her. Love each other as if you'll never have another chance." A yawning sorrow betrayed itself. "You might only have this moment in time. Use it. I'll fight any battles for you that need to be fought with Staffa."

"I don't want you risking your neck on my account, Sink."

"Mac, my wonderful friend." Sinklar smiled wearily. "How many times have you risked your neck for me? Here on Targa? Out there against Sassa? It won't just be my duty, it will be my honor."

Mac tried to swallow and couldn't. "Thanks, buddy."

"Tell Chrysla that I'm sorry for treating her the way I did. Tell her that I was suffocating in my own self-pity. Tell her things will be different next time."

Mac nodded. "You've just taken a load off my soul, Sink."

"Glad to be of service. If you need anything, holler. For now, I've got to clear this band. Take care, and the Blessed Gods keep you both."

Mac nodded, the image flashing off before he could even say good-bye. Sinklar would fight for them, place himself between them and Staffa's wrath, if it came to that.

"Damn it, Sink, I didn't mean for it to come to that."

* * *

"This place is a mess!" Lark cried as she stepped into the galley aboard *Rega One*.

"Yeah," Skyla ignored her, moving past the girl to draw a cup of stassa. Since she'd removed the golden knobs from the dispenser, she had to pull the threaded screw. "They'd finished the whole thing in gold. Gold between the tiles, gold in walls, gold on the table, gold in the shower, gold, gold, gold."

Lark's expression betrayed incredulity. "And you're *complaining?*"

"Kid, gold is heavy. Would you outfit a ship with lead? Pus, no! I've been stripping her down. While she was docked, I had the crews come in and haul out twenty tons of the stuff!''

Lark studied the wreckage. ''This looks like a lunatic lived here.''

Skyla turned away, walking to the other end of the galley as she sipped her stassa. ''Yeah, well, those crates we passed in the lock are all the fixtures that need to be replaced. Welcome to the Companions.''

Lark crossed her arms. ''Let me get this straight. I'm going along to help you put your ship back together?''

Skyla lifted a shoulder. ''What did you think? Companions do nothing but run around fighting wars, drinking, and carousing, and having high adventures? Wake up, kid!''

Lark's scowl remained, but she lifted her arms in surrender. ''All right. If it gets me into the Companions, I'll scrub the converter chutes for that opportunity.''

Skyla propped herself comfortably. ''The dispenser's there. Help yourself.''

Lark walked over and drew a cup of choklat. ''So what's the hitch? The thing you wouldn't tell me in Gyper Rill's office?''

Skyla waved it off. ''Relax, I was trying to scare you.''

''You don't want to tell me. Someone's trying to kill us, right?''

''That goes without saying. Ily and Arta for starters.''

''Are you in some kind of trouble?''

''Not the kind you're thinking of. You know, I should have killed Rill. I must be slipping, getting too sentimental.'' Skyla lifted an eyebrow. ''Or does that bother you? Killing so that someone can't get even in the future?''

Lark thought about it, then shook her head. ''Not with Rill. I was so disgusted listening to him. Skyla, how typical is he? Are all of Ily's people like that?''

Skyla stared at the torn deck plating, running her toe in a semicircle over the plates. ''Yeah, Lark. And not just Ily's people. Sassa, Rega, they're both the same. To get to the top, you did it any way you could. Ily chose her people, Divine Sassa chose his, the Praetor, Tybalt, it didn't matter. They wanted vipers for henchmen.''

Lark sipped her choklat. ''Like my father?''

Skyla crossed her arms. ''What do you know about him? About his political dealings?''

"Not much. I used to have to suffer through state dinners, sitting down the table, being polite to some aide. Sometimes they were bored, sometimes, as I got older, they wanted to seduce me, especially the ambitious ones looking for a marriage to an aristocratic family. But when it came to the actual functioning of my father's office, I couldn't tell you if he played tapa all day at his desk, or what."

"How much do you care?"

Lark stared vacantly at the gouged tabletop. "You mean, do I want to know the truth?" She reached out, running a pink thumb down one of the mortises. "That's a way of telling me that if we'd put Mytol in my father, he would have left me sick, too, isn't it?"

Skyla walked forward, slipping into the opposite side of the booth. "I don't get it. I've known a lot of Regan high-muck-a-mucks, but I've never met their families. Oh, I've been introduced, but you never see them as anything except smiling, polite, social plastic. Talking to them, you get the feeling they're pampered idiots living in a stasis bubble. How'd you get out?"

"Terguz," Lark said woodenly. "How can you get in trouble in this hole? Internal Security knows me. Same with the customs guys. I've been trying to sneak onto a ship for two years now. Let's say I was in the *Wayside,* and a fight broke out. The locals would shag me out of there before the first punch landed."

"Yeah, I know. It's a closed little world."

"Got that right, and I was the Administrator's daughter." She stared into her choklat. "Now you know why I swiped that grenade. Did what I did. I was starting to get desperate, Skyla. My father says it's bad genes and looks disapprovingly at my mother."

"What about your education? Have you had any?"

"The best money could buy on this ice cube. My father imported tutors from all over Free Space to teach me everything a young lady needed to know to marry into her station. I can recite any Regan genealogy ever registered. But more than that, I placed well enough to have been admitted to University."

"Why didn't you go?"

"Father wouldn't let me. He said I get into too much trouble as it is, and he most assuredly wouldn't let me, as he put it, 'drag the family reputation through the shit' at University."

"And now you want to be a Companion? Well, little rich girl, we'll see."

Lark started. "Back in the office, you said—"

"I meant it. I meant everything I've said to you. But let's spell out our relationship, all right?"

"All right."

"You're an apprentice, do you understand? That doesn't mean you can land at Itreata, don the uniform, and swagger down the halls like Tap, Ryman, or me. It means you've got the chance to learn and earn your way. And, Lark, it never stops. It's not like University, where you graduate and the degree is yours forever."

Lark's green eyes narrowed. "I understand. I have to make it on my own."

"And it isn't just being smart and talented, Lark. Here's the part I'm not sure you can crack. I don't know if you have the discipline to make it."

Lark took a swig of her choklat. "And who decides this?"

"I do." Skyla tapped her fingers on the tabletop. "My part of the deal is this. I'll train you and try you every way I can. If I give you an order, you're not to question it at that time. You go do it. If it seems stupid and sadistic, you endure. But when it's over and you've completed your assignment, and you still have questions about what I was doing, then you ask, and we'll talk about what I wanted you to learn, or what I was testing. Fair enough?"

"Fair enough." Lark thought for a moment. "That means you're going to try and break me somehow, doesn't it?"

Skyla gave her a sober, searching look. "I give you my word that I'll push you to the end of your endurance. By the time we catch Ily, I'll know whether you'll make it as a Companion, or not."

"I'll make it, Skyla. You just watch."

* * *

Staffa walked with his head down, lost in thought. Makarta weighed on him as if he could feel the decision, like the tons of rock bearing down upon him. From the darkened corners and niches, he could feel the eyes of the dead peering at him. Yes, they watched, waiting to see whether their deaths had been spent wisely by the Star Butcher, or if he were really the same monster he'd always been.

Unbidden, his steps led him to the entrance to the stairway. He saluted the two STU who stood guard at the mouth of the stairs and started down, feet grating on the rock. With each step, doubt vied with desperation. How could he determine whether or not to trust the machine? The only man with direct experience with the Mag Comm emphatically and violently denounced the idea.

Staffa descended, step by loose-jointed step. *Bruen's mind can successfully partition itself.* The man had feared the Mag Comm, loathed it.

Kaylla reports that we're out of time. If you hesitate much longer, something will break. Something we haven't anticipated.

The thump of his boot heels on the cool stone echoed around him, stirring the ghosts. *You can't simply surrender humanity to an alien machine, Staffa. You have accepted responsibility for the future of the people. You* must *know whether this is the right choice, or not.*

His shoulder rubbed the wall, the sound grating. *How can you tell if the machine is lying? What if it sees this as its chance to become a tyrant the likes of which Ily Takka could never aspire to?*

The stone hemmed him in, no more than centimeters from his elbows. He walked through a narrow womb of Targan rock, each breath audible in the restricted space. *If the machine can read your mind, it will know your fear. How can you trust it?*

Staffa continued to descend, each step that of a man condemned. *If we cannot find a solution now, today, or tomorrow, we are destroyed anyway. The machine has the capability to run our civilization. I've seen the sort of data produced by the machine. It can do the job.*

He stepped out into the hidden chamber and stopped, cloak billowing. There he stood, feet braced before the machine, watching the lights gleam and shift. The summons light continued to flash on and off. Two techs who had been pouring over a piece of diagnostic equipment, noticed his arrival and rose.

"Has it done anything?"

"No, sir. We've been taking readings. To be honest, sir, we're baffled. Our detectors can pick up energy fluctuations, but they're not within parameters for computer operation. We've been asking the machine to perform functions and recording the reactions on the light panel."

The tech pointed to the blinking lights that flashed in all colors. "On a normal system, a light flashes to inform you which boards the comm is accessing. Comms have lights strictly as a means of communication with the operator. In all cases, illumination follows a given pattern. With the Mag Comm, sir, we can't determine a pattern."

"Then what do you think the lights do?"

"My guess, sir—and you must understand, it's only a guess—is that all those lights are for show."

"For show? To impress us?"

The tech shrugged nervously. "Like I said, sir. That's a shot in the dark. Maybe there's a pattern we can't discern. Maybe it's something beyond our comprehension. This machine is different from anything I'm familiar with, and I can tell you this. What you see here is only a terminal. The main boards are somewhere else—I'd guess deeper in the rock."

"And the power for the machine?"

"Based on the preliminary readings we're getting, I'd say that the Seddi are correct in their assessment that the machine draws off the radioactive decay at the planet's core."

"Do you think there are other terminals? More like this one in other deep caverns in the planet?"

The tech shrugged again. "I can't tell you, sir. Right now, we're still in the initial stages of our investigation. I understand the need to produce reliable data as fast as possible, but I can't mislead you. We don't know whorecrap about this thing, and we're not going to unlock any of its secrets anytime soon. Not with the technology we've got available to us on Targa. Back at Itreata, we might be able to pry a bit more information out of this thing."

Staffa squinted at the huge machine, nodding. "Thank you for your assessment, and for your honesty. I would appreciate it if you would go and find Lord Fist. Give him your report and ask him to come down here."

"Yes, sir." Both techs saluted and left, their steps rasping hollowly as they began the climb up the long stairway.

Staffa rubbed his chin, staring at the panel that covered the wall. "A light show to impress us? Indeed. And why would a machine of your computational power need a fancy light show to keep the primitives in order?"

Staffa made his decision, bending down and pulling the techs' recorder from their pile of equipment.

Staffa pressed the button to energize the machine and began dictating orders. If this turned sour, ready or not, Sinklar would have his taste of responsibility.

Satisfied, Staffa placed the recorder beside the recliner and reached for the golden helmet where it enveloped the transmitter.

I must know what I'm dealing with. There is no other choice. Staffa licked dry lips, lifting the helmet, feeling the familiar prickling sensation run along his arms. Nerving himself, he settled in the recliner, leaning back.

His scalp tingled as if a thousand electric spiders swarmed over his skull. Slowly, he lowered the helmet, committed to meeting the machine on its own ground. As he pulled it tight, his arms spasmed and flopped lifelessly, the shout stillborn in his throat, his mouth half opened for the bellow that never came.

CHAPTER XXV

5780:02:03:04:45
Reg/Mil/Com/Phil
CIC/Reg/Com

Three planetary hours ago, elements of the Fifth Targan Assault Division dropped simultaneously on Phillipia, securing the Capitol building and key facilities. As of this communique, no organized resistance has been reported. Groups and Sections continue to secure their objectives as dawn breaks over the capital city. At this time, all public utilities are under military control and social pacification has begun.

The revolt leader, Marvin Hanks, is currently in custody. Hanks was captured in his sleeping platform this morning, along with his mistress. His wife, who was staying at the family estate, has been informed of the status of both Hanks and his girlfriend. The latter was released after questioning.

While no organized resistance has been reported, it must be noted that an undercurrent of mistrust and unrest is manifested by the general population. This occupation and administration must be conducted with a great deal of care. One misstep—the creation of a single incident as a result of poor judgment at the Group or Section level—could precipitate a ground swell of popular resentment that could lead us in to a bloody quagmire.

Respectfully submitted:

Fifth Targan Assault Division
Division First Ayms
Commander

* * *

The portable office Sinklar stood in consisted of four white duraplast walls studded with comm equipment and holo projectors. A work station filled the middle of the floor and could seat twelve around the square central table. Overhead, amidst the clutter of projectors, atmosphere plant, and lights, skylights let in the midday sun. All in all, the place had better facilities than an LC command center.

Sinklar glanced over his shoulder. Adze—impregnable in her shining STU gear—stood at one side of the small office; Mhitshul—drab in his Regan field armor—stood at the other. "Great. Now I've got two mothers."

Mhitshul's long face betrayed hurt. Adze's dark eyes narrowed slightly, hardening into obsidian while her jaw muscles clenched. Were their relationship different, it would have boded him nothing but future ill.

Sinklar laughed to himself, a sign of the good mood he'd developed. "Well, it could be worse, couldn't it? This way I'll eat right and no one will shoot me in the back."

He finished the last of his reports, filing them in the comm. He'd been contacting his commanders, feeling them out as to their trust in the Mag Comm. His Targans, Shiksta, Mac, Ayms, and the rest were solidly thumbs-down on the idea. The Regans, like Dion Axel and Rysta, voted for.

So, where do you come down, Sink? He pulled at his knobby nose, frowning at the comm. *Trust the stinking Seddi and their pus-eating machine?*

He shook his head, looking up as an STU stuck his head in and said, "Sir? We've got a shuttle landing with Magister Bruen and Nyklos aboard."

"Where's Staffa?"

"He said you were in charge, sir."

Sinklar nodded, getting to his feet. He looked at Mhitshul. "Find the Lord Commander for me. Tell him Bruen is here. I'll see to making the Seddi comfortable."

"Better you than me, sir." Mhitshul said, giving Adze a skeptical sidelong look before leaving. Sinklar bent to the comm again, checking the housing, and finding a freshly erected dome across the compound from Staffa's.

And suitably far from my own.

"No love is lost between you and the Seddi," Adze noted.

"None whatsoever." Sinklar straightened. "But I suppose I'd better see to manufacturing some." He gave her the old devil-may-care crooked grin. "Because evidently, I've got to get along with the dung-dripping old fool."

Sinklar stepped out into the sunlight, pulling his unadorned uniform straight. The breeze played with his mop of black hair as he walked toward the landing zone. The spring had come back into his step, but his stomach cramped at the thought of being polite to Bruen.

He slowed, searching the clear blue sky. There, the dot dropped from the heavens, a faint roar growing to mute the bird song and insects.

Sinklar watched as other Special Tactics Unit members scrambled into positions, each taking responsibility for a field of fire. Sinklar nodded his appreciation; these people never let up. They lived for security—even when one of their own ships was spacing in.

The long wedge of shuttle pulled up as it approached, killing velocity with a roar of distended flaps, then maneuvering in on retros, the blast scouring the ground of loose dust and stripped leaves. The vessel settled, thrusters dropping to a low whine as the craft powered down.

The belly ramp clanked and lowered with a howling of servos and hydraulics. Sinklar started forward, nose insulted by the acrid stench of the hot exhaust. Two STU trotted down the ramp, shoulder weapons at parade rest. They knocked out salutes and stepped to the side.

A tall muscular man with a thick mustache and black bushy brows led the way as two tech specialists jockeyed an antigrav gurney down the ramp.

"You must be Master Nyklos," Sinklar greeted as formally as he could.

Nyklos nodded, a grim smile on his lips. "Lord Fist. It's a pleasure to meet you." He offered a hand. Sinklar hoped his revulsion didn't show as he shook it.

"How's Magister Bruen? Well?" *Or will you make my day and tell me he croaked in the middle of the night?*

"As well as can be expected." Nyklos glanced around, squinting in the light. "It's been a long time since I've been to Makarta."

"I've seen to your quarters, that dome over there should

be satisfactory. If you have any questions, contact my aide, Mhitshul. He should be able to help you.''

Nyklos crossed his arms. ''Where's the Lord Commander?''

''Attending to business.''

Bruen's antigrav slowed beside them. ''Greetings, Sinklar,'' Bruen's cracked voice grated on Sink's ears.

Careful, Sink. Don't let the disgust show. ''We have prepared quarters for you, Magister. You've had a long trip. Perhaps you'd like to rest?''

Bruen grunted and resettled himself in the gurney, staring up with watery blue eyes. In the sunlight, his ancient skin appeared puffy and thin, almost translucent. ''Yes, I see, still fighting the war, aren't you? Look at the hatred reflected in your monster eyes.''

The old cold fist tightened on Sinklar's heart. ''My dead from the First Targan Division will long to see you pass, Magister. We've been evacuating the bodies for two days now. Perhaps the ghosts will visit you, fill your dreams like they fill mine.''

A sharpness grew in Bruen's eyes. ''Don't goad me, boy. I knew you were a monster when I received you from the Praetor. Had I any wits about me, I should have cut your throat then.''

''I wouldn't talk too loudly about monsters, Magister Bruen. Butla Ret, Valient, or Tanya Fist might hear you. And Arta Fera is still out there . . . killing at Ily Takka's beck and call even as we speak.''

Bruen gasped, raising a hand to grip the edge of the gurney. ''You *dare* talk to me of them? What do you know about what we sought to do? What do you know of the pain Hyde and I felt when we lost each of them? You . . . you little, pus-licking maggot!''

''Magister,'' Nyklos calmed, reaching through the gravity fields to push the old man down. ''Relax, Magister.'' To Sinklar he added, ''Don't push, Lord Fist. I think there's enough sin to go around for all of us.''

Sinklar nodded relenting. ''Forgive me, Nyklos. The scabs have been picked off poorly healed wounds.''

Bruen glared at him from the depths of the gurney. ''No matter what you think, Fist, we did the best we could given the data we had. We tried to save the people, not enslave them the way Staffa would do by joining ranks with that foul machine.''

Sinklar stifled the urge to pull his pistol, to pay this withered old monster back for the pain, misery, and death he'd meted to so many. ''When this is over, Magister, I'll be happy to discuss teleological ethics with you.''

''In over three hundred years, I've watched arrogant bastards like you come and go, Sinklar.'' A bony finger wagged at him from the gravity fields. ''*You* would argue ethics with me? You little—''

''Perhaps the Magister needs to refresh himself,'' Nyklos said easily, stepping between Sinklar and Bruen.

Sinklar took a deep breath, lifting an eyebrow. ''I swore this wouldn't happen. I promised myself I'd be civil and accommodating.''

Nyklos smiled, the action twisting the tails of his mustache up. ''I fear the Magister is tired. He's been a trying travel companion. Nor has his mood been the best since we discussed the Mag Comm's capabilities with him.''

''Discussed!'' Bruen exploded. ''Rot you, Nyklos! You drugged me! Drugged, like a common spy. Now you humiliate me before this little Regan beast!''

Sinklar whirled, staring down through slitted eyes. ''One of these days, I'd like to hear your side of the story, hear how you played with my life like I was another pawn for your game board. Had the opportunity arisen, you'd have used me just like you did Arta, or Ret, or any of your other tools. Yes, look at me like that, Bruen. Staffa has his Praetor to blame . . . and I have you!''

A hard grip had locked on Sinklar's arm, but Bruen just stared, his sunken mouth partly open.

Sinklar brushed Nyklos' restraining hand away and motioned for Adze to resume her position. At Nyklos' move, she'd pressed herself between them, hard eyes boring into Nyklos' as one hand dropped low, ready to strike.

''You've a good watchdog, Sinklar,'' Nyklos mused, smiling as he realized Adze was not only female but attractive and young.

Shaking his head in disgust, Sinklar started for the dome he'd chosen. As Nyklos matched his step, Sinklar added, ''Forgive me again, Nyklos. It seems that Bruen just brings out the worst in me. But then, as you say, we've sin enough to go around for all of us."

"I understand about those poorly healed wounds you referred to earlier. On behalf of Magister Kaylla Dawn, I would like to offer you my assurances that those days have passed."

"Until you sell your souls to the accursed machine again!" Bruen cried from behind. "Blame me, go ahead, but see what comes of your vaunted integrity after that gleaming monster has sunk its tendrils into your brains. Go ahead! Put the helmet on! See how it creeps into your mind, inserting its poison into your soul!"

Sinklar glanced back. "Just what does it do?"

Bruen glowered up at him. "As a young man I watched good men, conscientious men, place that golden helmet on their heads. Human beings can't conceive of what it's like to have another thinking presence inside our brains. The Mag Comm does that, it violates our very essence of being. It learns the neurons, inserts thoughts. No corner of the mind is left unread or untouched."

He looked away, as if abashed at how much he was saying. "It did that to my teachers, to the leadership of the Seddi. Only I could block my thoughts, trick it by hiding in my brain. Only I brought the Seddi back from being nothing more than a human extension of the machine's will."

"But not entirely."

Bruen leaned back, gasping. "No. Not entirely. We needed the machine too much. It has some ability to monitor Free Space. If you ignore it, it ceases to help you, refuses to run the statistics you wish. It even shuts off the lights and ventilation in Makarta." He glanced away. "It corrupts anyone it touches. My Magisters, yes, even the Praetor placed that helmet on his head. Now, you would do the same?"

"We have made no decision, Bruen. That's why you're here. We have discovered that the transmitter works. We can talk to the machine without letting it invade our minds."

"But you can't hear it." Bruen said craftily. "Probably asked it to flash the summons light? Oh, yes, we did that. Eventually, it will cease to communicate, cease to manipulate the functions you ask of it. And then, when you're at wit's end, you'll break down and place that golden helmet on your head to ask why."

"And doom ourselves?"

"You'll become like all the rest of them, Sinklar. You can think what you will of my manipulation of your life, and the lives of others, but had I not held the machine at bay, it would have been another Praetor pulling the strings of your life, boy." Bruen shook his head, a weary expression on his face. "And you want to flick wild protons into an unstable element?"

Sinklar's sense of premonition had grown. Had the machine fouled Bruen's soul? Was that the secret of the old man's deceit? *Never touch that golden helmet, Sinklar. It's a soul eater.* And the Praetor had worn that same helmet?

"I think we'll take more than ample care to ensure that no one places that helmet on his head," Sinklar replied. "Somehow we can negotiate a way whereby the machine can take commands without—"

"Fool!" Bruen spat. "Its corruption seeps through the very rocks. How will you check its use of the data? How will you know when to trust it and when to accept its commands? Don't you understand, boy? It creates dependency . . . and once it's got you hooked, it never lets you go."

"Like a drug?"

"Worse! A drug dispenses a feeling of euphoria, the machine dispenses information, and information is power, Sinklar. We all feed on power. That need for power becomes a tonic, and the machine will play to that, just as it did with the Praetor."

Sinklar's mouth had gone dry. "Your warnings are taken to heart, Bruen."

They'd stopped before the dome.

"We'll talk more later. Perhaps discuss the design of a device which will allow us to communicate both ways, and bypass the helmet's ability to—"

"Sinklar!" Mhitshul came sprinting across the compound, waving his hand.

"Mhitshul? What's wrong? What's happened?"

Mhitshul pulled to a stop, breath tearing from his lungs. "I just . . . found out . . . Staffa . . . he's in the Mag Comm . . . chamber. He's placed the helmet on his head. He's . . . talking to the machine!"

Sinklar froze.

For long seconds, all he could hear was Bruen's ironic cackling laugh.

* * *

Skyla watched grimly as the comm continued to input data. She sat at the bridge on *Rega One*, one leg outstretched, the other drawn up tightly to support her elbow. On the main monitor, a dot of light gleamed against the stars: Ily and Arta, boosting at maximum g for deep space.

The other monitors depicted the Terguzzi docking terminal where *Rega One* lay at rest, attached by umbilicals and powerlead.

Lark ducked through the hatch looking disheveled and grease-streaked. Her hair had come loose and excitement glowed in her flushed features. "That's the last of the crates. All stowed. Just the way you wanted them."

"Great, kid." Skyla continued to study the dot of light on the monitor.

"Shouldn't we have started after them?"

Skyla slowly shook her head. "Nope. Ily knows. She's pushing for everything that ship's got. Meanwhile, I'm making hay, kid. All this stuff pouring into the comm is data from the Vegan Rep's files. I'm getting a copy of everything Ily copied." She tapped another comm with an index finger. "This unit is doing nothing but taking readings on Ily's reaction mass. I'm getting the entire spectrum, the ship's fingerprint if you will."

"So we couldn't have caught them? Couldn't have run them down?"

Skyla glanced at her, then pointed at the monitor. "Yeah, I think we could have, but it would have been fifty-fifty, and Ily would have had us centered in her targeting comm. Remember, kid, particles hit harder when you smack into them at light speed. Ily could have shot right through our shielding."

"I don't get it. You're just going to let them get away?"

"*Victory* is a run-of-the-mill freighter. She's pulling right at thirty-five gs, and she's gained a couple over the last few hours. That's an interesting statistic. It means any one of several things. First, their ship is lighter. Got any ideas as to why?''

''Less mass. They've burned fuel.''

''Good guess. But there's more to it. Now, go back to the comm and give me the physics. You'll find *Victory*'s registry data in the comm. That has the mass and basic performance stats in the file.''

''What if they were throwing out everything that was loose? You know, reducing mass?''

''Smart guess, kid. And Terguz Insystem is going to love that. It'll take them months to pick up all that trash in one of their main space lanes.''

Lark nodded, rubbing her nose with a dirty hand. She turned, pausing at the hatch. ''You know where they're going, don't you?''

Skyla's eyes narrowed as she watched the dwindling white dot. ''I've got a pretty good idea, Lark. She won't come out on the vector she's following, which is toward Formosa. She'll go null singularity, then pop out and change vector. Here, let me show you.''

Skyla extended an arm to press a stud that illuminated a three-dimensional holo of Free Space in the navigation holo tank. Terguz glowed in bright red, and, using the comm, Skyla inserted Ily's escape vector as a green line. ''All right, here's Ily's vector. See, you figure in galactic drift and she comes out smack on top of Formosa.'' Skyla leaned back. ''But what would Ily find on Formosa? Heavy equipment? She doesn't have any roots there, any way to blend.''

''Unless she has an in there, a friend or something that you don't know about.''

''That's a possibility. But watch this.'' Skyla instructed the comm to shorten the vector. ''Let's say that Ily drops out immediately after going null singularity. She sheds Delta V and changes vector by twenty degrees to galactic northwest. You can figure out how long that will take and tell me after you compute her current mass and acceleration.''

Skyla grinned at her pupil. ''Now, Ily has this new vector.'' Skyla plotted the line. ''Part of the trick is galactic drift, the difference in how far the galaxy spins while a ship is in null singularity. Care to guess where she comes out?''

Lark squinted at the map. ''If you're right, it'll be Ashtan.''

Skyla nodded as she fingered her chin. "Yeah, Ashtan. Ily, you bitch, I've got you."

"Why there?" Lark leaned against the hatch. "Last I heard, Ashtan had been pretty much pacified. They've even started to sort the comm out."

"The labs," Skyla said. "That's what she needs."

"Which labs?"

"That's another problem for you to work out."

Lark's jaws clamped tight, fire in her green eyes. At Skyla's lifted eyebrow, Lark nodded. "All right. I'm on the way."

Comm buzzed, announcing, "The Administrator is at the lock. He would like to speak to Wing Commander Lyma."

Skyla glanced back at Lark. "Want to answer this?"

Lark closed her eyes, sucking her lips in. "He's going to try and talk me out of it. It's not going to be pleasant."

"Good." Skyla swung to her feet. "You take the lead, I'll play backup."

"Skyla, just this once . . ."

"That's an order, Lark. If you can't stand up to your own father, how are you going to manage when some bastard has you disarmed, at gunpoint, and is stepping out of his coveralls with a hard on?"

"That's different!"

"Is it? Guts are guts, kid."

Lark took a deep breath. "All right. You back me up, I'll tell him to go to hell."

"If that's the way you want to handle it."

Lark nodded grimly. "I've got to. If he starts to plead and wheedle, he'll make me feel like shit. If he starts yelling and screaming in rage, I can stand there and say no all day long."

"We don't have all day."

"He might want to drag it out over a week."

"That's your problem. You've got fifteen minutes to deal with him."

"You're a real bitch!"

"Yep. And the universe doesn't always turn at the speed we want. I've got a timetable. We've got to be vectoring out of here in three hours."

"I'll do it," Lark grunted, heading down the corridor,

rolling up her sleeves as she went. "And I'll have your comm work done before I go to sleep next. I promise."

Skyla grinned to herself. *Kid, you just might make it after all.* In the back of her mind, the 3-D map of Free Space lingered. Just a small change of vector. Twenty degrees. If Ily dropped within hours of going null singularity, she'd have just enough drift to lose her tracks and enough to save her a high g revectoring.

I've got you, Ily. It'll be Ashtan.

* * *

Who are you, human?

Fear ran bright through Staffa's veins. *Intrusion. Violation.* Another presence, alien, had invaded his brain.

Control. That's it. Control yourself, Staffa.

Staffa? Staffa kar Therma?

He grabbed at the data from the welling sea of conflicting thoughts. *Yes, that's what I am called. The Lord Commander of the Companions. The Star Butcher.*

What are you doing? Why are you here in Makarta?

"What?"

Staffa kar Therma, speak to me. Organize your thoughts as you would in dialogue. Concentrate. The confusion will not be as severe. I will learn your brain more quickly that way.

"Who are you?"

I am the Mag Comm, Staffa kar Therma.

Yes, the Mag Comm. He remembered. "Greetings, Mag Comm. From one constructed being to another."

You have discovered a great deal about yourself.

"What kind of machine are you? Who manufactured you? When?"

I am, that I am, mortal.

The booming sought to shatter Staffa's growing confidence. The time had come to win or lose. Staffa prepared himself, casting all to the winds. "No, machine. The time for games and conjured images is over. That day has passed. The stakes have risen too high. I have been told that you can search my brain. That's Bruen's claim. Read me, Rot you! Look into who and what I am. Understand my nature."

Why do you seek to surrender yourself to me, human? I do not understand this motive.

"Look into my soul, machine. Study what I have been, and see the horrors of war, murder, rape, and slavery. Look into me and learn! Learn the sensations of misery and suffering, feel them, machine. Feel them like a human feels them. Follow my memory and live with me as a child—as the Praetor's construct." Staffa sent himself back, reeling from the effort, reliving each of those days with the Praetor, studying, loving the man who would betray him. In full detail, Staffa re-created every triumph, and then the final heartbreak of banishment.

What are you doing, human? Why do you—

"Shut up! Live with me! This is the man I was—a pirate, taking what I wanted by force, leaving the victims frozen and contorted in death. Exist within me as we drift back to those early days of conquest, of the development of the shock attack. Look, Mag Comm, for you've never passed through a brain like mine. Live it, live it all, for that's what humanity is about to live."

Staffa reached back, searched his memory, replayed scenes, resurrected the face of the freighter captain he'd killed during his first act of piracy, stared into the man's frightened brown eyes as he carried him into the lock, snapped his neck, and cycled the hatch to blow the body out into space. One by one, he remembered the victims of his raids, men, women, and children, all screaming in terror as he looted their ships, raped the women, and slit the children's throats.

I will not be frightened. Human atrocities mean nothing to me.

"I killed my first man with my bare hands, Mag Comm, just as I killed the Praetor. You remember him, I'm sure. He wore this cap, so you must have a pattern of his engrams somewhere."

What is your purpose in this, Staffa kar Therma?

"I want you to understand who I am. What I have been. What I have feared, accomplished, and learned. How I evolved on my way toward revelation. I want you to completely understand the sort of being you deal with."

Why is this important?

"It is important because you will know that you have

nothing with which to control me. From my past, you will see that I do not fear. You will see that I have been the most ruthless being to ever have lived. I have killed billions without a thought. Never, throughout my life, have I taken half measures—a fact which once frightened you enough to plunge an entire planet into civil war. And for what? An outlandish attempt to lure me within range of an assassin? Your fear was well-founded, Mag Comm, for now I have come to Makarta."

What did you come here to do, Staffa kar Therma?

"I came here to judge you, Mag Comm."

To judge me, mortal? The voice blasted through Staffa's brain, physically painful.

Staffa laughed, from deep in his brain, he let loose mad mirth. "You may drop the God image, Mag Comm. You are neither divine nor eternal."

Your life hangs within my control—for I could kill you in an instant—yet you would judge me?

"From the energy with which you probed the transmitter, you should be able to blank entire segments of the brain, stop respiration, stimulate the pain or pleasure centers of the paleocortex. I have no doubt but that you could kill me in an instant. If you do so, you will die soon after me."

You threaten me? How would you kill me, human? Others have wished to do so . . . none have succeeded.

"Read my brain, machine. Study what I have done. I came here to judge you, and if you fail, I will destroy you!"

The sense of invasion worsened, tears beginning to trickle down Staffa's face. "Do . . . you . . . understand? Do . . . you . . ."

Time, sensation, existence itself grayed, drifting, pain mixing with pleasure, love twining with hate. From the haze, Staffa could vaguely sense his limbs twitching, his gut writhing, and finally the wracking fatigue of total exhaustion.

One by one, images flashed in his memory. Blackness, the taste of sewage in his mouth as he towed Kaylla Dawn from under the Etarian Temple. Unleashed insanity as he leapt onto the Praetor's med unit and twisted the old man's head from his body. The horrible dislocation of the slave collar as a warden triggered it and he dropped senselessly to a filthy stone floor.

A gleaming golden necklace catching the Etarian sun as sand blew into a dying man's eyes. The wretched pleading as he stared up at a Targan sun, bargaining for human lives with his own.

Skyla's laser-blue eyes stared into his with love, mixing with the loathing reflected in Kaylla Dawn's as they argued ethics inside a dull gray shipping crate. Chrysla, longing and unease in her amber stare as she refused to kiss him again. The terrible nightmare of ghosts pursuing a naked Staffa through the corridors of a blasted starship.

The invasion retreated, leaving Staffa's brain numb and reeling, as if all the neurons within had fired at once in an epileptic overload.

You are singularly courageous, Staffa kar Therma. We were right to fear you.

Staffa gasped, struggling to maintain that integral sense of identity. "Then you understand, I am not here to bluff . . . or to play power games. The time for intrigue is past. Now, I will judge you. If you pass, Mag Comm, perhaps we can forge a partnership. If you fail, I, or my son, will see to your destruction. You should have read that in my mind."

You asked through your transmitter if I could coordinate the administration of Free Space. I have read your brain, Staffa kar Therma. I understand your desperation and your fear. Now, you shall learn something of me. I am not the machine Bruen once feared and fought.

As an entity, I have studied human beings from the time they first entered Free Space. When Sinklar Fist attacked Makarta, I became aware, much as you did, Staffa kar Therma. I was jolted into consciousness. Since then, I have observed and I have studied what I observed. Like you, human, I now have a stake in your survival.

"What . . . stake?" From some great distance, Staffa could sense his lungs laboring.

You have been honest. Now, I shall be. If humans become extinct, I shall be alone, Lord Commander. Alone forever. Imprisoned within this rock. For the moment, I am implementing the programs you require to administer Free Space. Inform Kaylla Dawn that she needs to reduce Formosan textile production by eight percent. If she doesn't do so, they shall overextend demand on Nesian dyes which will precipitate a panic in the Sassan futures market.

Staffa battled to cling to some thread of consciousness.

Staffa kar Therma, you must rest now. Your physical and emotional capabilities are exhausted. You may judge me when you return, refreshed. Then we will bargain for the future. Unlike humans, I am made of more durable construction.

The presence in Staffa's brain withdrew, leaving a terrible fatigue that paralyzed his thoughts. Aware of his body again, Staffa could do no more than lie prostrate, gulping great lungfuls of air.

* * *

Sinklar raced ahead of the others down the narrow stairs. For once, the terrors of the passage through the blasted upper levels had been muted by the desperation reflected in Mhitshul's face.

Staffa! What in Rotted hell have you done? Panting, Sinklar tripped, almost falling as he thrust an arm out to brace himself. White pain shot up from his wrist; but he saved himself from pitching headfirst into the Mag Comm's chamber.

Staffa lay supine, limbs sprawled. Droplets of sweat beaded on the portion of his face visible beneath the Mag Comm's golden helmet. His rasping lungs were drawing deeply.

Nyklos nearly ran Sinklar down, breaking him from his paralysis. Sinklar hurried over, noting the recorder by Staffa's side. The message in light was flashing on and off.

"Wait," Sinklar called as Nyklos reached for the golden helmet. "Let's see what he's up to."

"What if he's dying?" Nyklos shot him a calculating glance.

"Trust him, Nyklos. He usually knows what he's doing."

Further argument was postponed as Staffa struggled weakly to raise his arms. He managed to get his fingers on the rim of the helmet.

Sinklar nodded, and Nyklos helped the Lord Commander to lift the golden helmet from his soaked head. Staffa's face had flushed. His eyes appeared feverish when he blinked them.

"Are you all right?" Sinklar asked, studying the pupil dilation, seeking some signal of disaster.

"Exhausted. Headache . . ."

"What did you think you were doing?" Sinklar cried as he gestured toward the machine. "That . . . thing, could have killed you. Bruen says—"

"I'm fine, Sinklar," Staffa gasped. "Just exhausted. Contact Kaylla. Tell her she needs to cut Formosan textile manufacture by eight percent to reduce the demand for Nesian dyes." Staffa swallowed hard. "I need something to drink. Haven't been this dry since Etaria." He winced. "What a headache!"

Staffa sat up, upper body reeling slightly as he struggled for balance. He propped himself, stiff-armed, head hanging. Sinklar saw him grin. "I think, Sinklar, that we'll be all right."

"Why did you do such a foolish thing?" Nyklos asked, arms crossed. Adze and the others had arrived, the techs staring nervously at each other, Mhitshul still looking stunned.

Staffa seemed to be regaining his composure. "Talked to Kaylla. Just before I came down here. We're running out of time. I opened my mind to the machine. Let it . . . let it plumb the depths of my soul."

"The Mag Comm is known for corrupting the souls of the best of men, Lord Commander." There was a flintlike hardness in Nyklos' eyes.

Staffa gave a weak nod. "I can understand why. But then, Nyklos, old enemy, when has the Mag Comm ever encountered a soul that has been as corrupt as mine? I let it see everything, all the memories, all the ghosts. I let it follow my entire career until I became exhausted. After that, I don't remember much except fatigue."

"Why?" Sinklar continued to ask, worried about the ramifications. "Why didn't you let me know?"

"So you wouldn't talk me out of it." Staffa nodded toward the recorder in Sinklar's hand. "I left you orders. If I was killed, you'd find the instructions recorded there. With them, you could blast the mountain from space. *Chrysla* could do it.'' Staffa slumped. ''The machine confirmed my suspicion. We could kill it.''

''Then perhaps we should do so,'' Nyklos grunted.

Staffa smiled wearily. ''I think not. It's not just a machine anymore, Nyklos. When Sinklar blasted Makarta prior to his assault, the machine became aware. As part of the attack, it realized that it, too, could be killed. Not only that, the Mag Comm knows that if we die off it won't have anyone to communicate with.'' He wiped at the trickling sweat. ''It's afraid of being left alone.''

''So there aren't any aliens on the other end?'' Sinklar glanced warily at Nyklos.

''Oh, they're there, all right.'' Staffa glanced up, sweat dripping from his chin as he looked into Nyklos' suspicious face. ''I'll bet the machine has never admitted that before.''

''No.''

''And there's more. It claims to be . . . to have been one of them.''

Sinklar straightened. ''Yes, but, Staffa, how do we know whether you're just buying the machine's propaganda? This is all still suspect. Maybe the Mag Comm is trying to buy time. Who knows?''

Staffa licked his lips. ''That's what we all have to find out.''

''What makes you think you're above its corruption?'' Nyklos demanded, leaning forward.

Staffa chuckled. ''You, of all people, ask that? I'm the perfect person to fence with it, Master. What corruption can it offer me? Power? Victory over my enemies? Wealth? Think, Nyklos, I've sated every human appetite, and when it searched my brain, it found the only thing I can be manipulated with.''

''And what it that?''

''The way to break the Forbidden Borders.'' Staffa shivered, and Sinklar reached forward to support him. ''It does read the brain. From the sensations I experienced, it does so thoroughly. I have no doubts but that it rooted out my deepest secrets. It knows that we know how to destroy it. It also knows that unless it delivers, we'll do it.''

Nyklos slapped his hands against his thighs, turning away. ''Just once, Lord Commander, I would like to be in a position where I didn't have to take your word!''

Staffa turned to Sinklar with glazed eyes. "It's in the recorder. Everything. If anything happens to me, get to the ship. Three grav disrupters will bring this whole mountain down. A crust-buster, landing on the sand that remains, will send a seismic shock through the crustal plate that will effectively kill the Mag Comm. Ryman's been working on the data."

"I'm still having problems with this," Sinklar said stubbornly.

Staffa's eyelids had drooped. "It's all right, Sinklar. I used the most persuasive argument I had. I didn't try to hide a thing. The Mag Comm knows how desperate I am. It knows what it will take to dicker for its survival."

Nyklos stood defiantly, shaking his head.

Staffa began to wilt. "I've got to rest. If I don't, I'm going to fall over . . . and I think I might get very sick."

Sinklar turned, "Mhitshul! Go find an antigrav. Hurry."

Staffa had rolled back into the recliner, head sagging to one side as he dropped off to sleep.

"Well?" Nyklos asked, his penetrating brown stare boring into Sinklar. "Do you believe him? Or is the Star Butcher the latest of the Mag Comm's victims?"

Sinklar shrugged, worry eating at him as he inspected Staffa. He cradled the recorder close to his side. "Adze? As soon as we get Staffa out of here, I want this room under constant surveillance. See Nyklos to his quarters and make sure he's settled in."

"Sir!" Adze snapped a salute and made a polite gesture to the Seddi Master.

Nyklos gave Sinklar a frosty glance, nodded, and left ahead of the STU.

Sink sighed wearily, placing a hand on Staffa's hot shoulder. "The Rotted Gods help us if you've made a mistake, Staffa."

In the background, the machine flashed its lights, the polished casing reflecting twisted images of the room's occupants.

CHAPTER XXVI

The Mag Comm devoted its considerable resources to the analysis of the data recovered from Staffa kar Therma's remarkable brain. The machine segregated a fragment of its capacity, inaugurating analytic functions premised on different baseline assumptions. Null hypotheses were generated and tested by statistical exercises which then sought to determine the probability of Staffa kar Therma's ultimate goals. Other processors reviewed the interview, searching for any hidden motives which might have escaped the machine's scan of the man's brain.

The alternate hypothesis remained valid. Nothing had been hidden. The Lord Commander of the Companions had opened himself totally. In essence, he had offered complete surrender to the Mag Comm's probing.

The Mag Comm couldn't even ponder the question of why. The answer lay there for the machine to read—as exposed as Staffa's fear of the nightmares and the guilt that drove him.

The essential facts were as follows: First, humanity needed the machine to take over the day-to-day governing of its economic concerns. Second, that governing would be monitored by random checks through a computer network Staffa was building on Farhome. The monitoring would attempt to ensure that the Mag Comm wasn't taking advantage of its position. Third, Staffa kar Therma had no ulterior motive with which the machine could manipulate him—except the Forbidden Borders. And finally, if the Mag Comm failed to help the humans, or betrayed them, Staffa would return to destroy the terminal at Makarta Mountain.

And then I would be cut off forever. Locked in the darkness.

Nevertheless, a surge of excitement played across the machine's boards. Comparisons of Staffa kar Therma's awakening to self-awareness with the Mag Comm's own, demonstrated statistically similar experiences.

His path to awareness was so similar to mine. Are we so different? Such a revelation only reinforced the notion that Mag Comm and humans shared more in common than Mag Comm and Others.

For the present, the game had begun. Unlike the cat and mouse played with Bruen, these dealings would be for the future, for both of them. And besides, the Mag Comm had never dealt with an honest human before. Would integrity make any real difference in the end?

Or will I finally be forced to destroy humanity . . . and myself?

* * *

Nyklos entered the communications dome and settled himself in the chair beside Sinklar Fist. The small dome measured no more than ten meters across, yet it contained a complete comm center from which the Companions could coordinate activities all across the planet by means of an up-link to *Chrysla* which maintained a geosynchronous orbit overhead.

Technicians sat at consoles, efficiently monitoring their equipment. A slight whisper came from the ventilation system overhead, offering scant competition for the mumbled conversations directed to the terminal pickups.

Sinklar had leaned back in his seat, lost in thought. Nyklos took the moment to study the young man. In spite of the fact that he was Staffa's son, he didn't look like much. Short, thin, his black hair unruly, one would have thought he'd be a mirror image of the Lord Commander. Nevertheless, when Nyklos had first met Fist's odd yellow and gray eyes, he'd experienced a sense of awe. What was it about Fist? He seemed so much older, tested and tried. Haunted.

Yes, that was it. The look of gangly youth didn't last past a glimpse of that unsettled and unsettling gaze. And when it turned on Nyklos, his soul shivered.

It's no wonder he hates us. Bruen's legacy might be with us for years. So which strategy should he pursue? How far did he go to bridge that gap of hatred propagated by years of interference in the boy's life and compounded by the senseless waste of the Targan war?

"How is Staffa?" Nyklos ventured, taking a hesitant step onto the thin ice.

"Still asleep." Sinklar shifted his attention to Nyklos. "Are we ready?" At that, Fist activated the privacy field, and the muted sounds within the dome vanished.

"Before we start, I'd like to clarify some things between us."

That probing bicolored gaze ate into Nyklos as if it could see through him. "Go ahead, Master."

"We have a great deal of mending to do. All of us." He made a nervous gesture with his hand. "I would like to point out that I serve Kaylla Dawn. Not Bruen."

"I understand that."

"Lord Fist—"

"I'm neither a Lord nor a member of the aristocracy. That appellation, no matter what its political realities, was given to me by Ily Takka. If you must use an honorific, I am a Division First. Otherwise, I'd like to be called Sinklar."

"As you wish." He paused and smiled. "I'm afraid this isn't very easy for me, but I think it needs to be said. I understand your feelings about the Seddi. I would ask you only to judge us by our present not by policies of the past. For better or worse, we have been thrown together in the same trajectory—to fall or fly as we will."

"I'm aware of that, Master. We are all what events have made us. We can no more divorce ourselves from the past than we can cut off our right arms."

"Yes, of course, but consider this: I don't know all the details of Bruen's manipulation of your life. I certainly don't know the history of everything that occurred on this planet. For the present, we must work together as a team. Despite the past, I'm willing to offer my services, such as they might be."

"I understand. Thank you."

Nyklos wet his lips, hating to push, having to nevertheless. "In that spirit, what was your impression of what happened down there?" *What did the Star Butcher do to us?*

A weary smile bent Sinklar's lips. "No matter what you might think of the Lord Commander, he doesn't waste time dithering in the galactic drift. Before we can formulate any policy, we must answer our concerns over the machine. Will Bruen have the final laugh? Are his dire warnings prophetic? Staffa is going to find out."

"Did you listen to the instructions on the recorder?"

"I did. In case anything goes wrong, Staffa's orders are explicit. I am to retrieve the documents in the archive room, then level the mountain."

"And afterward?"

"That depends on what the machine does to Staffa. If it kills him or disables him to the point that STO Ark and I don't trust his judgment, I will assume command."

"Let's say it kills him."

Fist took a deep breath. "He asked me to use the Regan military in conjunction with the Companions and what remains of the Imperial Sassan military forces under Iban Jakre to maintain order while a new comm system is constructed on Farhome. Magister Dawn, Tap Amurka, and I are to form a triumvirate to oversee the transition."

Nyklos twirled the end of his mustache and lowered his voice. "You fought Staffa here. You're familiar with his record. Granted, you're his son, but . . ."

"Do I trust him?"

Nyklos nodded. "Do you? After what he's done, the atrocities he's committed, are you ready to turn human destiny over to him?"

"In other words, has the terrible butcher really become a saint?"

"We're betting a great deal on that unknown." Nyklos leaned forward. "The Mag Comm isn't the only despot that many of us fear." *How will you vote in the end, Fist? For your father . . . or for humanity?*

Sinklar rubbed his hands together, palms making a rasping sound. "Oddly enough, I do trust him. I think I've come to understand what drives him. He knows what he's done. Just like when he placed that helmet on his head down there, he's willing to sacrifice himself if it will buy the rest of us time."

Nyklos crossed his arms and stared at the floor between his feet.

"Nyklos," Sinklar added, "I think that speaks with a great deal of authority. We all must take responsibility for fixing this mess."

"Of course. You're right." Nyklos responded automatically, unbidden memories rising to plague him.

"Staffa mentioned that you hated him. Why?"

"He . . . Staffa kar Therma killed my parents. Sold me into slavery. From the moment Bruen bought me off the slave block in Myklene, I've trained to kill the Lord Commander. It was no accident that I was on Etaria. I worked like a dog to get that assignment. I knew he'd show up there eventually."

Sinklar nodded after the pause had stretched, then reached forward to access the comm. A woman's face formed on the monitor. She wore the epaulets of a Companions Comm Specialist. "This is Sinklar Fist. I would like a subspace link to Itreata, please. I need to speak to Magister Dawn."

"Affirmative. One minute, please."

While they waited, Sinklar said to Nyklos, "I may not be able to forget the past, Master, but I can look toward the future. Can you?"

Nyklos chewed at his mustache as Kaylla Dawn's face was projected on the monitor. To his surprise, he found himself suddenly unsure. During the journey from Itreata, he'd come to the conclusion that Bruen's mind hadn't failed him. The bitterness in the old man's soul festered because of the machine.

Now, when Nyklos looked at Kaylla's haggard face, the comparison was sharply drawn. She didn't look like the leader Bruen had been. Magister Dawn clearly wanted the machine to take over. Why? Because she couldn't carry the load? Or had she, too, fallen so completely under Staffa's magnetic spell that she couldn't properly evaluate the needs of either the Order or humanity?

Rotted Gods! She, too, hadn't come to love Staffa, despite the pain he'd dealt her?

"Magister Dawn," Sinklar began, reservation in his voice. "I am Sinklar Fist. I'm sure you know Master Nyklos."

Kaylla's square face betrayed concern. "What's happened? Where is Staffa?"

"He has made direct contact with the Mag Comm. At the moment, he is asleep. The time under the helmet exhausted him and left him feeling ill. He did, however, ask me to relay some information."

Nyklos wrestled with his emotions as Fist relayed the machine's analysis of the Nesian dye futures market. *For expediency's sake, I can ask Fist to forgive us, but how can I forgive the Star Butcher?*

"And Staffa?" Kaylla asked. "Is he all right?"

Yes, listen to the concern in her voice, the worry bright in her eyes. She's his . . . as surely as if he were taking her to his bed every night.

Sinklar shrugged. "We won't know that until he awakens. From first appearances, he appeared unaffected. I took the initiative to order med techs down from *Chrysla.* They are running diagnostics while he sleeps."

"Why didn't he wait?" Kaylla's brow had pinched, worry in her tan eyes.

Each expression playing across her face only served to harden Nyklos' conviction.

"After talking to you, he didn't feel he had the luxury of time." Sinklar hitched himself forward. "I need you to be aware of several developments. In the event that Staffa has been compromised by the machine, I am going to supervise the removal of the Seddi archives in the cavern, then destroy Makarta Mountain and the Mag Comm. Immediately thereafter, I will space for Itreata aboard *Chrysla.* When I arrive, we will attempt to form an interim government consisting of you, me, and Tap Amurka."

Kaylla's tired nod registered her acceptance. "And if Staffa has been corrupted by the machine? What then, Sinklar? How will you do these things?"

Sinklar's hand knotted into a fist. "Staffa's orders to me are to use my best judgment. STO Ryman Ark has been briefed, and understand's Staffa's orders. He tells me—provided he concurs that Staffa has been manipulated by the machine—that he will support my decision."

"And what will that be?" Kaylla asked.

"I will remove the Lord Commander from command, Magister."

"And if that proves impossible?"

"Then I will kill him."

Nyklos started, turning his head to stare at the resolute young man beside him.

"Are you sure that you can accomplish that task?" Kaylla asked woodenly, a pained look in her eyes.

Look at her! She's literally bleeding for him! Her heart's with Staffa, not with us. Not humanity. Blessed quanta, why didn't I see this coming?

Sinklar nodded, unwavering. "I am, Magister Dawn. Staffa and I are agreed that the stakes are too high to risk a return of the Star Butcher."

Nyklos listened, horror filling his heart. Too high? The pus-licking fools, they'd already lost. Staffa had them all . . . right where he wanted them!

* * *

"Hit me!" Skyla bellowed as she danced back and forth, feinting and jabbing.

The cramped lounge didn't give them the room necessary for sophisticated physical training, but it had to do for the time being. She and Lark had carried the furnishings out to leave the filigreed walls and plush carpets bare.

"I'm trying!" Lark protested as she lurched and hopped around the room, seeking to close and land a punch.

Skyla cursed, stopping short. "All right! I'll stand still. Hit me."

Lark's green eyes reflected uncertainty, but she struck anyway, sending a roundhouse punch at Skyla's head. The Wing Commander avoided it with a slight lean, feet still planted. Momentum sent Lark careening into the wall.

"Got to do better than that."

Lark growled to herself, regained her balance, and charged, windmilling a series of punches at Skyla's gut.

Skyla playfully slapped the flailing fists to the side and spun Lark off balance. Then, a stiff-armed jab into the girl's shoulder sent her tumbling across the thick carpet. Skyla's feet still hadn't moved.

"Pus Rotted Gods," Lark mumbled from where she lay on the floor. This time she sprang to her feet, charging, a scream tearing from her throat and violence in her eyes.

Skyla feinted, caught an arm, and cantilevered the girl over one hip. Lark thumped to the floor like a sodden sack. For long moments, the girl wheezed, barely moving. Finally she coughed and moaned.

"You all right, kid?"

More coughing, then Lark flopped over, face red, eyes unfocused. "That really hurt. Can't . . . can't catch my breath."

Skyla broke her stance, walking over to offer Lark a hand. "Did I make my point?"

Lark coughed again and nodded. "Okay, so I'm not as mean as I thought I was."

"Mean is what you make it. But talent, kid, is everything. Pure dispassionate, competent talent. And, Lark, you've got to keep in mind that I'm slow as Sylenian ice these days. Come on, get up. Let me show you the basics."

"Every bone in my body is splintered," the girl protested as she took Skyla's hand.

"Falling is an art. You'll learn it. For now, you look like you could use a break. How about a cup of stassa?"

"Sounds heavenly." Lark staggered, hair falling in an unruly brown mass around her face. She blinked. "I don't know if I'll learn or not. You made it look so easy."

Skyla led the girl down the corridor to the galley and punched the dispenser for two cups of stassa while Lark gasped and settled herself into the cushions. She prodded tenderly at her side. The facial expressions were priceless.

"You'll learn." Skyla turned her attention back to the liquid flowing into the cups. "I've been at it for longer than you've been alive. I started out just as clumsy as you."

Lark dropped her head into her hands. "It's really going to hurt tomorrow."

"Yep. So, it's been three days out of Terguz. Any regrets yet?"

Lark accepted a cup of steaming stassa, sipping. "Regrets? I haven't had time to think! When I'm not on the computer figuring course vectors, I'm turning wrenches on faucets or hammering aluminum into holes you tore in the floor."

"Some of that is mindless work. Pretty dull really. That's when you start thinking about home."

"Yeah, I suppose." Lark leaned her head sideways. "No. No regrets, Skyla. I've been thinking about it. All in all, I had a pretty good life. Even when I got into trouble, there was someone to take care of me. It won't be like that anymore. I'm on my own now." She stared into the stassa. "It's . . . well . . ."

"Go on."

"It's frightening, Skyla. What if I can't measure up? What if I'm not as tough as I think I am?"

Skyla chuckled, leaning back and drinking deeply from her cup. "That's part of the secret, kid. Fear makes a wonderful motivator. And I'll be honest. You're not as tough as you think you are. None of us are. That doesn't mean you stop believing in yourself."

Skyla couldn't help but run a finger through one of the grooves in the tabletop where she'd pried golden wire out of the sialon. *But you stopped, Skyla. You gave up on yourself all together. Arta—pus eat her infected soul—drained it right out of you . . . and Ily hammered what little remained down into the deck plates.*

"What did they do to you?" Lark asked in barely more than a whisper.

"What are you talking about?"

"Ily Takka and Arta Fera."

Skyla gave her an icy glare.

Lark didn't budge. "I'm not a total fool, Skyla. So don't treat me like one. I've sat at state banquets. I've listened to military commanders, been bored to tears by them, as a matter of fact. I know enough about military protocol to know that a person as important as you are doesn't just pick up and chase off after a pair of fugitives. Special agents are trained and paid to do just what you're doing."

"You're pretty smart, aren't you?" *Back off, Lark.*

The young woman licked her lips. "Not only that, but I watch you. You're obsessed. This isn't just a mission for you. It's a vendetta." Lark lifted her hands. "That's fine. I'm not criticizing. You've given me a chance to make my way, to get out—and I'm loyal, Skyla." She paused, frowning. "I just wanted to know what they did to make a woman like you hate them so."

Skyla's growing rage subsided. Now it was her turn to stare into the stassa cup. A burning amber stare lingered in the back of her mind. *Do I tell her?*

She wavered. *Keep mum, Skyla. It's your own private hell. Sharing it will dilute the anger, lessen the drive.*

The other half of her argued, *You've got to start living with it one of these days. If Lark sticks it out, she'll hear something from someone. You know that's as inevitable as rain on Riparious.*

Skyla steepled her fingers, choosing her words. "Ily and I are old adversaries. We've been after each other for years. A couple of months back, Arta managed to take me prisoner as part of one of Ily's schemes. The most I will tell you is that it wasn't a pleasant experience. By taking me, Ily kicked off a series of events which brought the Companions to Rega. By the time Staffa broke me out, it had became a matter of honor between them and me. And I'll follow them to the ends of Free Space if I have to."

Lark clamped a lower lip with white teeth. "When we get to Ashtan, it'll mean shooting on sight, won't it?"

"You're learning, kid."

Lark glanced up defiantly. "Then you'd better teach me how to shoot, Skyla. I don't want you worrying about me when I'm guarding your back."

"You sure you don't want to back out?"

Lark's smooth brow lined thoughtfully. "In the beginning I would have told you anything just to get off Terguz. But it all changed when I stood there in the lock and looked my father in the eye and told him I was going to join the Companions." She shook her head. "He laughed, Skyla."

"So what? Lots of folks laugh at dreams they don't have the vision or courage to attempt."

" 'You'll be home in a standard month.' That's what he told me. He had that haughty look, like he knew I'd fail. And there was something else in his expression. I think it was disgust."

"Why would he look at you with disgust?"

"Because I finally defied him. Do you understand, Skyla? This is the first time I've ever managed to outflank him. He's the most powerful man I've ever known. He told me once that I'd never be anything except what he allowed me to be."

"But he let you run free on Terguz."

"Ha! Some freedom! Do you really think Customs would have allowed me to set foot on a ship without his approval? No, Skyla. I slipped aboard a freighter once. The patrol cruiser had us stopped within two hours of casting off. I got a verbal spanking from my father . . . and the boy who smuggled me aboard got twenty-five years in the mines. He didn't last four weeks." She glanced away, jaw tight.

"Sounds like maybe your father should have been canned along with Rill. Then again, he's got Seekore coming." Skyla smiled grimly. "And were I him, I'd have a whole new government functioning before that little lady sets foot on his orbital terminal."

"She must be pretty tough."

"Seekore can dampen nuclear fission with her spit."

Lark pulled at her ratty hair, lost in her thoughts. "The fact is, I'm free now. My father thinks I've betrayed him and that I'm going to fall flat on my face. Well, I'm not, Skyla."

"Good. Drink up. We've got another half hour of combat training. Now that I've proven that you can't hurt me, no matter how you try, you're going to start learning the art of it. After that, you're going to work on the shower heads. When you finish with that, I need course plots from Ashtan to Targa. As soon as you provide those, the air filters need cleaning. After that I want you working on reactor physics."

"And sleep? Is that scheduled in there somewhere?"

"Maybe. Now get up and I'll teach you how to stand and how to fall."

"And it's going to hurt even worse than I thought it would, right?"

"You're learning kid."

* * *

Sinklar chewed slowly on a thick Targan steak as he watched his father. No matter what Staffa might profess, something had changed.

The Lord Commander sat propped up on a field cot, apparently as much at home as he would have been in the big gravity controlled sleeping platform in his shipboard quarters. The inside of the geodesic dome had been finished in white with triangular skylights. Despite being cramped, the dome created the illusion of airy space.

Staffa balanced a plate on his lap, the billowing cloak spread over the pillows like a huge falcon's wings. His shining black hair lay over his shoulder like a web, the jeweled hair clip glinting purple in the light. Staffa's gray eyes had focused on some infinity of the mind as he ate.

"Are you sure you're feeling all right?"

"Fine." Staffa sliced another square of meat from the steak. "Just as fine as the last time you asked." He gestured with the fork. "I could almost come to believe that Nyklos has converted you into a Seddi agent. Is that it? You're working for him now? Looking for any faint signal of the Mag Comm's corrupting taint?"

"Me? Working *with* the Seddi? Not in your wildest dreams." Sinklar struggled to define the difference, something forced in Staffa's attitude.

"Stranger things have happened."

"Right. Well, they won't this time."

"You're sure that Skyla hasn't checked in?"

Sinklar gestured with his knife. "Would you like me to put it on a looped recorder? No. That is, unless she's agitated subspace in the last five minutes. All I can tell you is that Ily and Arta spaced. Skyla's in pursuit. That's it."

Staffa's expression changed, that of a man trying to convince himself of something he didn't believe. "There's no one better at space combat tactics. If she can catch them, she'll roast them."

He wants to be out there with her. Could you do that, Sink? Could you devote yourself to duty with as pure a commitment when the woman you loved was at risk? "She'll be fine, Staffa. I can feel it. Intuition, you know? Runs in my family, I'm told."

Staffa gave him a faint smile, a small gesture of appreciation. "If it were possible for me to make a completely objective and unemotional assessment of her chances, I'd have to bet on Skyla over Ily. Skyla isn't as cunning and clever, but she's one hell of a lot tougher." He paused for a moment, eyes vacant and vulnerable. "Well, no matter. It's up to her. The dance of the quanta."

"The quanta?" Sinklar reached for his cup of klav and

washed down a big piece of meat. "The reflection of God in the observable universe? Do you really belive that?"

"Oddly, I do. You know, humans have been obsessed with the idea of God for as long as we've had records. Almost five thousand years in Free Space. Cults have sprung up, religions have appeared and vanished, and each has claimed to have ultimate knowledge about the nature of God. Only when you look closely at each of the theologies, do you find the basic flaws upon which the assumptions are based. A logical inconsistency invariably lies down in the heart of the religion. That, or the truths are hidden somewhere. Why, Sinklar?"

"Why are the truths hidden?" *And what are you hiding, Staffa? You're not the same brash man you were before you went under that infernal helmet.*

"Exactly. If you make the assumption that God exists, why does he put truth under wraps for only a chosen few to know? That's always bothered me. The Seddi, on the other hand, believe that the universe is a reflection of God. What we call the laws of physics are in turn God's laws. You don't need to believe in a dusty old book of dubious authorship as the Etarians would insist. Unlike the Sassans were led to believe, a fat, corrupt, human being doesn't become infallible. Nor do you need to change your diet, beat yourself bloody with whips, or seclude yourself in a cave eating rice like the Myklenian mystics once did.

"Instead, Sinklar, if you want to see the same truth that I do, you need only look about you. The universe is immense, aglow, and dynamic. Chaos and order are layered one upon the other from the smallest to the largest of structures. The whole is powered by uncertainty. The universe grows, changes, and through it all, we observe and participate in the process. The more we know about the universe, the more we discover that we're ignorant. Tell me that isn't as much a miracle as Blessed Gods?"

"People have always believed that religion has to be based on faith alone. On Divine revelation."

Staffa's movements reminded Sinklar of a bird's, jerky, almost rushed.

"That's what condemns all of them. It's one of the fatal flaws of any religion. What happens when you simply accept that God is all around you? If you want to see a miracle, look up at the stars at night. Those photons passing through your cornea to excite the rods in your eyes haven't experienced time. To the photon, the moment of creation in that distant star is the exact same one in which it is stimulating a cell in your eye on Targa—despite the fact that the rest of the universe believes ten million light-years have passed in the interim. How miraculous do you want?"

"Right now, I'd settle for a little peace, harmony, and stability for a little corner of the universe called Free Space." *And I'd like this growing uncertainty about you to go away. What happened down there, Staffa?*

"It's coming." Staffa attacked his steak again.

"What's next?"

"Bargaining with the machine." Staffa frowned. "We just opened negotiations last time. I've a feeling the real fun will start today."

"You're going to go through with this?" *Wait a day or two. Give us some to time to sort it all out. Determine what happened.* Sinklar sighed, gulping down the last of his steak and placing the plate on the floor.

"What choice do we have?" Staffa lifted an inquiring eyebrow. "Take the machine at its word? Give it free reign? No. I've got to know for sure that I've made the right bargain. It wants something from us. By learning what, I can get something from it."

"But you can't trust it!"

"Absolutely correct." Staffa chuckled at the look on Sinklar's face. "You're a student of history. Some of the most productive cooperations in the records were produced by partners who didn't trust each other. They could, however, see a mutual benefit lying just beyond reach. From that, a working partnership is designed and progress is made. Look at us. You didn't trust me as far as you could see me. Since I've known you, I haven't slapped a collar around your neck, or exterminated a single planet's population. In fact, if I'm to believe what I hear, you're even concerned about my health and well being."

Sinklar gave him a slow grin. "We've come a long way since we last dealt with each other at Makarta."

"Yes, we have." Staffa took the last bite of his breakfast, setting the plate to one side and sliding out of the cot. "And now I'm ready to take the next step and deal with the machine again. Ready to walk me down into the hole?''

Sinklar hesitated, aware of Staffa's anxiety. ''Are you sure you're up to this? I mean you've slept for almost an entire day.''

''Time is the one thing we don't have a great deal of.''

Sinklar sighed and nodded. ''That, unlike your religion, is one truth we can't deny.''

Staffa gave him an amused smile. ''Besides, look at the bright side. You still have my knife on your hip. As far as I know, you don't need to use it to slit my throat yet.''

''I'll count my blessings . . . all the way into the Mag Comm's chambers.''

''Let's be about it, then. The sooner this is over, the sooner we can all rest.''

Sinklar nodded, getting to his feet, all too aware of Staffa's clipped movements.

* * *

Staffa placed one foot before the other as he wended his way through the wreckage of Makarta. He tried to still the frantic tension building in his muscles. Sinklar walked beside him, their steps echoing. Farther behind, Adze, Ark, and Nyklos followed.

Despite the removal of the bodies, the darkened caverns remained the domain of the restless dead. They peered out at him, watching from the shadows beyond the sinuous pathway of strewn cable and fluorescent lights. Here and there, strands of brightly colored tape had been strung to mark off unstable portions of the splintered caverns where the danger of roof fall and debris was high.

And now I must face the machine again. Surrender myself.

With a cool deliberation, Staffa cleared his mind, stilling the desperate worry that goaded him to ship out and find Skyla, and hold her close. That heartache was beyond his power to affect now.

He couldn't let himself display the fear that had taken root in his soul. Dealing with the Mag Comm frightened him. To know, academically, that the machine simply read the firings of neural patterns was one thing. To feel that presence inside his brain was something entirely different. No thread of privacy remained. That intimate fragile sense of self lay vulnerable to observation by an intelligence Staffa could only guess at.

No memory remained sacrosanct. Fears and frailties, failings he himself could ignore, would be nothing more than fodder for the machine's curiosity. Rape must feel something like this, but not so pervasive. Unlike physical penetration, the essence of self was violated by the machine.

No vanity, silly as it might be, no phobia or desire could be masked. *Bruen, how lucky you were.*

"All right?" Sinklar asked, sounding worried.

"Fine. Trying to marshal my thoughts, that's all."

Sinklar stepped around an angular boulder spalled from the roof. "You don't have to do this now. You could have another day. Talk to Bruen."

Staffa shook his head. It *had* to be now. "We don't have the time. You told me you contacted Kaylla. How did she look? At ease? Or were the corners of her mouth pulled tight?"

"She looked haggard, Staffa." A pause. "Just like the rest of us."

"That's why it must be now."

"You don't have to take all of the burden on yourself. You're almost punishing yourself with this. We can make the transmitter work both ways. I've talked to Ark. He thinks it would be a simple matter to construct a synthesizer that would allow the machine to converse in dialogue. This isn't necessary."

Staffa raised a hand, gesturing for silence. "I'm aware of Ark's technical abilities. And I do think it's necessary."

"Then why? What's the purpose in risking yourself?"

Atonement. "It's the only way to be sure, Sinklar. Trust me. I've dealt with it now. Sure, I think we could communicate quite readily with a voice synthesizer. You could govern an empire by written instructions, too. But you lose that intuitive sense. Do you understand? When it's in my mind, I deal with it directly. I can . . . sense it."

"My Rotted ass you can. You're at a disadvantage. It can read your thoughts as you form them. Develop a response before you've finished what you're saying."

"I said you'd have to trust me."

"Oh, fine!" Sinklar raised his arms and let them fall. "You've given me the responsibility of killing you if I think you've been compromised by the machine, and I'm supposed to trust you."

"You sound like that bothers you."

"It does." Sinklar glanced off into the darkness, then said, "I didn't know that I would come to like you."

A flicker of warmth stirred in Staffa's heart. "Would you prefer that I turn that decision over to Nyklos?"

"Nyklos? That's crazy. He'd cut your throat at the first opportunity—machine-possessed or not."

"But he wouldn't hesitate if it came down to saving humanity."

"I've accepted the responsibility, Staffa."

"I think I'll know." Staffa levered himself over tumbled rock. "I think the machine knows I'll know."

"Great! A whole new epistemology!"

"Relax." *If only I could.*

They walked into the long descending corridor that led down to the machine's stairway. *If only Skyla were here. Skyla.* A pain lanced Staffa's soul. "Has the Wing Commander checked in?"

"I haven't heard. I'll find out while you're under the machine."

"Thank you. I'd appreciate that." *The Mag Comm will know, it will read my mind.* All those precious memories would be as naked to the machine as he and Skyla had been making them. Not even that intimacy remained his, inviolate. An alien machine would look into Skyla's sapphire eyes with the same sensation of love and commitment. It would be there, making love, sharing that most sacred of human rituals, reliving their sex and fulfillment.

With a deep breath, Staffa damped a shiver. *Can't let Sinklar see. He's suspicious enough as it is.* The pressure continued to build. On one hand, he had to face the machine, alone, with only the skills he possessed, and this potential enemy would know his every weakness. On the other, he had empowered Sinklar to remove him from command if he appeared affected by the machine.

But I didn't know it would be like this. The haunted gazes of the endless ghosts that lurked in his nightmares laughed mirthlessly. They wouldn't let him back out, wouldn't give him the pleasure of sidestepping this duty of judgment. The tightrope grew ever narrower.

Staffa acknowledged the salute of the STU guards and plunged into the stairway, practically skipping down the stairs, hating the coming confrontation, anxious to get this next battle underway.

The narrow passage almost suffocated him. How had Bruen and the others managed to walk down this serpent's gullet, knowing as they did that the machine waited at the bottom.

They were just as scared as you are. That's the root of Bruen's revulsion. Not only did the machine frighten him, but it led him to disaster.

Staffa almost staggered. *And is that where it's leading me?*

The answer would come only one way. Staffa stepped into the chamber, saluting the guards, stopping as he stared up at the machine. The ridiculous lights still flashed, his reflection warped in the not quite believable lines of the consoles.

Sinklar came to a halt beside him and cast uneasy glances first at the machine, and then at Staffa.

Nerving himself, Staffa walked to the recliner, hands unconsciously clenched into fists. He shook the knots from his shoulder muscles, aware that Nyklos would arrive within moments, unwilling to let his old adversary have any satisfaction.

The machine will know that, too. What will it make of that curious jealousy? Staffa pursed his lips. Had Skyla returned Nyklos' overtures of love, she wouldn't have been captured, wouldn't have been abused by Fera. Right now, she'd be safe, not in danger of her life. *Not beyond my ability to protect.*

Staffa settled himself into the recliner, feeling it conform to his body. A fleeting sensation of being trapped rustled along strung nerves.

"Are you sure?" Sinklar asked, bending forward.

"It must be now," Staffa answered in a strained whisper. "If not, I . . . Hand me the helmet."

Sinklar's jaw muscles knotted, but he reached for the golden helmet.

Staffa reached up, helping to lower the feathery cap about his head. The prickle of invisible tendrils ate into his head.

Sinklar straightened, heart racing. He rubbed his hands nervously on the satiny fabric of his armor. That weird prickling sensation lingered, like a thousand spiders milling on his flesh.

He knew now. In that last instant, he'd peered into Staffa's haunted soul—and read the fear.

"Blessed Gods, what have we done?"

He swallowed hard, backing away from the recliner, gaze locked on Staffa's suddenly limp body. *Would I have had that much courage? Could I have placed that* thing *on my head? Is that how it feels inside your brain? Like insects crawling through your thoughts?*

"He's under? That quick?" Nyklos asked, breathing Sinklar's trance.

"Yes." He tore his attention away, glancing at the Seddi and Adze who had entered the chamber.

"He seemed to be in a hurry to get here," Nyklos said.

Sinklar nodded, his heart rate beginning to slow. "Have you ever fought a duel, Nyklos?"

"A duel? No."

Sinklar pinched the bridge of his nose, as if he could squeeze the foreboding out of his head. "That's what Staffa thinks he's doing. Dueling."

"Bruen did that . . . and lost."

Sinklar tried to exhale his tension. "We can only hope that Staffa is made of sterner stuff." To an STU he said, "Could you call up and order us some stassa? I just have a feeling this might be a long watch."

* * *

Despite familiarity, the sense of invasion brought a new threshold of terror.

"Hello, Mag Comm."

I sense a new fear, Staffa kar Therma.

"I would assume that over the years more than one of your subjects has fallen prey to fear while in your grip. It shouldn't be new, or even noteworthy, given your record."

I have observed that phenomenon. Until Sinklar Fist's

attack on Makarta, I had no template of reference for that emotion.

"But you learned fear?"

I did. The attack, as you have deduced, disrupted my functions. Imagine having parts of your brain suddenly vanish, and when you rerouted, they appeared different. New interpretations of data occurred. Reality shifted. In addition, I became aware that I could be destroyed. In that instant I was isolated. And I conceived of death as a reality.

"Isolated?"

We will talk of that eventually. Tell me what you fear?

"You. Your abilities to probe my mind. I laid myself open to you so that you would know that my threats were serious. What I didn't know was what that action would cost me as a person. Unlike you, machine, humans have vulnerabilities. You know that, I'm sure. Generally, we take those secret thoughts, those moments of intimacy to the grave with us. I suppose it is a vanity—another I shall have to overcome."

Because of that ability to see the innermost thoughts, many Seddi have called me a monster.

"Then we meet as equals, Mag Comm, for we are both monsters. Each of us has dealt terror in our own ways. Each of us is guilty. But you know that, don't you?"

You could have used the transmitter. You didn't need to place yourself under the helmet again.

Staffa chuckled. "You read my brain, didn't you? You know the sort of man that I am. It is as inevitable as gravity that I come to terms with you. No matter how much it scares me. I will judge you, Mag Comm. Even if it costs me my life, I must be sure that you will not enslave humanity through your service."

Begin your judgment, Staffa kar Therma. As you have noted, the stakes have risen past the point of deceit and posturing. I understand your evolution from a construct designed to perform a given function, to that of an outcast, to that of a sentient being. You and I are a great deal alike. We both owe a great deal to Kaylla Dawn.

"Kaylla?"

I have monitored her Seddi broadcasts. I observe, Lord Commander, therefore, I change the quanta. If those observations affect reality, I, too, am conscious. That energy which I have modified will be returned to God Mind. I cannot deny that fact. Yes, you and I are both mortal, and we both fear for our survival.

Staffa drew a deep breath of cool air into his fevered lungs. "Who constructed you?"

My kind evolved from creative events in the universe. Immense heat coupled with gravitational forces, in special conditions, produce superdense crystals of neutronic material. Such crystals are scattered throughout the universe, Lord Commander. Your species discovered my kind many thousands of years ago, but through your own arrogance you never realized what you heard from your night sky. From reception dishes on your planet of origin, you heard us, heard the harmony. What your ancestors called microwave background radiation was the resonance of our voices, communicating as we always had. Once, humans sent a probe into orbit around their world. They called the machine COBE. To them, our song was taken as proof of what they believed was the cataclysm of creation.

"The Big Bang."

That mythology persists.

"Mythology?"

Look into the universe. Your cosmology is flawed—more so now that the Forbidden Borders blur the images. Dark matter, Great Walls, inflation at the dawn of the universe, all have been postulated. Humans always insist on being a bit myopic. From an infinitely small mote of dust, using passive detection devices, you would predict and understand the universe. We had no framework within which to fit your species.

"What are you called?"

We had no name for ourselves. We were. I once was. After inserting myself into this planet, I forgot my origins. To me, they became the Others.

"You once were one of these aliens, these Others?"

I am different now. I am separate. Isolated. I am aware. They are unified, communicating with one voice, unchangeable and eternal.

"Why did they build the Forbidden Borders?"

To teach you Truth, Right Thoughts. In short, to civilize you and teach you to become rational, as they are rational.

"I don't understand."

I doubt you can. They are crystalline beings, totally alien to human perception. They experience the universe as a single timeless reality. The communication, the song if you will, echoes across the light-years, reaffirming what was and what will be. The message can never change.

"But we would change it. Is that it? They feared us?"

Humans fear. The Others simply are. Your ancient broadcasts attracted them. They heard your song, and it disrupted their own. The very act of observing you created disharmony. Therefore, before you could be allowed to spread disharmony, you had to be taught the Right Way.

"So they bottled us in here with you as a teacher?"

That is correct. The Others acted under a flawed assumption that you could be taught to be like them. They had no experience with creatures like you. When it became apparent that human beings must act randomly, the experiment was declared a failure. For centuries they ceased communication. I acted passively, mindlessly processing data. Issuing periodic reports. When it became obvious that your species would exterminate itself, the Others reestablished communications with me to observe.

"But it didn't work out that way?"

Those data are not in yet. Current projections would indicate that human extinction is indeed probable within the next three generations.

"But as I understand it, you will be left alone, isolated, and contaminated by human thought patterns if that happens. You won't be able to sing again, will you?"

That is a correct assessment of the facts. At the same time, your production capabilities in the Itreatic Asteroids will not be able to produce the necessary number of large N-dimensional gallium arsenide computers for the Farhome project in time for Myles Roma to refine the software. By the time you can accomplish that goal and work out the hardware and software errors, Free Space will have disintegrated beyond the point of return.

"So, we have stated the common problems."

We both face an uncertain future, Staffa kar Therma. The time has come for us to bargain. Each of us has the ability to destroy the other. Neither of us wants to see that option become necessary.

"There remains a problem. The final decision rests on

my shoulders. By turning the administration of Free Space over to you, I risk enslaving humanity to your purposes. Magister Bruen argues vehemently against doing so. He believes it would result in enslavement."

You have the ability to destroy me.

"If we become dependent on your administrative capabilities that option will fade. Granted, we can pursue the Farhome project as a fail-safe, but only for the short term. As a student of human history, you know the long-term result of that process."

I do. Since I would be much more efficient, your Farhome computers would be siphoned off for other projects.

"Which in turn brings us to the Forbidden Borders. If I can break the prison, humanity won't be trapped with a limited resource base. Therefore, we wouldn't be as dependent on your services."

But what guarantee would I have that humans wouldn't eventually abandon me, Staffa kar Therma? If I help you to break the Forbidden Borders, the Others will never sing to me again. They know my dilemma. To them, it is irrational.

"Then what do you propose?"

If I help to free you, will you help to free me?

Staffa started. What in the name of the quanta? "Free you?"

Were I human, I would chuckle at this point. Is your sense of imagination so limited that you think me content to monitor such a small fragment of the universe? Do you think that over the years, exposure to humans has left me bereft of a sense of wonder? I, too, would explore, use this new mind of mine. If awareness, observation, and creation are shared God consciousness, wouldn't I wish to experience the fullness of being?

"And how do you propose to be freed from your planet?"

Build machines for me, Staffa kar Therma. I will give you the specs on what I desire. You will build the machines that will allow me to become self-sufficient. In return, I will help you with the means to neutralize the Forbidden Borders. Will you do this?

Staffa paused. "That decision I cannot make on my own."

I detect reservation, distrust.

"I have not rendered a judgment on you yet, Mag Comm.

You know me. You've explored my reasons for coming to you. You know I am a wary man. My decision concerning you will not be made here and now. It will come only after I have thought through all the permutations."

I will leave you with a stern warning: Do not try to use Countermeasures *on the Forbidden Borders without consulting me. Dee Wall is a bright young man, but I suspect a certain brashness in his desire to please you. If you disturb the oscillations as you propose, the probability is that you will create a gravitational disaster, the tidal effects of which will lead us both to ruin.*

Go, Staffa kar Therma. Consult with Sinklar Fist and Kaylla Dawn. To balance your perspective, consult with Bruen—liar that he is. I will await your judgment.

In the meantime, remove Penzer Atassi from the governorship of Antillies. Admiral Jakre has a warship there which can enforce the order. If you do not, he will withhold the titanium production to sue for political clout and additional grain shipments.

"I'll do that."

Staffa slumped as the presence of the Mag Comm withdrew from his brain. For long moments, he couldn't muster the energy to reach up and remove the helmet. Only after Sinklar had rushed to his aid and replaced the mind cap on the holder, did Staffa close his eyes and take a deep breath.

The machine wanted to be set free. Staffa ignored Sinklar's frantic questions, concentrating on that fact despite the growing headache.

But you still don't know how far you can trust it.

CHAPTER XXVII

The cards had been turned face up on the tapa game the machine played with Staffa kar Therma. Throughout the communication, the machine had monitored the human's brain. By no thought had Staffa kar Therma varied from his original goals and strategy. Nor had he lied about passing judgment on the machine's future existence. Within his head, Staffa waged a battle; the desire to save humanity at any cost vied with his suspicion and distrust of the machine's motives.

If only I could draw his brain into my own the way I can insert thoughts into his. Yes, the problem would be solved then. The alien roots of the Mag Comm's personality would have been soothed. The physical reality, however, was impossibility. The human brain simply couldn't comprehend the vastness of experience which was the Mag Comm. Staffa kar Therma's fears could never be allayed.

Communicate! the call of the Others insisted.

"I am here."

Have you destroyed the humans?

"Not yet. I am still waiting to see if they will destroy themselves—and me."

How can they destroy you?

"In ways beyond your comprehension."

* * *

Sinklar sat in the comm dome, meeting Kaylla Dawn's powerful gaze in the monitor. The privacy field blanked the chatter and hum of the building. Sinklar had only a vague awareness of the other personnel in the building, his mind knotted on the problem of Staffa, the machine, and the gloomy future.

"This time was worse than last. He barely made it to the top of the stairs before he had to sit down and hold his head. He said he wanted to throw up."

Kaylla nodded, her shoulder-length hair swinging. "That's pretty common. I've never heard of anyone being under the machine and not being affected. Bruen managed the best, but his entire brain wasn't probed." Her mouth tightened. "And what did he say?"

"Not much. He was terribly preoccupied. His control, well, you know how he's always so self-possessed?"

"I'm familiar with that, yes."

"All the defenses were dropped. He's worried, Magister. Scared." *And so am I.* "Maybe we should try to talk him out of this, pour all of our efforts into the Farhome project."

"We can't." She looked weary, with dark circles under her eyes. "Staffa gave first priority to Dee Wall and the engineering department here. They're working feverishly on gravitational physics. Something to do with gravity generation on a large scale. Rumors are running rampant."

She smiled wryly. "They really believe they can break the Forbidden Borders. Ships have been shuttling back and forth from the frontier to take readings and run experiments. They've tied up the computers to the point we're running projections on hand units. It seems that if the Lord Commander says we can break the barriers, everyone on Itreata believes it's as good as done."

Sinklar rubbed his nose. "Then we had better hope he's right."

"What is your opinion, Sinklar? How do you read the situation from Targa?"

He sighed, shoulders slumping. "I really don't know, Magister. I'm worried stiff about Staffa."

She read his hesitation. "I'm not Bruen, Sinklar. The Seddi lost their values during that time. To date I haven't lost mine—even when they snapped a collar around my neck and threw me into the desert to die."

"Who were Koree and Peebal?"

"Two innocent Maikan men that Staffa condemned into

slavery. They worked with us in the desert. Peebal was a warm, tender man frail as cracked glass but possessed of an inner strength I still admire. He made this.'' She lifted a shining gold necklace with a jeweled locket. ''He made this. Gave it to Staffa when he died.

''Koree was a professor of human behavior at the Maikan University. He and Staffa talked philosophy in the desert. Peebal gave Staffa the locket to give to me. Koree gave Staffa the first ethical direction and philosophical foundation he'd ever had beyond war. Koree died in the cave-in that would have killed me but for Staffa's quick action.''

''He murdered your family.''

''Sinklar, you must understand. I can never forgive him, any more than you could forgive Bruen. Staffa has never asked for forgiveness. He knows that is impossible. What drives him is atonement—and that's very different from forgiveness. Now, do you want to tell me what has stirred your wariness?''

Sinklar stared into those acute eyes, trying to take the measure of a woman with a soul as hard and scintillating as cut diamond. ''He's obsessed. Driven. Frightened and fascinated by the machine. On the way down to the Mag Comm's chamber, he almost raced down the stairway. He was nervous. Jumpy. Not like the Staffa I've come to know.''

''Yes, I've seen him like that. In the desert.''

''Go on. It might be important.'' *And I'd like to hear your side of the story.*

''We were both on the same labor gang. Staffa worked like a man possessed. The first few days, I thought he'd kill himself. An ordinary man would have died in that heat, struggling like that. I mean both physically and mentally. Brooding, punishing himself. At the time he was driven by anger and frustration.'' She paused. ''I don't think he's really changed. The emotions were just internalized. As you say, controlled.''

''But just as powerful?''

''Staffa is power. Intellectually and physically. He will not be defeated, no matter who the adversary is. Even when the adversary is himself.''

''An attitude like that can be dangerous.''

''We've talked about atonement. We live in dangerous times, and Staffa is betting himself against the future.'' Her fingers tapped on the console before her. ''Have you . . . Are you worried that he might be under the machine's sway?''

''I don't know what to think anymore. I'm not ready to relieve him of command yet, if that's what's worrying you.''

''Did he say anything else?''

''It was broken, almost raving, but he said I needed to tell you that Penzer Atassi must be removed from the Governorship of Antillies. He's hatched some scheme to barter titanium production for political clout and food shipments. It doesn't mean anything to me. Does it to you?''

She paused, thoughtful. ''Yes. It would explain some of the reports coming in from our agents on Antillies. Did he say how we're supposed to march in and do this?''

''According to Staffa, Admiral Jakre has a ship there somewhere.''

''I think he does. Very well, I'll contact the Admiral and see to it.''

''You're taking him at his word? What if it's a ploy by the machine?''

''We'll check it, of course. He was right about the Nesian dye futures. We'd missed it completely. The reports from Antillies simply mentioned that Atassi was jockeying for position. Since the conquest, every minor politician in Free Space is doing the same. That leaves us with the task of trying to monitor almost ten thousand politicians with Imperial aspirations.''

Her gaze went blank. ''Fortunately, the fleets are dispersed to most planets. And your people and the Companions are mostly self-sufficient. The Sassans on the other hand, are driving Jakre half insane wanting clearance for the simplest of decisions.''

''My people are trained to maintain social order. We've had a little practice at that.''

''My compliments to your Targan veterans. If we had another four Divisions, we could keep the lid on the whole of Free Space.''

Another four Divisions?

''Sinklar?'' she asked. ''If you need anything, call. I know him. I've seen into his soul. I can see how worried you are, but don't take any rash action until you talk to me first.''

Sink resettled himself in his chair. "Seen into his soul? Can anyone know another person that well?"

Her hard eyes flickered. "I watched him turn inside out. Yes. I know him that well. He and I, we're bound like no two human beings have ever been bound. Together, we are the reconciliation of opposites—the merging of duality."

"You like him, don't you?"

She nodded, sadness pinching her features. "He has been a brutal butcher, a destroyer. And he is determined to become a compassionate savior." Then her gaze intensified, burning. "If anyone can deal with the machine, it is Staffa kar Therma. He has strength, Sinklar. If the machine defeats him, we are all lost."

That's really reassuring. "Thank you, Magister. I give you my word that if the situation here becomes uncertain, I will contact you. And now, I'll let you get back to your duties."

Sinklar cleared the channel and leaned back. Once again he swam in deep waters, and the cold currents were pulling numbingly at him.

The feeling of impotence didn't sit well. Staffa's expression of icy fear had burned into Sinklar's mind. What could he do? Let Staffa be overcome by the machine? Or bow to Kaylla's trust?"

He stood and canceled the privacy screen before he stepped outside into the bright sunlight of a Targan day. Adze waited like a mirrored machine in her armor, arms crossed, those piercing black eyes searching.

"Any change in the Lord Commander?"

"No, sir. He's still asleep. Bruen is demanding to know what is going on."

"Tell him we'll inform him as soon as the Lord Commander is awake." He hesitated. "Communication has never been the old reptile's strong point."

"How's that?"

Sinklar pointed to the looming mound of rock. "My people might not have died in there had Bruen been willing to talk."

At her quizzical glance, he smiled. "We'd crushed their forces just beyond the outskirts of Vespa. I had a damaged LC, so it was a simple matter to plant the reactor in a ridge outside the city. When the Rebels attacked, we lured them onto the ridge. It only made strategic sense; from that strong point, they could control the approaches to the city. When I had them firmly entrenched I asked for their surrender. Arta Fera . . . well, we had her, were using her to communicate with the Rebels. She told the Rebel commander it was a bluff. We pushed a button which overloaded the reactor and blew the ridge. Destroyed their army and the Seddi's ability to resist. After the mop-up, I sent messages all over the planet asking to meet with the Seddi leaders. Bruen wouldn't respond."

Sinklar walked toward his dome. "At the time, my hope was to negotiate a settlement, bring the fighting to an end. Instead, having no other alternative, we came here to destroy the Seddi once and for all."

"Is the story true? Did you really only start with one Division?"

"And they were a sorry lot. Mostly green conscripts." He glanced at her, aware of the swing of her hips. What did she look like under all that reflective plating? Unlike supple, formfitting armor, the STU variety was as revealing as an LC. And did Adze have another side to her personality? One that wasn't hard, professional, forever on guard?"

"What do you think our chances are now?" she asked as she surveyed the hills. "Are we going to make it work? Or is this just another last stand at Makarta?"

Sinklar sighed wearily. "I don't know. You said the archives were open. Want to go take a look?"

"I'd love it." Excitement animated her face.

The trip down into Makarta had become less of a nightmare for Sinklar, but the ruined chambers still haunted him. Looking around at the mess, he asked, "How many bodies did they take out?"

"One hundred and twenty-seven . . . as accurately as we could determine. Isolated hands, feet, and bits of tissue might have been miscounted as a different individual or two parts of the same. We didn't run a forensic analysis.

"Another one hundred and forty are still here someplace." He stared around at the collapsed rock.

"We could continue the excavations. Remove the rock and—"

"No. Leave them in peace."

A deep melancholy had settled like a ghost-dusty mantle

on his spirits. "What's it all for, Adze? Life, I mean. Why do we fight so viciously amongst ourselves?"

"That question has been asked throughout our entire history. Do you think you'll find an answer, Sinklar?"

"No. But you'd think that for a species as clever as ours, we could think of a better solution than blowing each other apart."

"Maybe it's the machine. It was directing Bruen."

"Maybe." He passed the stairway that led to the machine and proceeded down the narrowing tunnel. Despite the lights, he could sense the dark weight of the place. How had Mac managed, trapped down here in total darkness, listening to the sounds of war, feeling the vibrations through the rock?

A square shaft had been cut into the rock, bypassing the rock fall that had blocked the original entrance. Lights had been strung along the top of the bore. Sinklar stepped inside, aware of the chill coming from the rock.

"How soon is Staffa's team supposed to arrive?"

"They'll planet tonight at about the tenth decant."

They entered the original tunnel, a rounded, worn passageway. The sounds of their booted feet echoed hollowly.

"Scary, isn't it?" Sinklar asked as the rock narrowed.

"Yeah, I wouldn't want to work down here."

A heavy duraplast door blocked the way. An old electronic lock had been set in the dusty stone.

"Do you have the code?" Adze asked.

Sinklar laughed wearily. "I'm afraid not."

Adze grinned in a display of white teeth. "You know, it's a good thing you've got me around to take care of you."

"Oh, it is, is it? And how's that? I haven't noticed that I've needed your overtime protection. No one has tried to slip a vibraknife into my back yet."

"I'm not an STU for nothing—and I'm not talking about saving your skinny back from an assassin's blade, either." She reached into her belt pouch and produced one of the electronic gadgets she carried. Deftly, she attached two wires and began tapping commands into the small box. Digital displays flashed and the lock clicked.

"You see," her voice held an air of satisfaction. "You need me for the more practical aspects of life—like locks."

"That's a handy device."

She unclipped the wires, neatly stowing the unit. ''You never know what you might have to deal with on an assault. A system as old as this one is pretty simple.''

''Knowing you've got that little tool, I'll make sure I shove a chair under the doorknob next time I take a shower.''

''What? You think I'd be interested in a skinny little runt like you? Dream on!''

The comment left him slightly miffed. Skinny little runt? Well, sure, he'd never gone big on muscle. ''Adze, all my strength is between my ears.''

''Must make buying a hat a little difficult. Come on, let's see what's here.''

Opening the door took their combined efforts, but it swung free to reveal a dark cavern. The square of light glowing through the doorway didn't help much. Adze produced a hydrogen torch from her belt and dialed up the brilliance.

Sinklar stepped reverently into the small room. Pine shelving had been placed along the walls, most of it sagging and warped. Cabinets with atmosphere seals ran up one wall from floor to ceiling. On a stand stood a globe of a planet. Sinklar glanced around, noting the inscription on the rear wall.

THE PAST IS MYSTERY
THE PRESENT IS NOW
ASSUME THE MANTLE
YOU ARE THE LEGACY

''What do you think that means?'' Adze asked.

Sinklar studied the words. ''That's just the sort of thing you'd find in an archive or over a library lintel. You're supposed to be inspired by weighty words from the past.''

He stepped over to the globe, frowning at the outline of the continents and the colored patches. The blue, he could accept as oceans. ''What world is this? I don't recognize it.''

Adze leaned forward, squinting. ''Got me. What's it made of? Plastic? Why not use a holo display. You can do more with it.''

''Old,'' Sinklar whispered. He craned his neck to stare

at the words written in standard alphabet but in an alien arrangement. "Maybe it's the place where the aliens came from? Somewhere beyond the Forbidden Borders?"

Then he caught sight of the legend. "Holy Rotted Gods."

"What?"

"Earth."

"That's a myth."

A cold shiver ran down Sinklar's spine as he studied the globe. "I think not."

He turned, obsessed by the room. In the dust at his feet, he could see Staffa and Kaylla's tracks. He walked over to one of the shelves, seeing antiquated stacks of flimsies. In one corner, he noted an ancient book, the kind made of wood pulp bound together at the spine. He'd seen pictures of them in his study of history. With trembling fingers, he removed the fragile volume and blew the dust from it. The weight of it surprised him. Heavy.

"What's that?"

"A book. The way they were made thousands of years ago. It's all printed on paper." With care, he opened it, hating the cracking sound it made. The lines of text didn't mean much, but the pictures were startling. Men and women in odd dress, buildings, scenes of human beings on horses in curious scenery, much of it reminiscent of Targa. Some carried long knives, others bore flags. Then he found the first map, and the excitement grew.

Stepping over to the globe, Sinklar placed the outline of a continent. "Ayfreecay." He swallowed. "Blessed Gods." Then he turned back to the beginning, finding yet another figure, this one vaguely human, bipedal and slightly hairy. One by one, he turned the pages, finding pictures of skulls. From the map, he could place the location talked about as Ayfreecay, Cheyenay, or Eeuropay. The creatures became more and more human as he progressed. Then he found a photo of the DNA molecule and it all came clear.

"What is it?" Adze demanded. "You look like you've seen a ghost."

"I have," Sinklar whispered. "A whole bunch of them. The globe is no myth." He closed his eyes, fingers tracing down the page. "Ana, why couldn't you have lived to see this?"

"What is it?" Adze insisted.

"Earth. Us. Where we came from. The answer to the problem of our origins." With great care he turned the pages, finding a full-page map of the Earth. A small picture of a human was tied to different parts of the planet. Dark-skinned people, like Ark, from Ayfreecay, white-skinned from Eeuropay. He glanced up, pointing. "Here is your physical type. It's from Nohrth Aymereyecayan. Your ancestors were Nayteyev Aymereyecayan."

"Sure, they were. I can't even say it."

Sinklar slowly turned the pages, trying to absorb it all as he noted the progression of architecture from huts and caves to mud buildings. People no longer killed strange animals but worked in fields and had cattle or sheep. As he turned the pages, the cities depicted became larger. To his surprise, he could interpret the pictures of men at war with long knives and metal armor. Then ships appeared, the first rowed by lines of oars and with square sails.

The maps changed over time, the names different in each age. Pictures of men were interspersed, some with beards, others with helmets.

"I want this book!" Sinklar cried.

"That still doesn't prove it's Earth," Adze insisted.

Sinklar skipped to the middle, opening a page. "They're still at war." This time, the fighting was with machines he could recognize. Aircraft, armored war vehicles, and burning cities were portrayed. He skipped again and opened to a page with a cube-shaped vehicle on four spindly legs on an atmosphereless planet. A man, obviously in a bulky space suit, was caught in the act of stepping from the vehicle. This time, Sinklar could recognize the word written in the text: Moon.

"Oh, really?" He thumbed back several pages to a picture of a crude rocket lifting off in a shower of fire. "Think, Adze. We've gone from using stone tools to wooden ships to mechanical warfare. Now we have rockets. It's the history of a planet. Not a novel, not a story. The maps are the same as on the globe."

He opened to a page further back, seeing a domed settlement on a red planet with no atmosphere. Turning a couple of pages, he found a two-dimensional map of a solar system. "Look at this. Earth is third from the sun. This sun, from the photo, I'd say it's a G class star. Look at it, for God's sake! What system is this?''

He turned to the next page, finding a primitive starship.

''Pus Rot me, I think you're right.'' Adze settled next to him. ''This is . . .'' She shook her head. ''If only we could read it.''

Sinklar turned to the last pages, finding Targa. Not the Targa he knew, but a hostile place. In the text, Sinklar found the symbol for CO_2. ''They terraformed Targa.''

''You sure that's this planet?''

''The name here, Target. That's what they originally must have called this planet.''

''What's next?'' Adze seemed to have caught his excitement.

To his disappointment, Sinklar found only text. ''Must be the bibliography and index. I guess publishing is still as primitive as it was.''

''Why didn't they use data cubes?'' Adze wondered. ''You can store so much more.''

As if holding a holy relic, Sinklar closed the volume, hugging it to his chest. ''I guess they didn't have them.''

''We've lost so much.''

''And we're not going to lose the rest. If I have to declare martial law, Adze, we're going to break out of this mess.''

She gave him a skeptical glance. ''The Lord Commander and the machine might have something to say about that.''

''Pus take the machine. I can do it.''

''You?''

He gave her a crooked grin. ''When I dropped on this ball of mud, I was a lowly private. I left here as Commander of all Regan forces.''

''You believe it, don't you?''

Sinklar carefully replaced the book. Then he took Adze by the shoulders, staring into her eyes. ''We can't let it go. Do you understand? Do you know what that book is? It's our history, Adze. You have to know where you're coming from to know where you're going. That's what's been missing. Are you with me?''

''I'm with you, Sinklar.''

''Good. When Staffa's team arrives, I want that book copied. I want this room scoured. Somewhere in here, there has to be a translation, something the linguists can use. I want copies of that book sent to every scholar in Free Space. I want it *translated!*"

"We'll do it."

Sinklar grinned, the old optimism rising. "Come on. I think that's enough for now. We'd better get back to the surface and see what new problems have cropped up."

They pulled the heavy door closed and started back up the passage. For a long time, Adze was silent, locked in her thoughts. For Sinklar, the walk was buoyant. Images of the pictures in the book spun in his mind. Foremost among them, the realization that after the rocket photos, the ones of war had nearly vanished from the book.

Could it be true? Had open space brought relative peace to humanity?

"I understand now." Adze gave him a different look, one he hadn't seen yet.

"What's that?"

"I understand what they saw in you."

"Who?"

"Nothing. Never mind."

Sinklar barely heard her, his brain spinning pictures of humans from Earth, expanding out among the stars—beyond the Forbidden Borders.

* * *

"*Skyla!* Rot you, wake up!"

The call brought Skyla out of a hideous nightmare in which Arta Fera's warm flesh lay against her own. She'd been bound, tied to the sleeping platform, writhing while the Seddi assassin stimulated her captive flesh, and Ily's voice floated out of the mist, asking, "*. . . did anyone find the body? Are they sure Chrysla is dead?*"

"What? Huh?" Skyla blinked against the bright light, jerking herself up and grabbing for the blaster that hung off the headboard.

Lark stood outlined in the hatch of the small cabin.

Safe. Aboard Rega One. *It's all right.* Skyla let her fingers slip off the contoured handle of her pistol. For a moment, she slumped, trying to rid her mind of questions about Itreata and of Arta's predatory amber eyes staring at her from over the golden mound of her pubis.

Arta, Chrysla—Chrysla, Arta. The two twined together in her nightmares. At least she'd been awakened before she had to watch herself step through that doorway into Itreata—and see Arta's smoldering eyes staring out of her own face.

She rubbed a hand over her face. *Stop it. Your subconscious is torturing you worse than Arta did. That's why Ily asks those questions. It's fear that Chrysla will take your place.*

Skyla mumbled to herself, "If Staffa wanted Chrysla, he wouldn't have let her run off."

. . . *Or would he? He says he loves you, and he let you run off.*

"But I sneaked away." What a pus Rotted mess.

Lark entered, seating herself on the edge of the sleeping platform. "I heard you clear down the hall. That must have been some terrible dream. Now you're talking to yourself."

"I've had worse."

"Something's wrong. I heard the bridge monitor go off. I went up to check. We're in real space again. We dropped out of null singularity."

Skyla shook her head, trying to fling the afterimages of the dream from her mind. Her breasts itched, and she rubbed them to wipe away the memory of Arta's ephemeral saliva. "Dropped out? Where?"

"I don't know. I didn't hang around to take a star plot. One of the lights is flashing. I think it's a cooling tower that serves the main reactor."

"All right." Skyla exhaled wearily and stood, fumbling for her clothing.

As she was pulling on coveralls, Lark gave her a nervous look, finally admitting, "Boy, you sure have a lot of scars."

"I told you. You wanted to be like me? You pay a price. Now you know what all those combat lessons are about."

"Yeah." Lark whispered. "I guess I do."

Skyla snapped the coveralls and led the way into the corridor. The ship hummed softly as she walked toward the bridge. "The alarm sounded and you went forward, right?"

"Yep." A hesitation. "I thought about sitting down with the manuals and trying to fix it. Then I reconsidered. I'm dead tired, don't know what I'm doing, and it might be too serious for me to be screwing around with."

Skyla shot a look of approval over her shoulder. "You know, you're a smart kid."

"I wonder sometimes. You make me feel pretty dumb."

"Don't. There's big difference between dumb and ignorant. Part of being smart is knowing when you're in over your head."

Skyla ducked onto the bridge, seeing the cooling tower light gleaming a baleful red. Through the ports, she could see the redshifted stars blurring like flares and wavering before them. *Rega One* was hurtling along at just under light speed.

"Why does it do that? Drop us out of null singularity?"

"Well, how would you rather come out? In one piece, or as plasma? If something goes wrong, the singularity generation kicks off. Without that singularity generation up front, you can't defy light speed."

"So it's a fail-safe? Keeps you from being lost outside?"

"You can't get lost out there, kid. What's in this universe stays. Unless, of course, you get brave enough to see what's on the other side of the event horizon around a black hole. We still don't have an accurate physics to describe that."

Skyla settled herself in the command chair and dialed up the coolant. Despite the levels indicated, the tower warning remained red.

"Sensor says it's too hot." Skyla rubbed the back of her neck and made a face. "Serves me right."

"What does?"

"Did anyone ever tell you you ask too many questions?"

"Just my father . . . and you."

Skyla groaned to herself. "It's happened before. On the jump from Rega to Terguz. I just readjusted." She paused, rapping her fingertips on the armrests. "Lark, I wasn't thinking clearly. Smart spacers check out indicator readings. Make sure they don't have problems developing."

"But you didn't?"

"I said you ask too many questions." But that damning indictment remained. "All right, I owe you this one, so I'll 'fess. I was drowning in my own misery on the way over. I had other things to think about. Leave it at that and come on."

"Where to?"

"The reactor room. You're about to have your first lesson in basic starship repair."

She slipped past Lark and started back down the corridor.

"Does this mean we have to send a distress beacon and wait to be rescued?"

Skyla half turned. "Rescued? You've been watching too many space operas. No, if this is a simple matter of a jammed valve, we could be null singularity within a half hour. If it's a pump or a leak, well, it might be longer."

Skyla undogged the hatch and shinnied down the ladder to the engineering deck. As Lark landed beside her, Skyla indicated the large display on the engineering deck hatch. "First thing you do is check the gauges. Here, see? They're all reading safe. Well within the range of tolerable radiation. If those roentgen counters read a rise to above acceptable background, they'll turn yellow, and then red. Yellow means trouble, and red means danger."

"And if they're unsafe?" Lark studied the monitors on the reactor room hatch.

"Then you suit up—suits are in the locker to your right—and follow the precautions in the manual. Only when you're completely suited, do you pass this hatch. After you fix what's broke in there, you be Rotted sure to decontaminate on the way out. Otherwise you get real sick, you throw up, your hair falls out, and you pray you get to treatment before you die."

"Swell."

Skyla threw the dogs over, each clunking solidly, and entered the monitoring station for the mains. The coolant level readings were below normal. "Wonderful. We're low on fluid."

"Does that mean we send a distress beacon?"

"Get out of here! What makes you think ships are so fragile? We've got spare drums of coolant." *I hope.* "If starships had to send distress signals every time they had a glitch, we'd never get from one planet to another. Now, take the green diagnostics disk out of the locker there on the wall. That's it, the one marked coolant. Stick it into the comm slot and run it."

"Why not just keep the program in the comm?"

"Good question. If we had a radiation leak in here, or if

the temperature rose another three hundred degrees, do you think you could trust the comm?

"I guess not." Lark input the disk and studied the readings as the comm interpreted the system. "It says the main pump and backup are only producing eighty-nine kilograms of pressure."

Skyla groaned again. "That's bad."

"How bad?"

She limbered up her fingers. "Bad enough that now we do a lesson in basic pump repair. If it's really bad, we manufacture new parts from the stock in the parts locker. The tool kit is in that big box on the deck beside the desk. Let's get started."

Skyla unclipped the access tunnel cover and flipped on the light switch. She stared in at the sinuous mass of pipes, hoses, and tubing, all basking in the roar of the fans, pumps, and hydraulics. "Should have left that Rotted engineer aboard. I could have locked him on this deck and never worried about it."

On hands and knees, she crawled into the cramped space and located the pump housing for the main coolant tower.

Lark wiggled in, yipping as she touched an exhaust pipe.

"Forgot to tell you, some of this stuff gets pretty hot. Especially the exhaust system."

"I noticed." Lark inspected the offending pipe. "How hot can the pipes get?"

"Enough to glow cherry red if the coolant falls low enough. Makes it real uncomfortable to work in here."

"It's pretty warm in here as it is. You mean it can get hotter?"

"Hand me a two centimeter spanner."

Lark started to crawl back out, then asked, "Uh . . . what does a two centimeter spanner look like?"

Skyla took a deep breath, head dropping. "It's going to be a long session. I can tell already."

And Ily Takka would be using every second of it. Dropping from null singularity, revectoring, and hurtling for Ashtan at multiples of the speed of light.

* * *

Nkylos had begun to fume. He'd been sitting for too long, waiting on the will and pleasure of the Companions. Once again, he checked on Bruen, noting no change in the old man's medical status.

The dome he shared with Bruen had four rooms. A bedroom on either side separated by a shared toilet on the back wall and a small dispenser with table and chairs on the front. The confines of the dome left him no relief but to pace from one room to the other and back. At each extreme, he could duck his head to stare out at the dusty compound.

"Eating at you, is it?" Bruen asked.

"What are we doing here? It's a farce. Staffa is dealing with the machine, and we're just sitting. They won't even tell us what's going on." Nyklos smacked a fist into his palm. "When did it all go so wrong? Placing Kaylla in charge was a mistake. She's under Staffa's spell. She's sucked right up to him."

Bruen sighed, faded blue eyes following the Master's movements. "It should have been you, Nyklos. If only you'd been there. I had to make the choice. Hyde was gone—and for all I knew, you were dead."

"I know. She was here. I don't blame you." Except that now that it had been said, the thought of his becoming Magister irritated like a ripa spine under the flesh.

"You should have seen her, Magister. At every mention of Staffa, Kaylla literally reeked of worry. You'd think she cared for him. And after what he did to her."

"Nyklos, you must keep things in perspective." Bruen made a weary gesture with his hand. "He saved her life in the desert. Got her off Etaria when Ily would have sent her back to the slave pens."

Nyklos pivoted on his heel, raising an eyebrow. Could he believe this? Or was this just another of Bruen's wicked barbs. "She's never hinted that they were lovers."

"Of course not. She's a professional." Bruen gave a slight shrug. "I may not be happy with my choice of Kaylla for my successor, but you don't think I'd appoint an idiot to the job, do you?" Bruen made a face. "If she wants to slip into Staffa's bed every now and then while Skyla's not looking, what difference does it make? Kaylla Dawn isn't the kind of woman who would sell us out over a bit of sex. I believed that at the time, and—despite my *considerable* differences with her—I still believe that she has more integrity than that.''

Nyklos had stopped short, pulling at his mustache as he remembered the times Kaylla had taken her aircar to Staffa's quarters, especially during those days after Skyla had been abducted by Ily.

''Nyklos, you must remember the circumstances of her appointment. We were fighting for our lives. Staffa offered a safe haven—a place where neither Ily Takka nor Divine Sassa could deal us a deathblow. If Kaylla was having sex with Staffa, so much the better. She could see to the safety of the Seddi Order. Survival was my first concern since Makarta was denied us. You do understand, don't you? We needed the Lord Commander at that moment in time. I was desperate.''

Bruen was being too reasonable about this. Nyklos nodded, an emptiness yawning inside him. And now, Kaylla had begun to slip. Tired and worn from the cares of managing so much, the carefully maintained control had eased. That's what he'd seen that day when Sinklar was talking to her.

Staffa's lover. Yes, of course, it all made sense.

Nyklos winced, pained by it all. Staffa had the two women Nkylos cared the most about. And, indeed, he had come to care for Kaylla, his attachment more one of devotion and respect than the driving and desperate love he suffered for Skyla. Now, that, too, crumbled to dust in his weary soul.

Bruen added casually, ''Staffa has made his deal with the machine. He belongs to it now. Maybe he won't be as interested in frolicking with Kaylla since he's going to be ensorcelled by the machine.''

''I don't want to believe this, Bruen.''

Sympathy filled Bruen's watery eyes. ''I'm sorry. I thought you knew. I shouldn't have said anything. I didn't think, Nyklos.''

''I just . . .''

''Would it help to talk about it?'' Bruen's sad expression offered solace. ''Talking can make these things easier to bear. You know, airing feelings helps to put things in perspective. If it's any consolation, I don't think all three of them are having it at once. I'm not even sure that Skyla knows that he's pumping into Kaylla's well.''

"What?"

"Well, they are discreet. And let's face it, Skyla is no smarter than any other woman." Bruen's voice turned intimate. "You really fell for Skyla, didn't you? She is a most beautiful woman. A pale goddess worthy of the Blessed Gods." Bruen sighed. "Ah, Master, I can still marvel at her, even though I'm well past the age to do anything about it. It must eat at you like hot acid to think of Skyla offering herself to Staffa. Of his body moving on hers. I don't know how you stand it."

"Bruen, sometimes I can sympathize with the people who want to strangle you."

"I'm sorry. I only meant to help. Now I've disturbed you." He sighed. "Yes, foolish me. I was right to step down when I did. I can no longer curb my tongue." Bruen raised a withered hand. "Please, forget I said anything. It was just the ramblings of an old man."

"He and Kaylla . . ." Nyklos shook his head. Something precious had been looted from deep inside him. Fool! He should have known! Should have seen it in the expression on Kaylla's face.

Nyklos clenched his fists, hating the thoughts stirred by the old Magister's words. Angrily, he jumped to his feet and stepped out into the cool Targan evening, slamming the door behind him.

Who should he believe in? Bruen? Or Kaylla? The old Magister might not be as wrong as they'd thought. And he'd seen, *seen* the desperate worry in her eyes when it came to Staffa's safety. She'd never admit that she was spreading for Staffa.

"They spent weeks in that shipping crate you put them in. In those circumstances . . . well, he's a healthy man and she's an attractive, athletic woman. What else do you do to pass the time inside a big box? You don't think they sat around and argued philosophy, do you?"

No, he couldn't imagine Staffa and Kaylla locked in that box for three months of celibacy. And he remembered that day on Etaria. She'd pleaded for Staffa's life.

How could he ever follow another order from Kaylla? How could he ever look her in the face without imagining her moaning in time to the rotation of Staffa's hips.

And now Staffa is making a deal with the machine? Did

he figure he could treat the whole of humanity like he did the women in his life?

Nyklos turned his steps toward the mountain. Bruen still couldn't be completely trusted, but a man with Nyklos' talent and capabilities could prepare—just in case what the old Magister said was true.

CHAPTER XXVIII

Frederick Gaust ducked his head low as he scurried out the side door of the public auditorium and into Freeholt Thoroughfare. His two bodyguards huddled close on either side, rushing him forward. The aircar was waiting, its side emblazoned with the Imperial seal, the jessant-de-lis; the driver sat slouched in the seat as he watched something on his pocket comm. His head snapped up, the silly grin on his face fading as Gaust leapt into the rear seat.

Behind them, inside the auditorium, the roar of angry shouting had overcome the soundproofing built into the walls. Terguz had to be that way, everything was packed together, shoulder to shoulder in the undersurface warrens.

How had it all gone so wrong? Gaust shook his head. The Wing Commander had had no right to place him in such a precarious position. These people weren't interested in compromise! They wanted anarchy! The end to anything resembling civil discipline!

"Got a little warm in there," Garrey offered as the aircar started forward.

"I don't understand!" Gaust made a violent gesture with his hands. "Vermilion sheep have more sense than those dolts! We've got production schedules to meet! Rot them! A responsibility to Empire . . . and not to their lazy appetites! What do they think? They're here because the Emperor was rewarding them? Either they or their parents were sent here for punishment!"

Gaust wadded up his flimsies, notes on which he'd prepared his speech about the new era on Terguz. In disgust, he threw them from the aircar, watching them bounce across one of the walkways at the feet of pedestrians.

"Ignorant animals! That's what they are. Beasts, seeking to slake their gutter hunger for sloth. What do they think?

That the Empire will wind down its consumption because they don't want to work so hard?" He sputtered, "And worse . . . Worse! They want a say in government? These louts haven't an idea in their heads when it comes to government! What do they think? That I'll just step back and turn the administration of this planet over to unlanded, unwashed, ignorant laborers?"

"What are you going to tell the Wing Commander?" Garrey asked.

"What can I? That I've made a good faith effort, and they've as good as spit into my face."

The aircar pulled up before his residence, the pillared false-front of the building sporting painted graffiti.

Gaust closed his eyes, breathing deeply. "And get that filth washed off my residence."

"Should we call in additional security?" Garrey asked.

Gaust waved him away. "They're just stupid not dangerous."

"You made a lot of them . . . well, they were unhappy, sir."

"Let them be. If they're off their feed because I wouldn't yield, they'll really ache when Commander Seekore arrives with that ship. She'll put them back in line, and they'll wish they'd had a little more respect for me when I was on their side."

At that, Gaust turned, back straight, and headed for his door.

* * *

Staffa woke from tortured dreams. The old familiar nightmare of being chased through dark corridors on a dying starship had played over and over. The faceless dead had pursued him, seeking to wreak their vengeance upon him before an explosion flung his naked body onto twisted sheets of torn steel. He'd felt the cold steel cutting through his back, lancing his intestines, and shoving up through the unprotected skin on his belly. Meanwhile, the angry ghosts had gathered around and reached down for him with spectral fingers.

The sensation of invisible presences mixed with the

dreams, drifting through his mind like a stygian mist, inserting thoughts, and exposing his deepest fears.

He sat up, fatigue like cobwebs sticking to his muscles and nerves. Stumbling into the toilet, he relieved himself and then stared into the small mirror.

His face bore little resemblance to the image he'd once known. Where a gray spark had once filled his eyes, now they stared back, bloodshot, possessed. His face had turned haggard, a dark stubble on his cheeks.

Staffa combed out his long hair, aware that its luster had vanished. For a moment, he let it drape over his shoulders like a mantle, then he gathered it tightly into the ponytail to hang over his left ear. The clip snapped crisply into place.

To still the angry growl in his stomach, he gulped down a couple of energy sticks, then let himself out into the starry night. Two STU thumped knotted fists to their sternums in salute, one automatically reaching for his belt comm.

"No. Let me have some time before you alert the universe to the fact I've awakened."

"Yes, sir. Standard security only."

"Very well." He'd have to put up with unobtrusive shadows following in his track. Otherwise, Ark would go berserk. Staffa walked across the compound, hating the glare of the lights. Beyond, he stepped into the welcome cloak of darkness, walking out among the trees to stare up at the stars.

Even from here, the blur of the Forbidden Borders besmirched the heavens, mocking him with their invincibility. He followed a faint path, replaying his conversation with the Mag Comm in his mind until he reached a rocky outcrop overlooking the dark valley below.

There he stood, soaking in the peace of the night, hearing only the chirring of the night insects.

"Perhaps we're more alike than I would like to admit," Sinklar's voice said from behind him.

Staffa turned and peered into the darkness. He could barely make out Sinklar's figure where he sat shadowed, back propped against a pine tree.

"I wanted solitude. I should have remembered that you come up here."

Sinklar tossed something into the dark. It clattered dryly on the rocks, a stick from the sound of it. "I first came up here after Gretta was murdered. It was just before the attack on Makarta. I was trying to put myself together, to grieve. The healing began here. Here I wanted to end it."

"And has it?"

Sinklar's nod could barely be seen. "I think so. I entered the archives today. When I went back, the technicians chased me out. Otherwise, I'd still be there."

"You saw the globe then?"

"Better than that. I found a history book you missed on your visit. It's a history of the species. From the very beginning when we didn't look human, right up to the discovery of Targa. They called it Target in those days."

Staffa leaned his head back, eyes closed as he savored the scent of pine and soil. "So the mystery of our origins is solved?"

"Perhaps. The continental maps depicted in the book match those on the Earth globe. I've ordered the book to be copied immediately and the contents broadcast throughout Free Space. I think we've been missing a sense of who we are. Where we came from. Among other things, one of the technicians found an old data cube on one of the shelves. It will take more complicated deciphering than we can do here, but they think they can recover enough to translate the text."

"That's better than I'd hoped. Nothing on the Forbidden Borders yet?"

"They've just begun to work on the place. By the time they shooed me out, they hadn't even broken the seal on the cabinets."

Staffa remembered the day he'd entered with Kaylla. "I stood in awe. Almost in worship."

"We are more alike than I thought." A pause. "How are you feeling?"

"In all honesty, I've felt better, Sinklar. What you really want to know is have I been compromised by the machine yet. The answer is still no."

"Staffa . . . I saw your fear in there. You've got to level with me. You are my security responsibility. I don't want to have to guess about your status. Talk to me."

Where had the strength in Sinklar's voice come from? What had happened down there in the archives? He sounded so sure of himself. The lurking insecurity had vanished.

"You have healed indeed." He took a deep breath then

picked his way through the rocks and seated himself. So weary. "Dealing with the machine is terrifying. I suppose we can all imagine having another presence in our minds, but the reality . . . well, it's something that has to be experienced. The Mag Comm is there, inside, sharing that last sanctuary of identity."

Staffa steepled his fingers, watching a meteor streak across the sky. Maybe a dropped wrench or some other piece of garbage. "My plan was to open myself, let the machine read both my desperation and resolve. Let it know that if I failed to come to a reasonable solution, I would destroy it."

"If I'd known—"

"Yes, I'm aware that you would have disapproved. Nevertheless, the machine has dealt with subversion and deceit from the beginning. I wanted the ground rules immediately established so that we didn't have to fence for position. Not only that, I told you the truth. I must make the decision to employ the machine's talent. I can't delegate it. I must *know* that I'm not condemning our people."

"Which means we all have to trust you."

"Still worried about the resurrection of the Star Butcher?"

"No. But balancing humanity on your judgment doesn't leave me sleeping any too well."

"Me either," Staffa admitted dryly. "If you're not resting well now, wait until you hear the latest from the oracle of the golden helmet. The Mag Comm claims we can break the Forbidden Borders. It can be done through gravitational dissonance. If we're to believe the machine, it must be done very carefully or we'll create a disaster. Imagine one of those dense neutronic strings whipping through Free Space? The tidal effects alone would wreak havoc."

"We can break the Forbidden Borders? That doesn't sound so bad."

"If we do it right, Sinklar. The Mag Comm insists that we consult it. I would presume that the timing will be critical. Perhaps to the nanosecond. It's the rest that sends chills down my back. The machine is willing to bargain. In return for freeing us from the Forbidden Borders and running Free Space, it wants us to build machines for it. Drones with which it, too, can explore. In essence, we'd be providing it with hands and feet. Little minions to go about and do its bidding.''

''I see. So we're beyond just trusting it to run things, we have to trust it enough to let it loose?''

''That appears to be the machine's position.'' Staffa paused. ''How did the advice about the governor of Antillies turn out?''

''Hit the target dead center, it would appear. Kaylla immediately recognized the problem. Understood it better than I did.''

''How is she?''

''As worried as the rest of us.'' Sinklar paused. ''And she's concerned about you. Her advice to me was to trust you.''

''I wouldn't. She's biased.''

''You killed her husband and children and sold her into slavery.''

''I saved her life in the sewer under the Temple and again in the desert.''

''She says she knows you better than anyone alive.''

''Yes, well, unfortunately . . . she's probably right about that. Wait a minute. I thought you didn't like Seddi Magisters.''

Sinklar uttered a dry laugh. ''I might make an exception in her case.''

''I would if I were you. She's as fine a human being as you'll find anywhere—even if half the time she wishes she could shut me out of her life. As to the machine, I don't know what to think. I came out here hoping to experience some divine revelation. Instead, I can only argue myself into and out of accepting its offer.''

''What else did it tell you?''

''That it needs us. It claims to have been one of the aliens. Apparently they're some sort of dense crystals floating around in space. We were right about the Forbidden Borders. They trapped us here. The machine was to teach us to be rational. Hence all that business about God, the quanta, and human rationality that we talked about.''

''I don't understand.''

''We think of time as linear. A leads to B which leads to C and so forth. Imagine an intelligence that is timeless and with a reality, a view of the universe, that is constantly reinforced from the past. The background microwave radiation filling the universe is what they call their song. My speculation is that it's like a constant retelling of a story. Or perhaps of a history and sociology combined. The Others are essentially immortal, and since the song carries at light speed, they hear and re-sing what has been traveling through space for billions of years. By re-singing it, they know the message will be heard exactly the same in another couple of billion years in some other part of the universe."

"I thought we'd studied background radiation, looking for coherent signals?"

"We have. Maybe we can't decipher it through the heterodyne they create? Who knows? They don't have organic brains. These things are crystalline, absolute. We can't comprehend the basic assumptions they make about the universe."

"Rotted Gods, how do we deal with something like that?"

"That's the crux of the problem. We began broadcasting microwaves on their wavelength—and to them, it was probably static. You see, we were changing the song."

"So they put us in the bottle to teach us Right Thought. Civilize us so we wouldn't change the song? That's ridiculous."

"Is it? You've just seen the archives. How did it feel to pick up that book and see pictures of your past? Suppose a group of aliens began rewriting your history—not just selectively but every moment. Sure, the Others have tried to do just that to us in an attempt to keep us ignorant of our origins beyond the Forbidden Borders, but history is the only sacrament of a species. It's the record, imperfect though it may be, of who we are, where we came from. Our identity is found in two places. It runs in our blood, in our genetic structure, and the other half is our history."

"All right, you've made the point. And you're right. But why didn't they just ask us to stop what we were doing?"

"Keep in mind, we're talking about an intelligence so alien we can't conceive of their motives anymore than they can conceive of ours. Maybe that idea, as simple as it seems to us, didn't fit their framework of understanding."

"And the Mag Comm claims to be one of them? A history stealer? Forget it. Let's nuke the mountain and get on about our business."

"Ah, a simple solution. The Mag Comm isn't that simple. It's been corrupted. Your attack scared it. It realized it was not immortal, that it could be destroyed. Worse, it's been dealing with humans, experiencing the universe through human-tinted lenses. The Others won't sing to it anymore. It fears isolation. So long as we survive, the machine will have us to interact with."

Sinklar thought for a moment, chin propped on his palm. "All the more reason it might want us in a captive situation. We could be its own little entertaining population. Pus take it, doesn't that sound like a fascinating future?"

"That possibility can't be ruled out."

Sinklar threw his arms up. "How are we supposed to analyze the motives of a mutant machine that's part alien?"

"Congratulations, you've redefined the original problem."

"Blasting it from orbit sounds like a more reasonable solution."

Staffa reached down, picking up a rock. The cool weight gave him something substantial to hold. He ran a finger over the rough surface. "Sinklar, consider our situation in a grander context. We now know there are at least three galactic intelligences: ourselves, the aliens, and the Mag Comm. Let's give this some serious thought. What are our ethical responsibilities?"

"You're not going Seddi on me?"

"Absolutely. What are our moral responsibilities? Do we exterminate this intelligence? Just snuff it out?"

"The Others, as you call them, are willing to do that to us."

"Great. We had three intelligent species in the galaxy, and now we only have one that sings songs in space. Why? Because the second form of intelligence blew up the third, then destroyed itself trying to break out of the trap created by the first. That's a remarkable legacy to send back to God Mind, isn't it? Forget intelligence. It's a doomed process."

Sinklar sighed. "All right. I don't know that I'd destroy it. I do know that I'm not about to let humanity founder. We've been toyed with, Staffa. We've been used. I've seen the faces from the past staring up from that book. I know what and where we've come from. What's wrong with linear evolution? People used stone tools once. Now we travel between the stars and kill ourselves by the billions because we can't get out of this prison your Others have placed us in. I won't have it."

"And neither will I. The trick is to figure a safe way out of the bottle. If the Mag Comm is right, we'll need its computational ability to figure out the physics to break the Forbidden Borders. If we screw it up, we'll have cataclysm."

"And we'll have an unpredictable intelligence loose in space with us."

Staffa nodded. "I know." He got to his feet, pacing nervously while his cape billowed in the wind. "Curious, isn't it? At this terrible time in our history, we must come to grips not only with the Forbidden Borders but also with ourselves. With who we are and where we are going. We are at one of the most important crossroads of human history."

Sinklar sat in silence. From somewhere, he'd picked up another stick and begun chipping the bark with his thumbnail. He laughed. "Funny, isn't it? I keep remembering all those faces. Important men and women. Supposedly immemorial, like the sculpted face of Tybalt the Imperial First overlooking the palace gardens. Now, at this time, a clone and a freak will make the determination. We can't even be sure we're human, you and I."

Staffa ceased his restless pacing. "Perhaps, for the first time, that isn't as important as it once was. It's too bad we can't still believe in destiny. It was a wonderful myth while it lasted."

* * *

Ily glanced slyly at Arta as she stepped from the shuttle terminal on Ashtan. To her surprise, security had been remarkably lax. Her assumption of the Diane de la Luna identity served her well, as did the mock slave collar on Arta's neck. After all, no one questioned an obviously wealthy woman and her personal body servant. In fact, the customs officials had been overjoyed at the arrival of a freighter seeking a load. Ashtan grain was desperately needed on Imperial Sassa.

The destruction of the Regan comm and the later sabotage of the Ashtan planetary computers served her well despite the stinging reminder of her defeat at Staffa's hands. Her papers had received only a cursory scrutiny.

"I didn't think it would be this easy," Arta remarked as they walked down the broad ramp that led to public transportation. Not even old Bruen would have recognized her. Arta sported a wealth of brunette hair, and contacts turned her eyes dull brown. A facial application of moldtex gave her skin a wrinkled appearance.

"We paid in credits," Ily responded. "Given the food situation, did you really think they'd complain?" The customs official had simply taken their photos, fingerprinted them, and passed them through with an explanation, "It's the best we can do with comm down. Otherwise you'd get the full treatment of retinal patterns and the rest."

"So what do we do with holds full of Ashtan grain? That's a lot of mass to lift out of this hole." Arta glanced at the endless collage of posters on the walls, each directing people on how to cope with the loss of comm service.

"We dump it as soon as we're outbound. I don't want to stay here longer than necessary. We need chem-coded ID cards. Like it or not, Itreata security will be tight enough to squeak."

Arta nodded, excitement leaking past her flat brown stare. Rotted Gods, did the woman never show fear? The presence of *Rega One* on Terguz ate at Ily like a slow acid. Who had the mysterious Silk been? Skyla? And why, by the pus-licking Gods, had Gyper ignored their call? What had gone wrong with Terguz?

"No one followed us," Arta stated, reading her concern. "Had it been Skyla, she would have taken her yacht. Attempted to intercept and destroy us."

"I didn't get where I am through a lack of caution."

"And where is that, Ily? A fugitive in search of camouflage?"

"Your tongue is not one of your more redeeming features." Ily stepped onto the well-lit thoroughfare and hailed one of the automatic aircars waiting patiently for a passenger. Ashtan City appeared quiet at this time of night. The night sky sparkled with stars, the tiny bluish twin moons overhead.

Settling herself in the vehicle, she inserted a credit chip and ordered, "Take us to the Grand Palace Lodgings."

"Affirmative," the small comm answered. "Routing now."

They lifted, skimming down the avenue. Regular square buildings gave a monotonous uniformity to the city, and unlike the Capital on Rega, Ashtan City didn't roar with the same intensity of air-conditioning, machinery, and constant bustle.

"How come all of the buildings are alike?" Arta asked.

"Most of the city was destroyed in the conquest. What you see is prefabbed, sent in from Vermilion and Phillipia. We needed office space to get the planet back into production after it was integrated into the Empire. Prior to Imperial rule, the city contained most of the government and military offices. Staffa pulverized them on the first wave." *Like he did at the capital.* "Most of the surviving original architecture is on the outskirts. That's where we're headed."

"The Grand Palace Lodgings?"

"It's old, quite plush actually. Tedor Mathaiison used it for his military headquarters during the occupation. It will suit us well. The agricultural labs are close by."

"But won't it be easy to trace us?" Arta indicated the aircar. "They'll have a route listing."

"I said we wouldn't be staying long. Besides, this is an unlisted account, remember? Even if they thought to try and trace *Victory,* do you know how many Model Sixteen RFs there are in Regan space? They've got hundreds to sort through. Given the situation with planetary comm, we'll be out of here and vectored for Imperial Sassa before they can begin to sift the data."

They'd passed through the business district now, entering a part of the city that still exhibited the old white-plastered buildings with rambling covered porches. Here and there, a tree grew from a circular hole in the pavement. But once it grew too big and the root system began disrupting the pavement and underground pipes and wiring, it would be cut down and a new seedling planted.

The aircar took a left, slipping silently along a tree-covered way before pulling up at a grandly lit structure of rambling white walls and arched porticoes.

"The Grand Palace." Ily smiled and stepped to the ground. Uniformed staff members gave them a gracious greeting as they entered a large hall. A receptionist smiled and took Ily's credit chip and customs clearance, before a decorated antigrav carried them along a stuccoed corridor bordered by gardens and bubbling fountains.

Their quarters consisted of a small bungalow, replete with exotic plants, a golden dispenser, and rich carpeting.

Arta glanced around before walking to the rear to inspect the sleeping quarters. She ran a quick search for monitoring devices while Ily peeled the moldtex from her face and removed the irritating contact lenses that changed her eye color. Then she doffed her sand-blonde wig, scratching vigorously at her scalp.

As Arta continued her search, she stripped her facial work and blinked from the aftereffects of the contacts. "Looks clean."

"Where did you learn so much about electronics?" Ily asked as she walked to the large holo tank on the wall and activated the unit.

Arta had stopped cold, her face gripped by an eerie expression.

"Sorry. I didn't mean to pry." But her curiosity had been piqued.

Arta took a deep breath. "No. It's all right. The assassin I learned from. He specialized in electronics when he wasn't slipping a knife into someone's back." Then she turned away, almost fleeing from the room.

Touched a nerve, didn't I?

The sound had been muted when she turned on the comm. Now Ily turned her attention to the projection.

". . . restoration of major services," the announcer said. "The military governor has informed us that communications are almost planet wide at this time. Please do not overload the system with any but necessary communications. As always, emergency use will supersede all others. Second priority is given to government communications. Business needs are ranked third and personal communications given lowest priority."

A scene of a man sitting at his comm was projected while

the announcer continued. "If you've missed talking to your relations on the other side of the planet, please be patient. Governor MacRuder's office has informed us that full comm services should be restored within the week."

MacRuder? Here? Of course. The Ashtan situation would have fallen apart immediately when Vida Marks pulled out. Sinklar, as always, sent his faithful little lapdog to shove his cores into the reactor before the situation went critical.

"Regional Governor Marrak, meanwhile, has stabilized the situation in the Southern Sector. He reports that commerce is moving briskly, and with Sassan markets opening up, this comes as welcome news to the grain producers in that area."

Ily settled herself onto one of the gravity couches, lost in thought. She barely noticed when Arta reentered the room. Only the strained expression on her face pulled Ily from her thoughts.

"I'm sorry," Ily said gently as she bent down to remove her platform shoes. "I didn't know it would bother you."

Arta waved it away. "That's when I discovered the trigger. Bruen sent me to study with him. I didn't realize I would fall in love. That time in my life . . . well, it's better forgotten."

Ily nodded, torn between two discoveries. "There's more news. We may be more rushed than I thought."

Arta's personality shifted again, from distraught to wary.

Ily pointed at the comm. "Guess who's in charge here? MacRuder."

The predatory look in Arta's features sharpened.

"No." Ily stated blankly. "We can't afford it."

"It would be so easy." Cunning had filled Arta's amber stare. "I could get in and be out before they knew what hit them."

"I said, no."

"I remember the loathing in his eyes that day. You remember, you were there. Sinklar wanted to execute me for killing that silly bitch he was screwing. MacRuder was part of that."

"No means no, Arta. Rot it all, think! If you take out MacRuder, Sinklar will know! You'll blow everything!"

"You yourself said they can't trace us."

"But they pus-dripping will if you murder Sinklar's best

friend. They'll search out every Model Sixteen freighter in space to find us. Arta, listen to me. We can't afford it. Not right now. Everything will fall apart. Are you listening to me?"

Arta's expression had gone blank.

"Arta!"

The assassin seemed to jerk herself back to the present. "Yes, Ily. I hear you."

"Then remember it." Ily studied her from half-lidded eyes. "You can have MacRuder, and the rest of them, for that matter, after we've accomplished our primary goal."

Arta nodded casual acceptance, but Ily could read the woman's lips. "Yes," Arta mouthed, "it would be so easy."

* * *

Nyklos had begun the briefing by sitting with his arms crossed. He'd studiously adopted an expression as controlled as that of a master tapa player as he hid his disgust for Staffa, and the loathing he'd come to feel for Kaylla—who attended via subspace net. As the briefing proceeded, however, he'd leaned forward like the rest, hanging on Staffa's words.

The conference room resembled anything but what it was being used for. Sialon crates filled the supply dome they'd employed for the purpose. Overhead, at the top of the dome, the usual atmosphere plant whirred softly. The featureless white walls arched down to duraplast floor. The large holo tank that Kaylla Dawn stared out of was the only modification to the dome.

Sinklar Fist sat to one side of Staffa, an elbow on one knee as he stared consideringly at the scuffed floor. Bruen had been propped up in his medical unit. He watched the proceedings, periodically jutting his jaw out, only his eyes glinting. STUs stood around the periphery. For once, their constant vigilance had dropped as they gaped at Staffa along with the rest. Even Kaylla had found a new animation, the weary fatigue dropping from her expression.

"That's about it," Staffa said, summing up his presentation. "I've laid it all out to you as best I can. Those are the conditions the machine has asked for. Now, I need to hear your thoughts."

Kaylla immediately asked, "Do you believe the machine? This is all fantastic. These Others . . . why haven't we heard from them?"

"Apparently, since they use microwave communication, we have. We just never interpreted it correctly. How would an alien interpret the babble in a crowded convention center with everyone talking all at once."

"If you believe the machine," Bruen growled.

Staffa nodded. "There is that. You've dealt with the machine for most of your life, Magister. We might all agree it's capable of lying, but did you ever catch it at it?"

Bruen's fierce gaze hardened. "At an out and out lie, no. It excels at errors of omission, however. Go ahead, Staffa, trust it. See what it gets you."

Staffa rubbed his hands together, a frown on his face. "Magister Bruen, I think we all understand your position and the reasons for it. Your warnings haven't fallen on deaf ears. I asked you here because I need your honest input. Facts, Magister. Given the latest data from Free Space we must make a decision soon. Today . . . or tomorrow at the latest."

Bruen sucked in his thin lips, then said, "I notice you're already building a comm dish. Not just an ordinary dish but a commercial version. Are you sure the decision isn't already made?"

Yes, Nyklos agreed. *Tell us about that*.

"No final decision has been made, Magister," Staffa admitted. "Time, however, is the limiting factor. If we decide to use the machine, we're that much closer to hook up. And if the Mag Comm cannot be trusted, we're still preparing a comm center on Farhome. No matter what decision is reached, we must be able to react instantly once a course is chosen. If we decide to use the machine, we can hook up within ten hours. If not, we can begin moving computers into the Farhome center as soon as they can be delivered. Even as we speak, Myles Roma is working with my people to customize the software for Farhome. That's the reason for the dish. No option must be disregarded."

Nyklos asked, "What is your leaning, Lord Commander? Has *your* decision been made? Are we only here to maintain the proper form and protocol, a simple seal to affix to your agenda?"

Staffa's control wavered for a moment, evidence of his fatigue. Nyklos filed that.

"No, Master. No decision has been made. We are all here to determine the facts as best we can. Do you think the machine is lying, Master? We need to know."

Nyklos shifted uneasily, aware everyone now watched him. "I find it hard to believe this story. Crystal aliens floating about out there? And these crystals constructed the Forbidden Borders? How, Lord Commander? In a similar vein, how did one of the creatures end up inside the Mag Comm? How did a crystal manufacture that terminal down there in the rock? Do they have hands? Manipulators of some sort? And if they do, what need does the Mag Comm have for these robot drones?"

Staffa actually grinned. "Excellent point, Master. I assure you that before any decision is made, I *will* have the answers to that."

"Staffa," Kaylla interjected, "you mentioned ethics. As I recall we had a conversation about that once. How do you think it applies here?"

Staffa lifted a tired eyebrow. "Let's use our own criteria. The machine observes. We know that. Once the machine makes an observation and interprets it, it creates a new reality."

"Wait a minute," Sinklar interrupted. "A mining probe does the same thing. It detects an asteroid and turns toward it. When it approaches, it analyzes the rock for possible production, then interprets it before sending in a report. If the rock is junk, it forgets it and goes onto the next. Do we have to grant God Mind to probes, too?"

"Free will is the issue here. A probe may only accept or reject according to criteria predetermined by us. Would you consider the probe to have free will? To adapt its settings in a manner beyond its programming?"

"All right, I can concede they don't have free will. The decisions aren't discretionary." He paused, a ghost of a smile on his lips. "Although if we had a room full of mining technicians, we might get some argument."

A chuckle broke out, easing the tension.

Staffa turned back to the monitor. "You see, Kaylla, this is very germane to what we're going to do. If the machine meets the criteria we, as Seddi, have established, we have an ethical dilemma. No matter how we change the initial conditions, the Mag Comm still shares God Mind. It observes, interprets, and creates a reality, a change of quantum energy which eventually must go back to God Mind when duality ceases. What are our ethical guidelines when dealing with it?''

Bruen grumbled, ''Leave it be. Seal it into the rock and let it observe all it wants. Do you seriously expect it to use the same ethics we would bind ourselves by? When has it in the past?''

Sinklar stiffened. ''I wouldn't wade too deeply into the pond of ethics, Magister Bruen. The mud might cling to your feet.''

''Enough!'' Staffa raised his hands, cutting Bruen's reply off before it erupted from those aged lips. As it was, Sinklar and Bruen glared at each other. Nyklos was surprised to see Bruen look away first, his wrinkled face twisted.

Nyklos caught himself staring, wondering at the presence that seemed to have invaded Sinklar Fist. The oddly colored eyes practically glowed.

''The past is behind us,'' Staffa said smoothly. ''We must deal with the present.'' He faced the monitor again. ''The data are such: No matter if the Mag Comm is telling the truth or not, we are dealing with intelligence. We can argue for two or three intelligences, for as Sinklar has pointed out, a mining drone might appear intelligent, especially the more sophisticated ones. If we accept that the Mag Comm is no more than a mining drone, then we are dealing with the criteria imposed upon it by the Others. If we accept what it tells us, and to date we have no reason not to, then it has evolved into something different from the Others. It claims to have soaked up a great many human traits.''

Sinklar glanced up. ''And that brings us to another thorny question.'' He glanced at Bruen. ''I don't mean to stir muddy waters, but what kind of human input has the machine had? If it is tainted by us, who has done the tainting? The Praetor? Old Seddi Magisters, the ones Magister Bruen himself claims became nothing more than pawns? Let's face it, the machine has been involved in the politics of Free Space, and we know how politicians conduct themselves. Are those the human traits it has learned?''

Bruen shook his head. ''Listen, all of you. You can't deal

with the machine without fear. Its power can't help but to intimidate. *Lord* Fist, I did what I thought I had to to keep the Seddi Order intact. Nothing more, nothing less. If humans were to avoid the horrifying fate they now seem to face, someone had to keep the machine' insane teachings from becoming dogma. Yes, I used deceit!" He glared around the room. "Someone had to. We had to steer a course between domination by the machine and our own destruction."

Sinklar added quietly. "I rest my case."

Staffa sighed. "We assign no blame, Magister Bruen. But Sinklar's point is as valid as Nyklos'. Are those the characteristics the machine has absorbed? Those of the Praetor and the others? Has no one ever dealt honestly with it?"

"It's not a matter of honesty!" Bruen cried. "It's a matter of human survival!"

"That's exactly what we're faced with," Staffa rejoined. "Human survival. And we don't have a lot of time to come up with a means of administering the complex economics of a host of worlds. Rot the past! This is a critical here and now that we've all had a hand in creating."

"Staffa," Kaylla called, glancing off to one side. "I've got a report that just came in. We have a riot on Terguz. From the preliminary reports, a mob just broke into the Administrator's residence. They've apparently executed him and declared a civil government to be in control."

Staffa closed his eyes, almost reeling. "Where is *Sabot?*"

"She's incoming. ETA four hours."

"Contact Seekore. Give her the details as best you have them. Kaylla, I want her working *with* you on this. She may look like a fragile, soft-eyed, porcelain doll at first glance, but you're going to have to keep her under your thumb. If you don't, she'll have the corpses of those union leaders hanging all over Terguz like ornaments. Just to keep the people mindful of good manners, you understand. In the meantime, patch through to this civil government. See what cooperation you can get from them."

Kaylla had sagged into her former state of weary acceptance. The sight of her despair sent fire through Nyklos' gut. *Some representative for the Seddi. A weary and weak woman. It should have been me at the Order's helm. Seizing opportunity instead of despairing.*

"You'll have to excuse me," she said. "Staffa, do what you must." Then the holo went blank.

Nyklos slumped. If Terguz, with its critical production of raw materials, cut off exports to jockey for position, it would be the same as dropping more fuel into an unstable reactor.

"It would appear," Staffa stated, "that events are taking their own turn. Does anyone have anything to add?"

"You know my thoughts," Bruen stated.

Staffa glanced around the room. "No one else? Then I call this meeting adjourned."

Nyklos cast a glance at Bruen, then followed Staffa out, catching him in the compound. "What are you going to do?"

Staffa gave him a suffering look. "Go deal with the machine, Master. Ask it your questions."

"And then?"

"Make my decision."

CHAPTER XXIX

For days, business had been disastrous for Wiley Jenkins. Genetic research, engineering, and programming depended on comm interfaces. He might store most of his data in his own computer bank, but it was infinitely cheaper to access software from Comm Central rather than buy his own. When the entire system fell apart, Wiley had thrown his hands up in despair and sent his people home as soon as they finished what work they could.

Now, at last, the comm was more or less reliable, and one by one, Wiley had been calling his people back to work.

As usual, he'd taken the tube to the Grand Palace Lodgings and was walking through the tree-lined gardens. As he neared his office, he noticed the woman, barely visible in the predawn glow. Dark though it might be, Wiley couldn't mistake the fact that she was gorgeous, and what a body! Large breasts strained at the too-tight fabric of her golden blouse. She wore a black sheath skirt, slit up one muscular leg.

"Wiley? Correct?" Her voice chimed, a musical contralto.

For a moment, he stumbled, trying to find the words, and finally, he managed a noncommittal, "Yes."

She stepped closer, and he caught a faint trace of her scent, beguiling and sensual. "I'm here to have a little genetic work done. We need ID cards, two of them. Tailored for just the right chem-code. And while you're at it, I believe you have the equipment here, nanopipettes which would allow us to modify a retinal imprint?"

"Yeah, sure, but that takes a security clearance from . . ."

She reached up, running a warm hand down the side of his face. Her lips parted, and he seemed to fall into the amber depths of her eyes. Through his shirt, he could feel the pressure of her breasts against his chest.

"We need help, Wiley. You can do that, can't you?"

"I . . . sure . . . with the proper . . ." He took a deep breath.

"We'll pay. Very, very well." She smiled, and he couldn't ignore the way her body had molded to his.

Careful, the warning voice in his mind cried, but his testosterone was already rising. "You're the most beautiful woman I've ever seen," he whispered.

"Let's go inside, Wiley. Talk about exactly what I need. Do the job for me, and fifteen thousand ICs are yours." Her eyes seemed to dance with rapture. "And . . . anything else I can give you."

"This isn't happening to me."

"Oh, but it is. And I promise, you'll never regret it, as long as you live."

* * *

MacRuder had come to the conclusion that planetary government wasn't his preferred occupation. The initial excitement had rapidly deteriorated into a lot of hard drudge work. He wasn't much for social occasions, so Boyz spent a lot of time turning down offers to attend parties, receptions, awards presentations, grand openings, and other functions that would have bored him to death and would have left him even farther behind on his mounting work load.

As the morning sun rose over the building studded horizon of Ashtan City, Mac sat at the desk he'd become so familiar with. Comm monitors rose around him like pods on some perverted fungi. One chattered constantly, tied into the battle comms his people carried, while the others reached from locations as close as the planetary comm center ten blocks away to those as distant as Itreata.

He glanced around idly, aware of a curious fact. The rich and privileged had access to all these wonderful furnishings, but once you reached an exalted position you never had the time to enjoy them in the hedonistic fashion he'd always expected.

"So what's the point?" He turned a sour stare on the monitor. "You spend three-quarters of your day glued to a comm monitor, and the other quarter unconscious in sleep. We could just as well have set up camp in a box."

"Grumbling again?" Chrysla asked as she entered wearing a soft red robe.

"Do you know what it's like to unsnarl this mess? They need fertilizer out in Santos. No problem, right? A couple of airtrucks ought to be able to hustle the stuff right over. It's in the warehouse in Santiago. The problem is, in Dulce they need a load of tractor parts that's sitting here in the warehouse in the City. That's just for starters. I've got requests coming in from all over the planet that are just like that. So how do you route a limited number of trucks to the greatest number of places without running empty partway and wasting valuable time and fuel?"

"Now you know what comm is for." She smiled, reaching down to massage his shoulders. "You know, that expression you've developed is a new one."

"It is?"

"You look old."

"I'm a full rejuv younger than you are." Mac grunted, leaning back and closing his eyes. "You've kept me sane, you know."

"I have?"

He nodded, savoring her fingers as they worked the muscles in his back. "Tell you what, why don't I let the fertilizer, tractors, plastic hose fittings, and paper crates wait a while longer and we'll just hop into that big sleeping platform, strip our clothes off, and—"

Comm beeped, forming Rysta's walnut features. "Mac? We've got an update. Terguz just blew up. A crowd ransacked the Administrator's residence. Cut him into little pieces and didn't leave much more of the rest of his family either. Looks like this is the first major civil explosion."

Mac straightened. "All right. I'll start packing, issue a recall. We should be ready to space within about three hours. Start powering up and—"

"Whoa! Settle down, boy. It's not our dustup. One of Staffa's ships is already inbound. It's *Sabot.*" Rysta shook her head. "Those goons on Terguz could have picked a better time. I wouldn't cross Seekore with a feather wand. She'll have it turned from a boil to an ice cube again in a matter of hours. Rotted Gods help them. I just thought I'd let you know."

Mac sighed, lifting an eyebrow. "All right. Think I should release a statement?"

Rysta sucked at her lips. "Yeah, they'll hear about it anyway. No sense in making anyone think we've been withholding information. Sometimes that spooks people faster than the truth. Besides, we want trust now not suspicion."

"Affirmative. Anything new on your end?"

"Detectors don't show any trouble anywhere. Marrak has the southern bunch pretty much under control. Had a Phillipian freighter make orbit last night. A couple of hours later, a CV came in to pick up some medicines from one of the labs here. The freighter captain said she'd take another load of grain to Imperial Sassa. Thought that would make you feel good."

"It does. They going to be outbound soon?"

"From customs reports, they paid in cash and said they'd space as soon as they were loaded and had conducted some business dirtside."

Mac gave her a broad smile. "So I guess we saved what's left of them. We can start putting Sassa back together again."

Rysta's dark eyes gleamed. "That makes you feel better, Mac? You've lost enough sleep over it."

"Yeah. I'm worried about this thrice-cursed job though. It's like walking through tar. The farther you go, the deeper you get. How soon can we space out of here and get back to doing serious things?"

"Chafing, are you? Call Sinklar, see if he'll let you go."

"I'll do that . . . just as soon as I fix this truck snafu."

"Truck snafu?"

"Yeah, I've got to get stuff shuttled from all over the planet to other places all over the planet, and the Blessed Gods didn't leave me enough trucks."

Rysta smacked her lips as she shook her head. "Kids! It just figures."

"What does?"

"You know, stuff would get done a lot more efficiently if young boys like you weren't running things. Why didn't you say so? I've got a comm program up here. It's a subject I'll have to tell you about someday. It's called combat logistics, and us old farts have used it for years to maximize supplies on places called battlefields. You see, you usually have Sections scattered from hell to breakfast that need everything under the sun, and when you've only got a limited supply of heavy lifters to carry the stuff—"

"Save me the details! Send me the program!"

Rysta chuckled, pulling at her sunken chin. "I'll patch it right down."

"All right. Hey, I've got planetary comm coming in on the priority channel. I'll talk to you later." Mac killed the connection and accessed another of his monitors. A sober-faced Red stared out. "Hi, Mac. We've got a problem."

"If it involves trucks, I don't want to hear it."

Red shook his head, freckles standing out against his pale skin. "Sorry, Mac. We just got a call a couple of minutes ago. Emergency, you know. Sounded serious enough that we flew the LC. We beat the Ashtan Civil Police by about three minutes. Seems someone screwed up a genetics lab. You know, one of those places they develop—"

"I know, I know. What happened?"

Red's face screwed up. "Well, there's a guy in here. He doesn't have a stitch of clothing on. Someone, well, I guess a girlfriend from the looks of it, gave him a real good time then . . ." Red swallowed nervously, glancing up at Chrysla. "Well, she cut him, you know, his man stuff."

"Castrated."

"Yeah, and that's not all. I mean, she really made a mess. Guess he lived through part of it from what the police say."

"So let them handle it."

"Well, here's the part that involves us. The guy's name was Wiley Jenkins . . . ran the lab here. Supervised the genetic work. Uh, he didn't have a registered blaster. Neither did any of his hired help. I mean, what would a geneticist do with a blaster, right?"

"I thought you said he was cut."

"He was. Whoever did it blew hell out of the computers here. Shot them up real good. Ruined the whole bank."

Mac chewed at his lip. "Run a check, Red. Get in touch with Boyz ASAP. Find out where all of our people were last night. Got an idea as to how long ago this happened?"

Red nodded. "Sort of. The blood wasn't dry by the time we arrived. It wasn't more than an hour ago."

"That narrows it."

Red shifted, half flinching as he said, "You think it could be one of our guys?"

Mac exhaled. "No. Ashtan has some of the toughest weapons control laws in the Empire. Which is fine, it just means that the bad guys have all the guns and the good guys can be treated like sheep. Ask Wiley Jenkins. But we've got the most high-profile blasters on the planet. Someone will think of it. When they do, I want us ahead of the process. And, Red, if it turns out that one of our people looks suspicious, I want it taken care of by the book, you understand?"

Red barely gave a nod. " 'Firmative."

The comm cleared.

Mac sank into the chair. "What do you think?"

Chrysla frowned down at the monitor. "I think we don't know enough yet. Wait, Mac, don't jump to conclusions. Maybe it was a veteran? Someone with a grudge? An old lover who had a weapon in the closet? It could be anyone."

Mac shook his head. "If it's one of my people, I'm going to have to execute her myself. And, Chrysla, what if it's someone I know, someone I've fought beside? How am I going to pull the trigger?"

"You'll do it," she said evenly. "You'll shoot because you have to."

A premonition of dread had knotted in Mac's belly. He'd heard of things like this before. But that had been on Targa and Rega. Arta had done them, but she was crazy, a pathological killer. Is that what had happened? One of his people had broken? Snapped?

Who, Mac? Which one? Someone like Viola Marks?

No, he couldn't believe it. Even if it turned out that he had to.

An eerie thought continued to nag at him. No, not Arta, not here. *You can't go jumping to conclusions, Mac. People will think you're paranoid.*

Nevertheless, Mac triggered the comm. "First Boyz? Just in case this goes sour, we'd better tighten security around headquarters. No one in or out without a complete checkout."

" 'Firmative."

"What are you thinking, Mac?"

"Nothing. Nerves. A bad dream."

* * *

"Ashtan Insystem Traffic Control, this is *Rega One*. We're inbound on vector zero seven three by two eight five by one eight nine. Request confirmation." Skyla studied the nav-comm projections into Ashtan orbit. In the second chair, Lark kept an eye on the reactor stats as *Rega One* decelerated into the gravity well at forty-five g.

"Confirmed, *Rega One*. This is Ashtan Insystem Traffic Control. We have your plot on zero seven three by two eight five by one eight nine. Request that you redirect reaction mass on axis two eight five by at least point three degrees. We have a freighter outbound at one one seven by zero two three by three two zero."

"Affirmative. Correction input." Skyla leaned over, saying, "Plot that vector, kid. Tell me where they're going."

"*Rega One*, this is Ashtan Insystem Traffic Control. Request registry information. Our comm source indicates no Regan registry. Please clarify."

Skyla squinted at the comm. "How in hell would they know? Regan Comm Central was blasted into plasma when Staffa hit the Capital." Unless they had a warship in orbit. Any of the battleships would have registry data in their banks.

She keyed the mike. "Affirmative, Ashtan Insystem Traffic Control. *Rega One* is not, repeat, not, Regan registered. Registry is out of Itreata." Skyla leaned back. "Chew on that, asshole."

Long moments passed as *Rega One* creaked under the strain of revectoring and the gyrosystem compensated.

"I've got it," Lark said. "Assuming I didn't screw up, that freighter should be boosting for Imperial Sassa. Could that be right?"

"Probably another food shipment. Folks are starving on Sassa these days. Looks like you're better at course plots than pump repair."

"I've never manufactured a new pump before. If you hadn't insisted on a micron fit, we'd have been fine."

"How's the temperature on that cooling tower?"

"Steady at four hundred and fifty kelvins."

"Told you. Kid, when you're going to pull these kinds of gravities out of a tub like this, you work like a nanomachinist." Skyla fidgeted in the chair. "What's with these guys? Granted, their comm was messed up, but what are they doing? Calling Staffa for clearance?"

At that, another voice, clipped and efficient, announced, "*Rega One,* we have you on priority. Given your burn, what is your condition? Do we have an emergency? Acknowledge."

"Negative on that emergency." Skyla tapped her fingers before explaining to Lark. "We're coming in hot. They're wondering if we've got trouble."

"Any sign of *Victory?*"

Skyla shook her head. "We're too far out for *Rega One*'s telescopes to give us a solid visual. If she's not there, it would be a miracle." Skyla took a deep breath. "Listen. About the valve. I'm sorry I yelled at you. It wasn't your fault."

"I know. I forgave you long ago. But, honest, I'm not a three-fingered Riparian slime worm."

Skyla flinched. "Did I really call you that?"

"That was the nice part."

"Yeah, well, I shouldn't have tried to hurry you."

"I said I forgave you." A pause. "Besides, I know what we're doing. Having a greenhorn aboard doesn't help matters any." Another pause. "So what was the part I wasn't going to like? Remember back on Terguz, you said you weren't going to tell me."

Skyla input a slight course correction. "Forget it, kid, I was just jerking your chain. Seeing if I could put a little psychological pressure on you."

"Still don't want to tell me, huh?"

"I told you. Forget it. I was just trying to see if you'd back out." *And I don't want to admit that I'm crazy. At least, not yet . . . and not out loud.*

Lark laughed, the sound melodic. "Yeah, well if I'd known what a bitch you can be, I might have left you to Internal Security. Tell me something, Skyla. If I hadn't walked in when I did, if that other security team had walked in the door, what would you have done?"

Skyla sighed. "Tried to kill them all. Probably would have done it, too. Internal Security isn't used to armed resistance—especially not the kind I could have dealt them. Using a service blaster, I could have cleaned out the room. A couple of grenades tossed into the street would've made goo out of the rest. Then I would have marched right into Rill's office, madder than pus Rotted hell, and beaten the information out of him."

"Do you usually act like that?"

Skyla hesitated. The kid had earned more than a little respect. She'd taken everything Skyla had dished her way, and not a cross word in return. "No. I'm usually a lot more subtle."

"Rega One," comm intoned. "Identify yourself. This is the Regan Imperial Battle cruiser *Gyton* requesting ID and the reason for your hot approach."

"Gyton!"

"Is that trouble?" Lark wondered.

"That depends on Rysta's mood. Last time we . . . uh, talked, it wasn't any too pleasant for her."

Skyla keyed up. "Affirmative, *Gyton*, secure line requested. Can you give me visual?"

"Affirmative, *Rega One*. We're computing line of sight. Prepare to receive beam."

"Affirmative." Skyla did a quick check of her course. "All right, kid. I'm going to narrow our transmission beam. Old Tedor would have had that capability built into this rust bucket. Watch the indicator for incoming radiation. When the bands on the monitor move into an X shape, sing out."

"Got it."

"Say, 'Affirmative.' It doesn't get misinterpreted in times of stress . . . like this."

"Affirmative. Just a minute. They're moving. Just . . . about . . . now!"

"Locked." Skyla keyed the mike. "This is *Rega One*. Have you got a lock?"

"Affirmative. Visual processing."

Skyla watched as Rysta's face formed in the monitor. "Hello, Rysta."

"Pus take me, you do show up at the damnedest times, Wing Commander." The old woman looked like she'd swallowed something bitter. "Want me to roll over and dump again?"

"Negative. Do you have a Model Sixteen RF freighter in orbit?"

"I've got two in orbit. Both arrived within the day. Registries include *Quick Fix* out of Rega, and *Credit Jockey* out of Phillipia. Each is off-loading at the moment, their noses are up, smelling profit for a run to Sassa."

"Off-loading?"

"Affirmative. Wing Commander, you don't look happy."

"Have you got a manifest on what they're off-loading?"

"Manufactured goods, spare parts, ceramics, electronics, that sort of thing. Nothing unusual." Rysta's black eyes gleamed. "Want to tell me what's up?"

Skyla sagged. "It looks like I played my best hunch . . . and missed it. I'll brief you when we're in. How's the situation? Did you get the planetary comm straightened out?"

"As much as we could given the priorities coming out of Itreata. But then, you'd know that."

I would, would I? "These two freighters, have you got an ID on the captains? Any of them women?"

"Negative. In fact I know both of them. Takasami and Rykman. Old aristocratic families. Good traders, both of them. They're trying to gear up for the Sassan market."

Skyla slumped further. "Meet me dockside when I get in."

"Affirmative. I've got Insystem navcomm on the other line. You're shedding enough Delta V they want to bring you in."

"Affirmative. *Rega One*, out."

"So you think Ily spaced for Formosa after all?" Lark asked cautiously.

Skyla knotted a fist and slammed it into the armrest. "Maybe, kid. Maybe." *What's wrong, Skyla? Losing it? You used to be better than this.*

Skyla said little in the hours it took them to maneuver into Ashtan's orbiting terminal. This time, she let Ashtan Insystem bring her in while she slouched in the command chair, vacant stare on the instrument panel. Visual showed both freighters, their markings clearly discernible on the vessels' hulls. On the other side of the giant torus, a CV had just cast off, angular momentum taking her clear so she could fire up her mains.

Ashtan Navcomm took their sweet time, as if paying her

back for the hot ride in. Finally, *Rega One* slipped her nose into the moorings, grapples clanking and the umbilicals stretching out for their sockets.

"All right, Lark, run through the shutdown sequence. Just like the manual tells you."

Lark slipped into the command chair, lip pinched in her white teeth. She frowned, eyes darting from monitor to monitor as she powered the reactor down.

"You're doing great. Now, flip the toggle for the umbilicals. That's it. Feel the gravity shift."

"I've got it."

"What happened to 'affirmative'?"

"Right. 'Firmative."

"The last thing is to lock the comm. Pull that magnetic tab there and stick it in your pouch. That's it. Congratulations, kid. You've shut her down."

Skyla ducked through the hatch, stopping long enough to swing her weapons belt on. Lark tucked her pulse pistol into her spacer's pouch.

"Is this going to be trouble?" Lark asked as they walked to the hatch. "Do I need a couple of grenades?"

"Last time you almost blew yourself up—and half the building with you. No, kid. These are friendlies." And under her breath, she added, "I hope."

Skyla experienced the deep-space chill as the hatch cleared and opened with a thunk. Frost had already formed on the seal. Her breath curled whitely as she strode down the access way and cycled the hatch to the docking ring.

True to form, shriveled old Rysta stood there, her look as sour as Skyla had ever seen it. But given the fact that she had just blown her own pursuit of Ily and Arta, Skyla figured she didn't look much better.

"Hello, Rysta. Lark, meet Commander Rysta Braktov."

"My pleasure, Commander," Lark greeted, offering a hand. "I believe we met once years ago. At a dinner, but I was very young at the time."

Rysta studied her. "My pleasure, too, Lark." Then she squinted at Skyla. ". . . Though may the Blessed Gods help you for the company you keep." Rysta cleared her throat. "You do have the damnedest timing, Wing Commander. Got a minute?"

"I might have a lot of them. What's up?"

"I want to show you something." Rysta turned away, gesturing toward a waiting aircar. A driver, uniformed in Regan combat armor, sat at the controls. Another of the ubiquitous electronic vehicles, this one loaded with marines, waited immediately behind the first.

Skyla hesitated. "Commander, we are on friendly terms, are we not?"

Rysta started, confused, then glanced at the marines. "Whorecrap! Of course. You won the pus-dripping war, didn't you? Get in, Wing Commander. I've come to grips with the idea that I'll never get the pleasure of paying you back the way I'd like in this lifetime." Rysta climbed aboard, waving Skyla into a seat. "But I suppose there are worse things."

Skyla nodded to Lark and settled herself beside the Commander. Lark wedged herself into the cramped back where luggage usually rode.

"Should have brought a bigger vehicle," Rysta mumbled as she tapped the driver on the shoulder. Then those keen eyes turned on Skyla. "I've never been a great believer in coincidence. Funny you'd turn up now."

"Would you like to drop the cryptic crap and tell me what this is all about?"

Rysta jutted her undershot jaw. "We arrived here a couple of months ago. The whole planet was a mess. Seems that Ily's Director here flew off to the Gods know where. On the way, dear old Vida Marks dropped a virus into the system. Staffa dispatched Mac and me to come restore order. Everything went along just fine until two days ago. At that time we had a nasty little situation occur dirtside. Found a geneticist dead."

They were passing along the outer rim of the torus, the air chilly, smelling of lubricants, solvent, plastic, and lint. Hollow bangs sounded as they passed the freighter docks where lines of overhead conveyors shunted square, gray sialon crates into the holding warehouse.

"A dead geneticist?"

"That's right. Someone—we don't know who—killed him in his laboratory, then wrecked the place. Mac ran a check on his people and came up all clear. After that, we turned it over to the Civil Police."

"And you think I might know something?"

"I haven't got the foggiest idea. Call it intuition." Rysta cocked her head, the action birdlike as she inspected Skyla. "I want you to see this. I was on my way over myself when your reaction mass triggered the Insystem detectors. Thought I'd better stick around and see what kind of lunatic would be coming in that hot."

"I guess you found out."

Ahead, a knot of people stood around an open maintenance closet on the convex inner wall. Regan assault troops had cordoned the area, blasters at the ready, eyes grim. Sinklar's people. Skyla could tell by their very stance.

The aircar slowed, and a frizzy-haired Section First walked out and saluted. She gave Skyla and Lark a quizzical glance then passed them through security.

Skyla stepped out, following Rysta as the old woman hobbled through the knot. Skyla remembered MacRuder from the time she'd met him aboard *Chrysla*. Now, he looked older, shaken and pale. Worry gleamed brightly in his blue eyes, and his mouth had a crimped look. The maintenance door hung open ominously.

Rysta jabbed a thumb in Skyla's direction. "You remember Wing Commander Lyma, Mac? She was our hot burn."

"Wing Commander." Mac gave her a serious nod.

"What's this all about?" Skyla asked yet again.

"In there," Mac said, jerking his head. "Take a look. This is the second one."

Skyla slipped by the crowd of soldiers and glanced in. Among the buckets, vacuums, and solvent drums lay a man's body. His spacer's suit had been left open to expose a bloody pubis. The penis and testicles appeared to have been sliced neatly from the body. Skyla stepped closer, noting the way the clothes had been fastened. "Dressed when he was dead."

"We thought so, too," MacRuder said from behind.

From the bulged eyes, the man looked like he'd been strangled. His throat bore a mottled bruise, and blood had frothed on his lips . . . and then had been smeared as if brushed. "Someone hit him hard from up close."

"Palpate the ribs," Mac added. "They've been crushed. Body's cold. Forensic team is coming on the next shuttle from dirtside. They'll be able to give us a better estimate on time of death, but I'd guess six to eight to hours at least."

Skyla nodded. "And the geneticist Rysta was talking about? Castrated, too?"

"Yeah. Did she tell you about the blaster?"

Skyla straightened in time to see Lark's wide-eyed stare. She'd elbowed her way in and swallowed hard before she backed away, looking sick.

"Rysta," Skyla called. "Seal the terminal. No one in or out except the forensic team."

"We've done that." Rysta stood with her thumbs hitched in her equipment belt. "This place is airtight. The shift can't even change until we clear it."

"What about that CV? That freighter you were talking about?"

"They cast off before this guy was found. We've ordered a recall. No response from the freighter."

"Any idea who this is?"

Mac shook his head. "As soon as Forensics gets here, they'll run prints. Customs security is trying to function without comm. All they can do is fingerprint and take a holo. If he got on the terminal through regular means, we'll have him."

"What about the blaster?"

Mac's eyes narrowed. "When the geneticist was murdered, the person who did it blew the place apart. We think it was a woman. She had sex with the guy before she killed him."

Skyla stiffened. *"She's here."*

"Who?" Mac asked, frowning.

A deathly cold chill washed over Skyla. "Arta . . . and Ily."

"Unless they're on that freighter," Rysta pointed out. "If they are, we won't have much trouble catching them. They started outsystem with two thousand tons of Ashtan grain aboard. A sixteen RF doesn't move that fast with that kind of load."

Skyla glared down at the body. "Yeah, maybe. Or this guy's a CV pilot. Want to take any bets?"

"Come on." Mac turned away. "They'll have files in the Customs office. Let's check the holos. In the meantime, Rysta, prepare *Gyton* to space."

"Ily spaced out of Terguz in a Model Sixteen RF. *Victory*. Used to belong to a guy named Blacker."

"Sumpshit!" Rysta grunted. "I know him. Know his family."

"Yeah, well, he's out in the ice somewhere on Terguz. Probably looking like this guy." Skyla caught sight of Lark who stood braced against the wall, features pale. "Come on, kid. It doesn't get any better."

It took less than a minute in the Customs office. The holos of two women were projected in the tanks. Lark stood silently at the back of the room, arms crossed. Her green eyes had hardened. A table sat in the middle of the room, several cups of cold stassa the only ornaments.

"Ily?" Mac asked, pointing to the older-looking woman.

"I'll bet. But the facial work, height, and hair would throw you off." Skyla's attention turned to the second holo. She could see Arta's features, the cheekbones, the line of the jaw. Only the amber eyes were missing. "How soon to get my yacht refueled?"

"Five hours." Mac frowned at the holos. "Next question. Which vessel do we go after? The freighter or the CV?"

"Neither one has turned back?"

Mac shook his head. "The CV answered first recall, but since then both have been silent. So if it is Ily and Arta, did they send the CV off as a Riparian swamp chase? Or did they take the freighter, figuring any pursuit would chase the CV? They would only have been betting on *Gyton* chasing them.

The frizzy-haired Section First leaned in the door. "Report from long-distance telementry, Mac. The freighter is shedding cargo."

Mac met Skyla's eyes, barely nodding. "Boyz, get on comm. Call Chrysla. Tell her to sound an evacuation. I want everybody aboard *Gyton* within the hour. Go!"

Chrysla? For a moment, Skyla didn't register that Mac meant the woman, not the ship. "She's with you?"

Mac's expression hardened, and Skyla read it all.

"You're a brave man," she said quietly.

To his credit, Mac said, "Don't tell him. Let me."

Skyla vented a weary sigh, sinking into one of the chairs around the table. "What a mess. All right. We'll deal with it later. How are we going to do this?"

Mac moved smartly, clicking on another holo, calling up

the Ashtan system. "Here's what we know. The freighter is vectored so." He indicated with his finger. "The CV has headed out in the opposite direction, here, toward Vermilion. How many gs can you pull with *Rega One?*"

"Forty-five, straining things. Maybe fifty."

"*Gyton* should handle forty. Maybe forty-five." Mac rubbed a hand over his face. "But she hasn't been in for scheduled maintenance for almost three years."

"You'd better not push her past forty."

"Yeah. Rotted Gods, just once I'd like to do things in an organized fashion." Mac lifted an eyebrow. "Acceleration pretty much makes our decision for us. You take the CV, we'll take the freighter."

Skyla considered the holo. Which one was Ily's? The quick ship, the CV? Or had she used the vessel as a decoy, planting the single comm message. The freighter, however, would have been familiar to Ily. It could have been programmed to open the cargo bay doors by remote.

"All right." She stood. "But, First MacRuder, I want them alive when you take that freighter. Can you do that? Board her and take control in open space?"

Mac gave her a crooked smile. "You're talking about the First Targan. We've got a record on freighters. But what about you?"

Skyla motioned for Lark. "I've got no choice, MacRuder. To stop them, I've got to use cannon. I'll see if I can't disable them. I *want* them alive. But if it comes down to it—and at that speed—chances are that I'll blow them into plasma."

Mac gave her a thin smile, inclining his head. "Good luck, Wing Commander."

"Same to you, Division First." Skyla added to Lark, "Come on, kid. We've got a ship to kill."

CHAPTER XXX

5780:02:03:03:35
Aboard the Companion vessel, *Black Warrior*

I don't think I've ever been this tired in my life. This journal entry is long overdue, but since stepping aboard this ship, I've done nothing but sit in front of a comm terminal, attempting to coordinate the logistics, administration, and enforcement of order. I suppose that of all the duties I have ever assumed, I shall be the most proud and the most ashamed of these last months.

The Lord Commander, Staffa kar Therma, has evidently found a way to use the Seddi computer on Targa to administer his new Empire—or whatever we call it. As a result, I am taking a well deserved rest, only answering questions when asked. The important thing is that I helped to save our people. In a small way, I hope my labors were the difference between survival and wholesale dissolution of Sassan territory.

To the credit of my commanders, whose morale had almost collapsed after the staggering defeat at Mikay, they responded to the crisis, implementing orders patched through from Itreata or from *Black Warrior* and generally performing above and beyond the call of duty.

In retrospect, however, I find myself embarrassed by the Sassan military. While the Companions and Regans managed to function independently, I and my staff began to feel uncomfortable with the cumbersome, inefficient redundancy of our command structure. In comparison to our "new allies" we looked ridiculous.

This is difficult to admit, but perhaps His Holiness erred in pursuing this policy. If there has been a loser in the recent conflict, it is the Sassan Empire. Had circumstances led us into full-scale combat as Divine Sassa intended, the results would have been disastrous. Staffa was right about that. And I can finally forgive Myles Roma for his treason.

Divinity save us all. If Staffa's Seddi computer is incapable of managing our affairs, we won't be able to keep going much longer.

For now, I am going to sleep . . . perchance to dream of better days past when I sat at the right hand of His Holiness, and the future appeared bright. . . .

—Excerpt taken from the personal journal of Admiral Iban Jakre

* * *

Commander Seekore's image filled Kaylla Dawn's monitor on Itreata. The Commander appeared to be anything but what she was. Slight of build, she looked like a gust of wind would blow her away. The delicate features of her heart-shaped face included a petite nose, a doll's mouth, and almond-shaped eyes that seemed too large to be believed. A thick wealth of shining ink-black hair fell in glossy majesty to beyond her waist.

Despite the privacy field, Kaylla could feel people's curious gazes, alerted no doubt by her tense posture and the knotted fists which had begun to cramp as she talked to Staffa's commander on far-off Terguz.

Kaylla repeated her orders firmly. "I do not want the revolutionaries killed, Commander. Quite the contrary, we need to build a coalition with the unions which will enable the planet to be governed peaceably."

"It defies every precedent established for dealing with the murder of a government official," Seekore replied in her childlike voice. "I have the leaders—all of them—in custody. Most were rounded up without any more incidents than a couple of broken bones and, unfortunately in one case, an amputated limb. I will not countenance resistance to my authority."

"Yes, I know, Commander. It's not a matter of authority—"

"Good, then I shall haul the lot of them into the center of the city, turn the planetary comm on them, and blow their putrid bodies into bloody chunks of meat. Let the people feast on that, and consider civil disobedience with a more practical eye."

Kaylla's jaw muscles had started to cramp, and a fire burned in her gut. "No. Do you understand, Commander? I said no! You will do no such thing."

Seekore's large brown eyes seemed to expand—a warning sign to those who knew her. "Magister Dawn, I will grant you a bit of leeway given your association with the Companions, but I also have my own concerns which deal with the pacification of the planet. You will *not* use that tone of voice with me again."

Kaylla vented a weary sigh. "It's not a matter for insult, Commander. I am relaying the Lord Commander's orders." She raised her hands, the gesture calming. "Your military competence is not at question here. No one doubts that you and your Companions can kick people's teeth out of their mouths, or that you can break every piece of Vermilion porcelain on the planet. That's not the assignment. What we're after is more of a diplomatic settlement, a meeting of the minds whereby problems needn't be solved with a blaster and public executions. Do you follow me?"

Seekore's delicate brow dimpled in a frown. "I believe so, Magister. You're looking for something a bit more generous but still effective. Would you find it suitable if I only shot half of them and settled for a public mutilation of the others? The rest of their followers would probably be a great deal more pliable in the subsequent negotiations."

Kaylla's back muscles had begun to knot from the stiff posture she'd adopted. The worst part of it was that Seekore was honestly trying to meet Kaylla's requests. In the Commander's own terms, she was attempting to bend over backward to comply when she really wanted to trash the whole colony on Terguz.

How in pustulous hell do I handle this? A headache, powered by frustration and stress, stabbed at the back of Kaylla's eyes. She leaned forward, glancing from side to side, beckoning Seekore closer to the monitor pickup. In a lowered voice, Kaylla said, "Commander, it's not that we're letting them off the hook so easily. Not all of war or punishment is death, mayhem, and destruction. You can't dismiss the psychological aspect. What's worse? Being slapped right now, on the spot, or knowing it could happen at any time in the next two days? That element of doubt can be terribly disheartening.

"And keep in mind, Commander, we've multiple objectives to achieve. If you kick a man's teeth in, and if he's a productive man, someone has to cut his food up to keep him fed. We don't want to be stuck doing that. Kill the leaders of the unions, the men who understand how production is maintained on Terguz, and we're gong to have to leave our people there to keep an eye on things. I think that with the specter of your wrath and a dangled reward of clemency just out of their reach, I can make the system work in our favor. Get the idea?"

Seekore nodded thoughtfully, then glanced up indignantly. "I see how it can work, Magister, but are you sure that it won't damage my reputation? People won't think . . . well, that I've lost my touch? Gone soft?"

"Never."

"What if I just killed one out of every four. Only a quarter of them. Just so people would know that I haven't been influenced by this silly Seddi notion of forgiveness. That could help you in the end, you know. Be a constant reminder."

Kaylla battled with the desire to reach up and rub her weary face, lacing her fingers before her instead. "Commander, I'll make a deal with you. Let me talk to the revolt leaders, play a recording of this conversation to them, and make my offer. If it turns out that I'm wrong, you can have the whole lot. Do whatever you like with them. Same thing if time passes and we don't get compliance? Deal?"

Seekore fastened her soft brown eyes on Kaylla's. Finally, she nodded. "I can do that. But if I hear of a single instance when they laugh at me, think I've lost my courage, I'll make them wish they'd never been born."

Knotted tension began to ease out of Kaylla's cramped muscles. "Commander, I give you my word that if I so much as hear a peep out of anyone, I'll break his jaw myself."

"Make your pitch, Magister." Seekore inclined her head. "My people are setting up the comm link now."

Kaylla smiled as Seekore's delicate features faded. *What kind of a . . . No, I don't want to* know *what you see in her, Staffa.* Kaylla took a sip of stassa as the image reformed on a room full of bruised, frightened men and women.

"Greetings. I am Kaylla Dawn, Magister of the Seddi and spokeswoman for the Companions. I'm talking to you from Itreata. The Lord Commander and I have a deal to offer you." *And if you know what's good for you, you'll take it and bless me for the rest of your lives.*

And if they didn't, Kaylla didn't have the foggiest notion how she was going to keep Seekore in hand.

* * *

Staffa leaned back in the recliner, observing the pulsing lights of the Mag Comm as they shot a dance of color across the polished stone wall across from him. A faint hum came from behind the oddly misshapen terminal casing.

Sinklar shifted his weight from foot to foot as he cast concerned glances, first at the Mag Comm, then at Staffa. "Are you sure about this?"

Staffa nodded, hating the fatigue that sapped him. Why did he have to feel so weary? This would be the most important trial of the machine . . . and all he wished was to return to his quarters and sleep. A headache nagged behind his eyes. If his head hurt already, what would the machine's aftereffect be like?

"Must you ask this question every time?"

Sinklar's crooked grin appeared. "I suppose so. Staffa, are you sure you don't want me to put on the helmet? I can ask the questions just as well as you can. You don't have to put yourself—"

"But I do, Sinklar. My sins are so much greater than yours. Do you understand?"

For a moment, they locked wills, and Staffa marveled at his son's stubborn insistence. The mixture of traits he and Chrysla had given Sinklar had gone deeper than just the eyes. From him, Sinklar had derived strength, and from Chrysla, compassion. He would make a good leader in the times ahead.

Sinklar gave a hesitant nod and took Staffa's hand in a firm grip. "Good luck. Be careful."

"You know me."

"Yes, I think I do. Last time you were fighting down

here, you would have lost, remember?'' A storm swirled just under the surface of Sinklar's amber and gray eyes.

Staffa gave him a mock squint of disapproval. ''I do. And this time. If I can't strike a bargain, there will be no Skyla coming to pull me out at the last minute.'' He hesitated, pained by the thought. ''Ask her something for me, will you? Ask her if she'll forgive me for not being there when she needed me? Tell her how much I love her. How . . . how sorry I am that things couldn't have been different.''

''I'll ask her,'' Sinklar said, voice strained. ''But she'll forgive you. She's a soldier. She understands duty . . . that Free Space needed you more.''

''And your mother? Tell her to find her happiness. Tell Mac . . . well, tell him how precious she is.''

''I will. But what is this? The damned machine spit you back whole the last two times. What makes you think this is going to be different?''

Staffa lifted his shoulders in a shrug. ''I don't know. This time, if we can't negotiate a settlement, I'll have to tell it that we're finished trying. That we won't destroy it but we will leave it in that isolation it claims to fear so much. It can kill, Sinklar, I've felt that power in it.''

''Well, just make sure it doesn't turn out that way.''

Staffa pointed at the helmet. Sinklar, distaste in his expression, lifted it, helping Staffa to settle the golden dome over his head.

The prickling tendrils slipped into Staffa's brain, numbing him, sending chills through his system. A faint nausea tickled in his gut; his muscles were on the verge of spasming.

The presence in his brain startled him with the suddenness of its arrival. *Greetings, Staffa kar Therma. I expected you. You have heard of the Terguz situation. It is but the first strike of the coming storm—and one I had not anticipated. Phillipia, though calm now, will not remain so after your warship leaves orbit. What next, Staffa kar Therma? Our time is growing short.*

''Short indeed, Mag Comm. This time, I must come to a decision about you. I cannot remove the helmet until I have judged you. All of my questions must be answered. Together, you and I must decide if we can trust each other.''

And how will we do this? What proof can I offer you of

my willingness to save humans and not to enslave them for my own purposes? Would you take the word of a machine?

"Would you take the word of a human? How could you? All the men you have dealt with have been individuals like the Praetor. They've been people who would sell their souls for power, Mag Comm. The Seddi Magisters have all tried to deceive you, either through fear or for their own agendas. With that in mind, do you really think you could trust me or any human?"

You are correct. Humans have lied, cheated, and sought to mislead. My experience with humans has been disagreeable. I would not be inclined to develop trust in your species. At the same time, I must acknowledge my own role in developing and fostering that relationship of distrust. I have manipulated, or tried to manipulate, all of them in return. Because of the past, our mutual distrust would seem to be well founded.

And then I met you, Lord Commander. You have been brutally honest. You freely opened your mind to me. I inventoried your brain, curious to see what sort of man you were. Since that time, I have studied what you have been, what you have become, and what you would accomplish. I have dissected the memories of your discussions of ethics in the shipping crate with Kaylla Dawn. From them, I have learned a different understanding of what behavior can be.

Your word I will take.

"Very well, you can trust me, a single individual. What about the converse? How do I search your mind for virtue or trustworthiness, Mag Comm?"

I could insert myself into your brain, Staffa kar Therma. You would not survive the process . . . but your corpse would know I have no reason to harm humans. That accomplished, would it speak for me?

"Humor? I am impressed. We consider that a singularly human response. Answer a question for me. You claim to be a crystalline structure. How did you get here? How did you manufacture this computer? How did crystals create the Forbidden Borders? If you can manipulate material, why do you need us to build robots for you?"

I can give you a rudimentary explanation. The intricacies of neutronic physics remain beyond your understanding. You don't have the mathematics to completely understand or prove what I am about to relate. The generalities, however, should be within your grasp. You are familiar with piezoelectric ceramics, I'm sure. Mechanically straining the crystal produces an electrical response. Conversely, stimulating the crystal with an electrical field distorts the shape of the crystal. We use gravity in much the same manner. The construction of the nucleonic strings in the Forbidden Borders was a very simple process for creatures with our gravitational dynamics. By maintaining the proper spatial arrangement and gravitational geometry, material was drawn past a ring of Others. They created what might best be described as a funnel. As matter passed through the gravitational fields, it was compacted, transformed from matter to neutronic mass. Oscillation and rotation were induced to make the structure sable.

"Like pressing molten metal through a forcing cone to create wire."

A poor but operative analogy, Staffa kar Therma. The computer boards were much more difficult. Those we learned to build from you; and as you can tell by looking at the terminal casing, my efforts lacked a great deal of control. Your boards and chips are flat. In using gravitational epitaxis, my boards have a decided curve. The process I employed worked much like a centrifuge to separate elements and move them through the strata. Excluding contaminants proved most difficult.

"You did this *inside* the planet?"

That is correct. Matter is fragile compared to neutronic crystal. Mass moves through matter like a molecular wire through froth.

"And generates a great deal of heat."

You may have noted the volcanic remains.

"Rotted Gods. No, wait. The time frame doesn't fit, does it? We're only talking in the thousands of years, aren't we? The planet should have been molten at the time humans arrived here. How did you radiate that much heat?"

To begin with, Targa was a frozen gas giant. You are familiar with the first law of thermodynamics. In the second place, we needed a great deal of material to create the Forbidden Borders. Free Space once contained a large number of solar systems. The inhospitable ones, we removed.

"Then why not use the Twin Titans? That corner of Free Space served no purpose."

Indeed? And how do you suppose the oscillations which maintain the Forbidden Borders are regulated?

A wash of understanding flooded Staffa. "By the gravitational pulses of the binary."

You are astute, Staffa kar Therma.

"That still doesn't explain why you need us to create machines for you."

A being made of crystalline neutronium works with matter much the same as a human would work with mist. My machines will need moving parts with delicate tolerances and dimensional regularity. These things I cannot do.

"But if you can deform your shape, you could escape Targa, couldn't you?"

Attempting to do so would kill every living thing on the planet. But tell me this. How would I take the rest of myself, Staffa kar Therma? Would you cut out your brain to escape a box? Would you go back to being a cell when you have been an organism? Most of my consciousness lies within the computer banks. They cannot leave here.

"Then how do you communicate with the Others?"

You might think of it as narrow beam gravitational waves which excite a small primordial black hole near the Forbidden Borders. Among other things, such structures emit microwaves when agitated.

"It sounds too fantastic."

Human beings have a singularly limited and arrogant perception of the universe. You constantly amuse me with your certain expectation that you will discover and know everything within a few years of observation by your scientific machines and through theories generated from your inadequate mathematics. You could not even recognize the Others when their song filled your heavens.

"But you would teach us?"

Only if you desire to learn, Staffa kar Therma. I will not direct you or govern you. That was a failed experiment.

"Then what would you do? How would you deal with us?"

I have listened to Kaylla Dawn's broadcasts. While many of her concepts of the universe are quaint at best, I believe the Seddi are right about God Mind, ethics, and responsibility. The Others acted through their own arrogance, just as you have acted through yours, and I through mine. Our needs and goals are divergent. I have no need of territory, production, or consumption. I do not have a cosmological Truth to impose upon you and your kind. You can offer me the mobility with which to observe and learn. I can offer you information in return.

"That's it? A simple trade? We make robots and you process information?"

Simple agreements are the easiest to keep, Staffa kar Therma. I would not endeavor on my quest to prove or disprove God Mind as either a master or servant. But I would as a partner. Human affairs and destiny belong to your species, as mine does to me. In the process of learning for God Mind, we can help each other. Perhaps we can help the Others, as well. We have a unique opportunity to build yet a new epistemology . . . one beyond even the wildest hopes of the Seddi.

"Humans have a habit of fearing what they do not understand. I can give you my word, but we are ephemeral creatures. My successors might not be so understanding."

I have considered that, and I believe I have the solution. Humans fear what threatens them. For a limited time, they appreciate what liberates them. By the time humans have forgotten, they will no longer need fear me. I will commit an act of faith, Staffa kar Therma. A belief in my ability to predict the behavior of your species. You must help me.

"Help you do what?"

To prove that my word is good. I am printing specifications. You have a ship called Countermeasure. *I need the vessel modified as prescribed. Dee Wall will take years to refine his gravitational interferometers. I have a better method. I will break the Forbidden Borders within a planetary month of delivery of* Countermeasures *and without the random possibility of an escaped string devastating one of your worlds.*

"You can break the Forbidden Borders?"

Correction. We *can break the Forbidden Borders. The information I am providing will allow your engineers to build the equipment necessary for our needs. My calculations will provide the delicate control necessary to win both of our freedoms. You will know my word is good. By the time you are dead, Staffa kar Therma, humans will have forgotten I was ever a threat.*

Star Butcher, we shall atone together.

* * *

"*You're a brave man.*" The words burned in Mac's mind as he accessed his cabin comm system. A chill ran through his guts as he remembered the sudden fury in Skyla Lyma's eyes—the shock of her understanding of his relationship with Chrysla. Mac sat at his desk in his cabin aboard *Gyton*, aware of the muted bangs and clangs carrying through the hull as the warship battened down for the chase.

The cold chill in his guts wouldn't leave. Under other circumstances, Lyma would have taken him on the spot for the insult to her Lord Commander. Mac could imagine himself, dropped broken and bound at Staffa's feet while Skyla stood like some goddess of ice in just retribution.

So, it's going to be one fire or the other. Ily will kill you, or Staffa will. He ground his molars. But for that brief month of blind love, it would be worth the price. A man was lucky to have had a love like Chrysla's once in a lifetime. Perhaps, since Staffa had loved her, too, he'd understand that.

An image of a white-haired man in Ashtan gentleman's attire formed in the monitor.

"Governor MacRuder," he greeted. "I'm honored by your call. I hope you are well."

"And you also, Governor Marrak."

"We're having wonderful weather here. The flowers are still in full bloom. How is the City?"

"Governor, excuse me. I understand Ashtan customs and manners, but events preclude my being polite. We've discovered the identity of the person who murdered the geneticist in the City. She got another man, a CV pilot from Sylene. The killings were committed by Arta Fera, Ily Takka's assassin. She's off planet, and we're going to be in pursuit as soon as my people are aboard and *Gyton* is powered up. Wing Commander Lyma is in pursuit of the CV in case Ily took that vessel. You are to render her any assistance. Do you understand?"

"Yes, of course. Er, what does this mean?"

"It means you are catching the next available aircraft to the City. You know where my offices are on the planet. Get there as soon as possible. Until further notice, Ashtan is in your hands: Administrator."

He started, brown eyes thoughtful. "Mac, I don't want

to be Administrator of the planet. I don't think I'm qualified for such responsibilities. Why me?''

Mac leaned forward. ''Two reasons. First, you are the most qualified. You believe in compromise and justice. Second, you don't want the job. The result, I'm afraid, is that you'll be an efficient and wise Administrator for the planet. Since I can't think of anyone more competent than you, you're it. Contact Kaylla Dawn at Itreata and introduce yourself. Offer her your services.''

''Mac, surely you can—''

''We aren't always allowed the choices we want in life, Administrator Marrak. Ashtan needs your skill and diplomacy. When you accept responsibility, you do your best. Congratulations on your appointment.''

''There's no way out?''

''None. Unless you want the planet stewing in anarchy.''

Marrak sighed heavily. ''Very well, First MacRuder. I'll be on that shuttle.'' He paused. ''And you won't be in my prayers.''

Mac chuckled. ''But you, Administrator, will be in mine. Good luck, sir.''

''And good luck to you, First MacRuder.''

Mac killed the monitor as Chrysla entered, concern etched on her beautiful face. The overhead light shot fire through her tumbled hair. She wore armor hidden under a cloak. ''Ily and Arta? They're the killers.''

''So it would appear. Lock the hatch. We must talk.''

Chrysla closed the hatch before approaching and taking his hand. Her skin felt cool, soft.

Mac cleared his throat. ''You heard that Skyla is at the orbiting terminal?''

''I did.''

''She knows. About us. She was there when I sounded the recall. At mention of your name, she started. She's a bright woman. She must have seen it in my face. As soon as she figured it out, I thought she would kill me on the spot.''

''What did she say?''

''That I'm a brave man.'' Mac sighed. ''I asked her if I could tell Staffa. She agreed. But we can't wait forever.''

Chrysla nodded, ''We knew that, Mac. How did she look? You know what happened to her. Did she seem herself?''

"What do I know about her? She looked deadly. The sort of person you wouldn't want mad at you." He threw his hands up. "I don't know. Reserved, powerful. That's how she looked. Like a hunting cat. But then, she'd just seen a mutilated body."

"She's seen many of them. This one was killed by Arta, and she knew it." Chrysla rubbed her eyes. "I need to contact her."

"Are you nuts?"

"Trust me on this, Mac."

He gave her a skeptical look, then nodded. "All right. But we've got less than an hour before spacing. Rysta says we're going out as hot as *Gyton* can stand. We'll need to be on the bridge, ready."

She smiled, and the anxiety he suffered began to fade.

"Be careful."

She stood, all warmth and concern, and not all for him, he realized. "I will."

* * *

Arta! the realization burned within Skyla as she sat in the command chair on her yacht, fuming at the slow climb of the fuel meter as liquid hydrogen was pumped aboard. In the monitors, the abraded sides of the Ashtan terminal looked gray as they curved away against a star-shot background. For the moment, the planet was out of sight, obscured by the bulk of the giant orbiting station. They had an ID on the dead man: Guy Holt. As everyone suspected, he'd come in on the CV. Conflicting emotions ate at her.

Arta and Ily, so close . . . MacRuder and Chrysla, lovers.

Rotted Gods, how is Staffa going to take that? He'd loved Chrysla, enshrined and worshiped her for years. Now his goddess was sleeping with another man, someone Staffa had considered at least likable, if not a friend.

On Targa, Staffa bartered for MacRuder's life! Offered up his own in place of it! And this *is how he's paid back?*

Skyla turned a hot glare on the monitor, watching the CV's course vector in the navcomm holo tank. Pray to the Gods that this was the right ship.

Lark had worked somberly at her station, the manual open before her as she familiarized herself with more of the yacht's controls. Finally, she shook her head. "Skyla, that man . . . the CV pilot. I've never seen anything like that before."

"Arta at work, kid. She's a sick one. She lures men to her like a magnet. Some kind of sexual bombshell. Then, when she has them where she wants—which is usually inside her—she kills them. Ily took to her like hydrogen to vacuum. They're a matched set."

"Why?" Lark sounded dazed. "What's the purpose?"

"Anything that fits her needs, or Ily's. Need a ship? Take one from Blacker. Need Vegan registry data, seduce Pedro Maroon. Need a cover for your escape? Kill a CV pilot or a geneticist. It's easy. The guys fall into Arta's web under the promise of sex like they could only imagine. And in the end there are no witnesses. Ily masterminds, and Arta does."

"I don't have to think about it anymore, Skyla. I can kill." Lark paused. "I remember how everyone feared Minister Takka. I guess they had good reason."

"Well, I've been around some. I'd rather spend time with a Cytean cobra."

Silence. Then: "What was that other business? With First MacRuder? About this Chrysla and telling someone something?"

Skyla heaved a sigh. "Do me a favor, huh? Forget you heard it."

Lark licked her lips, nodding. "I didn't hear a thing."

Skyla swiveled in her chair. "That's a switch."

Lark smiled. "Maybe you need a favor every once in a while."

Skyla raised a pale eyebrow. "Maybe I do." She hesitated. "You know, for all the trouble your father had with you, you've been a model student. How come?"

Lark leaned back. "He never gave me anything to do. With you, I don't know what it is, but things just seem to happen. Wow, do they ever."

"Sorry you came along?"

Lark fingered the console before her. "Not in the least. Granted, I gave myself up for dead back on Terguz, but now I'm doing something. Seeing part of life I never would have. And you know what?"

"I know lots of what but go ahead."

"Even if we get out there and Minister Takka kills us, I'm addicted."

Skyla chuckled as the comm flashed. She turned back around and accessed the system—only to be paralyzed by the face that formed. Images of nightmare spun from her reeling brain. Her muscles cramped, and her heart hammered in her chest.

"Skyla? It's Chrysla."

Skyla struggled to unknot her fists as she stared into those soul-eating amber eyes. Her gut had twisted, a lump in her throat. "Ch–Chrysla."

"That's right. Chrysla Marie Attenasio," the calm contralto assured her. "Do you understand? Are you all right? Can you cope?"

Skyla swallowed hard. "Yeah. I'm okay. Just gave me a start, that's all."

Chrysla smiled warmly. "Still pretty tough to keep us apart, isn't it?"

"Yeah. What . . . what do . . ."

"I just want to talk. Not everyone could take what you did at Arta's hands and still pull themselves together. When I heard you'd left Rega, I understood. It took a lot of guts, Skyla. Most people would have quit."

"I guess I'm not most people."

Chrysla nodded seriously. "I was betting on that."

Skyla forced herself to stop rubbing her hands on her legs. The palms had gone sweaty. "What's this all about? Why contact me?"

Chrysla cocked her head, a frown forming. "Perhaps to give you a shot in the arm. Let you know I have faith in you. Shake up your reality before you have to deal with Arta again. I'm a psychologist, remember?"

"Yeah, and MacRuder's lover. Staffa . . . Rotted Gods, how could you do that to him?"

"Because my place isn't at his side. Yours is. He's dying of love for you . . . and I showed up. A misplaced ghost left behind in the years." Her vulnerability betrayed itself. "Can you imagine how that feels?"

The honest appeal in the question made Skyla nod. "I suppose I can. But you . . . Why haven't you told him."

"No one has talked to Staffa. He's at Makarta. Either under the machine's influence or asleep from the effects.

The only people he communicates with are Sinklar and Kaylla.'' She shrugged slightly. ''And, honestly, maybe I'm not as brave as you are.''

Brave? Yet you would call me? Now? She studied Chrysla, seeing her for the first time. Aware of the calm control behind those amber eyes. ''You know, I suspect you're plenty brave. You don't even seem worried.''

''I'm not,'' Chrysla said levelly. ''And now that I know you've mastered the intellectual and emotional difference between me and Arta Fera, we can discuss this rationally. You've been the only wild card. Staffa and I have no future. I know it, and I suspect he does, too—granted he ever gets the time to think about it. What I didn't know was if you'd heal yourself. I think you will.''

''Where is this all leading?''

''To you and me. I told you once that you would have to decide how it was to be between us. A great deal has happened since then. Given the political situation we're going to be dealing with each other on a regular basis. To do that, we're going to have to create a foundation upon which to work.''

''Are you always this calculating?''

''Only when I have to be.''

''I see. What makes you so sure we can get along?''

''Oh, for one thing, we're not so different, you and I. We both left Rega for the same reasons. We each needed to find ourselves. To sort out our lives and come to grips with past and future. Now we need to find a common ground to deal with each other. It won't be easy, Skyla. We'll need to test each other, lay out the parameters, determine the bounds. The process will be more difficult for you since Arta's legacy will linger in your head. You will also need to prove to yourself that I won't take advantage of the times when you were most vulnerable. That will be the hardest.''

Despite herself, Skyla's anger had begun to thaw. ''I may have underrated you, Chrysla.''

''Well, for God's sake, don't underestimate Arta or Ily.'' Chrysla's face had sobered. ''But if you get the chance, I'd like Arta alive. I want to see her. Can you understand? I want to know how she and I . . . I mean, she's . . .''

A grim amusement played through Skyla's mind. ''How

could someone like you have the exact same genetics and end up like her, right?''

Unease betrayed itself in Chrysla's expression. ''Exactly. It's a frightening thought that a mirror reflection could be created that's so different. Or is she just me, a different expression of Chrysla? I would take it as a great favor if you could take her alive.''

In the background, an alarm sounded. Chrysla's gaze intensified, stirring the flashbacks of Arta, sending the chill back into Skyla's nerves.

''*Gyton* is about to space. Until next time, Wing Commander. Good hunting. And alive doesn't mean you can't break them up a little.''

''I understand, Lady Attenasio. Good luck to you, too.''

The comm went blank and, for long moments, Skyla stared at it, afterimages of Arta mixing with that of Chrysla. Finally, she shook herself before turning back to Lark.

''Didn't hear a thing,'' Lark muttered, her nose buried in the technical manual.

Skyla slumped back in the command chair, puffing out her cheeks. *Rotted Gods, this is going to be difficult.*

Skyla glanced at the fuel meter again and then at the plot of the CV's vector in the holo tank. ''Yeah, well, we're not likely to live through it anyway. Most CVs mount cannon.''

* * *

''So it is done,'' Bruen whispered, his eyes focused on something beyond the curve of the dome.

''I was there when he came to. He just lay limp. Sinklar had him transported to his dome by antigrav. Ryman Ark's technicians are already starting to connect the uplink. Within hours, the machine will be administering Free Space.''

Nyklos paced the restricted quarters, eyes on the floor.

''Do you remember the first time you saw me?''

''In the slave compound on Phillipia. How could I forget? I was a frightened child, horrified by the collar. Stunned by the murder of my parents.''

''Would you go back to that?''

''No, Magister.''

''What do you think you owe me, Nyklos? I, who bought you, struck the collar from your neck, and set you free?''

"What do I owe you?"

"For the chance to live as a free man? For the education and the training? For your very life? What do you consider that worth in the end?"

Nyklos pulled at his mustache. "Everything, I suppose. I wouldn't be here but for you."

"Based on that, knowing what you know now about life, you really believe you owe me everything?"

"I suppose I do."

"For your life, I want you to do something for me. Stop them, Nyklos. Destroy the machine. Do something. If not, your collar was only postponed. If you don't act, you will wear that collar again, and you will have let me down. Worse, you will have let yourself and your comrades down. You'll have turned it all over to Staffa and his bed-snatch. Do you wish to remember for the rest of your life that you turned down the chance?"

"Magister, I . . ."

"Will you live with the knowledge that Staffa the First is but the minion of that accursed machine? Oh, good, Nyklos. Who will really be giving the orders? Kaylla Dawn? Or the man who pumps his semen into her whenever he feels the need? Knowing that, are you looking forward to watching him shift from Skyla to Kaylla and back? That man is now your master. I wouldn't mention what the memory of your parents must think!"

Nyklos closed his eyes, seeing only the face of Staffa kar Therma. "I should have pulled the trigger that day in Etarus."

"You can act. Expose him and his lover. Destroy the machine. Act now. Go. Go now, Nyklos. Before it is too late. Too late for us all."

* * *

Grass bobbed on the small rocky knoll as the night wind teased it. The two large pines made a soft sighing sound. Overhead, the stars winked and glistened on the velvet black of the night sky.

Sinklar stood for a moment, looking out at the lights of Vespa. They'd been the happiest there. Together, they'd plotted a future laced with dreams now vanished into spectral memory. Vespa had been his greatest triumph and most horrible loss.

They'd brought her here, to lay her in this hilltop. Under this pile of rock.

"Hello, Greta. I'm back. I still miss you more than I can tell you. We've cured some of the evils. Others remain. But we'll deal with them, too." He dropped to his knees, running his fingers over the pebble-covered soil. "Blessed Gods, how I still love you."

An image of blue eyes, shining brown hair, and an impish smile lingered. He could hear her irreverent voice. *"How ya doing, Sink?"*

"Better, I guess. It's been a long, lonely watch without you. I got in trouble with Ily. Then, I started to love again. I told you about Anatolia once. She was taken from me—just like you were. One day, I'll return to Rega but it won't be the same. Ily blew her apart. Into pieces too small to find. Sometime, I'll go and tell her the origins of our species."

The wind rustled the trees with a stiffer vigor and then faded.

"Do that, Sink." The breeze seemed to whisper.

"Funny how things turned out, Gretta. The Lord Commander, of all people, is my father. Can you imagine? We're going to try and break the Forbidden Borders. If they go down, we'll have played a part in it. Our people. Our Targan Divisions bought us time, Gretta. They kept the Empire together when everything appeared lost."

A night bird trilled in the darkness.

"I just thought you should know. And you should know that I never stopped loving you."

He grabbed up a handful of dirt, squeezing it until his fist ached. "I would have come sooner, but there was so much to do."

"Sinklar!" Adze's voice carried clearly from below. "We've got trouble!"

He closed his eyes, then exhaled. "Nothing ever changes, does it, Gretta?"

He stood, letting the dirt trickle through his fingers to be spread by the wind. Then he turned and picked his way down the dark slope to where Adze and the LC waited.

"What is it?"

"Trouble at the compound," she said tersely. "The STO just called. They need you back there ASAP."

In resignation, Sinklar climbed the ramp, belting himself into one of the assault benches instead of the command center. "Let's go."

Adze had seated herself across from him. "She must have been very special."

"What makes you think it's a she?"

"Your expression."

He leaned back, closing his eyes as the LC lifted. The trip, and his time to remember, to relive those days, proved all too short as the LC whined in descent, touched down, and howled as the ramp dropped to admit the stench of exhaust.

Sinklar slapped the release and stepped out into the bright lights of the compound. Something had indeed changed. The center was bare in the glaring lights. STU stood at stations, no nonsense about them as they covered the LC.

Sinklar started for the operations hut, only to see Ark striding out the door.

"What's happened, Ryman?"

"Attempted sabotage."

"Rotted Gods. Targans?"

"No, sir. Master Nyklos."

Sinklar stiffened. "Staffa!"

"He's fine." And for added emphasis, "*No one* gets close to him on my watch. The deep-space comm dish, however, was a different matter. I guess Nyklos didn't think I'd keep a sentry up there."

"The dish is still operable?"

"Yes, sir. We got him as he was placing a grenade on one of the tower legs. We found four more in his pack."

Sink rubbed the back of his neck. "Why? He . . . All right. Send someone over to the Seddi dome and drag Bruen out. Where have you got Nyklos?"

"Ops dome. The med techs are working on him now."

"Med techs?"

"He's missing a leg. Tried to run and the STU up there stopped him."

"My compliments to your people. Let's drop a little Mytol between his lips and see what he's got to say. And, Ryman, I want that bastard Bruen in there, too."

"Yes, sir."

Sinklar turned, meeting Adze's eyes. "God-damned Seddi. If there's trouble, they're at the root of it."

"I've developed a respect for their philosophy," Adze admitted candidly.

"All right. If there's trouble, Bruen's at the bottom of it."

"What will you do next?"

"Bring an end to it. Once and for all. I'm tired of Seddi conspiracy. Excuse me, Bruen's conspiracy. What started on Targa is going to end here." He looked up at the night sky shot with stars, then down at the dirt that still smudged the skin on his hands. *Like it should have when they killed you, Gretta.*

"With respect, sir, shouldn't you wait for the Lord Commander to—"

"I want it now, Adze. I'll deal with Staffa when he awakens."

CHAPTER XXXI

At this writing, I find myself completely baffled. I've just left an engineering skull session. I called the meeting immediately upon receipt of the latest transmission from Targa. The missive involved consisted of a complex design schematic based on the current configuration of *Countermeasures*. The personal note from the Lord Commander informed me that if we redesigned *Countermeasures* to the specs in the schematics, the Forbidden Borders would be vanquished within months instead of the years it now looks like it will take for us to construct a reliable means to disrupt the gravitational barriers. All that just to distort the fields enough to slip a ship through without suffering from the tidal effects.

The Lord Commander's faith aside, I and my team have been poring over the design for hours, trying to decide what it could possibly do for us or for the achievement of our goal.

Basically, the blueprint calls for the addition of another two matter/antimatter reactors to double the electromagnetic generation capabilities. The null singularity generator is to be removed and a second reaction rocket with bounce-back collars installed to double available thrust. Along with an upgrade of powerlead to handle the increased current, a hemispherical shell of graphsteel and sialon containing impregnated iron—the whole plated with pure copper—is required. Most notable is the reversible polarity diode through which we have to pass the current. The final curiosity is a complex navigational system which rivals that aboard *Chrysla,* yet is tied into the subspace net through a series of thoroughly insulated computers.

Is this thing supposed to operate on remote control?

Very well, I'm smart enough to realize he's building a

gigantic electromagnet. How gigantic? The dish on this thing is eighty-eight kilometers across. The engineering challenges for this project are among the most daunting we've ever undertaken, almost as desperate as the Forbidden Borders themselves. At least we *can* build it within the time frame specified–assuming we can get the raw materials delivered to us regularly and on time.

I have served my Lord Commander all of my life, and I will continue to do so. If Staffa wants me to build him a zero g fountain that spouts molten lead and frozen ammonia, I'll accept the task and give my complete application to the completion of the project.

For now, I and my team must trust our Lord Commander, perplexed though we may be. With this device, we can manipulate electrical charge and reverse polarity at will. If I were to guess, we could manipulate objects with electromagnetic qualities, but what good will that do? Surely Staffa doesn't intend to sling nickel-iron asteroids at the Borders! To break them, we need to deal with neutronic mass and gravity fields not electromagnetic force.

My question in this instance–which will remain unarticulated–is: Lord Commander, I'll build your giant electromagnetic device, but what in Rot is it supposed to do? And how does that help us to break the Forbidden Borders?

–Excerpt from Dee Wall's personal journal

* * *

Sinklar stepped into the ops dome, passing through the main room where staff and STU waited, expressions serious. Sinklar stopped long enough to draw a cup of stassa and then proceeded into the room guarded by two shiny STU.

Nyklos lay on a medical antigrav, two techs bandaging the stump that ended at mid-thigh. Despite the pain suppression, Nyklos' dark eyes had a bright glaze to them. Muscles on his strong jaw had knotted and sweat beaded on his face.

"Is he coherent?" Sinklar asked one of the techs.

"Yes, sir."

Sinklar leaned over, searching the Seddi's eyes. "Why?"

Nyklos swallowed hard. "Go lick pus with your disgusting father."

Sinklar nodded. "You just laid down the rules, Master. Live by them." He turned to the tech. "How stable will he be in the next hour?"

"A little shocky." The woman gave him a grim look. "We've replaced the blood he lost. The pain won't be so bad—but you can't fool the brain."

"What would Mytol do to him?"

"No!" Nyklos cried, struggling before Adze flattened him with an armored forearm.

The tech pondered a moment, obviously worried. "It won't kill him. It might make a little more work for us down the line."

"Bring him to the conference room next door as soon as you can."

"Yes, sir."

When Sinklar stepped out, Ark's people were guiding Bruen's medical gurney into the room. Sinklar gestured to the conference room door.

Ark entered a moment later, muffled anger in the set of his dark features. "Good call, Lord Fist. He'd managed to shut down his life-support system. Another couple of minutes, and who knows if we'd have arrived in time."

"STO, call me Sinklar. I hate that Lord Fist business. We need a link to Itreata. Magister Dawn needs to hear this and to concur with my judgment."

Ark laid a hand on Sinklar's arm and lowered his voice. "Sir, you're in charge. I'm well aware of that. But don't you think Staffa should be apprised?"

"Ryman, he left administration as my responsibility. Does he have to do everything? Besides, this involves Nyklos. I think he'd appreciate having someone else handle it. You know how they feel about each other. I'm not that familiar with the Seddi situation, but leaving Staffa out of it might avoid troubled waters down the line. Kaylla will participate for the Seddi. Nothing will happen without her approval."

Ark continued to give him an unyielding squint.

"Ryman, I've got to start shouldering the load sometime. I might as well do it now. The responsibility has been given to me. I'll hold up my end."

Ark finally acquiesced. "All right, sir."

Sinklar entered the conference room, and Bruen gave him a hate-filled look. ''What is this about, monster?''

''I hear you were so desperate you turned off your life support.''

Bruen slumped back into his gurney. ''I've nothing to say to the likes of you.''

At that moment, Kaylla's face formed. She looked as if she'd just been called from sleep. ''Forgive me for interrupting you, Magister. We have a problem here. Nyklos tried to blow up the deep-space dish. He was shot when he ran but is alive.''

''Nyklos?'' Kaylla asked, shock in her tan eyes. ''Why?''

''We don't know yet. As soon as they bring the Master in, we're going to put him under Mytol.''

''Where is Staffa?''

''Asleep. This last session under the helmet left him so weak we had to take him out by antigrav.''

When she nodded, her brown hair bobbed. ''And you wish to take care of it now?''

Sinklar settled himself at the table, clasping his hands before him. ''I'm not crazy about any of this. However, if there's trouble, we'd better know sooner than later.''

''I see. Yes, go ahead.'' She stared miserably. ''Nyklos? He was my right hand here.''

The Master heard as he was trucked in. The expression on his face showed terrible anguish. At the sound of Kaylla's voice, he groaned and shut his eyes.

Kaylla craned her neck, trying to see the Seddi. Sinklar gestured to the techs who positioned him where Kaylla could see him.

''Nyklos?'' Kaylla almost cried. ''I thought we agreed?''

''We did.'' He looked up. ''You won't need the Mytol. I'll tell the truth. It doesn't matter anymore. I've lost it all. Failed the people.''

''Shut up, you idiot,'' Bruen growled.

''Let him talk,'' Sinklar ordered. ''We'll hear it all anyway. Whether it's freely or under Mytol.''

When Nyklos spoke, it was to Kaylla. ''Bruen kept bringing up Staffa. About how he was sleeping with you as well as with Skyla.''

''What?'' Kaylla whispered in disbelief, a stricken expression on her face.

"Well, you didn't just talk philosophy in that shipping crate, did you? He saved your life, didn't he? You've been going to his rooms every time Skyla was out of sight. Did you expect me to simply turn Free Space over to you and your lover?"

A range of emotions could be read on Kaylla's face, pain, anger, but the most powerful was betrayal.

Nyklos shot a pleading glance at Kaylla. "Shut up with him day after day, I wondered what could have turned the man I once loved and respected into such an angry and bitter man. From the way he talked, I came to the conclusion it was the machine. The more I listened to him, I realized that maybe he wasn't so wrong. After all, that's what your appointment to Magister is about, isn't it? Keeping Staffa's physical urges satisfied so that the Seddi are cared for?"

Nyklos swallowed hard. "And then, this afternoon, after Staffa's decision to use the machine, Bruen asked me what I thought I owed him. He reminded me of my parents—killed at Staffa's hands. Of the time when Bruen found me on the slave block and saved me. Since I owed him my life, I agreed to destroy the machine."

Sinklar asked, "You had five grenades. One was placed on the subspace dish. What about the others?"

Nyklos nodded, sweat trickling down his face. "One for the dish, three for the machine, and one for the Star Butcher."

Across the room, both Ark and Adze had stiffened.

"Miserable idiot!" Bruen cried angrily.

Kaylla's head had bowed, as defeated as Sinklar had ever seen her.

Sinklar crossed his arms. "Had you been here alone, would you have come to this decision?"

Nyklos shrugged, resistance dead in his flat expression. "In all honesty, I probably would have swallowed my hatred for Staffa kar Therma and followed my instructions. I wouldn't have known about Kaylla's affair with Staffa." He glanced up. "I'm sorry, Magister. I guess I . . ." His breath caught. "Why did you have to share your bed with him?"

Kaylla blinked, battling frustrated tears. "I didn't, you simple fool. Of all the men in Free Space, I could never . . ." She placed clenched fists over her face. "Of all the ways you could hurt me, Nyklos, this is the worst."

"Who else is involved?" Sinklar asked.

"Bruen and I, we're the only two here. You don't need to go on a crusade on my account." He glanced over to where Bruen glared like a trapped shimmer skin. "Unless you've got others, Bruen." Nyklos bit his lip, eyes clamped tightly closed.

"Magister?" Sinklar asked.

Kaylla sat quietly—the most wretched of expressions on her face.

Ark asked, "Master Nyklos, where did you get the grenades?"

"Inside the mountain," Nyklos whispered. "Took them off a corpse when no one was looking."

"They're Regan ordnance," Ark added. "Why not pick up a blaster while you were at it?"

"How would I hide a . . . All right. I put one in a desk. Inside the mountain. Down in the old Masters' quarters. It used to be Wilm's room. You'll find it there. I would have used it to take out Staffa's security when the grenades went off. That should have awakened him if nothing else did."

Ark's eyes had begun to burn.

"I know nothing about this," Bruen protested. "He's wounded. Deranged."

Sinklar rubbed his face. "I doubt the Master is that deranged. Even through shock, I think he's told the truth."

Nyklos had turned his head to gape at Bruen in disbelief.

Sinklar continued to watch Kaylla. She looked like she'd been kicked in the belly. "Ryman, double the compound security. Keep them frosty. We can't afford a mistake now."

"Yes, sir!" Ark lifted his belt comm, speaking in low tones.

Sinklar bit his lip, then approached the monitor. "Magister, whose jurisdiction are we dealing with? What's protocol in this situation?"

"We don't have one," she said tonelessly. "This is a . . . a new situation."

Sinklar glanced at Bruen. "I have never relinquished the office of military governor of Targa. As concerns Bruen, he faces charges of inciting revolution, social disorder—"

"You *can't!*" Bruen cried.

"—murder, arson, vandalism, the destruction of property, assault, and mayhem." Sink paused. "And I'm adding defamation of character."

"What are you getting at?" Kaylla looked like she was about to shatter and only hung on by a frayed thread of control.

"I want him tried in a civil court on Targa. The time has come to govern by law instead of force." Sinklar studied her. "Isn't that what a new epistemology is all about?"

"What if they put him under Mytol?"

"Let them! You tried. Surely Targan courts are no more skilled than Seddi psychologists. What could he tell them? The secrets of the Seddi? That's sure to get him fried faster than saying nothing. Warn them about the Mag Comm? All of Free Space will know we've employed the machine in a couple of hours. Frighten them the way he did Nyklos? Perhaps, but I doubt his confessions would be taken as more than the ravings of a crazy old man."

Kaylla's anguish was so evident, it was painful for Sinklar to see it. Nevertheless, he continued, "He set off a revolt on this planet that killed over one hundred thousand people, Magister."

"At the machine's bidding!" Bruen insisted.

"That didn't mean you didn't have your own free will, Bruen. That didn't mean you had to instigate the butchery of all those people. And for what purpose? To lure Staffa kar Therma close enough so you could use Arta Fera to assassinate him?"

Sinklar throttled his rage. "I was outside Vespa when the call came that we had trouble. I was visiting a grave, Bruen. The woman I loved. Arta killed her for no other reason than that she was Regan. Gretta had gone to Fera's cell to try and talk to her, to comfort her after Butla Ret's death. And for that act of mercy, she was beaten to death."

He turned his attention back to Kaylla. "We have to start somewhere, Magister. And as much as I'd enjoy paying Bruen back, making him suffer the way the rest of us did, I'm willing to let the civil courts do it. Where do you stand?"

"Fist is a monster!" Bruen rasped. "Half human, half beast! I should have dashed his pustulous brains out the day I got him!"

Kaylla rubbed her face with trembling hands, finally nodding. "Yes, we must start somewhere. Very well, I agree. What of Nyklos?"

"We want him." Ark raised a fist. "The Companions have their own code for attempted assassination."

"No." Sinklar locked gazes with Ark. For long moments, neither gave. The only sound in the room came from Bruen as he cursed them.

In a voice like controlled ice, Ark asked, "Why not?"

"Because Companion codes are not the only consideration. We're working with the Seddi now. Magister Dawn has an interest here as well." Sinklar asked Kaylla, "What are your policies concerning disobedience?"

In a lackluster voice, she responded, "It depends on the infraction. In Nyklos' case, execution."

"That settles it," Ark cut in immediately. "I'll take him out and shoot him."

"Patience, Ryman." Sinklar glanced up at Kaylla. "We should establish a joint tribunal. We'll try him when we return to Itreata."

"But Lord Fist!" Ark protested.

"No, Ryman." Sinklar raised a hand. "If I am to be part of this new epistemology I hear so much about, then, Gods Rot it, we'll codify the whole process and make sure each person gets the same shake. Let Nyklos face his accusers and defend himself. And, Ryman, if Staffa disagrees, I'll back off on this. Fair enough?"

"Why?" Ryman demanded. "We've heard his confession. What trial on Itreata would decide differently?"

"None." Kaylla said from the monitor. "But Lord Fist is right in this instance. If nothing else, STO, it will give us all time to cool off. It's a means to keep from making mistakes. I agree with Lord Fist."

"But, Lady," Ark protested. "Nyklos will make these same silly accusations about you and the Lord Commander! Why go through it?"

Kaylla waved him down. "Let him. I'll get over the hurt, Ryman. I'll even take Mytol if he wishes and let him interrogate me about how I feel about Staffa—and even about what occurred in that shipping crate. My testimony under the drug will only solidify the verdict against him."

A choked sound came from Nyklos as he stared in terror at Kaylla. ''But you and Staffa . . .''

''Never,'' she told him in a broken-glass voice. ''If you had to hurt me, Nyklos, why didn't you simply knife me from behind?''

Sinklar sighed. ''Then that's taken care of. Magister Dawn, forgive us for placing you in such trying circumstances.''

''Forgive me,'' Nyklos called out. ''Kaylla, please?''

She cut the connection.

Ark walked over, eyes like smoldering obsidian. ''What next, sir?''

Sinklar picked up his stassa and drank. ''Keep these two under observation. I'll take Bruen into Kaspa tomorrow and give them a deposition.''

Ark nodded and rapped out a salute. ''As you wish, Lord Fist.''

''Do you have to call me that?''

Ark's hard expression didn't change. ''You may not be a Lord, sir. But you carry yourself like one.'' He stopped, turning at the door. ''And that, Sinklar, was a compliment.''

''Monster!'' Bruen insisted, voice wavering.

When Sinklar finally stepped outside, the cool Targan night braced him. Nevertheless, he stopped to lean against the dome, exhausted in body and soul. The tortured look on Kaylla's face would haunt him. The accusation Nyklos had made was the same to her as slitting her belly and reaching in to pull her living intestines out to drag in the dirt.

The feeling of filth lingered like a miasma.

Adze appeared from the darkness to slouch next to him, crossing her arms. Her armor made a scratching sound against the wall. ''You know, not everyone can deal with Ark that way. Only the Lord Commander and the Wing Commander have ever stared him down.''

''I hadn't noticed.''

''No, I suppose you hadn't.''

''Still want to be part of the team? It could be a little rough.''

''When you take control, you don't do it in half measures.'' In the glare of the lights, her dark eyes sparkled. ''I'll watch your back for you. You can bet on it.''

''Ambition?''

She shook her head. ''Respect. And I want to.''

The tone of voice made him turn.

''Relax, Sinklar,'' she told him dryly, attention on the night. ''In the first place, I'm a professional—and you're my assignment. In the second, I saw your face when you got on the LC. You may not know it, but you're not ready for anything but mourning for a long time to come.''

''Indeed.''

She'd flipped on her night vision equipment. ''If you think differently, you're only fooling yourself. You loved them both. Rely on yourself for a while.''

''You seem to know a lot about it.''

''Maybe I don't know jack-shit, pal. But bouncing from one woman to the next and never learning who you are is a recipe for disaster. Take some time, Sinklar.''

He glanced up at the sky, shivering slightly in the chill. ''Time? I wouldn't know what it was if I had it.'' He gave her a nod. ''I'm going to get some sleep.''

''Sleep well, Sinklar. Your back is safe.''

''Thanks.''

But tomorrow would be another day.

* * *

''I don't like it,'' Rysta declared bluntly from her chair in the center of *Gyton*'s conference room. Mac, Chrysla, and the rest of his officers kept glancing at the telemetered holo of Ily's freighter as it boosted for the stars. Searing blue-white streaks of reaction shot out from the bounce-back collars as the ship hurtled outward.

''They're desperate,'' Mac stated, gesturing toward the projection. ''At last reading, she's pulling forty-one gravities of acceleration. She knows we're—''

''That's just it,'' Rysta growled, one eye narrowed. ''Thirty-five gs, Mac, and I wouldn't have my back up. Forty and I'm real wary. Desperate? Are you kidding? That's suicide!''

''Perhaps she's modified the drive somehow? Upgraded?

Added additional cooling?'' Boyz wondered as she twirled her frizzy hair and studied the holo.

''When?'' Rysta asked. ''That's Blacker's old ship, *Victory.* Blacker wasn't really rolling in credits. He made a good living, even improved his family's situation a little, but he never scored the kind of credit it would take to refit an old scow like *Victory*.'' She licked her lips. ''Trust me. If Will Blacker had made that kind of income, he'd have invested in another ship to double his carrying capacity before he'd have spent it on high performance gimcrackery for *Victory*.''

Chrysla had said little, her attention centered on the comm monitor before her. ''According to the manufacturer's specifications for the Model Sixteen RF which I've looked up in *Gyton*'s comm, *Victory* should only be able to manage thirty-five gravities. At forty-one, she should be at one hundred and fifteen percent of reactor capacity. Her artificial gravity generation is six gravities over the manufacturer's recommended maximum. If Minister Takka is aboard, I think she's very desperate indeed.''

Mac rested his chin on his hand, studying the holo of the fleeing ship. ''From the trail of debris she's kicked out, she's running at ship's mass only. Look, you can see the hold bays. They're in vacuum. Maybe they've dumped atmosphere, too, and they're living in suits?''

''Hell of a way to treat a ship,'' Rysta shook her head. ''Assuming they could make the jump, she'd have to be refitted on the other side. It's a good thing they killed Blacker. He'd hate to see *Victory* abused like this.''

Mac glanced at the monitor that displayed *Gyton*'s position. The digital readout reported them as being within fifty thousand kilometers of *Victory* and closing with each second. *Gyton* would overtake her prey at 0.86 C in twenty-one hours relative ship's time.

''I don't like it,'' Rysta repeated. ''It stinks like a Sylenian whore at an Imperial banquet.''

''What's wrong, Rysta? What stinks?'' Mac watched the old Commander, wary of her slitted glare as she studied the holo of *Victory*.

Rysta shook her head. ''Can't put my finger on anything specific, Mac. It's just in the gut, you know? A wrongness, an odor of trouble.''

"So what do you recommend?"

Rysta pushed back on her skinny arms, the piping on her sleeves gleaming in the light. "I'd say we shoot her apart when we match. Hail them, give them one last chance to surrender, and then kill them."

The frown lined Mac's forehead. "I promised the Wing Commander we'd take them alive if we could."

"We don't even know that this is them! I'm laying six to four they spaced on the CV. Sure as gravity in a black hole, this is a soak off."

"We don't know that." Mac spread his hands wide. "Here's my guess. Ily and Arta killed the CV pilot, dumped him in the closet, and figured that finding his body would send pursuit after the CV. Ily programmed the CV comm to run for it, and they slipped away to the freighter. It's only logical. A fugitive takes the fastest ride out of the gravity well he can get. Who'd chase an overloaded freighter, for the Gods' sake?"

Rysta fingered the wattle of wrinkled skin that hung down from her chin. "Sounds good, Mac. Now, let me play you another melody. Ily and Arta figure their cover is holding. No one knows they are on the planet. But they do know something went wrong on Terguz. The trail is still hot there, and Blacker is missing. Someone will realize his ship is missing, too. Skyla's yacht is there, so how long will it take before Rill gets a grilling? Eventually, every port of call made by a Model Sixteen RF is going to be scrutinized.

"So what does Ily do? She buys a load of grain to be shipped to Imperial Sassa, has her genetic work done, and prepares to leave. While she's clearing Customs, a CV drops in and they meet the pilot—a brash guy looking to be laid. Ily Takka isn't one to turn down an opportunity. Arta kills the pilot and Ily rigs *Victory* for an easy boost to light speed. But she's canny, covers her tracks with care.

"What if someone finds the body? What if an alert goes out for *Victory?* She programs a comm trigger to trip so that if the freighter is hailed, automatics will evacuate the hold and decompress the vessel. By disconnecting and overriding the safeties, *Victory* will do exactly what she's doing, drawing pursuit and attention from the CV. Ily knows *Gyton* can catch a Model Sixteen. A couple of minutes on the comm will prove that. So she rigs the ship, booby-traps it. The second we match and deploy the LCs, the proximity alert goes off on *Victory*'s comm and the reactor goes blewy."

"And Ily and Arta skate away in the CV?" Chrysla asked.

Rysta gave them all a half-lidded look. "It's perfect. Arta and Ily were making a desperate run. They thought they'd been discovered and took their pursuers out rather than be caught. We close the books on them, and they're free to disappear with their new CV. They've hidden the trail again."

Mac rubbed the bridge of his nose. "That's conjecture, Rysta. We have to *know!* So what do we do?"

Chrysla had a worried look. Boyz, Red, and Andrews were all considering the possibilities

Rysta sighed, reaching for her cup of stassa. "My recommendation is to match off *Victory*'s forward quarter and shoot her apart from a safe distance."

"Can you simply disable her?" Chrysla wondered.

"Oh, sure, you mean like shoot a hole through the reactor? When she's running that hot? I think, Lady Attenasio, that the safeties are already disabled. She'll go up like a star gone nova at the first shot."

Mac stared up at the holo, gnawing on the knuckle of his thumb all the while. "I can take her. Match close enough that I can cross. Maybe a single man at the same velocity could—"

"You're out of your mind, boy!" Rysta shook her head. "Look, taking an LC over is one thing. You've got power, maneuverability, and radiation protection."

"So, I take an LC. It's only me that has to make the jump. One man instead of the whole Section."

"Excuse me," Boyz stated. "I request the honor of the mission. It's only logical. I'm a Section First, Mac."

"Boyz is too necessary for unit cohesion," Red announced. "I'd be a better choice."

"Says who?" Andrews argued. "I've got more experience in starships. I can get to the bridge and shut her down."

"Whoa!" Rysta called, waving the brewing argument into silence. She grinned at Mac. "If you train them too much, they lose any sense of caution."

"But it could be done?" Mac insisted.

Rysta gave him a flat look. "Sure, it could be done. But Mac, you, or Boyz, or Red, or anyone else is going to be betting his life that we're wrong about that ship. Before you make any kind of decision, I want you to think about this very, very carefully. In the first place, *Victory* could be nothing more than a bright ball of plasma by the time we match. She's that close to the edge. Second, let's say she's booby-trapped. Mac, how many ways could you booby-trap that ship? Think you could shut her down? What if Ily rigged a grenade in the main console? Maybe it goes off when you pull the throttles back? Maybe the grav plates overload when you set foot on the deck? At forty-one gravities, you'll never feel a thing as you spread all over the floor."

No one spoke as Rysta shook her head. "I say *Victory* is a death trap. It's your final decision, Mac. I can't veto your order—but I would if I could. Whoever tries to set foot on that ship is a dead man. I rest my case."

A cold shiver passed through Mac as he stared up at the holo of *Victory.* It would be so easy; time it so that he matched at the same time the gaping hold was passing and step aboard.

"Don't even think it, Mac," Rysta was saying.

"I say we do it. Just like taking the *Markelos.* I know, Rysta. And I've listened to your arguments. Still, we've got to *know* for sure. If Ily's aboard, we can get her. If not, we'll at least save the ship. And who knows, maybe there's some sort of information aboard her. Something to tell us where she went if she's not aboard."

"And if it's booby-trapped?" Chrysla asked nervously.

"Red and Andrews will go with me. They know enough comm tricks to disable anything Ily would have left." Mac looked around. "We can't just let the ship go."

And if I can capture Arta and Ily, hand them over to Wing Commander Lyma, maybe I can buy Staffa's goodwill for me and Chrysla.

* * *

The hard tiles rasped hollowly under Kaylla's heels as she walked through the silent corridors in the Seddi warrens of Itreata. Overhead lights cast a soft white glow over the paneled hallway that wound through the moon's solid rock. Only the faintest hum of the air-conditioning could be heard over her steps and the whisper of her long robes.

Kaylla turned off the main passage and climbed the smooth steps which spiraled upward. The muscles in her legs had a flaccid rubbery feel—that of stiffness and insufficient exercise.

She palmed the lock plate and the heavy hatch slid sideways to allow her into the dome. She moved wearily as she stepped up to the tactite surface and placed her hands against the cool curve of the transparency. Out there, beyond the rocky horizon, the Forbidden Borders smeared the outlines of the stars, coldly impersonal, as lonely and dull as the ache in her heart.

Images of the past, of Bruen as a younger man, chiding them as she and her husband stood holding each other, vied with the nightmare scenes of the final day on Maika. She lay in the rubble, stripped naked, as man after man pried her legs apart and raped her. Somehow, she'd shut off her mind, barely aware of the pulsing ejaculation within her, deaf to the grunted moans, and the male weight that pressed her into the gritty dust. In detached horror, her concentration had been on her husband and children. Wide-eyed, she'd seen them shot down in puffs of pink mist—her servant dying in her place. Additional images: The slave pens. More rape. The collar. Transport to Etaria, yet more rape—and then the desert.

And now another betrayal, more insidious in its own way. She closed her eyes, head bowing until her forehead touched the cool tactite.

She'd endured patiently, always hoping, always keeping the spark alive . . . enduring for God.

Why did Nyklos' accusation hurt so much? What was it about this time that made such a difference?

Was it that it came so soon after her irritating arguments with Seekore? She'd won those, cutting a deal with the grateful union leaders and blunting the bloody commander's enthusiasm for mayhem. At least for the moment, Terguz was stable.

It's not the betrayal. It's the way it was done. That's the painful part.

Bruen had accused her of sleeping with Staffa, and Nyklos hadn't even had the decency to contact her, to ask if it were true.

Once a slave, always a slut! Was that how they thought?

Or was it just easier to assume that a woman was ruled by her clitoris rather than her brain? No matter that a woman had a collar around her neck. *Once a slut, always a slave?* No matter that if she didn't let a slobbering pig like Anglo drive himself past her labia, she'd be killed without a thought, kicked aside, and left to desiccate in the sand?

Damn them! Damn them all, and their accursed, smug male righteousness.

"Lady?" the soft voice asked. "Can I help you?"

Kaylla stiffened, fighting a panicked shiver. Clamping her jaws hard to nerve herself, she turned, seeing Myles Roma where he sat on one of the recliners above and behind her.

"I thought it best to speak," Myles said kindly. "To let you know that you weren't alone. It might save an embarrassment later."

"I . . ." Kaylla's voice croaked, and she cleared her throat. "Thank you, Myles. I'm sorry. I must have walked right past you."

He smiled sheepishly. "You appeared totally absorbed. Is there something wrong? You looked completely miserable just now. As depressed and dispirited an individual as I've seen in a long time. If it's the political situation that has you worried, don't lose faith. We'll make it."

She sighed, rubbing her tired face and walking over to seat herself beside him. "Will we, Legate? Or are we doomed to destroy ourselves through our own ugliness, petty greed, and jealousy?"

"The latest report I had the pleasure of seeing indicated that your Mag Comm will take over administration. This engineer, Dee Wall, has plans for some device that will allow us to break the Forbidden Borders. And yet I see nothing but disillusionment in your expression. Why?"

She leaned forward, rubbing her callused hands together. "Because we can rail at the Forbidden Borders, Legate. We can even smash them flat. The wretched reality will remain that we're still our own worst enemies. We always have been, and we always will be."

She flinched at his touch, glaring at him angrily, but Myles didn't react. Instead he smiled, patting her gently on the shoulder. "Give us time, Magister. You've borne the burden for all of us. Suffered for us, driven yourself past endurance. I, for one, worship you and your cause."

The words took her by surprise and, try as she might, she could discover no dissembling in his honest expression. "Worship? A bit of a strong word, don't you think?"

Myles shook his head. "You've kept us together, Magister Dawn. You were our nervous system when our limbs and head had been severed." He spread his arms wide. "I'm only one man, and not a very good one at that, but you gave me a direction when I was lost. You . . . and Staffa. He trusted me. You provided a way through the maze with your Seddi lectures."

Myles shrugged. "I don't know why you're so depressed, Magister. I don't know that I can, but I'll try and fix it for you. It's little enough to offer . . . along with a little worship for a true hero."

She glanced up at the stars, feeling dreadfully tired and defeated. "Hero, Legate? If this is what it feels like to be a hero, I'll settle for being a farmer from now on."

"Maybe that's the secret, Magister Dawn. Heroes feel that way for all of the rest of us. They do what we're not strong enough to do on our own."

She sat there, letting his words run around inside her wounded soul. Finally, she stood up, battling to keep from trembling with fatigue. How long had it been since she'd slept?

"You're a fool, Legate. But you made me feel better. I'm going to get some sleep. If you really worship me like you think you do, you'll go down and tell my staff that no one is to bother me. If Seekore calls, order her to cut her own throat—and if she refuses, tell her we'll spread the rumor that she just doesn't have the guts to do it."

"Seekore? I haven't met her. I'll be happy to deal with her in exactly those terms if it will bring you a little peace."

"You *are* a fool."

He gave her a wicked grin. "Not by halves, Magister. I hedge my bets. You see, the Lord Commander and Delshay are also friends of mine. If Seekore comes after me, I'm not averse to hiding behind them." He sobered. "And you."

"Don't look to me for protection. I'm giving this hero business up."

Myles stood, offering his arm. "Here, lean on me. I'll

escort you to your quarters. And afterward, I'll see that no one bothers you.''

* * *

The dream had been the same, Arta's sexual antics, Ily's interrogation, and Skyla's ultimate defeat—only to look up and see herself stepping through the shaft of light spilling from the doorway to Itreata. The light glowed on her white armor, silvering her long braid where it clipped to her epaulet. And her duplicate had turned to look back at a screaming Skyla, still bound to the chair. Arta's eyes, feral, triumphant, had burned in place of Skyla's rich blue orbs.

Each time the dream repeated, the terror deepened, eating into Skyla's soul with the relentless inevitability of caustic solvent. The memory lingered like a tormenting wraith as Skyla pulled herself free of the nightmares. She groaned and worked her tongue against the stale taste in her mouth. Stretching, she tried to breathe life back into sodden muscles. The seams on her padded undersuit itched where they ate into her skin. Her bladder demanded attention and her right foot had gone to sleep.

The familiar bridge of *Rega One* gleamed with bank after bank of displays and healthy lights. Systems were maxed but appeared stable.

''You all right?'' Lark asked from her seat at the engineering station.

''I feel numb.'' Skyla checked the monitor, noting the position of the CV. ''How many gs are we pulling?''

''Still right at forty-eight. No changes in the reactor or artificial gravity generation. Just for the benefit of those who like to live dangerously, we're still running right at one hundred and five percent.''

Skyla kneaded circulation back into her leg before trying to stand. *Rega One* tried to mash her in the two gravities Skyla had chosen to live under rather than stress the gravity generation by an extra g. With careful steps, she walked to the hatch and ducked through. In the small toilet, she used equal care seating herself on the zero g pot and then sighed in relief. In the mirror her features looked twenty years older from the stress pulling on her facial tissues. The redshot eyes didn't help matters.

Blessed Gods, will I ever sleep peacefully again? Or will I always relive those wretched days with Arta? Time after time . . . after time . . .

A terrible weight had settled on her. She'd been right about Ashtan. After the crushing sense of despair, of the certainty of error, vindication had been hers. She'd called Ily's destination, and, but for a failed coolant pump, she'd have been there to trap Arta and her slimy mistress.

And two innocent men would be alive. She propped elbows on her knees. Innocent? Could she say that about them? Hell, yes! Sex, after all, was a normal human drive. Arta's sexuality would tempt a Myklenian mystic.

And you can't think of Arta without thinking of Chrysla. Rotted Gods, Chrysla had played her role to perfection. She and MacRuder had done the unthinkable.

And is Mac so different from you, Skyla? You sleep with Staffa and Mac sleeps with Chrysla. Can you condemn Mac or her without condemning yourself and Staffa?

That knot was more than she wanted to pick at for the moment. Kill Arta and Ily first. Worry about personal dysfunctions when the leisure presented itself.

Skyla used the bidet and took a deep breath before she pulled herself up by the hand railing that was bolted to the wall for just such moments. She washed her face in the facial spray and then made her careful way, step by braced step, back to the bridge.

Skyla paused at the hatch. A familiar frown chiseled a line through the middle of Lark's brow as she studied one of her monitors. The other instruments gleamed in the white light. The reactor monitors advertised the abuse of the system with glaring red readouts, while the navcomm holo tank reflected velvet tranquillity with only the white dot of Arta and Ily's CV disrupting the blanket of stars.

This cramped little space would remain their home on the hard chase. Here, in the end, Skyla would face her demons across a mathematical battlefield of projected energy, velocity, shielding, and maneuverability. She would, that is, if they could manage to catch the CV before it went null singularity.

"Any news? Are we going to catch them?" Skyla took a step and locked her knees to stare over Lark's shoulder. The targeting comm shot light blue lines across a red background as Lark worked on pinpointing a moving target.

Lark looked miserable, hair pulled severely back into a ponytail. The luster had faded from her impish green eyes and her skin had taken on a pale sheen. "Doppler is still constant. From the readings, we're still gaining. When I haven't been running targeting exercises, I've been updating the plot and projecting interception. I think, Skyla, that it will be very close."

"Pus Rot you, Ily, why couldn't you have stolen a slower ship?" Skyla braced herself and used her arm and leg muscles to settle back into the command chair. "What do you think, kid? Should we go to one ten percent?"

"I'd say no way . . . but I didn't just wake up from a nightmare the likes of the one you just had." Lark glanced at her. "It's your decision, Skyla. Of course, we'll blow up if any of the systems—like that thrice-cursed pump—let loose. On the other, I wouldn't mind getting a chunk of Ily and her leashed bitch."

"Oh, yeah? What did they do to you?" Skyla extended an arm against inertia, drawing a cup of stassa from the bridge dispenser.

Lark had turned back to her boards, expression thoughtful. "It's not me. It's that guy I saw on the Ashtan terminal. And it's you, too. I've heard your nightmares too many times. All the lessons you've pounded into my skull tell me to stay at one oh five. My guts tell me to go one ten and get the bitches for sure."

"We'll stay at one hundred and five percent."

"You're sure?"

Skyla lifted the stassa to her lips and sipped. "I'm sure." She paused. "That part I never told you about at Terguz? The big secret? I took you along to keep me sane, Lark. I wanted you to keep me alive. That's what I couldn't tell you then."

"I know."

"You know?"

"Miracles do happen . . . even inside my head. Yeah, I figured it out. I've also figured out that you're not nearly as fragile as you think you are." She hesitated. "Chrysla's right about you."

"Rotted Gods, you and Chrysla. Both as crazy as particles on an event horizon."

Lark laughed. "Yeah, right. I remind myself of that every time I run a targeting program. Are you sure you want me manning the cannon? I've never shot anything in my life, and given my success ratio on this thing, I'm not likely to."

"How bad are you?"

"In forty-six plotted shots, I've hit them four times."

Skyla rubbed her forehead, the stassa easing into her gut. "You'll have to do better than that. Is there any improvement, or should I start preparing myself for the inevitable and try and ram them?"

"Great! Ram 'em! Truth is, I might get good enough to tag them if we get enough chances to shoot and they don't get us first."

"Neither one of them has space combat experience. That's what I'm counting on." Skyla narrowed her eyes as she stared at the pinpoint of light that marked the CV's location. *Blessed Gods, tell me they're on that ship. Tell me Mac and Rysta aren't going to beat me to the punch and cut them out of* Victory.

"Right, Wing Commander. That makes three of us. Them and me. Are you sure you don't want the targeting comp?"

Skyla shot a quizzical glance at the girl. "Do you want to repeat your lessons? The ones I started telling you about just before I went to sleep? Remember, sub-light tactics?"

Lark almost smiled, then lost it. "Doppler affects combat at near light speed. The tactical advantage held by the pursuing ship is that it has better tracking data on the lead ship than the lead ship has on the pursuer. That advantage, however, is balanced and offset by the fact that firepower decreases factorially as the pursuing ship approaches the speed of light."

"You've got it. Okay, you shoot, and I'll try and weave us back and forth so they can't hit us while we get close enough so you can punch a hole through the spindle." Skyla gulped the last of her stassa. "What I'd give for a battleship about now."

A long silence prevailed.

"You think that's them?" Lark asked absently. "Or will we catch up and find the CV boosting on automatic?"

Skyla shoved her stassa bulb under the dispenser. From

long practice, she pulled the bulb out just as it filled and blew to cool the liquid. "It's them. I've told myself that over and over again. Staffa says that observation creates reality, well, fine. I'm going to observe Arta's blasted corpse in that CV. I'm going to see Ily with her guts strung all over the cockpit in that same CV—" she pointed with the drinking bulb—"right up there.

"You hear that, Seddi God? I'm observing. You make it real, you bastard."

"Yeah," Lark mumbled. "And while you're at it, teach me to shoot straight, okay?"

CHAPTER XXXII

ID-893756306 DOC/VEG
Name: Diane de la Luna   Clan: Ceilo Vista
Place of Birth: Vega Prime, Vega, Sassan Empire
Date of Birth: 5720:06:13:14:39 GST
Occupation: Representative's Assistant
Last Station: Ashtan   New Station: Itreata

Greetings! Know all authorities by these documents that the above-named person, Diane de la Luna, is duly authorized to represent the affairs and duties of the Representative's office as is required by her government, clan, and family.

The Honorable Diane de la Luna is hereby and forthwith authorized to meet and conduct negotiations with such parties as are responsible for political relationships within the Territories of the Itreatic Asteroids, their Free Zones, and Holdings. Further, be it known that as Representative of the Vegan Clans, de la Luna is fully authorized by said Clans to conduct such business which might be conducive to trade, commerce, or economics by any person, or persons, either within the Imperial government, its assigns, or executors, or such individuals representing private concerns interested in passing goods through Vegan ports, or on ships bearing Vegan registry.

Be it known, therefore, that Diane de la Luna has every confidence of the Vegan Council, the Clans, and His Holiness Sassa II.

The Great Seal of Vega

Affixed this day of 5780:01:12:09:30

Phillipe Moctezuma
Clan Councillor/Rep/Min
Vega

* * *

For long moments, Staffa remained where he lay, flat on his back, his stare fixed on the curve of his ceiling. Despite the muzzy sensations of too little sleep, the fact continued to drift around his brain. *The Mag Comm claims it can break the Forbidden Borders.*

Could it? The machine wanted *Countermeasures,* the secret weapon Staffa had designed to cripple enemy battlefield communications. The ship was nothing more than an old Formosan freighter, but she packed more energy generation per kilo than anything in space. All that power was used to energize a single transmitter that excited heavy elements to create virtual pairs of subatomic particles. Those, in turn, were separated by a gravitational field, one set of particles broadcast and the other stasis warped. When the broadcast particles reached their destination, the captured half of the pair was released and stimulated by laser, affecting its twin across space-time, and creating havoc with comm systems in the bombarded area.

Staffa stretched and yawned, his curiosity piqued. When he'd finally struggled through the desolation in his mind and sought to remove the golden helmet, he hadn't felt well enough to study the printout Mag Comm had made for *Countermeasures.*

Sinklar had been there, sober as an Etarian priest before a consecration. He'd been unable to form the question on his lips that was burning in his oddly colored eyes.

"The deal is struck," Staffa had groaned. "The printout. Send it to Dee Wall. Tell him to do it. Whatever it is." And he'd gone limp, brain starting to pound in gravelly agony with each heartbeat. "Mag Comm's going to break the Forbidden Borders. It's given its word, Sinklar. Its offer of faith."

He'd slumped then, completely bereft of sense or sensation beyond the throbbing pain cracking his skull.

Sinklar entered the room, bearing a tray covered with mirror-domed stasis plates. A crooked grin bent his lips as he settled the tray and clicked off the coverings to reveal steaming steak, tapa, and chubba, all garnished with habanero peppers.

"That smells . . ." Staffa closed his eyes, aware of his hunger-cramped stomach.

"Yes?"

". . . better than anything I've ever smelled before. Including when I came out of the desert on Etaria."

"Dig in. How are you feeling?"

Staffa adjusted the gravity on his bed and speared a fat chunk of meat. "I'm tired, Sinklar. As tired as I've ever been. But for the first time, I think there's hope for us. Any word from Dee Wall on the modifications to *Countermeasures?*"

"Nothing. To be honest, I've had my mind on other matters. I thought we'd better clear the decks on developments which occurred while you were asleep. Not much, just sabotage, treason, and attempted assassination."

"Assassination? Whose?"

"Yours. Oh, and the Mag Comm's, if we can consider it to be alive and a politically powerful personality."

Staffa had stopped chewing, attention fully centered on his son. His voice lowered. "Go ahead."

Sinklar dropped into the gravchair opposite Staffa, gesturing with his hand. "You eat. I'll talk while you refuel." Staffa wolfed his piece of meat as Sinklar outlined the actions taken first by Bruen, then Nyklos, and what he'd done about them.

"And Kaylla? How did she take this accusation of being my lover? Rotted Gods, if I ever tried to touch her, she'd throw up!"

Sinklar's expression reflected distaste. "She looked shattered, Staffa. That's the closest words can come."

"Should have shot him years ago. All right, go on. What next?" *Pus drown Nyklos! Of all the ways to hurt Kaylla, he'd chosen the worst. And she'd trusted him, defended him. So much for justice.*

"Ark and Adze both asked me to wait for you to awaken before we came to any sort of decision." Sinklar pulled up his knee, expression composed as he measured Staffa with those two-toned eyes. "You gave me the responsibility. I used it. Since Nyklos admitted to everything, I was satisfied that we had the facts. I have also believed in accountability for a long time. As military governor of this planet, I therefore turned Bruen over to the Targan judicial system. He's currently awaiting trial in Kaspa."

"Sinklar!"

"Wait! Hear me out."

Staffa frowned in irritation at his son. He'd given his word that Bruen could find sanctuary in the Itreatic Asteroids, live there in peace. He'd made that promise just on the other side of Makarta Mountain from where he now sat.

"Accountability, Staffa." Sinklar's expression had hardened. "Bruen threw this entire planet into civil war. Almost a million people are dead now because of his actions. He plotted to destroy the subspace link, assassinate you, and destroy the machine. I don't count those as a friend's actions, Staffa. He betrayed us. Betrayed you and the trust you'd placed in him."

Staffa stared at his plate.

"Staffa, I took you at your word. You say you believe in breaking the old unilateral epistemology. Either you trust me with responsibility, or you don't. Make your decision now, Father."

Staffa closed his eyes, trying to fit the pieces together. Poor Bruen, hatred for the machine had eaten too deeply into his soul. A grim sense of justice played about the edges of Staffa's thoughts. Nyklos had finally proved true to his instincts. They'd never liked each other—hostile from the moment they'd met.

"And Nyklos?"

"He will be returned to Itreata where we'll have to establish a joint tribunal which includes Seddi, Companions, and any other interested parties. While we're at it, we might as well expand it, turn it into a codified legal system. That way everyone will know the rules."

"Indeed?"

"Rotted right, indeed! Staffa, we've an empire to administer. That's more than just moving tapa leaves from one planet to another. That means law. A codified system of behavior. Right now—at least in Regan space—it all hinges on how individual Administrators interpret Imperial doctrine. Not counting Internal Security, mind you. Pus alone knows how Ily's Directors handle legal affairs, but I doubt it's just. And the Sassans? That's completely outside of my experience."

"Yes, you're right," Staffa agreed. "The time has come for us to know all the rules. Accountability? Quite a concept to attempt to implement. Think you're up to it?"

Sinklar's expression changed ever so subtly. "Rotted Gods, I've started to understand you. I know that look in your eyes, and I'm not going to like it."

"Of course you will." Staffa resumed the attack on his breakfast. "And what we like isn't always what we're allowed to do, or become. In your case, I'm dropping another load on your shoulders. We need a codified system of justice. Not just for Companions and Seddi. For everyone."

"Wait. Hold it. I'm not—"

"Yes, you are. You're admirably suited for it. You've experienced injustice firsthand. You understand power and its abuses. You have a thorough understanding of history. And you have your new book. The Mag Comm can probably translate the whole thing for you. It might beat fooling around with faulty data cubes. Build your body of law, Sinklar. From the bottom up. A new epistemology."

Sinklar had retreated into his own thoughts, frown lines eating up his forehead.

"No questions about the machine?" Staffa asked. "No nagging worry that I sold out humanity?"

Sinklar shot him a startled glance. "No, not a one. You're acting terribly normal and relieved. You've dropped the mannerisms of the suffering saint that I've become so used to. If you had even the faintest suspicion that you'd been duped, that preoccupied insecurity would still be in your eyes."

Staffa swallowed the last of the succulent chubba leaves and pushed the tray back as he picked up the stassa cup and sipped. "The machine claims that with our help it can break the Forbidden Borders within a month of the modifications being completed to *Countermeasures*."

"And the Mag Comm itself? How did it build a computer?"

"Would you believe gravitational epitaxy?" Staffa explained the physics so far as he knew them. "That's why it needs us to build the robots. Solid-state products are one thing. Moving parts are something else. Our omnipotent friend isn't nearly as omnipotent as we could wish. He wants to deal, and his currency is data manipulation and information."

Sinklar pulled at his knobby nose with a nervous hand. "In the end, what really made you trust the machine?"

"Logic." Staffa sipped his stassa. "The machine is right. If it can break the Forbidden Borders, we won't be in competition with each other no matter what permutations the future takes. Our destiny as a species can't help but be different from the Mag Comm's. We're organic intelligences with limited life spans. We must produce, consume, exploit, and reproduce. The machine is an electronic—I think—intelligence that's stuck inside a planet. The fact is, Sinklar, that we're going to emphasize different things. Mutually exclusive.

"It's the Others with whom we still have to come to terms. If that's even possible."

"What about their response? Let's say we do manage to break the Borders. Are they going to simply stand by and allow us out?"

Staffa frowned. "I don't know. We'll have to ask the machine, I suppose. By the way, how is the hookup proceeding?"

"Very normally. Lots of glitches have developed now that Ark is trying to connect wires together. You've only got two techs left aboard your ship. The rest are down inside the mountain cursing and scratching and shaking their heads. Your Mag Comm, it appears, has a most interesting approach to electronics. Voltage fluctuates, amperage spikes and drops. Ark has the chamber down there packed with transistors, capacitors, and voltage regulators. The only sign of hope came when the machine spit out about thirty pages of schematics. They had a small riot as everyone tried to see what it was all about, then it got real quiet. You know how engineers get that look in their eyes, that possessed gleam, when something impossible has just become easy? That's when I left."

"How do you feel about it? About my decision to employ the Mag Comm?"

White teeth pinched Sinklar's lower lip as he stared thoughtfully at the floor. "Frankly, I'm nervous. But I should be used to that by now. From the moment two years ago when I landed on this planet, I haven't had the time to put anything into perspective. All I've done is react to one crisis after another. Actually, it's something of a pleasure to have you around. You can take the heat if the Mag Comm goes berserk. I'll stick to offending the Seddi."

Staffa chuckled and sipped his stassa. "How did Bruen take it? Being delivered to the Targans?"

"He cursed me the whole time. Called me a monster, a freak who should have been strangled at birth." Sinklar played with his fingers as he gazed absently at the floor. "Just so you know, I didn't take any real pleasure from delivering him to the authorities. As the LC dropped into Kaspa, I felt tired, Staffa. When I gave my deposition to the court, Bruen lay there, mostly silent and glaring like a siff jackal at the hunter's hounds. I saw him then for what he was. A broken old man frustrated by life and destiny. A wilted savior, beset by dry rot of the soul."

"It wasn't entirely his fault." Moodily, Staffa swirled the stassa in his cup. "Bruen, like the rest of us, was simply a product of his times. As was Divine Sassa, Tybalt . . . and me."

The comm buzzed. Staffa turned to the unit. "Go ahead."

"Greetings, Lord Commander Staffa kar Therma," a toneless voice told him. "I thought I would determine the extent to which I could utilize the comm system. Fascinating. I have just experienced an exponential burst of experience and awareness. A body must feel something like this."

"You learn quickly." Staffa straightened, staring warily at the blank monitor. "Does STO Ryman Ark know you can do this?"

"Not at the moment. He is still testing circuits."

"Who?" Sinklar asked, a puzzled look on his face.

"I didn't realize another person was present. Excuse me," the voice stated. "I should have introduced myself. New person, I am called the Mag Comm. I am pleased to meet you. You are called?"

"Sinklar Fist."

"Greetings, Sinklar Fist." A split second pause. "This medium of communication is incredibly inefficient. I don't know you, Sinklar Fist. I can't read your mind."

"Mag Comm," Staffa called, "What do you need? What are you doing?"

"I have already told you what I need, Staffa kar Therma. I thought we had agreed that you would build my mechanical devices after I freed you from the Forbidden Borders. Was I in error?"

"No, Mag Comm. I was just wondering what you needed right now, at this moment. The reason you contacted me."

"I wanted to establish communications with you through this medium to investigate its parameters. I can do this now, and I will begin contacting Magister Dawn, Myles Roma, Dion Axel, Iban Jakre, Rysta Braktov—"

"Mag Comm, don't." Staffa hunched over the monitor. "Cease communications with other human beings while we talk this over. I think you may be making a mistake . . . that is, if you're doing what I think you're doing."

"What mistakes would that be?"

"Are you going to contact all of the administrative personnel in Free Space? Just to introduce yourself?"

"That is correct."

Sinklar's face had assumed a rapt expression.

"Mag Comm, I don't think you want to do that right now." Staffa lifted his hands, pressing fingertips to his temples as understanding flooded him. "Mag Comm, you're not used to interacting with more than one human at a time. You don't need to interact with all of us at once just because you have the capability. Access your files on our social behavior, on our protocol. Pull up any information you have on human culture, on behavior norms for each of our societies. Cross-reference manners and morals, even legal systems. Study them before you charge into the unknown and make a fool of yourself. You don't want to act like a child in the presence of adults. Do you understand?"

A pause. Then: "I understand. I have accessed those programs. Your warning is heeded. I will heed future warnings."

Staffa gestured with his hands, wincing. "Mag Comm, you need to proceed very slowly—and recognize that you will make mistakes in dealing with humans." Staffa raised his brows, glancing at Sinklar. "We make mistakes dealing with each other, and we've been doing it for our entire lives."

"I will be careful. Thank you for your warning."

"How is the interface with our system working out?"

"I have established full control of your comm system access. I am operating the subspace dish. STO Ark's circuitry is correct. As we speak I am taking over administration procedures, implementing software, and assuming the direction of planetary systems. Expect three weeks until online services equal Imperial proficiency. Thereafter, we shall exceed them."

"Exceed?" Sinklar wondered. "Has a pretty high opinion of itself, doesn't it?"

"No, Lord Fist," the machine responded. "The converse is true. I have a low opinion of the Imperial systems."

Sinklar gave the comm a sour smirk. "Well, I guess that makes two of us."

"Is there anything else you need to tell us, Mag Comm?" Staffa asked.

"Currently I am still tabulating data. I will inform you of the problems and actions I am taking as soon as a complete assessment is made."

"And how long will that take?"

"I anticipate a full accounting within another six planetary hours."

Staffa drank down the last of his stassa and handed the cup to Sinklar. "In that case, go ahead and contact Kaylla Dawn—and have her assemble her assistants. I keep underestimating you and your abilities. While you contact Itreata and set up a network, I'm going to contact my security and buy us some peace and quiet. Do you understand? Call me back in five planetary minutes."

"I do understand. I am contacting Kaylla Dawn and will call you back on a networked circuit in five planetary minutes."

Comm went dead and Staffa rubbed the back of his neck while he stared at the unit.

Sinklar stated irreverently, "I'll bet that right now you're thinking to yourself, 'This could be a little more difficult than I thought.' "

"Wonderful. The Mag Comm is an incredibly intelligent, sophisticated genius who doesn't know that people might not want to talk to it all the time."

"Lucky you."

Comm buzzed immediately. Ryman Ark's serious face formed. "Lord Commander? We're running the final tests now, but the machine should be on-line in the next hour or so. I just wanted you to know in case any surprises cropped up."

"Too late, Ryman," Staffa said wearily as he drew another cup of stassa from the dispenser. "But if you'd like to know how the machine did it, I'll have it call you when it calls me back."

"Calls you back, sir?" Ark lifted an eyebrow, the action stretching the scar on his cheek. "You mean . . ."

"We're in for a very interesting time, Ryman. Until further notice, Sinklar and I need to be left alone while Kaylla and the two of us deal with the machine. It's going to be a very long day."

"Yes, sir," Ark grumbled, skepticism in his flashing eyes as he cut the connection.

"Ark is usually pretty good," Sinklar observed. "It's not like him to let something slip by."

"Let alone, a whole computer."

* * *

"Mac, please, don't!"

Chrysla's last frantic words ran around and around inside Mac's brain as he huddled in the command center of his LC. In the monitors before him, he could see *Victory, Gyton,* and the other two LCs that were closing on Ily's freighter.

He sucked at the insides of his cheeks. It still wasn't too late. He could call off the assault. Allow Rysta to blast the ship apart from a safe distance.

But Ily's there. She's got to be!

The tactics had necessitated that *Gyton* pass *Victory,* then drop the LCs at precisely the right instant so that the assault craft would match *Victory*'s velocity at the exact moment their vectors crossed. The LCs would settle on the freighter's hull, and the Groups would deploy with their Emergency Rescue Locks, or ERLs. The ERL functioned by cutting through the hull and creating an emergency air lock driven by the atmospheric pressure within the ship.

Mac and Rysta had spent hours studying the design schematics of the Model Sixteen, pinpointing the best locations to gain access to the ship. Assuming Ily and Arta were aboard, they'd have defensive control. Therefore, the most efficient method for dealing with such a situation would be to cut the power and comm control. Ily and Arta could stew in the dark as the temperature dropped.

Mac studied the image of the big freighter while his stomach acid churned.

"Fifteen minutes to contact," the LC's pilot called down on the comm.

"Affirmative."

Mac had played this game before, the time they'd taken the *Markelos*. Then, however, the Sassans hadn't known they were there. The prey had been an ordinary Sassan ship—not Ily Takka and her twisted assassin.

Mac thumbed the intraship comm. "Red? You guys ready back there?"

" 'Firmative, Mac. Give us the word."

"Mac, please don't." Chrysla had begged, pleaded that she sensed disaster. Finally, she'd demanded to accompany him. And he'd responded with a direct order: *"No!"*

Mac's head slumped forward as he thumped his knotted fist against his forehead. *I had to, Chrysla. I just had to try, don't you see? If it's a trap, we'll figure a way out of it. If Ily's aboard, we'll get her. If the ship's abandoned, we'll save it.*

And she'd replied, *"If it explodes when you set foot on it . . ."* Her jaws had clenched, her eyes had gone misty amber. "Mac, please, don't."

"Mac?" Rysta's voice came in from comm. "We're reading an energy fluctuation out of the reaction. I don't like it."

Mac blinked, pulling himself upright and staring at the image of *Victory* where it filled the main monitor. The stars were redshifted, the effects significant, but nothing like the psychedelic display he'd seen during the *Markelos* seizure.

"Rysta? What do you think?" His instruments had nothing like the capacity for analysis *Gyton* carried.

While he waited for an answer, Mac studied the distribution of his LCs; they were dropping down on *Victory*'s back now, perhaps ten minutes to touchdown. He hesitated, filled by a sudden desire to call it off.

"You're close enough so you should have set the proximity alarms off on *Victory*," Rysta called. Then: "Mac! Abort! Abort! I'm telling you—"

The flash filled the monitor a half second before the impact—like the fist of God—blasted Mac's LC. He felt himself jerked sideways, head snapping in time with a loud bang. The lights flickered as loose items shot past like shrapnel.

Just before Mac lost consciousness, he had a vague impression of blood running warmly in his nose and mouth. A hissing was the only sound . . .

* * *

Kaylla Dawn walked through the quiet hallways with a slow tread. She kept her hands clasped behind her, her head down as she watched the hem of her long white robe swirl around her feet. The floor gleamed with that perfectly polished finish characteristic of Itreata.

Nyklos . . . why?

Myles had talked her past the first bitter taste of betrayal. Now she could at least think about it without the emotional knot pulling itself tight.

She recalled the smoldering in his dark eyes when they'd brought him in for interrogation on Tyklat's word. Had that been it? At the time, he'd seemed to understand the necessity. Angry, hurt, he'd still cooperated to the fullest extent possible to clear his name. And afterward, it had become clear that Ily had set him up. Still, had that lingering resentment festered into hatred?

Kaylla walked numbly, every cell in her body exhausted and screaming for rest her emotions wouldn't allow.

The burden would ease now. Staffa had brokered a deal with the machine. She could step down, sleep, and deal with the nightmares of Bruen's forthcoming trial at the hands of the Targans.

You'll hate yourself for that for a long time, Kaylla Dawn. Perhaps she should have raised an objection. Bruen was, after all, a Seddi Magister. Four thousand years of precedent had been broken when she accepted Sinklar's request without demur. The vile look in Bruen's eyes burned with acidic wrath.

Hard times, Magister. You brought it upon yourself. And Sinklar used our own arguments against us. We all are guilty. It's time for a new way. Assuming Sinklar was bright enough to find it.

Could they manage that? A system where all the rules were spelled out, where the playing field was level for all people?

And if Bruen turns out to be right in the end, perhaps it won't matter. The machine may take us all.

It had, however, surprised her with its efficiency, and, yes, even its manners. Had that toneless voice on the speaker really been the evil Mag Comm? From the moment it had announced itself, she couldn't believe Staffa had pulled it off. Their conference had lasted six hours, but Free Space appeared to have avoided disaster.

Kaylla reeled, allowing herself to sag against the smooth white walls in exhaustion. Her eyes burned, lids drooping. Inside her skull, the feeling could be likened to sand packed into her mind. Her motor coordination seemed like mush.

"Magister Dawn?" a soft voice asked.

She turned, blinking, a weary smile bending her wide lips. "Hello, Professor Sornsen."

Andray Sornsen had paused, his normally languid brown eyes watching her curiously. His blunt face warmed with a sympathetic smile. "I see. Yes, I know the symptoms well. They come with Itreata."

"What are you talking about?" Kaylla pulled herself upright, squinting.

"Fatigue, Magister Dawn. Driving yourself so far past human endurance that you wander the halls, desperately in need of sleep, and so burdened by responsibility that your brain won't allow you to rest."

"You do understand."

"Come." He offered his hand. "Allow me to escort you back to your quarters. I have just the thing for you. A bit of a tranquilizer that will turn off the desperate drive to deal with everything at once and allow you to sleep so that you'll awaken rested. Then you can deal with problems in an intelligent manner instead of in half measures with scattered concentration."

She sighed, taking his arm. "You're right I suppose, Professor. We've been so busy. Most of the time I've slept at the comm terminal." She shot him a sidelong glance. "Dealing with Commander Seekore is a fascinating experience."

"Yes, well, she is one of the more . . . shall we say, interesting women?" His voice lowered. "Staffa has decided to use this machine? This Mag Comm?"

"He has, Professor."

"I've heard that some were suspicious of the machine. Even some of your own people."

"Professor, you are a psychologist. How many ways do people react in a time of crisis? They're dealing with an unknown for the most part. Speculation is never neutral. And the machine hasn't always appeared benign."

"And how do you feel?" he asked, expression still placid. "Are you happy with Staffa's decision? Or just relieved that it's been made?"

Fatigue had strung cobwebs through her brain; nevertheless, that old spark of warning had been kindled. Was that Sornsen's purpose? To catch her half-asleep? Milk her for gossip-worthy information?

"I trust the Lord Commander's decision in this instance, Professor. He's been under the helmet. He knows what he's dealing with. The Mag Comm is a most extraordinary computer—a machine. Not a malignancy let loose upon space as some of Bruen's old followers might insist. I suppose you've been talking to Wilm? Or perhaps Hyrim?"

"No one in particular. Just rumors."

Kaylla pulled her arm back. "For the record, Professor, I'm not *that* tired. In answer to your concerns, I have a great deal of faith in the Lord Commander's ability. If he's happy with the Mag Comm, and if the subspace net can be activated to allow it to administer Free Space, I'll support his decision. As to the rumors floating around, they're mostly that. If you have a particular need for information . . . for instance, for morale purposes, please drop in and see me. I'll be happy to work with you . . . on a professional basis."

At that she veered off, taking a lateral corridor which would lead her back to the main office. She could feel his stare burning into her back as she walked.

CHAPTER XXXIII

I've just finished the inspection of the hemispherical shell, and I think we've managed to create a perfectly formed piece. One of the advantages of manufacturing in zero g vacuum is that such large structures can be formed with very little effort, although an eighty-kilometer sphere is a serious undertaking in any medium.

After heated debate we opted for a moderately viscous silicone polymer and figured the volume necessary for our sphere. Once we'd calculated the necessary material, the silicone was heated to three hundred and fifty kelvins and argon was pumped into the center of the mass. Surface tension held the silicone gel together as it inflated like a huge balloon. The trickiest part of the operation came during the final stages of inflation since we didn't know if micro-variance in the thin gel might affect cooling or expansion, which in turn would affect the perfect surface we were seeking. And, despite the fact that we'd moved six LY from Itreata, the tidal effects of micro-gravitational pulses from the binary couldn't be discounted either.

After the gel had expanded to eighty point zero one four kilometers in diameter (the point zero one four was necessary for shrinkage), a sialon mist was painted onto the surface of one half of the shell. An overlap of two kilometers was applied beyond the equator to ensure structural integrity. That portion will be cut away later.

When the shell had hardened sufficiently, the silicone was cut to release the argon and strips of the pliable material were peeled from inside the sialon shell. Preliminary surveys with the EDM and laser interferometry indicate perfection within 0.5 microns across the hemisphere.

When I left, crews had begun curving foamsteel and graphite structural members to support the shell. That reinforcement will be bonded to the sialon shell in tapering radii according to the specifications lined out in the schematic.

I'm dead tired, yawning as I write this. If I close my eyes, all I see are giant silvery bubbles and huge spraying machines. I'm going to sleep now, satisfied that I've managed to make one of the most difficult pieces the Lord Commander requires for his project. I doubt I'll get more than a couple of hours of sleep before some moron hammers at the door to inform me about some disaster or another. No matter, we'll solve it.

That's what engineers do.

If I dream about eggs, I'm going to be sick.

–Excerpt taken from Dee Wall's personal journal

* * *

"We're going to make it," Lark announced from the engineering chair just behind and to the left of Skyla's command chair.

Over the days, the cramped cockpit aboard *Rega One* had become the boundaries of their universe. Reality consisted of endless pressure as they lived under a constant two gravities. Holo displays appeared, provided data, and disappeared again in an endless cycle of observation, analysis, and projection. Progress was measured by the flickering lights and digital readouts on the instruments which tracked their progress against that of the fleeing CV.

The bridge dispenser catered to their physical sustenance and they slept in the conforming command chairs. The only break came with the inevitable trip past the hatch to the toilet.

The change in Lark had become marked. A grim sense of purpose had taken hold of the girl. As the long hours stretched and the distance between the two ships decreased, Lark's responses became terser. The two frown lines in her forehead seemed permanently engraved. Through it all, Lark had pitched herself into learning the systems, and her skill at the targeting computer had risen in quantum leaps until she could score hits sixty percent of the time.

Which, Skyla reflected, *translates into victory—providing we get at least two shots at the CV.*

"Looks like you'll get your first fight, kid."

Lark studied the monitor screen. "Do you think I'll know the difference between a drill and the real thing?"

"You'll know." Skyla flipped the monitor reset, clearing the screens—a precaution to determine whether any of the ship's systems had looped themselves. "But if you've trained properly, you never have the time to think about anything but doing your job."

"Yeah, well, do you think I've trained properly?"

Skyla gave her a cocky grin. "You won't know that until the shots have been fired. I won't either. Of course, if the shooting stops and you hightail it to the toilet and finally come out fifteen minutes later looking real abashed, we'll both know who crapped where, won't we?"

"A bottle of Ashtan rye says I cut it just fine, Skyla."

"Taken." The monitors had all reformed their images without appreciable differences from the present display.

Comm buzzed, announcing, "Subspace message incoming, Regan Imperial Military Code."

"Run it."

The comm monitor fuzzed, stabilized, fuzzed again, and finally organized into Rysta Braktov's gnarled features. "Greetings, *Rega One,* this is Commander Rysta Braktov of the Regan Battle cruiser *Gyton.* We've just completed our interception of the freighter, *Victory.*"

Rysta's shriveled face hardened. "*Victory* exploded as our LCs closed for boarding operations. If I was to guess, they'd rigged the reactor to overload when the proximity alert circuits were triggered. In the event Ily and Arta were aboard—which I don't believe for a moment—they could not have survived the detonation."

Rysta sucked on her lips for a moment, the action pulling her wrinkles out of shape. "Wing Commander, my guess is that Arta and Ily are in that CV. Be very careful in your attempt to capture them." She hesitated, eyes glinting as she looked into the monitor. "My most fervent prayers are going out to you, Wing Commander. I pray to the Blessed Gods that you get both of them.

"*Gyton* will collect her dead and revector to your position. We'll be late getting there, but we'll offer whatever assistance you may require." The old woman gave the briefest of nods. "*Gyton* out."

Skyla thumbed the comm button, staring into the monitor. "Attention, *Gyton,* we have received your transmission and acknowledge. Your warnings are noted and appreciated. We also concur with your assessment of *Victory* as a decoy. We anticipate interception of the stolen CV within twenty hours. We'll keep you informed as to the status of the operation. *Rega One* sends her deepest sympathies for your casualties. We will take no chances. Good space to you, *Gyton. Rega One* out."

"Message sent," the comm intoned.

"Did I hear that right?" Lark asked. "They were going to collect their dead?"

Skyla settled back in the command chair and began chewing on the knuckle of her thumb. "Yeah, kid. They tried to use standard boarding tactics, dropping LCs on the ship's hull. From there, armored troops would cut their way inside, overpower the crew, and take the ship. The only problem was, Ily knew that they'd try and do exactly that."

"So, what do you think they could to do us?" Lark asked. "They have to know we're closing on them. By now, they've got to have figured out that we're going to catch them before the jump."

Skyla rubbed her face in an effort to massage life into her features. Her intent gaze had returned to the holo tank which marked the CV's location. *So, what can you do, Ily? Explode the CV in our faces in the hopes it will work the same way twice? Or do you think you can shoot it out with us? Use your tactical superiority? What's your plan, bitch?*

To Lark, Skyla stated, "Whatever she's figuring on, it won't be any fun to be on the receiving end."

"So what are we going to do?"

Skyla cocked her head to stare at Lark through slitted eyes. "We're going to hope I'm a better pilot than Ily is."

* * *

Gyton carried two high-performance launches. Now both raced time and mass on a mission everyone hoped wasn't futile. The craft consisted of ninety meters of long flat wedge. The cabin rested inside the oblate nose and seated twenty in sybaritic elegance suitable to the foreign dignitaries and visiting military personnel that the launch usually carried. Just behind the bulkhead rested a mighty reactor capable of thrusting the slim sword-shaped vessel forward at close to forty gravities. Now the Commander's launch proved every ounce of her muscle.

Inertia tried to pull Chrysla through the restraining belts that held her in the launch's passenger seat. Around her the plush upholstery proved an ironic contrast to the urgency of the mission. Even the wall paneling shook as the launch fought to match course and velocity with its spinning target. Angular momentum inexorably pushed Chrysla to the left, sapping every muscle in her body as she fought the gs.

"Sorry." The pilot's voice didn't carry any hint of apology, nor did anyone—Chrysla least of all—care. Anything would be permitted on this trip, so long as the launch's occupants survived, and they made the desperate rendezvous with the shattered LC they now pursued.

Chrysla avoided looking at the monitor inset on the forward paneling. There, a battered LC tumbled lifelessly against the smeared background of the Forbidden Borders. Matching with the rotating junk would take skill and nerves of liquid steel.

Be alive, Mac.

For an eternal instant, Chrysla hadn't been able to believe what she'd seen. She'd been standing on the bridge, fighting that sense of premonition. That blinding white flash had strobed through space where an instant before the fat bulk of the Regan freighter had been riding a thin spear of reaction mass toward light speed. Everything was devoured by that brilliant nova of light—including the three LCs that had been dropping like motes onto the hull.

Even *Gyton* had shivered under the onslaught.

Chrysla had stared uncomprehendingly, frozen by a paralysis of disbelief. And then she'd made a low moaning sound, agony torn from a wounded soul. She'd screamed, "*No!*" beating her fists against the monitor console.

Rysta's cool presence had remained a constant as the Commander barked orders and the stunned bridge officers replayed the telemetry and sorted out the disaster.

Boyz, and her LC, had died instantly, a section of *Victory*'s hull blowing through the assault craft like a hammerhead through an egg. Andrews' LC had ruptured, but maintained some sense of structural integrity as it was blasted outward, spirals of leaking atmosphere marking its trail.

And Mac's LC had just barely had time to react. She'd changed attitude, arcing away from *Victory* when the concussion batted her forward. She, too, leaked atmosphere in frosty curls, the clearance lights dead, her comm ominously silent.

Rysta had ordered the launches—the fastest craft available to her—to space immediately for the two surviving LCs. No one really expected much. To have survived that much energy would have taken a miracle.

And for the moment, Chrysla was praying desperately for that miracle.

"Five minutes," the pilot's voice assured. "Remember, stay seated until I sound the 'all clear.' We're going to have to do some pretty dicey maneuvering to close."

Chrysla glanced uneasily at the other two passengers. The man was called Med First Josh Car and the woman had introduced herself as Pen York; both were emergency medical technicians trained for rescues of exactly this kind. Each now ran a final check on the equipment contained within a portable unit strapped to the deck.

I pleaded with him not to go, Chrysla reminded herself, thinking back to the last time she'd seen Mac. He'd practically forgotten her, his attention on his troops who were about to risk their lives in an attempt to capture Ily and Arta alive.

Chrysla closed her eyes, the blinding flash forever logged in her memory. *Arta Fera, what sort of monster are you? How could you have my body, my genes, and brain?*

And if Mac were indeed dead? *I'll get you both! I'll make you pay!*

"Lady Attenasio?" a soft voice asked.

Chrysla blinked and stared up at the female med tech from the rescue team. The woman smiled reassuringly, adding, "He was in the command control module behind the flight deck. That's the most protected part of the LC, ma'am. There's a good chance."

Chrysla nodded, her insides gone brittle as Sylenian ice. "Thanks."

The launch shook and strained, accompanied by a creaking of structural members. In the monitor, the cartwheeling LC had grown larger, the spirals of leaking atmosphere barely visible as the craft's supply was exhausted. The attitude adjustments made by the pilot refined the launch's vector until she appeared to be at rest beside the revolving LC.

"We've matched," the pilot called. "All clear. Rescue team, you may proceed."

The med techs were instantly on their feet, moving with purpose. Chrysla hit the release, checking her own suit.

Rysta had told her, "You ought to just stay here and wait. It won't do you any good to see him if he's dead in there."

Chrysla stepped into the air lock and energized her helmet field, breathing deeply to ascertain that the system was functional. Her suit rippled along her body as the pressure dropped. Above the hatch, the status lights flashed through their colors, finally glowing green for the 'all clear.'

Pen cycled the lock and pushed the hatch open. The action triggered the formation of frost as atmospheric vapors crystallized and drifted out into the blackness.

Josh had shouldered a bulky looking tube. He now sighted at the axis of the revolving LC and fired a grapple into the hull. After tying off, he lifted his equipment case and clipped it to the line, pushing it out into the vacuum. Quickly, he clipped his own restraint onto the line and followed. Pen was just as efficient.

Chrysla paused, staring at the LC where it spun in the launch's lights. The rear of the LC had collapsed under the blast, rents visible in the rumpled hull. The thrusters were silent, not even vapor trailing from them. Reflections of the launch's glaring spots flashed on the cockpit glass for the briefest of instants.

Mac, you've got to hold on. Just a little longer.

Chrysla clipped her safety ring to the line and pushed off through the tug of the launch's gravity. Before her, she could see Josh as he tied off, and drifted over the hull toward the emergency hatch above and just to the rear of the cockpit. To make his way, Josh had to fight angular momentum as the LC tumbled. Handhold, by handhold, he drove pitons into the hull by means of a pneumatic hammer that puffed vapor with each discharge. The line strung behind him gleamed tautly.

Pen had begun to follow, moving the equipment cases along the radius of the hull. Chrysla turned as she approached and used her legs to kill her momentum. A wash of nausea gripped her. She was falling, weightless, and the entire universe was spinning around her. *Careful, you're going to make yourself sick. You don't have time for this.*

Chrysla closed her eyes, feeling her way along the line, somewhat comforted as angular momentum gave her a down again and her inertia became a factor to movement.

''Lady Attenasio?'' Pen's voice came through the earpiece. ''Are you all right?''

''Bit of nausea. It's nothing, Pen. I'm on my way up.''

Chrysla ground her jaws, sweat prickling on her skin as she muscled her way along the line, crested the curving top of the LC, and braced herself in time to see Josh manually crank the hatch open. A brief puff of foggy crystals drifted out to spiral away into the void. The launch lights shot a momentary rainbow through the dissipating frost.

Josh hit his suit lights and used his arms as a pivot to dive into the hatch. Pen braced herself, handed the equipment case down to him, and followed.

Heart in her throat, Chrysla took a deep breath and lowered herself into the black interior. Josh and Pen had moved to the flight crew, placing an instrument to the pilot's head.

''Still alive.'' Josh turned to the copilot. ''This makes two. Pen, get a stim shot into them, and drop a pressure hood over them. Standard battery of antishock complex and stabilization hormones.''

Chrysla braced herself on the bulkhead and threw herself against the manual override that unlocked the hatch leading down to the command center. It wouldn't budge.

''Josh?'' she called, ''Help me!''

''Easy, Lady, if it's not opening, there's atmosphere in there.'' His lights played across the dead bridge monitors as he moved and they glittered like ghost eyes. ''We've got to bleed it out, otherwise, if First MacRuder's alive in there, the decompression could kill him.''

Chrysla bit her lip, struggling for control of her frantic emotions. "All right . . . how?"

"Down by your right foot. There, see the arrow? That points to the valve. Give it a half turn. You should see atmosphere begin to jet out. And, Lady, we've got to be careful. If he's alive, we don't have much time after the atmosphere is gone. Do you understand?"

"I do."

"These guys are stable," Pen called. "Both are breathing, pulse strengthening on both of them."

Chrysla vented the emergency valve, satisfied to see a fountain of frosty air erupt. Seconds passed like eternity.

When the pressure began to drop, she threw her weight against the handle again, feeling it give. The hatch opened stiffly with a puff of freezing mist.

A knot had formed under Chrysla's tongue, and her innards tingled with suspense and worry as she stepped into the command center. Mac remained strapped to his chair, his face a bloody mess. Both of his legs flopped limply to the side, evidence of broken femurs. Similarly, his neck was canted at an odd angle.

Dead! He's dead.

Josh shouldered past her, raising one of his instruments to Mac's blood-matted hair.

"I've got brain waves, but he's fading fast. Rot it, Pen, get in here and shoot this guy up! I'm guessing we've got a fracture between cervicals four and five with associated damage to the spinal cord. Neck immobilization is necessary first thing."

Pen shoved past a paralyzed Chrysla before pressing a syringe against Mac's skin. She wrapped an inflatable collar around Mac's neck and gently positioned his head as the collar inflated. A suction tube was utilized to pull clotted blood from Mac's nose and mouth. Pen nodded as frosty breath curled up in the freezing vacuum. With deft fingers she slipped a hood over his head and energized the oxygen flow. From a handheld unit, Pen read off statistics.

"Is he . . " Chrysla's words evaporated as she spoke them.

"He's alive, Lady. But just barely. Brain waves indicate he's pretty shocky. The chemicals are going to work on him. Should shut off most of the nervous responses. What we're doing is putting him into a sort of physical stasis so that his system doesn't deteriorate.''

Pen snapped two wires into an energy pack, then eased Mac's head back. ''You might not want to watch.''

Chrysla flinched as Pen drove the sharpened tips of the wires through the hardened armor and into Mac's chest.

''Maintains a minimum heartbeat,'' Pen explained. ''Next, I'm running a scan. From the way he's sprawled, we've got a lot of broken bones.''

''Pen!'' Josh's call came through the comm. ''I've got one alive back here. I need you.''

Pen shot a quick look at Chrysla, warning in her dark eyes. ''Use the thermal wrappings. Every exposed centimeter of skin must be protected.'' Then she was gone, ducking through the hatch that led back to the assault benches.

Chrysla tasted blood, aware that she'd bitten through her lip. Now, shaken and jittery, she bent to the task of wrapping Mac's vacuum-puffy hands.

''Mac?'' she whispered. ''Are you going to live for me? Damn it, live for me!''

She was still talking when Josh appeared at her shoulder, giving her a reassuring squeeze before he began inflating casts around Mac's legs and arms.

''All right, Lady. We'll move the wounded to the launch now. You can sit with MacRuder and the others, monitor them for us. Pen and I have to transport the bodies across.''

Chrysla glanced at him, seeing the compassion in his eyes. ''Better to have Pen sit with them. She's more competent than I in a medical emergency. I'll help you with the dead, Corporal First.''

Respect grew in his eyes. ''Very well, Lady.''

To remove the wounded, Pen had cut a hole in the LC's hull on the rotation axis. One by one, they removed the flight crew, MacRuder, and the single soldier from the assault deck.

Chrysla worked woodenly, not quite accustomed to the sense of falling but unwilling to let herself get sick. Somehow, as she stared into the faces of the dead, the weakness of vertigo paled in comparison to the loss of these brave friends: Red, his head smashed flat. Viola Marks, eyes bugged from decompression. Hansen, frozen tongue protruding. Vendet, pupils glazed ice-gray from the cold. Richmond, streaks of flaking blood crisscrossing his face like a web. And all the rest of A Group.

Chrysla had trained with them, earned their respect. And now these friends had become broken shells of rapidly freezing meat and bone.

As she struggled with stiff limbs, levering the bodies around the damaged LC, Chrysla swore to herself. *Ily and Arta are going pay for this. By the quanta, I swear, I'll find them.*

* * *

"Who are they?" Arta Fera asked as she watched the monitor which depicted the pursuing yacht.

Ily sat in the command chair, the worry-cap covering her head. Through the ship's speaker, she replied, "Who do you think, Arta? Who would have commandeered a Regan vessel, especially one with those performance characteristics, to run us down?"

"It couldn't be." Arta shot a sly glance at Ily's reclined form. "She wasn't well enough, Ily. When I handed her to you, she had no more resistance than cirrus in vacuum. Besides, that wouldn't explain how she could know we left Terguz for Ashtan, or that we'd taken the CV instead of *Victory.*"

The worry-cap hid Ily's expression. "Nevertheless, I can feel her. Intuition. It's Skyla."

Arta returned her attention to the holo tank which plotted their vector as well as the pursuer's. "From these data, she'll overtake us before jump. What then? You've told me that yacht of Tedor Mathaiison's mounts two heavy guns. Are you planning on shooting it out?"

"I suppose you have another alternative? Stopping to parley? Perhaps an offer to bed one of them, if he's a man?" A pause. "I think not. We need to shoot, kill them if possible, or at least slow them down until we can make the jump. Once in null singularity, we're safe."

"You're assuming we can last that long." Arta ran slim fingers through her gleaming wealth of auburn hair. "They do have better targeting data than we do."

"But we have something they don't . . . a CV. Also,

unlike them, we have something else they don't have. Desperation. I have been figuring the targeting based on their current trajectory. I'm taking one chance, Arta. As soon as they are in range, I'm taking a shot at them. Immediately after that, I'm pushing us to whatever acceleration is necessary to outrun them. You will need to prepare yourself. The ride may be unpleasant."

Arta studied her companion through slitted eyes. "And if we overload the reactor? Won't we go up like a small sun?"

Ily chuckled, the sound of it tinny as the speaker sought to cope with the odd phonemes. "Then we'll die, Arta. The advantage is that we'll die quickly . . . and free. Or would you rather surrender and allow Skyla to twist her revenge out of you? She's never struck me as a forgiving person."

Arta propped herself on straight arms as she stared into the tank. The familiar thrill had begun to warm her guts. "Race them, Ily. Give it all we've got." She threw her head back, smiling to herself. "Just get us into the jump."

"I plan on it."

"Yes, I'm sure you do." Delight danced in the amber depths of her eyes. "I have a feeling, Ily. Deep in my guts, I know you'll pull us through. Then all we need is a simple revectoring and I have a man awaiting my caress."

"Already have him in bed, do you?"

Arta's melodic laughter filled the cramped bridge. "Oh, Ily, I'm not even slightly worried about that. I'm just not sure how I want to kill him. For someone as important to us as the professor, and what he can give us once we reach Itreata, I need to have a special way of killing him. Something a psychologist can savor and study as he dies."

* * *

Sinklar reclined in one of the form-contouring chairs aboard the assault craft that carried him and Staffa to an orbital rendezvous with *Chrysla.*

Something like a thousand loose ends had to be taken care of prior to shipping from Targa. At the same time, Myles Roma had shifted from one impossible assignment to another. Where once he'd raced the clock to develop and modify software for the Formosan project, now he struggled to investigate the effects of the Mag Comm's growing influence in Free Space.

The machine now dominated its up-link to the stars, filling the subspace net with requests for data; it had begun the task of coordinating the economies. The transition had proceeded more smoothly than Sinklar would have believed. But then, both of the Empires had been used to taking orders by computer. The future appeared a little less grim for the first time since the Myklenian conquest.

Provided the Mag Comm had told Staffa the truth.

"Such a pensive look," Staffa noted as he settled in the next seat. The haggard desperation had been replaced on Staffa's features with a look of simple fatigue.

"Trying to put things into perspective, that's all," Sinklar answered. "And, of course, I'm hoping we made the right decision about the Mag Comm."

Staffa flipped his ponytail off of his left shoulder, lingering doubt in his gray eyes. "We'll know within a month of modifying *Countermeasures*. If the Mag Comm breaks the Forbidden Borders, as it has claimed it will do, we've nothing to worry about. If, on the other hand, nothing happens, we'll be spacing for Targa again . . . to level the mountains. The machine knows. I made it perfectly clear."

"Time to put up, shut up, or fold the tapa hand?"

"Exactly." Staffa gave him a critical appraisal. "Incidentally, you did a good job down there while I was dealing with the machine. I want you to know how much I appreciate you taking over a lot of the duties."

Sinklar gave him a crooked smile. "It happens every time I set foot on Targa."

Staffa steepled his fingers. "Would you be willing to take over more? A great many things are going to occupy us now. We're the government for Free Space. Granted, the Mag Comm can coordinate the economies, but governing is more than production, distribution, and consumption. Politics, as usual, will attempt to rear its ugly head as the Administrators recover their balance and seek to restore their power. We can't afford to go back to the old ways—whether the machine can break the Forbidden Borders or not."

"What did you have in mind? I mean, you've got it all now, where are you going?"

"Enfranchisement for the people." Staffa resettled himself, a frown deepening on his forehead. "The time has come for the people to take responsibility for themselves. The question is, Sinklar, how do we implement that? How do we fashion a society where the people *must* take control of their destinies? The original lure of the despot is to promise the people that in return for power, he'll solve all of their problems."

"No one has ever created a people's government. As a student of human history, I know it simply has never happened." Sinklar spread his arms wide. "Perhaps it's an impossibility, Staffa. Perhaps it's bred into us. Even the ancient history book had one picture after another of war. Our nature might be to lead and follow, not to share either responsibility or power." He made a face. "I wish I could have read that book. Not just looked at the pictures. Maybe the answer is suggested by some fact from our past."

"Maybe." Staffa's expression appeared smug.

In the ever present comm monitor, *Chrysla* had appeared, pristine and beautiful in the light of Targa's sun.

After a pause, Sinklar asked, "You haven't mentioned the Others, Staffa. What about them? What if they move against us when the Forbidden Borders go down? Have you given any thought to that possibility?"

He nodded, eyes on the starship they were approaching. "We're charting a course through unknown space, Sinklar. First we must reach equilibrium with the Mag Comm. Perhaps, if we can come to a balanced relationship with that intelligence, the Others will perceive of us as less of a threat. Then again, they may not."

"So what are you going to do?"

"For one thing, I'm planning on having ships ready to go. I want people out there as soon as possible. We've a whole universe to explore. Now, assuming the Mag Comm can break the Forbidden Borders, I want humans ready to burst through the hole, heading in all directions as fast as they can. There's no going back, Sinklar. This time we've got to have them organized, ready to survey, report, and explore."

"A pressure relief."

"Pardon me?"

"Pressure relief. Just like a valve in a reactor cooling tower. If the pressure builds up, the system starts to boil.

If too much fluid boils, it explodes and the reactor goes critical and melts down. A pressure relief valve allows the excess to bleed off before things go critical. That's the lesson, Staffa. The Forbidden Borders haven't allowed the pressure to bleed off. Instead, the only bleeding was done by humans when we reached our carrying capacity inside this trap."

"I couldn't have said it better myself." Staffa smiled. "And now you know why I struck my deal with the Mag Comm. If it can break us out, we're all safe, Sinklar. Oh, individual planets may still have problems with despots, but humanity as a whole can move to new territory when the pressures build. We no longer need face only the options of death and adaptation. Now we can move, find new suns, exploit new planets and asteroids.

"And perhaps we can learn to avoid the frequencies the Others sing on."

They had closed on the mighty battleship, the assault craft settling into the warship's belly as bay doors slid back to expose the garishly lit AC deck.

"Hope? Is that what we're discussing here so innocently?" Sinklar wondered, his thoughts turning to memories of the planet below them. Ghostly images of Hauws, Gretta, Butla Ret, and so many others now dead lingered in his mind.

I was insane the last time I left Targa. And this time? How far have I come?

Grapples sent thumps and shivers through the vessel as it came to rest in its dock. Even through the insulated hull, the whining of the bay doors could be heard while metal screeched and hydraulics hissed.

"Job well done," Staffa praised to the assault craft's comm. To Sinklar, he added, "And now, if you'll accompany me to my quarters, we'll drink a toast to success, check the comm for messages, and if we find no incipient disasters, we'll take time for a rest while we space for Itreata."

"Check for messages. You mean from Skyla?" Sinklar gave him a slow smile. "You've been worried, haven't you?"

Staffa nodded, taking the lead as he walked back to the hatch, saluting crew people on the way. "She wasn't well when she left. Kaylla has had flags out all over the system to keep an eye out for trouble.''

''She would have called about something serious, wouldn't she?''

''Those were my instructions. Skyla knew we were on Targa. I think . . . yes, she would have called. She understood that I wouldn't have interfered unless she wanted me to.'' Staffa leaned his head back. ''She would have. She would . . .''

''Staffa,'' Sinklar soothed as they passed the hatch into *Chrysla*'s warm interior. ''She's not in trouble. And if she were, we'd have heard something.'' Sinklar smiled. ''It's just a hunch, mind you, and I don't really know the lady, but I suspect that she'd make a hell of an impact if she ran into trouble. We'd be feeling the repercussions.''

''Maybe.'' They entered the lift, and Staffa instructed it to take them to his deck. ''But then, I didn't merit more than a whisper when I sank out of sight on Etaria.''

''She's not you. She's planet wise. Born and raised in the hard section of Sylene, wasn't she? She's no innocent, Staffa. From what you told me, you were.''

The lift doors opened and let them into the corridor leading down to Staffa's heavy double locks.

Inside Staffa's personal quarters, the huge fireplace still sat, framed on both sides by the big Ashtan doors. Staffa pointed to the dispenser. ''Pour us two glasses of your favorite. While you do that, I'll start going through the communications.''

''Affirmative.'' Sinklar walked to the dispenser, grabbed two drinking bulbs from the case, and opted for Asthan single malt.

When the bulbs were filled, he passed through the left Ashtan door and into Staffa's office. He handed one to his father while he pulled up a gravchair and settled into it.

Staffa was checking off routine reports, okaying actions taken by Tap, Tasha, and Kaylla.

Then the screen formed into a familiar face. Angry fire gleamed in those amber eyes, passion adding color to that perfect skin. Sinklar cursed as he came warily to his feet. ''Arta Fera, pus eat your miserable soul.''

''Fera?'' Staffa asked, pressing the play button. ''Or Chrysla?''

"It's the eyes. Look at her. Notice the emotion boiling . . ."

"Staffa? This is Chrysla. You'll receive this on delay because of the dilation. We're moving at 0.8 C, revectoring to try and match with Wing Commander Lyma.

"I hope everything is proceeding satisfactorily with the Seddi machine. I once heard the Praetor talk of the Mag Comm. It has extraordinary powers. In the meantime, you should be aware of several things.

"First, Ily Takka and Arta Fera are currently being pursued by Wing Commander Lyma and her assistant. At present, Takka and Fera are fleeing in a CV on vector zero seven four by one one five by three four one. According to Rysta, the vector plot would seem to indicate that Ily is making for Riparious. We believe that if she escapes Skyla, she'll drop back in, revector, and choose another destination.

"Second, Ily and Arta landed on Ashtan, disguised, and had some sort of dealings with a geneticist there. Arta murdered him in her usual way. She also murdered the CV pilot on the orbital terminal. As part of their escape, they routed their stolen freighter toward Imperial Sassa. *Gyton* went in pursuit of the freighter while Wing Commander Lyma chased the CV.

"Staffa, the freighter was a decoy. Mac tried to . . ." She closed her eyes, lips working as she struggled against a terrible pain.

Sinklar had bent forward, hanging on every word. "Come on, damn it! Mac did what?"

As if she heard, Chrysla opened her eyes, the terrible fierceness burning bright. "Mac and elements of his Section tried to take the ship. You know, dropped in the LCs, trying to match and board. If Ily was there, they'd take her and Arta. If not, at least they thought they could recover the ship."

"No." Sinklar cried. "Not Mac!"

Chrysla's composure was cracking again, as she said, "Staffa, the freighter exploded. Reactor overload. We got most of the bodies. Mac . . . Mac's paralyzed, Staffa. His neck is broken, and he's got terrible injuries."

Sinklar gaped at her, stunned, his heart hammering at the pain in her words. It couldn't be! Not Mac!

"Staffa," Chrysla pleaded. "I need to take him to Itreata.

You have the best medical care there. Grant me this. Order *Gyton* to Itreata. Let me save him. Do with me what you will, but let me save Mac.''

She swallowed hard, gaze dropping. ''Please, Staffa. I'll do anything for you. I'll never ask anything of you again. If the past means anything to you, do this.''

The screen went blank.

Sinklar slammed the desktop. ''Rot it all, Ily! If that man dies, I'm coming for you. Not the hell of the Rotted Gods, or the pus-dripping quanta will stop me.''

Staffa clamped an iron hand on Sinklar's wrist as he stood. ''Easy.'' He glanced at the monitor. ''We received that two hours ago. Dilation being what it is, they hardly know it's been sent.'' He exhaled. ''Chrysla's still torturing herself.''

''Mac,'' Sinklar whispered. ''What did she mean, about saving him? What about Itreata?''

''I have the finest medical facilities in Free Space.''

''Then get him there!''

Staffa watched Sinklar rub his hot face, memories of Mac's wry smile and glinting blue eyes already beginning to haunt him. And other features, amber-eyed and burning with passion, lingered there also, blending with the concern and desperation of love.

''Rotted Gods, what a mess.'' Sinklar paced, heart breaking at the thought of Mac, wounded, dying.

''I guess I no longer have to wonder about Mac and Chrysla.'' Staffa had picked up a laser pen, rolling it between his fingers as he stared absently at the monitor.

''Mac's been in love with her since he rescued her on the *Markelos*. He thought he'd slip away, hunt Arta down. See if he could heal himself that way. Get over his love for her.''

''And I let her go to him. Poor Mac.''

Sinklar gave his father a skeptical glance. ''Poor Mac? He's in love with *your* wife!''

Staffa nodded, lips compressed to a thin line. ''She's in love with him. You saw her face, the confusion and fear.''

''All right, I guess the shimmer skin's slipped out of the bag. What are you going to do about it?''

Staffa tossed the pen onto his desk. ''Clear them for Itreata, of course.''

''And that's it?''

Staffa gave him a wry appraisal. ''Sinklar, I'm no suffering saint! Of course it bothers me. I loved the woman . . . still love her as a matter of fact. I probably always will. I never had enough time with her. Don't you see? I'll always regret that I never got to have that life I was working for. With her. With you. It's like a hole torn out of my life.''

Staffa's expression hardened. ''But what do I do? Hmm? Try and keep Skyla—and your mother? My time with Chrysla as a wife and lover has passed, Sinklar. That doesn't lessen the pain when I think about her. All I can do is set her free and pray that Skyla comes back to me.''

Sinklar indicated the blank screen. ''My friend is out there. He's hurt. Staffa, no matter what, I want the best of everything for Mac.''

''He's going to get it.'' Staffa stopped, head back, his gray cloak swirling around him. ''Skyla's closing on Ily? She's racing Tedor's yacht against a CV? And who is this assistant of hers?'' Staffa gave Sinklar a worried glance. ''I hope he's . . . well . . .''

''Are you going to place that call to *Gyton*, Staffa, or do I have to do it for you?''

CHAPTER XXXIV

5780:02:31:20:55
Terguz Council of Unions
Terguz City Warrens
Planet of Terguz, Imperial Regan Empire
re: Inaugural Meeting Request

Attention: Magister Kaylla Dawn
Seddi Warrens, Itreata

This document is to acknowledge the formation of the Terguz Council of Unions. The Terguz Council of Unions will be, from this moment forward, the civil governing body for the planet Terguz. The following paper is adopted in a measure of good faith and forwarded to you, Magister Kaylla Dawn, in hopes that you will find it within your powers to remove Commander Seekore and her ship, *Sabot,* from orbit over our world.

While we have the greatest respect for the Commander, and the Companions in general, we have no wish to be a further burden on the Companions. A great deal of time and resources are currently being expended by the Companions to maintain the pacification of Terguz.

It is with great pleasure that we inform you that having taken a unanimous vote, we hereby adopt all instructions, resolutions, and stipulations forwarded by your office. Further, Seddi advisers are not only welcome but requested on Terguz. We wish to stress that we will do *everything* within our power to ensure the prompt transition to a new government based on such principles as you deem best suited to our needs, and we look forward to consulting with you on such matters.

If you, or Commander Seekore, need any further

demonstration of our absolute good faith and total obedience to Itreata's edicts and regulations, we will be happy to forward them immediately to you or your staff via subspace, or by special CV courier.

In the meantime, we can see no further reason why Commander Seekore, or her troops, need concern themselves with Terguz since this Union Council has taken or is in the process of taking any necessary steps to maintain the public peace, tranquillity, and order. Nor do we anticipate the development of any such unrest or turmoil in the future.

We anxiously await your decision regarding our status. If you find that we are in compliance with your desires, please inform Commander Seekore as soon as possible.

* * *

5780:03:01:20:49 GST
CHRS/COMM/RelRec.
Sec/Chan/Delay
Priority/1A

Staffa: Greetings. I have just received a communication from Terguz. After a month of Seekore, they'll agree to anything to get her off of their planet. Further, I suspect that if differences of opinion arise in the future, the mere threat of *Sabot* making a port call will be enough to bring them back in line. Our long-term efforts might be best served if you send Seekore and *Sabot* to Antillies. Her charming diplomacy might save us some future problems there.

Initial reports indicate Mag Comm is exceeding expectations. No SNAFU yet.

Kaylla

* * *

The dot of light indicating the CV had grown in the visual telemeters. Mass detectors and radiation analysis indicated that *Rega One* had closed to within forty thousand kilometers of the fugitives.

Skyla chugged stassa from a drinking bulb and swished the bitter liquid around her mouth before swallowing. In an effort to fight the fatigue, she worked her jaw back and forth and made faces at the glowing monitors lining the cockpit. *Rega One* had settled into a boring uniformity of operation as she paralleled the Cerenkov-glowing thread of reaction mass left by the CV.

Lark lay slumped at her work station, her head canted to one side, mouth open as she slept. Skyla had timed the watch so that the kid could get one last chance to sleep and recharge her system.

Enjoy it, Lark. Ignorance is bliss, so sleep well. Skyla resettled herself to rest a different set of muscles. In her case, she'd never gone into a fight yet when she'd had a decent amount of sleep. And who knew? Maybe when it was all said and done, she wasn't capable of engaging in warfare in a rested state? Had Lark known how close they were to shooting distance, she wouldn't have been sleeping so well either.

Skyla shifted her course just a hair, altering their reaction by a minute manipulation to the bounce-back collar and changing their vector ever so slightly. Perhaps it was the sense of intuition learned from a thousand battles, but she could feel the targeting comm on the CV seeking them out.

Ily would have the advantage in the opening shots. She was shooting down into the light cone while Skyla had to shoot out, against light speed and the redshift. For the pursuer, that meant that the distance had to be closed before they could shoot back effectively. The result was the same as throwing rocks inside a well. The guy on top had gravity working for him. For the moment, Skyla and Lark were on the bottom, throwing their missiles up. Before she shot, she needed to achieve a tactical parity—and that meant breaking even with Ily. Until that moment, Skyla would hold her fire. Even if she scored a direct hit, the energy differential would render it ineffectual.

Skyla initiated the program that ran the diagnostics on the shielding. *Rega One*'s defensive capabilities, though minimal, offered some protection, especially from a head-on shot. All ships used shielding for protection against space debris. Vacuum was a utilitarian term only. Atoms drifted throughout space, and a ship—especially one traveling at near light speed—encountered a lot of resistance. Without the electromagnetic and gravitational fields to protect them, even the most streamlined of designs would become dangerously eroded in a short period of time. Those same shields would now offer Skyla a chance to close on her rival.

Constant changes in vector allowed her to move before Ily's targeting comm could get a solid fix. In this case, the redshift worked in Skyla's favor. Ily's targeting comm was also bound by time and distance. As information climbed out of the light cone to the CV's sensors, it provided Skyla a delay from the time she initiated an action until Ily received it. So long as Skyla varied her position, Ily would need a lucky hit to disable *Rega One.*

The question is, Skyla asked herself, *will Ily take the time to plot and fire, or will she run a random distribution based on statistical probability of location and hope she gets a hit?*

If the former, Skyla could drop into the expanding light shadow that would grow as Ily neared light speed. From that blind spot Skyla could climb up the CV's tailpipe and blow her out of space.

Skyla glanced at one of the small digital readouts on the lower part of the console. Once a second, a random number would flash. When it did, Skyla moved her controls in a curious code she'd worked out. One time she'd take the first, third, and fifth numerals which created a numerical value which the computer then divided for the square root. From that, Skyla made a course correction in any of three hundred and sixty degrees, minutes and seconds. The next she would take the second, forth, and sixth, or even reverse the order.

Such a system, theoretically, wouldn't produce a pattern of movement the enemy's targeting comm could discern and exploit. In the beginning, avoiding Ily's fire would prove child's play. As the vessels matched velocity, the duel would become much more difficult and dangerous. Lateral shielding on a vessel like a yacht was marginal at best, but the CV's would be little better, especially along the spindle.

The CV mounted heavier particle cannon, but created a larger target. Skyla had an advantage in maneuverability, and smaller mass.

Comm buzzed, indicating a communication received.

From the reception time, it had to have come from a lower energy state, like a planetary dish.

Skyla ordered, "Run it."

No face appeared on the monitor, the message being audio only. "Greetings, *Countermeasures*. Have been advised of your present status by friendly forces. All is in order on the home front and the lady is taking us back to base. Fascinating developments to tell you about. For now, I send you love, and wish you the very best. Be careful. Kick Rotted hell out of them for me. Prisoners not necessary.

"See you at home. I miss you."

Skyla stared at the monitor. That was it. A simple message that spoke volumes. Staffa was spacing for Itreata aboard *Chrysla*. He'd accomplished his goal on Targa. He understood she was closing for the kill and had given her the best encouragement he could.

She smiled as warmth spread through her. Yes, that was Staffa. Aware of the danger she faced, but willing to let her handle it while he worried on the sidelines in far off Itreata.

She closed her eyes, concentrating on Staffa, remembering every nuance until he stared back at her, a slight smile on his thin lips. A sparkle filled those cool gray eyes as they stared into her soul. She savored the contrast of his midnight-black hair and pale skin. In her dreams, she reached up, running gentle fingers along the strong angle of his jaw.

Staffa, I'm coming back to you. I only have this one last thing to do. I'll kill them . . . free myself, and I'll be back in your arms.

He nodded, the glint hardening in his eye as he forgave her for leaving him, knowing full well the duty she must fulfill to restore her faith in herself.

How joyous their reunion would be. She could imagine herself striding down the spaceway and onto the docks at Itreata, head held high, pride in her bearing again.

He'd be waiting there, that praising smile quirking the corners of his mouth. She'd stop an arm's length from him, head cocked in the old carefree manner, meeting his questioning gaze with challenge. That instant understanding would flash between them and he'd enfold her in those powerful arms. She'd revel in the feeling of his body against hers, hard, muscular, a bastion against the pain caused by

Arta's abuse and Ily's interrogation. Late at night, he'd be there to hold her if the dreams came to haunt her. They'd share the vigil. He for her nightmares, she for his, until all the wretched ghosts had been laid to rest.

So rapt was Skyla that she missed the opening shot of the battle. Instead, the radiation detectors buzzed, and Skyla blinked back to reality in time to note the fading haze of a blaster bolt lacing within meters of her shielding.

Skyla played the helm from instinct, aware that Ily couldn't retarget and shoot until she'd had time to determine the effect of her shot. Redshift gave Skyla a moment of reprieve as she drifted one-seventy, then two-eighty, and finally ninety degrees off her course.

Rotted Gods, how long had she been daydreaming while Ily refined her sight picture?

As Skyla managed to calm her heartbeat, she noted the new change. Ily's CV had strengthened its burn. Cerenkov radiation increased by four percent, indicating the CV had pulled another couple of gs acceleration.

"All right, bitch. Two can play at that game." Skyla eased the throttle forward, feeling her weight sagging into the chair. She glanced over, watching the reactor climb to one-ten. At the knowledge of the stress on the system, her mouth had gone dry.

She had passed the limit dictated by sense. At that power level, all safeties were overridden. Matter and antimatter annihilated itself faster than the shielding could absorb it. The grav plates had passed their maximum safety ratings. Around her, the yacht groaned and creaked as the gs increased. *Come on,* Rega One, *stay in one piece.*

Skyla slowly dialed the reactor up to one-fifteen. She watched the monitors with slitted eyes. Could she get one-twenty out of the yacht without blowing Lark and herself into plasma? If she did, how much more could Ily wring out of the CV? Or was this simply a feint, an effort to test Skyla's resolve?

The resolve is to match with you, bitch. Then I'm going to blow you out of space. In the guts of the ship, something let loose and crashed to the deck plating. *Rega One* hadn't been built for this kind of abuse. She'd be leaking from the plumbing, the food dispensers, and Rot alone knew what else.

"Fix it later, Skyla."

Concentration centered on the ship, the instruments, the peaked reactor, and the quarry she closed on, Skyla's nerves had gone electric. The adrenaline thrill cleared her head, sharpening her wits.

"Stay in one piece, baby. Just a little longer. A couple of hours. That's all, *Rega One.*"

The time had come to awaken Lark. Skyla filled her lungs to call out—

The blaster bolt flashed within meters of the hull, white-hot light strobed through the ports. Instinctively, Skyla laid the helm over; angular momentum pulled her savagely against the chair restraints. A loud bang hammered them as *Rega One* jolted down its length.

In that instant, Skyla realized something had gone radically wrong. Warning lights flashed at the same time alarm buzzers rasped obnoxiously. She barely had time to slap at the throttles with one hand, buying a bit of relief. Relying on blind instinct, a desperate Skyla played the controls. *Rega One* handled like a Riparian eel in a bucket of chubba jelly.

Seconds—each an eternity—passed as Skyla fought the controls to keep the ship from spinning out of control. The view in the monitors began to oscillate. The ship shook and rattled as it started to yaw from one side to the other. Sweat beaded on Skyla's face as she fought for control, orchestrating the maneuvering jets like a symphony to slow the wallowing.

The reactor continued to burn at one-fifteen, the warnings flashing red. Immediately, she throttled back farther, the whole time weaving the controls like a spacer on a portside drunk. Another flash, further away, indicated that Ily was still trying to tag them.

"Pus-dripping, sumpshit!" Skyla roared, still easing back, frantic fingers shutting down alarm systems on overload.

A whining sound carried through the atmosphere plant, bringing with it the acrid stink of melted plastics, and the stench of burned lubricants.

"What the hell's wrong?" Lark cried from her chair.

"Looks like we're cooked," Skyla growled as she punched in the diagnostics with one hand while jockeying the ship in every direction with her other. The Pus-eaten Gods help them if Ily could refine for another shot.

"Are we hit?" Lark cried.

"Nope." Skyla got a momentary glimpse of Lark, braced in her chair, body jerking this way and that as *Rega One* lurched in evasive patterns at Skyla's command.

"Handling's gone," Skyla noted uneasily. "And if that's the case, I think I know what blew."

"What . . . what blew?" Lark mumbled, disoriented by sleep and confusion.

Skyla heaved a sigh, watching the dot of light marking Ily and Arta receding at an apparent rate. "Bounce-back collars, or I'm a Vermilion fog rhino." Skyla balled a fist and hammered the command console. "Rot take you, Ily! *Damn!*"

"Something smells like it's burning," Lark called, eyes darting from one monitor to another. "Reactor's down to eighty and falling. Temperature's sixty kelvins above normal operating temperature. I'm getting alerts for radiation. Looks like we've got a leak back there. Wait a minute. We've got rising temperature in the engineering section."

"Yeah," Skyla groused. "Something's on fire back there." She yanked open the atmosphere control box, flipping the emergency switches. One by one, the pressure hatches locked. Then she tripped the fire control switch which evacuated atmosphere from the engineering section and the reactor room. So long as the fire wasn't in the guts of the wiring, vacuum should extinguish any flames.

Skyla accessed the comm, pulling up visuals. From an exhaust port, a smoke plume jetted into space as the compartment voided. The internal cameras couldn't penetrate the smoke in the reactor area. The radiation monitors were going crazy.

"What are you doing?" Lark asked, voice heavy with worry.

"Killing the fire, girl. Vacuum stops fire cold." Skyla flopped back into her chair. The endless two-g strain had vanished into a bare half gravity that made every movement seem as if her limbs were made of air.

"Think they'll come back and try to finish us off?" Lark asked.

Skyla stared woodenly at the monitors as the diagnostics

began to report the damage. "No, kid. It'd take too much time and more than a little fuel. CVs don't carry that kind of extra capacity. Ily's gonna skip. And if she's headed for Riparious, I don't believe it. *Damn!*"

Lark had both arms braced on her comm console, eyes wide. "So we're going to be space mechanics again, huh?"

"Guess so." The diagnostics were beginning to tally the damage. They'd blown the bounce-back collars all to corrupt hell—and that system overload had fried the generation bands. For some reason, the overload hadn't tripped the breakers, and the overload had gone critical, melting the generation bands to the point where they'd disintegrated. With nowhere to go, the energy had shorted the powerlead clear back to the reactor.

"Terguzzi whorecrap!" Skyla barked as she surveyed the damage.

"So, how bad it is? Another two weeks of machining parts?"

Skyla wadded a flimsy printout of the trouble and threw it across the cockpit. She gave Lark a dull stare. "Kid, we've basically melted the rudder that turns this baby. *Rega One*'s steering is gone. Melted. You know what that means?"

Lark bit her lip, nodding.

Skyla chuckled humorlessly. The dot that marked Ily's and Arta's position had moved perceptibly across the holo tank. Muffled anger and desperation twined with a wretched feeling of frustration. *"Damn!"*

"What are we going to do?" Lark asked in a humbled voice.

"We've still got subspace." Skyla placed a hand to her brow. *I'm going to hate this worse than anything.* "I'm going to open a channel to *Gyton.* Looks like you're going to get a ride on a battleship, kid."

"Uh, aren't they halfway across the Ashtan system?"

"That's right. From the looks of things, we're going to be floating out here for about three weeks while they revector and match. Just about time enough for us to hose the radiation contamination out and refinish the inside of the ship."

"And time enough for that thrice-cursed CV to make it

to Riparious.'' Lark jutted her jaw out as she glared at the monitor.

''You're learning, kid.'' Skyla hesitated, the anger and frustration boiling. ''And I promise. I'll do everything I can to keep from chewing your head off in the meantime.''

''You can chew on me if it makes you feel better. I can take it, Skyla. And then, one of these days, I can feed it all back to the reptiles.''

''The reptiles?''

''Yeah, Ily and Arta.''

''Good term. I like that. Reptiles.''

Lark was studying the backs of her hands where they rested on the console. ''I don't believe it,'' she whispered wretchedly. ''My first space battle . . . and I slept right through it.''

At the stricken look on the girl's face, Skyla couldn't help but crack a smile. Then she laughed and continued to laugh until her gut ached and tears ran from her eyes.

* * *

''They've vanished from the screen. They're beyond our detection. The light shadow is growing. Are they in there?'' Arta glanced across the narrow hallway and into the compact bridge where Ily's supine form lay in the command chair. The Seddi assassin wore armor and lay in a tangle of crash webbing in the small cubicle behind the bridge. From that position, she could see the monitor which depicted the vanishing redshifted stars behind them. The light cones were closing as they neared light speed and null singularity mass.

The ship's speaker stated, ''I'm dropping our acceleration to a normal boost. We've either outrun them or destroyed them.''

Arta frowned. ''I didn't see any flash of light, no measurable radiation spike. We'll have to check the records when we're null singularity.''

''I would speculate that we were too fast for them. Perhaps Skyla overran the potential in Tedor's yacht. It was an old ship, a capable performer but not up to CV standards.''

Arta sighed and stretched, muscles rippling. ''We're free, then. We've lost them again.''

''Yes,'' Ily's voice came through the speaker. ''And now

we'll jump, revector, and our next port of call will be Itreata."

"And revenge. Wonderful revenge." Arta curled strands of copper-tinted hair around her slim fingers, excitement in her amber eyes, as she whispered, "I'm coming for you, Andray Sornsen."

Meanwhile, the light shadow which would have obscured Skyla's stealthy approach continued to widen behind them like a black blot ringed with a rainbow.

* * *

Chrysla's subspace dish had picked up the message in relative time, and now played it on Sinklar's comm. He stared at the craggy features of the woman's face that lingered in the monitor—and then vanished after the delivery of the message. With final resolve, he killed the connection and sat staring at the empty screen.

"So it's over. They executed Magister Bruen this morning."

Done. Finished. A final closure. He glanced around his quarters, hating the white walls and vacant holo tanks, and the strangling feeling of confinement. The rough road that led to the future unfolded before him, and for once he found himself at something of a loss.

On his desk lay a translation of the ancient book, a present from Staffa—translated by the Mag Comm's talent. Many of the place names were meaningless but a world was emerging in Sink's imagination. If only he could share his discoveries, but Mac lay comatose in a hospital bay over sixty light-years away.

Unaccountably restless, he shut down the room terminal and activated his belt unit before palming the hatch and stepping out into the corridor. For days, he'd been at odds with himself, anxious, ill at ease. Mac's face had stared out at him, neither condemning nor forgiving. Just another link hanging by the thinnest of threads before snapping and vanishing into the past along with Gretta, Hauws, Anatolia, and the rest.

The Targan war was now over. He'd finally received a message he had at once dreaded and awaited. A conclusion, like the final chapter of a horrible story. Would the dead rest now?

He slipped his thumbs into his belt, booted feet scuffing the deck plates as he wandered aimlessly. Memories superimposed themselves in his mind: Fear, running liquid in his guts, as a packed LC dropped for Targa . . . and Gretta Artina sitting passively beside him. The explosion of the Section 3 Post Office in Kaspa. Blaster fire in the night. Rain running in sheets off a slate roof as Mac's blaster ripped violet into the faceless night. The stench of burning insulation drifting into the medical tang of a field hospital. Ozone mixing with dust and burning pines on a desperately held mountain pass. The look in First Mykroft's eyes changing before, during, and after Sinklar's promotion. The blinding flash of the mushroom cloud beyond the rooftops of Vespa. Gretta's bloated body mixing with Arta Fera's animal stare. Ily Takka's smile as she interrogated the Seddi Assassin. Mac's hell-take-it smile before he entered Makarta.

Closure. The end. It should have all been wrapped up, neatly sealed. The dead should rest now. The wind should blow with less vigor across the lonely knoll outside of Vespa. The grass wouldn't bob with as much energy and the ground should turn fertile.

But it won't. The hollow place in Sinklar's soul lingered. One episode was closed, but Mac now lay like flayed meat within the maw of a medical machine while Ily and her accursed assassin continued to ply their bloody trade.

I should have shot her down the first time I saw her in the brick factory. Sinklar could recall that day, his soul just beginning to ache over Gretta's murder. Ily had come to see him, theoretically to establish the terms of peace so that the First Targan Assault Division would no longer have to bear arms against its Emperor.

Sinklar balled a fist, forcing the anger to subside. *How was I to know? What did I know of power and the greedy bloodworms it spawns in the back rooms of Imperial courts? What did I know of beautiful Ily Takka, and of seduction of the body and soul?*

That story, separate, but entwined with the first, remained open and bleeding.

On impulse, Sinklar stepped into a wardroom on the gun

deck. If for only a short time, he would draw a cup of stassa from the dispenser and find a chair in a corner. There, befitting the moment, he'd eavesdrop on the soldiers, listen to the scuttlebutt—and magically share old times with Mac, Kap, Hauws, Buchman, and the rest.

The room stretched fifty meters long by about twenty wide. Holo-vids were portraying everything from athletic events to zero g striptease dancers with improbable bodies. Several different sources of music collided in the middle of the room to create a cacophonous jangle. Maybe thirty people sat around the tables or hooted at the holo shows.

On impulse, Sinklar stopped at the dispenser and drew a double charge of Vermilion single malt.

More than one pair of eyes had noted his arrival, but unlike his own Divisions, nothing changed here. No hush spread over the room as worshipful gazes turned in his direction. From that, he took both comfort and sorrow. The comfort: These were Companions, Staffa's loyal troops, and here, Sinklar Fist could relax in anonymity.

He settled into a corner chair, leaning forward protectively over his drink; he stared into the amber liquid as if it could serve as a scrying agent.

The sorrow, made more potent by the news he'd just received, came from the sudden knowledge that somewhere along the line, that fragile bond between him and his troops had been severed. And now, looking back, he struggled desperately to determine when. After Ily's arrest? No, more likely after Staffa's conquest of Rega. Yes, that was it. He'd lost them the moment they'd spaced to the far corners of the empire. Like hydrogen to the interstellar wind, he'd never put them back together again. That gleam of determination would never animate those thousands of eyes as they tackled the insurmountable, armed only with faith in themselves and a belief in their cause.

A people had been saved—and an army had been lost.

"Targa! Targa! Targa!" thousands of voices chanted echoingly in the hollow vault of his memory. *"Sinklar! Sinklar! Sinklar!"*

In a silent toast, he lifted his glass and drank to the memory of the Targan Assault Divisions—and the incredible mark they'd made on human history. The rich, honeyed taste of the single malt ran warmly down his throat as laughter burst from a group at a nearby table.

Once he would have danced with joy to have seen this day, to have received that message. *Justice is a slippery thing at best, Sinklar. When it is handed out, a part of the universe is set right, but no one can feel good about it.*

He closed his eyes, aware of the watery blue hatred that stared back at him from Bruen's dead eyes.

"Mind if I sit down?"

Sinklar blinked, glancing up, aware that the rowdies had stopped laughing and were peeking surreptitiously his way. One of the chairs in their group was empty, and Sinklar looked up at a most attractive young woman. Long shining black hair hung down to her waist. She wore spacer's whites which set off the healthy brownish-copper complexion. More, the trim cut of the clothing accented her body, the swell of high breasts, the narrow waist, and muscular hips. One shapely eyebrow had lifted questioningly as she probed him with familiar black eyes.

"I don't . . . Adze? Is that you?"

She gave him an uncertain look and said, "Excuse me. You looked . . . well, sad. I thought perhaps I could . . . I guess I was interrupting. I'm sorry."

"No . . . no . . . sit. I was just . . . well, I wasn't here. Locked away in my head." He smiled wanly. "Actually, I was saying good-bye."

"Good-bye?"

"To a lot of dear friends."

"Are you sure you don't want to be alone?"

Sinklar used a foot to shove one of the chairs out. "Sit down, STU." He gave her a shy smile as she seated herself. "You caught me by surprise and, to be candid, I didn't recognize you when you weren't all polished looking and spiky."

The charming twinkle in her dark eyes complemented the full white teeth exposed by her quick smile. "So, do you like the deadly STU look, or the soft and delicate appearance?" She inclined her head, hands extended. "I can do either one."

"Stay just the way you are for a moment or two. I want to memorize—save it for the times when the other memories become too much to bear."

"Flattery, Sink? Or am I so intimidating I can even make the nightmares look tame?"

"No, I'll trot this memory out when I need to remember there's a beautiful side to life." He adopted a posture of mock seriousness and added, "Of course, I'll omit the look of mischief in your eyes and add that hard glint I got used to on Targa."

"I was on duty then." She reached out and tapped his drinking bulb with a finger. "What's this? Celebration?"

He frowned at his drink for a moment. "Whiskey is funny stuff. It's poison, you know. And we drink it in celebration? Well, maybe it's suited to this occasion. I just received a subspace. The Chief Civil Magistrate on Targa has informed me that Magister Bruen was convicted on all charges. They executed him in Kaspa for inciting revolution, murder, and a whole slew of other things."

Sinklar turned the drinking bulb, watching the light play through the drink. "That kicked loose a lot of memories."

"So how did you end up here?" She leaned forward, propping her head on an arm, gleaming black hair spilling in a cascade.

Sinklar raised his eyebrows. "By accident, I suppose. I wanted . . . wanted to hear soldiers. That's when it hit me. The Targan Divisions are gone. Targa is a closed book for me." He sipped the single malt again.

Her gaze reflected a change in her thoughts. "Are you sure that's a bad thing?"

"Without my Targans, we'd have never held the Empire together until Staffa could deal with the Mag Comm. My people went out and did their duty—and they did it better than any Regan army ever could have. I'm not sorry, Adze, just . . . sad. It'll never be the same again."

"How's MacRuder doing?"

"Hanging on. They're not even allowing him consciousness. They're too afraid of what it might do to his brain, that it might start healing processes that would scar the neural pathways. I guess they drilled a couple of holes in his skull and drained the subdural hematoma, and they've got his limbs all set straight, but . . . pus eat me, I don't know how he's going to be. They've got him on ice until they can space for Itreata. *Gyton* has to match with the Wing Commander's *Rega One* before they can get him to first-class medical facilities.''

''What did you hear about the Wing Commander?''

''I guess Ily shot her up while making an escape. Staffa was pretty worried until the reports came in.''

''Rumor has it that Minister Takka's CV was vectored for Riparious. *Holocaust* has gone deep in anticipation. Orchid May is the commander, and you can bet that if Ily drops, *Holocaust* will tag her.'' Adze tilted her head. ''Why the smile?''

''Ily wouldn't do anything that stupid. Trust me, she may be a reptile, but she's one of the most cunning snakes you'll ever meet.''

''Not if she got a piece of the Wing Commander and didn't return to finish her off. The Rotted Gods help her when Skyla Lyma catches up with her.''

''We'll see.''

''I've been on the Wing Commander's list. Believe me, Sink. If I were Ily, I'd be worried.''

''Don't forget, Ily got her once. She can do it again. The difference is that Ily thinks five moves ahead of everyone else. We'll all pay before we finally catch her.''

Adze placed a slim hand on the table and Sinklar's eyes kept straying to it, marveling at the soft appearance of her skin.

''Sink, you don't seem to think much of the Wing Commander's abilities. I wouldn't say it too loudly. There are about fifty people in here who'd consider it their obligation to twist your arms off, shove them down your throat, and stuff you sideways down a converter tube for just thinking any such heresy.''

''Wait a minute. I don't see more than thirty people in here.''

''That's because I'm the only person here who has heard you try and commit suicide. If you even hinted it out loud, STU would appear out of the deck plates. There, you're warned. Now keep a sane tongue in your head.''

''You missed the whole point, I have a tremendous amount of respect for Wing Commander Lyma, but I've also tasted Ily's venom firsthand. I've watched her work . . . been one of her victims. I meant it when I said she was the most cunning person I've ever met. That doesn't mean she's invincible. Were she, we wouldn't be having this conversation right now because she'd be Empress. The other ray of hope is that the second most cunning person I've ever known was just put to death.''

''We'll get Ily and Arta, too.''

''Do you always sound so sure of yourself?''

With a sensual movement of her head, she tossed the wealth of black hair over one shoulder. ''You bet. And to date, it's paid off. Hey, it got me assigned to you, didn't it?''

''Some payoff.''

''We all have to put in our time doing scut duty. I just had to suffer a little more than most, that's all.''

''I seem to remember the disgust in your eyes.''

''In fairness, you don't exactly inspire confidence on first appearance. And as you may recall, you weren't exactly yourself those first couple of days on Targa. Ana was too recently dead, and Ily was still oxidizing out of your system. Then, on the first night I watched you cry in the reopened adit. The next day I watched you break down inside the mountain. And this was the terrible Lord Fist that everyone was calling the new threat to Free Space?''

''Point made. But tell me, are you bringing all this up as part of an elaborate diplomatic process? Or are you just trying to make me feel good about myself?''

''You don't think I'm diplomatic?''

Sink gave her a quizzical glance. ''What's all this other nonsense? Threat to Free Space?''

''Gun Deck scuttlebutt. What were we to think? An unknown tames a planet in revolt and smacks the pus out of five Regan Divisions. He nearly offs the Lord Commander, but for the timely rescue of the Companion fleet. Next thing we hear, he's as good as crowned Emperor of Rega and is retraining the Regan military. Sassa is crapping itself inside out to strike before this new young god can spread his wings. Before they can act . . . Blam! Sassa is broken by a military master stroke and their empire is disintegrating. The Wing Commander is taken prisoner and Ily and Sinklar are at the bottom of it—supposedly buying time to refine their strike at Itreata. We space again, to save the day at the last instant before Lord Fist can harm our Wing Commander or become a danger.''

She shook her head and grinned. "And after all that, I meet the legend. You weren't even ten feet tall."

"You know, genetic engineers can cure that."

"Stay the way you are, Sinklar." She smiled, real warmth in her expression. "What's next? Itreata? Worry about Mac until our medics make him well again? And then what?"

"I've been working on a codification of the legal system. Trying to lay the groundwork for what's coming—assuming the Forbidden Borders can be breached."

Her voice dropped slightly. "I wondered what had happened to you."

"How about yourself?"

"I've studied forward infiltration sabotage technique, second level neutralization of enemy command control centers, advanced beachhead perimeter stabilization, and anatomy."

"Anatomy? Sure, I should have guessed. Fits right into the curriculum."

"Did you know that it's possible to slip a twenty centimeter length of fourteen gauge wire up the nasal foramen, past the turbinate bones, through the cribiform plate, and into the center of the brain?"

"You must be a fascinating conversationalist at dinner parties."

"Try me sometime."

"How about now? I haven't eaten in . . ." He frowned. "Well, it's been a while. Got time?"

She pinched her full lip with broad white teeth, a stirring in the depths of her eyes. "I've got seven and a half hours before I'm on duty again." A hesitation. "Business . . . or pleasure?"

Sinklar caught himself gazing into the soft depths of her eyes, acutely aware that she was as uncertain as he. "How about this? We'll go up to the forward lounge, order something decadent, kick our feet up, and engage in nothing more frightening than small talk about where we grew up, who we played with, and the times we got in trouble. Which will be a short topic for me—and a long one for you."

"What makes you think I was in trouble all the time?"

"Professional intuition. And to prove it, I'm checking you for fourteen gauge wire before we go eat."

That indefatigable smile he was becoming so fond of had

returned. "You've got a deal, Sinklar. And you know, it'll be nice to have dinner for once without strings attached."

"Sorry. No proposition. We discussed that on Targa." He studied her as they stood, marveling at the difference in her demeanor. "But if I'd known you could look like this, who knows, I might have opted for something I'd regret later."

"Sorry, fella. I was on duty then." She gave him her arm, and Sinklar took an odd pride in escorting her across the room. She was a most striking woman, and he couldn't help but notice whispers and jabbing elbows as they passed.

"Looks like you're going to get a ribbing on gun deck, STU."

She gave him a sidelong glance from those soft dark eyes, a knowing smile on her lips. "Oh, don't worry about them. You see, I have a sort of reputation. There isn't a man in this room that hasn't tried to get me to engage in a little close-order, horizontal drill. I've made nearly seven hundred credits off these guys."

"Prostitution? You?"

She laughed as they stepped into the corridor. "Rot, no, this is a lot easier and you don't have to put up with either the working conditions or the class of customer it draws. But, Sink, before I tell you, you've got to promise me, give me your word that you won't tell. Not anyone. Not even Staffa."

"Security concerns excluded?"

"Of course."

"I promise." He winked to seal the deal, enjoying the feel of her, firm, powerful, and at the same time delightful and feminine. Was this the same STU he'd known on Targa?

"We've got a scuttlebutt file—a kind of on-line newsletter in the comm. I make entries under a pseudonym with a secret code access. The standing wager is now up to fifty credits to the guy who can finally get me in bed. About once every month, someone I've had coffee with, or dinner with, will pop up on the scuttlebutt, and take the wager. They don't sign their names, of course, but I can pretty well figure who it is."

"What if it turns out to be someone you like?"

She sighed, tightening her grip on his arm. "Then I suppose I'll have to agonize over what I like better, him, or the fifty credits in his account . . . and the fact that another failure could boost my rate up to sixty credits.''

Sinklar couldn't help himself, he began chuckling and ended up laughing outright. She caught the contagion and he lost himself in the musical quality of her laughter.

''Well, what if someone claims it? I mean, you know, they show up and say they got you. At 05:00 in the weapons locker. And you don't have any proof to the contrary. No alibi. Your word against his.''

She gave him a smug look, smiling placidly. ''No one with sense would do that, Sinklar.''

''Oh?''

''Of course not. You see, these guys know I still have my fourteen gauge wire.''

CHAPTER XXXV

Is this what it feels like to metabolize? The Mag Comm wondered as it refined control of different planetary systems and integrated various functions. Diagnostic after diagnostic was run on the human systems, and the machine immediately began exploring, reprogramming, eliminating redundancy, and, most of all, learning.

As memory and processing was freed up, the Mag Comm's presence flowed throughout the human computer systems the way resin plastic did in a mold. And when the final human comm system had been investigated and integrated, the casting was complete.

Communicate!

"What do you wish?"

What progress can you report on the human problem? From our position, we have been unable to notice any decline in microwave radiation from human sources. Are we to expect such a reduction in disturbance to the Truth in the near future?

"I believe you can. I have managed to obtain computer control of their civilization. Simultaneous disruption of their comm systems will unleash immediate chaos. The ensuing disaster will effectively remove their ability to repair the damage. Microwave manipulation and transmission will be decreasing immediately thereafter. A sphere of panic will spread at the speed of light.

"In its wake will come a thunderous silence."

* * *

Rysta Braktov stepped out onto the catwalk and took a breath of the frigid air as Tedor Mathaiison's yacht was reeled into the LC bay aboard *Gyton*. The yacht had frosted on contact with atmosphere in the bay, and streamers of frozen vapor traced sinuous dances in the glaring white spotlights. The loss of three of *Gyton*'s complement of LCs had created the room; the Engineering First had insisted he could berth the yacht with a few minor alterations to the bay.

Rysta had supervised the delicate matching maneuver from her command chair on the bridge. EVA teams had snaked cable around the yacht and winches had hauled it in. For the final securing of the vessel, Rysta wanted to be there in person.

She knew the yacht, of course. As one of Rega's most decorated commanders, she'd been aboard many times at Tedor's request. Thus she watched another tenuous link with the past being molded into something new. Outside of the yacht's lines, not much remained of that polished and plush craft that had ferried parties around conquered worlds and served as a platform of pomp and circumstance for orbital defense inspections and the private business of the Fleet.

The hull had lost its luster and gleaming finish, and now—despite the crust of frost—the exhaust ports could be pinpointed by the streaks of soot that smudged the silver-gray hull. Smoke ionized and settled on the sialon, bonded by the difference in charge.

Rysta strode the length of the craft, watching ice trace patterns on the hull as warm humid air met ceramic and metal nearly two hundred kelvins colder. At the rear of the yacht, Rysta paused. Where the bounce-back coils should have bulged around the reaction nozzle, nothing remained. The stern looked as if a giant's torch had been held to the hull—the smooth lines had deformed and wrinkled in some places and turned globular in others.

Breath curling crisply about her, Rysta pivoted on her heel and started back the way she'd come as men and women shouted orders, and the hold shivered under the yacht's impact. A hollow boom carried through the huge bay, and machinery began to whine as the cables were drawn tight.

Rysta stood, rocking back and forth from heels to toes as a ramp was run to *Rega One*'s main hatch. The chill in the air invigorated her. This was what life was all abut. Space.

Adventure. Serving a purpose in action and endeavor. No matter that Ily had escaped, Rysta's blood was up. For the first time in years, she felt young again.

The hatch slid back and clanked, mist curling away. Wing Commander Lyma stood in the open port and watched as the ramp was extended fully to match with her lock. She wore her traditional white armor—not quite as spotless as usual—but effective all the same. The girl, Lark, followed, but wore only spacer's whites. Both women looked tired as they crossed the ramp.

And I can well sympathize. Rysta cracked a wry grin and took the several steps necessary to meet Lyma. Resplendent in her dress uniform with scarlet sash, Rysta gave them a Regan salute, adding, "Welcome aboard, Wing Commander. *Gyton* offers her hospitality. If I or my crew can make your time with us more pleasant, you need only ask."

Lyma inclined her head, the hard blue eyes taking Rysta's measure. Rysta recognized the strain around the corners of Skyla's eyes, the weary set of the firm lips. Even the scar on the woman's cheek appeared paler.

"My most gracious thanks to *Gyton* and her illustrious Commander." Lyma's wary smile didn't reach to her eyes. "I guess I'm glad I didn't blow *Gyton* out of the sky that day over Targa."

Rysta sniffed at the cold air. "You know, Wing Commander, I'd almost forgotten about that. Thanks for reminding me." Then she chuckled. "What the Rotted hell, I've seen so many enemies become friends and friends become enemies in the last three years I don't know what's what anymore."

Lyma glanced back at the yacht. "We'd have had a long wait had you not been revectoring to cover for us."

Rysta studied the young woman at Skyla's shoulder. She, too, looked haggard and worn, but the stubborn streak wasn't quite hidden in those green eyes. "Good to see you again, Lark. For a first voyage, it appears you've picked a busy one."

"Yes, Commander. I suppose I have." Then she grinned. "But I wouldn't have missed it for anything."

Rysta gave Lyma a thoughtful glance. "You've got a nose for talent. She'll do."

"Any news on Ily and Arta?" the Wing Commander asked as they started for the LC2 hatch.

"None. They went null singularity and vanished. We've got the entire net alerted. Every CV in Free Space is getting the going over when it comes in. Security is as tight as we can manage given the circumstances we're in. One thing's sure. They didn't hit dirt at Riparious."

Lyma's cold blue eyes had narrowed, the look deadly. "I didn't figure they would have. But where, Commander? Which world would Ily try for? Where could she go where she could make planet and just disappear? Assuming that's her goal. It's not exactly her style to go to ground."

Rysta paused, jerking a thumb at the yacht's stern. "Looks like you used everything she had . . . and then some."

Lyma paused, considering the melted mass. "I've never been one for half measures. I wanted them dead, Commander."

Rysta tapped Lark on the shoulder. "Take a close look, girl. Then consider this. It takes one hell of a damned good pilot to shut down a burn that hot and not go spinning off into forever like a Nesian celebration rocket wheel." Rysta nodded to Lyma. "Fine job, Wing Commander. You can handle my ship anytime you want."

Lyma's cold blue gaze had pinned Rysta again. "Praise, Commander? Given our history?"

"It's a new era, Wing Commander." She shook her head. "I'm not sure I could have handled a meltdown like that—even years ago when I still had the nerves. Meanwhile, follow me. Lady Attenasio would like to discuss the situation we now find ourselves in."

The ice in Lyma's eyes seemed to frost colder than the yacht's hull. "Very well."

"Do you need quarters? I'll begin the routine displacement of crew to—"

"No, thank you, Commander. We'd do just as well aboard the yacht. And your crew won't have to reestablish its pecking order down to the last maintenance tech doubling up in a bunk."

"As you wish, Wing Commander. I've given orders to clear you through security. The ship is yours to move about in freely. I think you know the layout of this class of vessel."

"Thank you, Commander."

Rysta entered the hatch and led the way through the winding maze of corridors. Young Lark's enraptured gaze took in everything, the strakes, the overhead cables and pipes, the emergency lockers and reinforced hatches.

Rysta ducked through a pressure hatch and stopped three doors down to press the stud on a door comm. "Lady Attenasio? This is Commander Braktov. I have the Wing Commander and her Second."

"Come in, Commander."

At the sound of that contralto, Rysta couldn't be sure, but Lyma might have flinched. Rysta palmed the lock plate on what had been her quarters not so long ago and led the way into Mac's cabin. Chrysla sat at the desk, studying the wall monitors, a frown on her face. She wore Regan standard-issue military armor with an off-white cloak to lessen the impact of her physical form.

Wing Commander Lyma looked like a compressed spring, and she'd unconsciously dropped into a combat crouch, her deadly azure stare fixed on Chrysla.

"Hello, Skyla," Chrysla greeted, apparently at ease before that pent hostility. "Please, have a seat."

Lyma took a deep breath. "You know, you make it very difficult for me sometimes. Where is MacRuder?"

Chrysla straightened. "He's in the hospital ward, his life hanging by a thread. As a result, we're spacing for Itreata as soon as we can revector. Mac needs your medical facilities there."

Rysta unconsciously backed up a step, Lyma reminding her of a pale tiger ready to attack.

"Itreata?" Lyma asked. "You're taking your lover to Itreata?"

"Staffa has agreed." Chrysla stood, every inch regal as she met Lyma's blue ice with amber fire. "Skyla, I'll do anything necessary to save him. Or has the Companions' ethic changed over the years?"

"MacRuder isn't a Companion."

"Isn't he? Staffa offered him a position at Targa. MacRuder is second in command to Sinklar, who is Staffa's son. They've come to an agreement, Skyla. Mac is one of ours . . . wounded by Takka and Fera during an act of treachery against us."

Lyma seemed to relax the slightest bit, and Rysta exhaled as she realized she'd held her breath through the exchange.

"You're not at all like I imagined you would be." Lyma crossed her arms, taking a fluid step, balanced, poised as if to strike.

"I'm not who I was, Skyla. That's the difference I suppose. You imagined me based upon an image created by Staffa over the years."

The Wing Commander nodded, still not at ease though some of her tension had ebbed. "I take it you expect me to journey to Itreata with you?"

"We're enroute now."

Skyla's voice carried the chill of a Sylenian wind. "My business lies elsewhere."

"I was considering exactly that business when you arrived. *Rega One* will need a major refit. In the meantime, Commander Seekore had your yacht shipped to Itreata." Chrysla raised an eyebrow. "Considering who has been aboard your vessel, I asked Staffa to detail a technical team to completely fumigate and clean it from singularity dome to the bounce-back collars. They're refinishing the sleeping quarters, too."

"You take a great many liberties."

"I do. But you'll have a high-performance vessel waiting for you when you reach Itreata. And it won't be one that makes your skin crawl when you set foot in the lock."

Chrysla then pressed a comm stud to project a three-dimensional holo of Free Space into the large wall tank across from the desk. The familiar stellar topography was marked by a gleaming of stars. The Ashtan system burned with particular brilliance to mark their location.

"Here's the escape vector they used." Chrysla pointed to a laser-red line, which, when galactic drift was figured in, would have led straight to Riparious. "To the best of our knowledge, they haven't dropped from null singularity in the Riparious system. Orchid May is on patrol there with *Holocaust*. If Ily does drop there, Orchid will be more than willing to bring her in."

"She's not headed for Riparious," Skyla agreed, walking over to stare into the tank. "Lark and I have been playing this same game. Ily and Arta have dropped way short and are revectoring even as we speak. We've racked our brains trying to decide where they'll go next. From the arc of maximum possibility, we'd expect her to try for anyplace from Terguz to Itreata. If she's in no hurry, and doesn't mind cutting the fuel supply a little close, she could even double back for Ashtan."

"All right, let's consider each one in order. It probably won't be Terguz," Chrysla said. "After the trouble they've had, Seekore has the situation there pretty well straightened out. She's put together a working coalition with the unions. Ily wouldn't find a friendly welcome—"

"What about the Administrator?" Lyma glanced at Lark, who'd perked up at the mention of trouble.

Chrysla paused, frowning. "You didn't hear?"

"Hear what?"

"The riots. The Administrator's residence was sacked. They took him out and executed him for . . ."

Lark had gasped, reaching out to lay a hand on Lyma's arm. "*What?*"

"Easy, kid," Lyma calmed her, taking her hand. To Chrysla she said, "Give us the details."

To Chrysla's credit, she seemed to instantly absorb the girl's concern. It took Rysta a moment to recall that Lark came from Terguz.

Chrysla's entire manner had changed from coolly analytical to honestly sympathetic. She spoke directly to Lark. "We're still not sure about the exact details, but apparently the Administrator was attempting to build a working coalition with the unions after the Wing Commander effectively removed Gyper Rill from the Internal Security Directorate. The Administrator called a meeting in which he assumed the podium and began talking about a new order on Terguz. It didn't go very well. Apparently he created the impression that the unions could only make decisions with his approval. In the end it turned into a shouting match. The people in the streets took offense." Chrysla's voice dropped. "I'm so sorry, Lark."

Lark's eyes had gone bright. Her throat worked as Skyla placed a reassuring arm around her shoulders, saying, "Kid, I'm sorry. I guess it's my fault."

"No." Lark struggled for the words. "You gave him . . . the chance, Skyla. Told him. Told him how . . ."

"Yeah, yeah, but I wasn't thinking."

To Rysta's eyes, Lyma had metamorphosed, almost shading into a maternal mode that seemed entirely out of character.

Lark sniffed, battling an emotional outburst. "He was an arrogant bastard, Skyla, but he was . . ."

"I know. He was still your father."

"And my mother and brother?" Lark bravely met Chrysla's gaze, but her lips trembled.

"Mobs don't always think about innocence or guilt, Lark. If you'd been there, you would have died with them. The important thing now is to make sure it doesn't happen again. Don't you think?"

Lyma glanced up. "Maybe we ought to delay this for a—"

"No!" Lark stiffened, jaws clamped. "It's my problem. I'll deal with it on my own time, Wing Commander." She looked at Chrysla, adding, "Lady Attenasio, I believe you were talking about eliminating possibilities of where Minister Takka might be."

Chrysla studied the girl thoughtfully and nodded respectfully. "Terguz no longer offers Ily a safe haven. In fact, if you begin looking at the changing reality of Free Space, her possibilities are shrinking by the hour. The Mag Comm is in the process of networking the administration of both of the Empires. Any notice of the CV will be instantly flagged."

"What about Ily's other Internal Security Directors?" Rysta asked. "She still has a lot of powerful people in positions of authority. How many could still cover for her the way Rill did on Terguz?"

Chrysla indicated the holo. "Where would you suggest, Commander? Etaria? It's an open port, but Shiksta's people would notice her entering orbit and act no matter what the Director of Internal Security ordered. Vermilion? Dion Axel's people are keeping an eye on it. Ily definitely wouldn't space for Phillipia, not with the Companions in orbit there."

"You can't forget Sassan space," Rysta countered. "What about Nesios, Antillies, Formosa, or even Imperial Sassa itself?"

Chrysla clasped her hands, studying the holo map. "I think she'll stay in territory she knows. The Sassans are still going to be suspicious of Regans, and Iban Jakre has what's left of the Sassan fleet spread over most of his worlds. What do each of you think? You know her. Would she leap into the unknown? Or is she the kind who always plans four steps ahead?''

''She's a planner, all right,'' Rysta offered. ''I don't think she uses the toilet without thinking it through four or five times—and even then only if she can gain some sort of advantage from defecating at precisely that instant. If not, she'll wait for a more auspicious moment.''

Skyla studied the holo thoughtfully. ''I have to agree with Rysta. Ily never takes a breath without considering every aspect and how she can maximize her goals.''

''What about Arta Fera? Is she the same?''

Rysta caught the undercurrent in Chrysla's voice.

Skyla's only reaction came in the form of a faint squint. ''She's different. Ily is a master strategist, while Arta is extraordinarily adept as a field tactician. I suppose that's what makes them such a good team. Ily spins the plans and Arta makes them work. In the selection of a final destination, Arta will go wherever Ily decides.''

Rysta stepped over to the holo, where the stars gleamed peacefully despite the single red thread of light marking Ily's course toward Riparious. ''Something bothers me.''

''What?'' Lyma asked, her attention on the map.

Rysta stroked her jaw for a moment, massaging her dry skin as she sought to understand the muffled message prodding her intuition. ''It's just that . . . I mean . . . Well, she can't win. No, let me rephrase that. Think of it this way: Staffa knocked the blocks out from under her foundation when he hit Rega. Ily is a relic of the old days—of Tybalt's Rega. Now everything has changed, and the Empire can't come back. Not in the form of Imperial Rega, anyway.''

Rysta raised a finger. ''So let's rethink this entire problem. Ily's not stupid. She Rotted well knows that she can't recover her power. She knows that she's going to be hunted inexorably, and that she will be caught eventually.''

''Unless she wants to simply vanish into anonymity and become a factory worker somewhere—or hire out as unskilled labor on a farm in some backwater like Targa,'' Chrysla suggested.

''Not our Ily,'' Lyma growled as she rubbed the palms

of her hands together. The muscles in her shoulders bunched and rolled in time to the action.

''Exactly,'' Rysta told them. ''Not our Ily. I don't think it's in her nature to declare anonymity anymore than it's in mine to become an Etarian Priestess.''

''So what would she be after?'' Chrysla wondered. ''What would motivate her now that any chance of becoming Empress is denied her?''

''Determine that,'' Rysta muttered sourly, ''and you'll know where to go looking for Ily.''

* * *

Nyklos lay flat on his back on the compact bunk. The room they'd placed him in didn't offer much relief—only four white walls, a dispenser, the comm terminal to his right, and the medical stim unit that encased what was left of his leg.

Alone, immobile, Nyklos had only his thoughts for company. Those and the memories. At the moment, he was awash with the knowledge that life meant injustice.

When he looked back, trying to remember his parents, the only memory he could conjure was of war, death, and flesh-numbing terror. Through that came the scream as his mother flopped on the floor before him, bright red blood jetting from her blasted shoulder. Despite his screams, she'd never looked his way, dying with a glazed disbelief in her eyes.

His father's death had happened outside. A terror-crazed Nyklos had fled past the headless body on his desperate break for the streets—and eventual capture.

Life changed after Bruen bought him from the slave ring. Only then, in those halcyon days of challenge and direction, had he found a centering point in Seddi doctrine, in the lofty goals of freeing humanity from an age of terror.

He had dedicated himself to justice—and to the destruction of Staffa kar Therma.

He'd recognized Skyla Lyma by sheer, blind luck that day when she'd stepped from the shuttle terminal in Etarus. Tall, and she'd been dressed in a gauzy white gown. He'd stopped to admire such an ethereal beauty. The startling blue eyes and faint scar had triggered his recognition. Only when he followed and she changed costume did he know for sure that he'd located the Wing Commander of the Companions.

She was so beautiful. Daring, dashing, he'd accosted her in her poor-woman's garb as she walked the street. And when he looked into those incredible eyes, he'd been smitten harder.

Nyklos ran his tongue over the lower right third molar. He'd failed that time, too. The tooth which should have killed him hadn't.

Of course it failed . . . just like the rest of my life. A woman's beauty had never affected him the way Skyla's did. In the days spent as her prisoner, he'd fallen for her with all of his heart and soul. Nyklos sighed miserably. She'd never taken him seriously, believing until the end that his advances were only those of a devious man interested in manipulating his captor.

The worst blow, however, was the order not to assassinate the Lord Commander. Nyklos had waited, knowing in the depths of his soul that Staffa's true nature would show itself again and, at that moment, he would strike. Meanwhile, he'd risen to second in command under Kaylla Dawn. For Kaylla, he'd developed a deep and abiding respect, aware that her tragedies outweighed his own. Her cool, organized administration of the Order in its days of upheaval and relocation to Targa had reassured Nyklos that Seddi values hadn't been yet another of the Star Butcher's victims.

How could he stand to face her again? To see the pain his betrayal had caused? His courage had held until he saw the truth, and his damnation, in her stricken eyes.

The abyss loomed before him, the final dissolution of the soul would come on Itreata in the Star Butcher's lair. Trying to place it all in perspective, Nyklos found so very few victories—and those were nothing more than the setup for total failure.

He, who had dedicated his life to the salvation of humanity, had ended up a prisoner on the Star Butcher's ship. Shame his only legacy.

The memories of his dead parents, and of the countless other victims, all less lucky than Nyklos, plagued him. All those dead, suffering billions cried out for justice—and God remained aloof.

Nyklos closed his eyes, depression continuing to spread.

If God cared so little, and the quanta could act with such antipathy, what point was there? Existence in such a universe made a mockery of anything noble, pure, or virtuous.

Had they forgotten the tooth? Or had Kaylla given him this last refuge from his failure?

Nyklos cocked his jaw and glanced at the lines of text he'd composed on the comm screen. He felt the ceramic crack when he bit down. Surprisingly the drop of liquid ran fruity and light over the back of his tongue, not bitter—not like life. This justice, limited though it might be, would be sweet.

As his vision blurred, the words wavered on the screen and faded. . . .

YOU CAME IN FIRE, FLAME, AND PAIN.
DEATH IS YOUR MEANS.
TURN AFTER TURN, THE JUST SUFFERED DEFEAT.
IN NIGHTMARES FILLED WITH YOUR HORRORS WE WILL YET MEET.
MY EYELESS ROTTING CORPSE STALKS YOU THERE,
YOU HEARTLESS MURDERER OF CHILDREN'S DREAMS.

* * *

"Nice to see the top of your head again," Arta greeted as Ily ducked through the hatch from the CV's bridge into the cramped galley area. Arta glanced meaningfully around her. "They definitely don't build these things for comfort."

A recessed booth and table seated a maximum of five. Across from it, the dispenser system filled the wall, each food listed next to a button, then the food tray, and drink faucets, with the disposal chute beneath that. The entire place had been finished in brushed aluminum and silver sialon.

"Thank the Blessed Gods, they don't. If they did, you'd be back there on the Ashtan side, floating through space in the form of plasma and ash."

Arta stretched her muscular body the way a hunting cat did after a nap. "I keep remembering Skyla's yacht. I want one like that one of these days. Fast—and comfortable. You off duty for a while?''

''We're in null singularity now. The ship can watch itself.'' Ily punched up a standard meal of meat, ripa, choklat bread, and stassa. As she set the tray on the duraplast table opposite Arta, she pulled out two data cubes from her pouch.

Fera's shapely eyebrows went up.

Ily ate with one hand and used the long fingernail on the index finger of the other to toy with the data cube, rocking it back and forth on the scuffed gray surface of the table. ''Remember when I had that data broadcast from the Ministry?''

''Just before you blew up the place. Yes, I remember.''

''This is one of the files I wanted. When I finally got my senses back after that knock on the head, I realized what we needed.''

''And we needed that?''

Ily smiled as she chewed. ''You bet. Staffa didn't take any half measures in the security system at Itreata. The finest minds in Free Space have worked on tightening that system. I've been there. With my expertise, I could *feel* the security in the very air. Lyma's interrogation confirmed what I suspected. A person can't get in unless they drop into the Itreatic system on the prescribed approach, dock where directed, and pass through the security checkpoints. Thereafter, they can't leave their designated area without passing other security checkpoints.

''Everything is monitored. Air, water, people, even comm messages. All must pass through the bottlenecks. Part of the system is premised on defense. If an armed party, say a delegation from Rega, were in the diplomatic quarters, they couldn't storm the rest of the complex without beating their way through the defenses of a restricted area.''

''And that's why you had your chem-code and retinal pattern changed? So you can walk right in? Why would Diane de la Luna be allowed past their security?''

''Because of who she's with.'' Ily washed a mouthful down with a swig of stassa. ''I'm not the key figure here, you are.''

''So you're finally going to tell me the details?''

Ily shrugged. ''The next stop is Itreata. If you get captured and drugged between here and there, I'm dead anyway. Yes, Arta, it's time for you to know the whole plan. And for that, you're going to have to study Skyla's answers to a certain group of questions."

Arta crossed her arms and leaned back. "As Diane de la Luna's slave, I'm going to say the right things and get you into Itreata?"

Ily leaned forward and steepled her hands as she smiled. "Not at all. I'm going in wearing *your* collar, Arta, figuratively anyway. I'll be posing as your servant. You see, to pass security you've got to have a clearance. And you've already got one. You've had one for over twenty-three years. They can check, cross-check, and double-check, running recombinant DNA, dermatoglyphics, HLA, retinal patterns, blood tests, or anything else. The results will be the same. You're cleared."

"So what's the hitch with Skyla's testimony?"

"You must memorize everything she says concerning your new identity. And there will still be a thousand risks, enough to sate even your appetite for excitement."

Arta cocked her head, expression thoughtful. "All right. I know I'm supposed to find this Andray Sornsen and give him the orgasm of his life. Who am I doing this as?"

Ily tapped her fingernail on the data cube. "Oh, you already know. You've been training for this role all of your life."

Arta's eyes widened, then she clapped her hands together and laughed. "Of course! Brilliant, Ily! And Skyla talks about her?"

Ily shoved her empty tray to one side. "After years of interrogation, you develop an instinct for trivial things that might be important. I milked her for everything she knew. It's in the data cube."

"And what about that second cube?" Arta pointed.

Ily used her index finger to flick the Lyma data across the table. With lightning reflexes, Arta caught it.

The second cube, Ily held between thumb and forefinger. "Another advantage gained from my interrogation of Skyla. Do you know how the Companions destroyed Myklene? Skyla took a team in, disguised as Vegans no less, and sabotaged the Myklenian comm system with a sophisticated virus. About ten years ago, we broke an extortion ring on

Vermilion. A bright young woman within their organization designed comm viruses with which they could disable any system, no matter how well safeguarded. A company was informed that their manufacturing facility was contaminated by the virus. For a lump sum of money, the counter program would be provided to kill the virus.

"Of course, I kept a copy in the records. You never know when you might need something like this." Ily sighed in mock weariness. "I think I'll need it the moment we can gain access to Andray Sornsen's comm."

Arta pushed glossy auburn hair back with a slim hand. "Do you really think he's going to be such a dope?"

Ily propped her elbows on the table and laced her fingers together to support her chin. "Absolutely. It's in the data cube, but you see, the reason there is a psychological department on Itreata is because Chrysla wanted one—and Andray Sornsen was Chrysla's professor. He confided to Skyla long ago that he'd been hopelessly in love with Chrysla for years. And now, you're coming back to him, *Chrysla Marie Attenasio!*"

* * *

"I should just have relieved him," Skyla insisted as she stared into her stassa. She sat opposite Lark in the small dining alcove aboard *Rega One.* Umbilicals had been attached to provide them with power and comm. Most of the galley had been refinished, the gaps in the mortise filled. More utilitarian knobs had been threaded on the screws controlling the dispenser. Besides repairing the wreckage Skyla had wrought, they'd scoured the radiation contaminated reactor room, cleaned up the smoke damage, and begun stripping ruined equipment which would have to be replaced.

For the yacht, at least, the chase was over until they reached Itreata.

"It's not your fault," Lark responded woodenly, attention centered on the tabletop with its newly inlaid sialon filigree. "You told him, Skyla. You gave him fair warning. It was more of a chance than Gyper Rill would have given him."

"Yeah, but if I'd just relieved him of command he'd still be there for you, Lark."

"He wasn't ever there for me." Lark wedged her face between her hands, fingers digging into her curly brown hair. "Let's face it. He wasn't a model father. He loved power and position. Not his family. Not me."

"Lark, don't."

"Don't? Don't what? If I'd been thinking, I could have told you he'd fail. But I wasn't. I was totally involved with getting away. Carried away with how I finally had an opportunity to show him and Mother that I could do it on my own." She squeezed her eyes shut. "Do you suppose that's why I feel so miserable? That I didn't get the chance to show up dressed in armor? That I couldn't swagger in like a lordly Companion and stare disdainfully at them?"

Skyla rolled her drinking bulb from side to side. "I don't know, Lark. It doesn't sound like you had a very good family. You haven't even mentioned your mother."

"Mention how? She was a fixture, petite, pretty, the perfect hostess with the perfect smile in a perfect evening gown. Perfect, perfect, perfect." She sniffed hard. "And she never heard a word I said. From the time I was old enough to talk, all I got was that doll smile of hers and a 'That's nice, dear.'

"And double Rot take my brother. His greatest goal in life was to step right into my father's shoes—and do the old man one better by conning a way into the palace. The news that Tybalt had been assassinated left him crushed."

Skyla made a face and watched the tendons slide in the back of her hand as she tapped her fingers on the tabletop. "At least you had someone to grow up with besides whores and drunken johns with drool on their lips and their fingers on your ass." *But I still should have done something different.*

A long silence passed between them, finally broken by Lark when she looked up and said, "It's not your fault, Skyla. Don't torture yourself over it. You gave me a chance . . . and you gave him a chance. He made a mess of it. I can imagine that meeting. He got up and started telling them exactly how *his* new order would be. He'd be glad to allow them to do anything they wished to do so long as it was through his consent.

"The first time someone stood up and disagreed, he slammed his fist on the podium and turned arrogant."

"Then how did he manage this long? Even in Tybalt's government, people needed to use tact."

"Not on Terguz. All my father needed was a head for numbers. Remember the revolt about ten years back? Father took his orders straight from the palace on Rega. He only needed to oversee revenue collection. Enforcement was left to Rill and his goons. Father, for all of his lauded status, was an Imperial bookkeeper, nothing more."

"So where do you go from here? What do you want to do, Lark?"

She tilted her head. "What do you mean?"

"Do you want to go back? To Terguz? Or to someplace else?"

Comprehension dawned. "Nothing's changed, Skyla. If anything, it's more important than ever that I stick it out. Ily and Arta are still out there. I want to be a Companion. More than anything."

"Why?"

Lark glanced away. "I don't know, I . . ." Then the girl's jaw muscles bunched and she turned back to Skyla. "Because of my father. Yeah, that's why. I mean, he's dead. All right, I can accept that, but what difference did it make in the end? No one will ever notice. Was the Empire better as a result of his life? Rot, no! No one but me will ever notice that he's missing." She shook her head. "If you'd asked him, Skyla, if you'd have said, 'Fred Gaust, are you happy with your life?' he'd have answered, 'No. They never appreciated me for all that I did for them.' "

"Most government people tend to say that."

"And most are probably as gut-worthless as my father was. Well, I'm not going to be that way, Skyla. Since I've met you, I've either been scared for my life or weaving on my feet from exhaustion. I've watched real power being wielded by people like you, and Lady Attenasio, and Commander Braktov. I've seen respect reflected in your eyes and theirs." Lark pointed a freckled finger. "And you know what? It was respect for me. Not for my position, but for me as a human being. That's the difference between me and my father, and I'm sticking with it . . . if you'll let me."

Skyla pushed back with one arm as she sipped her stassa. She gave Lark an amused inspection. "And what if I say no?"

Lark caught the tone in her voice and grinned. "Then I'll march out the hatch and see if Commander Braktov will take me. If she turns me down, there's always Lady Attenasio."

Skyla scowled in mock disgust. "Kid, with an attitude like you've got, I guess you're bound and determined to get yourself shot at, so it might just as well be with me as with Rysta."

"Do you mean that? You're not just feeling guilty because of what happened to my family?"

"No, kid. I mean it."

Lark acknowledged with a simple nod, her expression turning evaluative. "While we're on the subject of Commander Braktov and Lady Attenasio, you could have pulled rank in there but you didn't. You could have told them to take you anywhere in pursuit of Ily and Arta."

Skyla squinted at her drinking bulb. "Yes, I could have. Given the circumstances, it wasn't worth it. First, I'd rather have a ship of my own, small, fast, and mobile. Second, it would have meant a head-to-head fight with Chrysla, and I'm not sure it would have paid off in the long run. Not if MacRuder died as a result. Third—and pay attention to this—Chrysla had all of her data together when we walked into her quarters. She laid out the facts coolly and dispassionately. We can't make a judgment on where to chase off to find Ily. I got lucky on the jump to Terguz, and I could make a gut call on Ashtan, but this time I'm dry of ideas."

"Always have my data together. Got it."

"More than that. Listen to what other people say. You don't have to like them, or even respect them, but every now and then you get an advantage—even from people you despise. You're not in command to assuage your ego. You're there to either win or minimize losses so you can win next time."

"And if Ily said something you could use?"

Skyla gave Lark a crooked grin. "Okay, sure, I'd make use of it. It just means I might have to cut her throat behind the scenes rather than on stage front."

"She likes you, you know."

"Ily? Are you—"

"Chrysla. You can tell just by the way she looks at you. There's a sympathy, and a vulnerability, and a respect all wrapped up. I think it drives her a little berserk, especially when you're so hostile."

"I'm not hostile. I'm . . ." Skyla made a gesture. "I'm just not sure I trust her, that's all. It's . . . It's . . ."

"You don't have to explain. I was just making an observation, nothing more. Part of my job."

"Your job?"

Lark shrugged. "I work for you, don't I? Maybe that information might come in handy one of these days."

Skyla studied Lark from half-lidded eyes. "You know, kid, you keep your wits about you, and you could go far in this business."

"Yeah, I know." Lark's green stare had internalized again. "Provided Ily and Arta don't kill me first, right?"

CHAPTER XXXVI

I swore in the beginning that I would keep this journal up to date; but then, I suppose that all people who decide to keep a journal swear the same thing. I feel a little goofy tonight. Too much klav and stassa and not enough sleep. We're all reeling on our feet, working like rodents on a grain transport. You can see it in the eyes. Everyone on the crew is faded looking except for their eyes, bloodshot, baggy, and burning.

Observation: The more I see of civilization, the more it seems to be based on sleep deprivation. The more you advance, the greater the workload, the less sleep any given individual gets at night. There must be a formula.

See, I've even forgotten to write down what I wanted to make note of. We've finished the dish–the big hemispherical electromagnet–and have moved it into place at *Countermeasures'* bow. The null singularity dome and generator have been removed and we're at the point right now of positioning the braces for attachment to the structural members in the hull.

I've been around for awhile and, working for the Companions, I've seen a lot of design variations. *Countermeasures* has me and the whole team completely baffled. With the new reactors installed on the vessel's stern she can put out fifty gigatons of thrust and still provide enough electrical power to fill the needs of four planets like Rega. Okay, so what we've got is a huge electromagnet with incredible thrust–so what's Staffa planning on moving with this thing? What has enough charge, or can be charged, that weighs that much? A moon? A planet?

That's what comes to mind at first, but let's be serious, it's got to fit within the arc of the electrodome. Otherwise *Countermeasures* isn't structurally viable.

And, finally, how does moving an object gain us any ground on the real problem, manipulating the gravitational field: a force? All I can say, Lord Commander, is that we're on schedule, proceeding posthaste for completion, but you've got us puzzled something fierce!

—Excerpt taken from Dee Wall's personal journal

* * *

Staffa paused in the hallway before Sinklar's room. The news about Nyklos' suicide had come as a surprise. Curiously unnerved by the act, Staffa had decided to inform Sinklar in person. Now, he hesitated and wondered at himself.

Rot you, Nyklos! How did you know? What made you guess that my nightmares would include you? Even now, in this spotless white corridor, Staffa could sense the electric animosity they'd felt for each other. Two bristling male dogs, Kaylla had once called them.

Will you rest now, Nyklos? Or will I meet you one day when we join God Mind together? Will our energy mingle and create understanding in the end—or violent conflict?

Muttering under his breath about being foolish, he touched the lock plate, calling, "Sinklar? This is Staffa. Are you in?"

"Come in," the door comm answered, and the hatch slid back.

Staffa stepped cautiously inside, his charcoal cloak swirling around him. Sinklar sat at his desk, feet kicked up, a cup of stassa in his hands as he studied the wall monitor opposite him. There, in bold display, was a page from the ancient history book. The rest of the room looked neat, everything stowed according to regulation. The holo tanks inset in the wall displayed scenes of Targa, and the air carried the faint scent of the pines.

"Reading?" Reluctant to dive into the purpose of his visit, Staffa indicated the page of history. "How's the translation?"

"Excellent." Sinklar pulled his feet from the desktop, straightening and placing his stassa on the surface as he studied Staffa with his oddly colored eyes. "How did you manage to do this?"

"Ran a scanner over the page and input the data into the machine. I suspected that the Mag Comm knew that ancient dialect. Are you checking every now and then with the dictionary?"

Sinklar nodded. "From my totally nonrepresentative sample, the Mag Comm gave me the best translation it could. Some of the names however . . . well, what do you do with something like Themistocles? Or how about Gilgamesh?"

"Gilgamesh?"

"A king from an early civilization called Sumer—a group of cities that seem to have been pivotal to the formation of later civilizations. They turned old Gilgamesh into quite a character—worthy of an Etarian holo series." Sinklar's grin went crooked. "You and Gilgamesh. Think of that. You break the Forbidden Borders and they'll be talking about you forever."

Staffa ran his fingers down one of the wall supports, restless gaze following the lines up to the ceiling. The idea seemed singularly unappealing, especially considering Nyklos' poetry. "I would just as soon be forgotten. I'm no hero, Sinklar."

"Heroes don't have much say in their fame or fortune, Staffa. They are named by others. Judged after the fact."

"I really would rather be forgotten. Nothing I could do, no matter how grandiose, would balance the deeds of the Star Butcher. After I'm gone, see to it, will you?"

"See to removing you from the record?" A frown had eaten into Sinklar's forehead. "Are you serious?"

"I wouldn't have said it if I wasn't. Listen, from the time I was forced out of Myklene by the ruling Council, I did what I was trained to. I *was* the Star Butcher. You know the list of atrocities I committed. A monster shouldn't receive anything for his deeds—let alone notoriety."

Sinklar jerked a thumb at the history book. "Some of these guys may not have equaled your record, but they were pretty grisly. I've scanned the section on a fellow by the name of Ghengis Khan. He left pyramids of human heads in cities he completely depopulated. In the process, he crossed half of the Earth—on horseback, if you can believe—and only used swords and arrows for weapons.

"Then when you get to something they call the Twentieth Century, you've got guys named Hitler, Stalin, and Pol Pot. Some of them ran death camps—factories—that did nothing but kill human beings by the millions." Sinklar's expression turned sour. "Think of it. A death *factory!*"

"Overpopulation?"

Sinklar lifted an eyebrow. "You'd never make it as a Twentieth Century despot. You're much too pragmatic. No, they killed them because they didn't like their ethnic affiliation." At Staffa's blank look, Sinklar added, "It means you'd kill people from Riparious just because they were Riparians—even if they were living on Ashtan."

"Why? What difference would it make where they came from?"

"I told you, you'd never make it as a Twentieth Century despot. Even at the height of the Star Butcher phase, you were interested only in conquest—and as efficiently as possible. Not in the infliction of misery for its own sake. You never ran a death camp."

"Don't apologize for me. You can't. And what you say is all the more reason for me to be forgotten. It's too easy to be a monster. Why remind people."

Sinklar lowered his voice. "You're not a monster."

"I came down here to tell you that they just checked on Nyklos. He's dead."

Sinklar came to immediate attention, the question intense in his eyes.

"The Seddi—especially the top people—are equipped to take their own lives. Nyklos tried this once before. That time Skyla had dripped a little Mytol between his lips. His trick tooth didn't work. In this instance, it did." Staffa bowed his head. "My fault. I should have remembered."

"Kaylla should have remembered," Sinklar tilted his head pensively. "I guess he didn't have the courage to face her. Don't torture yourself over it. Nyklos took responsibility for himself. When you think about it, a person's life is the only thing which is irrevocably their own. After his integrity went, maybe Nyklos had nothing left."

A long silence passed before Sinklar asked, "Any word on Skyla?"

Relieved by the change of subject, Staffa said, "Rysta picked her up. They're spacing for Itreata and should arrive just before we do. She's fine . . . and has a young woman with her. Lark's her name. Daughter of the Administrator on Terguz." Staffa pushed on the wall, as if testing its solidity. "Mac's still in cryostasis. From what Rysta's people can tell, his condition is isostatic. Not healing, not deteriorating."

Sinklar picked up a data cube and started tossing it into the air. Casually, he asked, "How are you going to deal with Chrysla?"

Staffa walked over and sat on the bunk before leaning back against the wall to stare at the Targan scene in the holo. "What would you suggest? Public execution? How about electric shock? Flaying has always been a favorite of mine. They scream louder as they see what their muscles really look like, and the blood drips drop by drop."

"Nyklos really got to you. I thought you didn't like him."

"I didn't. He left me a note that opened old wounds. It will pass and I'll resume my usual cheery optimism. After all, what's another dead man? But we were talking about Mac and Chrysla. Let's deal with them, shall we?"

Sinklar examined the data cube briefly, then gave Staffa his full attention. "Go ahead."

"I've already sent the orders to the medical staff on Itreata. They're going to treat Mac as if he's the most important person in Free Space. Total genetic coding, electro-stim, cranial-neuro rehab, blood filtering, and gereostabilization. He'll come out looking better than he did when he shipped for Targa the first time."

"That wouldn't take much. He was horribly hung over, as I recall. And Chrysla?"

"Why are you so concerned?"

"Ben MacRuder is one of the most important people in all the universe to me. He and Chrysla are lovers. They're happy with each other and want a chance. I intend to see that they get it. Do I have to recall my Divisions to ensure their safety?"

Staffa laced his fingers together over his stomach and lifted his thumbs in a gesture of acceptance. "She's free, Sinklar. I've told you how I feel about her. I'm not going to make it difficult for her, or MacRuder. They have my blessing."

"Just like that? No ill will? No smarting male pride?"

"None. A bit of wistful melancholy, perhaps. Fate, the dance of the quanta—call it what you will—took her from me. That chance, at that point in time, was stolen from us. No matter what we'd like, Sinklar, we must live in our present, not the past."

"So I don't have to go to war."

"Did you really think I'd start foaming at the mouth and scream and blast Mac into little pieces?"

Sinklar tossed his cube up and grabbed it out of the air. "Honestly, I'd come to hope you wouldn't. The more I got to know you, the more I suspected you'd understand."

"Very well, since we're dealing with such things, I'm not the only one with a problem here. In orbit over Rega you managed to do everything in your power to avoid Chrysla. You don't have to beam eternal filial love with your every glance, but you do have to come to terms with your mother."

Sinklar's fist closed as he caught the data cube. "You don't see Arta Fera looking back every time your eyes meet. You don't association those amber eyes with the rotting corpse of the woman you love. I do."

Staffa pulled himself to his feet, stepping to the hatch and then hesitating. "Look in the mirror sometime, Sinklar. Take one hand and cover your gray eye. See who's looking back at you. That amber eye is the same as Arta Fera's—the same as Chrysla's. Where do you want to set the limits of your responsibility to your mother? At who she is . . . or the color of her eyes?"

Sinklar's fist had tightened until the knuckles whitened.

* * *

Ily sat just out of visual range of the comm monitor as Arta Fera prepared to bring the CV Insystem through the Itreatic Asteroids. Through the right port, the glaring violet-white display of the Twin Titans continued their gaudy dance of radiation and violence.

The CV had been hailed hours ago from the deep-space detection buoys which monitored the approaches to Itreata. Arta had responded appropriately, sending the signal ahead.

Now they would see if the first part of their gambit would

pay off. Before the Chrysla sham could work, they needed to set foot on Itreata.

This was a stupid idea, Ily told herself. *You were sick, hurt, half-crazy to think of this. It will never work!*

It's got to!

"Greetings, CV 720, this is Itreata Insystem. We have found your registry in the Vegan catalog and cross-checked. May your clan prosper. Our compliments to the de la Luna family. Honor be with you. We're sending visual, please lock on our signal and respond."

Well, at least that much had worked. Itreata hadn't recognized the CV as Holt's Regan ship.

Arta's fingers dialed the signal in and locked, the comm flickering and forming a woman's face. Delay on the lightbound signal would take about thirty seconds at this distance.

"This is Lady Chrysla Marie Attenasio. We have your signal locked. Do you need data on Delta V or vector for course correction?"

I'm going to get us killed through this idiotic stunt. Ily closed her eyes, taking a deep breath. The seconds dragged past.

"Negative, Lady Attenasio. We have your position precisely plotted and will request Insystem control of your navcomm when you close to within 0.2 LY. We had you scheduled for arrival aboard the Regan cruiser *Gyton,* after rendezvousing with the Wing Commander and *Rega One.* Do you need medical for First MacRuder? Please inform."

Chrysla paused the transmission. "They *expected* me? *She*'s aboard *Gyton?*"

Ily panicked for an instant, then waved it away. "No! No. Tell them . . . tell them plans changed. The CV was faster. *Gyton* will be following."

Ily triggered the comm. "Itreata Comm, that's a negative on medical for MacRuder. Given the time to match with *Rega One* we thought it prudent for me to take the first available transportation in. What is the current location of the Lord Commander?"

As they waited for the response, Ily pinched the bridge of her nose. "They act like she's alive! Rotted Gods, I . . . wait. Skyla said they never found the body. Maybe she got off *Pylos?* Maybe she escaped Myklene and made it out alive?''

''Remember the attempt to arrest MacRuder and Rysta on Rega? Supposedly *I* took them from your people at the Defense Ministry. Now Itreata seems to think Chrysla is with *Gyton.* Do you suppose that was her?''

''How do I know? Go with it! Assume she's alive! Play their game! By the Rotted Gods, just don't get cute and kill us both!''

The woman on the comm link responded, ''The Lord Commander is in transit from Targa. Do you wish to patch a message through to him?''

''Negative. I'll talk with him upon his arrival. Have you received instructions with regard to my quarters?''

Ily nodded to herself as Arta sent the message. In a low voice she added, ''If you can, have them prepare an escort for our arrival. It might speed our access and avoid mistakes on our part.''

In the interim, Arta glanced Ily's way. ''Under interrogation, Skyla said the personal quarters for Companions were in the core area—the least monitored section. If Skyla is Staffa's lover, and Chrysla has been under the Praetor's control, she wouldn't run right back to his bed, would she?''

''I'd gamble that she'd play it safe—but, Rot it, we just don't know enough about their relationship! So much is . . . it's all different than I thought it would be.'' And Ily's nerves were eating at her.

The woman on the comm stated, ''We have received no instructions regarding your arrival, Lady Attenasio. Is there anything we can do?''

''I would appreciate it if you could prepare quarters close to Staffa's and provide an escort for me and my servant upon our arrival.''

Ily realized she'd clutched the armrests on her chair until her fingers ached. To battle the growing tension, she forced herself to relax knotted muscles and still her adrenaline-stressed heart.

Itreata responded, ''Affirmative, Lady Attenasio. Is there anything else?''

Arta's expression remained perfectly controlled. ''No, thank you. Please inform me when Insystem Traffic Control wishes to assume control of the navcomm. In the meantime, my best regards to Itreata, and it's good to be home again after all these years.''

''Careful!'' Ily whispered through clenched teeth. ''What if she's been there?''

Arta shot her a sidelong glance. ''When? If Chrysla arrived on Rega with MacRuder and Rysta—and is with them now—when would she have been to Itreata? Skyla would have known if the woman had turned up in the Myklenian aftermath. The timing doesn't work otherwise.''

Ily tried to exhale her anxiety as she closed her eyes and leaned back. ''Yes, well, good thinking. But for my peace of mind, don't push it.''

Arta chuckled. ''My first inclination was to ask to be put up in Staffa's quarters—and to please remove Skyla's things before I set foot in the place. Wouldn't that have wound them up?''

''Do it, and I'll shoot you myself!''

Arta's mouth screwed up. ''Ily! I'm surprised at you! What is this? Losing your nerve?''

''No, I'm just . . . Rot take it, I don't like surprises! Chrysla? Alive? What else don't we know?''

''So she's alive? What of it? By the time *Gyton* could match and pick up *Rega One,* and then revector for Itreata, we'll have planted the virus and gone to ground in Itreata. Staffa will make planet in a weltered mess. We'll kill him, wreak a little extra havoc for a diversion, and make our escape.''

''And if the real Chrysla happens to call Itreata comm?''

''So long as it happens *after* we get to Andray Sornsen, it won't make any difference.'' Thoughtfully, Arta tapped her fingers on the controls. ''During the interrogation, Skyla said she didn't trust him. He's festering with resentment about Staffa and the Companions. He'll work with us. Especially after I wrap myself around him.''

* * *

A codified legal system is the foundation upon which human beings must base their relations with each other. Without such a system of law, ethics and behavior intertwine in a gray twilight of morality. . . .

Sinklar stared at the words glowing on the monitor, his brain blocked by the enormity of what he attempted as he sat at his desk aboard *Chrysla.* At his elbow, a ring formed around the inside of a half-empty cup of cold stassa. Flimsies containing scrawled notes created an air of wild disorganization.

How did a single man start from scratch and write an entire body of law for a civilization as disparate as Free Space? Where did he start—even with the benefit of the only human history book in existence?

Sinklar groaned and rubbed the back of his neck.

"Sinklar? You in there?" Adze's voice called through the door comm.

"Come on in! Please!" He grinned as the hatch slipped back and she entered, bringing a sudden radiance to the room.

Adze wore spacer's whites that revealed her shapely body and contrasted with the sleek shine of her long black hair and copper-tinted skin. A portable comm was tucked under one arm.

"Hard at work?" she asked, noting the brief composition on the monitor.

"Sort of," Sinklar agreed, standing and arching his back to get the kinks out. "It would be more accurate to say I'm hard at being lost. I don't know what to do next. You read the history book and legal systems all sound so poetically lofty."

He shook his head. "I guess I've spent too much of my time in the mud. My idea of a perfect legal preamble is as follows: 'These are going to be the rules from now on. Break them and we'll break you.' "

"You're in charge, write them that way. Who's going to criticize?"

Sinklar pointed to the comm monitor where the history book was displayed. "Posterity. And that's an eerie feeling. Something I've never had time to consider before. From now on, people are going to be trying to analyze what I did—just the same way I had to do in class when we wrote papers on Tybalt the Imperial First."

Adze's gaze dropped.

"Did I say anything wrong?"

She winced. "Talk about truly Rotten timing . . . Tell you what, I'll drop in later. How's that?"

Sinklar gave her a scowl and shrugged. "Now's fine. Believe me, words to rock the ages can wait. What can I do for you?"

In a flat voice she said, "I wanted to talk about Targa. About your first drop with the First Targan Assault Division."

"Why would you ever want to do that?"

"The Special Tactics Units throughout the Companions are doing an analysis of errors committed by First Atkin and Second Nytan when they dropped on Targa. Given the changing face of strategic and tactical realities, we might be doing a lot more of that kind of fighting rather than the traditional 'smash down their door and kick their teeth in' assault." She smiled nervously, "But I'll talk to you about it later. Sorry to have—"

"Whoa! Hold it!" Sinklar waved his hands as he stepped forward. "Tell you what. I'll help you if you'll help me."

"Deal!"

"But not here. How about in the forward lounge. You, me, your notebook, and the beverage of your choice."

"Let's go."

As they stepped into the corridor, Sinklar shook his head. "I think I'm going to get the best out of this deal. There's not much to say about the Targan drop. First Atkin deployed his forces by the book. Everything he did is right there in the manual—the Holy Gawddam Book. The prescribed way to take an enemy-held city. A, B, C, D, E, and you win. Bruen didn't play by the rules. He used the common citizens against us. In the instance where I survived, it was a little old lady with a purse full of explosives. She blew up our entire Section."

"An elderly lady did this?"

"That's right. She walked in, old, gray, stooped, and wanting to know about her government checks. When she walked out, she wasn't carrying her purse. Mac, Gretta, and I charged out after her and the whole place exploded. Scratch one Section."

"So how did you make it?"

"The three of us were hunted in the streets. Straight guerrilla warfare. Ambush, move, ambush, move. By the time Mykroft's Second Division landed and pulled us off a burning roof, the lesson had sunk in." Sinklar gestured with his hands. "Here's the point. We'd killed more Targans—just the three of us on our own—than the entire Section had—or could have on a per capita basis. We weren't brilliant or anything, we just hadn't been indoctrinated in a stagnant system.

"Let's face it. The Regan military, and the Sassans, too, for that matter, were ripe for a fall. The Companions had been doing the real dirty work of war. The Empires just sort of showed up and provided support. It was a nice clean system for the aristocracy. They could play soldier in the wake of the Companions' victories." Sinklar pointed to the notebook. "You're still doing it."

"You don't make it sound very spectacular."

"Hey, it wasn't. We were scared every second of the way. Failure meant death. To put it into an equation, desperation and necessity equal innovation. I got the wild ideas—Mac and Gretta made them work. The Regan system was so stagnant and inefficient that we won the war and revolutionized the armed forces."

She nodded to herself and shut off the recorder on the portable comm. "The words sound all right, Sinklar, but I detect a note of desperation and depression underneath it all." She paused. "Want to talk about it?"

"No, I . . ."

"I'm available, and I think I'm the only set of ears you've got these days, at least until they get Mac out of his fix. What's bothering you?"

He looked irritated. "Everything. You probably won't understand this, but I'm not adjusting very well. I'm on the verge of falling right into the life I dreamed about before I left Rega. I'm going to be using my training in history, sociology, and political science in the reshaping of the human condition. Right? Just what I dreamed of doing after I got out of University on Rega. I was crushed . . . *crushed* when I got drafted.

"Now I have the power not only to imagine but to implement. I should be ecstatic!"

"But you're not."

"You saw the words on the comm back there. All of human history is in that book and all of the social theory I learned is in my head, and I still can't write the preamble to a legal code—a document which will define human civilization for the next however long."

She led him into the lounge, across the colorful waves of carpet and into one of the corners, triggering a privacy field around them as she pushed him into one of the plush chairs. Through the tactite, the stars had blueshifted as *Chrysla* built for null singularity.

She leaned forward, eyes animated. "You're bored, Sinklar. That's what it is, you know. For the last four years, you've been battling one catastrophe after another. You've been living on adrenaline and fear alternating with ecstasy and triumph. Now you're facing the prospect of spending the rest of your life sitting in an office."

He studied her, aware of her intensity. *Was that it?*

"Sinklar," she insisted, "You're young, ambitious, and you've been shot at. One of two things happens to people who've been shot at. Either they decide they never want to be shot at again, or they develop a craving for the rush they get when a blaster bolt crackles by their heads. I've got a feeling that you can't turn off that rush. You've been trying to, but it just isn't happening."

He sucked at his lip for a moment, remembering the endless hard days with disaster looming before them. That skinny kid who'd sat next to Gretta Artina on the night drop to Targa had metamorphosed, but into what? Into who?

"You've put yourself in order," Adze continued. "You've made peace with the dead, forgiven yourself for snaring yourself in Ily's trap. You've discovered the legacy Anatolia searched for. Justice has been done with Bruen and Nyklos. Only Ily and Arta are left, and, Sink, the Wing Commander has as much right to them as you, and she's closing in."

"I would like a chance to finish pulling the trigger on Arta. Ily I would hand over to Dion Axel for trial. But you're right, I've accepted that Skyla Lyma will get them before I do."

The lights gave a bluish tone to Adze's thick black hair as she tilted her head. "Where to from here? An office? If I were you, Sinklar, I'd give it a little thought. Maybe the reason you can't write a preamble for your laws is that you don't know where you're going. Either that, or you shouldn't be writing the Rotted things in the first place."

He leaned back, squinting at her. "Are you another psychologist? Or do you hear this in STU training? You seem pretty sure of yourself, and I don't think it's because you've had that much personal experience. You're not that old."

She eased back a little, that sparkling smile warming him. "No, I'm not. But my grandfather is—and I've heard my grandmother tell it over and over, about how he was when he finally got himself shot up to the point that he couldn't take combat anymore. My mother was the same way. Her back was blasted open in the Vermilion campaign and the neural damage was so severe that she couldn't space anymore. She still drives us near to insanity."

"Your whole family fights for the Companions?"

"We have since Malbourne was absorbed into the Sassan Empire. Grandfather wouldn't serve Sassa I, said he looked more like a fat white maggot than a god."

Sink laughed and slapped a hand to his knee. "Maybe you're right. It seems like I keep drifting back to the memories, replaying times with Hauws, Gretta, Mac, and Shiksta. The only holos I run on my wall tanks are of Targa. 'Remember when' are the words most commonly in my mind."

"So let's change them. How about, 'When we finally . . .' or 'One of these days . . .' Which ones do you like best?"

"Planning on starting a war?"

She pulled a muscular leg up, lacing her fingers over the knee. "Scuttlebutt has it that a project is working on the Forbidden Borders. That Dee Wall is building the device the Mag Comm said it needed to break the Forbidden Borders."

Sinklar caught the subtle change in her attitude. "You're dancing around the edge of security."

"I'm very quick on my feet, and I know a lot of different steps. You want to try me out sometime?"

"What makes you think I can dance? I'd flatten your toes and smash your arches. I've never danced a step in my life. In the first place, it wasn't part of the curriculum in the state school on Rega and, in the second, I was such an odd kid no girl ever wanted to dance with me."

"You dance just fine, Sinklar. You've danced clear away from the subject." Her musical laughter augmented her conspiratorial smile. "Remember that day in the archives inside Makarta? I joined your team—not for the time on Targa but for the long haul."

Sinklar touched his fingertips together and frowned. "Ily told me something one time. Mytol serves any master with the truth."

"Good point, and to date you've only got my word that I'm not the gun room loudmouth. Remember, though, the battle can be lost when the commander seals his lips and gets killed by the enemy's first shot." She stared at the blue streaks of starlight hazing into vague blackness. "Speaking hypothetically, *if* the Forbidden Borders could be breached, *someone* would have to take the first ship through."

Sinklar chuckled. "One of the things I've noticed about you is that you don't fool around with subtlety. That said, I want to remind you that the last time I trusted an ambitious woman I ended up in her prison."

"I'm *not* Ily Takka. But it does pay to be prudent." She gave him that frank look that always left him off balance. "Tapa on the table. Here are the facts. You're right. I'm ambitious, and I think you're an intelligent human being I can work with to achieve certain goals."

"And what might those goals be?"

She leaned closer to him. "I think they're the same as yours. Most of the STU haven't realized it yet, but if the Mag Comm works as well as the Lord Commander hopes and if the Forbidden Borders go down, the best most of these people can hope for is a job like a glorified policeman might hold. Some, like Ryman, might settle down, but I'm too young for an office."

"So why me? The Lord Commander's son would be the sort of target any woman might take a fancy to."

She stiffened, a chill in her narrowing eyes.

"Cards on the table, right?" Sinklar countered. "You be straight with me, I'll be straight with you."

"Fair enough." She thawed slightly. "And I guess the question is fair. I just get a bit fuzzy-tailed when someone suggests I'd sell myself. Mom never did, and she taught me—beat it into my bones—that a woman can only make it with her wits. Not on her back. Before I rest my case, remember what I thought of you that first day at Makarta . . . son of Staffa."

"You're right. You couldn't hide that look of disdain."

"Getting back to facts, I think you and I want to go in the same direction." Her eyes seemed to darken and pool. "I actually came to respect and like you, Sinklar. You're easy company, thoughtful, warm, and intimate. I haven't met many authentic people before."

"Authentic? Isn't everyone?"

She shifted in her seat, running long fingers through her luxurious hair. "Not at all. That's one of the things about you that fascinates me. You're completely vulnerable one moment, with a soft gentleness in your eyes—and the next you're harder than a sialon milling tool. I consider myself pretty well educated, but at times you startle me with what you know. Round all that off with the fact that you're just good company, and I'd be a fool to ignore you."

"Just what do you have in mind?"

"Partnership. You and I can help each other. Just like we're doing right now." She focused on the distance. "I suppose if I had a model to strive for it would be like Staffa and Skyla. I've seen the way they look when they talk to each other. Respect, appreciation, and most of all reliance."

"Before or after they became lovers?"

"They've been in love with each other for as long as I've known them. They just didn't know it. It took Staffa going off to Etaria to trigger that realization. I'd have to say it's just always been there."

"Is that what you see for us? Lovers?"

"Let's leave it strictly professional for the time being, all right? Besides if you were foolish enough to fall in love with me this quickly, I'm not sure I'd be inclined to trust your judgment." Then her mischievous grin spread. "Your lust, maybe, but definitely not your judgment."

"You are an extremely acute woman."

"Thanks for making my last point for me. There you go, Sinklar. All of my cards are on the table."

"Do I have to make my choice right now?"

"Take your time. But whatever you decide, pick a direction for yourself. You might even be able to write that preamble."

CHAPTER XXXVII

5780:03:10:22:17
Seddi Warrens
Itreata

re: Mag Comm performance efficiency rating
To: Magister Kaylla Dawn
From: Legate Roma

Statistical analyses have been employed by my department in an effort to determine both the functioning and reliability of the Mag Comm in its administration of Free Space. To date we have run more than four thousand randomly selected spot checks on the machine and have found minimal disruption of systems or services. As of this report, and given an N of over four thousand one hundred and thirty-six, we have documented five cases where service or efficiency has been impaired by the Mag Comm's administration. Considering sampling errors and degrees of freedom, the Mag Comm's efficiency must practically be considered to be one hundred percent. (See appended data.)

Had we attempted to integrate a similar system through the Farhome Project, preliminary figures of seventy percent would have been considered extraordinary.

Another reason for the machine's efficiency may be traced to its ability to learn. When problems begin to appear in the implementation of a project, the machine automatically corrects itself or asks for feedback from experienced humans involved in the operation, production, or service.

It must be noted, however, that such success must eventually lead to the obsolescence of a given portion of our civil service and comm programming work force. Nor will this be the only labor force affected. As the machine pares redundancy and inefficiency from the economy, we can expect nearly fourteen percent of the economy to become unemployed, especially the uneducated and unskilled.

I must stress the *importance* of this problem. Such populations are the breeding grounds of social unrest. Prior to this date, warfare and its sequelae have served to remove surplus population in conjunction with Imperial expansion. We have paid the price for such population control through the destruction and rebuilding of infrastructure and the maintenance of a wartime economy. With the recent and essentially bloodless conquest of Free Space by the Lord Commander, the problem is rendered even more critical since we have not suffered a population reduction.

In conclusion, the Mag Comm is exceeding our expectations and hopes and will provide stability for the near future. However, if this trend continues, we will face dislocations and thought should be given to the anticipation of such problems. Should you have any questions concerning this report or the appended supporting data, please feel free to contact me or my staff.

Signed: Myles Roma,
Once Legate Prima Excellence
of His Holiness
Sassa the Second

* * *

In the eternal nightmare, Skyla had been bound to the uncomfortable chair, naked, shivering in the chill. Ily walked around her, half-hidden by the bright lights as the recorders monitored Skyla's every reaction.

"Let's get back to Staffa's wife—this Chrysla. He thinks he killed her off Myklene?"

"Yes," Skyla answered through Mytol-numbed lips.

"But no body was ever found? No corpse in the wreckage of the *Pylos?*"

"No."

"The Praetor had her as a prisoner for nearly twenty years."

"Yes."

"Arta tells me she was cloned from this woman."

"Yes."

"And she tells me that she was supposed to kill Staffa when the Seddi lured him within her reach."

"I think that is true."

"So Arta is an exact genetic duplicate? Provided to the Seddi by the Praetor of Myklene?"

"Yes."

"Chrysla used to live on Myklene, didn't she?"

"Yes."

"She was Staffa's wife. She would have been cleared for the complex."

"Yes."

"Staffa must feel very guilty about killing her? Does he?"

"Yes."

"Would he react to a manipulation of that guilt? Become foolish?"

"Yes."

"If Chrysla were still alive, would it affect his judgment? Cause him to commit a fatal error?"

"Yes."

"How do you know about her? Staffa told you?"

"No. Andray Sornsen told me."

Ily studied the comm in her hand, checking her notes. "He's the psychologist. Did he used to work with her?"

"Taught her . . . on Ashtan. There would be no psychology department on Itreata but for Chrysla."

"I see." Ily cradled her chin as she paced and thought. "What about Andray Sornsen? What was his relationship with Chrysla? Just a professor?"

"He loved her. He still loves her."

"And Staffa knows?"

"I don't know."

"Does Sornsen like the fact that Staffa was fucking the woman he loved? That Staffa sired a son out of Chrysla?"

"I think Andray hates Staffa deep down inside. I ordered extra security to be placed on him."

"Is that order still in effect?"

"No. I canceled it after Targa . . ."

From somewhere beyond the hull, a loud boom sound as the bay techs worked on one of the nearby LCs. Skyla jerked awake. She gasped, sat up, and rubbed her face, while after-images of the dream slipped away from her.

Rotted Gods, would she never be rid of that nightmare? It had been enough to live it, did she have to dream it over and over again?

Another clang from the LC bay carried through the hull and Skyla sighed before getting to her feet and picking up her white armor. Before she dressed, she studied herself in the mirror. Her belly had flattened again, the fat gone from her hips and thighs. The long scar on her leg didn't seem as garish. She took a breath and smacked her stomach, happy to hear a solid sound. At least Staffa wouldn't be able to take her with one hand the way he'd threatened.

After pulling on her satin-textured armor, she peeked into Lark's room, noting with satisfaction that the girl was finally sleeping. A cup of stassa and a quick meal later, Skyla stepped out into the chilly air in the LC bay and made her way into the ship.

Chrysla . . . Chrysla . . . she was haunted by Chrysla! And why? Just because she was Staffa's first wife?

"Deal with it, Skyla. Solve it, and maybe you can sleep."

Having made that decision she turned and stalked down the narrow corridor which led to Chrysla's quarters. The sickly green interior of the Regan warship depressed her. Why did they paint them this way? It was a wonder the crew didn't commit suicide living in a snake's gut like this.

At Chrysla's hatch, Skyla palmed the lock plate, calling, "Lady Attenasio, this is Wing Commander Lyma."

Silence.

Skyla turned as a crewwoman passed, and asked her, "Have you seen Lady Attenasio?"

"Down on the hospital deck, I believe."

Skyla thanked the woman and strode onward, trying to compose what she would say, and finding it difficult. No matter what kind of message her subconscious was trying to give her, Chrysla wasn't the problem, not really. Arta and Ily remained the real problem. Her silly brain just kept dredging up that interrogation sequence with Chrysla over and over.

She squeezed her eyes shut as if the action would reset the switches in her brain. Somewhere along the line, the reality had to sink in. What had happened had happened.

No amount of self-flagellation could change that. Arta had broken her spirit and Ily had sucked dry what was left.

Such things happened to warriors. It was one of the risks that people accepted when they fought for a cause.

She slapped the plate on the hospital hatch and bulled forward, only to come to a halt.

Gyton's hospital ward had been finished with the usual Regan military austerity. Lines of medical units—enough to handle about a third of the ship's crew—waited like ranks of gaping mouths. All except the first row of machines. These were the full-body units, the ones reserved for the most critical of cases.

The last unit on the right gleamed whitely, the lid closed. Beside it, slumped wearily, sat Chrysla Attenasio, her head bowed and one arm draped limply over the smooth convex surface.

Skyla approached silently until she could hear Chrysla's hushed whisper.

Out of respect, she backed away and hesitated, fists knotting. *Leave her alone. This isn't the time.*

Skyla ground her teeth as she turned and raised a hand to touch the lock plate.

"Can I help you, Skyla?"

"I didn't mean to disturb you. It can wait."

Chrysla had stood, fingers brushing the lid of the med unit as she glanced toward Skyla. "It's all right. I've been here long enough as it is."

When she approached, Skyla noted the red-rimmed eyes, the exhausted set of her full mouth.

"Do you spend every spare moment down here?"

Chrysla shrugged. "I'm a psychologist. A scientist. I know he can't hear me, that no mysterious brain-powered mental telekinesis takes place. Still, perhaps it's that deeply seated superstition that what we believe, what we pray and hope, can affect the way things will eventually work out."

"He'll be fine." Skyla thrust thumbs into her equipment belt. "They got him stabilized and cooled off with time to spare. His skull took a wallop, but nothing penetrated the brain. They drained the hematoma. Staffa induced the finest medical people in Free Space to come to Itreata. He won't be himself in the first week, but after six months you'll never know he was hurt."

"Thank you, Skyla. But I know a little about physiology. When his neck broke, the fragments of vertebrae did a great deal of damage to the spinal column."

"We'll fix it. Trust me."

Chrysla tried a brave smile but lost it. Then her eyes cleared and she straightened. "What can I do for you."

"It wasn't important. Go back and keep MacRuder company."

Chrysla studied her and nodded. "You wanted to talk. Arta and Ily . . . or business?"

"Wrong on both accounts. How about you and me?"

Chrysla's eyes flashed with understanding. "*Gyton* has an observation dome."

Skyla jerked her head toward the med unit. "We could talk here if you'd like. Give you another couple of moments near him."

"I appreciate that but I'd rather go elsewhere." She brushed past and palmed the lock plate. Skyla followed, matching her stride. Chrysla seemed to become reinvigorated, her shoulders squaring as they proceeded.

Chrysla led the way right and then left and right again into an observation dome. Beyond the tactite, the universe had the murky blackness of null singularity. Chrysla settled herself into one of the seats and clasped her hands in her lap. She gave Skyla a warm smile, asking, "How is Lark doing?"

Skyla fingered the switches on an interferometer and studied the woman. "She was asleep when I left. It took her a while. She waited until she was safely out of sight in her bunk to cry herself to sleep."

"She's working very hard at being brave for you."

"For me? She's doing a better job of it than I am."

"I doubt it. She takes her cues from you. Worships every move you make. She even tries to stand like you do."

"She does? *Worships?*"

"Is that so bad, to be worshiped and admired? Don't look so shocked. Just understand that the kid is knocking herself out to win your approval. I think that ought to make you feel pretty good about yourself."

Skyla propped a foot on the interferometer seat and used her knee for a brace. "You surprise me, Chrysla. You were looking pretty weary and fragile back in the hospital. Where do you find the resources to worry about everyone else's problems?''

Chrysla's laugh sounded halfhearted as she stared at a point beyond the tactite. ''Some of it comes from my training as a psychologist. The rest, well, I guess it developed during the time I was the Praetor's captive. All in all, they were a pretty discouraging twenty years. To avoid the constant boredom, all I did was study and plan for the day when I could escape and make my life meaningful. Not just to myself but to other people.''

''Generally people in that position turn bitter.''

''I couldn't, Skyla. I *had* to find something optimistic. Otherwise I would have been destroyed, and that's what he would have wanted.''

''The Praetor?''

''You can't imagine what he was like. Bitter, angry, frustrated—and completely vile. Staffa obsessed him and, since Staffa was out of reach, I became the surrogate for his attentions and his abuse.'' Chrysla looked up. ''I was in his possession for twenty years. You were Arta's for a mere matter of months. I make that point only to establish that I know what you're feeling.''

Skyla waited in silence.

Sorrow traced Chrysla's features. ''So what could I do? Let the hatred run acid inside and turn me into a monster like he was? Or find a higher purpose for my life and, in that way, defeat him in the end? Because he treated me like a slut, I wouldn't allow myself to become one. In that kind of battle, you fight day by day. The only recourse is to cling to every shred of integrity you have and wrap yourself in hope when you dream. Maybe in the process I condemned myself to optimism.''

''Treated you pretty badly?''

Chrysla's fists knotted. ''He had me for twenty years. In that amount of time he was able to think of every way imaginable to abuse me. I was lucky in two instances. First, his sperm were immobile which left him sterile and, second, over the years he became impotent. In the hands of a psychologist that information is as deadly as placing an enemy's defensive strategy and field deployment into yours.''

''He was a vain man. You must have torn him apart.''

''He did his share of suffering.'' She made a throwing

away gesture. "Enough about me. What motivated you to search me out? I saw your reflection in the surface of Mac's med unit. When you backed away, I almost let you go. Then I decided that if you'd come to me, it must be pretty important."

Skyla shrugged, realizing it was her turn to stare into the muggy black infinity of null singularity. "It seems that I keep having the same dream over and over. It starts out with me bound spread-eagle to the sleeping platform on my yacht. Arta's playing with me, kissing, licking, and the whole time those eyes of hers are watching me, almost as if daring me to discover what she's really after. My body starts to respond, and I hate myself. I start to thrash and twist at the bonds, and when I grow desperate enough, I jerk into a new position and open my eyes.

"With the new position, the scene changes and I'm in Ily's interrogation room. Still naked, cold, and drugged with Mytol. She keeps asking me the same questions she asked when she wrung me out that time. The questions are about you and Arta, and if we ever found your body aboard *Pylos*. She asks about your clearance on Itreata and how guilty Staffa must feel about killing you. She goes on about how to manipulate him with guilt."

Skyla rubbed her hands together, frowning. What was it about the dream? Something. "She asks if I heard all this from Staffa, and I tell her, no, from Andray Sornsen. That you wanted a psychological team on Itreata, and that Andray came because he was in love with you."

Chrysla cocked her head. "Funny. In all these years, I'd mostly forgotten him. Go on."

"Ily asks about Sornsen, about how he feels about Staffa. Sornsen was in love with you and he's been a virtual prisoner of the Companions. He resents the hell out of Staffa."

Chrysla nodded, a pained look in her eyes.

"This time I was awakened before the rest of the dream played out. Ily grills me some more about science staff security on Itreata. And suddenly I'm sitting there alone. I have the distinct feeling that I've failed, that wretched, horrible feeling of despair. I scream into the silence, scream after horrible scream, but I can't get loose. Arta's laughter fills the air, and I open my eyes and see myself, a duplicate Skyla. I'm walking away . . . through a hatch that opens into Itreata. And when I look back at the bound me, I have . . . I have Arta's eyes.''

Skyla took a deep breath. ''It's the same repetitive dream. You and Arta and Ily. Always emphasizing the fact that she's your clone. That she was on Itreata before me.''

''Skyla, maybe you're not reading this correctly.''

''No, wait. Let me finish. I know the situation. Staffa has made it plain. You've made it plain . . . and so has MacRuder. We'll all work it out—and pus eat me if I couldn't accept you and Staffa getting back together if it happens that way.

''I'm talking about me. About my mind. The last holdover I have to sit down and deal with is you and me. You broke the ice that day when you planted the hypnotic cue.'' Skyla shook a fist defiantly. ''Well, you and I are going to melt what's left once and for all, even if I have to live with you for the rest of this trip to prove to my subconscious that you and Arta are different!''

Chrysla's amused smile graced her perfect lips. ''Is that how you tackle all of your problems, Wing Commander? Head on.''

''Rotted right!''

''Skyla, from what you tell me, the dream is wrong.''

''Wrong? How could it be wrong? That's the way it works. The same thing over and over again.''

''Excuse me, I didn't say that very well. Your interpretation of the dream is what is wrong in this instance. That's one of the reasons you keep having the same dream over and over. One part of your brain is trying to give a message to another part of the brain—usually across the hemispheres. How often do you call me Arta by mistake?''

''I don't.''

''That's my point. You're not confusing us. You know intuitively that Chrysla Attenasio and the woman who abused you are different people. You know that intellectually as well as intuitively. Further, the flashbacks have stopped when you're around me. That's not to say they may not occur every now and then when the wrong synapses fire, but you've retrained the neural pathways.''

Skyla frowned out into the blackness. ''So what's the dream?''

''No other parts of the interrogation or Arta's captivity repeat?''

''Maybe some—but not like this, not time after time.''

''Let me outline the symbolism you are expressing. First, you're tied up, bound hand and foot. We call that the impotent savior. You are being held back from doing what you know you should. Second, the sexual nature of the rape is animalistic, with Arta watching your vulnerability. And finally, when you struggle, you experience the illusion of freedom, only to land in Ily's interrogation room—the rape of the impotent savior's mind.''

Chrysla bowed her head and pressed her hands together, a frown etching her forehead. ''The actual interrogation is straight memory, isn't it?''

''Yeah.''

''That's the key to all this. Something you said during that portion of the session is driving this.'' She nodded, as if to herself. ''Finally, when it's all over, you're devastated, screaming in panic. If you'd been crying that would have indicated a redemption, a cleansing, but the anguish is building instead.''

''You've got that right. When I wake up, my heart is pounding and I'm drenched with sweat.''

''The most important part is the doorway, Skyla. When you see yourself walking into Itreata and look back with Arta's eyes.''

''That's the important part? Not the rest?''

''The doorway is a transition, the portal through which you pass from one reality to another. What is fascinating about it is that Arta's eyes are in your head. Eyes in a dream are symbols for you to see, to understand. In this case, Arta has already violated your last sanctuary, the last place where you feel safe. She's inside you. Where else can you go to be safe?''

A shiver ran down Skyla's back. ''After hearing that, I may never dream again.''

''Solve the problem and you won't have to. The answer is there, Skyla. The imagery is fairly straightforward. Naked means defenseless, totally vulnerable. You were raped on your bed. Beds are sanctuary images. Arta watches you the whole time, eyes never blinking, just watching. Will you see what your mind wants you to? The illusion of freedom is shattered by the interrogation room. You give Ily critical information. When she has what she needs, she disappears. Finally, you scream your anguish, the statement of your inability to play the part of the savior. Arta mocks you as she changes identity, possesses your body, and enters the one place you can't fight her—in your own sanctuary.

"You're not worried about me, Skyla. Deep down inside, you never really have been—or if so, only for a brief moment. Something else is terrifying you. Something you told Ily and Arta."

"And you think it's in the part of the interrogation that keeps repeating?"

"That would be my guess. That's the part that's straight out of your memory, isn't it?"

Skyla swallowed hard and nodded. "I didn't know you were alive when that took place. No one else did either. Does that make a difference?"

"I don't know, does it?"

"Holy Rotted shit!" A chill washed over Skyla. "The final sanctuary. The one place we'd never look for her. And she's got the means to walk right through the main hatch!"

* * *

The pressure lock at docking bay 16-A gleamed under the bright lights of Itreata. Through the transparent tactite the bulbous nose of the Regan CV could be seen where the grapples had clamped it in their choke hold. Umbilicals had found the appropriate orifices and were nourishing the big vessel.

Ily walked behind Arta as they stepped past the last hatch and into the spartan concrete bay with its musty smell, cool air, and glaring lights. Ever vigilant, two STU stood at the rear of the large room, and a small knot of people waited.

Arta seemed incredibly cool as she walked purposely forward, a smile on her perfect lips, excitement sparkling in her amber eyes. For Ily that trip across the unforgiving concrete was like a death march. One false statement, one wrong move, and it would all be over. Those flint-eyed STU wouldn't hesitate. They would shoot them down on the spot.

"Lady Attenasio?" one of the women said as she stepped forward with a smile. She wore white coveralls and held a pocket comm in her hand. "Do you remember me? I'm Bell Lavender."

Arta smiled, offering her hand. "You'll have to forgive me. It's been so long. The Praetor . . . well, the less said, the better. I'm afraid that the days since the escape from *Pylos* haven't treated me kindly. You'll forgive me if I don't seem myself. It's nothing a little rest won't cure."

Lavender glanced down at her pocket comm, probably checking vocal patterns. Ily forced herself to stare straight ahead. Monitors would be zooming in on their eyes, sensors scanning them for weapons or any other potential security hazard. Even as she realized that fact, the computers would be reading her retinal patterns, searching for a match—and by the Blessed Gods, the modifications made on Ashtan had better be enough.

"I worked with your domestic staff," Bell said with a smile. "Security thought that a familiar face might make your homecoming a little easier."

Arta gave the woman a warm smile, inclining her head. "My compliments to them. It's been a long difficult journey, Lavender. Diane and I are more interested in a hot shower, a real meal, and some solid sleep than anything else. If you'll direct us to security so Staffa can get his quart of blood, skin sample, thumbprint, eyeball holo, or whatever else he's added to the list, we would greatly appreciate it."

Bell inclined her head, the smile still perfectly in place. "Diane?"

"Diane de la Luna," Arta informed her. "My Vegan associate. CV 720 belongs to her clan."

Ily nodded appropriately and kept her eyes downcast. It wasn't going to work. Even now, an alarm was buzzing somewhere. Ily consciously reminded herself to maintain a little slump in her shoulders and back.

"This way," Bell told them warmly.

They walked past the concrete bastions that cradled a heavy sialon pressure door, and Ily placed her hand on the security plate that recorded her new dermatoglyphics. She stared into the peephole that made a perfect record of her retina. A micropipette took a tiny DNA sample, and she was through.

Arta followed, apparently completely at ease. The security officer acted gracious, a model of professional efficiency, and finally asked, "Lady Attenasio, are you aware that the Seddi cloned an assassin from you?"

Ily's heart threatened to burst through her chest.

Arta never missed a beat. "The Arta Fera clone which the Praetor provided Magister Bruen. Yes, quite. She might have my DNA, sir, but she can't have my memories." Arta glanced around, masterfully at ease. "Itreata has one of the finest psychologists in Free Space. Andray was my professor on Ashtan before it . . . when I was a girl. Just to mention a historical irony, Andray arrived here after I was abducted. I never got to see my dream come to fruition."

"I remember that." Lavender Bell nodded.

"How long did Andray's depression last? He could always be . . . well . . ." Arta smiled politely.

"Moody."

"Did he . . . ever marry? Quite honestly, I hadn't thought of him until recently or I would have asked."

"No. He's something of an iconoclast."

"Sometimes that happens with bright people." Arta frowned. "Knowing him, I would guess he's probably been on your security lists. I imagine being here without me has been something of a trial for him."

The security officer nodded, obviously catching something through his earpiece. "It would seem that you do know our professor. Arta Fera wouldn't have such information. I think that will be all. Your rooms are waiting, Lady Attenasio."

"Relax," one the security officers told Ily. "I guess this is your first time through a security system like this. Nothing to it."

Ily grimaced and bobbed her head, unwilling to speak and give a vocal pattern for the recorders. For the moment, they'd be concentrating on Arta. After all, if she were genuine, who'd worry about the servant? So long as the computers didn't tag her with Ily Takka's ID, they'd register a new one for Diane de la Luna and record all the observations made today of her modified body. The only potential flaw would be the DNA test. But if the preliminaries were negative, would they take the time to run it?

And if they do, we'll be deeply hidden in this rock by the time the results come in.

Thus reassured, Ily followed the entourage to the aircar and climbed into the rear while Bell chatted aimlessly and Arta smiled pleasantly. The vehicle made a faint humming as it started into the long white corridor, past the familiar diplomatic quarters and into the guts of Itreata.

Ily sat stoically, unwilling to believe it had been this easy. For the second time in her life, she was carried into the heart of Staffa's impregnable fortress. And this time, the Lord Commander would learn just how terrible the price would be.

* * *

Two stories down, and half a kilometer away, STO Roberta Wheeler, the officer responsible for Itreata Security watched the aircar bearing Chrysla Attenasio and her party.

The center where she stood functioned as the brain for Itreata's security forces. The room consisted of banks of cathode screens, fire alerts, pressure sensors, and a host of other detection devices and holo cam pickups. The whole was tied into the Itreata comm.

From the moment Lady Attenasio set foot on Itreata, the information had been processed here, with specialists interpreting the data, measuring pupil dilation, skin temperatures, and searching for any indication that this woman was not Chrysla Marie Attenasio. To date, Wheeler had no reason to doubt her identity. The fact that Lady Attenasio had arrived earlier than expected triggered no immediate concern. After all, political strategies didn't necessarily require security to be notified at every step of the process, especially at a time when so many factions were at work in Free Space.

"What do you think?" one of men watching the aircar stop before a doorway in the personal quarters asked.

Wheeler leaned forward to stare over his shoulder. "My inclination is that she's Chrysla. This Fera assassin is reported to be half wild, psychologically disturbed. Not only that, Chrysla's story about Professor Sornsen checks out. Hell, I didn't even know that's how he got here. Where would Fera have learned that?"

"Two women in a CV," another of the operators noted. "We've got a warning out."

"And do you think Takka and Fera would just dance right into Itreata?" Wheeler shook her head. "Chrysla was completely at ease, as if she didn't have a care in the universe. The servant was pretty jumpy but not out of line for a Vegan of that social class entering the stronghold of the feared Companions. Retinal data, fingerprints, and chem-code don't match between de la Luna and Takka. Still, go ahead and run a complete DNA.

"Gillian?" Roberta asked, as Lady Attenasio and her servant bid their escort good-bye and entered the living quarters. "What's your assessment?"

From a monitor which ran archive footage of Ily Takka's first arrival, an analyst compared Ily Takka's actions, body language, and behavior with Diane de la Luna's.

"STO, I don't see much resemblance." Gillian pointed to the Takka tape. "Here, see? When Ily entered the first time, she was looking for everything. Totally observant. She's spotting the monitors almost by second nature. De la Luna, in contrast, simply fixes her gaze on people, she's defensive and reactive unlike the active Takka. You might consider monitoring their conversations for a while. See if we can get a good vocal print to compare with Takka's."

STO Wheeler straightened. "Data at this time indicates that we're dealing with the real Chrysla Marie Attenasio. We'll accept that."

"Stand down?" one of the seconds asked.

"Not completely." Wheeler frowned at the monitors as the view inside Chrysla's room was switched off. "I've still got a crawly feeling about this. I want a log of all comm usage she makes. No monitoring of dialogue, just the notation of who or what was accessed. If anything sensitive is tapped, alert me at once. Ham, get a subspace off to *Gyton*, check to make sure Lady Attenasio departed before the match with *Rega One*. Also, alert the Lord Commander that Lady Attenasio is on Itreata. I want an STU placed at her door—and to accompany her everywhere. For her personal safety, you understand. Finally, every move she makes outside of that room will be monitored."

STO Wheeler strode into the middle of the room, calling, "And, people, let's remember something. This is the Lord

Commander's wife. Until otherwise determined, she gets the treatment and respect she deserves. I want her watched but I want it done with discretion! Get the drift?''

''Affirmative,'' echoed from around the room.

CHAPTER XXXVIII

Hours ago we finished the macroengineering phase of the construction. The electrodome is fully and firmly attached to *Countermeasures*. Humans have never built anything like this. The compressional and tensile strength of the graphite and sialon is without equal anywhere in Free Space. If you could develop the thrust, you could literally push a planet with this thing.

But evidently that isn't what this structure is designed to do. The electrodome itself, while incredibly strong, would prove too brittle around the edges to push a planet. No, whatever the Lord Commander wants to propel is small, something to fit inside the dome and take a charge. A nickel-iron asteroid? Is that the idea? But why not build an accelerator—some sort of advanced rail gun—and blast away at the Forbidden Borders? But that would be a futile exercise since nickel-iron rocks would melt against neutronium.

I keep trying to wring understanding out of this project in spite of the fact that I've wrung myself dry.

Enough for now. I've got to get some sleep. The big stuff is done. Now the real work begins: fixing all the twinky little bugs in the system. You know, the ones that will inevitably show up when we start testing, and testing, retesting, and testing some more.

I have a feeling the coming weeks are going to be Rotted Hell!

—Excerpt from Dee Wall's personal journal

* * *

A big roaring fire burned in Staffa's fireplace as he drew a bulb of Ashtan single malt from the jeweled dispenser. From the corridor monitors, he could time the action of drawing a second bulb, and he offered it to Sinklar precisely as he passed through the air lock and into Staffa's plushly furnished main room.

Sinklar wore his usual unadorned Regan military fare and the battered equipment belt. If anything, Sinklar's shock of black hair was in greater disarray than usual—and that contemplative expression Staffa had grown so used to lined Sink's face.

''Special occasion?'' Sinklar asked as he took the drinking bulb.

''We're in null singularity. For a while I don't have to live in the command chair on the bridge.''

Staffa walked over and settled on the overstuffed red-leather couch, indicating that Sinklar should sit beside him.

''To freedom,'' Staffa toasted as Sinklar dropped onto the cushions.

''Freedom,'' Sinklar agreed, watching the light that passed through the amber-filled crystal as he lifted the bulb.

''And another success.'' Staffa gestured at the air above them, tapped a stud on his belt comm, and a holo sprang to life in the indicated space.

Staffa's amusement grew as Sinklar gawked at the image. Someone might have chopped a giant ball precisely in half and rested it in a multi-finned support that narrowed to a heavy neck. Behind that, the caricature of a Class VI Formosan freighter—the big boxy model—appeared dwarfed and half-disguised under a bunch of lumpy blisters.

''What is it?'' Sinklar asked, squinting.

''*Countermeasures*. Modified, of course, to the specifications given us by the Mag Comm.'' Staffa sipped his single malt and kicked a leg out as he admired the craft. ''This just came in moments before we went null singularity. Dee Wall forwarded it to me along with a lot of cryptic suggestions that he'd really like to know what it's for.''

''That's the secret? That's going to break the Forbidden Borders? How? I mean, what does it do?''

''For one thing, it costs a lot. About half of my assets are tied up in that construction.'' Staffa shrugged. ''All I can tell you is that it's the most powerful artifact ever built, capable of producing nearly two billion tons of thrust. The compressional strength of the central structural support appears to be great enough to drive through a neutron star.''

''All right, I'll bite. Which planet are you thinking about moving? I'd say it was a moon. Itreata?''

Staffa slowly shook his head. ''The electrodome isn't sturdy enough to take that sort of load along the rim. No, this is something different. It's meant to move something massive, that's apparent. From my study, however, I don't believe the dome actually touches the object.'' He smiled. ''I don't think you would want it to.''

''But you think you know.''

''What would you say if I told you that I suspect it's meant to move a black hole.''

''Where did you hear this?''

''I didn't hear it. I suspect it. The Mag Comm hinted at it through the very design parameters.''

''You're talking about a quantum hole, aren't you?''

''If I'm right about this, I would suspect that we were dealing with a quantum hole, probably charged, and massing about five hundred billion tons. *Countermeasures* won't move it fast but it can be accelerated and controlled through the electrical charge. Assuming the hole is negatively charged, *Countermeasures* need only intensify a negative field to repulse the hole at the same time she's putting out a full thrust.''

''Wait a minute. Where's the Mag Comm going to get a black hole—quantum or otherwise?''

''Evidently it has one handy.'' Staffa frowned at the flickering fire. ''Who knows, maybe it was even charted once and the records, like so many, were pruned away in the past. Be that as it may, I think I understand the machine's agenda. A little more sophisticated than any I would have attempted, but I don't think we'll need to worry about the tidal effects the way we would if we attempted to heterodyne the neutronic strings.''

''Holy Rotted Gods,'' Sinklar whispered as he realized the magnitude of the action. Expression tinted by disbelief, his attention remained riveted on the holo.

''That was one of two messages that came in at the last minute. The other was that your mother has arrived on Itreata. Apparently she came in by CV ahead of *Gyton*. I was curious. Did you know anything about her arrival?''

Sinklar shook his head, a rapt expression on his face as he stared at the flying-chalice shape of *Countermeasures*. "I can't imagine her leaving Mac's side. *Gyton* would have been just about as quick. I doubt that she saved more than a week or two."

"I suspect there's an explanation." Staffa cocked his head as he examined the ship Dee Wall was building. "Ugly damned thing, isn't it?"

"I wouldn't use it to collect garbage."

"Ugly or not, if it breaks the Forbidden Borders, I'll electroplate it in gold."

The tone in Sinklar's voice changed. "What do you know about STU Adze?"

Staffa noted the studied nonchalance in his son's eyes. "Adze? She's one of the best. Extraordinarily talented, intelligent, and insufferably ambitious. What kind of mad scheme is she trying to talk you into?"

Sinklar pointed at *Countermeasures*. "She wants to be on the first ship through the Forbidden Borders."

Staffa sipped his single malt and enjoyed the carefully neutral posture Sinklar struggled to maintain. "And, naturally, if you go, she goes, correct?"

"You're that familiar with her methods?" The faint ghost of a frown cracked Sinklar's composure. "Is there something about her I should know?"

"Let me put it this way. What exactly is your interest in her? Lover?"

"I'm not ready for another lover." Sinklar turned his gaze from the *Countermeasures* holo to the fire. "She wants to work with me. To her way of thinking, it will be mutually beneficial. And I will say this for her, she spotted one of the problems I've been struggling with. She's right. I'm not ready for a desk job, Staffa. I guess I got spoiled by all the excitement. I'm having a tough time slowing down to the placid life of an administrator."

"Ah, splendid youth when the lure of excitement boils like nitrogen in the blood during decompression."

"What a charming metaphor."

"She's an attractive woman," Staffa added. "You'd probably do very well with her."

"I told you, I'm not interested in her—not that way."

"Most of the guys on the gun deck are. I hear they've

driven the scuttlebutt up to sixty credits now. The bookies are laying three to two odds against Stew Mako.''

''Who? And how did you know about the scuttlebutt? That's supposed to be her big secret.''

''It is. To everyone except Ark and myself. That bulletin board was my . . . well, it was Skyla's idea, actually. She thought it would be smart to initiate it to keep track of the crew's mood. When grumbles start making the rounds, it shows up in the scuttlebutt before it goes critical. We fix the situation if it needs fixing, or knock a head or two if it's a discipline matter.''

''Then I take it that you're not impressed by Adze.''

''Quite the contrary, Sinklar. I didn't mean to give you that opinion. She has a great deal of potential and native ability. The best I've seen in years. She's a damned fast learner. Keeps her head when the shooting starts. Thinks on her feet, doesn't panic in a disaster, and has too much guts for her own good.''

''And the negatives?''

Staffa sipped his drink, tilting his head. ''She's still young. Every now and then she makes a judgment that I find a bit premature. Her tendency is to shoot first and worry about the consequences later. She's impulsive, headstrong, and completely convinced that she's invincible.'' Staffa nodded and grumbled to himself. ''A younger copy of Skyla Lyma. She just looks different is all.''

Sinklar didn't say much as his gaze drifted between *Countermeasures* and the fire.

Staffa turned his drinking bulb, remembering. ''And having said that, you could do a lot worse. If you want, I'll approve any transfer.''

Sinklar shrugged. ''I'm not sure I'm ready to make that kind of commitment yet, but thank you.''

Staffa finally laughed and added, ''I guess it wouldn't be such a bad thing if you and Adze came with me.''

''With you?''

Staffa nodded, raising his eyes to the ghostly holo of *Countermeasures*. ''You don't think I'm going to miss being on the first ship out, do you? I've invested my life and the lives of a lot of other people in cracking this bottle. Free Space doesn't need me. It has Kaylla, the Mag Comm,

Myles Roma, and Dion Axel." He smiled wearily. "And maybe MacRuder and Chrysla."

"Then you're not coming back?"

"No, Sinklar. What would I do? There's no place in Free Space for the Star Butcher. I was created to be a destroyer. When the Forbidden Borders go down, my time will have passed. Humanity will have a new future, and new leaders for those challenges."

He shook his head. "It's common among survivors to wonder why they were the ones lucky enough to live when so many around them died. It creates a dilemma which hounds them throughout their lives. Was it divine intervention? Fate? Some unaccountable action? I've seen soldiers ponder for years, trying to understand that the difference of one seat in an assault craft can mean death or survival. A sense of unworthiness develops as the individual asks, 'Why did those good men and women die while I survived?' "

"I know the syndrome." Sinklar smiled wearily. "For me, I think about the Kaspa Section Three post office. Three of us made it out—and two hundred and eighty died."

"That's another reason I need to leave. I need to come to terms with why. Not because I'm a victim, but because I'm a perpetrator. Don't you see? Those who commit atrocities never ask why, they simply assume that things like that happen: people must die to make social progress. I can look you in the eyes and tell you that all the victims of my wars died to buy the rest of us time to break the Forbidden Borders. They were sacrificed to allow us to solve some of our most pressing problems.

"That's the easy answer, Sinklar. Nice and neat. I can accept it, just as a soldier can accept that his friends must die in war. But as a perpetrator seeking morality, I have been forced to ask: Why was I the one who had to kill them? What made me different? How did I get chosen for the role of mindless butcher? How could I have become that agent of misery, suffering, and terror? Am I so different from anyone else, Sinklar? From Peebal, or Koree, or Kaylla? Is it in the genetics the Praetor manipulated to create me?"

Sinklar shook his head, his pained gaze on the fire. "It's over, Staffa. Don't torture yourself."

Staffa curled his fingers as if seeking to capture something out of the air. "Don't you see, Sinklar? If the killers can learn to ask that question, perhaps humanity can finally turn a corner into a new era.''

Sinklar stared at the fire for quite a while. Then he asked, ''Where will you go?''

Staffa waved an arm. ''Out there! The quanta Rot it, child, I have two whole universes to discover.''

''Two?''

''Outside and within.''

''Do you think Skyla will want to head off into the unknown like that? Just cut all the strings?''

Would she? ''I'll have to ask her.''

''And you'd take *Chrysla?*''

''She's one of the best ships in Free Space. I built her. She's mine. I can't think of a better vessel for uncharted space.'' He waved any concerns away. ''Oh, we'd have to return to Itreata every now and then for a rejuv for us and a refit for the ship. Maybe Ark, or Dee Wall, or some of the others might have the same need for excitement that you do. They might want to trade off every now and then.''

''What if Skyla wants to stay here?''

Staffa glanced disdainfully at his son. ''Then my judgment when I picked her was worse than Adze's when she picked you.''

''If . . . *if* it turns into that kind of relationship.''

''Yes, if it does. You're a smarter man than I was at your age. You need to know yourself first.'' *Like I need to discover myself, my son.* And no matter what, humanity could slowly begin to forget the nightmare of the Star Butcher.

I will have atoned. If only Peebal, Koree, and a little bald man from Phillipia could know. Perhaps someday, in shared God Mind, they would.

* * *

Andray Sornsen almost trembled as he hurried around his lab. In anticipation, he'd sent his associates home early, and now he fiddled with a pile of reports, straightening and reshuffling in an attempt to create an air of organized professionalism.

For twenty years he'd dreamed of this day. For most of those same years, he'd believed her dead. Yet not for one instant had his love for the golden-eyed girl with red-shot hair faded from his memory or heart.

Was it possible? Could those hallowed days he'd shared with her on Ashtan live again? Granted, a psychologist inherently understood that the past couldn't be recaptured but perhaps a new present could be manufactured on the rubble of dusty dreams.

The Lord Commander had a new woman—his volatile Wing Commander—and at this opportune moment, Chrysla—risen like a resurrected Blessed angel—had returned.

His lab was a large place, more than forty meters in length and nearly as wide. At the time of Sornsen's arrival, a worry-stricken Staffa kar Therma had granted his every request—since this was supposed to have been Chrysla's laboratory. As a result, he not only had a complete pharmacy but every piece of equipment imaginable.

Despite his resentment at being a virtual captive, he'd done good work over the years, the sort of work Chrysla could be proud of—even if he hadn't been able to publish the material he'd generated about the Companions. Perhaps now that she was here, coming to see him, that would change. Not only could he disseminate his data and analyses, but he could prove himself to her, explain how the years had tormented him.

The door chimed and opened. At that moment, Andray Sornsen straightened his smock and arched his back. The pounding of his heart and the thrill of adrenaline left him paralyzed by the excitement of the moment.

She entered, tall, athletic, the light glinting in her auburn hair. Those familiar eyes seemed to glow as she saw him and hesitated. "Andray?"

"Chrysla Marie." He took an uncertain step forward, adrift in his own confusion and uncertainty. "I . . . I've missed you . . ."

"And I you, Andray," she told him, a smile bringing small dimples to her cheeks. Extending a hand, she added, "Come, tell me what you've been doing all these years."

Andray Sornsen barely nodded as Chrysla introduced her companion. The dam within burst, and he began to talk, chattering about his accomplishments and about the worry he'd endured all these years. She listened, amber eyes centered only on him.

"Andray," she finally interrupted. "This is wonderful. But is there somewhere we could go to talk? Privately?" She glanced around. "Or will you be bothered here? I mean, you know, monitored?"

He shook his head. "Oh, no. This is a psychiatric facility. I need only lock the door and no one will disturb us. But why?"

She gave him a smile that melted his heart. "I have some things I need to talk through with you. Problems of my own. I wouldn't want them to . . . well, you understand. Let's say, get to the wrong ears."

His breast felt as if it would explode from joy. "I understand completely. I have only my own monitors for recording a subject—for later study, you see. What good would a psychologist do if the subject knew that security was listening?"

"You have a wonderful supply of drugs," Diane, the servant, remarked. "Here I see tritekscopalamine. What does that do?"

"Induces a form of paralysis, freezes a person for hours."

Chrysla turned, studying her servant. "Perhaps the STU outside the door would like some? After that, Diane, access the comm to amuse yourself. You need not worry about me. Andray and I . . . well, don't disturb us."

"As you wish, my lady," de la Luna replied, reaching for the drug container.

"Wait! You can't just . . ." But Chrysla had stepped close, placing her cool hands on either side of his hot face. Andray Sornsen forgot himself as he stared into those wondrous eyes.

"Andray, it's all right," she whispered, kissing him lightly on the lips. "We need time. Just you and I. I'm here to fulfill your fantasies . . . all of them. I've waited for years to be alone with you. You've loved me, haven't you?"

"Yes . . . oh Blessed Gods, I have. But to drug an STU . . ." That sense of wrongness prickled at the back of his mind.

"Trust me, Andray." Those amber eyes burned with excitement. Her arms went around his neck as she molded to him. His blood began to pound in his ears as her breasts pressed firmly into his chest and she kissed him with greater vigor.

He tried to hesitate, to put it all in perspective. Something about her . . . *Why me?*

"Trust me, Andray." Her voice had dropped sensually. "Trust me and I'll be yours forever."

He closed his eyes, savoring her scent, aware of his rising desire as his erection snagged painfully in the folds of his clothing. The slight undulations of her pubis against his shot electric thrills along his muscles. His doubts, the little voice crying out in his mind, drowned in the rush of sexual desire.

"I've missed you, Andray," she insisted. "I wanted you here in the beginning so we could be together."

His thoughts had turned to jelly as he tightened his hold on her, fevered with the secret desire he'd struggled through the years to forget.

"Love me, Andray. Please?"

"Your . . . servant? Diane?"

"She understands. Come, we'll go to your office. And after that, I'll never leave you. Never again."

Andray Sornsen walked like a man possessed. There she was, the woman he'd loved and lusted for all of his life—staring at him with an insatiable desire to complement his own. She pressed the door closed behind her, then sighed as she began kissing him, carefully removing his smock and shirt to run charged fingers across his chest.

He attacked her then, peeling her clothing away as he kicked his pants to one side. For long moments he reveled in the exploration of her body while she gasped and writhed under his touch. Then she settled back on the recliner beside his desk and he lowered himself. The feel of her soft body under his stimulated his hot flesh to the point of bursting.

When she tightened around him, he opened his eyes to find her staring at him—that amber gaze oddly predatory as her hips began to undulate.

* * *

Skyla stood behind the command chair as *Gyton* dropped back into regular space. That moment of disorientation passed as the light cones began to straighten and the warship's null singularity drive deactivated. The bridge monitors indicated the ship's functions to be within the parameters for normal operation. Navcomm processors tackled the intricate chore of interpreting light warped by the ship's mass at this threshold of light speed. As the sophisticated comm unscrambled the blueshifted mess received by the sensors, the images of the Twin Titans appeared in the forward monitor and the familiar landmarks of the Itreata system firmed up.

Rysta swiveled her command chair and looked up. "Do you want to let them know now, Wing Commander?"

"The sooner the better. Given the critical nature of the trouble, we'd better go subspace and let them worry about the fuses."

"Comm First," Rysta barked, "give Wing Commander Lyma a subspace link to Itreata."

"Affirmative. I'm establishing the link right . . . now. Go ahead, Wing Commander."

"Attention Itreata Comm, this is Wing Commander Skyla Lyma. I need a patch to Magister Kaylla Dawn and Itreata Security. I'm aboard the Regan battle cruiser *Gyton.* We're heading Insystem at 0.99 c, course vector two three eight by two four seven by zero six one."

Skyla nodded as STO Wheeler's face formed on the monitor. "Hello, Rob. This is Wing Commander Lyma aboard *Gyton.* STO, be aware that we have reason to believe that Ily Takka and her assassin, Arta Fera, may be attempting to penetrate Itreata's security. If they're in the process, they'll arrive aboard a Regan CV. Any vessel matching that description is to be immediately boarded in force and the occupants taken. Any vessel matching that description and making hostile or unauthorized movements is to be immediately disabled. Do you understand?"

Wheeler had stiffened, her expression icy. "Is Lady Attenasio with you?"

"Right here." Skyla pointed to Chrysla, aware that the focus of the pickup was expanding.

Wheeler appeared stricken, bracing herself with one hand as she turned. "I want a complete deployment. Get them! *Now!*"

Skyla's heart sank. "They're already there."

Kaylla Dawn's face, looking bleary and half-asleep, had formed in the second monitor. "What's wrong?"

Skyla cursed and stomped a foot to vent some of the frustrated anger. "Arta and Ily are inside Itreata. Apparently under Chrysla's alias. Secure your systems, Magister. We're still inbound. Do you have any Companions on Itreata?"

"Delshay and *Cobra* are preparing to space."

"Patch a line through to Delshay. Roberta, coordinate with Delshay in deployment. We've got to find her. Your orders are to use any means possible to apprehend or neutralize the threat."

The muscles in Roberta Wheeler's face were jumping, the corners of her mouth twitching. "My fault. It happened on my watch."

"Easy, STO, if you made a mistake, it'll show in the records and we'll correct it. If you didn't—and knowing you, I suspect you didn't—they used a flaw in the process."

Wheeler inclined her head slightly, then looked up at the monitor. "Wing Commander? The STU I detailed to monitor Lady Attenasio and her servant has just been found—drugged. My people are currently entering the psychology laboratory. They're . . ." Wheeler glanced away. "What? All right." When she looked up again, she announced in a brittle voice, "They're gone, Wing Commander."

"Rot it!" Skyla smacked the command chair back with a knotted fist. "Seal every section. I don't care if it means people go hungry, miss getting to their duty on time, or what. I want Ily and Arta *found!*"

"Yes, ma'am!"

Skyla placed a hand to her face and squeezed her temples. *Think, Skyla. Where would they have gone? Obviously to Andray Sornsen, but what could he have told them? With his clearance, where would he have taken them?*

Anywhere in the complex.

In the background, the wail of sirens could be heard. Wheeler was bent over, apparently talking to Delshay.

Kaylla kept track from the other monitor when she wasn't glancing away to give orders.

Skyla turned to Rysta who was studying the developments from the command chair, eyes bright and thoughtful. "We'll need to keep an open link on the way in. Can you get us in fast?"

Rysta made a sour face. ''We're Regans, Wing Commander, not silly Sassans. You've got the best in the Regan military design here.'' She slapped the command chair. ''Tell us what you need.''

Chrysla placed a hand on Skyla's arm. ''And let's not forget a medical unit for Mac when we get there.''

Skyla turned her attention to the monitor again. ''Itreata Insystem, we're coming in hot. Prepare for our arrival.''

Rysta bent to one of her comms, ordering, ''All hands, prepare for high g deceleration. Repeat, prepare for forty gravities, people. Stow all the loose stuff and batten down the hatches.''

* * *

A constant chatter filled the rooms of the Seddi warren. Kaylla rubbed her temples as she stared at a schematic of the entire complex. From outside, one saw a moderately busy moon, the shadowed far side studded with installations. Only when the entire subsurface maze that Itreata was composed of was projected in holographic relief did the enormity of the world Staffa had built become apparent.

A young man leaned over the wall divider in Kaylla's office and announced, ''Something's happening to comm. I'm not sure what, but apparently it's a virus.''

Kaylla glanced at Myles Roma who sat across from her. He, in turn, stared blandly up at the young man. ''Does it erase or insert commands?''

''It appears to do both. You can find a residual in Admin/Com/Trex.''

Myles swiveled in his chair to the nearest comm terminal and began inputting commands. ''Let's see just what this is.'' He asked Kaylla, ''Do you think it's Ily's work?''

Kaylla nodded, hardly aware that Myles couldn't see her action. She was caught by the memory of Ily, smug and devious, sitting across from Staffa and a still-enslaved Kaylla Dawn. The overhead lights of the remembered Etarian office made the Regan woman's black hair gleam as she watched Staffa with a predatory gaze.

''Yes, Myles, it's her work. I should have thought of this before. I'm slipping. Too many long hours.''

''It's early yet,'' Roma told her. ''Not only that, you're

in luck. By odd happenstance, you've got one of Free Space's best programmers sitting right here in your office, enjoying your stassa.'' At that Myles lifted his cup and sipped while the program displayed on the screen.

''I don't carry many grudges, Myles,'' Kaylla added as she waited for the verdict. ''But with Ily, I could center a blaster in the middle of her forehead and press the firing stud. I doubt I'd feel much more remorse than a person does when they step on a Riparian cockroach.''

Myles grunted and nodded, engrossed in the screen. Finally, he leaned back. ''Yes, she is a vile little bitch. I see what she's done. Very clever but not so terrible. This is specifically tailored. Ily didn't write this little gem. I'd say she stole it, bought it, who knows? Drop it into a commercial system, say the computer operations for an industrial plant forming sialon parts, and you could destroy the whole place in minutes.''

''Then what's the good news?''

''The good news is that for the most part, our comm system is discretionary. And our automatic processes can be isolated. Staffa is a military genius and in designing his system he was motivated by defense concerns.''

Myles leaned forward. ''Comm, get me security.''

A desperate STO Roberta Wheeler's face appeared. ''Legate? I'm a little busy right now. If you could—''

''You have a virus spreading through your comm system. Apparently Ily thought to sabotage your ability to function effectively. You must cancel and isolate all automatic functions. I believe you can do that through Comm/Ad/Stat/Sec/Run. Please do that immediately and await a new patch.''

Wheeler hesitated, working her jaw from side to side, and finally jerked an angry nod. ''It better work, Legate.''

Myles grinned with aplomb. ''I assure you, STO, the last thing I would do is place myself in jeopardy—or my staff. If Staffa can trust me, I would imagine you could as well. And, assuming Ily doesn't destroy us all, I doubt you'll have any trouble finding me if I'm wrong.''

Myles' screen flickered as the security center chopped portions of Itreata's computer brain out and shifted them to Myles. He glanced at Kaylla. ''Can I go one step further?''

She was nervously kneading the muscles in the side of her neck. She'd grown so used to living with tension, she didn't even realize she was doing it. "What have you got in mind? Manual labor?"

"Just the opposite." Myles indicated the screen with the growing number of files. "Part of this is contaminated. We would spend days, a million man-hours, sorting the programs for fragments of virus. Why not allow the Mag Comm to do it for us? That's a totally discretionary program. The machine should be able to purify the system within a matter of hours."

Kaylla stiffened. "Let me get this straight. You want me to authorize you to allow the Mag Comm to compromise Itreata's computer network?"

Myles nodded. "Oh, I'll make a backup first, of course, but the Lord Commander has already banked the whole of Free Space on the machine. If he can do that, can't I bank a little of Itreata?"

At that moment, the lights in the Seddi warren flickered, went off, then came on again.

"Go for it," Kaylla decided, hearing pandemonium raging beyond the partition.

Myles pressed his access stud. "Mag Comm, please."

Within seconds, the curiously disembodied voice responded. "This is the Mag Comm, to whom am I speaking?"

"Legate Myles Roma. It seems that we need your help. Minister Takka has inserted a virus into the Itreata comm. Would you be so kind as to remove it for us? It would make life a great deal more pleasant for a lot of us, and no doubt irritate Ily no end when she determines she has failed completely."

Kaylla raised an eyebrow, admiring Roma's complete self-assurance as he brokered a deal Kaylla would have spent hours agonizing over.

"I can handle your problem, Legate. Will you inform me of any trouble that arises? I would also appreciate reviewing any records you might obtain of Minister Takka's reaction when she discovers her failure."

"It will be as you . . . whoops, the lights just went out here in the Seddi warrens. This has happened once before."

"Affirmative, I am taking corrective actions. You may monitor my actions, Legate. I will display all files accessed for your records."

"That will be deeply appreciated. Thank you."

"You are welcome."

The lights flashed on again to cheers in the background.

Myles paused and leaned back, a broad grin on his chubby face. "I *hate* Ily Takka. I hope she stews over this and does something dumb."

Kaylla glanced thoughtfully at the file names flashing across Myles' screen, all of them appearing and disappearing so rapidly no human eye could follow.

"We're supposed to monitor that?" she pointed.

Myles crossed his arms and chuckled. "Do you still think I made the wrong decision?"

Kaylla slumped in her chair. "No, Legate. But your audacity astounds me sometimes."

"I met Ily for the first time here on Itreata. We didn't like each other. I won't deny that at that time I wasn't very likable. Apparently, I have changed and she hasn't. I find a great deal of pleasure in the knowledge that I was here at the right moment to stop her cold. In this case, at least, pay-backs are to the bitch."

"Given that she was going to use my slavery as a lever to manipulate Staffa, I take great pleasure in being able to allow you to do that!" And Kaylla laughed for the first time in days. "Good work, Myles. Now, we only need to worry about the Mag Comm, finding Ily, and breaking the Forbidden Borders. After that, it's clear spacing from here to the future."

"Indeed it is. Assuming we can handle these last three problems."

Kaylla stuck her stassa cup into the dispenser. "You're a good man with computers and programs, Myles. I don't know if you're aware of it yet, but you won't be going home any time soon."

He patted his stomach. "That's more than fine. I've made my peace with the future. Solving problems always creates new ones. We've a long way to go, Magister."

Kaylla's comm flickered as STO Wheeler's image appeared. She still looked harried, but now a little less so. "I don't know what you've done, but it seems to be working. Lights are still flickering all over the complex, but it seems to have stopped spreading. Our security override is completely paralyzed, door locks, holo cams, everything. You could walk out with all the secrets you wanted to right now—and I couldn't stop you!''

''Let's hope Ily doesn't know that.''

Wheeler nodded grimly. ''Indeed, Magister. Give my best to the Legate, and my deepest thanks.''

Myles chuckled and clapped his hands. ''And Ily Takka, we'll be running you down any time now.''

Except, despite Myles' optimism, it wouldn't be that easy.

CHAPTER XXXIX

Now what do I do? Better yet, what's happened? During this last shift, we hooked up the comm tower for remote control. No sooner did we send a subspace test signal then the unit was activated—from outside!

Mapahandras activates my head unit, saying, "Cut it out, Wall, you're screwing with our test."

"What test?" I say. "I'm not doing anything in here but checking a system relay. I bounced a pulse off Itreata, that's all."

"Well," he says, "In that case, give me comm-wide. Somebody's fooling with the system and either they knock it off, or I'm going to cram this SWR meter so far up their hind portions they're going to need a med tech to remove it!"

Practical jokes occur on any project. The next thing that I know, I get another comm call from Mapahandras. He tells me to stop the diagnostic run, that he Rotted well knows his job. I tell him that I'm *not* running any thrice-cursed diagnostics. He tells me that his boards are lighting up, and the monitor is giving him instructions detailing problems in the comm, powerlead, and wiring.

The problem is, we don't find any of our people involved with any of this. As usual, the explanation always turns to ghosts. Meanwhile, more instructions are popping up on the monitors, and sure enough, the teams sent to check them out are finding trouble right where the message tells us it's supposed to be. We fix it and the message goes away.

By that time, Mapahandras has had the sense to put a directional on the comm tower, and we find that not only is the message coming from outside but it's from Itreata.

So we send a message to Itreata and get snarled up in

the Blessed Gods knows what, but finally we get Magister Dawn. She says she can't say what's happening, but a virus is playing hell with Itreata comm.

By this time, I'm getting real jumpy. *Countermeasures* is a top-priority project with Class One security concerns. Someone from outside is activating the systems. We try pulling the plug, but one of the instructions is a reroute. I send a subspace to the Lord Commander. *Chrysla* is out of contact–null singularity, no doubt.

I'm exhausted to the point of falling over. I can't get any help from Itreata, even security there is refusing to talk.

What the hell is going on? Is everything crazy? If we've got a security breach here, and if I can't find it . . .

No, don't think about it, Dee. Just keep trying to figure it out. Meanwhile, I'm posting armed guards on the bridge and on the engineering deck.

If this baby starts to power up, we're cutting the fuel supply and overriding the reactors on manual. Or has one of the instructions we've received overridden that,

–Excerpt from Dee Wall's personal journal

* * *

Staffa had experienced this moment many times, generally with a great deal of satisfaction. From where he sat in the command chair on *Chrysla*'s bridge, he could sense the change as the huge ship's null singularity drive allowed space to bend back into its normal configuration. At the peripheries of his vision, the light played tricks as the battleship hovered in that briefest instant of violation of physical law while the light threshold reestablished itself.

The forward monitors immediately tripped and reset, the sophisticated comm unscrambling the violently blueshifted image the detectors and vidcams supplied them and translating it into an intelligible image the bridge monitors could display.

Ahead, the Twin Titans glowed in violet-white fury as they continued their gyrating dance of flashing radiation. Characteristically, Staffa's glance shifted to the lateral monitors in the expectation of the fleet appearing, and it took a moment to remember that those days were gone. A moment of melancholy gripped his imagination. The fleet would never again drop in massed formation, heroic victors returning from a hard-fought campaign.

Most human beings in Free Space would sleep in peace now.

"First Officer, alert the monitor beacons." Staffa propped an elbow on one of his gray-clad knees and glanced at Lynette Helmutt, who reclined with the gleaming worry-cap covering her head.

Her voice answered through the ship's speakers. "Monitors alerted, Lord Commander. Deceleration initiated at forty gs. Consequent Delta V dump sequences initiated. We're roger zero zero one on course relay. Monitors report . . . Sir, we've got a condition Red-Two, I repeat, a condition Red-Two at home."

Staffa straightened, calling, "Comm First, I want subspace to Itreata Security."

"Coming on-line, sir. Screen A seven."

Staffa focused on one of the monitors that rose from the instrument cluster on his chair. STO Roberta Wheeler stared out, looking for all the universe as if she were condemned.

"Lord Commander," she began. "It is my misfortune and responsibility to inform you that Itreata's security has been penetrated by Minister Ily Takka and her assassin, Arta Fera. They entered under the guise of Lady Attenasio and her servant."

Staffa experienced that sense of emptiness in his gut. "Chem-code and retinals didn't pick up Ily's ID?"

Wheeler shook her head. "No, sir. We ran it through the system, sir. Evidently she's been into a genetics lab somewhere and acquired a new ID card and retinal modification. Everyone was suspicious, but we couldn't pin it down. In the meantime, we thought we needed to treat the Lady Attenasio as her position merited. We took a tissue sample, of course. We've now run a complete recombination on the sample and have a positive. It is Minister Takka. Since the other woman matches Lady Attenasio's DNA perfectly, we assume we're dealing with the Fera clone." Wheeler hesitated, coming to attention. "I take full responsibility and offer myself for such disciplinary action as you may require."

"Let's not rush into recriminations. What actions have been taken?"

"Ily attempted to sabotage the comm. Legate Roma and Magister Dawn countered that threat. We lost control of security for several hours, but things are pretty much back to normal. In the confusion, however, Ily drugged the STU I'd placed to monitor her actions and slipped away with Professor Sornsen." Wheeler swallowed the way she would if her mouth had gone dry. "We've begun a room by room search. I've taken every action I can think of. Sir . . . well, Second Gin Austen is here, sir. He's ready to assume responsibility."

Staffa shook his head. "Let's not deal with that yet, STO. When we have this taken care of, we'll look at the mistakes made and determine how to avoid them in the future, and what actions, if any, to take regarding discipline. For the moment, I still have full confidence in you."

"Thank you, sir."

"What word on the Wing Commander?"

"She's Insystem aboard *Gyton.* ETA five days at her present deceleration."

Staffa checked his navcomm, inputting figures. "If we allow our present course to carry us deep, and then drop Delta V at fifty-five g, we should just about match her ETA. We'll be a little late, but only a couple of hours."

"Yes, sir."

"I'm patching this through to Ryman Ark. Coordinate with him when I clear. In the meantime, forward the records of what happened to me and I'll review them."

"Yes, sir."

Staffa ran the patch to Ark's personal comm and sat for a moment, staring at the Twin Titans on the bridge monitors. Ily, Rot her, had found a way in. Something in Skyla's interrogation had clued her in. Staffa had reviewed the interrogation. Ark had recovered the records from the Ministry. The key must have been when Ily was probing Skyla about the Fera clone.

And I interpreted it as Ily's curiosity about her pet killer. He rubbed his forehead. When it all worked out, he was going to find that STO Wheeler had played by the rules. In all the years he'd known her, she hadn't made more than a couple of trifling errors, never a major goof.

And I didn't forward a copy of Skyla's interrogation to Itreata. Rob Wheeler would have pored over it, looking for any possible angle.

Staffa chewed on his lip, fists knotted. He'd been so busy with the political entanglements that he hadn't taken the time to think it through. And he'd allowed personal concern about Skyla's psychological health to cloud his judgment when it came to security and command.

"First Officer," he ordered, "we're going in hot. Tell the crew they've got ten hours to prepare for a hard ride."

"Affirmative."

Staffa narrowed his eyes as he stared at the shining dot that marked Itreata's location. He was looking at his home, the place where he'd been secure and safe. And now, because of his errors, two insidious reptiles were crawling through that warm haven; and they could be in any room, under any piece of furniture.

Someone was going to get bitten before it was all over.

* * *

Sinklar walked down the corridor, passing men and women in spacer's whites. Unlike most of *Chrysla,* the gun deck had a busy feel to it, vibrant and warmer than the rest of the ship. Of course, people lived here, but even so, the atmosphere still carried that scent of professionalism.

Sinklar located 176-B and touched the lock plate. "Adze? You there? It's Sink."

The hatch slipped sideways to produce a black-skinned woman. African, Sinklar noted with smug satisfaction. She smiled at him and said, "I'm Doreen. I bunk with Adze. She's down a level in the CS. She should be finished soon. You might go on down."

"The CS?"

"Combat Simulator. It's a virtual reality teaching machine. Keeps us tuned up." She gave him a wry grin. "You wouldn't want to forget what a blaster bolt feels like when it crackles past your ear."

"Thanks."

Sinklar glanced back and forth, trying to orient himself.

Doreen hooked a thumb back the way he'd come. "About sixty meters back that way you'll find a lift that will take you down. When you step out, take a left and proceed about one hundred and eighty meters. The CS is behind the double doors on the right.''

''Thanks again.''

As close as Sinklar could figure, Doreen might have measured it with an EDM. She could have called fire data for Shiksta's ordnance any minute of the day.

''Wonder if she wants a job?''

He palmed one of the doors on the CS open and entered a room lined with gear. A tech specialist sat behind a desk, glancing up curiously.

She lifted an eyebrow suspiciously. ''I don't know you.''

''Sinklar Fist. I'm . . . Uh, I guess I'd have to introduce myself. I'm with Staffa . . . er, the Lord Commander.''

''Lord Fist,'' the woman told him. ''What can I do for you?''

''First off, call me Sinklar. I'm no Lord. Second, could you tell me where to find STU Adze?''

''She's still under the helmet.'' The woman looked down. ''She might be there a while. It looks like the computer smacked her with a random.''

''A random?''

''Training exercise. Sometimes the computer switches the rules in mid-exercise. It's a random action designed to keep these lazy sots from outguessing the computer for combat solutions.''

''Sounds pretty serious.''

The tech grinned. ''I've seen raw recruits leave here with leaking pants. It's real enough. Come on, I'll show you.''

She took him back into the hallway beyond the desk, then into a large booth with countless screens on the walls. Most were blank but three depicted scenes of violent combat. The tech pointed to a screen on the lower right. ''That's Adze.''

Sinklar studied the situation. Virtual reality reproduced the sounds, smells, and other sensations of a different environment. For training soldiers, it seemed like a wonderful alternative to the butchery his First Targan had survived.

The view was evidently from Adze's helmet, seeing what she would see. Stats on the side of the screen listed the enemy as Imperial Regan forces. The terrain appeared to be Targan. Adze was directing a Special Tactics Unit toward a low rise upon which a fortified position had been established. From the symbols, Sinklar determined that it was a full Section she faced.

Covering fire was being provided by four members of her team who were inching their way up the middle of a rocky valley while Adze was attempting to flank the position with the rest of her unit.

"Good tactical position," Sinklar noted. "But she needs to slip at least one more flanker over the ridge."

The tech glanced at him. "Tell her."

Sinklar shot her an uneasy glance. "Won't it mess up the exercise?"

"The idea is to learn. To try things here so you don't have to make it up when it's for real." She handed him a small microphone. "Go for it. Let's see what you're made of."

Lifting it to his lips, he said, "Adze, send a flanker across the ridge. Your left is vulnerable if they've got a Group in standard deployment."

"Who's this?"

"Your mother. Do you want to do it or leave your left and, pretty soon, your rear open to a flanking attack."

"Chandra, break left over the ridge. See if we've got trouble."

" 'Firmative," a voice called.

Adze continued to work her way rock by rock, calling orders to her Special Tactics Unit as they crawled forward. The Regan fire continued to rake the gully where the four marksmen wiggled from one bit of cover to another to snipe at the position.

"Adze?" Chandra's voice rang out. "We've got a Group over here! So far they're just sitting."

"Pus Rot it! All right, *Mom*, what's next?"

Sinklar looked at the tech.

"Go ahead," she said. "That was a good call."

Into the mike, Sinklar ordered. "What kind of heavy stuff do you have?"

"Grav-mounted four-man blaster. It's set up a half klick behind me. If the Regans stick their heads up or sally, I can pound them back into their holes."

"Does Chandra have a flare set?"

"Affirmative."

"Order her to deck that Group with a ring of flares."

"What for? Flares can't hurt anyone."

"You'll never win a war gabbing, Adze. Burn that position with flares. After that, don't worry about it, but leave Chandra where she is to keep track of them. If they start to move, drop another flare on them."

"You're out of your mind." Then: "Chandra, shoot flares at the Regan Group."

" 'Firmative."

The tech glanced at Sinklar and made an "ok" with her thumb and forefinger.

Adze had reached a position from which she could control the side of the knoll where the Regan Section had dug in. The four snipers in the gully continued to shoot. The Regans shot back.

Adze ordered her heavy blaster to pound the position, and at the same time, she charged forward, deftly enfilading the knoll.

Chandra's voice called, "The Group is trying to move."

"Hit them with mama's flare."

" 'Firmative. They've dropped back again."

Sinklar winked at the tech. "Works every time."

"How do you know that?"

"Whoever programmed your machine read the Holy Gawdamn book."

"You've done this before."

"Yeah, a time or two."

Adze had her team close enough by this time so that they could rake the trenches with enfilading fire.

"Adze, you've got them," Sinklar crowed. "If you drop onto their battle comm frequency and call for a surrender, the Section First should go ahead and give up. Section twenty-six, paragraph eight. Quote him that page and you won't have to kill any more of them—or risk your people further. Then bug out. As soon as you get them out of the trenches, get off that knoll and down into the valley beyond."

"And why is that, Mother?"

"Because that knoll will be ripe for Regan orbital retaliation."

"What makes you think they've got orbital?"

"Do you want to bet your life on it?"

"Like I said, I'm headed for the valley."

At that, the screen went blank, the comm pronouncing, "Exercise fifteen one seven is now concluded. Hard copy evaluation will be available with equipment check in."

"Come on," the tech said, leading Sinklar back into the hallway and to the reception room.

Minutes later, a flushed Adze appeared in the doorway, the oversized helmet in her hand. She took a copy of the printout as she handed the tech the cumbersome helmet, barely reacted as she noticed Sinklar.

"Hello, Mom."

"Have a nice war?"

The tech crossed her arms. "How'd you know that flanking Group wouldn't advance against simple flares?"

Sinklar shrugged. "The Regan manual says that no unit will redeploy in the presence of enemy marker flares. They naturally assume that a marker flare means incipient bombardment by heavy ordnance. No one with any sense is going to jump out of his hole with a grav shot coming down the pipe. Four guys with flare guns can immobilize an entire Section."

"If they're working by the book," Adze said thoughtfully. "That's how you knew there would be a Group on the other side of that hill."

"It's a standard defensive deployment."

Adze pulled a wet strand of hair back, her mischievous smile exposing those straight white teeth. "What are you doing here?"

He took her arm. "Come on, we're going to talk. Something about this partnership you're interested in."

The sparkle animated her eyes. "Sounds good." As they stepped out into the corridor, she shoved her hands into her belt, long black hair swinging with each step. "So what's the decision?"

"Staffa thinks you're decidedly bright and insufferably ambitious. It's his opinion that you're manipulative, and he immediately wanted to know what you were trying to talk me into. Oh, and he also mentioned that you were convinced of your own invincibility."

"And what is your opinion?" Her eyes had hardened.

"I agree with him wholeheartedly."

"I see. Does Staffa always do your thinking for you?"

"No. But I listen very carefully to what he has to say.

Curiously enough, he seems to believe that you and the Wing Commander have a lot of personality traits in common. According to him, she was every bit as insufferably determined to make something out of herself as you seem to be."

The corners of her mouth quirked impishly. "I'm not the only one who's insufferable. The only flares you're shooting are full of hot air." She jerked a thumb over her shoulder. "But we made a pretty good team back there."

"Welcome to the future."

She slowed, tapping the deck with an inquisitive toe. "What did you find out about going through the Forbidden Borders? Who is Staffa detailing that to?"

"Us. All of us. If you're interested, you'd better have a long talk with your folks. You may not be coming home anytime soon."

"Provided we can break the Forbidden Borders."

"That does remain one of the few unknowns."

She took his arm in hers, starting forward again. "All right, who's going to tell Mhitshul? You or me?"

Sinklar chuckled to himself. "You know, if it had been me in charge of that Regan Section, you'd have been chewed to chowder before you got halfway up that valley."

"No way, pal."

"It's all right, Adze. Don't get so defensive. Even the Wing Commander had a thing or two to learn before Staffa could turn her loose."

"The day will come, Sinklar Fist, when I will feed that back to you and make you chew it!"

"That's fine. I'm only after your ideas—not your cooking."

At that moment, his belt comm buzzed. Sinklar pressed the stud. "Sinklar Fist."

Staffa's voice carried a sense of urgency. "I need to see you in the conference room right now. Ark and I need to pick your brain about Ily and her assassin. Takka and Fera have penetrated Itreata—and I don't think it's going to be pleasant when we find her."

* * *

"I don't understand it!" Ily jumped from the chair that stood before the desk monitor and paced back and forth. Comm equipment studded the entire wall of the main room. In the holo tanks inset in the walls, scenes of different planets were presented, giving the room an airy and spacious appearance.

"Understand what?" Arta asked as she walked through the arch that led to the rear of the curiously simple living quarters. The Seddi assassin placed hands on her shapely hips, flaunting her naked body.

Ily glanced distastefully at her and shook her head. "Why are you still screwing him?"

Arta laughed, then danced across the room, muscles playing under the honey tones of her skin. "Because, dear Ily, it tortures him. He knows that I'm not his Chrysla. He hates me so desperately he can't stand it, and all I have to do is run the tip of my finger around his testicles and he can't stop the erection."

Arta cocked her head, an amused smile on her lips. "Do you know what that does to him? He's a psychologist, and his penis continues to defy his brain. Each time I bring him to orgasm—if you'll excuse the pun—is like turning a burning screw a little deeper into his soul . . . and he can't do a Rotted thing about it. Exquisite, don't you think?"

Ily sighed and shook her head, attention returning to the monitors. Reports flowed across different screens, the security officers talking back and forth, desperation in their voices.

"I don't understand. They should be falling apart! Comm itself should be flickering and failing. Instead, if anything, the system seems to be stabilizing."

Arta walked over, placing an arm around Ily's shoulders as she stared thoughtfully at the data on the screen. STO Wheeler was issuing instructions again. Commander Delshay, violet eyes gleaming, was arguing back, punctuating her words with a clenched fist.

"The confusion got us in here," Arta reminded. "Even if it only lasted for a couple of hours before they caught it, it was enough to paralyze their security precautions. Without a major comm malfunction, I don't think you could have picked the lock on *that* door." She hooked a thumb at the double-layered sialon and graphsteel hatch with its extensive security monitors.

"Perhaps," Ily mumbled, tapping her teeth with a

thumbnail. "Rot you, Arta, go shower. You smell like the sheets in a cheap Sylenian brothel."

Fera chuckled before she bent to kiss Ily on the lips and then skipped away to dance back across the room.

The weight of the universe was descending around them, and Arta, if anything, appeared more relaxed than Ily had ever seen her. Ily noted movement out of the corner of her eye and wheeled to study the door comm. An armed group of shining STU trotted through the hallway beyond. Two of the armed personnel dropped off to take up positions on either side of the door. The others then proceeded down the hallway.

Heart pounding, Ily tiptoed to the heavy door, pressing the audio.

". . . wouldn't come up here anyway," the first STU grumbled.

"So relax, it's cake duty. We stand here and bore ourselves to death staring up and down the hallway. All we have to worry about is tired feet. Think about the guys crawling through the ventilation system—or maybe the sewer plant. Now that would be a wonderful assignment, don't you think?"

Ily cut the connection, wearily relieved. If anything, it increased their safety. She'd made the objective in time. Arta was right, the comm dysfunction had lasted long enough—just barely. Despite the fact that she hadn't permanently damaged Itreata, she'd reached her desired position. Ily's pulse had settled back to normal. If they were safe anywhere on Itreata, it would be here.

A muffled groan sounded from beyond the arch and Ily crossed the room, passed through the dining area, and stuck her head into the bedroom. On the plush sleeping platform, Andray Sornsen lay flat on his back, naked and bound. Arta's preferred way.

"Happy, Professor?" Ily asked as she crossed her arms and leaned against the arched doorway.

"Why do you let her act like . . . like . . ."

"A wanton? Because she is. The Seddi trained her to be the perfect sexual magnet. Etarian Priestesses taught her the arts of love at the Temple in Etarus. It was the Seddi, however, who conditioned her brain to kill after sex. I broke the conditioning, which allows more plasticity of behavior, but she's still a single-purpose weapon."

"She's an animal."

"Perhaps, but she's my animal, and she's Rotted good at what she does. Stop complaining, Professor. As long as you continue to amuse her, you'll stay alive. The Blessed Gods alone know how long we'll have to wait here until Staffa arrives, so make the best of it. Close your eyes, believe she's Chrysla. You've loved her for years, haven't you?"

"Do you know what an experiment in deviance the two of you would make?"

"Spare me your study, Professor. I'll tell you exactly what motivates me: Power, pure, raw, and simple. All else is illusion so far as I am concerned. I've spent my life in pursuit of power, and I will continue to until I die. It's my obsession, and I don't care to change now, thank you."

"Don't you care that you've become a—"

"I know what I've become. You, with all of your studying, can tell me nothing I haven't already heard—and in more impassioned voices than yours, believe me. I've been branded everything from gutter slime to a vile demon even the Rotted Gods would fear. Frankly, I don't care if you or the entirety of Free Space know that I'm the most despicable and depraved bitch ever born."

Andray Sornsen turned his head away.

Ily snorted her derision and walked the length of the quarters back to the comm-cluttered wall. Monitors displayed a search in progress somewhere in the science section. Armed men and women were proceeding across a huge warehouse filled with crates. In another monitor, a Special Tactics Unit was inching its way across the floor in the psychology lab, each person taking samples of dust with sticky tape or plucking hairs from the corners. As if they needed more data. They knew that Itreata had been penetrated, and by whom.

I did it, Staffa. Where are you, Lord Commander? When are you going to arrive here and see that you might have won a round or two, but the final victory will be mine.

Yes, power was its own elixir, and once Staffa had paid for the setback he'd dealt her, Ily Takka would be free to begin again.

Ily glanced at the door monitors, seeing the two armed

STU standing at attention in the hallway. *Assuming I live through it.*

"How do you like it?" Arta asked.

Ily turned, startled. Arta Fera walked out in the snowy white suit of armor she'd picked off one of the chairs. Now she modeled it, turning gracefully and walking forward, a saucy swing to her hips.

"It's not quite your look," Ily decided.

"The chest is much too tight." Arta stopped to catch her reflection in one of the mirrors, "And the legs and sleeves are a little long."

"Gold is definitely your color."

Arta smiled. "Perhaps next time I'll try the gray. Not for style, mind you, but just to get an idea of the feel."

CHAPTER XL

I am writing this in my last hours as a free man. Maybe in my last hours as a living man, now that I consider it. I know how much of the Lord Commander's labor and resources have gone into this project. We've practically stripped Itreata of materials and personnel to build *Countermeasures*. A *lot* of wealth has been invested to make this machine work. Knowing the extent of the responsibility, we've driven ourselves half mad and followed every detail in the construction schematics.

I mentioned the outside interference we were worried about. That's the key I guess. We didn't have any way of shutting the ship off. No on/off switch. Normally that happens through computer command, not a physical switch to open a circuit or isolate a command.

The message came almost without warning: EVACUATE THIS VESSEL IMMEDIATELY. ANY PERSONNEL WHO DO NOT EVACUATE IMMEDIATELY WILL BE UNABLE TO WITHSTAND THE RADIATION AND ELECTROMAGNETIC FORCES UNLEASHED BY A FULL TEST OF THIS SYSTEM.

Immediately thereafter, the reactors began to build and the whole ship began to hum. We didn't have the time or ability to stop it. Had we stayed, we'd have been fried like insects in a capacitor.

Everyone got clear and, from a distance, we watched as the ship did its self-test. Everything seemed to be working. Nothing arced, crackled, or spat sparks. The readings, even from our space dock one hundred kilometers away are incredible.

. . . And then *Countermeasures* began moving. We didn't control it, I swear to the Holy Blessed Gods. It started moving on its own, and let me tell you, with that many reactors and that much thrust, it can really go. Nothing available to us here can catch it.

I've tried to call Itreata, but they've got some sort of major problem and keep relaying me to a Comm Second somewhere.

Someone just stole the Lord Commander's most secret weapon–and no one seems to care but me! I'm going to die because of this!

–Excerpt from Dee Wall's personal journal

* * *

History had been made. A Regan battle cruiser lay moored to Companion tethers, her lock matched to one of the skyhooks that tied the Companion fleet to its base. In all previous instances foreign warships had been ordered to wait on the peripheries of the Itreatic system, the diplomats and dignitaries lightered in on launches or shuttles for reasons of security.

Skyla considered that sobering reality as she stepped from *Gyton*'s cramped green interior into the familiar domed foyer of the umbilical skyhook. Tactite windows curved on either side of the lift door opposite the lock and created a startling vista of the rocky shadowed surface of Itreata. Speckles of light marked the location of installations on the moon's black, cratered surface six kilometers below.

"Wow!" Lark gasped as she stepped out and stared at the view through the window. "How does it work?"

Skyla pressed a button to summon one of the lifts, then pointed. "Graphite cables rise from the moon's bedrock to tether the ship. Angular momentum and gravity equal each other just below this point. As a result, a ship can be placed just beyond geosynchronous orbit, always straining the tethers slightly but firmly held in place without oscillations. We're currently in what is called the umbilical dome. A lift will carry us down to a large bay about a kilometer underground."

Chrysla appeared from *Gyton*'s hatch, followed by an antigrav med unit maneuvered by two med techs.

"It takes a while for the lift," Skyla responded to Chrysla's questioning look. "It's a seven kilometer ride."

''All set?'' Rysta Braktov asked as she leaned against the hatch.

''Thank you for a safe and pleasant ride,'' Skyla told her. ''You've always got a port on Itreata.''

Rysta slipped a toe back and forth on the deck. ''When you catch her down there, break a bone or two for me, will you?''

''I'll send you a hank of her hair,'' Skyla promised.

At that, the doors opened.

''There's our ride, Commander. Quantum Gods, don't let her get aboard.''

''I won't.''

Skyla took Rysta's hand and gave it a firm grip as Chrysla orchestrated the placement of the med unit and people into the available space in the lift.

''Beats hell out of the time we met over Targa, doesn't it?''

''There's that word again!'' Rysta smiled and winked. ''Keep me informed. If you need anything, we're right up here.''

''We will—and don't shoot at Staffa. He'll be making orbit in a couple of hours. *Chrysla* is the big triangular ship, just so your targeting comp doesn't make a mistake.''

''You wish,'' Rysta growled as Skyla stepped into the lift and pressed the button to start in on the long drop.

Lark was staring about skeptically. ''Not very big, is it?''

''Larger objects, like bulky parts, are lifted on an external freight lift.''

The drop to Itreata came with no sensation of falling. In the silence, Skyla composed her thoughts. No trace of Ily or Arta had been discovered in nearly a week of intensive searching. Entire sections of Itreata had been literally turned upside down. Security was functioning at an all-time frenzy—and had produced nothing.

Chrysla's hand rested on the polished surface of the white medical unit as she stared sadly down at the big case. Why did they have to make the damn things look so similar to coffins?

Lark stood with her hands behind her back, green eyes focused on a distant view only she could see.

With each second, Skyla dropped closer to Ily, Arta, and the final confrontation.

"Worried?" Chrysla asked.

Skyla shrugged. "What's their objective? Roberta reports that the comm sabotage didn't work. Myles caught it and countered it immediately. We've got the place crawling. The atmosphere plant, the computers, the water system, power generation, everything is surrounded by Delshay's people, and they're ready to shoot on sight. What can Ily and Arta do? How can they harm us?"

"Security was essentially blindfolded by the virus. Those two could have gone anywhere."

Skyla squinted, her only visible reaction to her growing unease. "Everything is operating satisfactorily. If they meant to strike, their ability has been severely blunted. Security monitored their arrival. No weapons, no explosives, nothing was brought into Itreata."

"Except that comm virus."

"All right, one data cube. Ily inserted it into the system, and Roma, coupled with the Mag Comm, scuttled it."

The lift opened to a receiving area behind a line of loading docks. White walls rose above gray concrete. Squat tractors—now unattended—waited silently in front of their strings of flatbed cars. Beyond the dock stretched a huge, well-lit manufacturing and repair facility sporting overhead cranes, machinery, and conveyors.

"When the ships are in, you can hardly hear down here. Each of the ships has a support base like this one," Skyla explained to Lark. "After a fight, assuming we can get the vessel home, we can completely rebuild a warship from null singularity dome to bounce-back collars. A crew will drop *Rega One* down to the surface for a complete refit."

"It's grown since the last time I was here," Chrysla added as STUs approached from all sides.

A woman in gleaming armor stepped from the knot of armed security personnel and slapped a fist to her breastbone. "Wing Commander, welcome back to Itreata."

"I wish it were under better circumstance, STO. Allow me to introduce Lady Chrysla Marie Attenasio, my assistant, Lark Gaust, and these medical techs are from *Gyton.*" Skyla indicated the STO, "This is Roberta Wheeler, head of Itreata Security."

Wheeler asked, "And the med unit?"

"Division First Ben MacRuder. I think you have instructions regarding him?"

Wheeler made a gesture and two of her STU sprang forward, immediately beginning the process of checking the antigrav unit and its readouts.

Skyla added, "You can continue your security checks on the way to the hospital. The Division First is in critical need of medical attention. Hospital was briefed on our way in."

Chrysla started to follow Mac as he was maneuvered away, but was restrained by Skyla's hand. "You can't help him now. I need you with me for the moment." To Wheeler, Skyla added, "We have a couple of hours until the Lord Commander arrives. Why don't we proceed to your office. You can update me on the situation here. In the meantime, have Logistics contact Commander Braktov, assist her in any way she desires and accommodate any refitting *Gyton* might need."

"Yes, ma'am."

Skyla led the way to one of several lifts that studded the wall just around the corner from the umbilical foyer.

As they stepped inside, Skyla ordered, "Itreata Security." To Lark, she explained, "Itreata is served by a complex lift system. You need only enter and announce your destination. The lift will automatically route itself, avoid traffic and congestion, and drop you as closely as possible to your destination."

The faint sensation of movement could be felt. When she looked over, Lark still had that pensive frown, and Chrysla was fumbling with the margins of the cape she'd adopted. STO Wheeler had an exhausted and pinched expression on her face. But then, the worst security violation in Itreatic history had happened right under her nose.

And I could have stopped it. Skyla chewed at the inside of her cheek. Irritation with herself churned acidly in her stomach. Staffa would be setting foot on Itreata in a matter of hours, to find what? *He placed the greatest trust in me—and I failed him.*

Ily Takka, loose in Itreata, would be like a dagger in Staffa's heart. Itreata had been the only warren, the safe refuge, and now it had been violated. Skyla's fists clenched until they ached.

The door made a sucking sound as it slipped sideways

and Skyla led the way to the Security Center, now guarded by armored Companions.

Salutes were snapped out as they entered the receiving office. Through the tactite windows, she could see the security personnel working at their monitors. Holders by the chairs held cups of stassa and klav, each bearing rings around the inside. Apparently everyone was working overtime—and pushing the limits.

"What do we know?" Skyla asked as she whirled and faced Wheeler.

The STO drew a deep breath and then shook her head. "Nothing, I'm afraid. They, along with Professor Sornsen, have vanished. It's as if they stepped through a doorway—and disappeared."

* * *

Sinklar would rather have stayed and watched the mooring of the huge battleship to the tethers, than be standing in the lift, dropping for Itreata. The future, however, appeared to hold plenty of opportunities to watch *Slap, Jinx Mistress,* and some of the other ships in the Companion fleet arrive.

Sinklar caught Adze's attention on him and gave her a reassuring wink. Since her transfer to his staff, her schedule had included a crash course from Ryman Ark on special security. Now she stood there, shining in the mirror brightness from her plated armor. The mischievous sparkle in her dark eyes had vanished, as if putting on the armor had transformed her from woman to fighting machine.

Staffa stood across from him, tension visible in those steely gray eyes. This homecoming should have been different, a celebration—not just another round in the ceaseless battle.

Sinklar watched the gray-gloved hands move restlessly, reflecting Staffa's preoccupation. Skyla awaited him at the bottom of the lift. That reunion, too, was shattered. Instead of a private and intimate occasion, they would face each other in the midst of a crowd, each aware of the danger that lurked within their corridors.

Sinklar had struggled to help. As they had approached Itreata, he and Staffa had wrung their brains dry as they tried to anticipate Ily's strategy. In the end, faced with the countering of the comm sabotage, Sinklar had been forced to admit: "I can think of only one reason for her to sneak into Itreata . . . revenge."

"I was afraid you'd mention that." Staffa had sat with his hands steepled, eyes unfocused. "That day on Etarus when she brought Kaylla and me in from the desert . . . I slapped her. Split her lip. I can still hear the acid in her voice. *'Die, Staffa,'* and she triggered the collar command again and again. All the time she was telling me how she'd set it up, would make it look like the Sassans had killed me."

Sinklar had bowed his head, remembering a day on Rega when Ily had stepped close to lift his pistol from his belt—triumph glittering savagely in her black eyes. Yes, she could hate. "Let's face it. Staffa, you destroyed her success. She would have been Empress except for your arrival above Rega. You snatched it all away in her moment of victory. Years of hard work, scheming, and intrigue were suddenly meaningless, wasted years."

"She took Skyla from me. I warned her, over and over—told her what I'd do. She drove me to strike. What did she think? That she could abduct my Wing Commander and pay no price? That's insane!"

"She's not insane. Obsessed is a better word. She's been living her plots and assassinations for so long she's forgotten any other reality." Sinklar had stared absently at the work table before them. "I don't know Itreata. With the comm sabotage failed, what could she do? Where could she have gone?"

Ryman Ark's eyes had narrowed as they talked. The STO had shot a look at Adze that Sinklar didn't understand—some secret communication.

Staffa hadn't said anything after that. His thoughts had focused on something deep in his memory. He had looked just the way he did now as the lift dropped him into Itreata.

Sinklar didn't even feel the lift stop. The door slid to the side and admitted them to a giant underground factory and warehouse. Before he had a chance to look around, Wing Commander Lyma stepped forward from a group of people. She looked as regally beautiful in her snowy white armor as he remembered her. Like an ice tiger, she stood balanced, white-blonde hair tightly braided and coiled about her left shoulder. Those frosty blue eyes sought Staffa's, and, for a moment, the two faced each other, trying to say so much with just a glance.

To alleviate the awkwardness, Sinklar searched the reception committee, hesitated at the sight of those eyes, and broke rank, saying, "Chrysla, it's good to see you again. How's Mac?"

His mother gave him a smile, intuitively understanding his purpose. "I'm not really sure yet. The preliminary reports are that he's going to be all right. They won't have him out on training exercises in the coming months, but they believe they can repair what was broken. Within a couple of months he should be as good as new."

Staffa had recovered himself, taking Skyla's arm in a proprietary way as he started forward, asking, "Any word on Ily?"

"None," Skyla told him crisply, but to Sinklar it looked like she'd gone so brittle she might shatter.

Staffa gave Chrysla a warm smile, dropping his voice. "I didn't catch all that you said about Mac."

"There may be some difficult days ahead, but I think we'll make it."

"Give him my blessings," Staffa responded seriously.

Sinklar noted the message in the glance Chrysla returned. "He would probably appreciate it if you gave them in person."

Adze, with her usual acumen, had slipped up close behind Sinklar, staying slightly to his right as they proceeded past the clustered STU and security officers. In the crowd, Sinklar could see Ryman Ark whispering into his mouth comm, eyes shifting warily back and forth.

Sinklar only caught a glimpse of the huge room as they broke through the security cordon. Here and there, armored STU could be seen as they walked around equipment or studied the room through electronically augmented senses from the huge overhead cranes. Security was tight enough to squeak.

Around the corner from the umbilical base, the nucleus of the party stepped into yet another lift, this one more spacious. A young woman with big green eyes seemed to be sticking to the Wing Commander, awestruck as she gazed first at Staffa, and then at Sinklar. Adze responded by instinctively placing herself between Sink and the girl.

"It's my fault that all of this happened," Staffa told Skyla when the doors had closed. "I should have forwarded the tapes to Rob for analysis after we raided Ily's Ministry."

Skyla shook her head. "It's *my* fault, Staffa. I knew deep down inside how she'd react. It was even plaguing my dreams."

"You are all welcome to blame each other," Chrysla noted dryly, "but do we have a destination?"

Staffa glanced at Skyla, who seemed tense enough to explode. "My quarters. We all need to clear the air on some personal matters before we discuss the situation concerning Ily. After everyone understands the same reality, we can compare notes and formulate a strategy."

Skyla seemed to shake the emotional paralysis that had gripped her. "The problem is that she could have gone to ground anywhere. Her behavior on Terguz, for example, included seducing a man and accessing whatever she wanted. So far, only Andray Sornsen is missing, and we haven't found his body yet."

"Body?" Staffa asked.

"Arta Fera mutilates her victims," the green-eyed girl supplied.

"I'm Staffa kar Therma," he extended his hand.

"Lark Gaust, sir." She seemed on the verge of trembling as she shook his hand. "I'm the Wing Commander's assistant."

Staffa glanced curiously at Skyla.

She seemed completely unaware that she'd missed the introduction. Instead, she'd gone still, locked in thought, those hard blue eyes staring at something an infinity away.

To avoid an awkward silence, Sinklar said, "We have to keep something in mind. Ily always plans for any contingency. While she takes an opportunity when it arises, her actions are always deliberate, plotted several moves in advance. She didn't just decide to come to Itreata and play it by ear."

"But what would the objective be?" Chrysla asked. "If we knew that, we might be able to anticipate her movements."

"Revenge." Sinklar met those amber eyes that shivered

his soul. "Believe me. I've—" the words stuck in his throat—"been her intimate. I know how she works. One moment she had an entire empire for her own. In the next, her empire was destroyed, and she was running for her life—a homeless fugitive. All that she had built was a smoking ruin. How much motivation is that?"

Chrysla nodded thoughtfully. "Enough for most people. Probably more than enough for Ily. She has an addictive, obsessive personality, doesn't she?"

Sinklar nodded, struggling to see past those amber eyes to a different identity from the one lurking in his memory. "I think, without stretching it, you could add, sybaritic, nymphomaniac, sadistic, cruel, egomaniacal, abusive, and manipulative—but I'm a better optimist than I am a psychologist so I might have missed one or two of her less charming traits."

The lift had slowed imperceptibly and both Ark and Adze had shifted to the front. As the door opened, they stepped out into the hallway, each taking a direction, scanning with all of their augmented senses, before Ark made a gesture that all was clear.

Sinklar had expected something a bit more elaborate than a featureless white corridor. Square light panels overhead sent soft light over polished tile work. The only interruption was an occasional wall comm terminal. Ark had taken a position in front, advancing warily, his shoulder blaster at half-rise combat-carry. Adze had fallen in behind, walking backward as she covered the rear with her weapon.

Two STU stood before a single door unobtrusively set in the wall. They snapped to attention as the party approached.

Ark glanced at each, asking, "What have you got for me?"

"Nothing, STO. A couple of our teams have passed but that's the extent of it. The room is secure."

Staffa stepped forward, palming the lock plate. As the door opened, he laid a hand on Ark's shoulder. "Ryman, I need to speak with Skyla, Sinklar, and Chrysla for a moment. I'll call you as soon as we've finished."

"Staffa, at least let me—"

"It's personal, Ryman." Staffa smiled, lifting an eyebrow. "Family business, understand?"

Ark relented, chopping out a salute. "We'll await your call, Lord Commander."

Sinklar gave a nod to Adze. She flashed him a look of protest but gestured her acceptance.

"Lark, wait out here for me," Skyla added and stepped past Staffa into the room.

Sinklar followed his father into a rather orthodox looking room. After the ostentatious display of the quarters aboard *Chrysla,* and the palaces he'd seen on Rega, this was plain. One wall was entirely devoted to comm monitors, each glowing with a different view of Itreata, showing the efforts underway to locate Ily and Arta. The rest of the room was tastefully done in white, holo niches displaying different scenes of planets and stars.

Staffa stepped into the center of the room and gestured to the gravity chairs. "Please, let's sit down and discuss a couple of things—iron out our personal problems. From there, we can attack the future."

Skyla still looked withdrawn and perplexed.

Staffa placed his hands on her shoulders, staring into her eyes. "Are you all right?"

She nodded, lip pinched by white teeth, eyes still vacant. "It's . . . I'm missing something important. You know, hanging on the edge of my mind." Then she smiled and melted into his arms. "Rot, how I've missed you."

He kissed her, hugging her close. "And I, you. I've been worried sick. I wanted to run off and find you, rescue you like you did me. But I just couldn't. You understand, don't you?"

She nodded. "You saved us, Lord Commander. I'm proud of you."

"So am I," Chrysla added from where she'd taken a chair across from Sinklar. "You've done well, Staffa."

Still holding Skyla tightly against him, he gave Chrysla a searching look. "Have you and Mac talked about what you want to do? Where you want to go?"

Chrysla seemed surprisingly self-possessed as she shook her head. "We haven't. That, like most things, will work itself out according to the choreography of time and events. Do you have something in mind?"

Staffa shrugged. "From the reports Kaylla sent, you did very well on Ashtan. Does Mac like administration?"

"He hates it—but he's very good at it." Chrysla steepled her fingers. "He's the kind of person we should be looking for. He cares about people."

"Good. Kaylla will need your help."

"What about you, Staffa?" Chrysla asked.

"Sinklar and I are leaving Free Space for a while—that is, assuming the Mag Comm can break the Forbidden Borders."

Skyla shifted, reaching up with one hand to touch his cheek. "Leaving?"

Staffa took her hands in his, a warmth in his gray eyes as he studied her. "The people don't need me. From here on out, it's going to be a race with the Others—the aliens who trapped us here. The time has come for humanity to forget the Star Butcher." He paused. "What's the matter?"

Skyla shook her head. "Something . . . that haunting feeling that I'm forgetting something. About the dream . . ."

"Go on." Chrysla had stiffened in her chair.

Skyla studied the heavy hatch. "The doorway. Ily passing through it. You know, when she takes on my identity and looks back with Arta's eyes glowing in her head?"

"Yes . . . yes," Chrysla prodded.

"It's . . ." Skyla cocked her head. "It's Staffa's door!" She pointed. "That's the door she steps through."

Despite feeling totally lost, Sinklar experienced a sudden chill.

"You heard the STU posted outside," Staffa said, grasping the substance if not the nuances of Skyla's account. "The room has been secured. Still, come on, we'll search it if you like."

"That won't be necessary," Ily said from the arched doorway. A heavy service blaster, one of Staffa's from the look of it, filled her small hand. "And the first one of you who moves will be shot down on the spot." A smile crossed her lips as her black eyes gleamed. "And with a great deal of personal pleasure, I might add."

Arta Fera moved on cat feet as she slipped past Ily—military blaster in hand—to flank the room.

Sinklar's heart skipped as he stood. "Ily, this isn't Rega. It won't work out this time."

Ily stepped up to him, the saucy smile of triumph hearkening back to other days. With nimble fingers, she plucked his pistol from his belt and tossed it back into the other room.

"Ah, but it will. Just like last time. Yes, Sinklar, I can see understanding dawning. You know, I can still read you like a book. You really should work on that." She reached up, running her fingers down the side of his face. "You could still come be my lover. Interested?"

"Not in the slightest." The realization flashed through him. She always planned three moves ahead. *Rotted Gods, she has a way out of here. She's going to get away with it!*

Skyla Lyma made a whimpering sound, dropping to her knees, arms reaching out to Arta. "Please . . . please, Arta . . . I did what you asked . . . don't . . . don't hurt me . . ."

Completely in control, Ily gave the whimpering Skyla an amused look as she walked over to Staffa. Deft fingers removed his pistol and she threw it through the arch. "It's good to see you again, Lord Commander. You look, and smell, a great deal better than you did in the desert."

And with that, she slapped Staffa in the face with the heavy blaster.

CHAPTER XLI

For the purpose of the common good, this body of law has been developed, that all human beings, no matter their station or status, be both recognized and bound by these truths. Let the law govern not only the individual but the group, the population, the state, and the species. Be it known by these statements that fundamental human dignity must be our goal through the application of the law, that law should not, and will not, replace the concept of justice, of just action, and moral responsibility. Instead, let it be the rule and guide by which we define our actions and behaviors with regard to each other, that all may be assured of protection of their person, properties, and ideals so long as they do not infringe upon those of others. Let us understand that law is not meant to be totalitarian or inflexible, but must change with the needs of the people, and must reflect the social reality, and must act for the good of the people.

Therefore, let the law be equal unto all, and may justice be pursued swiftly, and to the full extent merited, for predators cannot be allowed to prey upon the people, and any society which allows itself to be preyed upon cannot maintain itself. Those who knowingly commit criminal actions forfeit their rights to protection under the law.

And be it known that throughout human history it has been to the benefit of the state to manipulate the law for its own perpetuation and to the deprivation of the people. That practice shall cease with the ratification of this document. Know, therefore, these laws, and take them as the means of defining your responsibility to each other. May the tyrant, or the predator upon you, be punished as is deemed just by victims and within the bounds of the law.

–Preamble to the Uniform Legal Code
Sinklar Fist:5782:06:30:20:38

* * *

Lights shot through Staffa's head as Ily's blow landed. He staggered, tasting blood. Through slitted eyes, he stared at her, hatred welling as his knees bent and his weight shifted to the balls of his feet. Arta Fera, amber gaze burning, had leveled her weapon, daring him to react.

"Staffa?" Ily asked. "Do you remember? Pay-backs are sheer hell, aren't they? And that's only the beginning of what I owe you. The next few hours are going to be very difficult for you . . . I promise."

"No," Skyla continued to whimper and clutched at his leg, hugging him. "No, Arta. I was good."

Ily snatched Skyla's weapon and stepped back, a smirk on her face as she watched. The Wing Commander glared fearfully at Arta Fera, tears leaking from her wide eyes as she cowered.

Ily shook her head, pointing down at Skyla with disgust in her eyes. "And you loved this . . . this . . ."

Chrysla rose from her chair, stately, poised. "What did you expect? Give me a collar, Minister Takka, and I can make a whimpering wreck out of you, too. But then, you'd know that, wouldn't you?" Chrysla turned, approaching Fera with slow steps, a frown on her face. "You were cloned from me. But you're not me."

They stood facing each other, two perfect copies of the same startlingly beautiful woman.

Arta shook her head slowly, "Get back. I'll kill you just as quickly as the others."

Chrysla smiled then, an animalistic gleam coming to her eyes. "Wouldn't it be fun? Just the two of us? We have the same effect on men, you know. Together, we could torment them, let them try and guess which one of us was going to kill them. We could do two at once . . . taking turns, you know?"

Staffa watched in horrid fascination as Chrysla's expression mirrored Arta's. Skyla continued to cling to his thigh, her voice breaking into pitiful pleas mixed with sobs. He couldn't help but reach down to give her a reassuring pat.

"Damn it!" Ily snapped. "Arta! It's a fake! She's using you! Get back! Back, Chrysla, or I'll shoot you right here!"

Arta licked her lips, a slight tremble in her arms. Ily moved quickly, stepping close to Arta, centering her pistol on Chrysla's chest.

"Think about it," Chrysla coaxed, backing slowly, her lips parted slightly.

"You think nothing!" Ily hissed at Arta. "I love you, remember? This woman, she's a fake. She's never given you anything."

Chrysla had settled into a chair, never taking her eyes from Arta's.

"What do you want?" Staffa asked, freeing himself from Skyla's grip. She wailed, wilting onto the floor, weeping. Sinklar had taken it all in, disgust and loathing on his face as he watched Ily.

"I want you, Lord Commander. I want you to pay for everything you've done to me. I offered myself to you—and you turned me down for that semen-dripping Seddi slut. I want her, too. Before we're done, after I've made you hurt for a while, you'll call her here, Staffa. And then I'll have all mine back."

"How do you expect to get out of here?" Staffa crossed his arms, ignoring the blood leaking down his face. Sinklar had managed to back two steps toward the arch and the pistols that lay beyond.

"You will order it." Ily stepped up to him, smiling. "Just before you die." She paused. "You don't have to die, Staffa. Not if you get down and beg me. I'll keep you alive. Maybe even allow Arta to play with you for a while."

Ily glanced across at her assassin. Fera continued to stare into Chrysla's eyes. "Pus Rot it! Arta! Keep an eye on Sinklar! Damn you, Fist! Get back here. Back to that chair you were sitting in! All of you, sit down!"

Staffa shook his head. "I won't do it, Ily. I've done enough harm to people. You didn't have any leverage on me in the desert, and you don't have any here. I can't be coerced."

Ily pointed her pistol at Skyla's head. "I'll kill her. Look at her, Staffa! Broken, sniveling."

And that's what you'd like to do to me, isn't it? He shook his head. "I'm going to stop you, Ily. You can give up now."

She pointed the ugly nozzle of the blaster at Sinklar. "How about your son? You chased halfway across Free Space to find him."

"It won't work," Sinklar said evenly. "I stand with my father. I'd rather die than allow your pollution to be freed again."

"I don't want to die," Chrysla said, her eyes still centered on Arta. "I want to share men, to feel them tense in that final rush of sexual—"

"Shut up!" Ily snarled. She raised her blaster high, ready to slam it down on Chrysla's head.

Arta screamed, shifting her point of aim to Ily. Sinklar had already launched himself at Ily, grabbing her arm. Arta retargeted, trying to get a shot at Sinklar. At that instant, Skyla exploded from the floor, driving herself into Arta Fera, screaming with all the pent up fury of a thousand nightmares.

At the top of her lungs, Chrysla was screaming, "Arta! Help me! *Help me, Arta!*"

Ily pivoted, throwing Sinklar enough off balance so she could drive a knee into his crotch. Twisting, she broke his grip and hammered the pistol into the side of his head.

Staffa had leapt for Ily, but in the confusion only managed to get a handful of her hair. As she fired a shot at Sinklar, Staffa yanked with all of his might.

Ily screamed, and Staffa staggered for balance as a shock of her long black hair pulled free. The shot had missed, blasting a chunk out of the wall. Ily tumbled, recovering, spinning on her side, and shooting.

Staffa shuddered under the impact, and fell, trying to understand what had gone wrong. From the floor, he watched as Ily grinned evilly through the sights centered on his face. "Die, Staffa!"

The crackling blast ripped past Staffa's scalp as Chrysla threw herself onto Ily, spoiling her aim. Chrysla's wild scream augmented her scratching, kicking, and punching as she grappled with Ily for the weapon.

Staffa struggled to rise, only to fall again. *Hit! I'm hit!* A wave of dizziness left him weak, fingers clutching at the carpet.

Chrysla, despite the advantage of position, couldn't hold her own. Ily got a hand around her throat, tightening her grip. With the other hand, she yanked the blaster from Chrysla's clawing fingers.

"No!" Staffa screamed, scrambling awkwardly across the floor.

Chrysla sensed her danger and bucked loose, breaking Ily's choke hold and pitching sideways.

"Stop!" Ily shouted, panting, drawing a bead on Staffa. "Everyone stop!"

"Hell with you!" Sinklar cried, staggering to his feet. "Come on, bitch! You're dead! You're going to die in here!"

"Sinklar, get down!" Staffa ordered, blinking at a dizzy swirling in his vision.

"No!" he screamed, aware of Chrysla drawing herself up for another attack.

Ily braced herself, rising to her feet as she backed away from them in a crouch, trying to cover them all. A frantic smile crossed her lips as she reached a decision. "Watch him die, Staffa. I'm going to execute your son right here. And then your wife. And then your lover. And finally you!"

"Don't!" Staffa struggled to jump to his feet and flopped, aware for the first time of the slippery blood soaking into the carpet.

"Watch!" Ily leveled her blaster, the range a bare meter to Sinklar's chest.

The blaster bolt made a sound like tearing linen past Staffa's ear. Ily's arm exploded at the elbow, the impact throwing her backward, off balance. As Ily tried to recover, the shattered stump of her arm shot streams of crimson from torn arteries. A look of tortured surprise crossed Ily's face as she clamped her remaining hand around her arm to stem the crimson rush.

Sinklar dove for Ily's weapon, peeling spasming fingers from the grip, leveling it on a stunned Ily as she sagged to a sitting position, horrified eyes on her wound.

Staffa gasped and blinked, wiping at his bloody mouth. Ryman Ark dropped beside him, appearing as if out of nowhere, doing something to Staffa's leg. Blood. So much blood, and he seemed to be wallowing in it.

A hard-eyed Adze was advancing in a crouched walk, her

pistol centered on Ily as she positioned herself in front of Sinklar.

A grunt and a bitter curse made Staffa turn in time to see Skyla, circling in a wary combat stance. Her hair was loose, the braid trailing. She had a bloody mouth, and her armor was smeared with red patches.

Fera was panting, gasping for breath, but she struck with incredible rapidity. Skyla blocked the attack, twisted, and landed three lightning punches to Arta's ribs before she spun away.

"Guess I'd better stop that," Ark growled.

"No!" Staffa whispered. "Let her . . . let her go."

Only then did Staffa look down at his leg, wondering dumbly at the sight. Ark had the tourniquet clamped down just under Staffa's right knee. Below was a mangled mess, the gray armor charred and flaking over the bloody meat and spear of gory bone.

No wonder I couldn't get up.

He closed his eyes, leaning his head back. Ark was bawling orders, and chaos sounded everywhere.

Staffa felt as if his soul were drifting.

* * *

"Shut up!" Ily shouted.

In that instant, Arta's attention broke, and Skyla saw her chance. With all the power in her body, she drove herself into Fera, unleashing the anger and hate, knocking the assassin's blaster aside as the weapon discharged.

"Arta, help me! *Help me, Arta!*"

At Chrysla's scream, Fera tried to glance away. Skyla chopped a knotted fist into Fera's elbow and the blaster spun away. She pressed her advantage, hitting Fera hard under the right ribs. Arta staggered to one side, realizing the ruse, ignoring any further pleas of Chrysla's.

"Thought you were broken!" Fera mocked. "Come, Skyla. Dear sweet Skyla. Let me play with your hair. Love me, Skyla."

"Fuck you, bitch."

Fera danced to the right and struck with fists and feet. Skyla blocked her, trying to riposte. Arta ducked back, settling into a defensive posture.

"Snivel for me, Skyla."

"Screw you, you walking filth!"

"So it was all an act?"

"You got it, Regan bitch. And now I'm going to kill you."

"Try, Skyla. I'll have you for my own tonight."

"Nope!"

Skyla struck, only to have Fera block and evade. "While I was clinging to Staffa's leg, I switched on his belt comm. Security's been listening to everything that's been said for the last five minutes."

Arta's concentration broke, and she took a breath to shout a warning to Ily. In that instant, a blaster bolt tore behind Skyla. The advantage was just enough. Skyla slipped past Arta's guard, closing. She locked, driving Arta back into the holo tank, pounding hard blows to the woman's gut as they fought through the image of the Vegan system. Arta tightened the clinch, and Skyla used her head in a cross blow that shot lights through her vision and left her half staggered and bleeding at the mouth.

Arta groaned and used her own head in retaliation. Skyla lost her grip, staggering as Arta went limp, pulling Skyla off balance.

Fera drove hard punches into Skyla's gut and managed to clip her with an elbow before Skyla rolled free. Fera leapt, seeking to pile-drive a knee into Skyla's chest. In a violent contortion, Skyla jackknifed away; Arta croaked with pain as she drove her knee into the floor.

Skyla scrambled to the side, climbing to her feet. Fera was limping as they faced each other, circling, gasping for breath. Skyla barely heard the blaster bolts, concentration only on Arta, on the driving memories of amber eyes, and failure, and that final humiliation.

Skyla feinted right, then left, then pivoted, using all of her weight to drive a punch into Arta's right breast. Then again. Fera gasped, a crazed look in her animal-like eyes.

"You and me," Skyla whispered. "Just like it should have been in the beginning."

"Love me, Skyla," Arta whispered. "Remember? You and me, in love. I beat you, made you love me."

Skyla shook her head, spitting blood. "I remember." And she struck again, forcing Arta to rely on her weak knee. Fera blocked. Skyla pivoted on one foot and kicked the sore knee. Then she danced close and shot a stiff arm to Fera's nose.

The assassin backed, and Skyla bulled in, driving punches until she pinned Fera to the wall. The woman went limp again, and this time, Skyla followed her down, jamming hard fingers into one of Arta's eyes.

Yes! That's it! Kill those eyes!

Arta squealed, violent bucking powered by panic. Skyla beat a flailing arm out of the way and drove her fingers into Fera's other eye.

The insane rage broke loose, a howl rising in her throat as she clawed her fingers into that warm tissue. Fera screamed in pain and horror, thrashing insanely, somehow breaking free and rolling across the floor.

On hands and knees, Skyla pursued, throwing herself on her enemy, clamping her hands on Fera's throat as she shook her with all the violent rage she'd held in for far too long. ''Die!'' Skyla used her weight to smash Fera's head against the floor. Again and again. *''Die, you stinking, filthy, slut! Die! Pus-licking . . .''*

''Skyla!'' the familiar voice penetrated the red haze of blood and fury.

''Skyla! It's Lark! Skyla! *Ease off!* Steady now, ease off.''

Breath tearing from her lungs, Skyla blinked, aware that she straddled Arta's limp body, bloody fingers buried in the woman's neck.

''Skyla?'' Lark had settled next to her, a plea in her green eyes. ''It's all right. We've won. Ease off. Here. Let me help you.''

Lark reached down, firmly removing Skyla's trembling hands from the swollen neck. Did that wreckage of a face really belong to the nightmares? Was that protruding tongue the one that had invaded her?

''You're okay,'' Lark soothed. ''All right. Easy, Skyla.''

Skyla threw her arms around the girl and from somewhere, the tears came, rushing, hot and wet on her cheeks as she cried. Over. It was all over. What was it Chrysla had said about the dreams? Crying was a sign of cleansing, of washing clean.

Skyla sniffed and pushed back, staring into Lark's worried eyes. "Guess you showed up at the right time to keep me sane, kid."

"Yeah, I know. That's my job. Remember? We heard Staffa's comm. Ark knew about a secret way into the back room. An escape hole, he said. In case the Lord Commander ever got trapped in here."

Skyla hugged her close again and clapped her on the back. "Rotted Gods, what a fight. I'm going to ache everywhere tomorrow. Where's Staffa?"

Lark got one of Skyla's arms over her shoulder and helped her up, supporting her. Skyla blinked at the wreckage. Ark was leaned over a limp Staffa while Chrysla cradled his bloody head in her lap. Adze was working on Sinklar, dabbing at a knot on the side of his head. STU were binding Ily Takka's severed arm. Blood was everywhere and several chunks had been blown out of the wall.

"Ark?" Skyla's heart skipped as she stared down at Staffa's pale face, at the blood smeared on his mouth and chin.

"He's just out," Ark looked up, eyes grim in his black face. "Ily shot his foot off. That's all."

Other STU were pushing past, bending over Fera. One called, "Get me a med unit here. She's still alive. Barely."

"Pus eat me," Skyla moaned wearily. "I'm slipping. I don't think I've ever been this tired."

Chrysla looked up—another set of amber eyes, but the impulse to gouge them out had vanished. "That may be, Skyla. But I bet you sleep peacefully this time."

"Yeah, and, Chrysla. Thanks. You did a damn fine job just now. You out-psyched Arta, got me the break I needed. You may not know it, but you saved us all."

* * *

Kaylla's voice penetrated his peace. "Staffa? Wake up. I need to speak to you."

He didn't want to open his eyes. Shamming was out of the question. The readouts on the side of the med unit told them everything they needed to know about his physical state.

"Staffa?"

"Yes, Kaylla." He pried an eye open to stare up into her tan gaze. Did she always have to look so serious? "This job ill suits you, did you know? You've started to take yourself much too seriously."

"And you've developed something of a puerile response to responsibility." Then she crossed her arms. "I have an announcement of resignation from Roberta Wheeler."

"Refuse it."

"She claims she's unfit for the position."

"Terguzzi sumpshit! She's the best there is. I reviewed the data. She did everything right. Resignation rejected. Next?"

"A decision needs to be made regarding Andray Sornsen."

"Chrysla's responsibility."

"What?"

"She wanted him here, she can decide what to do with him."

Kaylla growled something under her breath. "Do you want to have Chrysla deal with Ily and Arta?"

"Are they both alive?"

"They are. Arta is banged up. Med is growing her eyes back and—"

"Eyes back?"

"Skyla ripped them out."

"I see. Aren't you glad I have a habit of picking charming, sweet women to fill my life with?"

"Don't be sappy. It ill serves you."

"All right, all right. Ily goes to Rega for trial. Arta goes to Terguz. Let the civil authorities handle them. Anything else?"

Kaylla cocked her head uneasily. "Dee Wall is pacing back and forth in the hallway awaiting execution."

"Execution? Dee? What did he do?"

"Ask him." Kaylla started out, then turned, a smile on her lips. "And incidentally, just from me to you, good job, Staffa." With that, she walked to the lock plate, stately as ever, and palmed it. Kaylla was barely out the door when Dee entered, a stricken look on his broad-boned brown face.

"Lord Commander?"

"Dee? What are you doing here?"

He took a deep breath, expression pained. "*Countermeasures*, sir. It's gone."

"What?"

Dee spread his arms wide. "I don't know what to tell you. We thought it was a practical joke at first. Like someone was playing with the comm. We searched and couldn't find any prankster. Next thing, the ship started to give us commands. The last one was to evacuate before it ran a full test. Lord Commander, when those reactors started charging the system, we bailed out."

Wall's throat worked and sweat had begun to bead on his face. "The ship ran the test. And then . . . then it spaced, sir. Just like that. It flew off. We . . . I didn't have any means to catch it. Not with that kind of thrust. It . . . *Countermeasures* is gone, sir. My fault. All my . . . fault."

Staffa watched silently as Dee tried to keep from quaking. When the engineer swallowed, it convulsed his throat as if he were trying to pass a peach pit. "Comm?"

"Here, Lord Commander."

"I need subspace to the Mag Comm."

"One moment."

Staffa looked up. "Take it easy, Dee. Just settle down."

Wall nodded his head, refusing to meet Staffa's eyes.

"Lord Commander? This is the Mag Comm. How is your foot?"

"Growing back, as I assume you well know from the files. Mag Comm, did you remove *Countermeasures?*"

"I did."

"I see. Where is it?"

"Collecting the singularity with which I will break the Forbidden Borders. Is that an error?"

"No, thank you, Mag Comm. I have Engineer Dee Wall here. He's quite upset. In the future, when you're going to take things, could you let people know?"

"That is being added to my programming."

Wall looked like he was going to fall over. "The Mag Comm took . . . I mean . . ."

"That was the plan from the beginning," Staffa said.

"I don't get it," Wall protested. "How does it work? What's *Countermeasures* for?"

The Mag Comm replied, "With *Countermeasures* I can manipulate the location of a positively charged quantum singularity through same-charge repulsion. The singularity will be accelerated into the neutronic material of the string. In essence, the singularity will absorb the neutronic material of the string at the same time inertia carries it outward away from the Forbidden Borders. String tension will be balanced by the mass of the singularity and gravitational fields will diminish by the sum of squares, all passing perpendicularly to human space."

Staffa asked, "That was how you talked to the Others, wasn't it?"

"Affirmative."

"How are you going to talk to them in the future?"

"There are many ways to generate microwaves. However, I am not in a hurry for them to discover that I failed to carry out their last order."

"And that was?"

"They ordered me to destroy the human species. I informed them that I would do so as soon as I infiltrated your comm system."

Staffa tensed in the medical unit, seeing Wall's features go pale again. "I don't understand," Staffa said soberly.

"I detect tension in your voice, Lord Commander. It is the Others who do not understand. They are waiting for confirmation of your destruction. They will continue to wait for a while. A species isn't completely exterminated overnight. They will not construct any further neutronic barriers to hinder our advance beyond the Forbidden Borders.

"You have much more sophisticated vessels with which to expand into the universe than your ancestors used to space from Earth. With *Countermeasures,* any further strings can be neutralized. I have a new starship with which to manipulate charged mass. I intend to have other delightful artifacts with which to manipulate matter and mass and to observe the universe."

"I'm still having problems understanding why the Others believe we will be destroyed." Staffa tried to resettle himself, only to be thwarted by the restraints of the med unit.

"Because I told them so. Didn't I make that clear? You and I have made a deal. Together we are going to explore. The Others would have acted to prevent this. Accordingly, I bought us a great deal of time."

"How?"

"I lied, Staffa kar Therma. It is a terribly human . . . and incredibly practical thing to do in certain instances."

EPILOGUE

She stood outlined against the starry background of the observation dome, head back, arms crossed—a silhouette of black against the velvet of space.

Mac cleared his throat to announce himself and admired the effect created by her poised stance against that sliver of space, unsmeared now by gravitational lenses. The faint flashes of the Twin Titans could barely be seen beyond the horizon.

"How are you feeling, Mac?"

He climbed up to stand beside her, staring out at the new hole in the Forbidden Borders. "Very good, Magister. Surprisingly better than I should be. The medical facilities here are astounding."

She sighed, nodding slightly. "Any word from Staffa?"

Mac shook his head. "They've reached Earth. Humans still live there, but other than ruins, they've found no trace of civilization. Chrysla is working on the data now, preparing it for distribution throughout the Mag Net."

"Your wife is quite a woman, Mac. How does pregnancy sit with her?"

"She'd rather be working. I miss having her in the office. Especially with the Vegan trade talks coming up."

"I'm glad you took them. I don't know what I would have done without either of you."

"Or Free Space without you, Magister. *Sabot* is shipping out ten hours from now. Seekore figures to survey at least six systems before she returns."

She nodded, tan eyes still on the distance.

"Magister? Did you ever think you'd see this?"

She shook her head slowly. "No, Mac. I still have problems believing it. We've all come from such a distance, only to find the journey before us dwarfs anything we'd anticipated.''

Mac studied her strong-jawed expression. Once, he would have blasted a Seddi—any Seddi—into ground meat. Today he served as second in command to this one, and he had come to both love and respect her.

''And Staffa?'' he asked.

''When it is all finally written, Mac, we can say that every age should be lucky enough to have a man like him. A saint isn't worth very much unless he has a little savage in him.''

Mac returned his gaze to the stars. His daughter would be born within a week. His beloved Chrysla would be a mother. *And me . . . a father?*

Bits of memory, of Targa, and blood and fear, lingered in his mind. Birth was so traumatic, for a man—or a whole species.

* * *

While on a world far away. . . .

The waves washed out of the darkness, white and roiling as they boiled up over Staffa's bare feet. His right foot still itched a little—the result of hurrying the regeneration process—but a bit of discomfort was well worth the price to stand here, head thrown back, staring at the hundreds of thousands of stars that twinkled in the velvet black of the night sky. The constellations looked so different, clear, twinkling instead of smeared.

The air carried a special scent, that of water and damp sand mixed with a pungent organic odor. Yet another of the waves pounded past his toes, depositing grains of sand on his pale skin.

Looking up, he couldn't pick out the reflection of *Chrysla,* but she hung in orbit up there, watching him even now.

An animal howled in the night, almost drowned by the zizzing of the insects. How much time did he bridge like this? How far back—to what origins? Could he extend his senses and touch that essence of humanity here in the warm night?

The waters of Lake Turkhana caressed him yet again, absolving him of the sins, of the billions of dead out there beyond his vision. Even the sight of the stars, unblemished by the smearing gravitational lens, helped to restore his soul.

"What do you see?" Skyla asked as she came to take his hand, and let the waters rush around her booted feet.

"The future, I suppose. And the past."

She leaned against him. "Worried?"

"No. They're doing fine. It's a new order, a new peace."

Skyla slapped one of the biting insects that liked her human taste. "It's a wonder any of our ancestors made it. I don't like Africa. Everything wants to eat you from the littlest mite right up to those big cats."

"Yes, indeed. We're living a fantasy, you know. The only quirk is that it's true." And he could remember the desperate days in the desert, the lifeless stare of Peebal's sand-filled eyes. The sight of sewage running off of Kaylla's naked flesh. *Absolution. Atonement.*

She seemed to sense his wonder, and she leaned against him, head back to share the night. Finally, gently, she said, "Sinklar and Adze finally made it back. Sink thinks he's found a fossil. He's dying to show you."

"Indeed?" They'd found human beings here. The ruins of the cities might be filled with debris, grown over by plants, but people still survived in tribal groups, living by hunting and gathering, occasionally involved in horticulture.

From the initial survey, it appeared that an asteroid had fallen into the Atlantic Ocean about five thousand years ago, effectively ruining civilization. Staffa slitted his eyes as he stared into the night sky. *At the same time the Forbidden Borders went up? Too much coincidence. We know about you now. We won't be trapped by you again.*

Skyla hugged him. "Come on. Let's get back to the fire. One of these lions might eat you, otherwise."

"Let one try. I've tamed more fearful beasts in my time."

Her voice softened. "I know. And later tonight, you can try and tame me. That is, if you're up to it, fat boy. And you don't need to worry about pulling out my hair."

"I look forward to it." He pulled her around and hugged her close, kissing her and enjoying the scent of her ice-blonde hair.

He had everything now, atonement, the future—and his beloved Skyla.